PARAGON PLACE

Paragon Place is a close-knit and diverse community: from its very own drunkard Alf Porter to his arch enemies, the prim and respectable Carey sisters; from Ginny Almond, courageously bringing up her five children on her own, to the voluptuous Muriel Taylor, the square's 'lady of the night'; from the local villains, the Dougan brothers, to the gossiping grannies, Lil Allen and Daisy Almond. All are drawn together, in laughter and in tears, in the never-ending fight against poverty, rationing and flying bombs.

From the author of *Ironmonger's Daughter*, *Paragon Place*, with its authentic London setting, powerful and compelling storytelling and wide cast of sympathetic and real characters, is sure to be another bestseller.

OTHER HARRY BOWLING TITLES IN LARGE PRINT

Ironmonger's Daughter

PARAGON PLACE

PARAGON PLACE

by
Harry Bowling

MAGNA PRINT BOOKS
Long Preston, North Yorkshire,
England.

British Library Cataloguing in Publication Data

Bowling, Harry
 Paragon Place.
 I. Title
 823.914 [F]

 ISBN 0–7505–0066–2
 ISBN 0–7505–0067–0 pbk

First Published in Great Britain by Headline Book Publishing plc
1990.

Published in Large Print 1991 by arrangement with Headline Book
Publishing plc, London and The Copyright Holder.

Printed and bound in Great Britain by
Redwood Press Limited, Melksham, Wiltshire.

To Shirley, Stephen, Sharon and Sally

PROLOGUE

1901–1903

IN January two young women sat together on a low wooden bench in a side room of the church. It was cold and the women shivered and pulled their cotton shawls tighter around their narrow bodies. The black and white marble floor had been freshly scrubbed and smelt of carbolic. There was a large, gilt crucifix on one of the white stone walls, and high up on the opposite wall a stained-glass window let in the pale sunlight.

The two women could hear muffled voices coming from behind a huge oaken door. They exchanged fearful glances and then looked hopefully in the direction of the silent figure who stood beneath the window.

'It shouldn't be too long now,' the church sister said kindly, smiling briefly at the two and then reverting her gaze to the high window.

The mumbling coming from behind the closed door went on, and when the sister had excused herself and left the room one of the women got up and paced the floor.

'This poxy waitin' is gettin' me down, Lil,' she grumbled, adjusting her grubby shawl around her shoulders. 'Why they takin' so long?'

'Gawd knows,' her friend replied, staring up at the crucifix. 'I didn't fink we'd be this long, Daisy. I've left a bleedin' suet puddin' boilin' in the copper. Me ole man'll go mad if 'is tea ain't ready when 'e gets in.'

In the adjoining room the church committee sat pondering the future of the two women and their families.

'What we have to consider is the whole question of eligibility,' the bearded member concluded, glancing around at his colleagues. 'The families are not members of St Joseph's. We must be seen to be observing and living up to the responsibilities which have been placed upon us, and we must be quite sure that all our tenants will live clean, orderly lives. We must be careful not to throw the homes open to the riff-raff from those riverside slums.'

Councillor Arnold Catchpole looked around at the nodding heads and felt the sudden urge to pull the chairman's beard out by its roots. The old goat has been prattling on for the past twenty minutes, he thought, flipping open the hood of his Ingersoll pocket watch and glancing at it. He coughed loudly, his usual way of gaining attention, and when everyone's eyes were on him he stood up, hooked his thumbs into his waistcoat pockets and cleared his throat.

'What we have here are people sorely in need of some Christian charity,' he began, staring hard at the chairman. 'We have two properties vacant and two deserving families who have each lost their youngest child to the fever. We all know of Salisbury Street and the terrible living conditions there. The families have been nominated by our welfare workers and their report shows that both families could be relied upon to maintain the properties to a good standard of cleanliness.' Catchpole's eyes glared at each member of the committee in turn. 'Now, gentlemen, and our good lady member, I would like you to agree to let these two properties to the Almond family and the Allen family forthwith. Let us be seen to be acting correctly, but let us also discharge our duties with some measure of compassion and social justice. After all, no family should have to endure life in those deplorable fever-ridden slums. We have the opportunity here to give hope to two families; modern homes in which their children can grow up healthy, free from the scourges of rickets and tuberculosis. I ask you to take the vote now, without more ado.'

Councillor Catchpole's passionate plea was warmly greeted by the lady member, who dabbed her eyes and smiled sweetly at him.

The vote was finally taken and the church sister carried the result out to the two women, who hugged each other in their delight.

'Jus' fink of it, Daisy,' Lil Allen cried. 'Runnin' water, a scullery wiv a real gas copper, an' a flush toilet. Gawd! I can't believe it!'

Daisy Almond retied the strings of her coarse apron and pulled her shawl up around her neck. 'C'mon, Lil,' she said. 'Let's get goin' or you'll 'ave no bleedin' puddin' left.'

One Friday night a couple of years later Jack Almond and Albert Allen left the tannery and took their usual route home through the gardens of St Joseph's Church. Halfway along the gravel path they stopped and looked around furtively.

'Well, go on then,' Albert said, thrusting his

13

hands deeper into his overcoat pockets.

'All right, Alb, gissa chance,' Jack replied, whistling tunelessly as he walked on to the grass and bent down beside a mound of newly dug earth.

Barely a minute had passed before the two men were back on the path, glancing behind them stealthily. 'Me ole woman loves plants. I reckon this'll look nice in 'er front parlour,' Jack said as they walked on out of the gardens.

As usual on Friday nights the two friends stopped off at the Railway Inn for a pint. When they had settled themselves at a table with drinks at their elbows, Albert glanced down at his hand at the slender sprig which had a few leaves sprouting from its tip and he grinned.

'It don't look much ter me. Yer sure it's an aspidistra?' he asked.

Jack wiped the froth from his moustache with the back of his hand and studied the plant. 'That's what the gardener bloke said when I asked 'im,' he replied.

Albert was not convinced and he scratched his bushy hair vigorously. 'Me ole lady 'ad one o' them aspidistra fings in 'er winder an' it didn't look anyfing like that bloody fing yer got there,' he said thoughtfully. 'Right proud of it, she was. 'Ad it fer donkey's years, she did. It broke 'er 'eart when it died. I remember the poor ole cow standin' in the parlour cursin' them mice.'

'Did the mice eat the plant then, Alb?' Jack asked, a comical look on his flushed face.

'Nah. The bloody moggie killed the plant. It used ter piss over it.'

'Why did yer ole lady curse the mice then?' Jack asked, becoming confused.

'Well yer see, we was runnin' alive wiv mice down in Salisbury Street an' the ole gel got this cat,' Albert explained. 'The moggie killed the mice, an' the bloody aspidistra in the bargain.'

'What 'appened ter the cat, Alb?' Jack asked. 'Did she chuck it out?'

Albert shook his head slowly. 'Nah. It got poisoned.'

'Poisoned?'

'Yeah, we started gettin' rats comin' in from the river an' me ole lady stuck some rat poison down. Yer can guess what 'appened.'

Jack felt that the conversation would soon begin to turn him off his dinner and he picked up his pint quickly. 'Don't tell me, Albert,' he said.

The bar was filling up and suddenly Albert nudged his friend. ''Ere, Jack. There's ole Isaac Porter over there,' he whispered. 'Look, 'e's readin' that bible again. 'E knows a lot about plants an' fings. Why don't yer ask 'im about that scrawny-lookin' fing yer got there?'

Two pints later Jack felt able to approach his strange neighbour, and he was surprised at Isaac's response.

'It's a sycamore sprig. Yer can tell by the leaves,' Isaac said confidently. 'See the pointed shape of 'em? I understand they're plantin' a lot o' them in the parks. That'll grow ter forty feet at least, wiv care, o' course. Where did you get it?'

'One o' me mates at work give it ter me,' Jack

15

said, mindful of his neighbour's religious convictions. 'I was gonna give it ter me missus. She likes plants.'

Isaac laughed. 'It wouldn't survive indoors. It needs air an' lots o' sunshine.'

Later, when Isaac had finished his drink he closed the bible as he prepared to leave, and then he caught sight of the unwanted sycamore sprig that his neighbours had left leaning against the wall. With a smile he picked it up and walked out of the pub.

PART ONE

1942

Chapter One

PARAGON PLACE in Bermondsey led off from the middle of Stanley Street, a long, narrow turning which threaded its way under railway arches in the general direction of the river. Paragon Place was a small square containing ten two-storey houses which had been built in 1880. Four houses were situated on each side of the paved square and at the closed end two more houses faced the entrance. The brick-built homes with their grey slate roofs were tidy-looking compared with many of the dwellings in the area, although some of the red chimney pots had become lopsided over the years. The two-up, two-down houses were identical, except that the four houses on the left-hand side of the square each had an extra room above the scullery. The other houses had a sloping roof over the scullery. No one had ever discovered why this should be, but rumour had it that the builders had run out of money and had taken it upon themselves to hastily revise their plans.

The houses in Paragon Place had been built with money put into a trust by one of the area's wealthy businessmen, who had found religion in later life and adopted the Catholic faith before he

19

died. The trust fund was administered by the church, who had engaged the services of a reputable estate agent to manage the property. It was the church committee who nominated prospective tenants and who upheld the wishes of the benefactor that the homes would be for God-fearing people of the area and their descendants. Paragon Place had survived the blitz, although one of the houses facing the entrance had suffered damage and its upstairs rooms were boarded up. The rooms of the houses were small, with stone-floored sculleries that had gas-lit coppers and iron gas stoves. From the scullery a door led out into a tiny backyard with a draughty toilet. In the early thirties electric lighting had been installed, but the gas lamps were still left intact. There was a Victorian gas lamp at the entrance to Paragon Place, and a sorry-looking sycamore leaned towards the brickwork of number 5, its leaves brushing the guttering.

It was back in 1903 that Isaac Porter, the grandfather of the present occupant of number 5, brought home a sapling and planted it in the space provided by a broken paving-stone. Isaac watered and tended the sapling every day and his neighbours shook their heads and mumbled that the thing would never thrive there, but to their surprise it took root and started to sprout. When the sapling had thickened up so that a child's hands would not meet around the bole, and its leaves were brushing the upstairs win-dowsill, Isaac Porter died. His tree had struggled skywards ever since, and when its branches spread above the grey slate rooftops and its roots lifted the paving-stones the council decided it would have to go. Workmen called round only to be met with angry protestations from the tenants of Paragon Place, who sent the men on their way with instructions to the council to leave the tree alone and replace the paving-stones.

Isaac Porter's sycamore survived, a memorial to its God-fearing protector, although his descendant, who had hardly ever set foot inside a church, had little interest in the tree. Alf Porter had lived alone at number 5 since the early days of the blitz, when the upstairs flat was gutted by a falling incendiary bomb. The tenants, an elderly couple, had escaped unhurt and had been taken off to a nearby rest centre. Alf Porter had reason to thank the tree on the occasions it had held him upright when he staggered into the square the worse for drink. There were also times when he had cursed his grandfather's tree, after he had walked full tilt into it on returning from a long session at the Railway Inn. The rest of the tenants in Paragon Place had grown fond of their tree and they felt that it added a little colour to their drab sur-roundings. Like the rest of Bermondsey's trees the sycamore had had a band of white paint applied to it when the blackout regulations came into force, and when the houses in Stanley Street suffered a direct hit during the height of the blitz the tree had had its bark torn and pitted with shrapnel. On its sheltered side a small, crude heart had been carved, enclosing the inscription 'B B loves S R'.

On a grey Saturday morning in early 1942

Sally Brady walked into Paragon Place clutching two heavily laden shopping bags. The queues had seemed extra long that morning and the walk back had made her feel rather tired. Sally noticed Blind Bob sitting on his windowsill, his head held to one side, and she knew that the sound of her footsteps had reached his ears. Bob was not an old man, but due to his handicap he had acquired a careful, deliberating manner that belied his age. His mongrel dog sat upright at its master's still feet, its leash slack and held around Bob's wrist. As she approached, Sally saw the man's sightless eyes darting from side to side and she called out to him, 'Mornin', Bob.'

The blind man pulled on his dog's lead. 'Mornin', Sal. 'E's ready fer 'is walk as usual,' he said with a chuckle.

The dog looked up at his master as if understanding what had been said and Sally smiled as she passed by. At the end of the square she stopped, put down one of the shopping bags and pulled on the doorstring of number 4. Inside, the passage was damp with steam and Sally could see her mother standing over the boiling copper in the scullery, pressing down on the clothes with a large stick. The woman replaced the lid and walked out into the passage rubbing her forehead with the back of her hand. 'You've bin a while,' she said. 'Long queues?'

Sally nodded as she carried the shopping into the front parlour and sat down heavily on a chair. 'Any tea in the pot, Mum?' she asked, unbuttoning her coat.

Mother and daughter sat sipping their tea in

silence. The ticking of the clock on the mantelshelf sounded loudly, and from outside they could hear children's laughter. Annie Robinson glanced at her daughter wondering whether or not she should mention seeing Ben Brady that morning. Her eyes returned to her tea cup and she decided against it. Annie was a small woman in her mid-fifties. Her greying hair was pulled tight around her ears and set in a bun at the nape of her neck. Her small dark eyes stared out from a thin face and her small mouth tended to droop at the corners. She looked older than her years as she sat slumped in her chair, her face hot from standing over the copper and her flowered apron wet and clinging to her narrow body. Sally was staring thoughtfully into the unlit grate as she sipped her tea. She had her mother's angular features, although her deep-set brown eyes were large and enquiring. Her dark hair was cut short and waved, barely touching her straight shoulders. Sally was taller than her mother, with a slim, shapely body that was hidden beneath her loose-fitting and rather shabby coat. She glanced at her mother and wondered why she did not mention talking to Ben. Mrs Mynott from number 6 had told her while they were standing together in the bread queue. "Ere, Sal. I jus' see yer mum talkin' ter that 'usband o' yours outside the paper shop,' she had said. 'I thought yer'd like ter know.'

Sally kicked off her shoes and leaned back in her chair. It was over a year now since she had left her husband Ben and taken a room in nearby Dockhead, and only a few weeks after the split

23

her mother had taken to her bed with pleurisy. Sally recalled the day her younger sister Lora called round and there had been harsh words. 'You can't expect me ter manage on me own,' Lora had said. 'Mum should be in 'ospital really, an' yer know Dad's useless about the place. Then there's Bill. I don't know why mum ever took a lodger. It's all extra work, an' I can't be expected ter do everyfink. Besides it's not fair on Bernard. I mean, yer can't expect 'im ter sit in nights. It'd be different if you were there. After all, you're on yer own now. You've got no one ter worry about.'

Sally felt her chest tighten in anger as she recalled her sister's words. She had agreed to come home to help out for a week or two and now she found herself trapped. The whole family seemed to be relying on her more and more.

Annie put down her empty cup and sighed deeply as she slumped back in her chair. 'See if that washin's done, will yer, Sal?' she said heavily. 'I'm fair whacked.'

Sally put on her shoes and walked out into the scullery. Hot steam rushed up into her face as she eased the lid from the copper. She turned off the gas and carefully lifted out the washing and put it in the tin bath. What could Ben have wanted? she wondered. Was he asking after her, or had her mother stopped him in the street? Whatever had been said she was determined there could be no going back. She was determined that her resolve would not weaken, despite Ben's very persuasive ways and her treasured memories of how good things had been

24

between them at first. The gas popped loudly and Sally jumped. She could hear her mother's voice calling from the parlour. 'I meant ter tell yer. Vera Mynott came over. She said can yer give 'er a knock this afternoon. Oh, an' can yer take Bill's clean sheets up when yer get a minute? It'll save me legs up them stairs.'

After she ran the washing through the wringer and pegged it on the line in the backyard Sally gathered the freshly ironed sheets from the chair beside the scullery door and hurried up the stairs. She tapped on the door and a rough voice bade her enter. The old man was sitting at a small table and he gave her a toothless smile as she placed the sheets at the foot of the bed. Beside him on the table was an open book and next to it a large magnifying glass.

Bill Freeman had lodged with the Robinsons for the past five years. A loner who was loth to encroach on the Robinsons' hospitality, Bill had but two passions in life. One was Western novels and the other was ducks' eggs. Every morning he had two ducks' eggs for breakfast and every evening he sat crouched over a lighted candle and read a Western novel through the large magnifying glass. Bill was a strange character who never wandered very far from Paragon Place. His past was a mystery. All the Robinsons knew about him was that he had once worked in a tannery nearby and was now retired. He never mentioned anything about a family or where he came from but his ruddy complexion and slow, unruffled manner indicated to the Robinsons that he might possibly have hailed from a

25

country area. Bill stayed in his tiny room and preferred to eat his meals alone. He never used the electric light or the gas jet over the small fireplace, instead he resorted to candles which he stuck into a metal candleholder. The only time he had ventured out from his room after dark was during the height of the blitz, when he sat with the Robinsons under the stairs. Bill's one outing of the week was when he visited the public baths in Grange Road on Tuesdays and then collected his pension at the nearby post office.

Bill's rheumy eyes fixed on Sally as she walked around the table. He enjoyed the occasional chats they had when she brought his meals up to him and he was hoping she would stay for a while. "Ow's yer mum, lass?' he asked, folding his hands on the table.

'She's okay, Bill,' Sally replied, sitting down facing him. 'Jus' tired.'

The old man pulled the coat closer around his shoulders and brushed a gnarled hand over his bald head. 'Yer sister was up 'ere this mornin'. She nagged me about the candle grease on the table.'

Sally laughed and tapped the old man's wrist playfully. 'You bin fallin' asleep over yer book again, Bill? You'll set the room alight one o' these nights.'

Bill pointed to a pile of dog-eared novels on a wooden shelf above the head of his bed. 'I've read 'em all, yer know. Next week I'm gonna change that lot. There's a little shop near where I get me pension. Yer can change books there fer a few coppers. Books is important, lass. When I was a young whippersnapper I was encouraged

26

ter read. I used ter read ter me farver. 'E never mastered readin', yer see. Paid a lot of importance ter books, though. I remember 'im sayin' once that books was second only ter bread on the table. Lot o' sense in what 'e said. You should read more. It's good fer yer.'

Sally grinned and rested her elbows on the table, cupping her chin in her hands. 'I'm too tired at night, Bill. I fall asleep over the evenin' paper.'

Bill shook his head. 'Yer work too 'ard, gel. You should let that sister o' yours do a bit more.'

Sally shrugged her shoulders. 'I'll come back later an' change yer bed, Bill,' she said, looking around the room. Bill had adopted his usual blank expression, his eyes staring towards the window. Sally got up and stretched. 'Oh well, I'd better get goin'. There's work ter be done.'

The old man eased his legs from beneath the table and stood up slowly. 'Afore yer go I wanna show yer somefink, Sally,' he said, fixing his watery eyes on her. 'It won't take a minute.' Sally looked puzzled as he went slowly over to the window and opened the drawer of a small cabinet. He retrieved an oblong tin and placed it on the cabinet's smooth surface. 'When I first moved in I didn't bring much wiv me,' he said, scratching the back of his hand. 'Most of it's in 'ere. I want yer ter know about this box. When I'm gorn yer can open it. I jus' want yer ter know where it is, lass.'

Sally laughed quickly. 'What d'yer mean, when yer gone? Yer got years yet, Bill,' she said, feeling suddenly uncomfortable.

He shook his head slowly and replaced the tin

27

box in the drawer. 'Jus' so's yer know,' he said, going back to the table.

Sally paused in the doorway. 'You jus' be careful with that candle, Bill,' she laughed, closing the door gently, but as she turned down the stairs, a shadow of concern darkened her expression.

The afternoon sky was heavy with rain clouds and in the small parlour Charlie Robinson was rousing himself. A nearly cold cup of tea stood at his elbow on the table and opposite him Annie was sitting darning a woollen sock that was stretched over an upturned teacup. She gave her husband a malevolent glance and tut-tutted as he yawned and scratched his corpulent stomach. 'You've bin snorin' fer the last hour,' she said. 'Why don't yer get up an' put some water over yer face.'

Charlie sat upright in the chair. He was a big man who had worked in the docks since he was eighteen. His thick grey hair was cropped short, and his pale blue eyes stared out from a wide, flat face. He was of average height and had powerful shoulders and large gnarled hands which testified to the work he did. Charlie had been working at the Surrey Docks that morning and after clocking off he had gone to the Railway Inn for a pint and a game of darts with some of his pals. 'It's bin a bloody 'ard week, gel,' he said, yawning again. 'I must've dozed off.'

Annie was not impressed. She knew that her husband had never gone into a pub without drinking at least three pints of ale and she knew that it was the drink which had made him sleepy. She looked down at the sock in her hand. 'I seen Ben Brady this mornin',' she said suddenly. ''E stopped me as I was comin' out of the paper shop.'

Charlie grimaced. He had never liked his son-in-law very much. They had on occasion worked together on the quayside and the young man's demeanour had irked him. Charlie considered Ben Brady to be just a little too sure of himself and loud-mouthed into the bargain. He had seen Ben grow up and follow his father into the docks and he had warned Sally about hanging around with him. Now it seemed that he had been proved correct. 'Oh, an' what did 'e want, then?' he asked.

Annie looked up over her spectacles. 'Not a lot,' she said quickly. ''E just asked 'ow our Sal was, an' said ter say 'ello fer 'im.'

'Did yer tell the girl you'd seen 'im?'

'No. It'd only upset 'er. Yer can see she still finks a lot of 'im.'

Charlie nodded. 'I warned 'er right at the start about that Ben Brady. She wouldn't listen, though. The flash 'Arry was always chasin' the girls round 'ere. I always knew our Sal was gonna regret gettin' involved wiv 'im.'

Annie put down her darning and took the cold tea out into the scullery. She returned with two clean teacups and filled them from the teapot which was standing in the hearth. When she had settled herself once more she looked across to her husband. 'That girl worries me, Charlie. She's goin' on thirty an' what's she got ter show fer it? It might 'ave bin different if she'd 'ave 'ad a baby. It might 'ave kept the pair of 'em tergevver.'

29

Charlie shook his head. 'It wouldn't 'ave made any difference whatsoever, Annie. 'E was jus' the wrong bloke fer 'er. She deserves better than that one.'

Annie sipped her tea. 'I can't 'elp finkin' 'ow different those two girls of ours are. I can't imagine our Lora bein' taken in by someone like Ben Brady.'

Charlie snorted. 'Leave orf, Muvver. Look at that bloody idiot she's runnin' around wiv. Toffee-nosed little cow-son. 'E's makin' 'er as bad as 'im. Did yer 'ear 'er last night goin' on about me drinkin' tea out o' me saucer when 'e's 'ere? She's gettin' a little too big fer 'er boots.'

Annie tried to hide a grin. 'Well, yer must admit yer did go on a bit when she brought 'im round, Charlie. Jus' 'cos the lad works in an office. We can't all be dockers.'

Charlie grinned. ''Ere, did yer see 'is face when I started talkin' about jellied eels an' pie an' mash. I thought 'e was gonna be sick.'

Annie got up and straightened the tablecloth. 'You're just a pig, Charlie Robinson. Now are yer gonna get that accumulator changed before the shop shuts, or are we gonna 'ave no wireless ternight? Yer know I like ter listen ter the news an' Sat'day Night Theatre.'

Charlie grunted as he got out of the chair and went to the sideboard. He unscrewed the terminals from the square glass battery and lifted it clear of the wireless. 'I fink it's about time we bought one o' those electric wirelesses,' he grumbled. 'This bloody fing don't last more than a few days at the most.'

30

Heavy rain spots were spattering the paving-stones as Sally Brady walked past the sycamore tree and knocked at number 6. Vera Mynott answered the door and beckoned her friend in. Vera was an attractive-looking redhead in her late twenties. Her hair was long and tied at her neck with a black band and her green eyes seemed to sparkle with mischief. The two girls had grown up together and both worked as machinists at a Tooley Street clothing factory. Vera had a boyfriend, a local lad who was in the merchant navy. She loved dancing and was forever attempting to persuade Sally to go along with her to the Town Hall dances on Saturday nights, but without success. While her boyfriend Joe was away at sea Vera was loth to remain quietly at home, and she was currently flirting with one of the lads at the factory where she worked.

Vera led the way up the winding stairs to her bedroom at the back of the house. Her elder sister Doreen had recently married and Vera had used the extra space provided to put in a gramophone and a washstand. She had also repapered the room herself and had smartened it up with cream paint. 'Well, what d'yer reckon?' she asked, showing Sally into the room. 'Don't yer fink I done a good job?'

Sally nodded. 'Is that yer dad's gramophone?'

''E said I could 'ave it,' Vera answered. 'Dad never plays the bloody fing. 'Ere, I've got some good dance records. Wanna 'ear 'em?' Without waiting for a reply Vera opened the lid of the gramophone cabinet and placed a record on the turntable. She wound up the motor and gently

31

eased the needle into the record groove. The metallic notes of a foxtrot sounded loudly throughout the room and Vera's feet tapped out the rhythm on the coconut mat.

Sally had seated herself on the edge of the bed and was looking around the room. 'When's Joe due 'ome, Vera?' she asked presently.

Vera pulled a face. 'Next week, I fink. I never can tell exactly since 'e's bin on them convoys.'

'It must be a worry, what wiv all them ships gettin' sunk,' Sally said.

Vera's head was shaking in time with the music and her dreamy expression did not change. 'Yeah, o' course it is, but 'e always turns up. My Joe's like a bad penny. 'E'll be 'ome soon, dyin' fer it as usual, an' I'll be fightin' 'im off – not too 'ard though,' she added, grinning slyly.

Sally smiled. She secretly envied her friend. She had good looks and confidence in herself, and she remained totally unaffected by everything that went on around her. It was the same at work. She never seemed to get ruffled or taken aback by anything that was said to her. Some of the women felt that Vera was a little too easy with the lads but Sally knew the truth. Joe was the only man in her life, and the only one who meant anything to her, although she did engage in mild flirtations while he was away.

The record had finished and Vera slumped across the bed. 'I wanted yer ter see me room now I've finished it,' she said. 'Now what about you an' me goin' ter the Town Hall dance ternight?' Her eyes widened. 'Come on, Sal, it'll do yer good.'

Sally shook her head. 'No fanks, Vera. I don't dance all that well, an' besides, you're goin' wiv Jimmy Kent. I'd only be in the way.'

Vera waved away her friend's excuses with a sweep of her arm. 'I'm meetin' 'im there. 'E's got friends. We might be able ter get yer fixed up fer the evenin',' she laughed.

'No fanks,' Sally said, shaking her head again and staring down at her laced-up shoes.

'You still carrying a torch, Sal?'

'No. It's all over wiv me an' Ben.'

'Is it?'

Sally's large dark eyes hardened as she looked into those of her friend. 'We've bin apart now fer over a year. It jus' didn't work out, that's all. Fings would still be the same if I got back wiv 'im. You know it'd be impossible fer us now, Vera. I'd still want kids an' Ben'll never be able to oblige. Then there was the medical,' Sally sighed sadly. ''E didn't 'ave ter go as 'e's a docker. But yer know Ben. I think 'im gettin' turned down 'cos of 'is ears an' not bein' able ter farver children made 'im change. It was as though 'e was always tryin' ter prove somefing. I'm sure that's what turned 'im ter the drink an' ovver women. We was 'appy as anyfink fer the first couple o' years.'

Vera could sense the rising emotion in her friend's voice and she went quickly over to the gramophone. 'Let's put anuvver record on, Sal,' she said brightly. 'C'mon, I'll show yer the steps.'

Sally smiled and ignored Vera's outstretched arms as the music filled the small bedroom. Vera sat down, disappointed.

Rain spots pattered against the windowpane as they sat listening to the gramophone. Vera studied her friend with a sense of sadness. She had noticed how Sally had let herself go since the breakdown of her marriage. Her clothes were shabby and she had taken to wearing old-fashioned low-heeled shoes. Her hair could do with a perm, too, she thought. Maybe it was her way of discouraging the opposite sex. She never seemed to go out anywhere, other than the weekly trip to the pictures. Sally can't be content to go on being a drudge to that family of hers, Vera thought. Maybe she still secretly hoped that she and Ben would be able to get back together, despite what she had said to the contrary. Vera's thoughts were interrupted by the sound of the needle stuck in the groove of the record and she went over to attend to the machine.

Sally got up and stretched. 'I'd better be goin,' Vera,' she said, buttoning up her coat. 'Enjoy the dance. I'll see yer tomorrow.'

The little square was deserted and the tree hung limp beneath the heavily falling rain as Sally made her way back to her house. Distant thunder rolled and a zig-zag of lightning momentarily lit the dark sky.

Chapter Two

MR AND MRS CAREY had been God-fearing people who had heeded the call to do Christian work in Bermondsey, and when their home was demolished along with the run-down mission the church committee which administered the trust fund nominated the couple for number 1, Paragon Place. The Careys had two daughters, Harriet and Juliet. Both children were brought up in the faith and Harriet, the elder, followed her parents in becoming a church worker. Juliet, however, was the more outgoing and less impressionable, but like Harriet she remained unmarried, and both sisters spent their young lives caring for the ageing parents.

After their parents died the Carey sisters remained alone at number 1 until they were paid a visit by the estate agent, who stated that he had another nominee to share the house. The sisters then agreed to move to the upstairs rooms leaving the ground floor to a family who had fallen on hard times and had been thrown out on to the street. The new arrivals in Paragon Place were a Mrs Taylor and her five children. The father, a drunkard and a bully, had met his end by falling under a bus one night on his way home from the pub. In the years that followed four of the Taylor children married early leaving Muriel, the youngest, who was reserved and devoted to her mother, at home.

The beatings and abuse by her husband and long years of struggling on her own to make ends meet finally took their toll on Gladys Taylor, and one night she put a sixpence in the meter and stretched out in the scullery with her head on a pillow in the gas oven. Nineteen-year-old Muriel found the body when she returned from work in the evening. The church committee met and after a long discussion they came to the decision that, the suicide notwithstanding, the tenet of their benefactor must be upheld, and therefore the young Taylor girl should be allowed to stay on at number 1. The committee were comforted somewhat by the fact that the Carey sisters lived above and would no doubt be willing to watch out for the poor unfortunate child.

Muriel Taylor was grateful for the roof over her head but she found staying alone in the house unbearable. She began to go out more often and soon got into bad company. Her character slowly changed after her mother's death. She started to wear make-up and her mode of dress became more loud. She visited pubs and often came home the worse for drink, much to the consternation of the Carey sisters. Harriet tried to talk to the girl but found it very difficult. Juliet on the other hand felt that there was nothing to be done and she argued with her elder sister that they should accept the way things were. When Muriel started to bring men home the sisters clashed again. Harriet became scared of what might happen, whilst Juliet, who was becoming more and more irritated by her sister's attitude, took the view that the Taylor girl was evidently in need of men's company, and after all, it was her life.

Now, at number 1, the Carey sisters were sitting together in their upstairs flat discussing the occupant of the flat below. 'Well, I think we should say something to the girl,' Harriet said, the corner of her mouth twitching with distaste.

36

'It's immoral the way she's behaving. She brings those men home without so much as leave nor bye. We don't know who they are. They could be anybody. Her poor mother would turn in her grave if she knew the goings-on.'

Juliet looked long and hard at her elder sister. 'We know who the men are, Harriet. She picks them up at the docks. They're seamen. But still, it's no concern of ours. It's her flat. I suppose she's got the right to bring anyone home she chooses, as long as they don't come up the stairs.'

Harriet was fussing with the tiny china ornaments on the mantelshelf. 'That's just it, Juliet. She could bring some maniac home. We could be murdered in our beds, or worse!'

The younger sister could not think of anything worse than being murdered in bed, but she understood her elder sister's fears. Harriet was terrified of men. She was fifty-two years old and only once in her life had she been with a man. The bad experience had turned Harriet away from sex for life and from that moment on she had lived a life of celibacy. Juliet had no such problems, although she valued her independent state. At fifty she was still involved with her boss at the insurance office in the City. The affair had been going on for the past twenty years. Basil Lomax's wife had been confined to a wheelchair since she contracted polio as a young woman. Basil's liaison with the younger Carey sister seemed to be an ideal arrangement for both of them. They made love in his office after work, or when she accompanied him on business trips.

Sometimes Juliet would go to his home with deeds or titles for urgent inspection, always when Basil's wife was spending time at a convalescent home. Harriet was ignorant of all the goings-on and as far as she was concerned her sister, too, had turned her back on men. Juliet leaned back in her chair and picked up the evening paper. 'I wouldn't worry too much, Harriet,' she said pacifyingly. 'We always put the bolt on when we retire for the night. Besides, who would want to molest two old creatures like us?'

Harriet was unconvinced and vowed to have a discreet word in Muriel Taylor's ear at the first opportunity.

In the downstairs flat the object of the two middle-aged ladies' discussion was busy preparing herself for a very active night. The flat had been thoroughly cleaned and Muriel had been around with the scented water which she dispensed from a bottle spray. The flower-patterned cushions had been tastefully placed about the front room and a bottle of whisky was left on the sideboard. The heavy brocade curtains were drawn tightly and a fire was laid ready for lighting. The bedroom, too, had been arranged carefully, with a new mauve eiderdown spread over the bed and new cushion covers in place. The ashtrays had been emptied and a firescreen was placed in front of the empty grate. When Muriel had satisfied herself that all was ready she set about the task of making herself presentable. By eight o'clock in the evening the rain had abated and Muriel was about to let herself out when Harriet Carey happened to come out on to the landing. 'Er, excuse me, Muriel,' she called down. 'Could I have a quick word with you before you go out?'

Muriel rolled the chewing gum to the side of her mouth, adjusted her fur stole and stood with her hands on her hips while Harriet came slowly down the stairs.

'I hope you won't think I'm being unreasonable, Muriel, but my sister and I have been talking.'

'Oh yeah,' the young woman said coldly.

'Oh dear, it's very awkward really,' Harriet stuttered.

'C'mon, luv, spit it out. I'm listenin'.'

'Well if you must know, my sister and I are concerned about the men you bring back.'

Muriel looked at her. 'Why, d'yer wanna borrer one?'

'Oh my God no!' Harriet gasped. 'You see, Juliet and I are worried one of them might find his way up the stairs. After all, we're just two ladies on our own. Supposing one of your visitors was the worse for drink or something. Why, anything could happen.'

Muriel tried to hide her amusement but a wide grin broke out on her round, well-rouged face. 'Don't you worry yer ole self, luv. I'm pretty careful, an' the men I bring 'ome won't be interested in anyone but me, I can assure yer. Jus' bolt yer door and sleep in peace. You'll be as safe as a Muvver Superior, take my word for it. Now if you're finished, I must dash. I've got some work ter collect.'

Near the railway arches in Stanley Street muffled sounds of merriment carried out into the dark, deserted turning. Inside the Railway Inn the local folk tried to forget the rationing, the depressing news broadcasts and the rainy night as they gathered together and sang their favourite songs around a battered upright piano. In the snug bar two old ladies sat with glasses of Guinness in front of them. Granny Almond took a pinch of snuff and blew loudly into her large stained handkerchief. Granny Allen nudged her friend as the door opened and Muriel Taylor flounced in.

The young woman gave them a wide grin as she leaned over the counter. 'Give us a gin an' lime, will yer, Bert,' she said breathlessly. 'I'm in an 'urry.'

Bert Jackson put the drink down in front of Muriel and gave her a sly grin. 'Got business ternight, gel?' he asked.

'Yeah,' the young woman replied, picking up the glass and swirling the contents around. 'I've gotta meet somebody at nine. Mustn't be late.'

Bert's eyebrows raised. 'Yer wanna be careful, young lady. There's some funny ole characters around these days.'

'Ain't I always the careful one,' Muriel said with a smile, downing the drink in one gulp.

As she turned and hurried out Bert grinned at the two old ladies. 'I dunno what this area's comin' to,' he said with mock seriousness.

Granny Allen snorted. 'It ain't what it used ter be, that's fer sure. Used ter be quite nice round 'ere one time.'

40

Granny Almond nodded her agreement. 'The bleedin' place 'as gorn right down the pan. It's the war what's done it. Used ter be right select in this part o' Bermondsey when I was a girl.'

Bert laughed loudly. 'Go on, Daisy. I bet yer used ter get up ter some tricks when you was a girl.'

Daisy Almond chuckled. 'Yeah, so we did, but we was more discreet. These youngsters do it right out in the open.'

The landlord of the Railway Inn picked up the empty glass left by Muriel. 'I don't fink that one does it in the open, Daisy,' he grinned, nodding towards the door. 'She likes it in comfort.'

Tobacco smoke hung in the air and both saloon and public bars of the Railway Inn had become packed. In the snug bar the two old ladies were warming to their regular chat together. 'I see they've put soap on rationin' now, Lil. That'll please the kids,' Daisy said, chuckling.

Lil took a sip from her Guinness. ''Ere, while I fink of it. I was talkin' ter Mrs Mynott terday. She told me she see that there Ben Brady talkin' ter Annie Robinson. I ain't seen 'im fer some time.'

Daisy nodded. 'It's a shame about 'im an' young Sally. I used ter fink they was well suited. They was always tergevver as kids, wasn't they?'

Lil shook her head. 'Well, ter be honest, Daisy, it doesn't surprise me one little bit that they split up. 'E was always one fer the girls. She's a nice kid as well. Very polite. I'm surprised she come back 'ome ter live, though.

41

She got a place of 'er own when she left 'im, so I 'eard.'

'So she did,' Daisy replied. 'Down at Dock'ead, it was, accordin' ter Mrs Mynott. She come back ter look after 'er muvver when she went down wiv pleurisy. Bloody painful, that pleurisy.'

Granny Allen took a sip of her Guinness. 'Strange she never went back ter the flat when Annie got better, Daisy.'

Granny Almond nodded. 'Yeah, funny that. Mind you, that girl's always workin'. She gets the shoppin', cleans the step, an' Annie Robinson told me once she does all 'er washin' an' ironin' fer 'er.'

Lil sipped her Guinness. 'Bloody drudge if yer ask me, Daisy. She'd be better off back at Dock'ead.'

The storm had passed over and rainwater ran along the gutters and gurgled down into the drains. Inside the Railway Inn the noise of the pounding piano and singing had become louder. In the quieter snug bar the two old ladies had finished their drinks and were arguing about whose turn it was to get the next round.

'You got the last one, Daisy. It's my turn,' Lil said, reaching down to the large handbag at her feet.

'No, you got the last one, Lil. I'll get this one,' Daisy replied, sorting out some silver from a small purse.

Bert had already replenished the ladies' glasses and was leaning on the counter, a look of resignation written on his large florid features.

His eyes went up to the ceiling. It's the same every Saturday night with these two, he told himself. They're a couple of con artists. "'Ere, girls, 'ave this one on me,' he said without much enthusiasm.

Daisy looked pleased with herself as she collected the drinks. "'E's a nice feller, is Bert,' she said loudly enough for the landlord to hear as he walked back into the public bar.

'Bloody crafty ole bats,' Bert groaned aloud to his wife Elsie. 'They've done it again.'

In the quiet after the rain had stopped Sally sat beside the fire with the evening paper resting on her lap. Her parents had gone to the Railway Inn and Lora had been out since early evening. Sally welcomed the opportunity of being alone in the house on this wintry night, and as she leaned back in her chair and listened to the dreamy music coming from the wireless she closed her eyes and let her mind wander. Her Saturday evenings had once been very pleasant, she remembered wistfully, especially during her courting days. After a hectic working week at Harrison's she had often looked forward to going to the pictures with Ben, and then maybe having a drink or two in a nearby pub before he walked her to her front door.

Sally sighed and let the sounds of the soft music flow over her. It seemed so long ago now since the two of them had first become more than childhood friends. They had never taken much notice of each other at school and it was not until Sally was in her late teens that Ben

43

began to pay her any special attention. She recalled how Ben had bragged to her about the girls he had taken out and she had sniffed contemptuously and tried hard to ignore him. He was just twenty and had only been working in the docks for a short time. He would wear his cap at a jaunty angle and knot his scarf the way the older dockers did. He had often stood talking to her in the square, his thumbs stuck through his braces, and his easy, infectious laugh would make her heart flutter. She had been nineteen and felt very grown up, but she was still slightly in awe of the good-looking lad who had suddenly started to take an interest in her. Her father was very strict and saw to it that she did not spend too much time talking with the 'flash young pup' as he called him. Sally recalled the time Ben had first asked her out and she'd refused. His reputation with the local girls was well known to her and when he offered to take her to the pictures she told him that she already had a date. Ben merely shrugged his shoulders and sauntered off, leaving her feeling red-faced and wild with herself for not taking up his offer.

That night she and her friend Vera were sitting in the Old Kent Picture House when they saw Ben. He was with Barbara Haines who had a reputation locally for being a flirt. Sally remembered how she had slunk down in her seat trying not to let him see her, but Ben spotted the two of them and when the show was over he gave her and Vera a big grin as he walked past, arm in arm with Barbara. Sally knew that Ben was bound to tease her and try to make her jealous the next time she saw him, and she vowed to herself that she would refuse him again when he asked her out, but for a long time he did not come around. When he finally made an appearance along with a few of his young friends he seemed reluctant to talk to her. Sally smiled briefly to herself as she recalled how her interest in him had begun to develop. She had gone out of her way to talk to him then, much to her parents' dismay. They had always felt that Ben was cheeky and disrespectful as a child, and a bad influence on the other children. They saw him now as being arrogant and too self-assured. But Sally ignored their warnings that he was the sort of young man who got girls into trouble and had let him see that she was interested in him.

It was her twentieth birthday when Ben finally asked her again for a date and she lost no time making up her mind to accept his offer. It had been a lovely evening, she recalled. Ben had given her her first real romantic kiss in the darkness of the cinema, and then after sauntering into the King's Arms pub with her holding tightly on to his arm and buying her a gin and lime he had walked her home. Sally remembered how her head had been swimming from the unaccustomed drink that evening, and she had allowed him to hold her tight and kiss her passionately as they stood in her doorway. They had been abruptly interrupted when her father had called out in a gruff voice for her to come in and shut the door. She had already fallen in love with Ben, although at first he would never admit to her what his true feelings were. Sally knew there was a sensitive side to him behind his swaggering image – she had never forgotten, when they were children, how he'd braved the sharp claws of a maddened cat to remove the tin can the local bullies had tied to its tail – and so that he would not feel he was becoming trapped she hid her feelings from him for a long time. Their relationship had developed slowly, but one sunny Sunday afternoon she discovered that he had childishly carved their initials on the sycamore tree in the square.

Sally smiled sadly to herself as she sat in the quiet room listening to the wireless and thinking about the past. Ben had always found it hard to put his feelings into words, and he would easily become embarrassed when he tried to talk about his own emotions, but like the crudely carved heart and initials on the tree he had always found touching little ways of letting her know that he loved her. She remembered with a deep sense of loss how happy she and Ben had been when they were first married, and how Ben had tried so hard to be a perfect husband, before their marriage fell to pieces around them.

A red-hot cinder tumbled into the hearth and Sally picked up the fire-tongs to replace it. The wireless crackled and distant thunder rolled. Sally leaned back in her chair and sighed deeply.

Later that dark, wet night, while the Carey sisters were listening to *Saturday Night Theatre* on the wireless, Muriel Taylor came back home.

46

Harriet heard giggling and the sound of an empty milk bottle being kicked over. She got up and peered carefully through the heavy curtains into the street below. She turned and looked at Juliet, her face grey with horror. 'It's her. Muriel. She's got men with her!' she gasped.

Juliet tut-tutted. She had missed hearing the detective announce the identity of the murderer. 'Really, Harriet. It's none of our business,' she said irritably, becoming secretly curious about just what Muriel had planned for that particular evening. She was still wondering when they both retired to bed.

The Robinson family were gathered together in their front parlour discussing the Prime Minister's speech which had just ended. It was a Sunday evening and the news was that Singapore had fallen to the Japanese. Charlie was sitting back in his chair beside the low-burning fire, a serious look on his face. 'It's bad news,' he said angrily. 'The bloody place was s'posed ter be impregnable. Jus' shows yer. I pity them poor bastards what survived. Them Japs are wicked gits.'

Lora was sitting beside her boyfriend Bernard and she winced at her father's strong language. Bernard glanced at Lora, his pale, weak face taking on a pained expression. His light blue eyes were heavy-lidded, and a strand of unruly fair hair hung down over his high forehead. Bernard was twenty-one and had just finished a college course in accountancy. He had had to register for military service and was very concerned about what the future held for him.

Annie was sitting in the other fireside chair facing her husband and she looked up from her knitting. 'I bet George Tapley's worried out of 'is life over them two boys,' she said. 'Young Laurie's in the Far East.'

Charlie nodded. 'I was talkin' to 'im in the pub yesterday. 'E ain't 'eard from 'im fer some time.'

'What about 'is eldest lad, Tony?' Annie asked. ''E's in the Middle East, ain't 'e?'

'Yeah. George told me Tony's a corporal now,' Charlie answered as he stretched his legs out in front of the fire.

Sally had been sitting at the table sorting through a pile of buttons and bits and pieces she had tipped out of the sewing basket. She looked up and caught the exchanged glances between her sister and Bernard. 'You gonna put the kettle on, Lora? I wanna get on wiv this,' she said sharply.

Annie got up. 'I'll do it,' she said, putting down her knitting.

Lora made no attempt to get up and Sally gave her sister a withering look. Charlie tapped his pipe against the heel of his boot and turned to Bernard. 'Yer know what that means, don't yer?' he said quickly.

Bernard looked at him blankly. 'What's that, Mr Robinson?'

Charlie jerked his thumb in the direction of the wireless set. 'Well, what they've jus' said about Singapore fallin'. It means we've lost

48

anovver base. We ain't got many in the Far East as it is, wivout losin' Singapore.'

Bernard's eyes widened. 'Oh,' he said simply.

'Bernard's registered fer service, 'aven't yer, Bernard,' Lora prompted.

The young lad looked embarrassed, and Charlie took advantage of his discomfort. 'I s'pose you're gonna volunteer fer the Pay Corps or somefing, you bein' a qualified accountant now,' he said mockingly.

Bernard sat up straight. 'As a matter of fact I've put down for the Air Force,' he answered proudly.

'Yer gonna fly then?' Charlie asked sarcastically. 'Yer gonna be a pilot?'

Bernard smiled at Lora. 'I've put down to be a navigator. You need to have a qualification in maths to be a navigator.'

Charlie looked into the fire. 'Oh, I see,' he said slowly, unimpressed.

Sally glanced over at her father and then over to Bernard. She felt sorry for the lad. He was forever being goaded by her father and his face showed his discomfort by flushing up a deep red. Lora was getting angry, and she did little to ease her boyfriend's discomfort by saying, 'Bernard passed the accountancy exam wiv top marks, didn't yer, Bern.'

Charlie ignored her indignant tone and leaned towards the fire with a rolled up piece of paper. He lit his pipe and brushed the shower of sparks from his waistcoat. His face took on a happy expression as he puffed on his briar, and when Annie appeared with the teapot and cups

49

balanced on a wooden tray he resumed his attack. 'Our Bernard's passed wiv flyin' colours, Mum. 'E's come top o' the class,' he said drily.

Annie smiled. 'That's nice for yer, Bernard,' she said, putting down the tray and laying out the cups.

''E's goin' in the Air Force, Annie. Gonna be a navigator, ain't yer Bernard?' Charlie went on, the sneer evident in his tone.

Lora looked at her father with disgust showing on her face. 'If you're not careful you'll catch yer boots alight,' she said quickly.

Charlie moved his feet back from the fire and glanced over at his younger daughter. He could see the anger on her pretty face and he felt a little sorry for goading Bernard, but the lad irked him. He seemed to have little spirit and was completely under his daughter's influence. Charlie thought how different his two daughters were. Lora was the more domineering, and he felt that she had been getting a little too above herself since she got her job in a City office. Sally, on the other hand, was quiet and patient and she very rarely complained about anything. They were different in looks, too. Lora was fair-haired and blue-eyed and the prettier of the two, but Sally had a kind face and a pleasant personality. She was easy-going and seemed to accept things for what they were. Charlie felt some relief that his eldest daughter had made a firm break from her husband, but he knew there was still much sadness that the girl kept locked up inside her.

Annie was pouring the tea and Charlie

watched her, puffing thoughtfully on his pipe. "'E's a nice man, that George Tapley,' Annie said, as if to break the silence. 'So was 'is wife Sadie. Shame the way she went.'

"'Ow did she go, Mum?' Lora asked.

'It was complications after young Laurie was born,' Annie said, adding sugar to the cups. 'George brought those two boys up all on 'is own. I must say they're both a credit to 'im. When they was kids they was never any trouble, was they, farver?'

Charlie nodded. 'I thought 'e'd 'ave got spliced again, jus' fer the boys' sake. I mean, they 'ardly knew their muvver.'

Annie passed around the tea. 'I fink everybody expected 'im an' Ginny Almond next door would 'ave got tergevver. I mean, there's 'er, a widow, wiv five young kids an' 'er ole muvver ter look after.'

Charlie laughed. 'She ain't a widow. Frankie Almond pissed orf years ago, an' Granny Almond is Frankie's muvver, not 'ers.'

Lora had gulped down her tea and was hurrying Bernard along. 'We'd better dash if we're gonna get in ter see the first picture,' she said, looking up at the clock on the mantelshelf.

Sally had finished tidying up the sewing-basket and was scanning through the *News of the World*. Charlie had said he was off to the pub for a pint before it closed and Annie was sitting listening to the wireless. The music ended and the announcer's voice introduced a talk on how to make the food rations go further. Annie groaned and twiddled with the knobs of the set. The sound of hymn-singing filled the room and she quickly turned the wireless off.

Sally folded the paper and looked over at her mother. 'Vera's mum told me she saw yer talkin' ter Ben yesterday, Mum,' she said suddenly.

Annie picked up her knitting. 'Yeah, 'e stopped me in the street,' she answered without looking up. ''E just asked 'ow yer was. Told me ter say 'ello. I didn't say anyfing, case it upset yer.'

Sally sighed deeply. 'Yer should 'ave told me, Mum. It wouldn't 'ave upset me. It's all over between us. It 'as bin fer some time.'

The room was quiet, except for the clicking sound of Annie's steel needles. After a while she said, 'Me an' yer Dad thought yer might 'ave got back tergevver again.'

Sally stared down at the folded newspaper on the table in front of her. 'No, it's final,' she said quietly.

'I was sayin' ter yer farver it might 'ave bin different if you'd 'ave 'ad a child,' Annie said, pausing in her knitting to pull a length of wool from the bag at her feet. 'Children keep a marriage tergevver, I always say. A marriage is no good wivout children.'

Sally felt the bitterness rising up and she ran her fingers down the back of her short dark hair. 'We tried, Mum. It jus' wasn't ter be. We both wanted children.'

Annie put down her knitting. 'It's the way it goes sometimes,' she said.

The clock showed ten minutes to ten and its

52

ticking sounded loudly in the quiet room. Sally watched as her mother picked up her knitting once more and started to count the stitches, her eyes squinting behind her metal-rimmed glasses. A suffocating feeling of depression weighed down on Sally as she stared into the fire. Was she destined to spend the rest of her life in this house, she wondered in a moment of despair, growing old slowly and without a man's love? She would have to make the break soon and leave the family home to find herself a flat somewhere or it would be too late to change anything. The clicking of the metal knitting-needles and the ticking of the clock seemed to become louder, counting out the seconds of her life as they slipped away from her for ever, and a sudden desperate panic welled up within her. With a sharp pang she thought of her decision never to go back to Ben. He wanted her to come home. He had told her often enough when they had first parted. He had often been waiting for her when she left work or when she went shopping at the market. He had said that she was the only one he cared for and begged her to forgive him, but she had made it clear how resolute she was and gradually he had stopped meeting her.

Sally breathed heavily. When the sudden moment of panic passed she began to think about the decision she had made. It had been hard, even though the hurt and anger at what he had done made her bitter. They had been blissfully happy at first. Ben had told her many times during their early days together that all his past girlfriends had meant nothing to him and he had eyes only for her. Sally had been convinced of his sincerity, and it seemed hard to believe now how everything could have changed so quickly as the war clouds gathered and Ben talked more and more of volunteering for the army. He had said that they should not consider having children the way things were and it was then that the rows started. Sally recalled the bitterness and disappointment she felt, and how she had accused him of being selfish and putting his pride before their happiness. He had been furious with her for not understanding that he would feel like a coward if he spent the war in a reserved job at home. Sally felt her anger rising as she thought about those early rows. She had not been able to make him see that he would be doing a vital job and it would at least be better than going off to fight and maybe getting killed or maimed.

On the day after war had been declared Ben volunteered, and he had been shocked and angered when he was turned down for military service because of a perforated eardrum. He became morose and angry at being rejected for the army, and it was only after much prompting by Sally that he reluctantly agreed to start a family. By the following spring Sally had still not become pregnant, and it was then that Ben turned to drink.

It had started slowly with him stopping off for a pint or two after work, but his drinking had soon got out of hand and often he had staggered home and fallen into bed after merely picking at his tea. The rows had become more frequent and

54

their lovemaking was by then a rare event. Sally remembered becoming convinced that Ben was seeing someone else, and she could still feel as if it were yesterday the pain and anguish she had suffered when she came home from work early one afternoon and found him in *her* bed with Barbara Haines, one of his past girlfriends.

It had been the end of their life together. She had hurried from the house and walked the streets for hours until, finally drained of all feeling, she had sunk exhausted on to a park bench and fallen into a fitful sleep.

As soon as she could collect her things she took lodgings in Dockhead and made a firm resolution never to go back to Ben after the terrible humiliation she had suffered. Sally shuddered as she recalled those weeks she had spent alone in the dingy flat. When Lora called to tell her of their mother's illness she had welcomed the excuse to return to her family home, if only to escape the sheer loneliness of her situation. Now she knew that being with her family could not help her to forget what she had lost, and as the days slipped slowly by she was becoming less and less able to face the future with any kind of confidence.

The clock chimed the hour and she saw her mother's head jerk and her sleepy eyes glance up at the mantelshelf. Without saying a word Sally left the warm parlour and climbed the stairs to her bedroom.

In the small back room Bill Freeman put down his large eye-glass and closed the book he was reading. The candle had burned low and was beginning to sputter. He got up and walked to the window to stretch his cramped legs and as he did so the candle went out. The room was in darkness, except for the small amount of light from the landing which came under the door. The old man peered through the curtains at the black night outside and then he turned back to the cabinet and fumbled for a new candle. When he had finally managed to light it Bill opened the cabinet drawer and took out his box. Seating himself at the table, he slowly opened the lid of the box and removed the contents. He shivered and pulled his shabby overcoat tighter around his shoulders as he picked up the magnifying glass and studied the old photograph that was lying on the top of the papers. It was of his father. The man wore baggy trousers which were tied beneath the knee. His collarless shirt was open at the front and the sleeves were rolled up over his brawny arms. The man's face looked stern and a thick moustache covered his mouth. He held a long pitchfork in his hand and behind him was a loaded hay wain. Bill put the faded photograph to one side and started to sift through the bits and pieces. He found the folded marriage certificate which was almost in pieces. He looked at the small blue envelope and took out the folded piece of matching paper. His tired eyes squinted in the light of the flickering candle as he read the letter once more.

The candle had burned for some time and a thin trickle of wax had run down to the holder. Outside the wind had risen and it rattled the small windowpane. The old man stared into the moving, conical flame and he saw her face clearly. She was young, with hair the colour of straw. Her eyes mocked him and her pretty mouth was parted, revealing her small white teeth. She stood, hands on hips, her long dress reaching down to her tiny feet. He was coming towards her over the grassy mound and her smile grew wider. He saw her, too, as she sat in the rocking-chair and he heard the rhythmical grating as the rails moved back and forth over the stone floor. The baby slept peacefully in her arms and her gentle crooning was sweet to his ears. The candle danced in the draught and he saw the men coming over the hilly mound. They wore long frock-coats and their black top hats were smooth and shiny. He heard the wailing as he led the small procession down the cobbled lane. He felt the icy wind on his face and saw the flakes of snow sticking to the men's hats as they led the way up the rising path. Bill sighed deeply as he stared into the flame. The distant sound of a night train into London Bridge station reached his ears and he saw the fields slipping by and the steam from the engine floating over the furrows like balls of cotton wool and evaporating. He heard the bustle and remembered his fear as people jostled around him and noisy traffic filled the strange London streets. All that remained of his past was the small bundle of papers he carried in his inside pocket, and the key to a new life in the big city was the one letter he had with him. He recalled the huge, frightening building, with its high dusty windows which turned the light of the sun brown as it filtered through the grimy panes. He smelled the stench of the tannery pits and saw the large animal skins hanging on the stretching frames. He felt again the sharp pain of his grief and the almost overwhelming desire to rush back again to the rolling countryside and the old stone cottage above the cobbled lane. Bill gave out a long, low sigh, and his head sank down on to his chest.

The first light of dawn was creeping up over the rooftops and the birds were awake when Bill climbed into his cold bed. The few words he had written were sealed in a brown envelope and safely stowed in the old tin box. He was satisfied that his affairs were now in order and he felt relieved. The old man did not sleep, instead he lay thinking of the many years he had spent in the Bermondsey leather trade and of various lodgings he had had in the area. It was in 1937, the year of his retirement, that he moved in with the Robinsons and he considered that the years he had spent with them had been happy ones. The family had allowed him to live his life the way he wanted and had looked after him very well. His meals had always been taken to his room and no one minded that he did not eat at the family table. Bill liked eating alone. He realised that it must seem rather strange to the Robinsons, his reading by candlelight when there was gas and electricity available. When he first moved in he had said that gas fumes tightened up his chest and made it difficult for him to breathe and reading by electric light caused him to suffer bad headaches, and his request to be supplied with candles had been complied with. Bill kept himself quietly to himself, but he enjoyed Sally's company now that she had moved back home. She said very little about her life and Bill understood. He himself preferred to leave the past behind, and the occasional chats they had together were happy and lighthearted. Now he had told Sally about the tin box he felt content, and his one simple hope was that he would live long enough to see the end of the war.

Chapter Three

SALLY left her house at seven-thirty on Monday morning and met Vera in the square. The two women usually went off to work together and on this particular morning Sally noticed that her friend looked a little long-faced. Most mornings it was Vera who did most of the chatting, but on this occasion Vera seemed unwilling to talk. They left the square and turned left along Stanley Street, walking arm in arm under the long arch. There were two wine bottling stores under the railway arches, and at this time of the morning vehicles were loading and unloading. The warehouse lads and drivers invariably called out and made ribald comments as the two women passed by and Vera usually had a quick answer, but this morning she ignored the asides.

Sally glanced at her friend as they emerged from the arch. 'You OK?' she asked.

Vera gave her friend a wan smile. 'I'm fed up, Sal,' she said. 'It's me mum. She's bin nagging away again about me goin' out while Joe's away. We 'ad a bust-up before I came out this mornin'. She reckons I'm not bein' fair to 'im. I couldn't make 'er see there was nufink in it. Jimmy Kent knows I'm almost engaged. It's all above board.'

Sally laughed. 'I thought yer was gonna tell me yer was pregnant or somefing.'

Sally felt the pressure of Vera's hand tightening on her arm. 'Don't joke, Sally,' she said. 'I might be.'

'You overdue?' Sally gasped.

'Nearly a week now.'

Sally looked at her friend's worried face. 'You an' Joe?'

'Who else?' Vera said quickly.

They had reached the Jamaica Road and stood waiting at the tram stop. 'It was a smashin' week,' Vera was saying. 'Me an' Joe spent a lot o' time tergevver. He'd bin away fer nearly three months. We couldn't keep our 'ands off each ovver. It was a long time ter go wivout, Sal.' Sally's bitter smile made Vera wince. 'I'm sorry,' she said, squeezing her friend's arm. 'That was a stupid fing ter say.'

Sally laughed. 'It's all right. It don't worry me now. I've got used ter bein' on me own.'

A number 70 tram drew up and the two friends clambered aboard. They found a seat on the lower deck, and as the tram rattled away from the stop Vera fished into her handbag for

60

the fare. 'I've got that feelin' I'm carryin', Sal. I'm never late an' I feel sort o' different.'

'It's yer imagination,' Sally said, grinning. 'It's too early ter feel any different – ain't it?'

The two laughed and as the conductor came along the aisle Vera held out four pennies. She seemed to have recovered some of her spryness. 'Gawd knows what me mum's gonna say if I am. She'll swear blind it's Jimmy Kent's,' she grinned.

The tram clattered around the bend at Dockhead and pulled up. The area had been badly damaged by the bombing and on either side of the road ruined houses and shops stood empty. On the wall of a wrecked house someone had chalked 'Second Front Now'. The tram pulled away from the stop and Sally stared out of the window. She recalled how only last year she had been desperate to get pregnant, and now here was Vera talking about having her first baby.

The tram had crossed the Tower Bridge Road and stopped outside the factory in Tooley Street. The two friends hurried down from the tram and in through the open doors of the Harrison factory. They joined the queue of women waiting to clock on and soon they were sitting at their machines.

Harrison's was a long-established firm which made military uniforms and the company was currently busy with a contract for army battle-dress. Inside the factory huge piles of khaki material were piled on wooden pallets set against the walls, and between the large industrial

61

sewing machines stacks of partly finished battledress blouses awaited completion. The two friends occupied adjacent spaces and although the clatter and din made it hard to talk they managed to make themselves understood. At eight o'clock exactly the factory whistle sounded and the machinery started up. Vera was working away, her head bent down over the noisy machine as she guided the thick material under the presser foot, her bottom lip constantly pouting as it usually did when she was concentrating.

High on a wall facing them was a large clock which the factory girls tried hard not to notice. For the past few weeks Sally had been finding it increasingly difficult to keep her eyes off it. The hands seemed to be moving backwards as she constantly glanced up at them. She was finding it harder and harder to apply herself to her work. She had been employed at Harrison's for the past five years and although the job was tedious she had always been able to cope. At first the pace had been slower and the tasks varied. When the war broke out, however, the work had been classed as essential to the war effort and things changed. An hour was added to the working day and government inspectors were appointed to increase efficiency. It was very difficult to leave for another job under the new regulations, unless it was other essential war work. Sally found herself trapped in a soul-destroying job which left her feeling exhausted by the end of the day. Her state of mind only made things worse. She often found herself going over and over the past, and as the anger and self-pity welled up inside her she wanted to scream out and run from the building. It was only Vera's lively mischievousness that drew her out of her misery. She was constantly chatting above the noise of the machinery, and during the lunch hour break when they went to the firm's canteen it was Vera who kept the laughter flowing.

At twelve noon the factory whistle sounded and the women hurried to the floor above for their lunch. Sally and Vera found a couple of places at a table near the window. Two of the older women sat at the end of the table and Maggie Chandler sat opposite them. Fat Maggie, as many of the workers called her, was the butt of Harrison's. She was in her early twenties and spoke in a dull, monotonous voice. Her straight black hair was held back from her forehead with hairclips and her brown eyes peered out through thick-lensed spectacles. Her face was flat and there were two red patches on her cheeks which grew larger when she got excited. Although Maggie was the laughing stock of the factory everyone knew that she was the fastest machinist there. The factory women were constantly trying to marry the poor girl off and any new male who arrived at Harrison's was quickly pointed out to Maggie, who would then flush alarmingly.

The two older women sitting at the table were not generally liked by the rest of the girls. They did not join in the fun and were considered to be rather strait-laced. Vera nudged Sally as the two women went on with their usual moaning. 'I think it's downright disgusting the way some of these young girls carry on,' the larger of the two women was saying. 'I mean to say, they've got their husbands away at the war and they're out and about at every opportunity.'

'You're right, Flo,' her friend replied. 'It's disgusting.'

Flo glanced at Maggie who was busy cutting her sausage in half and patted her newly permed hair. 'I wouldn't allow a girl of mine to carry on the way some of these young women do. They smoke in the street and wear lipstick and rouge. Proper little tarts, some of them.'

'You're right, Flo. Proper little tarts,' Doris said.

Jimmy Kent had spotted Vera and he came over with his plate of sausage and mash, sitting himself at the other end of the table. ''Ello, Vera. Good dance, wasn't it?' he grinned.

Vera's eyes had a wicked look as they flashed to the two women and back at Jimmy. 'It wasn't bad. I got told off when I got in, though,' she said in a loud voice. 'Me mum said two o'clock in the mornin' was far too late ter get in from a dance.'

Jimmy caught the look in Vera's eyes and he tried to hide his grin. 'Did she know it finished at twelve?' he asked, looking down at his sausage.

Flo gave Doris a meaningful look. 'Do you know, when I was a young girl I had to be in by ten o'clock,' she said severely. 'My father would take the belt to me if I was a minute later than ten. There's no respect for parents now.'

64

'You're right, Flo. There's no respect,' Doris said as she rearranged the food in front of her.

Vera had heard enough and a mischievous look came into her eyes. She pushed her plate back and looked at Jimmy Kent. 'Jimmy, I fink I'm pregnant!' she said suddenly.

Jimmy flushed slightly and Sally burst out laughing. Maggie stopped chewing her sausage and her eyes widened with surprise as she stared at Vera. The two older women looked at each other in shocked disbelief at what they had heard.

'Well, don't look at me,' Jimmy said, his face a bright red. 'It's nufing ter do wiv me. I didn't do it.'

Vera got up from the table, a petulant look on her face. 'I need some air,' she said haughtily. 'Comin' fer a walk, Sal?'

Jimmy had lowered his head over his plate, not quite understanding just what Vera was up to, and Maggie Chandler was still staring, her knife and fork held in the air over her forgotten plate. The two older women watched with shocked faces as the two friends walked away from the table, and then Flo vigorously patted her hair down once more. 'What was I saying to you? It's scandalous the way these young girls carry on,' she said, fiddling with the knife and fork on her plate.

Doris merely nodded and Jimmy hurriedly left the table. Maggie realised that the excitement was over for the time being and she suddenly remembered her last sausage.

Vera took Sally's arm as they strolled along

Tooley Street. 'Did yer see their faces, Sal?' she laughed. 'I thought they was gonna chuck a fit.'

Sally shook her head slowly. 'Vera, you're gettin' worse. They'll put it all round the factory. And poor Jimmy. Yer got 'im right embarrassed.'

Vera chuckled. 'Well, it made me so mad listenin' ter them two ole bats goin' on. Anyway, I don't care. If I am in the club everybody'll know soon enough.'

Sally glanced at her friend and saw the look of resignation on her face. 'What about Joe?' she asked. 'Will 'e marry yer?'

Vera sighed. 'Yeah. 'E wants us ter get married. We'll 'ave ter do it quick, though. Mum's gonna be upset about me not 'avin' a white weddin', an' dad'll jus' pull a face an' go back to 'is paper. Still, yer know that ole song, "It's the rich what gets the pleasure, it's the poor what gets the blame". C'mon, let's get back ter the treadmill.'

At number 3 Paragon Place Monday morning was just like any other for Ginny Almond. She had served breakfast for her five children, and the youngest of the brood, Jenny, who had just started school, had toddled off happily with Sara who was seven and Billy who had just had his tenth birthday. The two eldest, Frankie who was coming up twelve and Arthur who was thirteen, were at the local secondary school and they had gone off leaving Ginny worried about how she was going to find the money for two pairs of football boots. Money had been very short in the

Almond household since her husband left her. Ginny did early morning office cleaning and any other extra work which came her way.

Recently Ginny had heard about home work and one day she had hurried to a factory in Jamaica Road which had started sending out display cards. After waiting in the queue for over an hour she had come home with Sara's old pram laden down with heavy bundles of cardboard. All day long Ginny threaded the elastic through the punched holes in the display boards, breaking off only to get the children's meals, and late that evening after all her children had been tucked up in bed she took stock. By her reckoning she had earned the less than princely sum of two shillings and sixpence. Ginny was disappointed, but she decided to finish the work. The next day she started early and her mother-in-law Daisy offered to help. Ginny found that she had to constantly correct the old lady's efforts, and at the end of that day the two of them together had earned just two shillings. Ginny decided then to try some other means of earning a little extra money, and when she heard from one of her friends that a firm in Tower Bridge Road was sending out work she decided to give it a try. The work entailed painting faces on moulded toy soldiers. The soldiers were only an inch tall and the task was tedious. When the blob of cream paint was dry two dots of black ink had to be applied as eyes. Granny Almond's eyesight prevented her from doing the work but the two eldest lads were eager to help. Paint got spilled and some of the soldiers had faces on the backs of their heads and huge eyes. The firm paid one shilling and fourpence per box of one thousand soldiers, and after she had spent two days completing one box Ginny again took stock. Arthur had paint over his pullover and Frankie had blobs of ink over his only pair of school trousers. The younger children had been left to their own devices and had caused havoc. Ginny decided there and then that home work was not for her and she had resigned herself to office cleaning.

On that Monday morning Ginny sat in her front parlour darning a pair of young Frankie's socks. Ginny was in her mid-forties, a cheerful woman despite having been left to bring up her brood by a husband who had walked out on her not long after Jenny was born. Ginny was short and had a well-rounded figure. Her mousy hair was untidy and often gathered up carelessly into a hair-net, and her friendly blue eyes stared out of a round, rosy face. She was always popping into the Robinsons', and when she occasionally went out to do some extra cleaning jobs during the evening Sally would look in to make sure the children were all right. Ginny had one other friend who she often visited for a chat, and it had started the tongues wagging.

George Tapley, her next door neighbour at number 2, was a dapper widower in his early fifties. George was vaguely aware of Ginny's interest in him but he had become set in his ways over the years. An emotional involvement was out of the question as far as he was concerned. Ginny, on the other hand, felt differently. She had definite designs on the quiet man and had decided to play her hand very carefully. It had been a frustrating time since her man left her and she was a hot-blooded woman by her own admission. She felt that George could be tempted out of his celibate state if she handled him carefully. Be patient, Ginny, she told herself. He'll come around one day.

Granny Almond had been over to see her long-time friend Lillian Allen and when she walked back into the room she flopped down into her favourite chair and kicked off her shoes. "Ere, Ginny. I jus' bin talkin' to Lil Allen. She got stopped by that Carey woman,' she said, puffing as she reached down to put her shoes on the brass fender.

'Which one was that then, Daisy?' Ginny asked, not taking her eyes from her darning.

'Why, that funny one, 'Arriet,' Daisy said. 'She was tellin' me that Muriel Taylor brought two blokes back on Saturday night.'

Ginny looked up at her mother-in-law and grinned. 'Good fer 'er. She should 'ave brought one over ter me.'

Daisy folded her hands in her lap. 'It's not funny, Gin. 'Arriet's terrified of what's goin' on. That Muriel brings all sorts o' blokes back. It's frightenin' the life out o' the woman.'

'What's she got ter be frightened of?' Ginny asked. 'Long as they're not interfering wiv 'er.'

'What she's frightened of is in case they come up 'er stairs,' Daisy replied curtly. 'I mean, it's easy done. She was almost cryin' when she was talkin' ter me. She said 'er an' 'er sister could be

69

murdered in their beds.'

Ginny laughed aloud. 'C'mon, Daisy. The men wouldn't be interested in the Carey sisters, an' besides, I expect Muriel knows who she's bringin' back. It's one way of earnin' a few bob. I bin finkin' about it meself.'

Daisy looked shocked. 'Yer don't mean it do yer, Ginny?' she asked anxiously. 'It's not right fer a woman ter carry on that way.'

'What way, Daisy?'

'Well, sellin' 'er body. Men are animals where that sort o' fing's concerned.'

Ginny enjoyed shocking the old lady. 'It depends 'ow much it means ter yer,' she said thoughtfully. 'An' after all, some women are more broadminded than ovvers.'

Daisy pinched her lips together with distaste. 'Well, I'm against that sort o' carryin' on,' she said firmly. 'An' besides, it's givin' the place a bad name.'

Ginny snorted. 'Givin' the place a bad name? Paragon Place got a bad name years ago. What about that drunken ole sod Alf Porter at number 5? What about the time you found 'im layin' in the square wiv 'is trouser fronts all open an' showin' everyfing? An' what about the rows an' fights 'er at number 9 'as wiv 'er next-door neighbour? At least Muriel does what she does indoors.'

Daisy lapsed into silence, and after a few moments Ginny rolled up the sock she was working on. 'I'm gonna pop next door, Daisy,' she said. 'I wanna 'ave a word wiv George. Put the kettle on, will yer? I won't be long.'

A little while later Ginny was sitting in George Tapley's front room, a cup of tea balanced in her lap. George sat opposite her with a worried look on his pale, thin face. 'I'm expectin' the worst, Ginny,' he said sadly. 'I'm dreadin' the messenger boy ter come pedallin' down the square.'

Ginny looked down at the tea dust floating in her cup. 'I shouldn't worry too much, George,' she said comfortingly. 'Young Laurie's all right, mark me words. Letters take a long time ter get from the Far East, don't they?'

George picked up the poker and raked over the glowing embers. 'The last letter I got from 'im was back in November. It come from Bombay. Gawd knows where 'e is now. I'm worried case 'e got sent ter Singapore. I 'ad a dream last night, an' I don't dream very often, but I could see young Laurie large as life. 'E was layin' on a stretcher wiv 'is 'ead all bandaged up. I tell yer, it was clear as day. I woke up in a pool o' sweat. I don't like dreams, they can be omens.'

Ginny laughed. 'Yer don't believe all that twaddle, do yer, George? Dreams don't mean anyfing. It's only what's on yer mind. Yer was worryin' about the boy an' yer prob'ly went ter sleep finkin' about 'im.'

'P'r'aps you're right, Gin,' he said taking up his tea. 'It is bloody worryin', though. What wiv Laurie, an' me eldest boy Tony out in the Middle East.'

Ginny looked hard at the man and felt she wanted to take hold of him and squeeze him to

71

her. George felt uncomfortable under her steady gaze and he sipped his tea noisily.

'Are yer workin' ternight, George?' she asked suddenly.

George shook his head. 'No, I'm on again on Wednesday night,' he replied. 'The council's took over one o' those tannery ware'ouses fer storin' people's furniture an' I'm doin' me shift down there Wednesday.'

'It mus' be a miserable job bein' a night watchman, George,' she said.

He smiled. 'I've got used to it now. I take a good book an' me evenin' paper. I can brew me tea when I want to an' I get a visit now an' then from the night bobbie. It ain't so bad.'

Ginny had finished her tea and as her eyes travelled around the small room she noticed that the picture of George's wife was missing from its usual spot on the sideboard. Ginny wondered why it should have been removed. Maybe he had put it out of sight for her benefit, she thought. Maybe he was beginning to have feelings for her and wanted to let her know.

George's sharp eyes spotted her staring at the sideboard. 'I broke Sadie's picture last night,' he said sadly. 'I was tidyin' up an' it sort of fell out o' me 'ands. Course, that got me finkin'. Was it an omen, I asked myself?'

'You're a superstitious ole fool, George Tapley,' Ginny chided him gently. 'Yer shouldn't dwell on such fings.'

George laughed. 'P'r'aps I am superstitious,' he said bashfully.

'That job o' yours don't 'elp neivver,' Ginny

said, waving her finger at him. 'You've got too much time ter fink. Them gloomy ole ware'ouses are enough ter give yer the creeps.'

'Yer should 'ave bin wiv me last Monday night,' he said with a chuckle. 'I was at that big ole ware'ouse back o' the Grange Road. It's full o' people's furniture from the bombed 'ouses. There's beddin', wardrobes, sideboards, you name it they've got it. Now on the ground floor they've got a load o' pianers. Some's got the lids missin' and ovvers 'ave got the casin' all busted. Proper mess they're in. Mind you, some of 'em ain't got a scratch on 'em. Anyway, I was sittin' in the office readin' me paper an' I 'ears this pianer start playin' on the floor below. Now you know I'm not a nervous bloke normally, but I tell yer, Ginny, me old 'eart started goin' ten ter the dozen. I gets up an' grabs me torch an' a crowbar fer protection an' down I goes. The whole place is in darkness. The lights ain't workin' an' it smells sort of musty. Proper creepy, it was. Well, I shines me torch an' shouts out, "Who's there?" The tinklin' still goin' on. It wasn't a tune, more like somebody runnin' their fingers over the keys. So I shines me torch in the direction o' the noise an' all of a sudden I see it.'

Ginny's eyes were open wide. 'What was it?' she gasped.

'A bloody great rat. Big as this, it was,' George said, holding his hands out in front of him. 'Jus' runnin' over the keys, large as life. Was I relieved. Anyway, I aimed the crowbar at it an' it scampered away. I don't fink I did the

73

pianer much good. I was still a bit shaky when I got back ter me office so I decides ter make meself a nice cup o' tea. I was waitin' fer the kettle ter boil when strike me if I don't 'ear a wardrobe creak open. I reached fer me crowbar an' I suddenly realised I'd aimed it at the rat, so I put the lock on the door an' brewed me tea.'

Ginny shivered. 'What was it, anuvver rat?'

George laughed aloud. 'I don't fink so, Ginny. I don't fink a rat could reach the door knob. No, it must 'ave bin the furniture dryin' out. Wood shrinks when it dries. I s'pose the door was jammed an' as it dried out it freed itself.'

Ginny put her cup down and stood up. 'Well, I'd better get goin',' she said with a sigh. 'The kids'll be 'ome fer their dinner soon. 'Ere, I bin finkin', George. 'Ow about you an' me goin' out fer a drink one night. Who knows, yer might get pissed an' try yer arm,' she laughed, digging him playfully in the ribs with her elbow.

'Yeah, I'd like that,' he said, walking with her to the front door. 'It'll give the neighbours somefing ter talk about, won't it?'

She turned at the door. 'What about Saturday night, George?' she asked suddenly. 'Yer don't work Saturdays, do yer?'

'OK,' he replied. 'I'll be ready about eight o'clock, if that's all right wiv you?'

She gave him a big smile. 'Smashin'. Don't ferget what I said about you gettin' pissed.'

He laughed and as he reached for the door handle she kissed him on his cheek and walked quickly out into the square.

74

Sally Brady and Vera Mynott were walking home along Stanley Street that evening when Ben Brady stepped out from the corner shop in front of them. Vera squeezed her friend's arm. 'I'll see yer termorrer, Sal,' she said, giving Ben a quick glance as she walked on. Sally felt her face flush as Ben smiled at her. He looked heavier than she remembered him. His face seemed bloated and there was some puffiness around his pale blue eyes.

'I saw yer comin' along from the shop winder. 'Ow are yer, Sally?' he asked, looking her up and down.

'I'm fine,' she replied coldly as she started to walk on homewards.

Ben stood directly in front of her. 'I've bin finkin' about yer, Sal,' he said, fixing her with his eyes. 'I wanted ter see yer. I'd like us ter talk. We should talk.'

Sally smiled bitterly. 'There's nufing ter say, Ben. We've bin over this before.'

He winced and looked down at his feet. 'Is there somebody else?' he asked quickly, his eyes coming up to meet hers.

'There's nobody. I'm not ready ter start seein' anybody else, even if I wanted to,' she replied wearily.

'We can start again, Sally. We was 'appy once,' he said, reaching out and touching her forearm.

She drew back from his touch. 'I've got ter go,' she said firmly.

'Tell me you'll fink about what I said. We can talk it over,' he said, falling into step beside her.

She sighed. 'It's all bin said, Ben. What more is there ter say?'

As they reached the corner of Paragon Place Ben gripped her arm. Sally felt the strength of his grasp and she looked into his eyes. There was something there which frightened her. She sensed an anger in him, and an uncomfortable feeling gripped her in the pit of her stomach. She had never felt this way before. Even when he had found out where she was living and called round to plead with her, his eyes had not frightened her the way they did now. There was something very strange in his burning stare as he held her arm tightly. 'There's somebody else. You've got somebody else, ain't yer?' he asked in a choked whisper.

'I've just told yer, Ben. There's nobody else,' she said, her voice shaking with emotion.

He held her firmly in his grasp, his eyes narrowing and glaring into hers. She looked along the square hoping that no one was watching, but there were only some children playing around the tree. 'Look, Ben,' she said, twisting her arm so that he had to let go, 'I never wanted it to turn out the way it did. It was you. You played around, not me. You was the one who took somebody else into our bed. I've never bin wiv anuvver man. There was only you, an' there's nobody else. I couldn't face goin' out wiv anybody the way I feel right now, so don't get the idea I've found anuvver feller.'

He saw her distress and anger and shuffled uncomfortably.

'Just tell me you'll fink about what I've said,

and I'll go,' he said flatly.

She nodded reluctantly. 'OK. I'll fink about it,' she replied, in little more than a whisper.

She walked into the square, aware that his eyes were following her. As she reached her front door and pulled on the latch string she glanced back, but he had gone.

As Sally walked into the front parlour and took off her coat Lora looked up from her seat by the fire and gave her sister a quizzical stare. 'You all right?' she asked. 'Yer look white as a sheet.'

Sally sat down and kicked off her shoes. 'I've got a bit of an 'eadache,' she said. 'We've bin busy terday.'

Annie came into the room carrying plates and a tablecloth tucked under her arm. Lora got up to help lay the table and her eyes flashed a message to her mother. Annie looked over to Sally. 'Yer didn't see Ben on yer way 'ome, did yer, Sal?' she asked.

'Ben?'

Annie smoothed the cloth over the wooden table-top. 'Lora said she seen 'im 'angin' around at the paper shop as she came 'ome.'

'Yeah, I did,' Lora said, placing the plates around the table.

Sally stared into the fire. 'Well, I've got nufing ter say to 'im.'

Lora and her mother exchanged glances. The awkward silence in the room was broken by the sound of the front door opening. 'That's yer farver,' Annie said quickly. 'I'd better dish the food up.'

They soon finished the meal and Charlie was sitting back in his chair, an evening paper spread out on his lap. The clatter of plates sounded from the scullery as Lora and her mother got on with the washing up and Sally turned up the wireless set as the six o'clock pips signalled the news broadcast. A deep voice announced more Japanese gains in the Far East and a growing toll of merchant ships being sunk on the North Atlantic food convoys. As the news ended with the threat of more rationing Charlie puffed loudly and folded up his paper. 'It's all bad news, gel,' he sighed. Sally was leaning back in her chair, her eyes riveted on the glowing coals, and she did not answer. Charlie looked over at her, concern showing in his eyes. 'You OK, Sal?' he asked. 'Yer look a bit peaky.'

Sally smiled wanly. 'It's bin a busy day. I'm OK, Dad.'

Charlie sat forward in his chair and fiddled with his tobacco pouch for a while. 'Look, gel, I don't like keep bringin' up the subject, but I reckon you've got the right ter know.'

'Know what?' Sally asked quickly, raising her eyes from the fire.

Charlie fidgeted uncomfortably in his chair. 'Well, it's about that 'usband of yours.'

'What about him, Dad?' Sally prompted, irritation creeping into her voice.

Charlie started to fill his pipe, purposely averting his eyes from his daughter's. 'I got talkin' ter one o' the casuals terday,' he began. ''E knows Ben well an' 'e was workin' wiv 'im last week. This bloke told me that Ben's gone

78

back on the booze. There was a bit of a punch-up on the quayside an' your bloke was involved. I know 'im of old, Sal. Once Ben gets on the turps 'e's trouble. All I'm sayin' is, be careful. Yer mum said 'e's bin 'angin' around 'ere lately. I don't want 'im pesterin' yer, d'yer 'ear me?'

Sally groaned inwardly. She had felt that she was just beginning to get the man out of her system and now she was not being allowed to forget him. She could see more trouble and heartache heading her way and she stared back disconsolately into the fire. Her silence prompted Charlie. 'I never liked the bloke,' he went on, 'but it was your choice, gel. All I'm sayin' is, if 'e starts pesterin' yer, let me know an' I'll sort 'im out, OK?'

Sally nodded briefly. "E won't pester me, Dad. Whatever there was between us is finished. Ben knows that.'

Annie came back into the room and took up her knitting, her glasses perched halfway down her nose. A little later Lora popped her head around the door to say she was going out to meet Bernard. Charlie began to doze in front of the fire, his hands clasped over his middle and his head falling to one side. Sally picked up the evening paper and scanned through it. The news was depressing and the solemn music coming from the wireless did little to cheer her. She knew that her mother rarely had anything to say while she was engrossed in her knitting and she reverted to watching the glowing coals. The day seemed to have dragged terribly, and only the episode in the canteen had brought any relief.

The sudden confrontation she had had with Ben that evening had opened wounds that were far from being healed. Maybe it would be best to find herself a place of her own once more, she thought, or even volunteer for one of the women's services, if she could get her release from Harrison's. Anything would be better than the long grind at the factory and her miserable existence at home. Maybe she should smarten herself up a bit, have her hair done and go out with Vera. Her friend was always encouraging her to get out and enjoy herself.

The fire had burned low and Sally bid her parents goodnight. In the darkness of her back bedroom she lay in bed with her hands clasped behind her head and stared out through the open curtains. She tried to get to sleep but the noises of the house kept her awake. She heard her mother's light step on the stairs as she went to her front bedroom, then the heavy plod of her father and his loud coughing. Later she heard muffled voices and the sound of a key in the lock. She heard her sister Lora go to the bedroom beneath hers and the sound of Bernard's footsteps as he walked out of the square.

The night became quiet and Sally's mind began to race as she stared out at the dark, scurrying clouds. Why did Ben Brady have to show up the way he did? she asked herself. She felt suddenly angry at him for not being able to understand that there could no longer be any future for them together. He would keep on pestering her, trying to force her into talking with him, she realised with a sinking feeling.

Why had she said she would consider meeting him again? She could not imagine having real feelings for another man, but she couldn't go back to Ben, he would be no different than before; he might try to compensate for his failings for a while, but he was Ben. There would be other women. And he could not give her a child, which was the one thing she wanted more than anything on earth. Sally's eyes grew heavy as she tossed and turned, and the room grew darker as clouds covered the new moon. Finally sleep claimed her just as the nightly ritual began in the square below.

Alf Porter had staggered into Paragon Place, his coat unbuttoned and half of his shirt hanging out of his trousers. His trilby was pushed to the back of his head and his mouth hung open as he tried to mumble the words of a song. He progressed slowly, taking two steps forward then one step sideways and a step backwards. He could see his welcoming front door just to the right of the tree and his mouth contorted into a grin. Women had no place in Alf Porter's life. He took himself off to work in Fleet Street every morning and when the newspapers had ceased rolling from the presses Alf went straight into the nearest pub. He caught the last tram from the embankment every night and, with the aid of the conductor, he found himself staggering in the general direction of Stanley Street.

When he neared the Robinsons' front door he stopped and swayed alarmingly as he put his finger to his lips. Even in his befuddled state Alf remembered the time he had sat on the paving-stones beneath the Robinsons' bedroom window, too drunk to get up, singing his own version of 'Eskimo Nell'. Alf plainly recalled the bedroom window flying open and the contents of Charlie's chamber-pot landing on top of him. Ever since that occurrence Alf Porter, master printer, had been very careful not to antagonise the family. He tiptoed past and into his own home.

A few days later Ginny Almond had given her children their tea and was trying on a dress which had been hanging up in her wardrobe for over a year. It was of black satin, calf-length, and had clusters of sequins sewn around the bodice. 'I must 'ave put on weight, Sal,' she said with a long face. 'Just look at it.'

Sally Brady smiled. 'It looks nice. I wish I could fill a dress out like that.'

Ginny twirled around in front of the mirror inside the wardrobe door and brushed a hand down her front. 'I got this orf the tallyman. Gawd knows why I bought it, I've only wore it twice. You sure it looks all right? I don't wanna look like a bundle o' rubbish.'

Ginny's younger daughter Jenny popped her head around the bedroom door. 'Sara won't let me play wiv 'er,' she moaned.

Ginny glared at her child. 'Jenny, go down an' sit quiet. Sally'll be down in a minute.'

The child pulled a face and toddled off down the stairs. Ginny raised her eyes to the ceiling as the sound of loud voices came from the parlour. 'Are you sure yer don't mind keepin' yer eye on 'em?' she asked. 'I shan't be too late. Don't stand no ole truck wiv the boys. The girls won't be no trouble. Jenny an' Sara are always in bed early.'

Sally stood up from the edge of the bed. 'Don't worry, Gin. They'll be OK. You 'ave a nice time.'

Ginny sat at the dressing-table to put on her black high-heeled shoes and then glanced at herself in the mirror. She had used the curling tongs on her thin mousy hair and dabbed her red face with a touch of talcum. Moving nearer to the mirror Ginny wiped a smear of lipstick from the corner of her mouth with her little finger and pulled a face. Well, it's not made much improvement, she sighed to herself.

'Give us a kiss, Mum,' Jenny cried, holding out her arms as her mother came down the stairs.

'Me too,' said Sara, jostling Jenny to one side. 'Now mind me make-up, kids,' Ginny said, reaching down to Jenny. 'Now you be good, all of yer. If I get a bad report from Sally I'm gonna take the belt ter yer, understood?' The boys grinned, and both Sara and Jenny looked serious as their mother went to the door. 'Thanks, Sal. I won't be late,' she said, holding up her crossed fingers. 'Wish me luck.'

Sally smiled to herself as she closed the front door behind Ginny. Only the previous evening Ginny had confided her plan to Sally, who hoped that tonight her friend would realise her long-cherished desire. Seeing Ginny dressed up and getting excited over her night out reminded her of when she and Ben were doing their courting. Sally recalled one Saturday evening when she wore a new outfit. It was a tight-fitting dress in pale blue cotton glaze with a matching half-coat. She remembered feeling very smart as she walked out of the square. Ben had been complimentary and said she looked like a film star. It seemed such a long time ago.

Ginny knocked on George Tapley's front door and glanced furtively around the square, thankful that it was deserted. She was aware that the tongues had already started wagging over her frequent visits to George, and she guessed that a few of her neighbours were probably peeping through their lace curtains that very minute, but Ginny was not too worried. While they were talking about her they were leaving somebody else alone, she reasoned. George had not answered the door, and Ginny brought the knocker down harder this time. Still there was no answer. She moved to the window and tried to peer in, but the curtains were drawn tight. She banged the knocker once more and this time she heard a shuffling in the passage. Slowly the door opened and Ginny gulped at the sight of George. His eyes were darkly ringed and he was trembling noticeably. 'Oh my Gawd! Whatever's wrong, George?' she gasped.

He stood back to allow her in and she followed him into his front parlour. He picked up a crumpled piece of paper from the table and his hand shook as he gave it to her without saying a word. She opened it out and read the typed message. 'The War Office regret to inform you and your son, Rifleman L. Tapley, has been reported missing in action.' Ginny groaned aloud. 'Oh no!'

George sat down in his easy chair, his head sunk low and his shaking hands clasped as though in prayer. 'I knew it,' he mumbled. 'I knew it was gonna come.'

All Ginny's feelings for the man welled up inside her. She sat on the chair-arm beside him and pulled his head into her breast. 'You poor man,' she whispered. 'It's not right. It's jus' not right.'

She could feel his body trembling and then he broke down and sobbed violently. For some time she held him to her, comforting him as his grief flooded out. The front of her dress was wet with his tears when she finally released him and stood up slowly. 'You need a strong cuppa, George,' she said softly. 'We both do. I'll get us one.'

'It came this afternoon,' he said in little more than a whisper. 'I 'eard the boy ringin' 'is bell an' I was at the door before 'e knocked. I knew it, Ginny. I told yer I 'ad that dream. It was an omen.'

Ginny found herself trembling as she made the tea. When she had filled two large mugs she opened the sideboard door and looked in. 'Yer need somefing in it, George,' she said.

He pointed a shaking finger towards the cupboard in the recess beside the fireplace. 'There's a bottle o' whisky in there, Gin,' he said quietly.

Ginny took out the bottle and poured a large

measure in each mug.

George sat bowed in his chair, the mug clasped in his shaking hands. Only the loud ticking of the clock interrupted the silence as they sipped their tea. Ginny noticed how the man seemed to have aged in the very short time since she had last seen him. His eyes kept straying to the buff-coloured telegram lying on the table and his shoulders rose and fell heavily as he cried.

They had been sitting together for some time before Ginny got up and took the empty mug from his hands. The spirit seemed to have steadied him somewhat and he had leaned back in his chair. She took the empty mugs into the scullery merely to compose herself, and when she returned she stood beside him and put her hand on his shoulder. 'Yer mustn't give up 'ope, George,' she encouraged him gently. 'Young Laurie could be a prisoner. After all, they've only said 'e's missin'.'

'I know, Ginny,' he said, looking down at his tightly clenched hands. 'I've gotta pray the lad's still alive. I won't give up 'ope – not yet.'

'Good fer you, George. All the people in Paragon Place will be prayin' fer yer boy, I'm sure of it.'

He looked up at the clock. 'It's gettin' late, Ginny. I don't want ter keep yer.' He paused for a moment. 'Fanks fer, y'know, talkin' an' that.'

Ginny smiled briefly. She felt she should stay and comfort him, but she knew he wanted her out of the house, away from being party to his private torment and suffering. She patted his head in her motherly way and made for the door. 'If there's anyfing yer want, George yer know where ter come,' she said. 'Try an' get some sleep. I'll look in termorrer mornin'.'

He nodded slowly as Ginny left the room, and when she had gone he buried his head once more in his hands.

Chapter Four

ANOTHER week had slipped by, and now in the first few days of March the weather had grown mild. On Saturday morning Sally went to the market, and after the Robinsons' usual Saturday lunch of pie and mash she popped in to see Vera. The Mynotts' daughter was pegging out the washing in the tiny backyard and Sally sat on the window-ledge, her feet on an upturned beer crate. Vera wore a headscarf which was tied at the nape of her neck and her face was flushed from running the wet clothing through the wringer. She was a little short of breath as she told Sally yet again about the phone call she had received the previous afternoon at Harrison's. 'I was worried out o' me life when the forelady told me I was wanted on the phone, Sal,' she said, puffing. 'Me 'eart was poundin' away as I was goin' ter the office. I didn't know what ter fink, an' when I 'eard Joe's voice all the way from Liverpool I wanted ter scream down the phone at 'im fer frightenin' me.'

'Still, it was good news,' Sally laughed. 'I was surprised yer didn't tell 'im yer was pregnant, now yer know fer sure.'

Vera took a clothes-peg out of her mouth and clipped it to the last of the washing. 'Like I said, Joe's bin wantin' us ter get married. 'E got the nod from me Mum an' Dad an' we agreed ter talk about it when 'e got back from sea. I don't want ter put 'im under any obligation, Sal. I mean, who knows, Joe might 'ave 'ad a change of 'eart. 'E might 'ave found 'imself a girl in a grass skirt. I wouldn't like ter fink 'e married me jus' 'cos I'm in the club.'

'So you're gonna wait till 'e gets down on 'is 'ands an' knees, then,' Sally said, grinning.

Vera snorted. 'I can't imagine Joe doin' that. 'E'll be more likely ter say, "Well, what about it then?" an' I'll say, "What about what?" then Joe'll give me that funny look, an' 'e'll say, "Yer know what." D'yer know, Sal, we could go on like that until 'e got the needle, an' then 'e might well storm off ter the pub. After a couple o' pints 'e'd most prob'ly ferget what 'e was tryin' ter say, so yer see, I've gotta be careful.'

Sally was laughing aloud at Vera's impersonation of Joe's gruff voice. 'Wait till yer tell 'im you're pregnant!' she said.

Vera pulled a face. 'I 'ope 'e don't fink it's somebody else's. 'E won't, will 'e?'

Sally shook her head. 'Vera, you put me in stitches. Of course 'e won't.'

'What, fink it's 'is?' Vera said in mock horror.

Sally looked at Vera's flat stomach. 'As long as

88

yer don't leave it too long ter get married nobody's gonna know you're carryin'. By the way, I don't fink yer should be usin' the wringer. Me mum was sayin' that's 'ow a lot o' women get the cord twisted.'

Vera ran the back of her hand across her forehead. 'Yer should 'ave bin 'ere when I told me mum I was like this. She started bawlin' 'er eyes out. She said she always wanted me ter 'ave a white weddin' in church, jus' like our Doreen. Me dad told me what a silly girl I was, an' then 'e went off up the pub. They're all right now, though. They both fink the world o' Joe. I s'pose they'll be glad ter see me get married at last.'

Sally followed Vera back into the house and stood in the scullery while her friend put the kettle on the gas stove. 'I bin wonderin' why that 'usband o' mine 'asn't tried to see me lately,' she said suddenly.

Vera lit the gas and flopped down in a rickety chair. 'Yeah, it's funny that. P'r'aps 'e got the message.'

Sally shook her head. 'Not Ben. I'll never ferget that look in 'is eye. I was really frightened.'

"Ave yer said anyfing indoors about 'im pesterin' yer?' Vera asked.

Sally sat down on the edge of the copper. 'They don't know about 'im speakin' ter me, but they know 'e's bin 'angin' around. Lora saw 'im outside the paper shop. Me dad told me ter tell 'im if Ben starts gettin' a nuisance an' 'e'll sort 'im out. That's all I want,' Sally groaned. 'Ben an' me farver comin' ter blows.'

Vera took the tea-caddy from the shelf above the gas stove and spooned the tea into the china teapot. 'I was gonna ask yer, Sal,' she said. 'Would yer stan' fer me when I get married?'

'Stan' fer yer?'

'Yeah. I want yer ter be me maid of honour,' Vera said.

'Course I will,' Sally grinned, getting up and hugging her friend.

'Well, that's settled then,' Vera laughed. 'All I've gotta do now is 'ope Joe boy asks me.'

'When d'yer expect 'im 'ome?' Sally asked.

''E reckons 'e'll get inter London about seven o'clock ternight. 'E's comin' straight round, so I reckon about eight o'clock.'

The kettle started to boil and Vera poured the water into the teapot. She looked thoughtful as she stirred the tea-leaves around in the boiling water. 'D'yer know, Sally, I've not bin able ter get Laurie out of me 'ead all week,' she said suddenly.

Sally sighed. 'Nor 'ave I. I keep finkin' about when we was all little. D'yer remember when we all used ter go up the open-air swimmin' pool at Southwark Park?'

Vera nodded. 'What about that time when Ben picked on Laurie an' Laurie's bruvver Tony went lookin' fer Ben an' they 'ad that fight.'

Sally smiled. ''Ere, an' what about when we all went up the Trocette and bumped in. We only 'ad the price of one ticket between us, an' Tony went in an' opened the back door fer us.'

Vera was still stirring the tea. 'I saw ole Mr

Tapley this mornin'. 'E looks really ill.'

Sally sighed and ran her finger along the wide split in the table. 'P'r'aps Laurie's a prisoner. Ginny said somebody she knows got a telegram sayin' 'er son was missin' an' then she was told 'e was a prisoner.'

Vera finally removed the spoon from the teapot and put on the lid. 'I was really 'appy a few minutes ago, Sal, but I'm all miserable now.'

Sally's eyes had filled with tears and she tried to blink them away. 'So am I,' she faltered.

The two girls hugged each other spontaneously and tears ran down their cheeks. 'I wish the war was over an' Laurie an' Tony were back in the square,' Vera said, wiping her eyes.

Sally gulped hard. 'They will be, one day, you jus' wait. They'll be OK. I've got that feelin'.'

At number 1 the Carey sisters were in the midst of a serious discussion. 'Well, I don't see any other answer,' Harriet was saying. 'We should go and see Mr Cuthbert at the estate office. He always said he'd be ready to listen if we had a problem.'

Juliet was not too keen on Mr Cuthbert. He reminded her of a strutting peacock, and his eyes had that crafty look, she thought. 'Do you think we should, Harriet?' she asked, pinching her chin between thumb and forefinger.

'Yes, I do,' Harriet replied firmly. 'That girl's shameless. She's using her flat for immoral purposes and we've got to live over it all. God knows what she gets up to in there.'

Juliet had often fantasised about Muriel Taylor's nocturnal activities and occasionally she had become ashamed of her own thoughts. She attempted to look suitably disgusted as she bit her bottom lip. 'Maybe we should have another word with Muriel,' she suggested. 'She seems a reasonable sort.'

The older of the Carey sisters slid her half-moon glasses down on to the tip of her nose and looked over them at Juliet. 'A reasonable sort? The woman's nothing more than a common tart,' she said with venom. 'That young vixen brings those merchant seamen back night after night. She'll be putting up a red lamp before long.'

Juliet sighed. She did not want to get into a discussion about Muriel Taylor on this particular evening. The subject always distressed her sister and she often became unwell. When she had one of her turns Harriet invariably took to her bed, leaving her younger sister to act as nurse, house-maid, and guardian against a possible visit from one of Muriel's mariners. Juliet was praying that her elder sister would not get too worked up on this particular evening, as she was looking forward to one of her clandestine meetings with Mr Lomax tomorrow. It was late on Friday afternoon when he had given her the good news that his wife was being taken to see her sister early on Sunday and would not be back until late that evening. Juliet had brought home a sheaf of old deeds suitably tied up with red ribbon and shown them to her sister, saying that they had to be delivered to a client on Sunday morning. Harriet had had her usual moan about the situation. 'Mr Lomax is just using you, Juliet,' she declared. 'You should tell dear Mr Lomax that Sunday is supposed to be a day of pleasure.'

Juliet had put on her usual pained expression. 'I suppose you're right, Harriet, but he does rely on me, and after all I do get paid for it.' The explanation had seemed to suffice, and Juliet could barely suppress a wry smile. She had a strong feeling that Sunday would certainly prove to be a day of pleasure.

The morning sky was clear and Sunday promised to be fine and dry. The ice cream man had pushed his brightly coloured barrow along Stanley Street and set it down at the end of Paragon Place, and later the winkle stall opened up for business outside the Railway Inn. Sally had cleaned the front doorstep and had popped up to the corner shop by the railway arches for the Sunday papers and a packet of Daisy powders for her mother's headache, and on her way back she saw Vera standing by her front door with Joe. Her friend was smiling broadly. 'What d'yer fink, Sal. We're gettin' married!' she called out.

Sally grinned slyly at Vera and, looking suitably surprised, held out her hand to Joe Copeland. 'Congratulations, Joe,' she said. 'When's it gonna be?'

Joe's wide face broke into a grin. 'I'm 'ome fer a couple o' weeks – they're taking their time mending the ship. We gotta sort it out wiv the registry office.'

Vera clasped his arm happily and smiled up at his rugged face. ''E finally got round to it, Sally. 'E didn't need any promptin' neivver.'

Sally looked at the two of them standing close to each other and was suddenly filled with envy. They made a good couple, she thought. Vera was bubbling over with personality and forever making light of things. She was pretty, too, with a nice figure and red hair that curled naturally. Joe was a good six inches taller than Vera, with broad shoulders and a straight back. His short-cropped hair accentuated his high forehead, and his deep-set blue eyes had a dreamy look about them. Joe Copeland had joined the merchant service at eighteen. Although he was now in his twenty-fifth year, Joe still retained a boyish look, and he was completely dominated by the persuasive powers of Vera Mynott.

Sally listened while Vera chatted away happily about their wedding plans, glancing at Joe now and then and catching a subservient look on his handsome face. They had all grown up together in and around Paragon Place. Like her and Ben, the two of them had always been together and it seemed only natural that they would get married one day. Sally secretly hoped that Vera and Joe would find more happiness together than she and Ben had.

'If we can get married next Saturday I'm takin' the next week off,' Vera said, interrupting Sally's thoughts. 'We'll go away fer a few days, won't we, Joe?'

Joe nodded and broke away from Vera's

grasp. 'I've promised ter meet the family up the pub. I better be goin',' he announced, licking his lips in anticipation. As he walked away along the square Vera gave Sally a wide grin. 'It was easy. I got 'im on the subject an' 'e asked me ter get married – in 'is usual romantic way,' she joked. 'When I said all right Joe nearly fell off the chair wiv surprise.'

Sally laughed as she gripped Vera's arm. 'I'm really pleased fer yer. Mus' go now. We'll talk later.'

That Sunday promised to be like any other in war-time Paragon Place. The smells of cooking drifted out from opened windows and children played in the square or sat by the tree sucking on ice cream cones. At exactly twelve noon Vera's father Fred Mynott knocked at number 7 and together with Ted Bromley, Granny Allen's son-in-law, he strolled up to the Railway Inn. Charlie Robinson was hot on their heels, although Granny Almond, in company with Granny Allen, followed on at a more leisurely pace. Both the ladies were looking forward to their constitutional Guinness and their usual chat about the current situation in Paragon Place. Blind Bob left the square soon after, his faithful mongrel dog straining at the leash. Harriet Carey had recently returned from Mass and was already pottering about with a duster in her upstairs flat at number 1. She was still fretting over the continuing antics of her downstairs neighbour, and bemoaning the fact that Paragon Place was not the square it had once been.

95

At two o'clock the Railway Inn closed its doors and the tenants of Paragon Place returned for their Sunday lunch. The little square became quiet and peaceful. Even Alf Porter refrained from singing as he staggered home later, and he was careful to avoid the old sycamore as he advanced erratically, key in hand, towards his front door, clutching a bag of winkles. The tranquillity of the little square was about to be shattered.

At number 10 Mrs Fuller was seething. She was a big, freckle-faced woman with bright ginger hair and a squint in one eye. She was in her mid-thirties with three young children and a meek husband ten years older than her who worked away from home in a munitions factory. Maurice Fuller was home for the weekend and was beginning to regret it. The children had been playing up and Ada had not stopped moaning since early morning. Now she was threatening to go next door and punch Mrs Botley's head in.

For over a year now relations between the two women had been deteriorating. It had originated when Clara Botley accused Ada Fuller of having an affair with her husband Patrick. The aggrieved man had been at pains to point out that Ada Fuller was not his idea of a desirable woman and if he had wanted to stray it would more likely have been with someone like Muriel Taylor. Patrick's problem was that he was a softhearted man who was always ready to help his neighbours, and when Ada Fuller wanted a line put up in her backyard or needed a patch put on

96

a saucepan he was happy to oblige. Patrick felt sorry for the woman. Her husband was very rarely around, and as Ada was quick to point out, 'That silly bleeder o' mine can't even bang a nail in the wall.' Patrick worked as a crane driver in the docks. He was nearly fifty, tall and with a mop of dark, curly hair and deep blue eyes. His blonde wife Clara was obsessed with the idea that many of the local women wanted to bed her husband, and Patrick's good neighbourliness only served to fuel her excessive suspicions. Whenever he stopped to pass the time of day with anyone of the opposite sex she would accuse him of chatting the woman up. Patrick became resigned to Clara's unnatural obsession, and when things got too bad he would retreat into the backyard to tend his chickens and rabbits.

It had all started when Ada Fuller had found she needed a new washer on the scullery tap. Maurice volunteered to do the job and Ada had gritted her teeth. It would be a disaster, she knew, but the way things were with Clara Botley she dare not ask Patrick to do the job. It took Maurice some time to find the stopcock and then he encountered his first problem. The stopcock was beneath the sink and it was jammed tight. After sweating and fuming for some time he decided it might be better to unscrew the tap and replace the washer without turning the water off, providing he was quick about it. He found a rusty spanner and loosened the tap thread, then he placed the washer on the wooden draining-board. Slowly he unscrewed the tap.

His tongue was hanging out and his eyes bulged as he concentrated. Gingerly he made the last few turns and suddenly water spurted out with incredible force. The tap flew off under the pressure and a jet of water hit the ceiling. Maurice tried to stem the flow with one hand while he reached for the washer with the other. Water poured over the draining-board and the washer floated out of the scullery. Maurice was holding on with both hands as water spurted everywhere. There was nothing he could do. 'Ada!' he screamed. 'I can't move!'

His long-suffering wife had been hovering in the passage holding her breath, and she held her hand up to her mouth at the sounds of impending disaster. She strode into the scullery, her feet splashing in the water. 'Can't yer do anyfing right, yer dozy git?' she screamed.

Maurice was dripping wet. His hair hung over his eyes, his hands were slowly going blue and water was creeping up around his ankles. 'What am I gonna do, Ada?' he groaned.

Ada sighed. 'Stay where yer are. I'll get Patrick,' she shouted.

Things returned to normal after the good Samaritan had turned off the stopcock and helped Maurice find the washer. Ada had scooped up most of the water from the stone floor and was soaking up the remainder with a house flannel when her youngest ran in to ask for money to buy an ice cream. As Danny skipped into the scullery he slipped on the wet floor and cracked his forehead on the scullery step. A large bump grew on Danny's forehead, and he buried his head into Ada's apron sobbing loudly. The harassed woman took her son out into the backyard and sat him down on an upturned box while she applied a cold wet flannel to bring out the bruise. It was then that she heard Clara Botley's ranting.

'Yer can't wait ter get inter that 'ouse, can yer!' she screamed at her husband. 'Can't that silly bastard do anyfing? What did she 'ave ter call you for? Anyfing ter get yer in there. Wait till I see the boss-eyed cow. I'll give 'er a piece o' my mind.'

Ada gritted her teeth and stamped her foot in anger. 'You just wait, yer ugly-looking mare. I'll sort yer out,' she raved to herself.

The tap-washer episode had meant that the Sunday lunch was delayed, and it was after the Railway Inn had closed its doors and the tenants of Paragon Place had returned when Ada put the vegetables on to cook. 'Oi, you! Keep yer eye on that dinner,' she shouted out to a very subdued Maurice. 'I'm gonna sort that scatty mare out.'

'Don't take any notice of 'er,' he pleaded. 'Yer know what she's like.'

Young Danny was sitting on the front doorstep, his face still tear-stained and the bump on his head beginning to turn blue as his mother brushed past him and rat-tatted on number 9's door. The lad took one look at his mother as she stood arms akimbo with her mouth screwed up angrily and he ran indoors.

'Come out, yer scatty whore!' Ada yelled. 'I'll give yer callin' me a boss-eyed cow!'

The front door opened and Clara Botley faced

her rival. She stood in the portal, her arms folded, glaring at Ada. 'Jus' leave my ole man alone! Get yer own 'usband ter do yer dirty work!' she shouted.

Ada stood back a pace. 'Nobody calls me a boss-eyed cow. Least of all you!'

Clara snorted. 'I don't know what my ole man sees in yer, yer scruffy prat!'

Ada jerked her thumb over her shoulder. 'Get out 'ere an' say that!' she said, her voice choked with anger.

The big woman stepped over the threshold and immediately they clashed. Clara grabbed at her rival's apron and Ada took hold of Clara's blonde locks. They swayed and staggered into the middle of the square, snarling and screaming obscenities at each other. Patrick had heard the scuffle and he ran out and tried unsuccessfully to separate the two antagonists. The women staggered sideways and then fell in a heap. Ada's apron and blouse were torn and Clara had lost a tuft of hair. The women were now rolling over and over, each trying to get on top. Ada finally managed to straddle her enemy and was proceeding to bounce Clara's head against the paving-stones when Patrick grabbed hold of her around the waist and pulled her off. Maurice was standing at his front door, a horrified look on his gaunt face. He was holding his sobbing youngster and wishing he had stayed in Leicester. Patrick still had hold of Ada who was screaming for him to let go of her. Clara pulled her tangled hair from her face and gave her husband a wicked stare. 'Go on then. Go wiv 'er.

I know what's goin' on,' she snarled.

Patrick let go of Ada as his wife turned on her heel and walked into the house. Ada straightened her dishevelled apron and rubbed a grubby hand over her ginger hair. 'She's a bloody lunatic. The woman should be put away,' she growled, hurrying in to serve up a very belated Sunday lunch.

At number 1 the elder of the Carey sisters had witnessed the brawl and she was searching for her smelling-salts. 'I wish Juliet were here,' she groaned to herself. 'I can feel one of my turns coming on. Why does that man keep giving her those jobs to do at weekends? If I didn't know my sister better I'd think there was something going on between them. Oh dear, where did I put that bottle? I can't stand much more of this. The sooner we get to see Mr Cuthbert the better.'

Another witness to the fisticuffs was Alf Porter. He had been sitting in his front parlour busying himself with a darning needle and a plate of winkles when he heard the commotion. Peering through his filthy lace curtains he had seen threshing arms and legs, and a sorry-looking Patrick attempting to part them. Alf grinned to himself and got on with the dewinkling. He considered himself to be a very fortunate man not to have got married, although he very nearly had once, he recalled. As it was he could leave for work in the mornings without a woman screaming into his ear, and then when his labours were done he could sit himself in a pleasant pub and have a few drinks, and maybe a few drinks more, without worrying over the consequences.

Living alone had never worried Alf Porter. He had been alone for most of his life. As a youngster his early recollections were of being left with his ageing grandfather while his mother went off to work. Alf had never discovered the identity of his father, and he was not particularly worried. He had never got to know his mother very well either. She had gone out to work one day and never returned. Rumour had it that she had run off with a merchant seaman, and the last anyone heard of her was when Isaac got a letter from his daughter postmarked Liverpool. The old man had brought up his grandson and Alf had grown to love him and think of him with gratitude and fondness, despite the fact that it was his grandfather who had planted the tree which kept the light out of his parlour and blocked his view of the square, the tree which had often sent him sprawling on nights when he was a little the worse for drink.

It was late evening on that same March Sunday when Sally took the Robinsons' lodger his cup of cocoa and two dry biscuits. Her parents had gone to the Railway Inn and Lora was out with Bernard. The quiet of the house had been broken by the sound of Bill coughing. Sally felt a little apprehensive as she climbed the stairs to his room. Bill was a hardy soul who rarely ever caught a cold, despite his spartan existence. His cough seemed to be harsh and prolonged and it worried her. As she entered the room Sally was shocked to find Bill slumped over the table, his face grey. He was holding his side and grimacing as the cough attacked him again. She put down the mug of cocoa and leaned over him. 'You all right, Bill?' she asked. 'I don't like the sound o' that cough.'

'It's all right, lass,' he grunted, pulling his shabby overcoat around his frail shoulders. 'I must 'ave caught a chill.'

Another spasm of coughing wracked his body and as he recovered Sally could see beads of perspiration breaking out on his forehead. 'I'm gonna get the doctor, Bill,' she said firmly. 'Now you get into bed. Yer shouldn't be on yer feet,' she added, frowning at his weak protestations.

Doctor Bartholomew felt irritable at being called out on a cold night and he urged Sally to lead the way with an impatient gesture. As soon as he had examined the old man, however, Doctor Bartholomew's attitude changed. He beckoned to Sally to follow him and when they had gone down into the parlour he looked at her with a serious expression on his large face. 'It's pneumonia,' he said quickly. 'I'm going to give you some tablets to help with his breathing, and if you can get a steam kettle it would be beneficial. Make sure you get a fire going in that room, too. The place feels cold and damp.'

Sally took a half-crown from her purse and handed it to him. The doctor slipped the coin into his waistcoat pocket and fished in his well-worn black bag. He took out a phial of white tablets and put them down on the table. 'Give him one every three hours and keep him warm,' he said. 'I'll call in sometime tomorrow.'

When the doctor had left Sally hurried up to her room and removed one of the blankets from the bed. Bill looked up at her as she entered his room. His face seemed to be the colour of old parchment and his rheumy eyes were like two burning coals. She could hear his laboured breathing and as she put a match to the already-laid fire Sally heard the front door open. Loud, laughing voices carried up to her and she felt a wave of anger at their ignorance. She hurried down the stairs and confronted her mother in the passageway. 'It's Bill,' she said with a frown. "E's ill.'

Annie looked surprised. "E was all right when I took 'is clean clothes up. Wassa matter wiv 'im?'

'It's pneumonia. I got the doctor in,' Sally answered shortly.

Charlie was standing behind Annie, his hands hitched through his wide braces, his eyes bleary and heavy-lidded. 'Bloody ole sod neglects 'imself. We're always gettin' on ter 'im ter come down an' sit wiv us. It's enough ter kill 'im up in that bug-'utch of 'is.'

Sally gave him a cold stare and turned to her mother. 'The doctor said 'e should 'ave a steam kettle. Where can we get one?'

Annie walked wearily into the parlour and sat down heavily in her easy chair. She took off her stiff black hat and threw it down on the table.

104

'Sure as I go out fer an 'alf-hour somefing 'as ter go wrong. Put the kettle on, Farver, will yer?'

Sally sat down at the table and glanced at her mother. She seemed to show very little concern for the old man. Lora was as bad. She always seemed to consider Bill a burden and never had a kind word for him.

Annie had loosened her coat and she stared gloomily into the dying fire. 'I'll knock at Mrs Almond's in the mornin'. She 'ad a steam kettle fer one of 'er kids. It's too late ter knock ternight.'

Sally got up and left the room. Without putting on her coat she slipped out into the dark square. She could hear the wireless playing softly in Ginny Almond's front room and she tapped lightly on the door. She saw the curtains move slighly then the sound of bolts being drawn. 'What's wrong, luv?' Ginny asked, surprise showing on her large features.

"Ave yer got a steam kettle I could loan, Gin? It's ole Bill. 'E's got pneumonia.'

Chapter Five

THE tram was late. As the queue got longer people started to moan and Sally sighed irritably. She was only half listening as her friend talked incessantly about her coming marriage. Sally felt uncomfortable. She had spent most of Monday night in and out of Bill

Freeman's room giving him sips of water, keeping the fire going and replenishing the steam kettle. Annie had stayed up for part of Sunday night and yesterday she had told Sally that another night without sleep would surely finish her. Lora had been little help, saying that she felt she was going down with the flu, and she had turned in before ten o'clock. Early that morning the fever had broken and Bill had settled down to a more peaceful sleep. Sally had woken up to find she had been sleeping with her head resting in her arms over the table and she had staggered down wearily to make the morning tea before rousing the household. Now as she waited for the tram she felt exhausted, but she took comfort in the knowledge that at least the old man was on the mend.

'You've not been listenin' to a word I've said,' Vera moaned.

'Sorry. I was jus' finkin',' Sally replied. 'What was yer sayin?'

Vera pulled a face. 'It doesn't matter. I was only sayin' that me an' Joe are goin' away fer a few days after we're married. Joe's uncle owns a little place in Kent an' 'e's gonna let us use it. It's not a mansion, but I don't s'pose we're gonna worry too much about the look o' the place. We'll 'ave ovver fings on our minds,' she laughed, nudging Sally playfully.

Sally grinned mirthlessly. As the tram shuddered up to the stop she felt the strong urge to turn around and go back home.

On the factory floor stacks of khaki material were ready and waiting to be sewn. More stacks of the material were lying beside each worker's seat and Sally shuddered inwardly as she hung up her coat and took her place at the long row of industrial machines. The hours seemed to drag past very slowly and she found herself fighting sleep. During the early afternoon Sally's machine suddenly ground to a halt and she said a little prayer of gratitude. The forelady came up and scratched her head. 'Well, the needle's all right,' she said.

The shopfloor manager came up and pulled a face. 'Well, the motor looks OK,' he said, touching the machine gingerly. 'Better get Jimmy Kent.'

Jimmy arrived, his face wreathed in smiles and Vera glanced over at him. 'You're all cheery terday,' she remarked. 'Somefing must 'ave 'appened.'

Jimmy put down his toolbag and slipped his thumbs through his overall braces. 'I'll be leavin' this dump soon,' he replied, giving Sally a big wink.

The shopfloor manager put his hands in his trouser pockets and glared at the young mechanic. 'Any chance o' gettin' that machine fixed 'fore yer go?' he growled.

Jimmy cast his eye over the idle contraption and scratched his spiky hair. 'Yeah, I should fink so,' he grinned cheekily.

Sally got up from her seat. 'I'm away ter the loo,' she whispered to the forelady.

After examining the machine for a while Jimmy straightened up. 'It's the main bearin',' he announced. 'Gotta strip the 'ole fing down.'

'Well, 'ow long are yer gonna take?' the manager groaned.

''Ow the bloody 'ell do I know?' Jimmy said with spirit. 'I'll give yer a shout when it's fixed.'

The manager walked away grumbling to himself and Jimmy dived into his toolbag for a screwdriver.

Vera had been working at a fast rate attempting to finish her quota of back seams on time. She leaned back in her chair and wiped her brow with the back of her hand. ''Ere, what's all that about you leavin'? Yer can't, can yer?' she asked, puzzlement showing on her pretty face.

Jimmy sat down on the edge of the workbench and faced Vera. 'There's bin a few changes in the regulations, so I've 'eard,' he said, wiping his grimy hands on a piece of cotton waste. 'Yer can get de-reserved. That means I can volunteer fer the Navy.'

Vera still looked puzzled. 'I don't understand. Yer job's classed as essential work. We're all on war work. 'Ow comes yer can leave?'

Jimmy's boyish features broke into a wide grin. 'Look. The way I understand it is, there's a shortage o' manpower fer the services, so the government 'ave said that certain people can apply ter get de-reserved. All I 'ave ter do is get the guv'nor ter sign me application an' I'm free ter go in the Navy. It's what I wanted ter do in the first place.'

Vera snorted. 'The guv'nor won't let you go. Who's gonna fix the machines?'

Jimmy leaned forward. 'It's already bin taken care of,' he said in a lowered voice. 'Ole

Murray's gettin' somebody ter take me place. 'E's an older bloke who ain't liable fer military service. 'E's startin' next week, an' Murray's gonna sign me application before I finish work ternight.'

Vera glanced at the young mechanic with affection. He looked too young to get involved in the fighting, she thought sadly. 'Well, good luck, Jimmy. When yer come 'ome on leave yer can take me dancin' again – as long as Joe's not 'ome,' she added. Over Jimmy's shoulder she caught sight of the manager walking towards them. 'Careful, Miserable Bob's on 'is way,' she whispered.

Jimmy was feeling pleased with himself as he got on with the task of stripping down the machine. He had been trying for some time to get his release from Harrison's but on every occasion he had been refused. With the new regulations which had recently come into force Jimmy had felt that he might have a better chance of persuading the manager to sign his application form and he had decided to wait until the right opportunity presented itself. It was soon in coming, but not in the way he had expected.

On Monday afternoon things had been going wrong at the Harrison factory. Machines broke down, sewing needles snapped and there was a power failure. Jimmy had been feeling particularly harassed as he hurried about the factory floor and when he'd gone along to the manager's office to get a chit signed for spare parts John Murray was nowhere to be seen. His secretary

109

had said that he was about somewhere and got on with filing her long fingernails. Jimmy had next tried the various offices, but there was still no sign of the manager. Everyone he had asked shook their heads and one or two voiced the opinion that as far as they were concerned John Murray could disappear permanently. It had been one of the canteen workers who finally pointed Jimmy in the right direction. 'I saw 'im goin' down ter the basement about an hour ago. There was somebody wiv 'im,' she'd said, grinning slyly.

Jimmy had hurried down the twisting stone staircase and at the entrance to the main stores he'd paused. Normally the door was padlocked, but on this occasion the lock was missing. Jimmy had heard muffled laughter coming from inside and very gently he'd turned the handle and eased the door open. The light was on and he'd seen the various parcels and bundles stacked on the high shelves. The stifled sounds of giggling had seemed to come from the far corner of the large room. Jimmy had coughed loudly and called out, 'I'm lookin' fer the manager.'

There had been a scrambling sound, then John Murray appeared from behind a stack of boxes, his face flushed and his normally well-combed hair in disarray. 'What is it?' he'd growled, a guilty look on his bloated features.

Jimmy had caught a glimpse of another person who appeared from behind the boxes and stood half-hidden by the manager's bulky frame. Maggie Chandler had blinked at him through her thick-lensed glasses and Jimmy had seen that she was holding the top of her blouse together in her clenched hand. 'Can yer sign this chit, Mr Murray?' he'd asked, trying to hide a grin. 'I gotta get some spares on the quick.'

The manager had quickly signed the piece of paper. 'Look, I don't want this getting around,' he'd whispered, jerking his thumb in Maggie's direction.

Jimmy had folded the chit carefully and put it into his overall pocket, then his eyes had narrowed slightly. 'Oh, while I fink of it. About that release form,' he'd said, an expression of dignity on his face. 'Can yer sign it fer me, Mr Murray?'

The two had stood eye to eye for a few seconds, then the manager had puffed. 'OK. But I'll need time to get a replacement. Bring the form along to my office before you go home tomorrow evening.'

The Carey sisters were busy preparing to visit Mr Cuthbert at the estate office. Harriet was fussing over whether she should wear her navy-blue hat or the white one with the half veil, whilst Juliet sat patiently waiting for her elder sister to make up her mind. Harriet had been full of the incident in Paragon Place that previous Sunday and she had been insisting at great length that something should be done to prevent the little community from 'going to the devil', as she put it. Juliet had reluctantly agreed to take the day off so that she could accompany her sister to the estate office. Harriet was adamant

111

that her sister should join her in the crusade. 'After all, you must have some time owing to you,' she said. 'Look at all those visits you have to make out of working hours.'

Juliet had enjoyed her last so-called 'visit' and as she watched Harriet carefully sliding a hat-pin into her tightly drawn-up hair she felt sad for her sister. Harriet had led an even more sheltered life than she had. At least she had Mr Lomax. He brought excitement into her mundane existence. Poor Harriet spent most of the daylight hours working as an assistant in that dusty reference library, and then there was the voluntary work she took on for the church. It must be so dull and unexciting, Juliet reasoned. If only she had met the right man when she was younger, but then neither of them had wanted to get married when they were younger.

Harriet had by now become hysterical over the declining morals in Paragon Place and Juliet knew that her sister would not be able to rest until some action was taken. 'Are you nearly ready, Harriet?' she sighed. 'We don't want to be late. Mr Cuthbert did say ten o'clock sharp.'

Harriet finally settled for the navy-blue hat, and she glanced at herself in the wall-mirror once more before picking up her handbag and slipping it over her gloved hand. 'We've plenty of time, Juliet. If we're too early we'll have to wait in reception with that awful secretary,' she said with distaste.

The two sisters descended the winding stairs and Harriet's face took on a haughty look as she glanced back into the scullery. 'Just look at the state of that room, Juliet,' she whispered.

The younger sister nodded compliantly and followed Harriet out into the square. Instead of turning right into Stanley Street Harriet turned left and started to walk further into the square.

'Where are we going?' Juliet asked quickly.

'I just want to knock at number 4 to see how poor Mr Freeman is,' Harriet answered.

'What's the matter with him?' Juliet asked, frowning.

'He's very poorly and Mrs Robinson's had to have the doctor in,' Harriet replied. 'I heard that awful man Porter shouting the news to that woman opposite as I was getting ready.'

Annie Robinson came to the door and Harriet put on her sweetest smile. 'Hello, Mrs Robinson. My sister and I have just knocked to inquire how Mr Freeman is feeling this morning.'

Annie had never had much time for the two 'stuck-up ole biddies' as she called them, and until her lodger was taken ill she had only ever passed the time of day with them. ''E's all right,' she said unfeelingly. 'It's me what's feelin' queer. I've bin up an' down them stairs like a blue-arsed fly. It's fair wore me out.'

Harriet's mouth trembled at the corners and she blinked for a moment or two. 'Don't your daughters help you at all, Mrs Robinson?' she asked, delicately touching the back of her head with the palm of her hand.

Annie felt a strong urge to shoo the two busybodies away from her front door. 'I'll 'ave ter go. I fink that's Bill shoutin' out fer me,'

113

she lied.

'Well, tell him we called, and give him our sincere wishes for a speedy recovery,' Harriet said, smiling sweetly once more.

Annie nodded briefly. 'All right, I'll tell the ole f-feller,' she replied, realising that she had nearly slipped up.

The two walked quickly out of the square and as they turned towards the railway arches Harriet looked at her sister with a frown. 'She does look ill. You'd think those two girls of hers would do a bit more, wouldn't you, Juliet?'

Mr Cuthbert was sitting at his large desk at Ashworth Estates fretting over the impending visit from the Carey sisters. He was a rotund man with side whiskers and spiky grey hair which prompted some of his subordinates to liken him to a Dickensian character. His puffy eyes were small and tended to dart from side to side when he got excited, and he had bushy eyebrows which curled up and met in the centre. Mr Cuthbert enjoyed his job of managing a number of the local estates and properties, with one exception. The effective management of Paragon Place depended solely on the whims and wishes of the Catholic Church committee, and in Mr Cuthbert's opinion they were far too lax. He had on more than one occasion suggested to the religious body that they might consider moving more families into the square, in certain cases where the houses were under-occupied, and that the low rents could be raised to a more practical figure. He had had his supporters amongst the

114

members, but the majority had declined. Now, as he sat waiting, Mr Cuthbert felt powerless to provide any practical answers to the problems the two ladies were likely to present him with.

On the stroke of ten the Carey sisters were shown into the large office and invited to sit down. Harriet put her large handbag down beside her and folded her gloved hands in her lap as she attempted to remain calm. She smiled shyly at the portly figure of Mr Cuthbert while Juliet crossed her slim legs and gave him a cold stare.

'Now, ladies. What exactly can I do for you?' he said smiling patronisingly.

Harriet took a deep breath. 'Well, Mr Cuthbert, you know that my sister and I have lived at Paragon Place for a number of years, as did our parents before us. It was always such a respectable place to live . . .'

'Was?' the manager interrupted.

Harriet began to twiddle her fingers. 'The young lady who lives beneath us at number one has got into the habit of bringing men home,' she said with embarrassment.

'Merchant seamen,' Juliet added.

Mr Cuthbert ran his eye down a list of names at his elbow. 'A Miss Taylor, I believe. You say she brings men home?'

'Yes.'

The manager sighed to himself and quickly wrote the words 'knocking shop' on a notepad. 'We have to be certain that this Miss Taylor is using her premises for immoral purposes before we can act,' he said in a tired voice. 'As you are

115

aware, anyone has the right to bring a guest into rented property, providing it falls within the terms of that person's tenancy. In many cases of furnished accommodation the rules forbid guests. However, in this situation the tenancy is unfurnished and no such restrictions apply. What we have to establish is that in this case the house is being used as a brothel.'

Harriet felt her cheeks getting hot. 'Well, apart from being present I don't know how we can get the proof needed,' she said, surprised at her own words. 'All I know is that we're perfectly sure that the house is being used for that purpose. Why, only last week the young lady brought two men back.'

'Together?'

'Yes,' Harriet asserted. 'Together.'

The manager wrote the words 'sex mad' beneath his previous entry and rubbed his brow in perplexity. 'I suppose I could have a word with the Church committee,' he suggested. 'They may decide to send a visitor around to see the young lady.'

'Well, something's got to be done,' Harriet said quickly. 'And while they're visiting Miss Taylor maybe they should call in at numbers nine and ten.'

Mr Cuthbert's face took on a look of exasperation. 'Nine and ten?'

Harriet took a deep breath and related the events of that previous Sunday leaving nothing out, while the manager occasionally jotted key words into his rapidly filling notepad. Juliet merely nodded occasionally and her eyes

116

reverted to one corner of the room as she watched the long brass pendulum of a grand-father clock moving slowly backwards and forwards in its glass case. Harriet added a postscript by mentioning that one particular tenant of Paragon Place was permanently in a state of intoxication and was in the habit of sitting beneath tenants' windows and mouthing obscene verses.

Juliet had to intercede. 'He hasn't done it since that time—'

'Juliet, please!' Harriet gasped, her hand going up to her mouth.

'What happened?' Mr Cuthbert asked, a sudden look of interest showing on his face.

'It doesn't matter,' Harriet said quickly. 'At least we have explained just what is going on in Paragon Place. We sincerely hope you'll be able to do something. It's all getting too much.'

Mr Cuthbert was doodling on his filled notepad and he glanced up as Harriet brought a hand up to her forehead and leaned sideways on the arm of the chair. Juliet leaned over to comfort her sister. 'Don't have one of your turns here for goodness' sake, Harriet,' she said quickly.

The manager looked down at his notepad and studied his entries: 'Knocking shop, sex mad, female fisticuffs, drunkenness, obscene behaviour.' Good God! he thought. If I take all this to the Church committee they'll be down to re-consecrate the place. 'All right, ladies. Leave it with me,' he said, getting up and pointing his open hand in the direction of the door.

Juliet linked arms with her elder sister as they left the office and stepped out into the busy street.

Harriet sighed. 'I feel much better now, Juliet. Mr Cuthbert seems a very nice man, and I noticed he was writing a lot down on that notepad of his. I'm sure he'll get something done.'

Juliet nodded. Well, that was a waste of time, she thought.

The week wore on and Paragon Place settled down to normality. Bill Freeman was able to get out of bed for a spell and do a spot of reading, and he had reverted to his favourite breakfast of two ducks' eggs instead of the thin broth which Annie had been preparing for him. A fragile truce was operating at numbers 9 and 10, and when the two ladies accidentally met they both pulled long faces and averted their eyes. Patrick Botley came home from his job at the docks each evening with a resigned look on his rugged features, and as soon as possible he retired to his little backyard and tended his chickens and rabbits. Maurice Fuller from next door had gone back to his job at the Leicestershire armaments factory with a huge sigh of relief, and the unshakable conviction that he was not cut out to be a practical handyman.

The week passed slowly for Sally. The meeting with Ben Brady worried her and she found it more difficult than ever to concentrate. He had frightened and disturbed her and she found herself dwelling on the way things had once been between them, before they become so helplessly estranged. Vera had tried to raise her spirits on a couple of occasions, hinting that maybe she should get her hair done and use a little make-up. One morning Sally stood in front of the dressing-table mirror in her room and studied herself carefully. She knew that something needed to be done if she was not going to let herself become a dowdy, dried-up old maid. She studied her face and saw that her skin was dry and there was a look of tiredness around her eyes. Her face had a mournful look about it, she thought, and her thin, shapely lips tended to droop at the corners. She stretched her mouth with her thumb and forefinger, gargoyle-like, as she stared at herself and she pulled on her dry, dark hair. She then stood back suddenly and stripped naked in the sanctity of her bedroom. She straightened her shoulders and studied her small, firm breasts and her flat stomach. She ran her hands slowly down from her narrow waist over the curve of her hips and slowly along her smooth thighs. She brought her hand up and lifted her hair away from her neck, and turning sideways she glanced serious-faced at her outline in the dressing-table mirror. She smiled. Her figure was still trim and her body was unmarked. She ran her hands along her ribs and cupped her breasts in her palms, feeling their firmness and recalling the almost forgotten sensation she had so often experienced with Ben, when his rough hands had gently caressed her whole body. She dressed quickly, guiltily stifling her feelings as

119

she hurried down into the room below and went about her chores.

Chapter Six

IT was Saturday and people stood at their front doors in Paragon Place as the wedding party hurried out of the square. Granny Almond stood next to Granny Allen, holding a small handker-chief to her face. 'Weddin's always make me get upset,' she said. 'Don't she look nice?'

Lil nodded. 'So does Sally. That's a nice dress she's wearin'.'

Blind Bob was at his front door with his upstairs neighbours the Chapmans. They said something to him as the party passed by and he tilted his head. 'Good luck, girl!' he shouted loudly.

The Carey sisters were leaning on their upstairs windowsill and they called out, 'God bless you both!'

Vera smiled and she squeezed Sally's arm tightly. She wore an emerald-green two-piece suit that hugged her shapely figure. The coat was tailored at the waist and the calf-length skirt was pleated. She had on a matching wide hat with a small set of flowers attached to the top edge of the brim. Her red hair was neatly done and fluffed out around her ears. She wore high-heels, seamed stockings and grey gloves, and she clutched a small handbag to her side.

Sally walked beside her, equally well attired. She had spent a considerable time getting ready that morning, and her sister Lora had been surprisingly helpful by volunteering to do the shopping. Sally had washed her hair carefully the previous evening and had slept in curlers. The curl was tight and her dark hair sat neatly on her neck. She wore a long flowered dress and a short navy-blue jacket with a pill-box hat to match. Her slim calves looked shapely in her sheer stockings, and the tight-fitting jacket made her waist appear tiny against her well-rounded hips. Sally had spent some time with an excited and bubbling Vera the previous evening fussing over what they would wear, and Vera had lent her friend a pair of her high-heeled shoes for the occasion.

During the morning Sally had been filled with apprehension. She had gone over to help Vera get ready and her friend had insisted on doing her make-up. She had sat perfectly still as Vera applied lipstick, face powder and a faint trace of rouge. She had darkened Sally's eyelashes and plucked her eyebrows, then playfully told her to wink seductively for effect. They had giggled and laughed loudly, and then Vera had suddenly become emotional, shedding a few tears and confiding in Sally about the fears she had for the baby growing inside her. 'What sort of a world is it comin' into wiv this war an' all, Sal?' she had said, dabbing her eyes on a crinkled handkerchief.

Sally had quelled her friend's fears with a few well-chosen words. 'Look 'ere, Vera. Yer should fink yerself lucky. Joe's a good bloke. 'E finks the world of yer an' I know 'e's gonna really spoil that baby o' yours. I'll tell yer somefink else, too. I wish I 'ad a child. I'd change places wiv yer any day. Now shut yer silly row an' let's get ready.'

The two left the square with Vera's mother and father close behind, both dressed in their Sunday best. Other guests, including Vera's sister Doreen and her husband, were going directly to the registry office at the Town Hall. Vera's intended had woken up that morning to much shouting and banging and found himself sitting in the backyard toilet. He gave out a low groan of discomfort and recognised his mother's loud voice as she hammered on the door and screamed out for him to rouse himself. Breakfast was a very tricky operation for the young merchant seaman after his heavy stag-night session, and as the queasiness grew with each mouthful he knew he was going to bring everything back up. He felt a little better after a visit to the local public baths and the barber's, where his short spiky hair was trimmed and the clippers were run up the back of his neck and then found himself sufficiently recovered to pay a quick visit to the Railway Inn, where he gingerly sipped a pint of ale with his docker brother Dave before going on to the Town Hall.

The wedding of Vera Mynott and Joe Copeland had created a great deal of interest within the small community. The two youngsters were popular with everyone in Paragon Place and the event was seen by the tenants as a chance to make merry and forget for a while the food rationing, the consistently bad news from the war fronts and the terrifying memories of the heavy bombing during the previous year. There had been various suggestions and ideas for the best way to proceed, and Mrs Mynott's neighbours had rallied round with donations of food from their own rations. Trestle tables were borrowed from the local school, and Granny Almond found a large white tablecloth at the bottom of her metal trunk, which she freshened up by starching it in her copper. Crockery was scrounged from various sources and a tub of ice cream had been purchased for the children from Mr Rossi at a reduced price. Everything was at hand, and as soon as the wedding party had left the square their friends and neighbours got busy with their preparations.

There was one major problem and it was Ginny Almond who drew everyone's attention to it. 'What we gonna do fer music? We gotta 'ave music,' she asserted.

'What about askin' Blind Bob ter play 'is squeezebox?' someone asked.

'Leave orf. That always sets 'is mongrel off 'owlin',' someone else piped in.

While the discussion amongst the tenants of Paragon Place was progressing from the sublime to the ridiculous, Ginny Almond glanced up the square and spotted Alf Porter sauntering along with his usual rolling gait. ''Old up,' she said. 'It's pissy Alf. Don't keep 'im talkin'.'

Granny Allen was having trouble hearing and

she missed Ginny's words. As the square's inebriate drew level Granny Allen said in a loud voice, 'I'd loan yer my pianer, but it weighs a ton an' it's on them there glass stands.'

Alf's hearing was about the only part of him which was in perfect working order and he heard the remark. ''Ello, girls. What's the problem, then?' he said, rocking back slightly on his heels.

'We're tryin' ter sort out some music fer the celebration,' Ginny replied, lifting her eyes to the sky.

'What about a pianer?' Alf asked.

Granny Allen shook her head. 'Me pianer's too 'eavy ter move. Besides, it's on glass stands.'

Alf rocked back again and stepped forward a pace as he steadied himself. 'What about my ole joanna? Mind you, it ain't bin played fer years, but it still goes – an' it's on castors,' he added, grinning.

The impromptu entertainments committee believed the problem had been solved and they decided to recruit volunteers. 'My daughter Rene's Ted won't mind 'elpin,' Granny Allen said.

'Patrick Botley an' ole Charlie Robinson'll give an 'and,' added Ginny.

'An' me,' Alf volunteered.

'C'mon then,' Ginny said. 'Let's get started or they'll be back afore we're ready.'

Alf stood at his front door for a few minutes, swaying slightly as he tried to untangle a bunch of keys from the lining of his coat. By the time he had got into his house and removed the bits and pieces from the top of the piano with a sweep of his arm the labour conscripts had arrived.

'Right, now you get one end an' I'll 'old on ter this end an' we'll swivel it round,' Charlie said in an authoritative voice.

Patrick pulled his end of the piano away from the wall just as Alf attempted to lift the lid. Alf was sent sprawling across the room and collapsed in the corner with his legs in the air. 'What the bloody 'ell was yer tryin' ter do?' Charlie moaned. 'Jus' keep out the way.'

'I was jus' wonderin' if I locked that lid,' Alf groaned, rubbing his back and burping loudly.

Patrick heaved and Charlie pushed until the contraption was halfway out of the room. 'It's no good. It won't go no farver,' Charlie announced.

'We'll 'ave ter up-end it,' Ted Bromley said, scratching his head thoughtfully.

Alf got up and started to scramble on to the piano.

'What the bloody 'ell d'yer fink you're doin'?' Charlie shouted.

'If I get out first I can guide yer out,' Alf replied, grinning sheepishly.

Ted gave Alf a leg-up and the inebriate carried on going head first over the opposite edge, slithering down into the passage with a thud and a groan.

'Gawd almighty, take a look at it, will yer,' Charlie muttered.

'I've 'it me crust on that poxy stair,' Alf said, rubbing his head ruefully.

'Right, now do us all a favour an' get out the

125

way,' said Charlie, spitting on his large hands. 'Up we go.'

Outside in the little square the tables were being set up and at number 3 Ginny was busy preparing the food with Granny Allen and her daughter Rene. Annie Robinson looked in and Ginny handed her a plate of cheese sandwiches. 'Could yer take these out, luv? 'Ere, 'ave they got that pianer out yet?' she asked.

Annie walked over to number 5 and heard a variety of obscene comments before she saw the piano in the passage, tilting forward at a sharp angle. 'What's 'appened?' she asked innocently.

Charlie's head appeared over the top of the piano. 'What's 'appened?' he shouted. 'We up-ended the poxy fing and swung it round ter get it out o' the room, then when we lowered it the bloody front went right frew the poxy floor-boards. See if yer can get us somefink ter lever it up wiv, Annie.'

Annie pulled at her chin thoughtfully. 'What about a broom-'andle?' she suggested.

Charlie raised his eyes to the ceiling. 'A broom-'andle's no bleedin' good. We'll 'ave ter 'ave somefing 'eavier.'

'Ain't Alf got anyfing in there?' Annie asked.

Charlie leaned forward on the piano and clasped his hands. 'Listen, Annie,' he began in a measured tone. 'Alf got knocked over, then 'e cracked 'is bonce. Now 'e's got 'imself wedged down the side of the joanna. Unless we can get somefing ter prise up the front 'e's gonna stay there.'

A muffled groan came from the narrow space

126

between the piano and the wall and a pained expression appeared on Charlie's face as Alf called out, "Urry up an' get me out, fer Gawd's sake.'

'Shut yer noise, Alf. We're doin' the best we can,' Ted yelled at him.

Annie returned to Ginny's house and began relating the events at number 5. 'They're in a right ole state,' she moaned. 'The floorboards 'ave give way an' poor old Alf's trapped under the pianer. They want somefing ter prise the fing up wiv.'

'Well, they'll 'ave ter fend fer themselves. We've got all these sandwiches ter do yet,' Ginny stated.

Granny Allen looked up at Annie. ''Ow they doin' wiv that joanna Annie? 'Ave they got it out yet?'

'Alf's trapped under the floorboards,' Ginny said patiently, dipping her bread-knife into the margarine.

Granny Allen carried on slicing the bread. Soon Daisy Almond came into the room with fresh supplies. ''Ow they gettin' on wiv that pianer, Ginny?' she asked.

'They're takin' the floorboards up,' Lil Allen cut in.

'Why's that then?'

'Alf's fell down an 'ole or somefing.'

Ginny laughed aloud. 'We'll 'ave ter leave 'im there an' get Blind Bob ter play that squeezebox of 'is.'

'Bloody idiots,' Daisy chuckled. 'They couldn't organise a piss-up in a brewery.'

An hour later a battered piano was wheeled out into the square. Charlie and Patrick were pushing and Ted was guiding it from the front. Behind them came Alf, one sleeve of his coat almost hanging off at the shoulder. They turned the contraption so that it was positioned next to the tree facing the entrance to the square, and Charlie wiped his brow. 'C'mon, lads, let's get a pint in the Railway before it shuts,' he said. 'I fink we deserve a drink.'

Ted looked around. 'Where's that bloody idiot disappeared to?' he asked.

Patrick grinned and pointed to number 5. ''E's gone back fer the stool.'

Alf appeared with the seat and set it down. 'Luvverly ole pianer, this,' he said, patting the lid.

Charlie was getting impatient. 'C'mon then, we gonna get that drink or not?'

Alf licked his lips. 'Good idea,' he grinned. 'Before we go, though, let's see 'ow it sounds.'

The women had come out into the square and stood around watching as the piano was being put into place. 'Go on, Alfie. Give us a tune,' someone shouted to him.

Alf lifted the lid and clicked his knuckles together in an exaggerated gesture. With a grandiose flourish he raised his arms above his head and thumped down hard on the keys. Everyone groaned. Not a sound had come from the piano. Charlie kicked the contraption and looked hard at the drunk. 'Well, I ain't gonna cart that poxy fing back in there,' he shouted at Alf. 'It can stay there.'

128

Patrick scratched his head thoughtfully. 'Let's 'ave a look inside. There might not be much wrong wiv it.'

'Nufing a box o' matches wouldn't put right,' Charlie growled.

Patrick opened the top and looked inside. His face brightened and he reached down and took out a tattered, dust-covered overcoat.

'I wondered where that got to!' Alf exclaimed. 'I used ter put that ole coat on me bed in the winter.'

After a few strains of 'Swannee' the men disappeared to the Railway Inn for some welcome refreshment, and the women set about putting the finishing touches to their preparations.

At number 1 the lace curtains moved and Harriet Carey turned to her younger sister. 'I do hope they don't have too much to drink, Juliet. They get so noisy when they're drunk.'

High billowy clouds presaged a dry evening as the wedding party returned from the Town Hall. Joe had a look of relief on his broad features, whilst Vera was still flushed with excitement. Sally walked a way behind the pair in company with Mr and Mrs Mynott, and a further distance behind came Vera's sister Doreen holding on to her husband's arm.

'Cor! Look, Joe, they've even got a pianer out in the square!' Vera exclaimed, squeezing his arm.

Joe grinned happily as the folk from Paragon Place gathered around them, offering their congratulations and giving the two advice on how to

129

prolong married bliss.

''Ow d'yer get that fing out in the square?' Vera asked, nodding in the direction of the piano.

'Don't ask,' Ginny said, grimacing. 'They nearly done away wiv Alf Porter in the process, and Charlie reckons 'e's nearly ruptured 'imself.'

Joe's family and friends had started to arrive as well as a few invited guests. Drinks and food were quickly handed around and after Fred Mynott said a few words of thanks to the organisers the party got under way.

Sally had slipped thankfully into the background. She stood beside a table talking to Ginny and glanced over to the newlyweds. Vera looked radiant as she stood in the centre of a group, laughing happily and holding on to Joe's arm. Sally felt a twinge of sadness as she recalled her own wedding. She had been married in white at the local church, with two of Ben's younger sisters acting as bridesmaids. The reception had been held at his house, and soon after the two of them had left for a few days' honeymoon in Ramsgate the celebrations had turned into a brawl. Her father had had too much to drink and took offence at something that was said. He had received a black eye, and someone else had fallen through the downstairs window and had been rushed to hospital for stitches to his face and arms. Sally recalled her mother saying that it was a bad beginning for a married couple, and now she smiled ruefully to herself.

Crates of ale were stacked beneath the barren

sycamore tree and at one of the tables Ginny was kept busy serving ice cream and lemonade to the children. Alf was coaxed into playing the piano but he began to irritate the revellers by continuously stopping midway through the melodies to take a swig of ale.

Granny Almond hobbled over to Blind Bob, who was sitting beside his front door. 'Get on that pianer, fer Gawd's sake, Bob,' she implored him. 'That soppy git Alf ain't played one song all the way frew yet.'

Bob allowed himself to be led over to the piano by Daisy, who prodded Alf in the back. ''Ere, you. Get orf that joanna an' let Bob 'ave a go.'

Alf was only too keen to oblige and as soon as the blind man struck up with 'Dear Old Pals' he scurried away to get a refill.

By the time the weak sun had slipped down behind the leaning chimney pots the food had all but disappeared. Folk sat around chatting together in groups. Granny Almond turned to Granny Allen. 'I wonder if the two bible-punchers'll show up.'

Lil's eyebrows went up. 'Who punched who?' she asked, turning her good ear towards Daisy.

'The Carey sisters,' Daisy said in a loud voice. 'I wonder if they'll show up.'

Lil shook her head. 'I don't fink so. Them two don't drink.'

'What about that Taylor girl? D'yer fink she'll show up?' Daisy asked, mouthing her words carefully for her friend's benefit.

'I shouldn't fink so, Daisy. She's got ter go

ter work.'

Daisy nodded and then spotted Fred Mynott nearby. 'Gonna top us up, then?' she grinned, holding out her empty glass.

Children darted in and out of the tables and around the tree while others, too full of ice cream and lemonade to move far, sat around together and giggled at Alf's antics as he tried to dance a jig. Outside Ginny's door her children were having a serious discussion.

'Why did they get married?' five-year-old Jenny asked.

''Cos they luv each ovver, stupid,' said Sara, a knowledgeable seven.

Ginny's ten-year-old son Billy sat with his back to the wall, hands cupping his chin. 'Yer gotta get married if yer want babies,' he said.

'No yer don't,' Jenny piped in. 'My friend at school ain't got no dad. 'Ow comes she got born?'

'She's different. She's a widder,' Sara replied.

Billy laughed aloud. 'No she ain't. She's an orphan.'

Frankie, who was a grown-up twelve year old, was rearranging a pack of dogeared playing cards. 'She ain't an orphan neivver,' he declared. 'She's a bastard.'

The two girls gasped and held their hands to their mouths. 'You swore! We'll tell Mum,' Sara cried.

Frankie pulled a face. 'Look, you two. Bastard ain't swearin'. It means yer mum ain't married, so yer got no dad. It says so in the diction'ry. I seen it in the one we got at school.'

132

Jenny was watching the revellers milling around near the piano and she suddenly sighed. 'Poor Mr Porter. 'E's one, too.'

''Ow d'yer know?' Billy asked.

''Cos I 'eard Mummy tellin' the lady next door Mr Porter's a soppy bastard.'

At eight o'clock Vera and Joe took their leave of the wassailers. Joe was carrying a tatty-looking suitcase, and as the two reached the end of the square they turned and waved back to their tipsy friends and relations. Granny Almond put a handkerchief up to her eyes and Ginny looked sad as the newlyweds disappeared from sight. 'Gawd 'elp 'em,' she said to Annie Robinson. 'It's gonna be 'ard fer 'er when 'e goes back ter sea.'

Sally had hugged both Vera and Joe when they went round saying their goodbyes. She had forced a happy smile and wished them every happiness, though her heart was heavy and her thoughts were elsewhere. Now, as she stood gazing along the square, she saw George Tapley leave his house and walk slowly out into Stanley Street, his head bowed.

Dusk was settling over the little square when Bill Freeman came to the front door and stood propped against the door post as he watched the dancers. Charlie brought out a chair and Bill sat crouched, his hands clasped over his knees. He had his shabby overcoat pulled around his shoulders against the growing cold and Sally could not help noticing how frail and ill he looked. She had been reluctant to join in the dancing and as soon as she could disentangle

133

herself she went over and sat beside him. "Ow yer feelin', Bill?' she asked, puffing from her exertions.

'I'm OK, lass,' he replied. 'I 'eard the music an' I thought I'd take a look. It's nice ter see everybody enjoyin' themselves. What about you? Are you enjoyin' yerself?'

Sally nodded. 'I'm not one fer dancin', Bill. It's a nice do, though.'

The old man looked at her and she felt as though his old eyes were seeing right into her mind. 'I like ter see yer 'appy, but I don't know as yer are,' he said quietly. 'You've got a sad face, Sally.'

She forced a laugh and touched his clasped hands. 'It's me natural look, Bill. I'm OK.'

'Yer still missin' that feller o' yours, ain't yer?' he said, looking into her dark, troubled eyes.

She was taken aback by his directness and she flushed slightly.

Bill's gaunt face broke into a grin. 'I know what you're finkin'. You're sayin' ter yerself 'e's a nosy ole goat. Yer see, lass, it's one o' the comforts o' gettin' old. Yer can ask those sorts o' questions. I've watched yer lately. I noticed yer when yer was backwards an' forwards lookin' after me when I was ill, an' I said ter meself, that girl's got a sad face. Young people should be 'appy. Us old 'uns don't like ter see yer young chickens sad.'

Sally grinned. 'I can see you've recovered all right, Bill. And in answer to your question, yes, I s'pose I do still miss Ben, but it's over between us, Bill. I've got ter get used ter the idea. It jus'
134

didn't work out fer the two of us.'

He leaned back in his chair and looked at her, his head tilted slightly. 'Yer wanna know somefing? Fings are gonna change fer yer. Yer gonna be very 'appy. I can tell.'

Sally crossed her slim legs and leaned towards him, her chin cupped in her hand and her elbow resting on her knee. 'Tell me, Bill. 'Ow d'yer know? 'Ow can yer tell?'

He inclined his head towards hers. ''Cos it's written on yer star.'

'On me star?' she queried.

He chuckled and raised his face to the dark heavens. 'D'yer see that little group o' stars?' he asked, ignoring her confusion. 'There, just above the chimney-pot? That's the Seven Sisters. See that very bright star over there? Well, that's Sirius, the dog star.'

'I didn't know yer knew about the stars, Bill,' she said, a surprised look on her face.

He smiled faintly. 'When I'm not readin' me Westerns I read about the stars. It's a fascinatin' subject, the stars. Mind you, though, it's very 'ard ter see the star patterns in London most o' the time. Too much fog and smoke. Now, in the country yer can see 'em clear as anyfing. When I was a lad I used ter spend hours watchin' the stars. Very interested in astronomy, I was.'

Sally smiled and her eyes widened. 'Yer still 'aven't told me about me star,' she grumbled affectionately.

Bill pursed his lips and grunted. 'Well yer see, it's like this. We've all got a star, but what yer gotter do is claim it.'

135

'Claim it?'

'Yeah.'

'But 'ow do I claim it, Bill?'

He smiled and raised his eyes to the dark sky once more. ''Ave yer ever looked up there an' seen a shootin' star?'

Sally nodded. 'Course I 'ave. They say that when yer see a shootin' star, a baby's born.'

'That's right,' he replied, still staring skyward. 'A shootin' star is a lucky star, an' that's the star yer claim. When yer see it dash across the night sky yer just say ter yerself, I claim that star. Yer 'ave ter be quick, though, it's gone in a flash o' light. What yer do then is shut yer eyes and count ter ten. It's as simple as that.'

Sally laughed aloud. 'Bill Freeman, you're 'avin' me on.'

His tired old eyes looked into hers, and a serious look replaced the smile. 'What I'm sayin', lass, is that yer gotta claim yer 'appiness. We all 'ave to. Trouble is, before yer can claim it, before yer really know it, yer gotta know misery. It's the only way it works, believe me.'

'Did yer claim yer 'appiness, Bill?' she asked.

'I did, lass,' he said.

A chill breeze had sprung up and it was now too dark to continue the festivities outside. Most of the revellers had drifted off and the Mynotts invited the few who were left to continue the party at their home. Sally helped Bill up to his room and took him his cocoa and biscuits. Annie and Charlie Robinson were at the Mynotts and Lora, turning her nose up at the party, had been

136

out with Bernard since the afternoon. Sally sat alone in the house thoughtfully staring into the low fire. She wondered what it was that Bill had been trying to say. Perhaps the only happiness that was real was born out of abject misery. She wondered whether she would find true happiness, or whether it would elude her. If she was destined to live a life without love and without knowing the joy and pain of motherhood, how could she go out and claim her star?

The fire had almost died when footsteps sounded outside. Sally heard giggling and then Lora's low voice in the passage. 'Sounds like the party's still goin' on,' she said.

Lora and Bernard walked into the room and Sally saw the disappointment written on Lora's face. 'I thought you'd be at the party,' she said quickly.

Sally shook her head. 'No, I didn't feel like it.'

Lora sat down in the easy chair leaving Bernard standing beside the door. 'Did the weddin' go off all right?' she asked flatly.

'Yeah, it was very nice,' Sally replied.

Lora looked up at Bernard. 'Well, don't stand there like a dummy. Sit down.'

Bernard moved into the room and sat beside the table. 'I've got my call-up papers, Sally,' he said suddenly. 'I've got to report next week. Up in Lancashire.'

Lora kicked off her high-heeled shoes and picked up the heavy poker. 'I s'pose 'e'll be datin' all those Waafs once 'e gets that uniform on,' she said without humour, prodding at the

137

dying coals.

Bernard grinned sheepishly. 'I expect I'll get leave after a few weeks.'

Lora's face showed her displeasure. 'What am I s'posed ter do while you're away?'

Sally felt irritation welling up inside her. Lora was being her usual self and Bernard looked ridiculous, sitting upright in his chair with a fixed grin on his baby face. 'I s'pose yer could do what everybody else 'as ter do – like stoppin' in,' she said sardonically.

Lora snorted. 'It'll drive me mad, stoppin' in this dump every night.'

'This dump's yer 'ome,' Sally said with feeling. 'Maybe yer'd feel better livin' in a rest centre. Yer should fink yerself lucky we didn't lose our 'ome in the blitz. Thousands did.'

Lora looked up sharply. 'Who's upset you?' she said quickly.

Bernard fidgeted in his chair. 'It's getting late. Maybe I should be getting off home,' he said hesitantly.

'Goodnight then,' Lora said, her angry eyes still on Sally.

Bernard got up and backed towards the door. 'Well, er, goodnight then,' he stammered.

'Goodnight, Bernard,' Sally said, feeling sorry as she saw his embarrassment. She listened to the sound of the front door closing and then she rounded on her sister. 'There was no need fer that,' she said in a low voice.

'Need fer what?'

'Makin' the feller feel small,' Sally said angrily.

138

Lora laughed mirthlessly. 'Well, 'e annoys me at times. 'E's so immature.'

'Yer knew 'e was younger than you when yer started goin' wiv 'im. I don't know why yer bothered.'

'That's my business,' Lora snapped.

'Well, yer should at least treat 'im better,' Sally said quickly.

'That's ripe – comin' from you.'

'What d'yer mean by that?' Sally said quietly.

'Well, you certainly know 'ow ter treat a feller, don't yer,' Lora snarled. 'Maybe if you'd 'ave bin a bit more understandin' towards Ben 'e wouldn't 'ave looked elsewhere.'

Two spots of anger showed on Sally's pale cheeks. 'Yer don't know what yer talkin' about!' she snapped. 'There was no cause fer 'im ter jump inter bed wiv any little tart 'e fancied.'

Lora grabbed up her shoes from beside the chair and puffed loudly. 'Well, I'm not stayin' 'ere arguin' wiv yer. I'm off ter bed.'

Sally sat back in the chair trying to calm her cold anger by breathing deeply. She could hear faint voices singing and muffled laughter coming from the Mynott's house. The mournful sound of a tug whistle reached her ears, and then she heard Alf Porter's loud voice saying goodnight. Sally got up from her chair and put a few small pieces of coal on to the fire before going up to her bedroom. At the bend of the stairs she listened at Bill's door for a second or two, and then, satisfied that he was sleeping peacefully, she continued on up to her room.

Chapter Seven

IN Paragon Place life went on at a slow pace during the mild April days of '42, with the local folk deploring the growing food shortages and the bad news which continued to come from the war fronts. George Tapley had become increasingly concerned for his elder son, Tony, who was serving in the Middle East, when news came over the wireless that Rommel had launched a big offensive. He had felt a little easier when he finally received a letter from Tony, but he continued to grieve for Laurie, of whom he had still received no word.

For Sally life had become a dull, monotonous existence and she found herself growing more and more depressed as the days dragged by. After Ben confronted her in the street she had been dreading the next contact he would make with her, but nothing had happened. Instead of feeling relief at his disappearance she had found herself becoming increasingly worried about him. When she finally heard the news she was gripped by an almost overwhelming anxiety. It was Patrick Botley who had told her father and Charlie blurted it out one evening as soon as he set foot in the house. 'Ben's inside,' he announced. ''E got six months for assaultin' a publican.'

Sally could not hide her concern as she questioned her father, and Charlie told her he had learned that Ben had been making a nuisance of himself around some of the local pubs, and one or two publicans had barred him. It was after one heavy drinking session when the landlord of a Dockhead pub told Ben he had had enough to drink and refused to serve him that the trouble had started. Ben had thrown a chair across the bar which shattered a large mirror, and he had been subdued only after beating up the publican.

The bad news made Sally feel guilty. She felt as though she were partly to blame for what had happened, and she confided her feelings to Vera. 'I feel terrible about it,' she sighed. 'If only I'd talked fings over wiv 'im it might 'ave bin different.'

Vera leaned back in the chair and ran a hand over her rising belly. 'That's stupid talk,' she asserted. 'Yer couldn't be expected ter know what 'e was gonna do, an' yer can't blame yerself. Besides, 'e's bin on the turps fer ages. Yer said yerself 'e was drinkin' 'eavy before the two of yer split up. It was on the cards that 'e was gonna get 'imself inter trouble. It 'ad ter 'appen sooner or later. Ben was always a bit wild, Sal.'

Vera's words did not console Sally. 'I know, but 'e wasn't always on the booze,' she said sadly. 'When we first got married 'e 'ardly touched a drink. If only—'

'If only nufing,' Vera cut in. 'Look, Sal. Yer gotta get it inter yer bonce that you're not responsible fer what 'e gets up to. What 'e does now is no concern o' yours. S'posin' yer found anuvver feller, what then? Would yer ask 'im if it was all right? Course yer wouldn't.'

'There's no fear o' that,' Sally snorted.

'Don't yer be so sure,' Vera said quickly. 'You're not gonna go on ferever wivout a bloke, are yer? You'll end up like those two creaky ole sisters at number one.'

'Bein' on me own don't worry me,' Sally said defensively.

'P'r'aps it don't now,' Vera countered, 'but in time, when yer really got that piss-artist out o' yer system, you're gonna get the urge again. What yer gonna do then, love 'em an' leave 'em like Muriel Taylor? No, Sally. That ain't yer nature. You're not cut out ter be a dried-up ole prune, neivver. One o' these days you're gonna find a feller who you're gonna go overboard for, mark my words.'

Sally had listened to her friend's advice, but she could not fully absolve herself from blame for what had happened to Ben. It was no comfort to her that her father considered Ben to have got what he deserved, and she knew that she would not be able to talk to her mother or Lora about the affair. Sally grew more withdrawn, embarrassed at her feelings of concern and her sense of guilt, and it became a strain to remain in the house. She had considered moving out but her mother seemed to be ailing again of late and was leaving more of the running of the house to her. There was Bill, too. He had become more of a recluse and had to be coaxed into going out for his pension and his weekly bath. At Harrison's the days passed slowly. The numbing monotony of work felt as if it were killing her, and even Vera's bright and breezy nature could not dispel her gloom and despondency. Sally began to realise that there was only one thing she could do to break out of her depression. She would have to visit Ben in prison.

It was a sunny spring day when Sally made the trip across London to visit Ben but her heart was heavy and she felt a growing sense of unease. She caught a bus to the Elephant and Castle and then took the underground, changing from the Bakerloo Line to the Central Line at Oxford Circus and anxiously watching as the train rumbled into each station for fear of getting lost. When she finally stepped out into the bright sunlight at East Acton she sighed heavily, trying to calm her unsteady nerves.

The tree-lined Du Cane Road was quiet and shady, and Sally soon came upon the prison which stood back from the thoroughfare. She took a deep breath as she walked up to the reception office, fearful of how Ben might react when he saw her. He would be expecting one of his brothers but his family had been only too happy for her to use the visiting card.

Sally was shown into a waiting room and she seated herself amongst the other serious-faced visitors. Some of them had brought young children with them, and many seemed as nervous and worried as Sally, staring up at the ceiling or watching the prison officers who strolled around self-importantly with heavy key-chains fixed to their belts. Children became irritable from waiting and one harassed mother was trying desperately to quieten her bawling baby without much success.

At last Sally was called into a small, high-ceilinged room and as she slipped into a chair at a heavy wooden table a metal door swung open and Ben walked in accompanied by a warder. Surprise showed on his pale face as he seated himself opposite her and rested his hands on the polished surface.

'I didn't expect yer ter come in,' he said off-handedly, his eyes unblinking.

Sally forced a faint smile and shrugged her shoulders. 'I wanted ter see yer, Ben. I was worried,' she said simply.

Ben's eyes went down to his clenched hands and then he glanced briefly at the prison warder who was standing in a corner of the room staring out of the high barred window.

'There was no need fer yer ter come. It's a bit of a journey,' he said quietly, his voice sounding hoarse.

Sally noticed how pale he looked as he sat slumped at the table, and how his hands seemed to be constantly moving.

'Are yer feeling well?' she asked.

He nodded and a bitter smile played around the corners of his mouth. 'Yeah, I'm OK,' he replied. 'The food could be better an' the accommodation ain't first class, but it's OK.'

Sally clasped her hands on the table. 'Look, Ben,' she said, leaning forward as she spoke. 'I didn't come all this way ter gloat. I blame meself for you bein' 'ere. If I'd 'ave . . .'

'Why did yer come, then?' he asked with hardness in his voice, his eyes widening. 'Will it make yer feel better now you've seen me? Will it

144

make yer more satisfied you've got shot of yer no-good, drunken 'usband?'

Tears started up in Sally's eyes and she swallowed hard. 'Whatever 'appened between us don't mean that I wanna see yer in prison, Ben,' she said in a low voice. 'I jus' wanted ter say that if we'd 'ave talked yer might not 'ave done what yer did, that's all.'

Ben glanced across to the warder whose eyes were still fixed on the window, then he looked back at Sally.

'Jus' get one fing straight,' he said. 'I don't 'old you responsible fer me goin' garrety. I done wrong an' I'm payin' fer it. There's no need fer you ter lose any sleep, an' there's no need fer yer ter come in any more. You've made it clear in the past me an' yer are finished. Leave it at that, will yer?'

Through her tears Sally saw the cold look in Ben's eyes and she suddenly stifled a sob, dropping her gaze and easing her chair back from the table.

Ben had already stood up and he glanced at the warder. 'Look after yerself,' he said to her quietly, then he turned his back on her.

Sally walked out of the prison quickly without looking back, and as she turned and hurried along to the underground station she burst out crying.

The lengthening days of spring slowly gave way to summer, and with the hot June days came cool pleasant evenings. The introduction of Double Summer Time brought a few changes to Paragon Place. Folk found it difficult to sleep while it was still light and they took to sitting around at their front doors chatting until very late. The children, too, had taken to staying awake longer, and when the toffee-apple man pedalled his bike up to the top of the square and rang his bell late in the evening parents raised their eyes to the sky and called up to their clamorous offspring, 'No it's not the toffee-apple man, now get ter sleep.'

'I 'eard the bell, Mum. It is 'im.'

'No, it's the warden.'

'No it's not. Wardens 'ave whistles.'

'Well, this one's got a bell.'

'Ah, Mum. Let's 'ave a toffee-apple.'

'Now shut up an' get ter sleep. Toffee-apples rot yer teef, an' besides, you'll get the toffee all over the bedclothes.'

The argument was almost lost, but the children were persistent. 'No I won't, I promise. Cross me 'eart an' 'ope ter die. I'll clean me teef after, Mum. Honest.'

'This is the last time, understand?'

'Cor, fanks, mum! 'Urry up or 'e'll be gone.'

'All right, now shut yer row.' The harassed mother clenched her teeth. 'If 'e comes round again termorrer night I'll stick a bleedin' pin in 'is tyre,' she added to herself.

Ginny Almond usually sat chatting with George Tapley after she had settled her brood for the night. She had given up trying to persuade him

146

to go out for a drink since he received the bad news about his younger son; instead she made small talk and felt pleased whenever she could bring a smile to his sad face. On one very warm evening when they were sitting together George suddenly said, 'I 'ad a dream about Laurie last night, Ginny.'

'Did yer?'

'Yeah, it was a strange dream,' he began. 'I was in a big room an' it was all white. It was like an 'ospital ward, but there wasn't any beds. A lot o' people were sittin' around an' they all 'ad bandages on. Some 'ad their legs done up an' ovvers 'ad their arms in slings. I could see one or two wiv their 'eads bandaged up, but I couldn't see the faces. It was like all their faces was covered in mist. Suddenly I see Laurie. I knew it was 'im, even though I couldn't see 'is face. 'E 'ad 'is back ter me an' I could see that 'is 'ead was covered in bandages. I went up to 'im an' touched 'im on the shoulder an' when 'e turned around 'e was smiling. I could see 'is face was pale an' drawn and 'is eyes were starin', but 'e 'ad this big smile on 'is face. It was like 'e was tryin' ter tell me somefing, an' as I looked at 'im I started ter drift backwards. Laurie was gettin' smaller an' smaller an' the mist was all round me. I woke up suddenly an' me 'eart was poundin'. I couldn't get back ter sleep after that, Gin. I got up an' made meself a cup o' tea an' sat finkin'. What did it mean? Is 'e alive or dead?'

Ginny had been listening intently and she touched his arm gently. 'I'll tell yer what it means, George,' she said. ''E's safe. You'll 'ear

147

soon, mark my words.'

George looked down at his feet. 'It's bin a long time, Ginny. Surely I would 'ave 'eard by now if 'e was a prisoner or somefing?'

'You'll 'ear soon,' Ginny said smiling. 'I've got that feelin'. You'll 'ear good news soon, an' I tell yer what. When yer do 'ear the good news you'll 'ave ter take me out fer that drink. OK?'

He nodded. 'We'll get drunk tergevver, gel,' he replied, his serious face relaxing slightly.

It was during the hot summer months when word began to get around Paragon Place that all was not well at number 8, and when the Robinsons sat down to tea one evening Annie broached the subject. 'They seem such a quiet couple, Charlie,' she said. 'I was talkin' ter Mrs Mynott this mornin' an' she said it's bin goin' on fer some time.'

Charlie stuck his knife into an opened packet of margarine and spread a generous helping on to a thick slice of bread. 'I ain't surprised, ter tell yer the trufe,' he said. 'I always reckoned there was somefing peculiar about the bloke. I never forget when the air raids was on. We couldn't get 'im outside that 'ouse ter do 'is share o' fire-watchin'. Petrified, 'e was.'

Annie pulled a face. 'Well, the blitz was bloody frightenin'. I s'pose the poor feller was scared,' she said.

Charlie dipped the bread into his mutton stew and took a large bite. 'We was all frightened, but if we'd all sat under the stairs like 'im the ole bloody place would 'ave burnt down. Look

148

when we smuvvered all them incend'ry bombs wiv sand on that Sunday night.'

Annie grimaced. 'Wipe yer chin, Charlie,' she sighed.

'Well I'm right, ain't I?' he asked, running the back of his large hand across his mouth. 'We was all doin' our bit an' there was Sammy Chapman sittin' under the stairs playin' wiv 'is rosary.'

'You're a wicked git, Charlie,' Annie admonished. ''E couldn't 'elp 'imself. The man was jus' terrified. Don't yer know every one o' them beads is a prayer? 'E was prayin'. Freda Chapman told me 'e always 'ad 'is rosary wiv 'im when the raids was on.'

Charlie laughed aloud and looked around the table. 'Bloody 'ell, Annie. We was all prayin'. I said a prayer or two when I was puttin' the sandbags on those incend'ries. What was 'e prayin' for? Did 'e expect Gawd Almighty ter put the fires out for 'im?'

Sally had been listening and she stifled a grin. Lora gave her father a look of disgust and went on eating. Charlie was warming to the subject and he gulped down another spoonful of broth. 'Look at that time the bomb landed over in Stanley Street an' we 'ad ter dig the Murphys out. I didn't see Sammy Chapman gettin' 'is 'ands dirty. Christ! We could 'ave done wiv a few more 'elpers that night.'

'Well that's as it may be,' Annie retorted. 'I'm just tellin' yer what Mrs Mynott told me this mornin'. She said Freda Chapman told 'er that she reckons Sammy's goin' orf 'is 'ead.'

'What's 'e doin' then, eatin' the soap or some-fing?' Charlie asked grinning.

'It's nufing ter laugh at,' Annie replied. ''E started goin' funny at work an' they ended up givin' 'im the sack. Freda coaxed 'im inter goin' ter the doctor's but all 'e's done is put 'im on tablets. Ole Bartholomew reckons it's nerves. Freda said the tablets ain't doin' 'im much good. In fact she told Mrs Mynott 'e's gettin' worse.'

Charlie wiped the last of his bread around the plate. 'Well, if 'e was goin' a bit scatty at the gas-works I reckon they 'ad a right ter sack 'im,' he said, his eyes widening. 'They've gotta be careful. I mean, 'e could 'ave blown the bloody place up, an' 'alf the Ole Kent Road wiv it!'

'Well, I feel sorry fer poor ole Freda,' Annie said. 'She's such a pleasant woman. It mus' be a terrible worry fer 'er. She can't get 'im ter wash 'imself or change 'is clothes, an' 'e's started talkin' to 'imself.'

'I bet Blind Bob ain't too 'appy neivver,' Charlie remarked. ''E's livin' under it all.'

When the meal was over Charlie settled down in his favourite chair and lit his pipe. Annie turned on the wireless for the news broadcast while Sally gathered up the plates and took them out to the sink. She had almost finished the washing-up when Lora walked out into the scullery and picked up the tea-towel without say-ing anything. Sally glanced at her once or twice before asking, ''Ave yer 'eard from Bernard?'

Lora shook her head. 'I've not 'ad a letter fer two weeks. I'm not stoppin' in any more, that's fer sure. I'm goin' dancin' ternight wiv some o'

150

the girls from work. Anyway, I'm finkin' of writin' Bernard a letter ter tell 'im I don't want ter see 'im any more. 'E's too young fer me.'

Sally glanced quickly at her younger sister. ''E's gonna be upset.'

'Too bad,' Lora replied. ''E'll get over it. Besides, 'e was gettin' too serious fer me. 'E wanted us ter get engaged before 'e got called up. I'm not in any 'urry ter get married. I don't wanna be lumbered wiv screamin' kids. I wanna see a bit o' life before I get tied to a kitchen sink.'

'Well, I 'ope I 'ave kids one day,' Sally declared.

Lora shook her head. 'You're welcome to 'em. Me, I wanna meet somebody wiv money. I want good clothes an' a nice 'ouse away from this dump. I don't wanna spend the rest 'o me life scrapin' an' schemin' an' gettin' old before me time. Jus' look at 'alf of 'em round 'ere. Look at Ginny Almond. 'Er an' the five kids were left in the lurch by 'er ole man. No fanks.'

Sally saw the hard glint in her sister's eyes and felt somehow sorry for her. There was something about her sister's attitude she could not quite understand. Lora had a hard streak in her make-up, and she seemed somehow aloof and unconcerned with other people's feelings. The look of angry determination on her face made Sally suddenly think of Ben. He would be sitting in his prison cell that very moment, she told herself. She tried to imagine what he could be thinking, and she became aware of Lora's eyes watching her. She turned to the draining-board

151

to hide her face and gazed out at the night sky above the backyard, feeling weak and lonely.

Sally and Vera walked into Paragon Place one Friday evening in early August and saw immediately that something was wrong. They had left work together with Vera holding on to Sally's arm as they made their way from the tram stop and through the arches in Stanley Street. Vera was beginning to feel the effects of her pregnancy and she was puffing slightly. The heat made her feel tired and listless and they had walked slowly. Vera could now feel the movements inside her belly and she was looking forward to leaving Harrison's soon. They paused as they entered the square and Sally looked quickly at Vera. A few yards away Ada Fuller stood with her arch enemy Clara Botley and the two women were whispering to each other as they stared up at the window of number 8.

Vera nudged her friend. 'Look at those two,' she muttered out of the corner of her mouth. 'That's a turn up fer the books.'

Further along the square folk stood at their front doors and Sally could see her mother talking to Ginny Almond and Granny Allen's daughter Rene. Annie was standing with her hand cupped to her chin and her elbow resting in the palm of her other hand. Sally knew her mother always adopted that position when she was worried. 'What's up?' she asked as she reached her front door.

'It's Sammy Chapman,' Annie replied, a frightened look on her thin face. "E's just poked 'is 'ead out the winder. 'E was 'oldin' Freda by 'er 'air an' 'e 'ad a bloody great carvin' knife in 'is 'and! 'E said 'e's gonna cut both their froats at nine o'clock ternight.'

Vera shivered despite the warmth of the evening and she went quickly to her house. Sally stood beside the little group staring up at the bedroom window. ''As anybody gone fer the police?' she asked.

Ginny nodded. 'Yeah, somebody's run round the station. Trouble is, if they try an' break in Sammy'll do what 'e said. Yer should 'ave seen 'is face when 'e come ter that winder! It frightened the life out o' me. 'Is eyes were all stary an' 'e 'ad the knife up against Freda's froat. Yer could see she was cryin'. It was really 'orrible.'

They heard the sound of a dog barking. 'Is Blind Bob in the 'ouse, Mum?' Sally asked.

Her mother nodded. ''E's sittin' on the landin' tryin' ter talk ter Sammy, though Gawd knows what 'e can do.'

It was very quiet in the square. Small groups were whispering together and occasionally they heard the barking of Bob's mongrel. A police car squealed to a halt at the end of the square and two uniformed policemen walked quickly up to number 8. They stood hesitantly at the front door and glanced up to the window. Suddenly the window was thrown open and Sammy's head appeared. 'If yer come in that door I'll kill 'er now,' he shouted, his wild eyes bulging.

The policemen stepped back and one of them shouted up, 'Let yer missus go an' we can 'ave a chat.'

Sammy's answer was to slam the window down and draw the curtains.

'Can we get in round the back?' one of the policemen asked Granny Allen, who was standing nearby.

'What yer say?' she shouted, turning her head towards him.

Granny Almond came over. 'She can't 'ear yer,' she said to the policeman. 'She's deaf. Yer won't be able ter get in round the back. All the yards are separate, an' all these 'ouses back on to the paper sorters. It's a big 'igh wall. You'll 'ave ter go in the front, it's the only way.'

'P'r'aps if one of us kept 'im talkin' the ovver one might be able ter slip in the door,' the officer whispered to his colleague, stroking his chin.

Daisy overheard the remark. 'That won't be no good,' she said quickly. 'Those stairs creak like anyfing. 'E'll 'ear yer, sure as Gawd made little apples.'

'It's a tricky one, this,' the other officer said, taking off his helmet and scratching his head.

'Well, yer better fink 'o somefing quick, or 'e's gonna slice 'er,' Daisy said abruptly.

Inside the house Blind Bob sat hunched on the stairs beside the bedroom door with his dog next to him. He had been talking quietly to Sammy, urging him to let his wife go at least, but with no success. Now as he sat with his ear pressed to the door-panel his hands gently ruffled the dog's coat. He had heard Sammy's last threat and the bang as he slammed the

154

window shut. While he waited patiently for the tormented man to settle himself Bob talked in a low, reassuring voice to his faithful mongrel. 'We're gonna sort this out, boy. Me an' you tergevver. That's it, boy, stay.' The dog had slumped down against Bob's leg with its head resting on its paws. Occasionally it gave out a low whine, as though aware that all was not well. Bob's sensitive fingers found the dog's head and patted it gently. 'There, boy. We gotta be patient,' he said quietly. 'Our Sammy's not goin' anywhere.'

There was a scraping sound from within which Bob took to be a chair moving. A plan was slowly forming in Bob's head and he bit on his bottom lip. 'We gotta try it, boy,' he whispered. He leaned his head against the closed door. 'Sammy. Can yer 'ear me, Sammy?' he called out loudly.

There was a pause, then Sammy shouted back, 'Yeah. I can 'ear yer.'

'Yer gotta let Freda go, Sammy. At least let 'er go.'

''Ow many more times 'ave I gotta tell yer?' the gruff voice sounded from behind the door. 'No! We're goin' tergevver. The Germans ain't gettin' us. I'm doin' away wiv the both of us like I said – at nine o'clock.'

'The Germans won't get yer, Sammy. We're gonna win. They won't get yer.'

A low moan came from within. 'Can't yer see? The war's over. They're tellin' us ternight. We're givin' in – at nine o'clock. They're tellin' us on the wireless.'

Bob leaned closer to the door. 'Is it true, Sammy?' he asked, a note of anxiety appearing in his voice. ''Ave we really lost the war?'

'You'll know ternight. You'll all know ternight,' came the voice. 'They're tellin' us on the nine o'clock news. We know already, though. Don't we, Freda?'

Bob could hear Freda sobbing and he took a deep breath. 'I don't want those Germans ter get me. Let me in Sammy. I wanna go wiv yer.'

'Go away from the door, Bob. Leave us alone,' Sammy shouted.

'Would yer leave a blind man ter the mercy o' those German bastards, Sammy? Won't yer take pity on a blind man. Let me go wiv yer – please.'

There was complete silence for a few seconds, then Bob heard the bolt slip. The door creaked open a few inches and Sammy's wild eyes stared through the opening. 'All right then, but you'll 'ave ter leave yer dog outside.'

Bob stood up and felt the blood rush to his cramped legs. He held out his hand and Sammy gripped it tightly, pulled him roughly into the room and closed the door quickly.

Out in the square folk were standing around, their serious faces staring up at the Chapmans' bedroom. The Carey sisters were looking out of their window and people were beginning to congregate around the entrance to the square.

'What's 'appened?' someone asked.

'Bloke tryin' ter kill 'imself an' 'is missus,' another answered.

'Who is it? D'yer know 'im?'

156

'Sammy Chapman, by all accounts.'

'Gawd A'mighty. Who'da thought it?'

The two policemen had been joined by another officer and they stood talking quietly beside the sycamore tree. 'Well, we can't stay 'ere all night,' one of them said. 'I fink we should try the roof. If one of us could get down in the back bedroom an' out on the landin' we'd 'ave a chance of shoulderin' the door and grabbin' the bloke before 'e could do any 'arm.'

'It won't work. 'E'd 'ear the noise fer sure,' another said.

'Well, we'd better wait fer the inspector an' let 'im sort it out,' the first officer replied.

Blind Bob stood in the middle of the room, a thin, wiry-haired man whose sightless eyes darted around in their sockets. He knew he had to get his bearings quickly if the plan had any chance of succeeding. 'Is the curtains drawn prop'ly, Sammy?' he asked.

The balding, heavier-built man looked at Bob quizzically. 'What yer ask for?' he snapped.

'Well, we don't want anybody gawkin' in, do we?' Bob replied, moving slightly until he could feel the very faint heat of the electric lightbulb on his head.

'Sit 'im down, Freda,' Sammy said irritably.

As the terrified woman took Bob's arm and guided him into an easy chair he could feel her hand shaking violently. He was now forming a picture of the room in his mind. Sammy was sitting beside the door, he had decided. Freda was now sitting near enough for Bob to hear her anxious breathing, and he guessed she was about

157

an arm's length away. He could smell black-lead and soot, and he moved his foot slightly until it touched the fender. He knew he was sitting beside the unlit fire. The table was to his right and directly above the edge of the table nearest to him was the light-bulb. Bob had been blind since his early twenties, but he could still imagine how dark the room would be for sighted people without the electric light. Experience of the blitz had taught him that everyone had heavy blackout curtains which effectively kept the light from filtering out. If the curtains were drawn in daylight then the reverse would apply. There was nothing else for it. He had to take the chance. How much time was there? he wondered. Sammy had repeatedly said he was going to kill them both at nine o'clock. Bob could still hear Freda's anxious breathing and he refrained from asking the time. He knew that it would only add to the woman's anxiety, and he did not want to provoke Sammy into doing something prematurely. Bob remembered that he had been listening to a talk on home vegetable-growing which followed the six o'clock news. It was during the programme that Freda first screamed out and begged her husband to put the knife down. Bob calculated that he had been sitting on the landing for well over an hour. Maybe an hour and a half. It must be nearing eight o'clock. He had an hour, maybe even less. If the police stormed the house now the three of them would be done for. Sammy had shot the bolt and it might well delay entry long enough for him to carry out his threat.

Outside, Paragon Place folk stood in a now silent vigil as the hour grew late. At the entrance to the square there had been a scuffle when Arthur the Hat strolled up and offered six to four against Sammy doing the deed. It had distressed some of the women, and a couple of burly dockers had grabbed the bookie, frogmarched him over to the bombsite and threw him on to a heap of rubble. At eight o'clock a police car pulled up at the entrance to the square and Inspector Harris climbed out. He walked quickly into the square and began consulting with his officers. 'I don't like that roof idea,' he said finally. 'It'd be impossible to scramble up there and get into the back room without making a racket. It's too risky. No, I think we've got to get the man to the window and then go in through the front door. Yes, it'll have to be the front approach. Get ready, lads. We'll call him now,' he announced gravely.

Blind Bob tried to keep calm although he could feel his heart beginning to pound. Sammy would obviously be sitting with the knife in his hand, he thought. He would have to get that table between them. Bob crossed his fingers and said a silent prayer.

'I fink I'll loosen me boots,' he said casually, and with an exaggerated sigh he bent slowly forward. While he fiddled with the laces his hand moved silently into the fender. It was there, just as he had hoped. Grasping the poker he suddenly straightened up and in the same movement leapt sideways out of the chair. He heard Sammy spring forward as he swung the

159

poker at where he hoped the light would be. Freda screamed as the bulb shattered. Bob felt the glass shower down on his arm as he gripped the table and shoved it sideways with all his might. He felt a soft thump and knew he had Sammy pinned against the door. He felt the wind as his opponent swung at him with the knife. 'We're even now, Sammy,' he shouted. 'You're as blind as I am!'

'Oh no! No, Sammy, don't!' Freda was screaming.

Sammy was growling like a trapped animal. Bob felt the pressure against his arms as the crazed man tried to push the table away and knew that he would lose a trial of strength against the heavier man. With a quick movement he slipped sideways and let the table go. As he heard the thud of Sammy falling forwards Bob reached out and found the door. He slid silently around until he had his back to it. He knew he dare not open the door for the landing light was on. His groping fingers found the bolt and slipped it just as Sammy was picking himself up. Bob knew that Freda was still beside the fireplace and he had to protect her somehow. His breath came quickly as he unbuckled his leather belt and twisted the ends around his fists. ''Ere I am, Sammy. Beside the door,' he called out, hardly recognising his own voice.

The tormented man staggered forward in a desperate rage at being cheated. His foot caught the table-leg and as he tried to regain his balance Bob moved sideways. He could smell the sweat on Sammy's body and he positioned the man in his mind. With a quick movement he lifted his arms and brought the belt down around Sammy's neck as the man brushed past. Bob could not tell whether Sammy still had the knife in his hand and fear gave him extra strength. He arched his body backwards and felt the strap tighten around his opponent's throat. Sammy gurgled and fought for breath as the two of them crashed to the floor. Bob gave out a gasp as his head caught the wainscoting, and with a sickening feeling his strength faded from him and a searing pain ran through his side. There were loud noises as the threshing body above him moved away, and he heard the crashing sound of breaking glass and a loud scream before he lost consciousness.

Down in the square one of the policemen had been standing in front of the house while the inspector and the other officers were positioning themselves near the front door. The inspector gave the signal for the officer to call out and at that very moment a faint sound of breaking glass came from the upstairs room followed by shouts and a woman screaming.

'C'mon!' shouted the inspector, throwing his weight against the front door and stumbling into the passage with the two officers rushing in behind him. Folk screamed as the din increased, and then suddenly a body came hurtling through the window and landed head first on the pavement below. Annie Robinson groaned and looked away quickly from the twitching body.

Sally grabbed Ginny and they buried their heads in each other's shoulders. A policeman's face appeared shortly at the shattered window and an eerie silence filled the square. Only one person moved towards Sammy. She leant down and slid her hand beneath his head, cradling it to her breast. Blood stained her apron and dripped down on to the stones. The inspector walked slowly out from the house and looked down at the large, ginger-haired woman. Her squint was pronounced as she stared up at him.

''E's gorn, ain't 'e?' Ada Fuller said quietly.

As night closed over Paragon Place the Robinsons sat talking in their front parlour. Charlie was subdued, feeling slightly guilty at his earlier defaming of the dead man as he listened to Annie's account of the tragedy. Sally and Lora sat beside their mother, wide-eyed and serious-faced as she spoke. 'Blind Bob managed ter talk 'is way in there, so 'e told the copper. 'E grabbed Sammy an' 'e got stabbed in the side. The copper told Ada Fuller 'e's gonna be all right. Christ! That must 'ave took some guts fer Bob ter go in that room. When the coppers broke the front door down they tried ter grab Sammy, but they were too late. 'E run straight at the winder and chucked 'imself frew it. Gawd! I'll never forget it as long as I live. It was just like a sack o' coals landin' on the pavement. I couldn't look. Ada went over to 'im. She cradled 'is 'ead in 'er lap, but the man was stone dead. Poor Ada was covered in blood. It was all down 'er apron. What must 'ave made the poor sod do it? Why?'

Charlie winced and put his hand on Annie's shoulder. 'I dunno gel,' he said softly. 'P'r'aps 'e's better off now. We all reckoned 'e was a bit gutless the way 'e carried on durin' the blitz, but I s'pose nobody knew the torment 'e was sufferin'. All that bombin' must 'ave played on 'is mind, Gawd rest 'is soul.'

Annie dabbed at her eyes. 'Freda's gone ter stay wiv 'er married daughter. She was in a terrible state, poor cow.'

Charlie took out his pipe and tapped the bowl against the heel of his boot. 'When this war's over an' they start reckonin' up, I wonder if they'll include Sammy amongst the victims? They should do, by Christ.'

Chapter Eight

THE tragedy at number 8 haunted the folk of Paragon Place during the long August days. Newspaper reporters called round and the story made the front page of the *South London Press*. Blind Bob had become a local hero and the news was that he would be spending some time in hospital. The knife had penetrated his kidney and although he was out of danger he needed careful nursing back to full fitness. Bob's dog was being looked after by Freda Chapman for the time being, who felt it was the least she could do for the man who had undoubtedly saved her life. Number 8 remained shut tight, and the boarded-up upstairs window was a stark reminder of the terrible happening there. Granny Almond was quick to point out to everyone that at least some good had come out of the tragedy. Ada Fuller and Clara Botley had become the best of friends. Clara was full of praise for the way Ada had reacted on the terrible evening and they visited each other's homes for cups of tea. Clara had even suggested to her husband Patrick that maybe he should offer to put a new shelf up in Ada's scullery. "Er Danny was swingin' on it an' it fell down,' she said. 'It won't take yer long, Pat. After all, 'er bloke ain't there, an' in any case 'e wouldn't be able ter do it, 'e's as silly as a box o' lights.'

Patrick winced as he thought of the last time he had done some work at the Fullers' house but he nodded and went to get his tool-bag.

At the end of August Vera decided to give up work. 'I reckon I've got an elephant in 'ere,' she joked with Sally. "E's kickin' the life out o' me.'

'You've made yer mind up it's a boy then, Vera?' Sally asked with a smile.

'Course it is,' Vera replied, patting her bulge and pursing her lips. 'If it's a girl Joe said I can sell it.'

They were sitting in Harrison's canteen at lunch time and their conversation was overheard by Maggie Chandler who had plumped herself down at their table, scoffing her food and pausing only to push her glasses up on to the bridge of her nose.

Vera leaned back in her chair and winced noticeably. 'There 'e goes. It feels like an elbow.' Maggie was fascinated by Vera's comment and she paused with a forkful of cabbage held up to her mouth. Vera laughed and nodded to the girl. 'Wanna feel it, Maggie?'

'Ooh, no,' Maggie shuddered. 'It frightens me.'

'What does?' Sally asked.

''Avin' babies do. I'd be scared,' Maggie said, looking down at her plate.

Vera laughed again. 'Well, if yer want the pleasure, yer gotta take the pain, Maggie me girl.'

The stocky machinist looked down at what was left of her food in embarrassment. She could not quite understand just what Vera meant. Her first experience of sex was not at all as she had imagined. In fact it was not very nice at all, she decided. Mr Murray had been rough and it had hurt, she recalled sadly. He had also told her to keep her mouth shut about going into the basement with him or she would get into trouble. Maggie remembered hearing the two older women talking about young girls getting into trouble and she decided to do as Mr Murray told her, especially as he wanted her to go down to the basement with him that afternoon. Maggie was not too happy about the arrangement. She fretted about getting pregnant like Vera. Her mother had threatened to send her to a convent if she got into trouble. She would lose her job, too. That would be terrible, she thought.

Vera was dabbing her hot brow with a hand-

165

kerchief and she puffed hard. 'I'll be glad when Friday comes, Sal,' she said with a sigh. 'Then I'll be able ter lay in bed an' fink of you sweatin' away in this dump.'

'Don't remind me,' Sally said, grimacing. 'I'm gonna miss yer. It's not gonna seem the same. What wiv Jimmy Kent goin' as well.'

Vera nodded. 'Yeah, I miss 'im. 'E's a nice feller. It was a bit mysterious 'ow 'e suddenly got 'is release.'

'P'r'aps 'e 'ad somefing on ole Murray,' Sally suggested with a mischievous grin.

Vera laughed aloud. 'Yer could be right, Sal. P'r'aps Jimmy caught the dirty ole git wiv 'is trousers down.'

Maggie suddenly jumped up from the table with a flushed face and hurried off without a word.

'What's the matter wiv 'er?' Vera asked.

'Gawd knows,' Sally replied. 'I expect she's goin' fer seconds.'

Vera snorted. 'The way she scoffs it's like watchin' coal bein' shovelled in a boiler. I dunno where she puts it, honest I don't.'

The factory whistle sounded and there was a loud scraping of chairs. 'Oh well. Two an' 'alf more days,' Vera said, rubbing her hands together.

The rat-tat on her front door frightened Ginny Almond. That sort of knock usually meant trouble. The school board man rapped on the door when he came inquiring after her eldest boys, and the police rat-tatted when they called to ask after her absent husband. Ginny wondered who it could be on this Saturday morning. It was early and her children were not up yet. She went to the door and was faced by a beaming George Tapley.

''E's all right, Gin!' he shouted. 'Laurie's alive!'

Ginny felt the tears rising. She opened her arms and they hugged each other on the doorstep. She stepped back, her arms on George's narrow shoulders. 'What did I tell yer!' she croaked between tears and laughter. 'I knew it all along. That was a good dream yer 'ad, George. I jus' knew it.'

He dabbed at his eyes with a red-spotted handkerchief and then blew his nose loudly. 'I got the telegram from the War Office a couple o' minutes ago, Ginny. Laurie's a prisoner in Japanese 'ands.'

She kissed him on the cheek and threw her arm around his shoulders. 'C'mon in an' I'll make yer a nice cuppa. I'm so pleased. All right, 'e's a prisoner, but the war won't last fer ever. 'E's alive, that's the main fing.'

The good news travelled fast amongst the Paragon Place folk and soon people were knocking on George Tapley's front door to offer their congratulations. Daisy Almond and Lil Allen called together. They had both seen George's lads grow up in the square and they shed a few tears with the elated father. Later Harriet and Juliet Carey paid George a visit. 'We've prayed for your son, Mr Tapley, haven't we, Juliet?' the elder sister said, smiling sweetly.

'Yes, we both prayed,' Juliet said, nodding.

'I know it must be a worry your son being a prisoner, but I'm sure they'll treat him well,' Harriet went on. 'Quite a lot of the Japanese people are Christians, I believe.'

George thanked the sisters and when they had left he slumped down in his favourite chair. He felt suddenly deflated. Harriet's well-meant comments had had the opposite effect, and he began to fear for his younger son.

Maybe Ginny was right, he thought. Maybe it would do him good to have that long-promised drink with her. She was a good, kind woman, and her support and encouragement had kept him going during the terrible time of uncertainty. Maybe he should let himself go a little. She had hinted more than once how she felt about him. Perhaps he should repay her kindness by showing her a bit of affection. After all, he had been a widower since Laurie was born. He could not be expected to mourn for ever. Maybe he should lay the ghost to rest and learn to live a little.

On that Saturday afternoon a stranger called at number 1 Paragon Place. She gave one knock, and getting no answer she knocked again. Normally the Carey sisters ignored single knocks as it was usual for their visitors to knock twice, but on this occasion Harriet looked out of the window and saw a uniformed figure standing patiently below. 'Juliet! It's someone from the church,' she said excitedly.

Harriet's younger sister looked up

abstractedly. 'I heard the Taylor girl go out some time ago,' she said, dropping her eyes again to the novel on her lap.

'I think we should answer the door, don't you, Juliet?'

'If you like,' Juliet sighed irritably, eager to get back to the seduction of Lady Abercrombie's daughter by the fiendish Lord Quinton-Selby.

Harriet hurried down the stairs and opened the door. The caller was dressed in grey and wore a purple habit which seemed to take the colour from her stern face. 'I'm from St Joseph's Church,' she said, smiling faintly. 'I've called to see Miss Muriel Taylor.'

Harriet felt instant relief. Her entreaties to Mr Cuthbert had at last been duly noted. 'I'm afraid Miss Taylor went out some time ago,' she said. 'I'm Harriet Carey. I live upstairs.'

The pale-faced woman smiled. 'I wrote to Miss Taylor a few weeks ago, but she didn't reply to my letter. I was hoping to catch her in.'

Harriet's brow knitted. 'My sister and I went to see Mr Cuthbert at the estate office some time ago about Miss Taylor. I would have thought that someone would have come round before now.'

The visitor looked bemused. 'I'm sorry. The church hasn't been in contact with Mr Cuthbert. I think you might have misunderstood the reason for my visit.'

Harriet was dismayed that the woman was not on a mission from Mr Cuthbert. She wanted to ask just why the woman had decided to call, but she resisted the urge. 'Maybe you should call

169

back,' she said weakly.

The visitor smiled and was about to leave when Muriel flounced into the square. She was wearing a tight-fitting dress and high-heeled shoes which sounded loudly on the pavement, her dark hair was flowing loosely around her shoulders and her face was heavily rouged. She carried a large handbag and a cardigan which was slung over her free arm. She gave the visitor an easy smile and then glanced briefly at Harriet.

'Miss Taylor?' the church visitor inquired.

'That's me, luv,' Muriel answered with a grin.

'Can you spare me a few minutes? I would like to have a few words with you.'

Harriet returned to her flat with her face showing anger. 'I just don't understand it, Juliet,' she declared. 'We took the trouble to go along and see Mr Cuthbert and he's done absolutely nothing.'

'How do you know, Harriet?' her sister asked. 'I'm sure he would have informed the church committee. He promised us he would.'

'Well, the young lady from the church told me otherwise,' Harriet retorted, getting more angry. 'She said there's been no contact with Mr Cuthbert. Really, this is not good enough.'

Juliet had been absorbed in her novel. Was Quinton-Selby going to succeed, or would the maiden choose death before dishonour? She put the book down with a sigh. 'Well, I'm sure I don't know why, Harriet. We'll just have to wait and see what happens.'

Harriet gave her sister a hard look. 'Well, I'll be wanting to have words with Mr Cuthbert. It's so worrying.'

Juliet sighed again and slipped a book marker into the novel. It seemed she would never be allowed to discover the maiden's fate. Harriet was working herself up into a state and she was sure to have one of her turns very shortly. 'Sit yourself down, Harriet,' she said pacifyingly. 'Try not to get too worked up. I'll make us a nice cup of tea.'

In the flat below Muriel was listening with some degree of irritation as Sister Josephine went on. 'Father O'Donnell has been going through the church records and he has decided that we should visit all the Catholic families who no longer attend our church. Your mother always attended our church, Muriel, until the last few months before she took her life. We were all very sad about that. It was awfully tragic. Your brothers and sisters were married at St Joseph's and you yourself were baptised there. We'd be very pleased to see you at Mass on Sunday. Won't you think about it?'

Muriel shook her head. 'I'm not a Catholic. I ain't bin inside yer church since I was a kid, Sister.'

'But your family are Catholic, Muriel,' the Sister suggested.

'That's as may be,' Muriel replied. 'But I ain't a Catholic. As a matter o' fact I thought yer was callin' about somefing else.'

Sister Josephine looked puzzled. 'Yes, it's strange you should say that. I was talking to the lady upstairs. Harriet Carey, I believe. She seemed to think I was sent on behalf of the

171

estate agents. Of course I told her I wasn't, but why should she think that?'

Muriel nodded her head slowly and a wry smile appeared on her face. 'Well, if yer really wanna know, Sister, that ole busybody upstairs is concerned about me morals. She don't like what I do fer a livin' an' she's bin makin' complaints. She finks I'm givin' the square a bad name.'

Sister Josephine looked quizzically at the young woman. 'What exactly do you do for a living, Muriel?' she asked.

'I'm on the game.'

The church visitor's face froze momentarily in shock. 'You mean you're a – a prostitute?' she stammered incredulously.

Muriel grinned. 'That's right, Sister. I'm a fallen woman. I bring men back 'ere an' charge 'em fer me services. Yer see now why I don't come ter yer Mass. You people wouldn't like a prostitute sitting wiv the congregation, would yer?'

Sister Josephine was taken aback by Muriel's forthrightness, but she straightened her habit and said with magnanimous dignity, 'We're all sinners, Muriel. You know what Jesus said about casting the first stone. You'd still be welcome at Mass.'

Muriel was somewhat surprised at her response. She sighed. 'Maybe so, but I don't fink those two busybodies upstairs would want ter sit wiv the likes o' me.'

Sister Josephine stood up, feeling that there was little more she could say. 'Well, God bless you, Muriel,' she said with a sweet smile. 'Do think it over. We'd love to see you on Sunday mornings.'

When her visitor had left Muriel made herself a cup of tea and sat staring into the empty grate deep in thought. She realised that she had been a little indiscreet in the past when bringing her clients back to the house. Mr Cuthbert had warned her about Harriet Carey and how difficult it would be for him to hold her off. Muriel smiled mirthlessly as she recalled that afternoon in Cuthbert's office. She had received a letter from him asking her to call in as soon as possible as there was a serious matter he wished to discuss with her. She had dressed down and left her make-up off especially for the visit, guessing that the serious matter concerned her nocturnal activities. Mr Cuthbert had been ill at ease, and as he told her of the Careys' complaints he had fidgeted and stammered, his eyes avoiding hers in his embarrassment. Muriel remembered his reaction when she went into her routine. She crossed and uncrossed her legs, revealing just enough to get his attention. She took out her handkerchief and dabbed at her eyes as she told him of her struggle to make ends meet and how she hated selling her body. She told him how impressed she was with his understanding, and thanked him for being so kind. He had been snared and Muriel had then played her ace card.

'I'm very careful about the men I bring 'ome, Mr Cuthbert,' she had said. 'I'm very discreet and careful. When a lady's workin' from 'ome she's gotta be. You'd be surprised at some of me

173

clients. They're respectable, mature men – like yerself. They're jus' lonely, or wiv wives who don't understand 'em. It's sad, really.'

By the time the young woman had finished her monologue Mr Cuthbert was completely captivated, licking his lips at the prospect of getting to know her a little better. Muriel had been quick to respond. 'I 'ope yer don't fink I'm bein' too forward, Mr Cuthbert,' she had said with exaggerated shyness, 'but you're a respectable man, an' if yer ever feel the need for me services I fink we could come to an arrangement.'

The estate manager's eyes were wide open now, and he fiddled with his fountain pens. 'I couldn't come to see you, Miss Taylor,' he said, looking down. 'I've got to be careful in my position.'

'Call me Muriel,' she said, smiling coyly at him. 'I could come 'ere, if that would be suitable.'

A deal had been struck there and then, whereby Muriel would grant her favours, and in return Mr Cuthbert would not proceed with the Careys' complaints.

As Muriel sat staring into the grate she realised that the church woman's visit would probably stir things up. The woman had told Harriet Carey her visit was nothing to do with the estate agents and the old busybody would certainly wonder why no action had been taken. Maybe she should try to cultivate a friendship with the younger sister, she thought. She seemed much the nicer of the two. It was Harriet who

174

seemed to be doing all the complaining, and Juliet appeared to be siding with her sister just to keep the peace. She often went out alone, too. Perhaps she had a man friend, Muriel thought. If that were the case she would be more inclined to understand how things were. Muriel got up with a sigh and proceeded to tidy up the flat. She must remember to ask Mr Cuthbert how much he knew about Juliet, she told herself. It would not be too difficult to get the information out of him.

On a Saturday afternoon in late August Sally called in to see Vera. She was hoping her friend would agree to go to the Old Kent Picture House with her that evening but she was disappointed. 'I couldn't sit still that long,' Vera said. 'I'm gettin' these bad backaches. The doctor reckons the baby's layin' on a nerve. 'E said it's nufing ter worry about, but it makes me so uncomfortable.'

Sally laughed. 'Yer gettin' ter look like a little podge. Yer sure it's not twins?'

Vera pulled a face. 'I 'ope not. One'll do ter start wiv!'

'Sure yer don't wanna come?' Sally asked raising her dark eyebrows. 'It's *Reap the Wild Wind*. Ray Milland an' John Wayne.'

'I'd love to Sal, but it's no good. I'd 'ave ter walk out 'alfway frew. Yer can tell me all about it termorrer.'

Sally remained with her friend for a while chatting and joking, and then she suddenly became serious. 'Lora's got 'erself a new bloke,' she said. 'It's all a bit mysterious.'

'Oh, an' why's that?' Vera asked.

'Well, normally Lora's always gone on about 'er fellas, but with this one it's different. She's very secretive. Mum's bin pumpin' 'er about 'ow old 'e is an' what 'e does fer a livin', but she couldn't get a squeak out of 'er. The ovver night me mum asked 'er when she was gonna bring 'im 'ome an' Lora got all moody and stormed off out.'

'P'r'aps 'e's married,' Vera said, getting up to ease her aching back.

''E might be,' Sally replied, her dark eyes widening. 'I wish I could talk to 'er, Vera, but she cuts me dead, too. If Lora is involved wiv a married man it can only end up wiv 'er gettin' 'urt.'

Vera sat down again and slid her hands over her midriff. 'Yeah, an' the bloke's wife.'

Sally smiled mirthlessly. 'Yeah, you're right.' She stood up and sighed. 'Anyway, I better get goin'. Can't keep Ray Milland waitin'.'

Dusk had settled over the backstreets as Sally walked home along Tower Bridge Road thinking of the film she had just seen. Normally she would have taken the tram or a bus but the night was balmy and her legs felt stiff from sitting for over two hours in a cramped cinema seat. As she crossed the thoroughfare and turned into Grange Road she became aware that someone was following her. The heavy, hurrying footsteps behind her were quickly coming nearer. She glanced fearfully over her shoulder and her heart raced as she saw him. He trotted up to her, a smile playing on his pale features. "'Ello, Sal. I 'ope I didn't frighten yer,' he said, panting slightly.

She smiled back nervously as he slipped into step beside her. "'Ello, Ben,' she said quickly, trying to hide the note of fear in her voice.

"'Ow are yer keepin' now, Sal?' he asked, giving her a sideways glance.

'I'm all right, Ben,' she replied, returning his stare. He was thinner in the face than when she had last seen him, and his fair, curly hair was still cropped short. He seemed to have lost some of his boyish look, and as he strolled beside her his shoulders were hunched. "'Ow long 'ave yer bin out?' she asked.

'Last week. I got a couple o' months off fer bein' a good lad.'

She smiled again quickly as she looked at him. 'You've lost weight, an' yer 'air's still too short,' she remarked, looking away from his eyes.

He put his hands into his trouser pockets as they crossed the Grange Road and turned into a side street. 'Yeah, the food was bleedin' lousy,' he said quietly.

Sally was ill at ease. She had dreaded meeting him after the way he had behaved when she visited him at the prison, but she would never have expected him to be so subdued. There was a different look in his eyes. They seemed larger and less accusing. 'It must 'ave bin bad in there,' she said in a soft voice.

'It wasn't too bad,' he replied. 'I jus' kept out o' trouble an' counted the days.' He looked at

177

her suddenly, a serious expression on his face. 'Sally, I – I'm really sorry about the way I acted when yer come ter see me,' he said, looking down at the pavement. 'I thought a lot about the way I behaved, an' I wished like anyfing that I'd get the chance ter 'ave anuvver chat wiv yer.'

Sally looked at him quickly as they approached the railway arches. 'We didn't 'ave much ter talk about, Ben – did we?'

He shrugged his wide shoulders. 'Maybe you never, but there was a lot I wanted ter say. I wanted ter tell yer what a stupid idiot I'd bin, an' I wanted ter tell yer 'ow much I was missin' yer. Most of all I wanted ter tell yer I was sorry fer all the 'urt I'd caused yer, an' 'ow I'd give anyfing ter be back wiv yer.'

Sally fell silent and a distressing feeling of hopelessness gripped her stomach. Despite all the bitterness that had grown between them she still loved him, but it was too late now to tell him how she secretly shared his longing. After all that had happened she knew there could be no future for them together any more.

They walked under the dark arches, their footsteps echoing beneath the metal girders, and as they emerged they could see the eerie bombsite and the unlit gaslamp opposite the entrance to Paragon Place.

'D'yer fink it was my fault?' she said suddenly. 'D'yer fink yer wouldn't 'ave got inter trouble if I'd agreed ter meet yer that time?'

He shook his head. 'I jus' wanted the chance ter talk, but I don't blame yer fer what 'appened, Sal. I was stupid drunk. It was me feelin' sorry fer meself. D'yer know, I used ter sit in me cell an' look out frew the tiny winder at night. I could see a few stars twinklin' up there an' I wondered what yer was doin'. I wondered if yer was lookin' at those same stars right that minute. I wanted ter write yer a letter. As a matter o' fact I did, but I tore it up.'

'Why?' she asked, slowing down as they reached the entrance to the square.

He laughed nervously, and as she turned to face him she could see that he was trembling. 'Yer know what I'm like,' he said with a slight smile. 'I read the letter an' it sounded ridiculous. Yer would 'ave laughed if you'd 'ave read it. There was so much I wanted ter say but I couldn't get it ter sound right on paper.'

They were standing beneath the gaslamp. The square was deserted and overhead a few stars looked out from gathering clouds. Sally felt panic rise up in her and she felt a sudden desire to rush into her house and leave him there, but something about his manner kept her. He had never really expressed himself properly before, yet now he seemed to be talking more openly than she would have thought possible. She began to feel afraid. 'Look, it's gettin' late,' she said defensively, trying to stay calm.

He nodded, his eyes searching hers. 'Look, Sally. I know what's done is done. I know that yer can't forgive me fer all the pain I've caused yer, but will yer do one fing fer me?' As her pained eyes stared into his he searched them for an answer. 'Will yer meet me sometime, when you've 'ad a chance ter fink over what I said? I know yer can never ferget what I did ter yer, but I wanna try ter make it up ter yer. I've changed, Sally. I'm off the booze. I wanted yer ter know that. Will yer at least fink about what I said?'

She nodded. 'I'll fink about it.'

He backed away, and as she turned to walk into the square he called out to her. 'I'm still at the flat, Sal, if yer wanna leave a message.'

Sally hurried to her front door, her mind in a whirl. She knew it had been inevitable that she would meet him sooner or later. She had resolved to be firm. She had prepared herself to face his anger and had gone over the words she would say time and time again. She had been determined to make him understand that what had happened could never be undone and they had no future together. Instead, he had been calm and repentant, and she had listened to him and allowed him some hope. She reproached herself for being weak and silly and allowing him to feel he still had a chance of getting back into her life. She would have to meet him again now. Sometime in the future she would have to confront him and close the door on him forever.

Chapter Nine

THE day had been a long, thirsty one for Alf Porter. He had finished his Saturday shift at the *Evening News* and decided to water his dry throat in the King's Head, a little pub just off

Fleet Street. He had intended to have only one drink and then get home to spend a quiet evening with his feet up listening to the wireless. But throughout his life Alf's best intentions never quite materialised. He had met a few pals quite by chance in the pub, and the talk turned to the bad news from the war fronts, rationing, and most important of all, the state of the watered-down British pint of ale. Nevertheless Alf had not forgotten his decision to get home in a sensible condition and he decided to buy a round and then leave. The small group of printworkers began to increase and Alf was per-suaded to stay for one more pint. When every member of the gathering had bought a round Alf finally made his getaway. He staggered out into the evening air and immediately fell over what he considered to be a dangerously placed kerb. He swore as he picked himself up, tucked in his shirt, straightened his tie and found his trilby hat, which had rolled into a heap of fresh horse manure. Cursing his inability to say no to a pint and mean it, he walked carefully along to the Embankment and stood holding on to the swaying tramstop sign.

At that time in the evening it was nothing unusual for the conductor of the number 38 tram to see Alf talking to the tramstop, and he sighed as he helped the inebriate printworker aboard. Alf was usually no trouble, and quite often the conductor had to wake him up when the tram pulled up at the Bricklayer's Arms. On that Saturday evening, however, Alf did not feel like sleep. Instead he sat on the lower deck staring out of the window, trying to remember the words of 'O'Reilly's Daughter'. How did it go? he wondered, racking his addled brains. 'As I was sitting by O'Reilly's fire, drinking—'

'Oi, you! Shut yer noise,' interrupted the conductor. 'We don't want none o' that on 'ere. There's women up front.'

Alf removed his fertilised trilby and nodded to a large bespectacled woman who was sitting beside a small man on the front seat. 'Shorry, lady,' he slurred. 'No offenshe meant.'

The conductor trotted up on to the upper deck and when he returned Alf was in the process of negotiating the aisle, much to the amusement of the other passengers. 'Oi you! Where you goin'?' the conductor shouted. 'Now sit down where yer was an' be'ave yerself.'

A florid-faced woman tugged at the conductor's arm. 'I told 'im ter move somewhere else,' she said assertively. ''E's got 'orse-shit all over 'is 'at. It stinks to 'igh 'eaven.'

The sorely tried conductor sighed and steered Alf into a seat behind the large woman and her small companion at the front. 'Now stay put, or I'll chuck yer off at the next stop,' he said in a stern voice, winking at the other passengers. 'D'yer 'ear me?'

Alf blinked and tried to focus his bleary eyes. 'OK, Sid. I – I'm shorry,' he slurred.

'All right, now shut up – an' my name's not Sid,' said the conductor, hiding a smile.

The tram had crossed Blackfriars Bridge and was clattering over the criss-cross of tramlines at the Elephant and Castle when Alf decided he wanted to address the large woman. He prodded her on the shoulder and was rewarded with a wicked glare. 'Do you mind?' she hissed.

'Are we at the Brick yet, missus?' he whispered. 'I wanna – I wanna get off at the Bricklayer's Arms, yer see.'

The small man turned round. 'This is the Elephant an' Castle,' he said in a quiet voice.

Alf gave him a crooked grin. 'Fanks, Sid. Yer name is Sid, ain't it?'

'No, it's Reginald, actually,' the little man replied, looking embarrassed.

The woman prodded Reginald in the ribs. 'Don't get talkin' to 'im. 'E's pissed,' she growled, sniffing the air and pulling a face.

'Who's pissed?' Alf said with a look of mischievous indignation in his bleary eyes. 'I'm not pissed, am I, Sid?'

The little man gave Alf a sickly smile and turned to face his front.

At the Bricklayer's Arms Alf was hustled off the tram by a thankful conductor, who pointed him in the general direction of Stanley Street and pulled on the bell-cord before Alf had time to change his mind and get back on.

'It's a bloody disgrace. Why they let people like that on trams is beyond me,' the large woman complained to her small companion. 'I've a good mind ter write ter the Passenger Board. Did yer smell 'im? I fink 'e must 'ave shit 'imself.'

The small man sank lower in his seat and the large woman folded her arms in disgust. 'Yer should 'ave told 'im ter shut up, Reginald,' she barked. ''E was drunk, an' yer jus' sat there. Yer should 'ave told 'im.'

Reginald stared ahead without replying and wished that he was drunk.

The scourge of London Transport was weaving an erratic path as the pavement moved up and down, and when his watery eyes caught sight of a pub sign he straightened up with some effort and staggered through the door. Alf's way home from the Bricklayer's Arms never varied. He knew the route backwards, and when he was incapable his instinct kept him from veering. He found the backstreet pubs by instinct, too, and the publicans were usually ready for him. If he was not too drunk they would serve him a pint, then send him on his way, but tonight there was no chance of Alf getting another drink in his condition. He had just steadied himself by the counter when his arm was grasped in a firm hold and he was led to the door.

It was getting late when Alf Porter finally reached Paragon Place. He grabbed at the gaslamp by the entrance and peered down the square to reassure himself that he had not taken the wrong turning. Satisfied that he really was home he staggered into Paragon Place, his trilby sitting on the back of his head, his shirt-tail hanging out and his coat buttoned askew. He had taken two or three paces when his befuddled brain recalled the time he had been irrigated with the contents of Charlie Robinson's chamber-pot. He stopped and turned to face the first house on his left. His forefinger came up to his lips as he focused on the door number.

That's the Carey sisters' house, he thought. They wouldn't do what that miserable Charlie Robinson had done to him. The Carey sisters are civilised, he decided. Maybe they would appreciate a nice song.

Saturday Night Theatre had just finished and Harriet Carey got up to switch off the wireless. 'It's been a long day,' she yawned. 'I'll make us some cocoa and then I'm going to turn in.'

Juliet put down her novel, happy that the detestable Lord Quinton-Selby had finally received his just deserts at the hands of The Honourable Dickie Smythe. She stretched, smiling to herself at the thought of having to deliver some very important deeds on the morrow. Suddenly there was a growling sound in the square below, and then a strange, out of tune singing carried up into the quiet room. Harriet paused in the doorway and came back into the room, a look of horror on her thin face. Juliet sat up straight and frowned as her sister went over to the drawn curtains.

'As I was sittin' by O'Reilly's fire,
Drinkin' some of O'Reilly's water,
Suddenly a thought came ter me 'ead,
I'd like ter marry O'Reilly's daughter . . .'

Harriet peeped through the curtains and then quickly turned to Juliet. 'It's that disgusting man Porter,' she said with horror. 'He's half-undressed and staggering about down there.'

Juliet got up and joined her sister at the window. Harriet pointed over to the light-switch.

'Turn that light off,' she said. 'I'm going to give him a piece of my mind.'

Juliet did as she was bid and came back to the window. Harriet threw back the curtains and slipped the catch. Down below Alf had spotted the sisters and he grinned. "'Ello, ladies. 'Ow the bloody 'ell are yer?' he shouted, staggering backwards as he looked up and almost losing his balance.

Harriet had opened the window. 'Go away you disgusting man,' she cried.

Alf laughed and started to unbuckle his wide leather belt, intending to tuck his shirt back into his trousers.

'Oh my God! He's taking his trousers off,' Harriet cried. 'Do you hear me? Go away, you horrible man!'

Alf had unbuttoned the front of his trousers and as he took hold of his shirt the stained trilby hat slipped from his head. Alf forgot what he was doing and made a grab for his favourite hat. The trousers fell around his ankles, revealing a pair of baggy, knee-length undershorts. Harriet had seen enough and she recoiled in horror, but to her surprise Juliet was still staring down at the drunken character.

'Come away from that window, Juliet. The man's exposing himself!' Harriet gasped.

Alf had managed to tidy himself up and he began to stagger towards his front door. He was thinking about something funny and chuckling to himself without properly watching where he was going, and as he neared his house Alf collided with the sycamore tree. He staggered back, rubbing his forehead and growling.

'I'm gonna do fer yer, see if I don't,' he mumbled, waving his forefinger at the tree. 'I'm gonna get me an axe an' I'm gonna chop yer down, d'yer 'ear me? I should 'ave done it years ago. What d'yer 'ave ter keep bumpin' inter me for?'

While Alf Porter was sleeping late on Sunday morning his Saturday night antics were the subject of discussion amongst his neighbours. Paragon Place was coming to life and at numbers 9 and 10 the former antagonists were already out and about. Ada Fuller had just whitened her doorstep and Clara Botley was sweeping the area around her front door.

'That looks nice,' Clara said, nodding to Ada's step. 'I should do mine, really, but I'm out o' whitenin'. I'll 'ave ter send one o' the boys up the shop fer some.'

Ada got the square biscuit-tin in which she kept her cleaning materials and handed it to Clara. ''Ere, yer can borrer this, luv,' she said. 'There's plenty there.'

Clara set to work, and when she had finished she took the tin back to Ada. 'Fanks, luv. I was worried about that step. 'Ere. I know what I was gonna ask yer. Did yer 'ear that drunken ole bastard last night?'

'Who, Alf Porter?'

'Yeah.'

Ada shook her head. 'I 'ad the wireless on an' I dropped off ter sleep. It must 'ave bin after twelve when I woke up, 'cos all the programmes

187

was finished.'

Clara jerked her head in the direction of Alf's house. "E was pissed as a newt last night. I looked out me curtains an' I see 'im drop 'is trousers ter the Carey sisters. Yer should 'ave 'eard that 'Arriet go off at 'im. She told 'im ter piss orf, or words ter that effect.'

'Christ! I bet she was shocked. She's a churchgoer, that one,' Ada said.

Clara folded her arms against her large bosom. 'Funny couple they are. Mind you, they don't interfere wiv anybody. It must be a bit awkward for 'em, what wiv that Muriel Taylor livin' underneath.'

Ada nodded. 'I reckon that one's on the game, don't you?'

'Yeah, I reckon so,' Clara replied. 'Funny 'ow she turned like that, though. She was such a quiet, shy girl when she was younger.'

'If yer ask me it was findin' 'er muvver dead what turned 'er,' Ada said. 'Must 'ave bin a terrible shock.'

Clara aimed a kick at the scruffy mongrel that was sniffing around her freshly whitened doorstep. 'Yeah, it must 'ave bin. Oh well, I s'pose I better get back ter work. I ain't shelled me peas yet.'

Sally was up early that morning. She strolled up to the corner shop for the Sunday papers and on the way back she bumped into Muriel Taylor. The two girls had never been close friends but they often passed the time of day, and Sally had always had a sneaking regard for Muriel. Fate had dealt her a tragic blow with her mother's suicide but the girl had picked herself up and got on with her life. Sally had heard the street gossip but paid little attention to it. The girl's life was her own. If she chose to be a prostitute it was her affair, Sally reasoned.

Muriel smiled as they drew close. 'Did yer 'ear the rumpus last night, Sally?' she asked.

'No,' she replied. 'What 'appened? I went ter the pictures an' as soon as I got in I went ter bed.'

Muriel flapped her hand in mock exasperation. 'Yer should 'ave seen it,' she said, grinning. 'Alf Porter staggered inter the square blind drunk an' 'e flashed it at those two ole biddies above me.'

Sally laughed aloud, her hand going up to her mouth. 'I bet they was shocked.'

Muriel laughed with her. 'I 'ad somebody wiv me an' I 'eard the drunken ole goat outside the winder singin' one of 'is dirty songs. When I peeped out o' the curtains I see 'im droppin' 'is trousers. Cor! 'E did look a sight.'

When they had finally managed to stop laughing Sally tucked the papers under her arm and wiped her eyes. ''Ow d'yer get on wiv them two upstairs?' she asked.

Muriel shrugged her shoulders. 'They're a bit of a pain in the arse. Well, that 'Arriet is. The ovver one's not so bad. They reported me ter the estate agents once fer bringin' men 'ome, but I sorted it out,' she said, smiling slyly. 'What about you? 'Ow's yer love life at the moment, Sal?'

'What love life?' Sally grinned.

'Ain't yer gonna get back wiv your bloke, then?' Muriel asked.

Sally shook her head. Normally she would have resented that sort of question but Muriel asked it in an innocent, disarming way. 'No, there's no chance o' that,' she said quietly.

The Taylor girl grinned mischievously. 'Come out wiv me one night, I'll get yer a nice feller,' she said with a conspiratorial wink.

'Fanks fer the offer, but I don't fink so,' Sally replied, moving away in the direction of her house.

Muriel laughed. 'If I get overworked I'll unload one o' me blokes on ter yer, 'ow's that sound?'

'As long as 'e looks like Gary Cooper,' Sally laughed back to her.

It had been threatening rain earlier that morning but the clouds had now passed over and an autumn sun lit up the Bermondsey backwater. The houses had fresh lace curtains up at the windows and clean doorsteps, the square had been swept clean and even the sycamore tree seemed to have perked up, its large, drooping leaves brushing the roof guttering as they caught the slight breeze. A few people stood around at their front doors and some children began to play in the square. The ice cream man had set up his barrow by the bombsite and the winkle and shrimp stall was already outside the Railway Inn as Bert and Elsie Jackson opened the doors. The public bar started to fill up very quickly and the two Grannies took their seat in the snug bar. 'Give us a couple o' Guinnesses when yer get a minute,' Daisy Almond called out to the landlord. 'An' mind 'ow yer pour 'em.'

Bert Jackson growled under his breath as he reached below the counter for the bottles. When Daisy said 'when yer get a minute' she usually meant immediately, and she liked her drink poured very slowly. 'A Guinness should only 'ave a little 'at on, not a bloody great load o' froth,' she once told him. 'Some publicans should learn 'ow ter pour a Guinness.'

Bert set the drinks down on the counter and gave the two ladies a big grin. 'There we are, girls. Now drink it slowly, an' no singin' or upsettin' any o' me customers.'

Daisy picked up the drinks and scowled at the landlord. 'Gercha, yer saucy git. If everybody was like us two yer'd 'ave nufing ter worry about. That's right, ain't it, Lil?'

Granny Allen turned her head to one side. 'What yer say?' she asked, pulling a face.

Daisy turned to Bert. 'Poor cow. Deaf as a post, she's gettin'. It's gettin' bleedin' 'ard ter 'ave a conversation wiv 'er.'

'What about them there new 'earin' aids?' he asked. 'They're s'posed ter be pretty good by all accounts.'

Daisy shook her head vigorously. 'She won't 'ave nufing ter do wiv 'em. She's frightened o' gettin' 'lectric shocks in the 'ead. I've tried ter tell 'er, but it's like talkin' ter yer when you're pissed. I might as well talk ter that pint.'

Bert laughed aloud. 'Enjoy yer drink, girls.

191

I'm gettin' smoke signals from Elsie.'

A strong smell of stale wine drifted out from the padlocked bottling stores as the younger Carey sister hurried through the arches, her shoes echoing in the ironwork above her. She was dressed in her Sunday best and her flowered hat was perched at a jaunty angle over her permed hair. She carried a flat brown parcel under her arm and as she emerged into the watery sunlight her thin, angular face had a worried look. Why did Harriet have to get so boiled up? she asked herself. It made things very difficult. She had fretted over that nasty man Porter and had woken up with one of her sick headaches. Harriet was unable to attend Mass that morning and she had sat back in her chair with a sorrowful look on her face. Juliet had been made to feel guilty about leaving her sister, and when Harriet said, 'You go if you must. I'm sure I'll be able to manage – if I'm not sick', Juliet had wanted to make an angry retort but she bit on her tongue.

'Maybe I should ask Muriel to pop up to see if you're all right?' she suggested instead.

Harriet's response had been sharp. 'I wouldn't have that woman in this flat,' she had uttered in such a way that Juliet almost felt sorry for Muriel. At least the girl was out in the open in her dealings, she admitted to herself. She wasn't sneaking off to meet someone with ridiculous excuses about delivering important papers. What would Harriet's reaction be if she found out her sister was carrying on with a married man? She would no doubt take to her bed in shock. Juliet smiled bitterly at the prospect. Maybe it would be better to get it all out into the open. Sooner or later her sister was going to find out. It was amazing that she had accepted all those silly excuses so readily. Perhaps Harriet had her suspicions and chose not to voice them. If only she would get out a bit more instead of hiding herself away in that depressing flat of theirs. Juliet sighed sadly and hurried to the tram stop. She had better put on her happy face, she reminded herself. It upset Mr Lomax to see her looking worried.

Back in Paragon Place Alf Porter had finally roused himself. He sat up in bed with a feeling of dread. Had he disgraced himself last night? he wondered anxiously. His head was banging and trying to think only made it worse. He struggled into the scullery and put the kettle over the gas-ring. Slowly the events of the previous evening started to come back to him. He could recall a window going up and someone shouting at him. Alf's head hurt and his shin felt sore and he desperately needed a cup of tea. He turned his attention to the kettle and realised with a curse that he had not lit the gas. He got up and found the matches, noticing how his hand shook as he finally managed to light the gas-ring. He turned and looked into the cracked mirror over the sink. He saw the purple bump in the middle of his forehead and suspected that it might have something to do with the tree. Yes, it was all coming back now. He sat down and pulled up the leg of his trousers. There was a long graze running along the shin-bone and he leaned on the edge of the table as a wave of giddiness flowed over him. He remembered now. He had upset those old biddies with his singing – and worse. He sat down and groaned.

He wondered if he should tidy himself up and go to see the Careys. Perhaps he should take them a bunch of flowers or something and tell them he was sorry for making a fool of himself. Yes, that was the answer. As soon as he had finished his breakfast he would go along to the florist in Jamaica Road. They were usually open on Sundays.

It was nearly one o'clock by the time Alf had pulled himself together enough to venture out of his house. Breakfast had consisted of a hard-boiled egg and a dry slice of toast, washed down with a strong mug of sweet tea. He had then dipped his head under the tap, used the egg-water for his shave and quickly snatched a clean shirt from the backyard clothes-line. He had been unable to find his favourite trilby at first but the smell led him to look under the scullery table and he decided it was too filthy to wear. As he walked unsteadily along the square and out into Stanley Street a few faces broke into a grin at his appearance. Alf had a piece of cigarette paper stuck to his face where he had cut himself shaving and he wore a grey, chequered cap which was a size too large. Unknown to him there was a large mud stain across the back of his coat, and another one on the seat of his trousers.

Alf hurried to the florist but found the shop was shut. Well, the intention was there, he thought, as he licked his dry lips. Maybe a pint would get rid of the dry taste in his mouth. He made his way back to the Railway Inn and entered the public bar fifteen minutes from closing time. The first pint was consumed with much face-pulling, but the second one tasted much better. As the last bell sounded and Alf stepped out into the street he felt more comfortable. The winkle man was now selling jellied eels to the pub customers and Alf scratched his head thoughtfully. It was unfortunate that the flower shop was shut but maybe he could take the ladies back a nice carton of jellied eels. They would probably like that.

Muriel had just gone into the scullery to see if the pork chop was cooked when she heard the double knock on the front door. When the knock was repeated she hurried out to see who it was. Alf looked embarrassed as he stood on the doorstep, the carton of eels held in his shaky hand. 'Is the sisters in?' he asked hesitantly.

Muriel tried to keep from smiling. 'Juliet went out early,' she answered. ''Arriet should be in. She might 'ave fell asleep.'

Alf looked down at the carton in his hand and back to Muriel. 'I wanted ter give 'em this,' he said, holding out the jellied eels.

Muriel grinned widely. 'Is that a peace offerin'?'

He winced. 'Was I – I mean, did I upset 'em last night?'

'I dunno about upsettin' em,' she laughed. 'I

reckon yer scared the bleedin' life out of 'em, standin' there in those plus-four underpants an' singin' that filfy song. Look, stay there, I'll call up the stairs.'

Muriel went up to the bend of the stairs and shouted up to Harriet but there was no reply. 'She must be asleep,' she said. 'If yer wanna leave the carton wiv me I'll take it up an' stick it on the landin'. Yer can come back an' see 'er later.'

Alf nodded and handed over the jellied eels. Maybe it was better he never got the chance to talk to the woman after what the young lady had just told him, he reasoned, as he walked slowly along the square. Muriel meanwhile had crept up the stairs, not wishing to disturb the sleeping Harriet, and left the carton of eels on a small table which stood next to the gas-stove on the landing.

Harriet Carey awoke and looked at the alarm clock beside her bed. It showed ten minutes past the hour of three. She was not in the habit of taking solid foods when she had one of her bad turns. Juliet had told her she had prepared some soup which was in a pot over the gas. Harriet put her feet over the edge of the bed and held a hand to her head for a few seconds. Maybe she should try some of the soup, she thought. Getting slowly to her feet Harriet walked out on to the landing and lit the gas-jet. Maybe just a small slice of bread would be nice with the soup, she decided. It was then that her eyes suddenly caught sight of the carton. Harriet smiled. How considerate of Juliet, she thought. She knows how much I like fresh cream. Maybe I'll try some later with one of those soft pears.

Muriel had finished her meal of new potatoes, peas and pork chop and was sitting quietly in her armchair listening to the wireless. Sandy Macpherson was playing a melody of popular tunes on the theatre organ, and just as he struck up with 'Lazy River' a piercing scream rang out. Muriel jumped from her chair and hurried to the stairs.

'What's up?' she shouted, her heart pumping with shock.

'Take it away!' Harriet screamed out. 'Take it away! I can't stand the things!'

Muriel rushed up the stairs and saw Harriet standing on the landing clutching her hands to her face, her wide eyes staring through her fingers at the opened carton.

'I thought it was cream,' she cried. 'When I opened it I saw those revolting things. The sight of them makes me ill.'

Muriel picked up the carton and backed away down the stairs. 'Alf Porter left 'em fer yer,' she said. 'It was a gift, 'cos 'e thought yer didn't like 'is song last night.'

'A gift!' Harriet shouted almost hysterically. 'The man's mad! I know what he's trying to do. He's trying to drive me mad, too. Take those revolting things out of the house. Do you hear?'

'All right, all right. I'm not deaf,' Muriel shouted back, angry at being disturbed by the distraught woman. 'It's only jellied eels. They go down well wiv a drop o' vinegar.'

Harriet returned to her room and threw herself down on the bed. Mr Cuthbert is going to hear about this, she vowed.

When Juliet returned from her day with Mr Lomax, she found her sister in a state of near-hysteria and from what she could gather it seemed that Alf Porter was engaged in a campaign of terror against Harriet. When she calmed her sobbing sibling and made her a cup of strong cocoa laced with two aspirins she went down to have a talk with Muriel.

'You'd better sit yerself down,' Muriel said in her most pleasant voice after Juliet had given the reason for her visit. 'It must 'ave bin a nasty shock ter find yer poor sister in that state. Is it one or two sugars?' Juliet took the tea from her and sipped it while Muriel went on. 'It was jus' a nice gesture that went wrong. 'E was so upset at frightenin' the pair of yer 'e wanted ter make up fer it. 'E told me 'e went ter get yer a nice bunch o' flowers but the shop was shut.'

Juliet looked abashed. 'Dear, dear. I'm sorry I troubled you, Miss Taylor. I just had to get to the bottom of it.'

'Call me Muriel. It sounds better,' Muriel said, smiling sweetly. 'It was no trouble. I 'ope yer sister feels better in the mornin'.'

Juliet finished her tea and Muriel took the cup from her. 'Would yer like anuvver one?' she asked.

Juliet shook her head. 'No, that was very nice, thank you.'

Muriel sat down facing her guest. 'Look,
198

Juliet – yer don't mind me callin' yer Juliet, do yer?'

'No, of course not.'

'Well I've bin finkin',' Muriel went on, assuming a caring expression. "Ow would it be if I went ter see Alf Porter? I'll make sure that 'e doesn't worry yer sister again. 'E'll listen ter me.'

'Would you really?' Juliet asked. 'It would be a great help.'

'Course I will,' Muriel gushed. 'After all, we are neighbours, ain't we?' She was determined to cultivate a good understanding with the Carey sisters.

Juliet stood up to go. 'Well, thank you, Muriel. I appreciate your helping us.'

'That's all right, Juliet. I'm only too glad to 'ave 'ad the opportunity of puttin' fings right. I've bin told I've gotta mend me ways,' Muriel said, putting on her little girl face.

'Oh, and who told you that?'

'Mr Cuthbert from the estate office called round ter see me some time ago. 'E said if I wasn't careful I'd be evicted,' Muriel lied. 'They wouldn't evict me, would they, Juliet?'

Juliet felt consumed with guilt. 'Don't you worry about it, Muriel,' she said in a confidential tone. 'They won't evict you. As long as you're discreet no one need complain. I'll have a talk with Harriet. I'm sure things will work out just fine.'

Muriel's look of strained anxiety disappeared and she smiled happily at the older woman. 'I fink you're very nice, Juliet,' she said sweetly.

'It's bin lovely talkin' ter yer.'

Muriel waited until the footsteps on the stairs faded, then she collapsed into her favourite chair with a large-size grin on her pretty face. 'Silly ole mare,' she said aloud, feeling rather pleased with her own performance.

Muriel inadvertently became the subject of discussion amongst the tenants of Paragon Place, and Granny Allen voiced the opinion that the girl must have run out of men. 'I was in me front room an' I see 'er out o' the winder,' she told her friend Daisy as they sat together at the Almonds' house. 'She was knockin' at Alf Porter's door an' I see 'er go in there wiv me own eyes.'

'Gawd 'elp us, she's gotta be 'ard up knockin' at 'is door,' replied Daisy.

Ginny chuckled. 'I fink yer bein' a bit 'ard on the girl, Mum. She might 'ave bin goin' there ter get change fer the meter or somefing.'

Daisy snorted. 'Well she wouldn't walk all the way down the square fer change, would she? What's the matter wiv 'er goin' next door?'

Muriel's visit was innocent enough. 'All I'm sayin' is, yer wanna give the woman a wide berth, Alf,' she was saying. 'She's a bloody neurotic. I'm sure she reckons yer was out ter frighten 'er ter death.'

Alf scratched his head and put on one of his sad faces. 'I was only tryin' ter make up fer frightenin' the woman on Saturday night, Muriel. Bloody 'ell, 'ow was I ter know the silly ole cow was terrified of eels?'

Muriel laughed aloud. 'Well, you jus' take my tip. Steer clear of 'er. She'll get over it.'

Alf went to his sideboard and took out a bottle of whisky. ''Ere, fancy a drop o' this?' he said with sudden enthusiasm. 'Just ter show me appreciation, yer warnin' me like yer did.'

Muriel took the proffered glass and held it up. ''Ere's to yer, Alf.'

He grinned and tapped her glass with his. ''Ere's ter good ole chivalry, an' long live jellied eels.'

Chapter Ten

PARAGON PLACE had settled down to a quiet, untroubled existence as the days grew shorter and the autumn leaves began to drop. Muriel Taylor had become the soul of discretion, and whenever Alf Porter came home drunk he would walk unsteadily past the Carey residence with a serious look on his thin face and a forefinger held against his lips. The two grannies had left Muriel and Alf alone, having found new topics to discuss, and Ginny was persisting doggedly in her bid to eventually bed the reluctant George Tapley.

For Sally Brady the days had been long and tiring, and as she walked home from work through Stanley Street's railway arches one Friday evening late in September her thoughts were troubled. She pulled her coat collar up against the keen wind as she passed the corner shop and glanced down the small side turning. Sally was dreading the prospect facing her that evening and she gritted her teeth, angry with herself for not being able to control her nervousness. She had been indecisive, and now she was going to have to face him and spell it out once and for all.

It was almost three weeks now since he walked up to her as she left the factory. Ben had been waiting for her that evening and had taken her by surprise. He had followed along as she made her way home and had asked again that they should go for a drink to talk things over. Her excuse that she needed more time had only served to make him more determined, and she had finally, nervously, agreed to see him this evening.

Instead of talking to someone about the situation she was in Sally had kept everything to herself, and she had grown increasingly nervous. She had felt that there was no one she could turn to for help. Vera was her best friend and she was always ready to listen, but she was going through a rough time herself. Her pregnancy was proving to be very trying. The baby had turned and she was facing the prospect of a difficult birth. Vera was also very worried about Joe. She had not heard from him for some time now, and the news broadcasts did not do anything to allay her fears. More and more merchant ships were being sunk in the North Atlantic, and the reporting both on the radio and in newspapers caused her a great deal of concern. She tried to put on a brave face, but Sally knew that behind her outward cheerfulness Vera was struggling with her own very real fears and she did not intend to worry her with her problems.

Sally had considered talking to her family but had decided against it. Her father disliked Ben and he would only have ranted and raved. Her mother would have adopted her usual worried frown and gone on about how the worry of everything was making her ill. Sally knew that attempting to confide in Lora would be a waste of time. She was wrapped up in her new romance and very rarely spent any time in the house. Sally knew she would have to work things out for herself. She would have to be firm and refuse to be taken in by Ben's promises. He had told her he was now off the drink, but his appearance had suggested otherwise. His face seemed to have become somewhat bloated again since his release from prison, and his eyes had the all-too-familiar bleary look about them. Ben was not going to change, and she would have to make him see that getting back together would only cause more heartbreak for both of them.

Sally entered her house and immediately saw the troubled look on her mother's face. 'Bill's bin taken bad,' she said flatly. 'I found 'im collapsed by the side o' the bed when I took 'is tea up to 'im. I couldn't lift 'im. I 'ad ter get Ginny ter 'elp me.'

Sally quickly took off her coat and went to the stairs. 'Did yer call the doctor?' she asked.

"E's bin,' Annie replied. "E said it was Bill's

age. Apparently 'is 'eart's not too good. The doctor left some tablets an' 'e's callin' in ter-morrer. I dunno, it's all bleedin' worry lately.'

Sally hurried up the stairs and went into the small back room. Bill was lying on his back, the bedclothes pulled up under his chin. Sally walked over and saw that his eyes were closed, but as she stood looking down at him he opened them and gave her a faint smile.

'Sorry ter be a nuisance,' he managed to say.

She smiled down at him and stroked her hand very gently over his forehead. 'You jus' rest, Bill,' she whispered. 'A few days in bed an' you'll be yer ole self.'

He pulled a face and slid a bony hand from beneath the bedclothes. 'Yer remember that tin, lass?' he whispered, his watery eyes blinking.

Sally nodded. 'Don't worry about the tin, Bill. Try ter get some sleep.'

Bill's face seemed to cloud and he struggled to go on. 'Just in case anyfing 'appens. I want yer ter know where it is,' he mumbled.

'I know where it is, Bill,' she replied. 'Now don't worry. You're gonna be OK. Jus' rest fer now.'

Bill sighed and closed his eyes. Sally looked down at him for a few moments and then tucked his cold hand beneath the bedclothes and crept from the room.

The autumn light was fading as Sally walked along Jamaica Road. She had arranged to meet Ben at the Yachtsman, a small riverside inn at Dockhead, and as she took a side street towards the Thames her troubled thoughts turned to Bill Freeman. He seemed so frail and ailing and Sally feared for him. She wondered about the tin box and why he had been so insistent that she should know where it was kept. What secrets did it hold of the old man? He had never been one to dwell on his past, and maybe he had good reason for not doing so.

Ben was there, seated at the counter as she entered the smoke-laden bar, and he got up as she walked over to him. 'Fanks fer comin', Sal,' he said, a smile breaking on his ruddy features. 'What can I get yer?'

Sally looked across the counter. 'A gin an' lime, please.'

The pub was quiet, with only a few regulars seated beside a coke fire. Ben took the drinks and led her to the table farthest from the door. 'It gets packed in 'ere after nine,' he said, putting the drinks down on the table. They seated themselves and Sally took a sip from her glass. It was some time since she had tasted gin and she pulled a face.

'D'yer want some more lime in it?' he asked.

'No, it's fine,' she replied, glancing at him and then studying her drink.

He took a gulp from his pint of ale and set it down again. Sally noticed the slight shake of his hand and the tenseness in his body as he rested his arms on the round iron table. He glanced around the bar and she stole a brief glance at him. His fair hair had grown and it curled about his ears. His face had a reddish look about it and there was a slight puffiness beneath his deep-set

205

blue eyes. He seemed to have put on weight, but his mouth was still firm, his thin lips framed by a clean-shaven, square jaw. He was still handsome in a roguish way, she thought, although he seemed to have lost that carefree, boyish look which had first attracted her to him. He looked older, more mature, and there were lines she had not seen before in the corners of his eyes.

A few customers had come into the pub and were laughing with the landlord. Ben suddenly turned to her, breaking the awkward silence between them. ''Ave yer considered what I said about gettin' back tergevver, Sally?' he asked her.

She looked down at her glass. 'Yes, I did. I've thought a lot about it.'

'Well?'

Sally slid the palms of her hands down the top of her legs and clasped them tightly together beneath the table. All the dithering and indecision were gone, and in their place was a firm resolve that here and now she would end their association. There could be no other way if she were going to start a new life for herself. She realised that going back to live with her family had been an unreal kind of escape, for it had allowed him to cling on to the idea that one day she might return. What she was about to say had to be said, and she brought her eyes up to face his.

'I'm not comin' back, Ben,' she said slowly. 'I want a divorce.'

His face tensed and his blue eyes burned into hers. 'What you're sayin' is that yer not prepared ter forgive what I've done?'

She took a deep breath and her knuckles whitened beneath the table. 'What I'm sayin' is that we can't 'ave a future after what's 'appened. I'm not prepared ter argue the toss, Ben. I've said it, an' I mean it. I wanna get a divorce.'

He looked intently at her. 'I know what I've done can never be undone, but I've changed. I can see fings in a different light now. I know I've 'urt yer bad but it was never really meant that way. I'd never deliberately go out ter 'urt yer. Tell me, Sal, 'ave I ever slapped yer? Yer know I 'aven't. I wouldn't lay a finger on yer. What I did was stupid. I s'pose I needed ter prove somefing ter meself, an' I realise now that I must 'ave bin mad. Look, I'm not askin' yer ter forget. I know yer can't. What I'm askin' for is yer forgiveness. I'd never do it ter yer again, Sal. We'd 'ave a chance ter be the way we was. It was good once, yer know it was.'

She sighed deeply, moved almost to tears by his words. 'I know it was good once,' she said quietly. 'That's what makes it so 'ard. I sometimes wish yer 'ad laid yer 'ands on me. That would be easier ter forgive. But I find it impossible ter forgive your betrayal. No, yer wasn't brutal in a physical sense, Ben. What yer done ter me was far more brutal than if you'd just slapped me around. Bruises on the body 'eal, but my sort o' bruises can't be seen an' they'll never 'eal. I'll always carry them around inside me, so don't try an' talk me out of it. Me mind's made up.'

He stared down at his half-empty glass for a

moment and then his eyes came up calmly to meet hers. 'It's gonna be painful fer both of us,' he said. 'A divorce is gonna rake up a lot o' dirt.'

Sally shook her head. 'It needn't be that way. Me parents don't know why I left yer, Ben. They fink we just couldn't get on tergevver. They don't know the real truth. I jus' couldn't tell 'em. We could get a divorce fer desertion. All right, it could take a couple o' years, but it'd be cleaner. Nobody else would get 'urt.'

Ben pushed back his chair. 'All right. Yer can 'ave yer divorce, Sally,' he said quietly as he got up. 'I won't stand in yer way. Jus' remember, though. I'm still gonna be around, an' I'm never gonna forget yer. If yer ever feel the need ter come ter me fer anyfing, I'll be there. Will yer remember that?'

She nodded. 'I'll remember, Ben.'

He had gone, and Sally sat for a few minutes staring down at her empty glass. It had been easier than she could have hoped. There had been no hard anger, no fierce argument, only a plea for her to forgive him, and then his parting words which she found very sad. He must have known in his heart that there would be no reconciliation, she told herself, but there was an ache in her heart. She and Ben had played together as children, flirted as teenagers and then experienced adult love. Sally felt then that part of her had died and she wiped a tear away. She was suddenly aware that the customers were staring at her, and she quickly got up and walked out into the night.

Chill October winds had begun to sweep across the square. Doorsteps did not get whitened so frequently and blackout curtains were pulled across the lace earlier as winter settled in. The Paragon folk banked up their coke fires and drew doormats up against the draughts. Long evenings were spent in front of the hearth and people listened to the news broadcasts with growing interest as reports came through that a large scale battle was taking place in the Middle East.

At number 2, George Tapley listened to the broadcasts with a mixture of elation and dread and his eyes constantly strayed to the small photograph of his son Tony.

''E's in that, Ginny. That's why I ain't 'eard from 'im lately,' he said, staring down into the fire.

''E'll be all right, George,' Ginny replied. 'Fings seem ter be movin' now. Please Gawd they'll all be 'ome before long.'

George's eyes strayed to another photograph on the mantelshelf and he sighed. 'I wonder 'ow that poor sod's gettin' on, Gin? Gawd knows when I'll 'ear from 'im.'

She sipped her tea, her large eyes looking over the top of the cup. ''Ere, when are we goin' out fer anuvver drink?' she asked with a smile. 'The folk round 'ere ain't 'ad much ter talk about recently.'

George grinned as he kicked a red cinder back into the grate. 'I know I ain't bin much company lately, Ginny. It's just that I can't get them boys out o' me mind. They're all I've got. They're good boys. Their muvver would 'ave bin proud of 'em, Gawd rest 'er soul.'

Ginny nodded sympathetically but inside she felt a mixture of pity and anger. She had gone out with George on one or two occasions, and later in the privacy of his home they had kissed and cuddled, but it had always ended there. She felt as though the ghost of his wife was for ever in that room with them. Ginny had hinted and encouraged him, but with little success. George was a dapper, fit man who took pride in his appearance and still retained a sense of humour, and she had often wanted to take him by the hand and lead him to the bedroom, but always she had resisted the urge. He would have to make the first move, she decided. He would have to lay the ghost. When he put his arms round her and kissed her she had sensed that he was struggling with his thoughts and desires, and she resolved to be patient for a little longer. She would give him a little more time.

At number 4, Annie Robinson was grumbling as she spooned hot broth from a large iron pot into a china basin. ''Ere, take this up ter Bill, will yer, Sally? I can't keep up an' down them stairs. I've 'ad ter 'elp 'im down when 'e 'ad ter go out the back an' 'elp 'im up again. Me legs are playin' me up as it is.'

Sally put the basin on a small wooden tray and cut a thick slice of bread which she laid beside the broth. 'Bill's gettin' weaker, Mum,' she said. 'E's feelin' the cold terrible.'

Annie puffed. 'Well, there's not much more I

can do. There's a fire goin' night an' day an' yer dad's blocked the winders up. Trouble is, the ole boy don't eat enough ter keep a sparrer alive. 'E can't go on livin' on scraps. 'E should stay down wiv us. At least 'e'd be warmer.'

Sally climbed the stairs with the tray and pushed open the door with her elbow. The old man was sitting at the small table and as she entered he smiled weakly.

'I don't want anyfing ter eat, lass. I fink I'll turn in soon,' he said to her quietly.

Sally put down the tray and stared at him with a stern look on her face. 'Now look, Bill. I ain't takin' this down till yer've emptied it, an' I don't mean yer tippin' it in that chamber-pot neivver.'

Bill sighed and eased the old overcoat higher on to his shoulders. 'Yer a good girl, Sal. You'd make a good nurse. All right, I'll try some.'

She stood over him while he spooned the broth into his mouth. 'C'mon, eat that bread. It'll give yer strength,' she said firmly.

His hands were shaking and at each spoonful he swallowed Bill pulled a face. Sally watched him with sadness in her dark eyes. She realised that he was fading away gradually. Even lifting the spoon seemed to be an effort.

When he had finished Sally picked up the tray. 'Can yer get inter bed OK, Bill?' she asked.

He nodded. 'I can manage, lass. Fank Annie fer the soup. It was very nice.'

Sally smiled. 'Get yerself sorted out an' I'll be up later ter tuck yer up fer the night.'

He looked up at her, his rheumy eyes

searching hers. "'Ave yer got a minute, lass?' he said.

She sat down at the table. 'Course I 'ave,' she replied. 'What is it, Bill?'

His bony hands were clasped in front of him and his lips moved over his toothless gums. 'Annie told me terday that you an' Ben was gettin' divorced,' he said slowly.

Sally nodded. 'Yeah, that's right, Bill.'

'Well, I'm sorry ter 'ear of it,' he said, his eyes staring into hers. 'I always reckoned you an' 'im was well suited.'

'We was, once,' she said quietly. 'Fings change, though. It's best we make the break now, Bill.'

He nodded. 'Well, you're young yet. Yer got yer whole life in front o' yer. One day you'll meet somebody else. Jus' don't waste yer life bein' on yer own. We all need somebody. It's the worse fing in the world bein' lonely. Jus' remember that, lass.'

She looked at him, the affection she felt for the old man shining in her eyes. 'I won't forget it, Bill. Claim a star, yer told me.'

'That's right,' he answered, a grin appearing on his lined features. 'I see yer remembered.'

Her hand went out to his. 'When I see the next shootin' star I'll squeeze me 'and tight, shut me eyes an' count ter ten,' she laughed.

'Don't forget ter claim it, though,' he chuckled. 'Yer gotta claim it, lass.'

At Harrison's clothing factory in Tooley Street work had been stepped up after the management

212

secured a new government contract for army overcoats. From eight in the morning until six o'clock every weekday the machines ran at full speed and the workforce found themselves under pressure from the management to keep up the output. At first things went well, but soon the supply of raw materials started to flag and the ageing machines began to break down under the strain. The contract started to fall behind schedule and tempers began to get frayed. Shopfloor supervisors harried the workforce and they themselves were pressurised by the management to keep up the output. Even Maggie Chandler, the firm's most efficient machinist, found herself hard put to reach her targets and one morning after a telling-off from one of the supervisors she ran from her workplace in tears. Maggie sought comfort from Mr Murray, who regretted ever having taken her down into the basement. His abrupt words only served to inflame the simple girl's passion and she threatened to tell her mother he had interfered with her unless he was more sympathetic in future. Maggie had no intention of informing her mother, but her threat worked. She was sent back to her machine happy that she would be spared the supervisor's wrath in future – and with the knowledge that Mr Murray would try to find the time to take her on another guided tour of the basement as soon as possible. For the rest of the workforce things were not so rosy, and arguments often blew up on the shopfloor and in the canteen at lunch times.

Sally was missing Vera's companionship and

bubbling sense of humour. Her replacement on the adjoining machine was Brenda Foster, a surly looking girl of about Sally's own age who was reluctant to engage in any form of conversation. She had taken an instant dislike to Maggie and seized every opportunity to goad the simpleton. Sally avoided sitting near the two at lunch times but Maggie had taken a liking to her and often sought her out.

It was on one of those occasions when Maggie sat down opposite Sally that Brenda also decided to sit at their table. All through the lunch Brenda eyed Maggie, and when the simpleton spilled gravy down her chin the surly Brenda was quick to react.

'Yer eat like a pig,' she snarled. 'Can't yer eat sensible? If you're not careful you'll swaller the knife an' fork.'

Maggie pushed her glasses up on to the bridge of her nose and carried on eating without comment. Brenda's irritation grew and she continued to watch the girl closely as she finished her food. Maggie's appetite was never quite satisfied by the canteen meals and she usually rounded off her dinner by wiping the plate clean with a piece of bread before starting on her sweet. Brenda watched as Maggie fed the last forkful into her mouth and then picked up the bread.

'Christ! Why don't yer lick the plate?' she said cuttingly.

Sally puffed in annoyance and gave Brenda a hard stare. 'Why don't yer leave the girl alone. She's not 'urtin' you, is she?' she asked.

Brenda snorted. 'She ought ter be sittin' at a trough, not a table. She's got the manners of a pig.'

Maggie had had enough, and her confidence had been boosted by Sally's interjection. She pulled her plate of jam tart and custard towards her, looked at it for a moment, and then slowly got up. Without saying a word she walked around the table and tipped it over Brenda's head. Within seconds the canteen had erupted. Maggie lost her glasses as she and the custard-covered Brenda grappled. Sally sprang up and tried to separate the two only to be sent sprawling. Workers gathered round as Maggie grabbed two handfuls of Brenda's messy hair and pulled her to the floor. The simpleton was crying with temper and the luckless Brenda screamed as she lost a tuft of hair. Maggie had her opponent pinned to the floor, and it took the combined efforts of two supervisors to drag the combatants apart and march them off out through different doors.

When the canteen incident reached John Harrison's ears he brought his fist down heavily on the desk. 'That's it! I'm calling a meeting!' he exploded.

Low morale and bad output figures were top of the agenda and the white-haired and ageing managing director sat at the head of the boardroom table listening to the reasons and excuses which were readily forthcoming.

'It's the machines,' Mr Murray said. 'It's difficult to get spares these days.'

'It's the workforce,' said Mr Cornbloom, the

chief supervisor. 'They're a lazy lot at the best of times. Put them under a bit of pressure and they go to pieces.'

'I disagree,' said Mr Brown, the chief accountant. 'The targets are too high. We need an extension to complete the order. At least another two weeks, I would say.'

Mr Sackville, the production manager, shook his head. 'We're having trouble getting the cloth delivered on time. It's putting production under a lot of pressure.'

Mr Carmichael, the personnel officer, coughed nervously. 'Maybe it would be a good idea to remove that factory clock,' he suggested tentatively. 'It's very distracting, and in my experience it doesn't do to have a clock on the factory floor where everyone can see it.'

Mr Renshaw raised a bony hand in an effort to attract attention. He was the most senior of the managers, both in age and service. General opinion around the table was that he had out-lived his usefulness but because of his seniority he had to be tolerated and humoured.

'Yes Mr Renshaw?' said the managing director.

'It's the food,' the old man said, nodding his head slowly as if agreeing with his own diagnosis.

'The food?' everyone chorused.

Mr Renshaw sat back in his chair, happy in the knowledge that at last he had been noticed. 'Yes, the food. I've been in that canteen at lunchtime and I've seen those meals they serve up. If I had eaten one of those portions I'd have slept the afternoon away. They're too big.'

Mr Carmichael ground his back molars together. Silly old fool, he thought to himself, why the firm don't put him out to graze is beyond me. 'I'm afraid I've got to disagree, Mr Renshaw,' he said, smiling pleasantly at the elderly manager. 'You have to realise that those portions served at lunchtime are necessary to sustain the workforce. It's all a question of calories, supplementation and coefficients, you see. It's all in the Government paper issued by the Ministry of Food for factory canteen meals. We have to abide by their directives, or we'll find ourselves in trouble if their inspectors pay us a visit.'

Mr Renshaw scratched his head in bewilderment. He was not at all sure what calories, supplementations and coefficients had to do with large helpings of meat pie, jam tart and custard and treacle pudding. The rest of the management felt a little bemused too, and they turned to Mr Harrison for guidance.

His response was not what they had expected. He leaned forward, his hands resting palms down on the highly polished surface. 'Well, I've listened to your arguments,' he began, 'and I've got to say that I've never in my entire life heard such a pathetic load of codswallop. I think you're making this business out to be a subject for a Mack Sennett comedy. What have you come up with?' he asked, his eyes narrowing. ' "Get rid of the factory clock and cut down on the meals." Good Lord! How the hell do the workforce know if they're falling behind with their targets

217

without a clock to go by? And as for smaller meals. If we did that we'd have more to worry about than someone getting custard poured over them and two silly women rolling around over the canteen floor. We'd have a full-scale riot on our hands. So much for your inspired suggestion. Now what about the excuses? Let's take the machines.'

'I wish you would,' Mr Murray mumbled to himself.

'I want them all thoroughly serviced after working hours. Overtime for the mechanics,' Mr Harrison declared. 'Agreed?'

'Agreed,' concurred Mr Murray.

'I'll personally talk to the Ministry of Supply about replacements. Sir Basil Phillips might be able to help on that one. As for the cloth, I'll deal with that, too. There's a proviso in the contract. I'll make use of that if I have to.'

Mr Carmichael felt angry and deflated at the response to what he thought was a perfectly good idea of removing the factory clock, and he was moved to hold up his hand.

'Yes, Mr Carmichael?'

'I'm sure you'll be able to sort out the supply problem, Mr Harrison, but what about the question of low morale?'

Mr Harrison gave the personnel officer a hard look. 'I'm coming to that. We've got to look at a bonus structure. Mr Brown, I want you to do a feasibility study. I want it on my desk as soon as possible. Mr Carmichael, I want you and I to put our heads together. Let's see if we can get the military to pay us a visit. The sight of some

218

servicemen being shown around might help boost morale. I also want you to organise a function.'

'A function?' Mr Carmichael almost gasped.

'An evening social, man. A dance. If we hurry it along we might be able to give our military visitors a few complimentary tickets. That should please the workers.'

The personnel officer gulped hard. He had visions of the workforce fighting over partners and rolling around the dance floor in mortal combat. 'Right, sir. I'll look into that straight away,' he said.

Mr Harrison looked around the table. 'Right then. Now there's just one other thing I want to say. I think we need to look at our method of approach with regards to our workforce. A little encouragement doesn't go amiss.' He looked directly at Mr Murray. 'I'm looking for good, relaxed management of our staff, but I don't expect you to become too familiar. Is that understood?'

Mr Murray felt as though his whole private life had been suddenly exposed and he wilted under the firm gaze of the managing director.

'Well, I think that's all,' Mr Harrison said, adding, 'Oh, Mr Murray. I'd like you to remain, if you please.'

The winter took grip and cold northerly winds brought the threat of snow. On a mid-November evening Sally and Vera sat talking together at number 6 Paragon Place.

'I'm a bit nervous,' Vera said, rubbing her

219

hands over her very noticeable bulge. 'Still, it'll be nice ter get inter one o' me dresses instead o' this bloody smock. I feel like a hippopotamus in this bloody fing.'

Sally laughed. 'I dunno. Yer look better in that than I do when I'm dressed up.'

Vera sat down on the edge of her bed. ''Ere, when it's all over 'ow about you an' me goin' dancin'? I used ter love goin' up the Town 'All.'

'Yer won't find time once the baby's born,' Sally replied. 'You'll be up ter yer eyes in dirty nappies and bottles. 'Ere, talkin' o' dances. They're 'avin' one at the firm next month. There was a notice up in the canteen about it.'

'Bloody 'ell. What's got inter 'Arrison's?' Vera said, raising her eyebrows. 'I've never known 'em ter lay on a dance. Who they gonna get ter do the music, the Salvation Army?'

'No, it's bein' 'eld at the church 'all in Dock'ead,' Sally answered. 'Some o' the girls was talkin' about it yesterday. They reckon the band's pretty good.'

'What's the name o' the band?' Vera asked.

Sally put her hand up to her mouth. 'I can't remember. I fink it was Joe Miller, but I can't be sure.'

'If it's the Joe Miller band yer can count me in,' Vera said enthusiastically. 'Yer gonna go, ain't yer?'

Sally shrugged her shoulders. 'I dunno. Yer know I can't dance all that well.'

'I'll teach yer a few steps,' Vera said encouragingly. 'Anyway, yer don't 'ave ter worry. Jus' 'old on tight ter yer fella an' let 'im take yer round. That's what I do.'

The wind howled as it swirled around the deserted square and Vera shuddered. 'I don't like the sound o' the wind. I fink it's creepy,' she said, pulling her cardigan round her shoulders.

Sally laughed. 'D'yer remember when we was kids an' yer used ter come over my 'ouse on Sat'day nights? We used ter frighten the life out of each ovver by tellin' ghost stories on windy nights.'

Vera nodded. 'Seems a long time ago now, don't it?'

'Yeah, it does,' Sally replied, a thoughtful look in her eyes. 'It's funny 'ow fings work out. There's me gettin' a divorce an' you almost a mummy. I can remember the time yer told me yer never wanted kids, an' I said I wanted six.'

Vera got up from the edge of the bed and rubbed her side with the palm of her hand. 'Are you gettin' broody again, Sal?' she asked her friend.

Sally studied her fingernails for a moment or two then her eyes met Vera's. 'No, I was jus' finkin',' she said quietly.

Vera went over to Sally and took her by the arm. 'C'mon, no more finkin',' she said with mock seriousness. 'Let's go down an' make a cuppa. I wanna listen ter the nine o'clock news.'

It was Monday morning when Bill Freeman passed away. Charlie had taken the old man's morning tea up to his room and found him lying dead beside the bed.

'We can't leave the poor ole sod layin' there,' Annie said, dabbing her eyes with a handkerchief.

Charlie shook his head. 'Best ter leave 'im where 'e is till the doctor gets 'ere. It won't make no difference ter Bill.'

Sally sat down in the easy chair, feeling as though icy fingers had gripped her stomach. ''E was such a lovely ole man,' she faltered, fighting back her tears.

Annie was managing to compose herself. 'I don't fink 'e really got over that there bout o' pneumonia,' she said. ''E was so weak. I could see it comin'. It's still a bloody shock, though.'

When Doctor Bartholomew had finished his examination he washed his hands in a bowl of hot water that Annie had made ready, then took the glass of whisky that Charlie had poured for him.

'He's been dead for some hours,' he said, puffing heavily. 'At a guess I'd say it happened when he was getting ready for bed. The poor old chap's heart was very weak. Does he have any family?'

Annie shook her head. 'I don't fink so. 'E never mentioned 'avin' anybody, at least not ter us. 'E might 'ave mentioned somefing ter our Sally. She got on wiv 'im really well. She's bin livin' 'ere wiv us since she split up wiv 'er 'usband. 'E wasn't much good. Always on the beer. 'E can be trouble, too, when 'e's sloshed. Now, Doctor, I wanted ter chat ter yer about me insommia.'

Doctor Bartholomew put down the empty

222

glass and took hold of his bag, eager to get out of the house before Annie started talking about all the ailments she had suffered over the past twenty years.

'You'll need to take that to the undertaker,' he said, quickly pointing to the death certificate he had left on the table. 'I think he'll be able to collect the body this afternoon. Well, I'd better be off. You've still got some of those pills I prescribed, haven't you, Mrs Robinson?'

'Yeah, they're up on the mantelshelf, doctor,' she replied.

'Well, see that you take them. They'll help you sleep.'

The Robinsons had finished their tea and were sitting around the fire. Charlie puffed away on his pipe, deep in thought, and Annie tried to occupy herself by knitting. Lora was reading the paper and suddenly she looked up.

'Will the parish 'ave ter bury 'im?' she asked.

Annie shook her head. "E 'ad insurance. I paid it wiv ours. It was only coppers, though. Just about enough ter cover the cost. Me an' yer farver's gonna sort it out termorrer.'

'You got on wiv 'im pretty good, Sal. Did 'e 'ave any relatives?' Lora asked.

Sally looked across to her sister. 'No. At least I don't fink so.'

'I never got ter know 'im like you did,' Lora went on. "E never talked ter me much. Well, not like 'e did ter you.'

Sally got up quickly, her eyes burning into her sister's. "E? 'Im? 'Is name was Bill. Can't yer

223

call 'im by 'is name?' she shouted.

Lora looked abashed and stared down at her hands. Charlie looked hard at Sally and Annie put down her knitting. 'Lora didn't mean no 'arm,' she said quickly.

Sally felt tears flood into her eyes and the words stuck in her throat as she tried to speak. She looked around at her family and hurried from the room.

'What did I say?' Lora asked, picking up the paper with a sigh.

Charlie tapped his pipe against the fender and studied the bowl for a moment or two. 'Yer gotta realise, Lora, she thought a lot o' the ole man,' he said quietly. "E used ter talk ter the girl 'cos she 'ad time fer 'im. I don't fink the rest of us give 'im much of our time. Yeah, we fed 'im an' made sure 'e 'ad clean clothes on the bed. We took 'is tea up to 'im an' 'elped 'im up an' down the stairs when 'e wasn't too well, but 'e paid 'is keep. It was the least we could do.'

'Well, I couldn't stand around chattin' all day,' Annie said. 'I 'ad me work ter do an' the meals ter get.'

'Yeah, we all 'ad fings ter do. So did our Sal, but she managed ter find time ter chat wiv 'im. She thought a lot o' Bill so it's only natural she's takin' it 'ard.'

'Well, she didn't 'ave ter jump down me throat,' Lora said, turning the pages of her paper with energy.

Charlie reached up to the mantelshelf for his tobacco pouch without answering. Annie got on with her knitting, occasionally glancing down at the glowing coals, and Lora was silent, staring at the newspaper. Outside the wind howled, and strong gusts rattled the windows and shook the bare branches of the sycamore.

Sally had gone up to the small back room and stood looking around for a while, hardly believing that she would never see the old man again. Her mother had stripped the bed and removed the candle holder. The books had been cleared from the table and the grate was empty. It felt icy cold in the room and Sally shivered violently as she went to the cabinet. Bill had told her often enough that she was to have the box, but it seemed wrong to remove it so soon. She opened the drawer hesitantly and picked it up, clasping it to her as she stared sadly around the room once more. A whole lifetime, she thought, and all that was left were a few tattered books and a small tin box.

Tears came to her eyes and she hurried out to her own room and sat down heavily on the bed. For a few minutes she stared down at the tin box she clasped in her hands, almost fearful of what secrets it might hold. Slowly she lifted the lid and turned the contents out on to the bed. Amongst some folded papers and opened letters she found a faded photograph and a sealed letter addressed to her. As she tore it open and took out the contents her eyes widened with surprise. Folded inside a large sheet of paper were ten large white banknotes. Sally read the message on the sheet of paper, written in a spidery scrawl.

To Sally,

Thank you for all your kindness to an old man. Please use the money as you wish and remember what I said. Your star is out there somewhere. You only have to claim it.

God bless,
Bill

She looked down at the banknotes, dry-eyed but swallowing hard against the lump that was rising in her throat. She put the money to one side and picked up one of the folded sheets of paper.

The bedroom became colder as the night wore on and Sally was shivering as she slowly went through the vestiges of Bill's life. The secret history of their lodger's life and times was slowly unravelled as she scanned each sheet of paper and each letter. As the details grew and shed increasing light on the old man's past Sally began to feel very close to him, but she could not help experiencing a sense of guilt at such an intrusion into his privacy. Bill had never volunteered any information about himself while he was living and any questions had always been rewarded with a blank stare and a wry smile. Now, in death, he had afforded her the opportunity to peer through the veil and share his past. She felt humbled, almost overcome with sadness as she folded the last sheet of paper and put it back into the box.

★ ★ ★

The funeral took place on a bitterly cold
226

morning, with just a few neighbours standing huddled at their front doors. When the Robinsons returned home, cold and sad-faced, Ginny Almond provided them with steaming hot tea and sandwiches which she had ready. Later that evening the family sat huddled together around a roaring fire in the front parlour. Sally had told her folks the morning after Bill died about the money he had bequeathed to her, and she had said that there were lots of papers that needed sorting out. Now, as they sat together in silence, Sally felt it was time she told the family all she had pieced together of the old man's life.

'It's all in 'ere,' she said, placing her hands on the tin box that was resting in her lap. 'Bill was born in Suffolk an' the family were farm labourers. That's Bill's dad,' she indicated, handing round the creased and dog-eared photograph. 'Bill married a local girl by the name o' Kathleen Carmody when 'e was nineteen, and apparently they lived in a cottage belongin' ter the farmer Bill worked for. They were married less than a year when their son was born. They christened 'im Simon. There's the marriage lines an' birth certificate in Bill's papers. There's a death certificate, too. Both 'is wife an' son died o' typhoid fever on the same day. The boy was just a year old when it 'appened. That means they were married less than two years. They didn't 'ave much time tergevver, did they?'

Charlie and Annie both shook their heads. 'What a terrible fing ter 'appen, losin' 'is wife and child like that,' Annie said sadly.

'Times must 'ave bin 'ard then,' Charlie said

grimly, puffing on his pipe.

'Bill 'ad ter get out o' the cottage after 'is wife an' child died,' Sally went on. 'It seems 'e left the country an' come ter London. There was a letter amongst 'is fings from a Reverend Purdy ter the manager o' Brandon's leather factory.'

'That's the place in Long Lane what burned down right at the beginnin' o' the blitz,' Charlie interrupted.

'Be quiet, Charlie. Let 'er finish,' Annie said quickly.

'The letter was a sort of introduction,' Sally continued. 'Bill was given a job at the factory an' there was anuvver letter from the vicar sayin' 'ow pleased 'e was that Bill 'ad settled down in London. Yer can read the letters if yer like, they're all in the tin.'

'It must 'ave bin bloody 'ard fer the poor sod, 'im bein' from the country,' Annie said.

Sally stared into the fire for a few seconds and Lora exchanged glances with her parents. 'Bill was in the leather trade when 'e retired, wasn't 'e?' she asked. ''E must 'ave bin in the business all 'is life, then.'

Sally shrugged her shoulders. 'Well, most of 'is life, anyway. There's also a letter from a firm called Marchant Leather Factors wishin' Bill an 'appy retirement, an' it mentioned 'im doin' thirty-five years wiv the company. I've bin workin' all the dates out. The vicar's letters were dated 1894. That means Bill must 'ave come ter London when 'e was twenty-two. The retirement letter from Marchant's mentions that Bill first started work for them in 1902, when 'e was thirty. I assumed 'e worked at Brandon's up until then. But then I read this letter.' She opened the box and took the top envelope out. 'It's a reference Bill got from Brandon's, an' it's dated November, 1897. That means 'e left there when 'e was twenty-five, five years before 'e started work at Marchant's.'

Charlie had been listening intently and he flipped open his tobacco pouch. 'It seems strange when yer come ter fink of it,' he said. 'Bill come ter live 'ere five years ago. I remember 'im tellin' us then 'e'd just retired. That's 'ow long we've all known 'im, jus' five years. I'm beginnin' ter feel I've known 'im all 'is life now.'

Sally nodded. 'When I started lookin' through this box I felt the same way. Then I got ter finkin'. What did 'e do from the time 'e left Brandon's until 'e started at Marchant's? There was a five-year gap. There's nufing in this box that covers those years. It seems strange, really.'

Annie picked up the poker and prodded the fire. 'P'r'aps 'e was out o' work. There must 'ave bin a lot of unemployment then,' she offered.

''E might 'ave joined the army an' bin in the Boer War,' Lora said.

Charlie shook his head. 'The Boer War started in 1899. Bill might 'ave joined up but surely 'e would 'ave left somefing, like medals, or 'is army papers.'

Annie pulled on her lower lip. 'Ain't there nufing else in there?' she asked, looking at the tin box.

Sally shook her head. 'No, that's about it.

229

Like yer say, Bill could 'ave bin out o' work or doin' different jobs until 'e went ter Marchant's. 'E might 'ave gone back ter Suffolk fer a time. I don't s'pose we'll ever know. P'r'aps it's just as well,' she said quietly.

Annie leaned back in her chair. 'Well, at least the poor ole sod's past ain't too much of a mystery now,' she sighed. 'I can understand now why 'e didn't like ter talk about 'imself. Too many bad memories.'

Sally took the envelope containing the money from the tin box and separated the banknotes. She handed two five-pound notes to each member of her family, waving away their protests. 'Bill told me to do what I liked wiv it,' she said firmly. 'I know 'e wouldn't 'ave expected me ter keep the 'ole fifty pounds ter meself.'

The hour was late and the fire had burned low. Charlie stood up and stretched. He took a key from the mantelshelf and wound up the clock, then looking at his pocket-watch he moved the minute-hand on to the hour. There was a whirring noise and then the dull chimes sounded.

At the midnight hour the chiming of the clock at number 6 was drowned by a baby's first cry. In a few moments Vera was cuddling her new son to her breast.

'Wait till daddy sees yer, Gawd 'elp 'im, wherever 'e is,' she whispered before closing her eyes and letting sleep engulf her exhausted body.

PART TWO

1943

Chapter Eleven

THE new year started cold and wet, with dreary mornings and long dark nights. The war-time Christmas had been austere, and a quiet one for the Paragon Place folk, although Bert and Elsie Jackson at the Railway Inn felt that it had been the best Christmas for business since the outbreak of war. Many of their customers had voiced the opinion that the tide was turning and things were soon going to look up. Food shortages, long queues at the shops and stalls, the blackout, and all the war-time restrictions were looked upon as 'bloody inconvenient but not to be helped' by the Jacksons' clientele. At Christmas they had gathered at the counter and sat at the tables, singing loudly as the pianist played their favourite melodies. Everyone had sensed that the new year would bring new hope. Charlie Robinson and Alf Porter both got drunk on Christmas Eve, and Alf was discovered later snoring loudly with his back propped up against the sycamore tree. He was picked up and carried into his house by Charlie and Patrick, who threw him unceremoniously on the bed, removed his boots, loosened his shirt collar and left him to sleep it off. Annie Robinson sent Alf over a Christmas dinner, and later she gave him a telling-off for the noise he had made coming into the square the previous evening. Now, as the new year got under way, Paragon settled down to face the worst of the winter.

Vera Mynott was making preparations for little Joe's christening and was feeling sad at her husband's departure. Joe had managed to get home two days before Christmas and had had to leave before the year was out.

'It wasn't long enough,' Vera moaned to Sally. ''E went crackers over little Joe.'

Sally smiled down at the tiny bundle. ''E's a little smasher. 'E's gonna be ginger like 'is mum, ain't yer, Joey?'

The baby screwed up his face and started to bawl. Vera sighed as she lifted him from the crib and sat down in a chair beside the fire. 'Are yer 'ungry, then?' she cooed, offering him an engorged breast.

Sally watched with amusement as the baby's open mouth searched for the nipple and then latched on to it greedily. ''Ow's 'e sleepin'?' she asked.

Vera leaned back in her chair and relaxed as the pressure pain in her breast began to ease. 'I'm still up in the night feedin' 'im, but 'e soon settles. I wanna keep 'im on the breast as long as possible, although it does tie yer down. Mum's good wiv 'im, though. She's spoilin' 'im already.'

Sally continued to watch with interest as Vera winded the baby and put him to her other breast. 'You've stopped yer mum's gallivantin' fer a while, 'aven't yer, Joey?' she laughed.

Vera pulled a face. 'I was choked I couldn't make that firm's dance. Never mind, I'll try an'

234

get ter the next one, that's if they 'ave any more. Yer gotta come, too, Sal. And I'm not gonna take no fer an answer, neivver.'

'They reckon they're gonna 'ave one every month,' Sally said. 'Everybody seemed ter enjoy it. Maggie Chandler found 'erself a chap, so I 'eard. 'E's the new ware'ouseman. Seems a bit dopey ter me, but Maggie's gone a bundle on 'im.'

Vera put the baby over her shoulder again and gently patted his back until he gave a loud burp. 'Let's get Bonzo settled an' me an' you can 'ave a nice chat,' she smiled. 'I ain't seen much of yer since Christmas.'

The January days were busy ones at Harrison's. The firm had secured a new contract and Mr Harrison watched the firm's progress very carefully. The supervisors were aware they were under scrutiny and discharged their tasks with new-found diplomacy. Mr Murray was very careful not to attract the attentions of Maggie Chandler, and was very relieved when he discovered that she had now transferred her passion to the new warehouseman. He had not forgotten the lecture he had had to endure at the hands of his employer, who had ended by saying that any more indiscretions would mean the sack.

In the canteen things were quieter. Brenda Foster sat as far away from Maggie Chandler as possible and had set the tongues wagging by her obvious interest in one of the supervisors.

'Just look at that Foster girl. She's all over 'im,' one of the women said, patting her permed hair. 'It makes yer sick ter see it.'

'Well, I blame 'im, Doris,' Flo replied. ''E's a married man wiv kids. I know 'is wife. If she knew what was goin' on she'd be up 'ere like a shot.'

'She's anuvver Vera, that one. D'yer remember 'ow Vera used ter be all over that Jimmy Kent? I reckon that was 'is baby, don't you, Flo?'

'I dunno, Doris. She used ter flirt wiv all the lads. I don't fink there was any 'arm in it, though. Mind you, she did go dancin' a lot wiv that Kent boy.'

Doris felt her dislike for Brenda growing as she watched the huddled conversation taking place on the end table. The new girl's arrival had put an end to her own aspirations with regard to Tommy Carlton. He had always been so attentive until that slut came along, she thought. 'This one's just as bad, Flo,' she said. 'Did yer see the way she was actin' at the dance? An' that dress she 'ad on. There was more out than in. Proper little tart.'

Flo nodded, knowing the full reason for her friend's dislike of the girl. 'She'll be the next one ter get 'erself in the puddin' club, Doris. Jus' look at 'er, she's all over 'im.'

Doris snorted. 'Well, it's their affair. I couldn't care less,' she lied. 'C'mon, Flo. Time ter get back.'

Sally had had the sad task of taking Bill's remaining books round to the Salvation Army hostel in Spa Road. Her parents had decided not to take in another lodger, and for the time being his room became a junk room. Things had become a little strained in the Robinson household since Lora had informed her parents that she was going away for the weekend. Charlie was against it and Annie had tried to spell out the dangers, but Lora had flown into a rage.

'I'm over twenty-one an' what I do is no concern of anybody's,' she shouted.

Sally had seen her father's reaction and had decided not to get involved. Charlie had stood eye to eye with his daughter, his wide face flushed with anger.

'It's our business while you're under this roof, me gel,' he raved. 'An' I don't want yer talkin' ter yer muvver like that, d'yer understand, or I'll take me belt ter yer, old as yer are.'

'Anybody'd fink I was goin' ter some 'otel wiv 'im. I'm only goin' ter stay wiv 'is family in the country fer the weekend,' Lora complained, her voice shaking with emotion.

'Well, that's as it may be, but keep a civil tongue in yer 'ead or yer gonna answer ter me, young lady,' Charlie declared.

Lora had run from the house in tears and since then she had adopted a moody silence in front of her father.

The atmosphere in the house was beginning to upset Sally, and her thoughts turned to finding a place of her own once more. Now that Bill had gone she found herself becoming increasingly bored and depressed. She missed his company and the cosy chats she had had with the old man. Her mother seemed to tire even more easily now and she often feel asleep in the fireside chair during the long evenings. Her father had resorted to going along to the Railway Inn most week-nights and as soon as he got back he would go to bed. Sally began to spend more and more time in the company of Vera, who was beginning to feel the strain of motherhood.

'Don't get me wrong, Sal,' Vera said to her one day. 'I wouldn't change fings fer the world, but I'd just like a bit o' time ter meself now an' then. All it's bin lately is washin' shitty nappies and makin' up bottles. Since me milk dried up I've 'ad a job gettin' 'im used ter the powdered milk. I really fancy a night out. 'Ere, when's the next dance at the firm?'

Sally shrugged her shoulders. 'Next week, I fink.'

'Yer fink?' Vera mocked. 'Don't yer know? They must 'ave put a notice up. Find out fer sure, Sal. Me mum said she'd get Joey's bottle an' tuck 'im up fer the night if I wanna go out. Don't forget you're comin,' too. It's about time yer started goin' out. Yer gettin' a right ole stick-in-the-mud. Jus' take a look at yerself. Work all day, an' sittin' around all night. You're gonna be old before yer time if you're not careful.'

Sally smiled at Vera's admonishment. She knew that her friend was right. It had got to the stage now where her depression and daily exhaustion had smothered her physical needs. It was easy to go to her room and let sleep wash over her. Only very rarely did she lie awake and let her mind drift back to happier times, but then in a welter of self-pity, anger and confusion she would always shut the memories out of her mind.

'Yeah, I'll come wiv yer,' Sally said suddenly, surprising herself.

'Cor! That'll be really great,' Vera gushed. 'We can find ourselves a couple o' fellas fer the evenin', or we can jus' dance an' 'ave a few drinks,' she added, eager not to appear too keen. 'We don't 'ave ter worry about the fellas. I don't s'pose there'll be many good-lookers there any'ow. P'r'aps I might try an' get off wiv Maggie's boyfriend,' she said, a comically distracted look on her face.

Sally laughed. 'Anyfing but that, Vera. Our Maggie's turned inter a little demon. If yer flirt wiv 'er bloke she's likely ter pull a few o' those red locks 'o yours out.'

They both giggled at the thought of Maggie Chandler in a mad rage and suddenly Sally became serious-faced. 'I don't know what I'd do wivout yer, Vera,' she said with sincerity. 'It's the only time I get a laugh when I'm wiv yer.'

Vera put her arm around her friend's shoulders and their heads came together. 'We're old friends, me an' you,' she said quietly. 'That's why I'm concerned fer yer. It's important yer let yerself go sometimes, Sal. Yer gotta get out and about. Yer can't sit mopin' all the time. Yer got a smashin' figure an' when yer do yer 'air an' put on a bit o' make-up yer look the part. Jus' go out an' let it all 'appen. If a feller fancies yer play 'im along, that's what I do. They're bound ter take a few liberties, but all

239

yer gotter do is make sure yer don't let 'em get ter Paris.'

'Paris?'

'Yeah, yer know what I mean, Sal,' Vera laughed. 'Look, I'll tell yer somefing. When I go out wiv a feller I'm the perpetual virgin. I make sure they know it, too. Mind you though, it was different wiv Jimmy Kent. I used ter tell 'im I'd put my Joe on 'im if 'e took liberties. Anyway, what I was sayin' was, if they fink yer still intact an' don't know anyfing they get all superior, an' besides, they know you're not gonna be an easy conquest. I give 'em a little come-on an' then go all virginal. They get a bit confused that way. It usually works – well, most o' the time.'

'What about the times it don't work?' Sally asked, her eyebrows rising.

Vera grinned. 'Well, then I use the oldest trick in the book. I chuck the curse at 'em.'

The year started badly for the erstwhile foes at numbers 9 and 10, and Patrick Botley was forced to seek sanctuary in the backyard amongst his furry and feathered friends. The fragile truce had ended rather abruptly when young Danny Fuller was led in crying by his elder sisters Lena and Joyce.

'What's 'appened?' Ada asked, her hair sticking to her neck with the steam from the copper.

'Mrs Botley smacked 'im, Mum,' Lena said.

Ada felt her temper rising. 'What did she smack 'im for?' she asked angrily.

240

Joyce shrugged her shoulders. 'Dunno, Mum. We was playin' skippin' by the tree an' we see Danny cryin'. 'E said she smacked 'im.'

Ada put the lid on the copper and took off her soggy apron. 'C'mon, Danny, stop that silly cryin',' she said, bending down to him. 'Now, what did Mrs Botley smack yer for?'

Danny wiped his eyes with the back of his hand. 'Me an' Terry Botley was only playin' on 'is doorstep, Mum, an' she come out an' smacked me,' he said tearfully.

'Did she say why she smacked yer, then?' Ada asked.

'She jus' told me ter piss on me own muvver's doorstep.'

'Yer mean yer weed on Mrs Botley's clean step?' Ada asked incredulously.

'It wasn't clean, Mum,' Danny replied, sniffing. 'Me an' Terry caught a big spider an' we 'ad it in a matchbox. Terry let it loose an' I tried ter drown it 'cos it was tryin' ter run away.'

Ada raised her eyes to the ceiling. 'Well, yer 'ad no right ter piss on 'er doorstep, but she 'ad no right ter smack yer. I'm goin' ter see 'er. You lot stay 'ere.'

Clara Botley was in one of her black moods. She was sure that Bert Jackson's new barmaid had designs on her husband. She had been making eyes at him on Christmas Eve and her husband had seemed very keen to go back into the Railway Inn on Christmas morning. Clara had also seen Patrick and Ada laughing together and she was sure that he was up to his tricks again. Patrick's excuse that they were laughing over the children cut no ice with Clara and her mood got blacker. They're all conspiring against me, she told herself. Danny Fuller's attempt to drown the spider was the last straw as far as she was concerned.

'That boss-eyed cow's put 'im up ter this,' she raved to Patrick. 'Everybody's 'avin' a go at me. Well, I'm not standin' fer it, d'yer 'ear?'

'Don't be so silly,' he countered. ''E's only a kid.'

'Kid nufing. She's be'ind this, mark my words.'

'Well yer shouldn't 'ave smacked the boy, Clara. Yer should 'ave told 'is muvver an' let 'er punish 'im.'

Clara poked at the fire with a vengeance. 'Don't yer tell me what I should an' shouldn't do. I know what's goin' on be'ind me back. She was only bein' friendly ter me so's I wouldn't suspect anyfing. I ain't silly.'

Patrick knew it was useless to argue with his wife while she was in her present frame of mind and he made his exit.

The urgent knock on Clara's front door was repeated.

'All right, all right, I ain't deaf!' Clara shouted, opening the door and glaring at Ada.

'Oi you! What d'yer clout my Danny for?' Ada growled.

'I smacked 'im fer pissin' on me clean step. An' I tell yer somefing else. I reckon you put 'im up to it,' Clara answered menacingly.

'Oh yer do, do yer,' Ada replied in an equally menacing tone. 'Well, all I can say is yer ought

242

ter see a doctor. Yer goin' orf yer bloody rocker!'

'Who you callin' mad, yer boss-eyed cow!' Clara screamed. 'I ain't mad. In fact I'm a little bit too clever fer you. I know yer game. Fink I couldn't see frew it? I know yer runnin' after my Pat again.'

Ada stepped forward angrily. 'Runnin' after Patrick?' she said with ridicule in her voice. 'Do talk sense, yer bloody imbecile. I've got enough wiv me own dozy 'usband. I don't want another one in tow.'

'Oh, so 'e ain't good enough fer you then?' Clara snarled.

Ada put her hands through her apron sleeves. 'I tell yer what, silly cods. That man's too good fer the likes o' you. It's a wonder 'e ain't pissed orf years ago. My ole man's a bit dozy but 'e wouldn't stand fer what your Pat's stood fer. 'E must be a man in a fousand.'

Clara was taken aback by the sharpness of her neighbour's abuse. 'You jus' keep yer bloody eyes orf 'im,' she spluttered, her mouth screwed up with rage.

'I don't want 'im. You keep 'im,' screamed Ada.

'I bloody will,' Clara retorted. 'An' tell yer boy ter stop pissin' on my doorstep.'

'Don't yer start givin' me orders, yer poxy ole cow,' Ada said, choking with anger. 'They should lock yer up in Colney 'Atch an' chuck the key away.'

Patrick sat in his backyard wincing as he listened to the fiery exchanges, and the mention

243

of Colney Hatch made him laugh bitterly; the way Clara was going she would soon be a prime candidate for the place, he thought. He wondered whether he should go out and try to break it up, but then thought better of it. The last time he had intervened he had got a nasty kick and been off work for a few days. Maybe he should just let the two of them slug it out until they came to their senses, he suggested to himself. While Patrick remained in the backyard undecided there was a momentary ominous silence, and then he heard a sudden scream and Ada's voice ring out.

'Gawd almighty! The cow's tryin' ter blind me!' she bawled.

Patrick ran to the front door just in time to see Ada Fuller holding her eye. 'She's punched me in the eye!' she screamed.

Clara stood on the doorstep, her clenched fists held up in a boxer's pose. 'C'mon, then. Want some more?' she snarled.

Ada took her hand away from her eye and looked at it, as if to reassure herself that her eye was not in her hand. 'The daft whore's tried ter blind me,' she moaned to Patrick.

Clara was not finished. 'C'mon then, yer got anuvver one,' she sneered. 'It might not be all that straight, but yer can see out of it, can't yer?'

Patrick placed himself between the two women just as Ada decided to rush her opponent. He saw the large body come full tilt towards him and he shut his eyes. Arms were flailing around him and suddenly he fell in a heap, clutching at his chest. The women stepped

244

back at the sight of Patrick writhing at their feet.

'Oh my Gawd! 'E's 'avin' an 'eart attack!' Clara screamed. 'Patrick? Talk ter me, Pat!'

Ada bent down and loosened his shirt collar. 'Quick, roll 'im over,' she shouted, looking down at the gasping man. 'That's it, now sit 'im up gently, case 'e chokes.'

'We can't leave 'im 'ere,' Clara said, panic in her voice.

Ada reached down and grabbed his legs. 'You get 'is top 'alf an' we'll carry 'im inter the front room. That's it, easy does it.'

Patrick opened his eyes as soon as he was settled in the chair. 'What 'appened?' he asked in a whisper, looking at his wife in apparent surprise.

'I fink you've 'ad a bit of an 'eart attack, luv,' she answered, dabbing Patrick's forehead with the bottom of her apron.

Ada shook her head vigorously. 'Yer don't 'ave a bit of an 'eart attack, Clara. Eivver yer 'ave one or yer don't. No, I fink that's worry.'

'Worry?'

'Yeah, worry, Clara. 'E's bin worryin' over yer. 'E fainted wiv nerves, didn't yer, Pat?'

Patrick nodded, not wishing to add to the confusion. 'I'll be all right, if I could just sit 'ere quiet fer a few minutes,' he said breathlessly.

Clara patted his head and then turned to Ada. 'I'm sorry fer 'ittin' yer, luv,' she said with a sad expression on her face. 'C'mon, let's me an' you go out in the scullery. I'll make us a nice cuppa. Yer deserve a cup o' tea fer 'elpin' me. I don't know what I'd 'ave done wivout yer.'

Even though he had had to suffer the indignity of being carried into the house by the two women, Patrick grinned to himself when the ladies had gone away. It had worked.

Harrison's forthcoming January dance was eagerly awaited by the workforce. The December dance had been a success, although some of the girls had complained that there was a shortage of male partners, and everyone felt that this one would be even better. Word was out that a coachload of soldiers was coming to the dance and the girls reckoned that they could expect at least one dancing partner each. Early in January a group of army officers had been shown around the factory, and as they left to wolf-whistles and bawdy comments from the girls they were given a batch of dance tickets to circulate among their men. A few days later Harrison's was informed that thirty soldiers would be bussed to the dance from a camp somewhere in Sussex. The firm had hired a church hall in Abbey Street, and to the delight of the girls, Joe Miller and his band had been hired again for the evening.

On the Saturday of the dance Vera was becoming excited. 'Cor! It'll be me first evenin' out since Joey was born,' she exclaimed, rubbing her hands together and grinning at her friend.

'Well, jus' watch yerself, Vera,' Sally cautioned jokingly. 'Remember what yer told me.'

'Don't worry, Sal. I'm gonna enjoy meself, an' if I get pissed jus' prop me up in a corner an' send over a nice-lookin' soldier.'

'If there's no 'andsome soldier available will Mr Murray do?' Sally asked, grinning.

'Oh no! I'd sooner die,' Vera drawled, gliding across the room with thumb and forefinger held to her brow and her other hand resting on her hip in an impersonation of Bette Davis.

They giggled as they carried on with their preparations. 'Come 'ere, let's see if yer perm's took,' Vera said, gently laying her hand on Sally's pipe-cleaner curlers.

'I'm scared,' Sally said suddenly, as her friend began removing the curlers.

'Don't worry. It's took OK. Yer got nice 'air fer permin',' Vera remarked.

'I don't mean me 'air, stupid. I mean the dance,' Sally grumbled.

Vera laughed. 'What yer scared about? You'll look a dream when I've finished. You'll 'ave all the fellas queuin' up fer a dance.'

Sally was sitting in front of the mirror and she watched anxiously as Vera removed the last of the curlers and started to comb out the curls around her forefinger. 'S'posin' somebody comes up an' asks me ter dance the foxtrot or the quickstep, Vera?' she asked, with a worried look on her face.

'Jus' get up an' 'old on like I said. Once the feller feels yer pressin' against 'im 'e'll forget the steps 'imself.'

'Vera, you're a scream,' Sally said, shaking her head slowly. 'Ain't yer nervous?'

'Nervous? What for? I'm just excited finkin' about all those smashin' fellas,' Vera said,

247

pursing her lips sensuously. ''Ere, by the way. Wanna borrer that green dress o' mine?'

'It's a lovely dress, but it's a bit low at the front,' Sally said, looking sideways in the mirror at Vera's endeavours with her hair.

'Don't be such an ole prude, Sal,' Vera scolded her. 'You're goin' dancin', not ter some bloody muvvers' meetin'. I tell yer, wiv that dress an' yer new uplift you'll set 'em alight. It'll show just enough ter get the fellas dribblin'. Now come on, let's get yer barnet fixed. I've got mine ter do yet.'

At seven-thirty that evening the two friends left Paragon Place arm in arm. Under her coat Sally was wearing the green printed cotton dress with the plunging neckline. It fitted closely at the waist and hung full from the hips, swirling around her calves as she walked. She wore black high-heeled shoes and a precious pair of dark-seamed stockings, and carried a white cardigan and a small black patent-leather clutch-bag under her arm. Her dark hair was loosely curled and shaped neatly around her forehead, covering her ears and barely reaching her shoulders. Vera had insisted on doing the make-up, accentuating Sally's small mouth with carefully applied lipstick and highlighting her dark, deep-set eyes with mascara. Vera had agonised over her own figure since having the baby and she had decided to wear a black dress, cut low and square at the front. Like Sally she was wearing a coat and carried a clutch-bag. Vera was slightly the shorter of the two and wider in the hips. Her long red hair hung down around her shoulders and she wore green clip-on earrings in a leaf design. The two young women exchanged self-conscious smiles as they walked briskly along the square and out into Stanley Street, aware that a few of the neighbours were eyeing them curiously.

It had been a mild day for the time of year and the evening had brought just a light wind. The two friends walked under the railway arches and then veered off into the maze of backstreets. They had decided it would be quicker to walk than wait for a tram, and as they neared Abbey Street Sally squeezed her friend's arm. 'Don't go leavin' me soon as we get in there, Vera,' she said nervously.

The red-haired girl pulled a face. 'Now what did I tell yer, Sal? Jus' take a deep breath an' walk in there like yer own the bloody place. You'll be OK.'

Sally sighed nervously. 'I feel all funny inside. It's bin such a long time.'

'Too long,' Vera said with passion as they hurriedly crossed the thoroughfare.

The church hall stood back from the road and already people were milling around as the two friends reached the entrance.

One of the girls nodded to Vera. 'I 'ope the soldiers are comin'. There's no sign of 'em yet,' she said with a hungry look on her face.

'Give 'em a chance. They've gotta ponce themselves up, ain't they?' Vera replied, glancing at Sally and grinning as they handed over their tickets and walked into the large hall.

The band had already struck up with a lively tune and one or two uninhibited members of Harrison's workforce were moving around the highly polished dance-floor. As Vera led the way to an empty table Sally pulled on her friend's arm. 'Look, there's Maggie Chandler over there,' she said.

Vera groaned. 'Bloody 'ell! Don't let 'er see us, Sal. If she sits at our table we'll never get invited ter dance.'

Sally laughed. 'It's all right, she's wiv 'er man.'

Vera draped her cardigan over a chair. 'I'll get the drinks, Sal,' she said with a mischievous glint in her eye, 'then I'm gonna grab the best-lookin' fella in the place.'

The evening got under way and gradually the dance area became packed as the band played a medley of waltzes. Sally was slowly beginning to relax as she sat with her back to the wall, content to watch the revolving dancers. Vera had already been on to the floor and she was now standing beside the table renewing acquaintances and laughing cheekily with her old workmates. Suddenly there was a commotion and a cheer rang out.

'It's the soldiers! They've arrived!' one of the girls shouted over to Vera.

Sally glanced over to the entrance. She could see the mass of uniforms as the soldiers walked self-consciously into the hall and stood in a group near the door. One or two of the bolder men walked over to the tables to claim a willing partner and gradually the initial excitement began to die down.

Vera was determined to involve Sally in the dancing and she brought over one of the supervisors. 'C'mon, on yer feet,' she laughed. 'Albert wants a dance.'

Sally found herself being pulled around the floor by the extrovert supervisor. Albert was eager to show off his newly mastered steps and as he led her into the centre of the floor he did a quick shuffle. Sally winced as he trod on her toes and then kicked her ankle. Albert was oblivious to the discomfort he was causing and he stared over her shoulder, a dreamy look in his eyes. The band finished the waltz and immediately struck up with a foxtrot. Sally began to feel beads of perspiration breaking out on her upper lip as she tried to keep in step with her partner. Again he kicked her ankle and, worse still, he had started to hum the tune loudly. Sally felt that everyone's eyes were on them and she secretly cursed Vera for talking her into coming to the dance.

It happened quickly. One moment Sally was gritting her teeth and wishing Albert would stop humming, and the next moment she found herself dancing in the arms of a tall soldier who had tapped Albert on the back just as the band struck up with a waltz.

'I 'ope yer didn't mind,' he said, a slight smile showing on his face.

Sally returned his smile. 'Fanks fer rescuin' me. I was gettin' trampled on,' she said.

'Yeah, I noticed,' he laughed.

They were swirling around together and Sally

251

felt herself being whisked into the centre of the floor. He was holding her firmly and she found it easy to follow his lead. They moved confidently, avoiding the other couples, and as they reached the edge of the floor he looked at her.

'Fancy a drink?' he asked.

She nodded, following him to the bar counter. The soldier raised his eyebrows inquiringly as he took a handful of coins from his pocket.

'I'd like a light ale, please,' she said.

He was leaning forward over the counter waiting to be served and Sally had a chance to study him. He was tall and heavily built, with cropped fair hair, his face was broad and square-jawed and his large blue eyes were widely spaced. He wore a sergeant's stripes and above them the words 'Rifle Brigade' emblazoned on a shoulder-flash. His hands were large, and Sally noticed that he wore a plain gold band around his ring finger. She looked away quickly as he took the drinks and glanced at her inquiringly.

'Where're yer sittin'?' he asked.

She led him to her table and as they made themselves comfortable Vera came over.

'Oops! I didn't know yer was wiv somebody. Where d'yer find 'im?' she said with a smile, looking approvingly at the soldier.

Sally grinned sheepishly and made room for Vera. 'This is me best friend, Vera,' Sally said to the soldier. 'By the way, I'm Sally.'

He smiled and held out his hand. 'I'm Jim. Pleased ter meet yer, Sally, an' you too, Vera.'

'Where're yer from, Jim?' Vera asked, her eyes appraising him.

252

'I'm from Stepney. A lot o' the lads in our regiment come from the East End,' he said, glancing around the hall.

'Where're yer stationed?' Sally asked.

'We're trainin' down in Sussex. I'm not allowed ter say where, though. It's all a bit 'ush-'ush.'

Vera had been whisked on to the floor once more and Sally watched her gyrations, aware of Jim's eyes as he studied her.

Jim cast a glance at Vera. 'She's a good dancer,' he said, tapping his fingers on the table in time to the music.

'Yeah, she loves dancin',' Sally answered, nervously toying with her drink.

'A waltz is about my limit,' he said, picking up his glass.

'Me too,' she laughed.

'D'yer go dancin' much, Sally?'

She shook her head. 'This is the first time fer ages.'

He nodded and became quiet for a while as he watched the dancers. Sally leaned back in her chair and occasionally stole a shy glance in his direction. There was something sad about those large blue eyes, she thought, as she sipped her drink.

'Are yer married, Jim?' she asked suddenly, her eyes going down to the gold band on his finger.

'I was,' he said quietly. He paused for a moment. 'That's a weddin' ring, ain't it?' he asked, looking down at her hand.

Sally nodded. 'I'm separated.'

'Sorry. I shouldn't 'ave asked,' he said quickly.

'It's all right,' Sally reassured him with a disarming smile, amused at the expression on his rugged face.

Jim fidgeted in his chair and looked around the hall. Sally noticed that he was becoming preoccupied with what was going on directly opposite them on the other side of the dancefloor. She followed his eyes and saw that there was a group of soldiers sitting around a table who seemed to be arguing. A waltz struck up and Jim turned back to her, a comically eager look in his eyes.

'It's a waltz,' he laughed.

Sally followed him on to the floor and as he took her hand and slipped his arm around her back he smiled and said, 'Let's see if I can avoid treadin' on yer feet.'

They moved easily together around the floor and Sally felt comfortable as he gently pulled on her hand and pressed against her with his body to steer them in and out of the dancers. It was a long time since she had been in the company of a man and it seemed strange, although his easy manner had helped to dispel her initial nervousness. He had not forced conversation and Sally struggled to relax. She wanted to enjoy the evening and his company. After all it was just a very brief interlude, and tomorrow she would no doubt chat with Vera about the tall sergeant she had danced with and it would seem then like a mere fleeting dream.

A loud clatter and a shout startled her and she

felt Jim's grip on her hand tighten suddenly. A soldier was on his feet, swaying slightly as he faced an angry-looking civilian.

'C'mon then,' he snarled, rolling his belt around his clenched fist.

The young man seemed unsure of what to do and he shaped up with his fists. The music was still playing, although everyone had stopped dancing and people were backing away from the two men as they faced each other.

Jim had moved quickly. He stepped between them and turned to the drunken soldier. 'Put that belt back on, Duffy,' he said quietly.

The soldier glared at the sergeant. ''E started it, Sarge,' he growled.

Jim looked past him to the group of soldiers who were standing in the rear.

'Johnson, Smith. Get 'im outside,' he barked. 'Keep 'im there till 'e cools off. Move!'

The soldiers hurried their friend from the hall and slowly the dancing got under way once more.

Jim led Sally back to their table. 'I'm sorry about that, Sally,' he said. 'Fings are bound ter 'appen when squaddies are let loose fer an evenin'. They've bin cooped up fer a long while now an' this is their first night away from camp. Anyway, it's all over now. Let me get yer anuvver drink.'

Sally reached for her handbag. 'Let me get you one,' she said quickly.

He laid his hand on hers. 'No. This drink's fer puttin' up wiv me dancin'.'

The evening wore on and the hall became

stuffy and full of smoke. Vera flitted back and forth, fluttering her eyelashes at Jim in an openly outrageous manner and then hurrying away to find herself another partner. Her speech was slurred from the amount of alcohol she had consumed and her face was flushed with her exertions on the dance-floor. Sally smiled to herself as she watched her friend dancing a quickstep with Albert the budding vocalist. Vera had a dreamy look on her face as her partner serenaded her clumsily, drawling the wrong words to the song.

Jim had also been watching Vera's antics and he turned to Sally with a smile. 'Yer friend's gonna 'ave a large size 'angover termorrer,' he said.

Sally laughed. 'She'll prob'ly moan about what a rotten dance it was.'

They had finished their drinks and Jim stretched. 'Would yer like ter get some air?' he asked.

Sally nodded, picking up her cardigan as she followed the sergeant out into the small courtyard. The night was cool and the wind had dropped. Above them clouds moved slowly across a deep violet sky and a crescent moon shone down. Jim took Sally's cardigan and slipped it over her shoulders as they walked slowly towards a large plane tree which stood just inside the yard. Other couples were sitting on the low wall or standing around in the courtyard. Jim lit a cigarette, cupping the lighted match with his hands.

'Well, it seems ter be goin' off OK now,' he

said quietly. 'All the lads are enjoyin' it, except Rifleman Duffy, of course.'

Sally laughed and then turned to him as they reached the tree. 'I'm enjoyin' it, too,' she said. 'Fanks fer bein' me partner.'

He looked into her dark eyes. 'Maybe I asked yer ter dance because yer reminded me of someone.'

She stood facing the tall sergeant, shadowed by the leafy tree. 'I won't spoil it by askin' yer who,' she said.

His face was set and he shrugged his shoulders. 'It's the past. I shouldn't dwell on the past. It's done with. It can't be changed, Sally.'

She looked into his serious face and saw something tragic in his eyes, as if he were haunted by something he wanted to forget. He had become silent as he studied the cigarette held between his fingers and Sally searched for something to say.

'It's nice out 'ere,' she remarked, looking up at the night sky.

His face relaxed into a smile and she noticed the lines in the corner of his eyes as he puffed on his cigarette.

'Yeah, it was gettin' stuffy in there,' he answered, holding on to her elbow as they walked away from the tree.

'It'll be the last waltz soon,' she said. 'I s'pose we'd better go back in.'

Jim stopped and turned to face her. 'Look, I'd like ter see yer again,' he said suddenly, his eyes looking into hers intensely with an expression almost of helplessness.

Sally dropped her eyes for a second, then raised them to meet his anxious stare. 'I'd like that, too,' she replied.

His face lit up. 'If yer give me yer address, Sally, I'll write ter yer,' he said smiling. 'Soon as I can get a weekend pass I'll let yer know. I'll be stayin' wiv a pal o' mine an' 'is family over in Bow.'

The band was playing the last waltz and Sally let her body relax against Jim's as he led her slowly around the floor. She could see Vera clutching her soldier partner tightly, her head resting on his shoulder. Everyone seemed to be on the floor and couples rubbed shoulders as the sounds of 'We'll Meet Again' filled the hall. Jim held her close and she could feel the warmth of his firm arm around her back. She sighed as they moved around slowly. Would he write to her? she wondered. Perhaps she would never see him again.

The tune ended and the dancers stood applauding the band for a while, and then they began to leave the dance-floor. Outside the soldiers were starting to say their goodbyes and couples were locked in passionate embraces. Jim and Sally walked slowly to the army bus which had drawn up at the entrance. He turned and held out his hand.

'I'll write soon,' he said as he clasped her hand in his.

She smiled and watched him climb aboard. He turned at the top of the steps and gave her a wide smile before disappearing inside the bus.

Sally turned away as the bus moved off and

immediately spotted Vera walking towards her. Her friend looked as though she had been crying. Her mascara had run and her eyes seemed puffed.

'You OK, Vera?' Sally asked, slipping her arm around her friend's shoulders.

Vera laughed as she held on to Sally giddily and gazed at her with red eyes. 'Wasn't it smashin',' she said.

'Yeah,' said Sally quietly.

Chapter Twelve

SALLY had arisen early on Sunday morning and when she knocked on Vera's front door at midday the girl's mother beckoned her in.

'She's in the front room, Sal,' she told her with a wry smile. 'She's just recoverin'.'

As Sally walked into the parlour her friend looked up from the easy chair. Her face was pallid and her eyes heavy-lidded.

'Don't ask me 'ow I am, Sal. Jus' don't ask me,' she groaned.

Sally laughed as she sat down facing her. 'Well, 'ow d'yer feel?'

'Terrible. I've bin sick twice,' Vera replied. 'Mum's took Joey upstairs. 'E was bawlin' an' I thought me 'ead was gonna explode.'

'So yer enjoyed yerself?'

Vera grinned briefly, then pulled a face. 'I drank too much. Made a fool o' meself, didn't I?'

259

'Course yer didn't,' Sally replied dismissively.

Vera leaned back in her chair and gave a deep sigh. 'It was nice, wasn't it? What got me was the last dance. This soldier grabbed me up an' as we danced round I kept finkin' o' Joe. I imagined it was 'im 'oldin' me an' I come over all soppy. Mind you, I always get like that when I drink gin. I shouldn't touch the stuff really. It always makes me depressed.'

Vera's mother popped her head around the door. 'Joey's gone ter sleep, Vera,' she said. ''E took all 'is bottle.'

Vera smiled with effort. 'Fanks, Mum. You're a treasure.'

Beryl Mynott raised her eyes to the ceiling and looked at Sally. 'Gawd knows what she drank last night. I couldn't get any sense out o' the girl.'

Vera shook her head and puffed loudly at the mention of drink. 'I was jus' tellin' Sally. I 'ad a few gins. That's what done it, Mum.'

Beryl snorted. 'They don't call it muvver's ruin fer nufing, young lady. It was a good job Sally stayed sensible. She was 'oldin' yer up when yer walked in.'

'Don't remind me,' Vera groaned. 'I'm never gonna touch the stuff again.'

Beryl shook her head. 'I'd better see if that boy of yours is okay.'

When her mother had disappeared Vera turned to Sally. 'I see you was doin' all right last night,' she said with a sly smile. ''E was a nice-lookin' bloke yer was dancin' wiv.'

Sally grinned sheepishly. ''E was all right.'

260

'All right? 'E was better than all right,' Vera said, her eyes widening. 'I wouldn't 'ave minded 'im meself. Tell us about 'im, then. Yer gonna see 'im again?'

'I dunno,' Sally replied, studying her fingernails.

'Yer dunno? What d'yer mean, yer dunno? As 'e asked ter see yer again, or 'asn't 'e?'

"E said 'e'd write,' Sally replied quickly.

Vera looked at her friend, a crafty smile growing on her pale face. 'Well?'

Sally could not help smiling back at Vera. 'Well what?'

'Did yer like 'im? Did 'e get yer clock tickin'?' Vera prompted.

'Yeah, 'e was nice,' Sally blushed.

Vera winced and pressed her hand to the top of her head. 'So we could 'ave anuvver romance in Paragon Place?'

Sally stood up. 'I'll keep yer posted on developments, Vera. I'd better get goin', I've got the spuds ter do.'

Vera waited until Sally reached the door. 'Sal?'

'Yeah?'

'Did 'e kiss yer goodnight?'

Sally stood with her hand on her hip. 'Vera. D'yer know yer trouble? Yer wanna know the ins an' outs of a nag's arse. Now mind yer own business and I'll see yer later.'

The tenants of the little square had been mystified by the continuing absence of Blind Bob. Rumours abounded, and according to the latest gossip Bob had had a relapse and was at death's door. Other rumours had it that he had moved to a home for the blind or gone to live with his brother in the country. Meanwhile number 8 stayed locked up and the lace curtains became grey and dusty. The square's two pugilists were still enjoying their delicate truce and they exchanged their own versions of the story.

''E won't be back, Clara,' Ada said to her friend one day. 'I 'eard from ole Mrs Pope that 'e's in a wheelchair.'

Clara put her hand up to her chin. 'Mrs Pope? Who's Mrs Pope?'

'You know Mrs Pope,' Ada went on. ''Er wiv the club foot. She gets in the Railway sometimes. She only lives roun' the corner.'

'I know 'er,' Clara said, taking her hand away from her chin. 'Wasn't she the one who 'ad all that trouble wiv 'er insides?'

'That's right,' Ada continued, eager to impart her extensive knowledge of Mrs Pope's varying fortunes. 'She went in fer appendix an' they took 'er gall-bladder out. Mind you, though, she always looks ill. She's 'ad a lot o' trouble, that one. There was that ole man of 'ers. Always pissed, 'e was. I fink 'e used ter knock 'er about as well. Then there was 'er two boys. Bleeders, they was. One's doin' time fer robbery an' the ovver one's bin in an' out o' Borstal. She's a nice woman, though. Always got time fer a chat. As I say, it was 'er what told me about Bob. I don't know 'ow true it is but Binnie Pope told me she 'eard it from 'er neighbour. Paralysed, 'e is.'

'What, 'er neighbour?'

'No, Bob. Can't get out the chair. 'E can't even take that dog of 'is fer a walk.'

Clara shook her head sadly. 'Surely 'e can get somebody ter take the dog out?'

''E's 'ad ter 'ave it put down. Shame really. 'E loved that dog.'

Clara nodded. 'It was gettin' on, though, wasn't it. Bloody fing was full o' fleas.'

Ada tucked her hand through her floral apron. 'It's a wonder they've kept that 'ouse shut up, what wiv all the people who's bin bombed out.'

'D'yer know I thought those Carey sisters might 'ave put in fer it,' Clara remarked. 'They've 'ad a lot o' trouble wiv 'er underneath.'

Ada shook her head vigorously. 'They wouldn't move in there. Not after what 'appened. Church people don't like that, do they.'

'What, suicides?'

'Yeah. They frown on that sort o' fing, Clara. It's a sin in their eyes.'

Clara jerked her head in the direction of number 1. 'Didn't that Muriel's muvver do away wiv 'erself? Why didn't they get out then?'

Ada shrugged her large shoulders. 'That was before me an' you moved down 'ere. I 'eard they agreed ter keep an eye on the Taylor girl. Mind you, they was a lot younger then.'

Clara brushed her hands down the front of her apron. 'Oh well, this won't do,' she said, puffing. 'I've gotter get a meat pie in the oven. My Pat loves 'is meat pie.'

The following Monday morning all speculation about Blind Bob ended when he suddenly walked into the square on the arm of a stern-faced young woman. Bob's faithful mongrel trotted by his side, sniffing the air and yapping excitedly. A few minutes later a removal van pulled up at the entrance to the square and men started to carry Bob's possessions to the van.

'Where yer movin' to, Bob?' Ada called out.

'Camberwell,' he shouted. 'Nice place it is. Church-run. There's ovvers like meself there.'

'Well, good luck, Bob, and don't forget ter come back an' see us,' the neighbours called out, genuinely sorry to see the blind man leaving them.

Bob's sightless eyes moved around in their sockets and he held his head sideways to catch the folk's good wishes. 'Cheerio all,' he shouted out. 'Gawd bless yer.'

On Friday of that week the tenants of Paragon Place met their new neighbours. A slim woman of middle age walked confidently into the square on the arm of a large man who sported a walrus moustache. The woman's hair was pulled tightly around her ears and gathered into a bun at the back of her head. She wore a flowered hat and silver-buckled shoes, and a long dark dress showed below the bottom of her black coat. Her huge husband was dressed in a grey suit that had become shiny with constant wear. He wore a silk scarf which was knotted over a collarless shirt, a brown trilby hat and light brown boots. Behind them came their three sons. The two older boys

264

wore long trousers and blue shirts beneath their open coats and the youngest of the three had on short trousers and a baggy pullover beneath a heavy coat that was a few sizes too large.

Ginny Almond was standing at George Tapley's front door when the family arrived. "Ello, missus. You our new neighbour, then?' she asked.

The woman walked over. 'I'm Maudie Cox,' she said in a strong voice. 'This is me ole man, Arfur. That's me eldest son, Ernest, who's seventeen. That's Richard an' e's thirteen, an' that's me youngest, Derek.'

Arthur nodded to Ginny but the boys remained impassive. Ginny gave the family a friendly smile. 'Well, pleased ter meet yer I'm sure. My name's Ginny Almond, an' this is me good friend George Tapley. I live at number 3. If yer need anyfing jus' give us a knock, unless it's money yer want. I'm a bit short o' that at the moment.'

Maudie returned the smile. 'Well, c'mon you lot,' she barked to her family. 'There's fings ter be done.'

The family walked over to number 8 and Ginny watched with some amusement as they disappeared inside.

'Well, that's a strange-lookin' crowd,' she remarked to George. 'Yer can tell who wears the trousers there, can't yer?'

George grinned. 'They look like a coster family ter me. Well, she does, anyway. 'Er ole man looks like one o' those picture-palace attendants on 'is day off.'

Ginny laughed. 'I can just imagine 'im. "One an' nines this side. Queuin' all parts." '

George smiled. 'Well, at least she made 'erself known. Quaint-lookin' though, wasn't she?'

Their speculation was interrupted as the door of number 8 suddenly opened. Arthur Cox stepped out, followed closely by his wife. 'Get straight up there,' she said loudly. 'Tell 'em ter get down 'ere right away. An' while you're at it, get us a bundle o' firewood from the corner shop.'

Arthur walked quickly along the square and Maudie Cox looked across to Ginny. 'They've turned the bloody gas orf,' she raged. 'The place is damp as anyfing.'

''Ave yer got any coal?' Ginny asked.

'Yes, fanks. There's some in the coal cupboard,' the woman replied as she went back inside the house.

At six-thirty that evening Sally returned home from work to be told that a letter had arrived for her. Her spirits rose as she took the small envelope down from the mantelshelf and quickly opened it. The letter was written on a single sheet of lined paper and as she read the few scrawled words Sally's heart leapt. She had begun to think Jim had changed his mind about writing, and now she had a letter from him telling her that he was coming home on a week-end pass and wanted to see her. She folded up the piece of paper and put it back into the envelope, aware that her mother was eyeing her curiously.

266

'Yer don't usually get letters, Sal,' she remarked, looking at her daughter inquisitively.

'It's from a soldier I met at the dance,' Sally replied quickly.

'That's nice. Does 'e wanna see yer, then?' Annie asked.

'I'm meetin' 'im next weekend.'

Annie spread the clean linen tablecloth out and proceeded to lay the table. 'Lora won't be in fer tea,' she said, busying herself with the plates. 'She's goin' straight out wiv that bloke of 'ers. Yer farver's late. I s'pose they're finishin' a ship orf.'

Sally looked at her mother. 'Don't say anyfing about me gettin' that letter, Mum,' she said quietly with a sudden intimacy.

'All right, Sally,' Annie replied, giving her daughter a quizzical look. 'There's nufing wrong in gettin' asked out, is there?'

'No, there's nufing wrong in it, Mum, but yer know 'ow Dad goes on. 'E might get all worried, 'cos 'e's a soldier.'

Annie shrugged her shoulders. 'You're old enough now ter look after yerself. All yer gotta do is be careful. Soldiers are 'ere today an' orf termorrer. Jus' don't get too serious. It don't do these days.'

Charlie arrived home at a quarter to seven and Annie became sulky when she smelt beer on his breath. The meal was eaten in stony silence and afterwards Charlie made himself comfortable in his favourite chair, having decided that conversation with Annie was out of the question. Soon his head dropped on to his chest and Annie got up from her chair and turned up the wireless to drown out his loud, rhythmic snoring.

When Sally had finished the washing up she went straight up to her room. She sat at the small dressing-table staring into the mirror, her mother's words echoing in her head. 'Soldiers are 'ere terday an' orf termorrer', she had said. Maybe she was right. Perhaps it was wrong to get too attached to a serviceman, Sally fretted. Maybe she was giving too much importance to it. After all, he might not turn up, or might not enjoy the evening out. Her thoughts raced as she sat in the quiet room thinking of him. She had to admit that he was an attractive man. It had been hard to tell his age; he was probably in his mid-thirties, or maybe a bit younger. He had told her he had been married. Perhaps he was separated from his wife, or maybe she was dead. He had not been forthcoming, and he had not pressed her about her husband, either. There was something about the man that intrigued her. Since parting from Ben she had not allowed herself to become interested in any men that she met. Her attitude very quickly stifled any opportunity to get to know anyone, and consequently the few eligible men who worked at the factory had left her alone. Now she could not deny that this reserved stranger had excited her; she felt it growing within her as her mind went back to the night of the dance. He had held her close as they danced together and made her feel comfortable and happy. It had been nice, too, when she stepped out into the courtyard with him. He had been considerate and polite, and when he became serious and talked about not dwelling on the past Sally had sensed an echo of her own misfortunes. She had sensed in his large, brooding eyes, sadness and misery.

A rumble of thunder sounded in the distance and rain-spots pattered against the window. Sally got up and turned off the light before pulling back the curtains. The rain was becoming heavy now and it bounced off the paving-stones and hammered against the roof-slates. She undressed quickly and climbed into bed. She had always liked listening to the rain, and as she nestled down a sense of wellbeing flowed over her. The storm gradually came closer but Sally slept soundly.

At number 5 Alf Porter was sleeping in the chair beside his bed with a blanket draped around his shoulders, unaware that rainwater had penetrated the bomb-damaged roof of the house and poured into the empty upstairs flat. As the storm increased and more water poured in through the roof it puddled over the bare floor-boards and started to seep through the ceiling of Alf's bedroom. It started with a steady drip that bounced off his forehead and he turned on his side. The water then dripped into his ear, and he began to dream that he was being subjected to the water torture by an evil, monocled German who laughed wickedly.

Alf woke up with a start, and he saw that his bed was soaked. The steady drip of water continued through the ceiling as he sat shivering, a dejected look on his thin face. Slowly he gathered his thoughts and tried to work out what he could do. His first idea was to place a bowl or a bucket on the bed to catch the drips but he realised that it would not do much good. The water stain was growing and soon the whole ceiling might well collapse. He listened to the rain and felt that nature would not come to his aid in the next few hours. 'It's on fer the night,' he groaned aloud to himself. There was only one thing to do, he decided. The hole would have to be plugged.

Alf scratched his wet head and tried to think where he had put his torch. He dressed quickly and found it in the sideboard, only to discover that the battery was useless. Cursing to himself he lit a candle and climbed the stairs. He opened the door of the room above his own bedroom and peered in. The candlelight gave the room a ghostly appearance. Wallpaper hung down from the blackened walls and the bare floorboards were sodden with water. In the rafters above, Alf could just make out the round hole where the incendiary bomb had crashed through the roof. A steady trickle of water was running down on to the floorboards, and as he took a step into the room Alf found himself looking at dark clouds and waves of driving rain through the gap where the tarpaulin sheet should have been. 'The bloody wind's shifted it,' he said aloud as he stepped further into the bare room. There was a cracking sound and as the charred wooden planking suddenly gave way under his weight Alf fell through the floorboards.

When he had stopped falling with an abrupt

bump Alf thought for a moment that he must be dead. Fortunately he had landed on his soggy bed. He slowly disentangled himself from blackened timbers, pieces of sodden plaster and bedclothes and inspected his injuries. Apart from a few scratches and a lump on his head he had escaped unhurt. There was only one thing to do now, he decided angrily, and he went out to the sideboard to pour himself a stiff drink.

The week passed very slowly for Sally. The large wall-clock at Harrison's seemed to stand still and the piles of khaki material beside the machine grew larger. The social evening had been almost forgotten by most of the workforce and misery had replaced the euphoria. Supervisors gradually slipped back into their old ways and moans and groans filled the long, dreary days. In the canteen workers ate their meals in silence or moaned about the slave-driving management, and the managers complained about the low output. A few of the older women sat together discussing the declining morals of the younger women and the young women moaned about the lack of understanding on the part of their elders. Maggie scoffed her food and made eyes at her new young man, while Brenda Foster ignored the sniggers and derogatory remarks of all and sundry as she openly flirted with her favourite supervisor. All day the noise of machines prevented conversation between the workers, and when the *Music While You Work* programme was relayed over the crackling loudspeakers it was almost drowned by the din.

Sally kept her head down over the machine and concentrated her mind on the coming weekend with some trepidation. What could she wear? she wondered. Where would they go? She wondered what they could possibly talk about. What if he didn't turn up? she thought suddenly. Of course he would. He had written to her. Sally began to worry about how Jim would treat her. Would he escort her in a gentlemanly manner and give her a goodnight kiss, or would he assume that she wanted him to make love to her? Perhaps he saw her as an easy target, a young girl missing the love of her husband who would gladly allow herself to be loved by a stranger. The questions raced around in Sally's mind and she tried to calm her growing fears. It was just a date, she told herself. She would have no expectations, no preconceived ideas. She would be dignified, calm and self-assured. She smiled to herself at the idiotic notion. She knew that she would more likely be a bundle of nerves, unsure and faltering. She would let him kiss her and hope he did not take advantage of her. She felt nervous at her lack of experience. There had only been one man in her life. She and Ben had played together as children, and they had discovered love with each other after growing up together. Everything would be so different with Jim. The sudden sound of the factory whistle rescued Sally from her tangled thoughts and she got up from her machine with a sigh of relief.

There were several comings and goings in

Paragon Place during this time. The gas men called on Mrs Cox, and builders called at number 5 with ladders and planking to repair the Porter residence. Alf took the day off to supervise, and after getting under the workmen's feet and making a general nuisance of himself he retired to the Railway Inn, leaving his key with Annie Robinson. When the pub shut at three o'clock Alf walked back in his usual unsteady way and found that the workmen were in the process of replacing the passage floorboards which had been damaged by the piano. The day was cold and Alf decided to spend the afternoon at the local library. At least it would be warm there, he thought. He could not remember the last time he had been to the public library but he was aware that they had the daily papers there, so he would be able to have a read.

Alf puffed as he climbed the few steps to the entrance and strolled into the hall. He stroked his chin as he looked around, and then he saw the arrow pointing to the reference library. Assuming the papers would be in that department Alf climbed the wide stone stairs and stood for a minute on the landing before going through the swing doors. One or two people were seated at the large wooden tables, their heads bent over open books, and Alf sat down to catch his breath. There were no papers on show but the large room felt pleasantly warm and cosy. He caught sight of an elderly looking librarian eyeing him over the top of his glasses and Alf decided he had better look studious. He got up and reached for a large volume without bothering to consult the title and took it back to the table. He sat down again, opened the book and put on his glasses. Alf placed his elbows on the polished surface, rested his head in his hands and closed his eyes.

Harriet Carey had finished her afternoon tea in the staff room and she glanced at the clock. It was time to relieve Mr Wilson, she realised, picking up her handbag and making her way back to the reference section. Her elderly colleague was polishing his spectacles as she came in and he motioned to her with a slight movement of his head. 'There's a man over there who came in just as you left,' he said to her with a frown. 'He looks like he's asleep. Just keep your eye on him. I won't be long.'

Harriet got on with her cataloguing and occasionally glanced across the room. Mr Wilson was right, she thought. The man had not moved or turned the page. She applied herself to her task once more and she had almost completed the list on wild birds of the British Isles when the sound of snoring reached her ears. The other readers had heard it too, and there were a few tut-tuts directed towards the end table. Harriet got up with a sigh of disgust and walked over to the slumbering figure.

'Excuse me,' she said, in her most authoritative voice.

There was no answer, only the low, uneven sound of snoring. Harriet laid her hand on the sleeper's shoulder and he suddenly jerked awake.

'Sorry,' he mumbled, his bleary eyes coming

up to meet Harriet's. 'I must 'ave fell asleep.'

Harriet stepped back in horror as she stared at him. 'My God! It's you!' she gasped, hardly believing her eyes.

''Ello, gel,' he grinned. 'I didn't know yer worked 'ere.' Harriet turned abruptly on her heel and rushed off to find Mr Wilson, leaving Alf scratching his head in surprise. He got up and stretched, aware that the other readers were watching him. He walked to the door, winking at a stern-looking woman whose eyes were following his progress.

'Good book is it?' he grinned, walking out on to the landing.

Down in the staff room Mr Wilson was comforting the distraught Harriet. 'There, there. It's all right, my dear. You stay here. I'll deal with him,' he said firmly.

Harriet was twisting her lace handkerchief into a tight knot. 'When I saw that awful man I was so shocked. I'm sure he's trying to frighten me.'

Mr Wilson patted her hand. 'It's all right. Just you leave it to me, Miss Carey. I'll throw him out of the building,' he said, becoming breathless at the thought of it.

Harriet watched from the door of the staff room while her colleague walked determinedly up the stairs. He looked into the reference section, then leaned over the banisters.

'It's all right, Miss Carey. The man's gone,' he called out.

Still feeling shocked Harriet walked up the stairs and went back into the room. The large red volume was still open on the end table and she went over to replace it. Her eyes widened as she read the title and she flopped down heavily into the chair.

Mr Wilson hurried over. 'Are you all right?' he asked, concern showing on his lined face.

She was staring at the large book. 'Look what he was reading,' she said almost in a whisper.

'*Chemical Compounds, part one. Poisons and Irritants*,' he recited.

'That awful man's plotting something!' Harriet exclaimed. 'I'm sure of it!'

Saturday evening arrived with Sally feeling increasingly nervous. She had busied herself with the household chores during the day attempting to stay calm, but as the time for her meeting with Jim drew near she felt the butter-flies fluttering in her stomach. Vera had been full of dos and don'ts, adding to her feelings of panic by giving her earthy advice on how to fight him off should he get too ardent. Sally had spent time with her hair and makeup, and as she walked out of the square her heart was pounding.

The night was cold and she wore her best coat, dark grey with a high collar, over a lemon blouse and a tight-fitting oatmeal skirt. She had laddered her best stockings as she put them on and had hurried to Vera in panic. Her friend had lent her her only pair of sheer stockings and a grey clutch-bag. 'It'll go better wiv the coat, kid,' she had said. 'Yer gotter look yer best ternight. 'Ere, an' when yer see 'im ask 'im if

276

'e's got a friend fer me, will yer?'

Sally shivered as she walked along Stanley Street and through the railway arches. The wind caught her hair and strands blew into her face. She was going to look a mess. Her clip-on earrings were pinching and so were her shoes. At the tram stop she turned her back to the wind as she adjusted her lemon chiffon scarf and pulled her coat tighter around her body. The tram was late, she fretted. Jim would be waiting. Maybe he would think she wasn't coming and go back home. Keep calm, she told herself, glancing anxiously at the clock above the pawnbroker's shop. Eventually a tram came along and squealed to a halt at the stop, and as she climbed aboard she looked back at the clock. It showed ten minutes to the hour.

At exactly eight o'clock Sally alighted from the tram opposite the Trocette Picture House and crossed the road. Jim was nowhere to be seen. She walked casually along by the cinema entrance and saw a blue-uniformed commissionaire removing the queuing signs as a few late-comers hurried into the foyer. Sally turned on her heel and walked back to the tram stop. He was coming from Stepney, so he would either get the 42 bus which came over Tower Bridge or travel through Rotherhithe Tunnel and catch the 68 tram, she reasoned. From where she was standing Sally could see both the stops and she walked up and down to keep warm. She shivered, worrying that her nose had gone red, and she turned her back to the strong wind. She was beginning to feel that all her efforts to make herself look nice had been in vain. Her hair was swirling around her face and grit was getting into her eyes.

She turned again as a bus pulled up and she saw him. Her heart leapt as Jim hurried across the road, a big smile showing on his handsome features. He was wearing his service overcoat with the collar turned up and his forage cap was perched on the side of his head.

'I'm sorry fer bein' late, Sally. The bridge went up,' he said breathlessly as he reached her.

'It's all right,' she replied. 'I've only jus' got 'ere meself.'

He took her arm as they walked off. 'Yer look cold,' he said. ''Ow about somefing ter warm yer up?'

Sally imagined that she must look a mess. 'Yeah, OK,' she answered.

'You look very nice,' he said, smiling as if to reassure her, and she felt a little cheered by his words.

The wind gusted as they turned the corner and Sally grabbed at her hair.

'Will this pub do?' he asked, pointing to the swinging sign over the door.

She nodded and followed him into the warm interior.

The Horseshoe was crowded but they soon found a seat. Jim took off his overcoat, throwing it carelessly over the back of a chair.

'What can I get yer?' he asked.

'A light ale, please,' she said, loosening her coat.

He went to the bar and soon came back with

the beer and two small glasses containing a dark-coloured liquid. His face broke into a smile as he saw Sally's puzzled frown. 'It's brandy,' he said. 'It'll warm yer.'

She watched as he swallowed his in one gulp and then she picked her glass up tentatively. 'I've never tasted brandy,' she said, looking at him over the top of the glass.

Jim laughed. 'It won't 'urt yer. Drink it.'

Sally followed his lead and downed the drink in one gulp. She gasped for breath and her eyes watered as she brought a hand up to her chest. 'Phew! That's strong,' she spluttered.

'It's good fer a cold night,' he replied, watching her reaction with amusement.

Sally felt the warmth radiating in her stomach and she leaned back in her chair, letting her eyes wander around the bar. He was watching her, a ghost of a smile playing around the corners of his mouth.

'Tell me about yerself, Sally,' he said suddenly.

Sally met his gaze and smiled. 'There's not much ter tell, really. You already know I'm married but separated. I'm livin' back 'ome wiv me parents an' younger sister. I work as a machinist an' I don't go out much. That's about it.'

He sipped his drink. 'No boyfriend?'

Sally was slightly taken aback by his direct approach and shook her head. 'What about you?' she asked.

He shrugged his broad shoulders and stared down at the glass by his elbow. She saw a

279

faraway look come into his eyes and she followed the movement of his hand as he toyed with his glass. The bar was filling up with customers and a piano had started to play in the adjoining bar. Sally felt comfortable in their secluded corner and her eyes studied him as she waited for his answer to her question. He looked up after a while and then he sighed deeply.

'I told yer I was married once, didn't I?' he asked her.

Sally nodded, her eyes fixed on his.

'I 'ad a son, too,' he went on. 'They were both killed in an air raid.'

Sally winced noticeably. 'I'm very sorry,' she said softly. 'I shouldn't 'ave bin inquisitive.'

Jim's face relaxed and he smiled faintly, his eyes looking directly into hers. 'It's OK. I'm glad you are. It seems a long time ago now. I was stationed in Kent when it 'appened. It was just after the blitz started. We could see the fires lightin' up the sky an' 'ear the continual roar of planes flyin' over. I remember sayin' ter the lads it was a bad raid. We were all worried 'cos a lot of us came from London. Anyway, the next mornin' I was called in front of the commandin' officer. There was a padre wiv 'im an' I didn't 'ave ter be told. I already knew what they were gonna say. I got compassionate leave an' I was on the next train ter London. I tell yer, Sally, I'll never forget that mornin' when I walked inter my turnin'. It was 'ard ter reco'nise. I could smell the brick dust and charred wood, an' there was ambulances waitin' around fer the victims ter be brought out from the debris.

There was this ole copper. D'yer know 'e 'ad tears in 'is eyes. 'E'd bin a copper in that neighbour'ood since I was a boy. 'E knew everybody in that little street. It was 'im who told me about Janie an' little Billy. They'd bin taken ter the local church 'all. I 'ad ter identify 'em. Less than an hour later I was on me way back ter camp. There was just nufing ter 'ang around in London for. Everyfing was gone. I felt a stranger on me own manor.'

Sally's eyes were still fixed on his and she saw the deep pain reflected in them. She wanted to say something but she could not find the right words. Her silence prompted him to continue. 'I 'ardly knew the lad,' he said. ''E was only six months old when I got called up. That was at the outbreak o' war. I went ter France wiv the Expeditionary Force an' I was one o' the lucky ones. I got out at Dunkirk wivout a scratch. Yer can imagine what a shambles it was. They was tryin' ter sort us all out but our regiments 'ad bin almost wiped out. I got made up ter corporal when they re-formed our regiment. Most of the lads are new recruits, although there's a few o' the old ones left. Most of 'em were at the dance.'

Sally was listening quietly, her chin resting on her clenched fist. It surprised her how he was suddenly so full of words, his eyes expressive and his hands clenching tightly on the table. She watched as his mouth occasionally twitched in the corners and his shoulders shrugged as he talked: his voice deep and resonant. She tried to draw him away from the tragic story of his family.

281

'You've got three stripes. That means you're a sergeant, doesn't it?' she asked.

He nodded. 'I got me third stripe a few months ago. They must be gettin' 'ard up.'

Sally smiled. 'I bet you're a good sergeant. I saw the way yer sorted that argument out at the dance. What did yer do before yer was called up?'

'I was a cooper,' he replied.

'A cooper?'

'I made barrels. There's a lot o' cooperages in the East End. I took an apprenticeship when I was fourteen. It was me farver's idea. 'E'd bin a cooper all 'is life.'

'Is 'e still livin'?' Sally asked.

Jim shook his head. ''E died jus' before the war started. There's jus' me bruvver. 'E married a Lancashire lass an' 'e lives up there. I ain't seen 'im fer years.'

'I s'pose you'll be goin' overseas soon?' Sally prompted.

He shrugged his shoulders. 'It all depends. Anyway, that's enough o' me. I'll get us a refill an' then yer can tell me a little bit more about you.'

It was comfortable in the warm pub as they sat with fresh drinks on the table. Sally felt strangely at ease in Jim's company. He was prompting her, subtly trying to draw her out of herself, and he listened quietly, occasionally nodding his head and smiling at her words as she told him of her family, her friend Vera and her boring job. And she told him about Ben.

'Won't it be difficult ter get a divorce?'

282

he asked.

Sally looked down at her fingernails. 'It'll take a couple o' years. We've both agreed it'll be fer desertion. I left 'im, so 'e'll start the proceedin's.'

Jim was silent for a few moments and then he sipped his drink. 'We're casualties o' war, me an' you, Sally,' he said without smiling. 'We're carryin' our scars where it don't show. They're the worst ones.'

The last bell had sounded and Jim took Sally's arm as they left the pub and crossed the road. The wind had dropped and the air was chill. They walked slowly along the Grange Road, her hand resting lightly on his sleeve. A moon shone down fitfully from a cloudy night sky and one or two pencil-beams of light darted about as searchlight teams from the local park started their nightly exercises.

'Did yer enjoy the drink?' he asked suddenly.

'It was very nice,' she replied, glancing sideways at him.

They lapsed into companionable silence, their footsteps echoing on the empty pavements. Sally wondered if he would ask her out again. Had she been too open about her personal life? she worried suddenly. Perhaps she should have been more secretive. She had to admit to herself that it would have been difficult in his company. He had a certain way with him. He was easy to talk to and he seemed able to draw her out almost without her realising.

They had turned into the backstreets and Jim broke the silence. 'D'yer know, I've enjoyed this evenin', Sally,' he said, looking at her with an awkward smile. 'It's bin a long time since I've talked so much about meself. I was wonderin' if you'd like ter come out again?'

'Yes, I'd like to,' Sally answered, trying to control the excitement in her voice.

'I've gotter catch a late train,' he said. 'Maybe we could go ter the pictures termorrer afternoon. We could go up west if yer fancy it?'

'Yeah, that'll be nice,' she replied.

They had reached St Joseph's Church and they cut through the small gardens that ran alongside the tall, grey stone building. Sally pulled on Jim's arm as they reached a wooden bench which was set back from the path and sheltered by vine-covered latticework.

'Look, Jim. I'd better leave yer at the gate,' she said. 'I only live round the corner an' you can get a bus or tram at the end of the road.'

He led her to the bench as the moon disappeared behind heavy clouds. In the darkness he took her by the shoulders and smiled down at her.

'Fanks fer comin' out,' he said quietly. 'I'll meet yer 'ere, if yer like. Four o'clock OK?'

Sally nodded and then felt Jim's lips on hers in a soft fleeting kiss. She remained rigid for a moment, surprised by the suddenness of it, then she smiled shyly up at him and they walked hand in hand to the gate.

'Four o'clock, then,' he smiled and walked away into the dark.

Chapter Thirteen

SUNDAY morning dawned bright and cold. A wintry sun looked down on Bermondsey as the little square slowly came to life. Clara Botley and Ada Fuller shared a block of hearthstone and their children played happily together. Patrick Botley was preoccupied in his backyard and Maurice Fuller was home from the munitions factory for the weekend. He sat in his front room reading the morning paper, hoping that the peace and quiet would prevail at least until it was time for him to take his leave. Charlie Robinson was cleaning his best boots and Annie stood over the steaming copper, pressing a pair of sheets down into the boiling water with a rounded stick. Alf Porter had roused himself and was munching on a slice of burnt toast and sipping his strong tea, trying to remember if he had upset any of his neighbours when he staggered home the night before. At the Mynotts' house young Joey was exercising his well-developed lungs while Vera busied herself with running a batch of freshly-boiled napkins through the wringer.

At number 8, Maudie Cox was sitting listening to the wireless while Arthur stropped his open razor and hummed tunelessly to himself. Harriet Carey was wearing her best hat as she left the square for Mass, and about the same time Muriel Taylor opened one eye at the alarm clock, then buried her head beneath the blankets once more.

It was a usual Sunday morning in Paragon

Place, although for Sally Brady the day promised to be excitingly different.

Vera was eager to discover just how Sally's date had gone and as soon as she had Joey settled in the pram she knocked on number 4. The two friends took a brisk walk to the nearby park, Vera pushing the pram and Sally ambling along beside her with her coat done up tightly against the cold.

'Well then?' Vera asked as soon as they had left the square.

Sally grinned. 'Well what?'

Vera puffed. 'Don't keep me in suspense. 'Ow did it go?'

'It was all right,' Sally said, non-committally.

'Did 'e kiss yer, then?' Vera asked excitedly. 'D'yer like 'im? Are yer seein' 'im again?'

Sally kept a straight face. ''E got me drunk, made mad passionate love ter me in a shop doorway, an' I'm not seein' 'im again.'

Vera bent down and took the pram-cover from Joey's mouth. 'All right then, be like that. I was only askin'. If I never said anyfing you'd fink I wasn't interested.'

Sally laughed at Vera's show of petulance. 'We went fer a drink, an' e's asked me out again this afternoon.'

Vera's eyes widened. 'Are yer goin'?

'Yep.'

'Did 'e kiss yer goodnight?' Vera asked, easing the pram down the kerbside.

'Sort of.'

'What d'yer mean, sort of? Did 'e or didn't 'e?'

286

'Well, 'e gave me a peck on the lips.'

They crossed the road and entered the park gates. An avenue of leafless trees arched over the gravel path and on either side circular flower beds sprouted with crocuses. Vera pulled the pram up beside an empty bench sheltered by large overhanging bushes.

'What d'yer fink of 'im, Sal?' she asked, kicking the pram brake on.

''E's nice. 'E makes yer feel sort o' comf'table,' Sally said, sitting down beside her friend.

Vera rocked the pram as Joey started to fidget. ''E's a nice-lookin' fella,' she remarked. ''E'd make me feel right uncomf'table. 'Ow long's 'e 'ome for?'

''E goes back ternight,' Sally answered, pulling faces at Joey as he started to bawl.

Vera got up and kicked off the brake. ''E don't like bein' still,' she said, brushing away a loose strand of red hair from her face.

They walked through the park and went out at the far gate. The morning air on their faces was still chill as they crossed the road and walked back slowly to Stanley Street. Vera was quiet and Sally could see the worried look on her face. 'Not 'eard anyfing from Big Joe?' she asked.

'Not a word. It's bin over two months now,' Vera replied. 'I'm really worried.'

Sally laid her hand on Vera's and gave it a little squeeze. 'Joe's all right,' she said. 'You'll 'ear from 'im soon.'

287

The Railway Inn was filling up and Bert and Elsie Jackson were being kept busy. Charlie Robinson was sitting with Fred Mynott and Ted Bromley in a corner, and their conversation centred on the square's new arrivals.

'Where they come from?' Ted asked.

Fred sipped his pint. 'Arfur Cox used ter live in Tower Bridge Road,' he said. ''E 'ad a salad stall fer ages. 'E used ter stand in Bermondsey Lane. Always a bit peculiar 'e was.'

'What d'yer mean, peculiar?' Charlie asked, taking a large gulp from his glass of ale.

'Well, Arfur used ter live wiv 'is ole mum,' Fred went on. 'My family used ter live a few doors away from 'em. There was only the two of 'em. Arfur always took 'is mum ter the muvvers' meetin's at the church 'all, an' then 'e'd escort 'er back 'ome again. 'E used ter wait outside fer 'er.'

'Well, I should 'ope 'e did. Look silly goin' in a muvvers' meetin', wouldn't 'e?' Ted piped in.

Fred grinned. 'I dunno so much. There used ter be a lot of ole boys goin' ter the meetin's. Jus' 'cos 'e wasn't as old as them don't mean 'e couldn't 'ave gone in. They used ter get cups o' tea an' a chance of forty winks durin' the service. They used ter get looked after at Christmas, too. Nice big 'ampers an' a few bob as well. I mean ter say, fings were 'arder them days. Yer 'ad ter take from where yer could.'

Charlie wiped his hand across his moustache. 'Waitin' outside the church 'all fer 'is ole muvver don't mean ter say the bloke's peculiar, does it?'

Fred lit a cigarette. 'It wasn't only that. Arfur

Cox was right under the ole lady's thumb. 'E couldn't move wivout 'er. Daren't take a bit 'o stuff back 'ome. Blimey, she'd 'ave 'ad 'is guts fer garters. It was all work an' no play fer Arfur. She 'ad 'im boilin' them beetroots in the evenin's ready fer the next day, an' 'e was up early fer market every mornin'. Poor old Arfur. The lads used ter take the piss out of 'im somefing chronic. I never see 'im go in a pub. Always wiv 'is ole muvver, 'e was. Arfur used ter do all the 'ousework as well.'

"Ow did 'e get tied up wiv' 'is ole woman, then?' Charlie asked.

'It was after the ole girl died. Not so long ago neivver,' Fred went on. 'Bit of a turn out, it was, too. All the costers went ter the weddin'. It was in the local rag. Pictures an' all.'

'So them three boys ain't 'is kids, then?'

'Nah. Maudie Buckhurst was a coster, too. She an' 'er ole man ran a veg stall in the Tower Bridge Road. 'E was a piss artist. Burst ulcer killed 'im. Maudie married Arfur about a year after 'e kicked the bucket. Bit of a surprise, it was. Mind you, it's wicked ter laugh, but poor ole Arfur jumped out o' the fryin' pan inter the bloody fire. She's got 'im runnin' from pillar ter post. Funny fing, though, the boys all fink the world of 'im. 'E's a nice bloke, when yer can get a word out of 'im.'

The conversation was interrupted by the entrance of Alf Porter, who staggered into the pub and almost fell against the bar counter. When he finally managed to make himself articulate enough to order his pint Alf joined the party.

''Ello, chaps,' he said, grinning. 'Who are you lot schemin' against?'

Ted was gathering up the empty glasses for a refill. 'We've jus' bin talkin' about the temperance paper they're bringin' round,' he said, winking at Charlie.

Alf took a swig from his glass and pulled a face. 'Christ! That tastes 'orrible. What's that about temperance papers?'

Charlie grinned. 'Yer better ask Ted.'

When Ted came back with the beer Alf nudged him. 'What's all this about temperance papers then, Ted?'

Ted shook his head sadly. 'We don't 'arm anybody, do we?' he asked, addressing the gathering. 'We don't stagger inter the square blind drunk in the middle o' the night or sing filfy songs, do we? 'Ow comes they're tryin' ter ban us from drinkin'?'

'Ban drinkin'!' Alf spluttered into his beer. 'Who's tryin' ter ban drinkin'?'

Ted's face was a picture of contrived misery. 'Why, the landlords, o' course. They're puttin' it in the lease, by all accounts.'

'They can't do that!' Alf spluttered. 'It's against the law. It's more than they dare do. They'd 'ave the brewers up in arms.'

Ted sipped his beer, a solemn look on his broad face. 'Yer gotta remember, Alf, the church is a powerful force,' he said in a defeated voice. 'They've gotta lot o' sway, 'specially in Bermondsey. If they wanna ban drinkin' in Paragon Place they can do it. Who's gonna

290

oppose 'em?'

Alf looked around the group in disbelief. 'You're all 'avin' me on, ain't yer?' he asked anxiously. 'They wouldn't, would they?'

Charlie was finding it difficult to keep a straight face. 'Paragon Place is owned by the church, Alf,' he said. 'They 'ave the say who goes in an' who don't. If they wanna keep us boozers out they can do it. It's easy ter write it in yer tenancy. All it means is we'll 'ave ter be careful. No comin' back pissed or we'll get notice ter quit. We'll 'ave ter find ourselves annuver pub too. It stands ter reason, we won't be able ter use the Railway any more. It'd be like shittin' on yer own doorstep.'

Fred Mynott had been sitting quietly enjoying the joke and suddenly he got up. 'I won't be a minute,' he said. 'I'm goin' fer a jimmy riddle.'

Alf did not notice the hilarious exchange between Fred and Bert Jackson at the bar, and when Fred returned to the table he caught Ted's eye.

''Ere, Ted. If we can't drink in the Railway ain't ole Bert an' Elsie gonna get upset? I mean, can't they do anyfing?'

'I dunno. Yer better ask 'im,' Ted replied, staring down at his pint.

Fred looked over at Bert who was waiting to take his cue. ''Ere, Bert. Any chance o' you writin' ter the landlords about this temperance business?'

Bert pulled a face and stared at Alf. 'Can't do that,' he said, stern-faced. 'I can't go against 'em, can I? I mean ter say, the church

291

committee use me upstairs rooms fer their monthly meetin'. I can't afford ter upset 'em. They spend a few bob in 'ere, one way an' annuver.'

Alf was by now becoming irate. "Ere. Am I 'earin' 'im right?' he spluttered, addressing the group. 'That church mob come in 'ere once a month ter make their bloody rules an' get pissed in the bargain, an' there's us in 'ere every bleedin' night o' the week. Where's the justice?'

Bert shook his head. 'Charlie an' Ted don't come in 'ere every night o' the week. Nor does Fred, fer that matter.'

'Well, I do,' Alf said indignantly.

'So, what do I do? You tell me, Alf?'

Charlie pulled on Alf's arm. "Ere, I know. What about if Alf comes an' talks ter the committee next time they sit, Bert? 'E could plead our case or somefing.'

'I ain't talkin' ter no poxy committee,' Alf ranted. 'Anyway, it wouldn't do no good. It's those bloody bible-punchin' sisters what's be'ind all this, you mark my words.'

Bert looked over to the group. 'Look, lads, all I can say is yer welcome in 'ere any time, long as it's only lemonade yer drink. I mean ter say, I gotta be careful.'

'Lemonade! Lemonade! I can't believe it!' screamed Alf. 'I ain't drinkin' no poxy lemonade.'

The group erupted into laughter. 'It's all right, Alf. We was only 'avin' yer on,' Ted said laughing.

Alf slumped back in his chair. 'All right, you

292

lot,' he said with a wry face, a malevolent look in his eye. 'You've 'ad yer fun. I'll get even wiv yer, see if I don't.'

Charlie stood up and ruffled the inebriate's hair. 'It's only a joke, Alf. Now what yer 'avin'?'

At two o'clock the Railway Inn closed and the merry drinkers walked back to the square. Charlie and his friends were laughing at Alf Porter's reaction to their little joke, but the victim was in a less than happy mood. He had sat brooding for the last half hour about the attitude of his neighbours, and as he walked home he was feeling angry. There was that silly cow at number 1, he recalled. She had called him names and then left him in no doubt that he was not welcome at the public library. Then there was Charlie and his cronies. They were always trying it on. He had been doused with a chamber-pot, almost maimed by their clumsy efforts to get his piano out into the square, and now he had been made to look ridiculous by their silly joke. Well, they were all going to get their come-uppance one way or another, he vowed. Just let them wait and see.

Sally had helped her mother peel the potatoes and prepare the cabbage. The leg of lamb was roasting in the oven and the morning's washing was hanging out on the line. Annie was slicing the parsnips and she looked up suddenly.

'It's none o' my business, Sal, but yer wanna be careful about bringin' that fella 'ome,' she said in a concerned voice. 'There's a few of 'em round 'ere know Ben's family. They'll be bound ter tell 'im.'

Sally put down the iron and wiped her brow. 'It's none o' Ben's business what I do now, Mum,' she replied. ''E's agreed ter give me a divorce.'

'Well, that's as may be,' Annie said, putting down the vegetable knife. 'Yer wanna be careful anyway. 'E might get a bit stroppy.'

Sally stared down at her father's shirt that was spread out on the ironing blanket. 'I know that, Mum. Jim's goin' back off leave ternight. I'm meetin' 'im, 'e's not callin' fer me.'

Sally's answer seemed to pacify her mother and she got on with slicing the parsnips. After a while she looked up. 'Are yer serious about this Jim, Sal?' she asked.

Sally put the iron back over the gas and picked up the freshly heated one. 'It's only a date. 'E just asked me out, that's all. It's too soon ter know. 'E's a nice bloke, but I'm not rushin' fings.'

Annie put the sliced parsnips in a pot of water and sat down heavily at the table. 'I dunno, what wiv you an' yer sister. It's all worry.'

'What's wrong wiv Lora? Is she 'avin' problems?' Sally asked, running the hot iron over the shirt collar.

'She's not 'avin' problems as far as I can see, but she's givin' me an' 'er farver problems. She's off again this weekend. We don't see much of 'er at all these days,' Annie said, resting her chin in her cupped hand.

Sally hung the ironed shirt from the open scullery door. 'Lora's over twenty-one. She can please 'erself now, Mum. It's no good you an' Dad worryin' yerselves over 'er. She can look after 'erself.'

Annie sighed. 'I'd just like ter see the pair of yer settled down. I'd like ter be a granny before I peg out.'

Sally had been looking forward to her afternoon out but her mother's words only served to dampen her happy feelings. She picked up the ironed laundry and walked out of the room without a word.

Sally left the square at ten minutes to four and walked quickly along Stanley Street. At the corner shop she turned left, pulling her coat collar up against the wind as she made her way to the church gardens. Her high heels sounded loudly in the quiet turning and she could hear the muffled sound of a gramophone playing in one of the houses. The backwater was deserted except for a mangy mongrel who trotted along the pavement in the opposite direction. At the gate Sally paused to adjust her coat and then walked as casually as she could along the gravel path.

Jim was waiting. His service overcoat was pulled up around his ears and his forage cap pressed down on to the side of his head. He stamped on his cigarette butt and walked towards her, a smile breaking out on his face.

'That's good timin'. I've just got 'ere meself,' he said, proffering his arm.

Sally slipped her arm in his as they walked out into the street and made their way to the main road. 'I thought I was gonna be late,' she said. 'Me dad never 'urries back from the pub on Sundays.'

He smiled. 'I thought women were the ones s'posed ter be a bit late.'

'Only sometimes,' she laughed.

They had to run for the tram and when they had climbed aboard and found a seat he reached out and touched her hand. 'OK?' he asked.

She nodded, smiling at him with her eyes. She could feel his body pressing against hers and she noticed the faint aroma of cologne. His hand lingered on hers for a moment or two and she felt pleased at his show of concern. As his eyes appraised her she gave him a coy smile. The conductor was standing over them, a pained look on his face.

'Where to?' he asked in a tired voice.

Jim reached into his pocket. 'Two ter the Elephant an' Castle, please.'

The conductor clipped the tickets and handed them to Jim, yawning as he walked away up the aisle.

'We can grab a number 36 at the Elephant. It'll take us ter the Embankment,' Jim said, rubbing his chin.

Sally settled down in her seat as the tram rocked and swayed along the Jamaica Road. She noticed how large his hand looked gripping the seat-rail. She smiled at his light-hearted remarks and occasionally glanced out of the window at the bomb-scarred streets and the shuttered shops in the Tower Bridge Road, a feeling of excitement growing within her.

Soon the tram shuddered to a stop at the Elephant junction. They stepped down and Jim took her hand as they hurried to catch a waiting number 36. As they climbed aboard the conductor ambled out of a café carrying two enamel jugs of tea and handed one to the driver before clambering on to the rear platform and pulling on the bell-cord. The tram clattered over the criss-cross of tracks at St George's Circus, trundling into the Blackfriars Road, then crossing Blackfriars Bridge before it finally swung round into the tree-lined Embankment.

The wind gusted as the two young people walked briskly up Northumberland Avenue into Trafalgar Square. A few servicemen and women strolled beside the fountains and one or two warmly clad children were feeding the strutting pigeons. Sally held on to Jim's arm as they skirted the sandbagged entrance to the National Gallery and walked a little way up Charing Cross Road, turning into Irving Street to reach Leicester Square. Although it was a Sunday afternoon the signs of wartime readiness were no less evident: uniformed figures seemed to be everywhere; sandbags lined the large buildings and signs pointed the way to shelters; war posters stared down from hoardings and walls, and strolling policemen carried steel helmets strapped to khaki gas-mask packs slung over their shoulders; red-capped military policemen patrolled in pairs and high in the cold clear sky silver barrage balloons floated, anchored with steel hawsers.

Sally was quiet as she took in the scene around

her and Jim made no attempt at conversation until they had reached Piccadilly Circus.

'I wonder where 'e's gone,' he said suddenly.

Sally looked at him, puzzlement showing on her face. 'Who?' she asked.

'Why, the God of Love,' he grinned, pointing to the poster-covered hoarding around the Shaftesbury Memorial.

'Evacuated, I s'pose,' Sally laughed.

He sighed as they walked around the memorial steps. 'D'yer know, it seems like everybody's waitin'. There's a lot o' movement takin' place, yet nobody seems ter be goin' anywhere. I got that feelin' all 'ell's gonna break loose soon, Sally.'

'Yer mean this Second Front everybody's talkin' about?'

He nodded. 'Yeah, sort of, although I don't fink it'll 'appen this year. There's a lot o' trainin' goin' on an' a lot o' troop movements along the South Coast. There's a load o' Yanks comin' over as well, but it's early days yet. Everyfing seems ter be buildin' up fer it, though.'

Sally shivered and he looked at her with concern showing in his eyes. 'I'm sorry. I shouldn't go on about the war.'

She tightened her grip on his arm. 'No, it's all right,' she hastened to say. 'I was jus' finkin'. There's gonna be a lot o' lives lost before it's all over, an' a lot o' grievin'.'

He looked at her and for a moment Sally saw a question in his deep-set eyes. Her thoughts seemed to be laid bare to his searching gaze and for an instant she felt panic.

He smiled, his eyes reassuring her. 'Let's get out o' the cold,' he said.

They stepped down from the tram and walked slowly through the Bermondsey backstreets, chatting cheerfully together as if to hold back the imminence of their parting. Sally had sat in the warm cinema and felt a shiver of excitement run through her as his hand searched for hers and held it in the darkness. She had gripped his arm tightly as Humphrey Bogart faced Claude Rains on the runway in *Casablanca* and then laughed in embarrassment at her childish excitement. They had walked back out into the cold evening and found a small cafe where they sat in a corner talking lightheartedly about the film. It was Jim who had first become serious and his words lingered in her mind. 'I'm glad yer agreed ter come out wiv me, Sally,' he had said. 'As a matter o' fact I thought yer was gonna say no. I felt sort o' clumsy when I asked yer. It seems like I'm gradually finding me way. I need time ter come ter terms wiv what 'appened. I 'ope yer can understand that.'

Sally recalled how she had blushed slightly at the time. 'I can understand that, Jim. I need time ter find me way, too,' she had said, hoping he would feel reassured. It was the same for her. She had been anxious that he might find her cold and distant. She realised that they had a lot in common. They were both trying to pick up the pieces of their lives after the unhappy experiences they had suffered, and they each carried many memories and feelings locked up inside them. It would take time to lay the ghosts of the past, and in a brief moment of doubt Sally wondered whether they would both truly want to.

They reached the church gardens and he slipped his arm around her as they walked up to the secluded seat where they had met earlier. They stood beneath the overhanging leaves and he pulled her to him, looking down into her dark eyes.

'Did yer enjoy our time tergevver, Sally?' he asked.

She sighed and smiled up at him. 'It's bin really nice.'

'Can I see yer again?' he asked.

'I'd like that, Jim. Will yer write ter me?'

He laughed gently. 'I'm not one fer writin', but I'll manage it.' His face became serious. 'Look, Sal, I don't know when I'll get any more leave. It might be a couple o' months, it's 'ard ter tell. Will yer write ter me as well? Just a few lines'll do.'

She nodded and saw the look in his eyes change. He leant towards her and slowly lowered his head and his mouth touched hers. She slipped her arms around his neck as she felt the pressure of his lips and her eyes closed. His arms seemed to engulf her and she let her body relax against his. It felt delicious as he held her to him, and he caressed her back.

She eased back from his kiss. He was gazing down at her, his eyes glancing across her flushed face. 'You will write?' he asked in a whisper.

She nodded, a smile forming on her lips.

'Will you?'

In answer he kissed her lips once more and she closed her eyes as he hugged her tight.

They said goodbye at the gate and after she had gone a few yards Sally turned back to wave to him. Jim was still standing beside the garden railings and he raised his hand, then he turned and walked off into the night. When Sally reached Paragon Place her thoughts were still lingering on the kiss. It seemed so long since she had felt a man's arms around her and his lips pressed to hers. Her dormant feelings had been aroused. The need for him was strong in her belly and she shivered with pleasure as she remembered the sensation of his fingers stroking her neck. Vera had been right. One day she would feel the urge, she had said. The warm glowing feeling grew within her and Sally smiled, remembering how she had doubted her friend.

Heavy rain beat against the windowpanes and spattered up from the flagstones of the little square. Sally turned over and glanced at the alarm clock beside her bed. It was six-thirty and she could hear her father moving about in the room below. She stared out at the grey morning and stretched leisurely. She tried to guess what Jim was doing at that very moment. Was he thinking about her? she wondered. Did men harbour those delicious feelings or was it just a physical thing with them? She wondered whether he would write, and tried to imagine how soon they would be together again. The alarm made her jump and she quickly clicked it off. Work would not seem so bad this morning, she thought, as she swung her feet down on to the coconut mat beside her bed, and in her mind she would compose her first letter to him.

'You awake?' her father called out.

'Yeah, I'm gettin' up,' Sally replied, slipping on her dressing-robe and hurrying down the steep stairs.

Charlie was standing in front of the sink, his face covered in lather. 'Tea's made,' he mumbled, guiding the safety razor down the side of his face.

Sally cut two slices of bread and put them under the grill, and she began to hum as she poured out the tea and unwrapped a packet of margarine. Charlie eyed her inquiringly in the cracked mirror, a little surprised at her cheerfulness.

'You're chirpy this mornin', Sally,' he said, dipping his razor in the hot water. 'Did yer 'ave a nice evenin'?'

She nodded. 'We went ter the pictures up west.'

Charlie ran the razor around his chin once more and then splashed cold water over his smooth face. 'Muvver tells me 'e's a sergeant.'

Sally looked up as she removed the toast from beneath the grill and nodded. ''E's in the Rifle Brigade. 'E was at Dunkirk.'

Charlie sat down at the rickety scullery table and sipped his hot tea. 'Yer muvver told me she warned yer about Ben,' he said. 'I know she goes on a bit but I make 'er right. Yer wanna be careful, Sal. Don't give 'im any room ter cause

302

trouble. Less said sooner mended.'

Sally swallowed down the hard toast with a gulp from her tea. 'It's OK, Dad,' she replied. 'I didn't bring Jim back ter the square, an' I don't s'pose I'll be seein' 'im fer a few weeks yet.'

Charlie stood up and tightened his thick leather belt before reaching for his heavy working-coat. 'I'm glad yer found yerself a bloke, Sally. Yer should get out a bit more, but all I'm sayin' is, be careful. Ben might've agreed ter give yer a divorce but yer know 'ow 'e gets when 'e's 'ad a drink or two.'

Sally nodded and planted a kiss on her father's cheek. 'Don't worry, Dad,' she said with a smile. 'It'll all work out all right, you'll see.'

'Well, I 'ope so, fer your sake,' he replied, putting on his cap as he made for the front door.

Sally sat for a while thinking over what her father had said. He could be right. Although Ben had agreed to a divorce, she was sure that once he found out there was another man in her life he might try to stop her finally leaving him forever. She would have to be careful, try to avoid him and hope that he did not change his mind or make trouble. It was early days yet anyway, she reminded herself. Maybe nothing would come of her new romance with Jim. But with a thrilling feeling in her belly she hoped very much that their relationship would develop. For the first time in a long while she felt excited and happy.

Chapter Fourteen

AT number 8, Arthur Cox was leaving for his job at the Town Hall. Arthur had sold his salad business when he married Maudie and taken a job as attendant at the municipal offices. He found the hours more compatible with married life, since he did not have to get up at four o'clock to go to market twice a week. The council had supplied him with a navy-blue serge uniform and a peaked cap, and a shoe allowance was thrown in as well. All in all Arthur was very pleased with his new position, although he missed the market camaraderie, the banter and the hustle and bustle. Maudie, too, was pleased that he had given up the stall. Now she could fuss over his appearance and always make sure that he went to work with knife-edge creases in his trousers, well-polished shoes and a shiny peak to his cap. On rainy mornings Maudie dug out her trusty umbrella and insisted he use it to save getting his uniform wet. Arthur felt a little silly walking to work under a flower-patterned umbrella, but it did keep the rain off.

As the rain beat down Maudie dusted Arthur's coat collar with a stiff clothes-brush, straightened his tie and handed him the umbrella. 'Right, off yer go,' she said, turning her cheek and receiving a quick peck. 'Now, don't forget ter fetch me shoes from the menders on yer way 'ome.'

'Yes, dear.'

'Well, come on then, off yer go,' Maudie said, shooing him out of the front door.

She watched him disappear out of the square, his umbrella held up against the rain, and then she went back in and called up to Ernest. 'C'mon or you'll be late.' Her eldest son hurried down the stairs and darted into the scullery. He was a big lad for his age, dark-haired and with deep-set brown eyes. Maudie felt that of the three he was most like his late father. Ernest worked at a saw mill, and as he was coming up to eighteen he was preparing himself for call-up. Richard followed his elder brother down the stairs. A slightly built lad with fair hair and blue eyes, he was shy and quietly spoken. Richard had just started work as an office junior with a shipping firm. Derek, the baby of the family, had already got himself a paper round since the family moved into the square and had been out since seven-thirty. At twelve years old Derek favoured Richard, with the same colouring, features and the same quiet nature. Only Ernest gave his mother any reason to worry; he was moody and inclined to run around with an undesirable crowd. She had hoped that her marriage to Arthur would give the boys some stability, but she was not altogether sure that she had done the right thing by them. They had taken to Arthur, it was true, but he lacked authority. He was a good provider, honest and level-headed, but he was a little simple-minded. He needed to be prodded constantly, she felt.

The boys had gone off to work and young Derek had come in to change his sodden clothes before hurrying off to school. Maudie had finished her chores and now she sat down to await her visitor, trying to control her anxiety. At ten o'clock a man hurried down the square carrying a large laden shopping-bag. He disappeared into Maudie's house and left soon afterwards. His arrival was duly noted by a few of her neighbours as they watched through their lace curtains. After her visitor had left Maudie took stock. The shopping-bag contained ten pounds of Brooke Bond tea in half-pound packets. She stowed the produce in her back bedroom and then unwrapped the large roll of cloth that her visitor had had concealed under his coat. She rubbed her hand over the material and screwed one corner up in her fist for a few seconds, letting it spring out of her grasp. She studied the creases and decided it was first-quality worsted. Satisfied with her morning's delivery Maudie made herself a cup of tea. If the weather brightened up she would start her door-knocking, she decided.

Ernest Cox hurried through the rain to the saw mills at Dockhead, his mind centred on the girl at number 1 who had given him that big smile only the night before. He had overheard his mother talking to one of the neighbours who said her name was Muriel Taylor and she was on the game. He had stared at the young woman as she left her house and had been rewarded with a big smile and a suggestive wink. Ernest was worried, and as he hurried to work his mind was racing. He would be eighteen in June and it would not be long before he was called up. He could be killed in action without ever knowing what it was like to make love to a girl. He had bragged to his pals about his conquests and was always ready with the fast talk when they congregated at the pub, but he kept his secret and it worried him. He would have to do something about his lack of experience before long, just in case. The problem was, how would he go about it? He could go up west like his pal, Jackie Smith. Jacko had said it was really good, even though the prostitute would not let him kiss her on the lips in case it smudged her lipstick, and even though she had ushered him out through the door before he caught his breath. No, that was not for him. Ernest wanted it to be the way those flashy actors did it in the films. He wanted to learn all about it without being rushed. Perhaps if he played his cards right he might get Muriel Taylor interested, although he was not going to pay for it, he vowed.

The morning dragged on for Ernest and as he sliced the heavy nine-by-four timbers and stacked the planks against the wall he kept thinking about that big smile Muriel had given him. Perhaps she did that with everyone, he thought. Perhaps she wasn't on the game. She might just be sex-mad and go with a lot of boys. The neighbours might have jumped to the wrong conclusion. She wouldn't have told them she was on the game, and even if she was she wouldn't take the money from her clients in the square, so how did they know? People were always jumping to conclusions, Ernest thought. Well, he would just have to play his cards right and see what transpired. He might be able to get her talking. Maybe she wanted a shelf put up or a new lock fitted. That would be no problem for him. Who knows, she might be grateful enough to offer him money. He could wave it away and give her one of his best looks. That should do it, he thought. She would get the message. Ernest switched off the circular saw, picked up his mug of tea and opened his packet of cheese sandwiches. One thing was certain, he told himself as he sipped his tea. If he did get killed in action he wasn't going to die a virgin.

Maudie Cox had realised that the rain was not going to ease off and time was pressing on. She could not put off her door-knocking any longer. She decided to try Ginny Almond's house first. The woman had made herself known and had said she was always ready for a chat. Maudie put on her coat, pulled the collar up around her neck and donned her headscarf. Ginny would be the ideal person to try, she thought. She would know the neighbours and would probably give her a bit of advice about which doors not to knock on. Maudie had already decided not to approach the ladies at number 1. She was not too sure about the drunken man at number 5 and the two scruffy-looking individuals at the end of the square. Still, Ginny would be able to put her right, she thought, as she stepped out into the teeming rain.

Ginny opened her door with an irritable sigh. She was in the middle of cleaning out her parlour grate and was covered in ashes and soot.

'Sorry if it's inconvenient, Ginny, but I got a

bit o' tea if you're interested,' Maudie said, looking left and right as though someone might be watching her.

Ginny stepped back. 'C'mon in, Maudie,' she said, a little surprised. 'I'm just gonna put the kettle on, when I've washed me 'ands.'

Maudie walked into the passage and Ginny motioned her into the scullery. 'I can't take yer in the front room, there's soot everywhere. I 'ad a bleedin' great brick come down me chimney last night.'

Maudie sat down and waited while Ginny washed her hands in the stone sink and then put the kettle on. 'I got some 'alf-pound packets o' tea,' she said. ''Alf a crown a packet. It's Brooke Bond's Dividend.'

Ginny reached up to a shelf and took down a small tin box. She took out two half crowns and laid them on the table in front of Maudie. 'We drink gallons o' tea in this 'ouse Maudie,' she said. 'I'll take one fer George Tapley as well. Yer know ole George next door?'

Maudie nodded. 'I'll bring 'em over in a minute. 'Ere, by the way, what are them two like at the end? I don't like askin' 'em unless I'm sure.'

Ginny smiled. 'Yer mean Ada Fuller an' 'er sparrin' partner, Clara Botley? They're good as gold. The only trouble wiv Clara is she finks everybody's tryin' ter bed 'er ole man. Mind you, 'e is a bit tasty!'

Maudie laughed. 'I was gonna give the sisters a miss at number 1. I don't s'pose they take any black-market gear.'

309

'Bloody 'ell, Maudie,' Ginny exclaimed. 'Don't knock on their door fer Gawd's sake. That 'Arriet's a funny ole cow. She'd be down the station before yer could blink.'

Maudie pinched her chin between her thumb and forefinger. 'What about that Alf Porter? Would 'e be interested, d'yer fink?'

Ginny pulled a face. 'Alf's all right but the trouble wiv 'im is, 'e's never sober. 'E might start blabbin'. I mean, yer gotta be careful. They'd put yer away fer knockin' out black-market gear.'

Maudie nodded. 'I fink I'll give 'im a miss, too.'

Ginny took the steaming kettle off the gas-ring and filled a teapot with the boiling water. 'Everybody else is OK,' she went on. 'That Muriel at number 1 would no doubt buy a packet but yer can't afford ter let those two ole creatures know what's goin' on. I'll tell yer what. If I see Muriel shall I tell 'er ter give yer a knock?'

'That's a good idea,' Maudie said. 'There's only one fing. Tell 'er that if me ole man opens the door she'll 'ave ter ask fer me. I don't let 'im know about the stuff I get. 'E'd worry 'imself ter death.'

Ginny poured out two cups of tea and sat down beside Maudie. 'Yer don't get any salmon by any chance, do yer?' she asked, sipping her tea. 'I ain't tasted salmon fer ages. I used ter love it wiv a couple o' slices o' cucumber. Jus' finkin' about it makes me mouth water.'

Maudie shrugged her shoulders. 'I 'ave ter

take what I can get. The bloke what brings it used ter be a good friend o' me first ole man. I s'pose 'e finks it's 'elpin' me out. Mind you, I don't put anyfing on the price. I gives 'im the money an' 'e chucks in a couple o' free packets fer me.'

Ginny nodded. 'Yer wanna be careful. I was readin' in the paper only the ovver day about that shopkeeper who got six months 'ard labour fer floggin' black-market bacon.'

They sat chatting for a while and then Maudie put down her empty teacup and gathered up her handbag. 'Well, fanks fer the tea, luv,' she said. 'I'll pop the stuff over later.'

Ginny went with her to the front door. ''Ow are yer boys settlin' in 'ere?' she asked. 'Do they like livin' in Paragon Place?'

'Yeah, they like it all right,' Maudie replied. 'The place is a sight better than the gaff we lived in before. It was bomb-damaged. We 'ad one room wiv 'alf the ceilin' missin' an' the boys was all packed in one bedroom. Every time a tram or bus went past our front-room winder bits o' plaster fell down on us. Last winter it was sheer murder. We all slept wiv old overcoats on the beds. At least they've got their own rooms 'ere, an' it's dry, fank Gawd.'

'Oh well, that's somefing ter be fankful for,' Ginny said as Maudie moved away from the door. 'Annie Robinson at number 4 should be in if yer wanna knock there.'

Maudie nodded and gave her new friend Ginny a wink as she went next door.

Ernest Cox walked home from work that evening with the nagging problem still uppermost in his mind. After listening to Lofty Arrowsmith going on about his life history and army experiences for over an hour while they were unloading a timber lorry Ernest was more than ever determined to get himself sorted out. He had heard the saga of how Lofty had been a territorial in the East Surreys and had gone to France at the outbreak of war. Lofty had got bombed, strafed and almost drowned, but managed to get back to England without a scratch. He then decided that he had had enough of the war and was quite content to let someone else have a go. The problem was that the army had not finished with Lofty and when he was told to report to his depot he rebelled. 'I've got shell-shock,' he had told the company sergeant. The sergeant was not impressed, but knowing Lofty had been at Dunkirk he told him to report sick. The medical officer was not impressed either and he sent the reluctant soldier to the military hospital for tests. Lofty was interviewed by a team of doctors who he described as 'nutcrackers'. They asked him personal questions and one of them slyly dropped an empty biscuit-box on the tiled floor behind him. Lofty had heard all about their devious carryings-on from a pal of his and he was ready. At the sound of the tin box clattering on the floor he immediately dived under the table and shouted loudly: 'Take cover!'

They wrote copious notes and prescribed certain tablets which Lofty said reminded him of white cartwheels. He did not intend to be fooled by the enormous tablets which he knew were made up entirely of chalk and he flushed them down the toilet. After a week he was taken back to see the 'nutcrackers' after he had been caught trying to throttle a floor-mop.

'Did the tablets help, Arrowsmith?' the chief 'nutcracker' had asked.

Lofty shook his head. 'No sir. I doubled the dose but it didn't 'elp.'

The doctors exchanged glances and wrote in their note pads while Lofty put on a show of indifference by twirling a little toy in the palm of his hand, trying to centre the tiny ball-bearings in the eyes of the clown. Lofty's persistence had paid off and after more tests he was declared physically unfit for further service. His pals at the saw mill looked up to the Dunkirk veteran, and he was always ready with advice on how best to deal with the call-up notice.

As Ernest walked home that evening he recalled the conversation he had had with Lofty.

'Yer can always plead insanity, or make out yer stone deaf,' Lofty had said.

'No fear. I wanna go in. I wanna do me bit,' Ernest replied.

'What yer puttin' down for, Ern?'

'The Army.'

Lofty shook his head. 'Mm. I dunno. It all depends on what mob yer go in, me ole son.'

'What d'yer mean?' Ernest asked.

'Well, if yer go in the infantry yer get put right up the sharp end. Mind you, the signals ain't much better. Yer 'ave ter climb up

313

telegraph poles an' you're likely ter get picked off by snipers. The tank corps ain't a bundle o' laughs eivver. Yer like a sardine in a tin in those bloody fings. Nah, if yer gonna go in the army go in the caterin' corps. As long as yer don't do anyfing terrible ter the food you're all right, unless they get short o' troops, then they stick yer alongside the infantry anyway. No Ern, it ain't much fun bein' a soldier, take it from me.'

Ernest pondered on what Lofty had said. Maybe he should put down for the Navy. That wouldn't be any good, he decided. He had never learnt to swim. The RAF might be the thing although Lofty had said they were pretty strict about who they took in, education-wise. It would have to be the army, he concluded. One thing was certain, he told himself. He would get sexually initiated before he got shot at.

Ernest was still deep in thought when he walked into the square and Muriel Taylor spotted him immediately as she was cleaning her windows. 'Tell yer mum I'll be over later, luv,' she called out, giving him a big smile.

Ernest could only nod quickly and he cursed himself for being caught unprepared by the woman. 'I should 'ave chatted 'er up,' he groaned to himself. 'At this rate I'll never get it.' What could she want? he wondered, as he pulled on the door-string and let himself into the house. Maybe she wanted a shelf put up, or maybe it was only an excuse to make him notice her.

Ernest walked into the front room and glanced at himself in the wall mirror which hung over the mantelshelf. He looked sideways, smoothed down his hair and pulled faces. Richard was sitting in the armchair reading the evening paper. Ernest shook his head slowly.

'Wassa matter, Ern? You got an affliction or somefing?' he said smirking.

Ernest took off his coat and sprawled down in the chair opposite his young brother. 'Don't yer reckon I look a little bit like Don Ameche?' he asked, pulling a face.

'Donald Duck more like it,' Richard answered, dodging one of Ernest's shoes.

'I've just seen Muriel Taylor. She's comin' over later. I fink she fancies me,' Ernest said, slipping his thumb through his braces and puffing out his narrow chest.

Richard put down the paper. 'She's on the game, didn't yer know?' he said.

''Ow d'yer know?'

'It's common knowledge. She takes men in 'er place.'

'So do lots o' people, that don't make 'em prossers, Richie.'

'What's she comin' over for?' Richard asked suddenly.

'I dunno. She wants ter see Muvver,' Ernest replied. 'I fink it's just a blind. She's got the twitches fer me. I could tell by the way she smiled.'

'She smiles at everybody. It's all part o' the business,' Richard said, picking up the paper again. 'You'll never see a miserable prosser.'

'What d'you know about such fings?' Ernest snorted. 'You've only just left school.'

The threatened argument was cut short as

Maudie came into the room. 'Right, you two. Get yer 'ands washed. I'm dishin' up the tea soon,' she barked.

When Arthur came in from work the family sat down to tea. Ernest ate his in silence, his mind flitting between what Lofty had said and the impending visit of the square's siren.

Arthur was in a talkative mood and he went on at length about his responsible position with the Bermondsey Council. 'There was a bit of a ter-do at the lib'ry not so long ago an' there was a complaint put in,' he was saying. 'Anyway, they 'ad a meetin' about it an' it was took ter the full council meetin' only last week. The result was I've gotta patrol the lib'ry as well now.'

'Why's that then, Arfur?' his wife asked.

Arthur leaned forward over the table. 'Now, keep this ter yerself, 'cos it's about that Carey woman an' Alf Porter.'

Maudie pushed the empty plate away from her and leaned her elbows on the table, hoping for some choice titbit of gossip. 'Go on then, Arf,' she said quickly.

When Arthur had finished his tale of the librarian's confrontation with Alf Porter Maudie shook her head. 'The woman must be goin' round the twist,' she said, making a wry face. 'All right, 'e might be a piss artist, but yer only 'ave ter look at 'im ter see 'e wouldn't do anybody any 'arm.'

'Well, that's as it may be, Maudie, but I've bin told ter keep me eye skinned fer any suspicious-looking characters. Yer can't be too careful. Anybody could . . .'

316

A knock on the door interrupted Arthur's observations and Maudie made to get up. Ernest had been listening to his father's story, one ear trained on the front door, and he jumped up quickly. 'All right, Mum, I'll go,' he blurted out.

Richard smiled to himself. She'll eat him for breakfast, he thought. Ernest opened the door and saw the heavily made-up Muriel standing there. 'Can yer tell yer mum I'd like ter see 'er fer a minute, luv?' she said, smiling.

Ernest stood rooted to the spot for a few moments before he could compose himself. 'You're Muriel, ain't yer?' he said, rolling his shoulders the way he had seen James Cagney do it.

'That's me name.'

'I'm Ernie. I see yer this mornin' when I was on me way ter work.'

Muriel grinned. 'Yeah, I was up early this mornin'. I 'ad ter get some shoppin'.'

Ernest's eyes strayed down to Muriel's ample bosom and he tried desperately to think of something to say. 'I work in a saw mill,' he blurted out. 'I'm waitin' fer me call-up.'

The square's siren looked at him, a friendly smile hovering on her face. He looked little more than a child, she thought. 'Are you goin' in the army, Ern?' she asked.

'Yeah, I've put down fer the Marines,' he replied, puffing out his chest.

Muriel raised her eyebrows. 'That's a tough lot. What does yer girlfriend fink about it?'

Ernest blushed. 'Well I, er – I ain't got one at
317

the moment,' he stammered.

Muriel was moved by his boyishness, and she was about to say something when she caught sight of Maudie hovering at the parlour door. ''Ello, luv. 'Ave yer got a minute?' she asked.

Ernest backed away. 'If yer need any jobs done, like shelves puttin' up or anyfing, give us a knock,' he said.

Muriel nodded. 'OK, Ernie. I'll keep it in mind.'

Early spring flowers burst forth in window-boxes and in the public gardens, and the sun shone down warmly. In Paragon Place the sycamore tree opened its wide leaves and cast a shadow over the grey flagstones. People listened to the morning news broadcasts and then went off to work or to the market with a mixture of elation and dread. For Vera the news was bad. In the North Atlantic the attacks were reaching a climax and she had received only one short, scribbled letter from Joe. The news was more promising for George Tapley. He had heard from his son Tony and the news broadcasts told of sweeping Allied victories in the Middle East. One morning Sally had received a letter from Jim saying that he was hoping to get some leave very shortly and she went off to work in a happy frame of mind.

Clara Botley and Ada Fuller had remained friends and their neighbours began to think that the periodical confrontations between the two women were now a thing of the past. Alf Porter continued to come home drunk most evenings, although he made a point of not dallying too long beneath the Carey sisters' window, and on the second of June Ernest Cox celebrated his eighteenth birthday.

Ernest was increasingly convinced that Muriel had a crush on him, but had he known her true feelings he would have been very disappointed. She had taken a genuine liking to the tall, thin lad, and his childish manner and shyness brought out the mothering instinct in her. He would soon be going off to fight and he was still only a child, she thought. He had probably not yet been with a woman and she felt sad for him. Maybe she could find him some job to do for her. He was always asking. It would no doubt make him feel grown-up. She looked around the small flat and decided there was not much that needed doing. Perhaps he could put a longer lead on the standard lamp, she thought. She could then move it into the opposite corner of the room. At least it would be out of the way.

Ernest walked home from work on Friday evening with Lofty's latest pronouncement ringing in his ears. 'I tell yer, Ern, once yer get in uniform yer got as much chance o' pullin' a bit o' skirt as gettin' a pork chop out of a synagogue. In the garrison towns the women are all spoken for. The sergeants an' bloody officers get all the birds. All the decent girls ain't allowed out at night anyway. Nah, it's bloody 'opeless. Look when yer come 'ome on leave. All the civvies 'ave got the birds. The girls don't wanna know about servicemen. I tell yer, I'm glad I'm back in civvy street.'

Ernest had been surprised at Lofty's outburst. 'Didn't yer get a bit o' stray when yer went ter France, Lofty?' he asked innocently.

'Do me a favour,' Lofty answered, a mirthless smile on his lips. 'I tell yer somefing. When we went ter France they gave us all a load o' French letters. I thought ter meself, 'ello Lofty, you're gonna get pounced on soon as yer land out there. They're givin' us these in case we all get dosed up. It didn't take me long ter find out what those French letters was really for.'

'What was they for, Lofty?'

'Ter keep yer poxy gun-barrel dry, that's what. We 'ad ter stick 'em over the nozzles of our rifles when we waded frew water. I tell yer, cocker, it was a dead let-down. You get yer end away before yer pull yer uniform on, 'cos yer certainly ain't gonna get any when yer go in the Kate Carney.'

When Ernest got home there was a message waiting for him. 'That Taylor girl's bin over,' his mother said, eyeing her son suspiciously. 'She asked if yer could put a longer lead on 'er lamp. I said I'd ask yer. Yer don't know anyfing about electricity. Mind what yer doin'.'

Ernest slipped his hands through his braces. 'I mend all the fuses at work,' he said proudly. 'I've learnt a lot about electricity since I've bin workin' at the saw mill.'

Maudie shrugged her shoulders. 'Well, jus' be careful. I don't know why she can't get one of 'er fancy men ter do 'er repairs for 'er.'

Ernest decided to wash and change before tea.

It was going to be now or never, he thought. Like a spider Muriel had beckoned him into her web and he was going willingly. Maybe he should adopt the nonchalant tack, or perhaps he should be masterful and sweep her off her feet. He glanced into the scullery mirror and winced as he saw the spot on his nose. He would have to do something about his spots before he got called up, he thought. Lofty had said the army was fond of giving soldiers nicknames. He could be called Spotty Cox, or Ernie Pimple. Worse still, they could find out about his lack of experience and call him Ernie the Virgin. Well, we'll see, he said to himself as he glared into the mirror.

As soon as he dared Ernest left the tea-table and went to his room. He combed his hair, opened the top button of his shirt and spread the collar-wings down over his shoulders. With a final scowl into the dressing-table mirror he hurried down the stairs, picking up a pair of pliers and a small screwdriver from the dresser drawer and avoiding his mother's questioning look as he went out into the square.

Muriel opened the door and smiled at him. 'I 'ope yer didn't mind me bovverin' yer, Ernie,' she said. 'I can't do it meself. I'm frightened of electricity.'

Ernest shrugged his shoulders nonchalantly. 'It's OK if yer know what you're doin',' he said, following her into the parlour.

Muriel reached into a cupboard and took out a coil of insulated wire. 'Is that enough?' she asked, looking suitably perplexed. 'If yer could

321

put the lamp over there I'd be very grateful.'

Ernest rolled up his sleeves and set to work, aware that Muriel was watching him from the easy chair. She crossed her legs and from his position on the floor he caught a tantalising glimpse of her white thighs. He gulped and turned back to the job in hand. He'd soon attached the new cable and he got up to try the switch.

'Oh, you are clever,' Muriel said, standing up with her hands on her hips. 'Would yer like a cup o' tea?'

Ernest nodded. Be nonchalant, he told himself, smiling at her the way Clark Gable would have smiled at Claudette Colbert as he sat down at the table.

Muriel brought two cups of tea into the parlour and joined him at the table. ''Ave yer got yer call-up papers yet, Ernie?' she asked.

He shook his head. 'It takes a time when yer put in fer the Marines,' he answered.

Muriel sipped her tea, her eyes watching his youthful features. He returned her gaze, attempting to stay calm as he looked into her dark eyes. He could feel his face becoming hot and his palms sweaty. She noticed his growing discomfort and put down her cup.

'What do I owe yer, Ernie?' she asked.

He could feel his chance slipping away and he took a deep breath. 'Yer don't 'ave ter pay me,' he said in a faltering voice. 'I like yer, Muriel. That's why I said I'd do little jobs fer yer.'

Muriel saw that his face had reddened. 'That's nice of yer, Ernie,' she said, smiling sweetly.

322

'Yer don't mind doin' fings fer somebody like me then? People might talk.'

'They don't worry me,' Ernest said with a show of bravado. 'Let 'em talk.'

Muriel got up and walked round to him. 'You're a sweet boy,' she said softly, planting a kiss on his cheek.

The young man rose to his feet, his breath coming fast and his face flushed bright red. He reached out and clasped her by the shoulders, pulling her to him. Muriel brought her hands up and pressed them to his chest to keep a distance between them.

'Ernie. I believe you're making a pass at me,' she said, smiling and gently mocking him.

'I fancy yer, Muriel,' he said huskily, trying to draw her to him.

She pursed her lips and breathed heavily. 'Ernest. I didn't know, honest I didn't. I bet yer fink I've led yer on.'

'I fancy yer like mad, Muriel. I fink you're real nice,' he whispered, his hands tightening on her shoulders as he tried to pull her closer. She pushed against his chest but he brought his head down and kissed her roughly on her lips. Muriel pulled away.

'Ernie, you're fergettin' yerself, ain't yer?' she said in surprise. 'I wasn't leadin' yer on, honest.'

He suddenly relaxed his grip and stepped back, his cheeks glowing with two bright red patches. 'I'm very sorry,' he said, crestfallen. 'I jus' thought . . .'

Muriel looked at him and felt a wave of sorrow sweep through her. She should have known, she told herself. He was young and confused. He was going away to fight soon and he was trying to grow up in five minutes flat. She watched him gather up his tools and turn to the door and her heart went out to him.

'Just a minute, Ernie,' she said.

He turned, a sad look on his young face. She walked over to him and gently took the tools from his hand and laid them on the table.

'Tell me if I'm wrong, but don't lie to me, Ernie,' she said quietly. 'You're worried about goin' off ter maybe get killed wivout knowin' what it's like ter take a woman ter bed. Am I right?'

He nodded slowly. 'I'm eighteen. I've never 'ad sex. I wanted it ter be good, an' wiv somebody I liked. I'm sorry if I've offended yer. I didn't mean ter do anyfing yer didn't want me ter do.'

She took his hand without saying a word and led him out of the parlour into the passage. In the darkness she turned to him and moved close. 'Put yer arms around me, Ernie,' she whispered. 'Now hold me tight. Tighter. That's right. Now kiss me.'

His head came down and his lips discovered hers. She felt a gentle pressure and she pressed harder, opening her mouth and gripping her teeth gently on his bottom lip. She could feel his breath coming faster now and she moved back from his grasp, her hands on his shoulders.

'I love yer, Muriel,' he croaked, trying to pull her to him.

'No yer don't,' she said, smiling in the

darkness. 'Yer wanna make love. Yer wanna know what a woman feels like. Give me yer 'and, Ernie.'

Muriel pulled on his arm as she opened the bedroom door. As she led him into the room he could smell perfume and he saw a frilly pink eiderdown spread over the bed. The curtains were drawn and a soft diffused light came from a small bedside lamp. Muriel closed the door and moved close to him. Slowly she unbuttoned his shirt, her hands warm against his shaking body. He could feel the flood of passion threatening to overwhelm him and he gasped as he stared into her laughing eyes.

'Remember this,' she said in a low, sultry voice as her hands moved down along his body. 'Remember it well.'

Muriel gently pushed him backwards on to the bed and Ernest found himself sitting on the edge of the eiderdown, his eyes open wide as she stood before him slowly and deliberately unbuttoning her blouse. The smile never left her face as she stripped naked and slowly stepped towards him. Ernest gulped hard, his eyes startled by her smooth, heavy thighs, her full breasts and her flat belly. His heart was banging loudly in his chest as she pushed him back down on the bed.

'Easy, Ernie. There's no rush. Easy, easy.'

The room was quiet and he could hear her even breathing as she lay next to him, her hand slowly stroking his chest.

'Was that good?' she whispered into his ear.

He turned his head and saw her dark eyes, warm yet mocking, and he nodded. 'I never knew it was gonna be so good,' he said, resting his open hand on hers and smiling at her.

She lifted herself on to her elbow and looked down on his boyish face. 'I want yer ter remember this evenin', Ernest,' she said quietly. 'It's our little secret. Jus' keep it that way, an' when yer get older an' knows lots o' women you'll remember the first time.'

He looked into her eyes. 'I could never forget, Muriel, an' I'll keep it our secret – always.'

Chapter Fifteen

GINNY ALMOND'S patience was wearing thin and she decided to take advantage of George's happier frame of mind. He was full of the letter he had received from Tony and he made a point of showing it to her when she called round for her usual chat. He had also been cheered by the news that the International Red Cross were trying to get the Japanese authorities to allow their prisoners of war to send letters home, and he was optimistic that he would hear soon from Laurie.

Ginny broached the subject with her usual aplomb. 'When the bloody 'ell are us two goin' out fer a drink, George?' she asked. 'It's bin ages since we went out. If I didn't know yer better I'd be finkin' yer was frightened of what the neighbours might fink.'

George laughed and slipped his arm around her waist. "'Ow about termorrer night?"

Shortly afterwards, Ginny knocked at number 4 and spoke to Sally. 'Can yer mind the kids termorrer night, Sal?' she asked. 'I've bin asked out, would yer believe.'

'It's not that George Tapley, is it?' Sally laughed. 'Yeah, sure. What time d'yer want me ter pop in?'

'Can yer make it eight o'clock? Oh, an' Sal . . .'

'Yeah?'

'Look, I might be a bit later than usual, so don't wait fer me,' Ginny said with a slightly embarrassed look. 'If yer just make sure they're all settled in bed and then leave about eleven. Is that all right wiv you? I wouldn't ask yer, but if I left 'em wiv Daisy she'd let 'em stop up all night. They know they can't mess you about.'

Sally nodded, a smile playing on her lips. 'Don't worry. Just 'ave a good time, an' if yer can't be good be careful.'

Ginny tapped Sally's arm playfully. 'Jus' fink of it, me gettin' in the puddin' club at my time o' life! That'd give the neighbours somefing ter talk about, wouldn't it? No, we're jus' gonna 'ave a couple o' drinks, an' then I'm gonna seduce 'im, please Gawd.'

'Well, good luck, Gin. Just read 'im the riot act. That should do it,' Sally said, grinning widely.

'Yeah. The bloody fella needs ter be reminded what 'e's got it for. I'm fed up wiv wet-nursin' the silly ole sod,' Ginny joked. 'See yer termorrer night, then.'

★ ★ ★

Saturday morning remained dry, with a furtive June sun slipping in and out of quickly moving clouds. Children were out early, and as the morning wore on women carried their laden shopping-bags into Paragon Place and groaned about the growing food shortages. Alf Porter walked out of the square to buy his racing paper and sup a pint or two of ale, while at number 10 Ada Fuller shook her head and wondered why she ever bothered to keep up appearances.

'Just look at that bloody step,' she groaned to her next-door neighbour. 'It's only bin done an hour, an' now look at it.'

Clara Botley glanced down at the black footprint and shook her head in sympathy. 'It makes yer sick don't it?' she said. 'I've bin tryin' ter get me washin' out an' there's Patrick under me feet cleanin' the palsy rabbit-'utches out. The yard stinks ter 'igh 'eaven, what wiv them an' those chickens of 'is. It's like a bloody farmyard out there. It's gettin' right on me nerves.'

Ada slipped her hands through the front of her flowered apron. 'That's like my ole man,' she said. ''E come 'ome fer the weekend an' what's 'e do? Ter start wiv 'e treads on me clean step, then 'e chucks 'is case on top o' me fresh

328

ironin' an' 'as the cheek ter say, "Gotta cup o' tea, gel?" I tell yer, I can't get nufing done while 'e's under me feet. I'm gonna get 'im ter take the kids up the park fer an hour or two so's I can get on.'

Clara moved closer to her friend. "Ere, did yer 'ave any o' that tea Maudie Cox was knockin' out?'

Ada nodded. 'Yeah, I did. Bit of all right, wasn't it? I 'ope she can get some more, we drink a load o' tea in our 'ouse. 'Alf a crown a packet wasn't bad. It's one an' fivepence in the shops.'

At number 3 Ginny handed out dinner-money to her eldest. 'Now make sure yer all keep tergevver, an' no muckin' about in the pie shop,' she told her children. 'I'll find out if yer 'ave.' She turned to Sara. 'You cut Jennie's pie up fer 'er, luv, an' make sure she eats it all up.'

The children hurried off and Ginny sat down to catch her breath. There were the children's clothes to wash and iron, socks to darn, and the beds to change.

Daisy poked her head round the door. 'I'm just orf ter see Lil, Gin,' she said. 'If yer get a chance can yer iron that white blouse o' mine? It's split under the arm. It'll need a few tacks in it as well.'

Ginny nodded, hoping she would have enough energy left for her evening out with George.

On Saturday afternoon Vera tucked Joey into his pram and clipped down the cover. The child slept peacefully and his mother tried to rid herself of the anxious feeling in her insides. The letter from Joe had sounded cheerful enough but she was not altogether satisfied and she puffed nervously as she buttoned up her coat and knocked at the Robinsons' house. Sally was ready and the two walked slowly out of the square towards the church gardens, pushing Joey along in the pram.

'I'm glad yer could come fer a stroll,' Vera said, still thinking about the letter she had received. 'It's nice ter 'ave a quiet chat wiv yer now an' again.'

Vera lapsed into silence until they were seated on a wooden bench beneath the high church wall. 'I got a letter from Big Joe this mornin', Sal,' she said suddenly. ''E's in 'ospital down in Southampton. 'Is ship got torpedoed.'

Sally gasped. 'Oh Vera! Is 'e injured?'

Vera shrugged her shoulders. ''E said it was jus' fer precautions. They was in an open boat an' they were all sufferin' from exposure. 'Ere, you can read it.'

Sally gave Vera a questioning look as she handed her the letter.

'It's OK, there's nufing sexy in there,' Vera said with a smile. 'Joe finds it 'ard ter string two words tergevver at the best o' times.'

Sally took the folded slip of paper from the envelope and read the small, sloping hand-writing, a serious look appearing on her face. 'Five days in an open boat. It must 'ave bin terrible,' she said concerned.

The baby stirred and Vera rocked the pram. 'I'm worried, Sal. Joe's not one ter make a fuss.

330

'E could be badly 'urt fer all I know. This bloody war. Why don't it 'urry up an' end?'

Sally squeezed her friend's arm. 'Joe said in the letter 'e'll be 'ome in a few days. 'E can't be 'urt bad or they wouldn't send 'im 'ome.'

As they sat in the peaceful surroundings of the church grounds Sally was sad to see how her friend's usual carefree confidence had deserted her. She had a worried frown on her face and she bit on her lip as she rocked the pram.

'I got this terrible feelin', Sal,' she said suddenly. 'I can see 'im walkin' down the square on crutches, or wiv one of 'is arms missin'. I jus' know somefing's wrong. I can feel it in me insides. Me stomach's bin goin' over ever since I read that letter.'

Sally looked hard at her friend with a mock sternness. 'It's not like you ter get all appre'ensive, Vera,' she said gently. 'You're the one who always tries ter cheer me up.'

Vera sighed. 'Yeah, I know. Maybe it's 'cos I got little Joey. I don't want 'im ter grow up wivout a farver. Every time Big Joe comes 'ome from sea I joke about it. I've always said 'e's like a bad penny. I don't want 'is luck ter run out, Sal.'

Sally saw the tears forming in her friend's eyes and she took a handkerchief out of her handbag. ''Ere, c'mon, Vera, blow yer nose,' she said, putting her arm round her friend's shoulders. 'Big Joe'll be all right, I know 'e will. C'mon, cheer up, you'll 'ave me cryin' in a minute.'

Vera took the handkerchief and wiped her eyes. 'D'yer know what, Sal?' she said in a

331

shaking voice. 'I dunno what I'd do wivout that fella. All right, I know 'e's a dummy at times, but 'e rings my bell. 'E always 'as done.'

Birds chattered in the trees and the low rose bushes on each side of the path were beginning to show patches of yellow and red bloom. An old man came towards them. His head was bowed and he helped himself along with a stout stick, his polished boots making a crunching sound on the loose gravelstones of the path. He gave the two friends a quizzical glance as he passed them and Vera watched his progress with some interest before she turned to her friend.

'Yer know, when I see ole people like that I fink of all the young blokes who might not 'ave the chance ter grow old,' she said sadly. 'There's Joe, Tony an' Laurie Tapley, an', that Cox boy. 'E's goin' in the army soon, so I 'eard. It's a wicked world.'

Sally looked down at the sleeping child, a distant expression in her dark eyes. 'I used ter say that ter our ole lodger, Bill, an' 'e used ter say the world's OK, it's the people in it. I miss ole Bill. When I was feeling a bit down I'd go up an' chat wiv 'im. 'E always made me feel better.'

'That's why I wanted yer ter come out wiv me this afternoon,' Vera said, slipping her hands into her coat pocket and stretching her legs out in front of her. 'We all need somebody ter talk to at times.'

Sally sat up straight on the seat. 'I don't fink there's nufing ter worry about, Vera,' she said with decision. 'Joe's gonna be all right. 'Ere, I know. I've found out somefing that'll cheer yer up.'

Vera looked at her friend, a faint smile forming on her lips. 'Oh, an' what's that?'

Sally put a hand up to the side of her mouth in an exaggerated gesture and looked at Vera out of the corner of her eye. 'Ginny Almond is 'avin' it off wiv George Tapley,' she said with a giggle.

Vera laughed aloud. 'Well, I know she always goes in there, but I can't see ole George raisin' a gallop, can you?'

Sally was still giggling. 'I dunno so much. 'E's a smart man, is George. Trouble is, ole Ginny's 'avin' an 'ard time gettin' 'im ter take 'er ter bed. She's a scream. I'm mindin' 'er kids ternight. She's goin' up the pub wiv 'im. I 'ope she finally gets 'er way. The poor cow deserves it, she's tried 'ard enough.'

Joey had woken up and started to bawl as hunger pains grew in his tiny stomach. Vera got up and kicked off the brake. 'Oh well, I'd better get back,' she said with a sigh. ''Is lord an' master wants 'is dinner.'

They walked along the path and when they reached a secluded bench Sally glanced briefly at the hanging vines. 'That's our meetin' place there,' she said.

'You'll be seein' 'im soon, won't yer?' Vera asked, giving her friend a sly smile.

Sally nodded, catching Vera's amusement. 'What you smirkin' for?'

'Oh nufing. Jus' thoughts.'

'What thoughts?'

'You an' Jim. Yer look good tergevver, Sal. I 'ope it works out fer the two of yer.'

Sally shrugged her shoulders. 'We're jus' friends at the moment. I don't wanna rush fings, an' nor does 'e.'

Vera laughed aloud as she leaned forward and tried to appease her baby with a dummy. 'Famous last words. I fink you've got it bad.'

'What makes yer fink that?' Sally asked, pretending to be indignant.

'Oh, I dunno. Yer jus' look different.'

'Different?'

'Well, fer one fing, yer got a sparkle in yer eye,' Vera remarked. 'An' fer anuvver, yer don't seem so jumpy.'

Sally smiled to herself. Vera must be right, she thought. Jim had been on her mind constantly, and she had felt much happier since she met him.

'We're not lovers, Vera,' she said as they left the gardens and walked along the quiet turning. ''E 'asn't given me that 'ungry, ravishin' look.'

'Not yet, maybe, but give it time,' Vera laughed. 'Give it time.'

The Saturday evening sky was a canopy of red as Ginny and George walked out of the square together. Ada Fuller and Clara Botley were standing talking together at number 10 and they nodded to the couple as they passed.

'Nice evenin'. Goin' out, then?' Ada asked, with a meaningful look.

'Just fer a stroll,' Ginny answered. 'No, we're stayin' in ternight, yer scatty mare,' she added under her breath.

George grinned. 'Now now, Ginny. Don't let

'em annoy yer,' he said quietly.

Ginny smiled back at him. 'I bet they're 'avin' a right ole chin wag about us two,' she said. 'Well, I don't care. I wanna get drunk ternight, George.'

'Oh, an' why's that?' he asked, feeling a little uncomfortable as Ginny slipped her arm through his.

'I jus' feel like it,' she said, pouting her lips in imitation of a naughty child. 'I'm a little bit fed up wiv washin' an' ironin', an' bein' on call every minute o' the day. I wanna enjoy meself fer a change.'

George glanced at her and felt a sudden compassion for the woman. It was a pity she was so put upon, he thought. She looked nice tonight, too. Her hair was waved and she had put on powder and lipstick, and she was wearing her new black coat which made her look slim. She had a chiffon scarf tied loosely around her neck, and she was wearing pearl-drop earrings and a large marcasite brooch on the lapel of her coat. George had seen that she had on her black patent high-heels which brought her height up to his. He had always thought how those high-heel shoes made her legs look shapely and George had to admit he was an admirer of shapely calves on a woman. Ginny had taken the trouble to look nice and George felt guilty at his recent behaviour. He had been wrapped up in his own troubles and had not really appreciated just how much comfort and support she had given him over the past few months. If it had not been for her constantly calling in to see him and spending her valuable time talking him out of his morbid state he would have been a nervous wreck by now. Well, he intended to make up for his lack of feeling. Tonight was going to be very enjoyable for both of them, he vowed.

They had walked for some time chatting together when they suddenly found themselves staring up at the high sweeping structure of Tower Bridge.

'I've not bin this way fer ages, George,' Ginny said turning to him. 'I used ter bring the kids up 'ere at one time.'

He smiled. 'I know a nice little pub over the bridge. 'Ow's yer feet?'

'Fine. I'm enjoyin' the walk,' she replied, squeezing his arm.

They saw the flowing water of the Thames below them and the massive white stonework of the Tower of London looming up ahead in the evening dusk as they strolled slowly over the bridge. George sighed contentedly. 'It all looks so peaceful,' he said.

She nodded, her eyes glancing briefly at him in the fading light. He was a dapper man, she thought. He was wearing a nice grey suit with an immaculate white shirt and neatly knotted blue tie, and his black shoes were highly polished. His hair was brushed and parted at the side and his pencil-thin moustache and thin face gave him a military look. Ginny felt a little thrill inside her and she smiled to herself.

They found the pub which looked over to the Tower, and after George had bought the drinks they seated themselves in a secluded corner.

336

Small copper pots and blue glass bottles hung from smoke-stained oak beams, and around the walls there were pictures of clipper ships in ebony frames. An old man wearing a sailor's cap and a knotted red scarf sat on a high stool playing an accordion. People sat drinking at round iron tables or leaned on the polished bar counter, and wisps of cigarette smoke drifted towards the ceiling.

'It's nice 'ere, George,' Ginny said, hunching her shoulders and smiling.

He laughed. 'Yer look about nineteen when yer do that.'

Ginny's face became serious. 'I'm a middle-aged woman, George. Me ole man's bin gone fer years an' I've bin left ter look after the kids an' ole Daisy. It's not bin easy, but I've managed. It was a case of 'avin' to. I'm gonna tell yer somefing else,' she said, leaning forward and fixing him with her brown eyes. 'I've not 'ad a man since 'e left me. Not that I didn't 'ave me chances, yer understand. I've devoted me time ter those cherubs o' mine but I've bin doin' a lot o' finkin' lately. What's it all about? Am I gonna turn inter a bitter ole woman, or am I gonna start pullin' meself tergevver?'

George picked up his glass of whisky and swallowed it quickly. He put the glass down on the table and he studied it for a moment or two.

'Ginny?' he said.

'Yeah?'

'Would yer consider – I mean, would yer fink – ow, sod it. Will yer marry me?'

She looked at him wide-eyed, hardly believing
337

what she had heard and then tears formed in her eyes. 'Course I will, yer silly ole sod,' she said, laughing with surprise. 'As soon as I free meself from that ole bastard o' mine I'll walk up the aisle wiv yer, George. Now get us a double, will yer? I'm in shock!'

A pale moon shone down as they alighted from the last bus across the river. They walked arm in arm along to Dockhead, past the grim warehouses and the bomb-damaged buildings in Tooley Street. They made their way through the little backstreets towards Paragon Place and as they walked through the dreary damp arches Ginny squeezed George's arm.

'C'mon, George,' she said excitedly. 'We've got time fer one in the Railway before it shuts.'

'Why not?' he grinned. 'Let's set the tongues waggin'.'

Chapter Sixteen

JUNE flowers were in bloom and the warm days grew longer. The Carey sisters now wore their flowered hats when they took their evening walks, and Alf Porter sported his summer blazer. The children of Paragon Place sat in the sun eating sticky toffee-apples and sucking on equally sticky Golly bars. The girls giggled at the boys as they hopped over skipping-ropes, and the boys pulled faces at the girls and frightened them with captured spiders and

338

beetles which they carried around in match-boxes. Lil Allen and Daisy Almond brought out chairs and sat at their front doors, nodding off to sleep in the peaceful early afternoon while the children were at school. Joey slept in the pram outside the house and when the sun moved over-head Vera would push him under the shade of the sycamore.

She had received another letter from Joe say-ing that he was delayed at the hospital and her fears were growing. Sally tried to reassure her friend but she was inconsolable.

''E's not tellin' me,' she said tearfully. 'I know there's somefing wrong, Sal. Why don't 'e come 'ome?'

In the second week in June her prayers were answered, and when Big Joe Copeland ambled into Paragon Place on Saturday morning carry-ing a large travelling-bag Vera ran to meet him and threw herself into his arms. Joe grinned sheepishly and blushed while Vera looked him over carefully.

'My Gawd, I thought yer was gonna walk in the square on crutches, or somefing. Don't yer dare scare me like that again. Are yer listenin' ter me?' she nagged.

Joe slipped his arm around her waist. 'Don't go on so, Vera,' he laughed. ''Ow's little Joey? Where is 'e?'

Vera leaned her head on his shoulder, her red hair falling over her face as they walked happily past the welcoming neighbours. Beryl Mynott came to the door holding the baby and Joe took his son gingerly and planted a kiss on his forehead as they went in out of the square.

Joey started to bawl and Big Joe became increasingly uncomfortable as he sat upright in a chair, his large hands holding the tiny bundle tenderly. Vera fussed and her parents plied Joe with questions until he began to feel a little breathless. Joey was finally taken away to be changed and fed and Beryl went out into the scullery to make yet another pot of tea, leaving her husband Fred with Joe.

Fred puffed on his pipe as he sat stretched out in his favourite armchair and listened to his son-in-law's account of the sinking.

'We got it in the boilers,' Joe began. 'There wasn't many of us got off before she went down. It all 'appened so sudden. I went over the side and swallered a load of oily water. Luckily I 'ad me life-jacket on an' I could 'ear voices callin' out. There was a few o' the lads that 'ad managed ter get in the lifeboat. I kept shoutin' out an' finally they came alongside. I remember bein' 'auled inter the boat an' bein' sick, then I must 'ave passed out.'

'Was it pitch black, or was the moon out?' Fred asked curiously.

'It was as black as Newgate's knocker. Yer couldn't see an 'and before yer face,' Joe went on. 'The next fing I remember it was gettin' light an' there was an 'eavy swell. It was rainin' an' squally. All of us were soakin' wet an' shiverin' wiv cold. There was six of us in all. One poor sod was badly burned an' 'e died the first night we were in the boat. There was anuvver bloke who was rantin' off all the time.

340

Bill Crossley, 'is name was. 'E was always doin' 'imself a mischief an' we nicknamed 'im Billy Blunders. Anyway, Bill 'ad a gapin' 'ead wound an' one o' the blokes who knew a bit about first aid reckons 'e'd damaged 'is brain. It was terrible ter see. Poor ole Bill was talkin' to 'imself an' ravin' on about everyfing. The next night 'e went all quiet an' this first-aid bloke reckoned Bill was slippin' into a coma. The next mornin' Bill was gone. Gawd knows what 'appened ter the poor bastard. 'E might 'ave fell asleep an' gone over the side, or 'e might 'ave jumped. Well, there was only four of us left then, an' we took it in turns ter row. We didn't seem ter be makin' much 'eadway in the swell an' we were takin' a lot o' water. We baled out when we wasn't rowin' an' we snatched sleep when we could. The food an' water was gettin' low an' we rigged up a tarpaulin ter catch the rain-water.'

Fred tapped his pipe against the heel of his boot. 'Did yer know where yer was goin'?' he asked. 'Did yer 'ave a compass or somefing?'

Joe shook his head. 'All we 'ad ter go by was the stars. Trouble was it was heavy cloud. All we could do was steer wiv the wind at our backs. That was anuvver problem. It was squally an' the wind seemed ter be comin' from all directions most o' the time. We began ter lose all sense o' time, too. I couldn't 'ave told yer what day o' the week it was. I started ter 'ave dreams. I could see Vera an' little Joey. I was back 'ome wiv me family, then I was back on board ship. I s'pose it was lack o' water. Anyway, the night

341

before we was picked up one o' the lads dropped over the oar. 'E jus' collapsed. We managed ter get 'im down in the boat an' put the tarpaulin over 'im ter keep the rain off. One o' the ovver blokes 'ad a septic 'and, so that left two of us ter row. I tell yer, Fred, that was the time I thought I was a goner. The next morning we spotted a ship an' fired off our only flare. It turned out ter be the *Wanderer* out o' Liverpool. It 'ad dropped back from the convoy wiv engine trouble an' was makin' fer Southampton. It come alongside an' 'auled us aboard. When we docked they took us straight ter the 'ospital.'

Fred shook his head slowly. 'It must 'ave bin terrible. They kept yer in 'ospital fer quite a spell, Joe.'

His son-in-law nodded. 'The ovver lads got discharged after a few days. I fink they was worried about the oil I'd swallered. Trouble was I couldn't keep any food down.'

'Are yer OK now, Joe?'

'Yeah, I'm fine now I've seen Vera an' young Joey,' he replied with a smile.

Beryl brought in the tea and the family gathered around in the small parlour. There was a sudden knock on the front door and Vera jumped up quickly. 'I'll get it,' she said, hurrying down the passage.

When she opened the front door she was greeted by Alf Porter's maniacal grin as he handed her a bottle of Scotch whisky.

"Ave a drink on me, gel. All of yer 'ave a drink,' he said, swaying slightly and blinking as he tried to focus his bloodshot eyes on the happy young couple.

'That's very nice of yer, Alf,' Vera said, taking the bottle quickly as he staggered backwards.

The merry printer regained his balance and dismissed her thanks with a theatrical sweep of his arm. 'It'sh OK. We've gotta be fankful ter boys like Joe. Good luck ter the two o' yer,' he slurred, turning with a comical smile on his face and walking unsteadily towards his front door.

As June wore on Sally was becoming more and more anxious, for she had received no word from Jim. Every morning as she got ready for work the postman came into the square and Sally anxiously watched his progress round the houses, willing him to deliver the letter she was waiting for, but it did not come. She went to work unhappy, dreading the boredom and the unpleasant atmosphere at Harrison's. The workforce were struggling with their targets and bad feeling was beginning to grow once more. Arguments started over minor things and a lot of the younger girls were disappointed that no more dances had been planned.

Rumours became rife on the shopfloor after John Murray suddenly left the firm. Word had it that he had been caught in a compromising position with one of the workers and had been sacked on the spot. Just who he had been consorting with was not clear to the workers and a few names had been mentioned. A lot of the girls gave Maggie Chandler funny glances, however, and she was made prime candidate for suspicion, especially as her passion for the new supervisor had seemed to have cooled somewhat. Maggie ignored the glances and got on with her work, careful not to let anything slip whenever her workmates tried to wheedle information from her.

Sally left work in the evenings knowing that she was leaving one depressing situation for another. Her mother had taken to her bed with another attack of pleurisy and her father had become morose and ill-tempered, spending even more time at the pub. Lora, too, spent little time at home. Most evenings she would hurry out after tea and she was never home at weekends. Usually Sally would have called in to see Vera when she was feeling miserable, knowing that her friend could always be relied upon to cheer her up, but Joe was home now and Vera was obviously preoccupied. Sally found herself spending her odd moments in the company of Ginny Almond who told her in confidence of her planned marriage to George.

'I'm not tellin' anybody else fer the time bein', Sal,' she said. 'They'll find out soon enough. Anyway, I wanna get meself sorted out first. Until I can find out what 'appened ter that ole goat o' mine I'm stumped. 'E could be dead fer all I know. 'E's bin gone fer over four years now an' I ain't 'eard a fing from 'im.'

Sally felt a kinship with the woman. Like herself, Ginny's marriage was over and she had plans for the future. She had devoted her time to the children and to Daisy, never going out or meeting friends until her friendship with George developed. Now Ginny had to obtain her freedom, and it was not going to be an easy matter.

'Trouble is, Sally, I dunno where ter start lookin', or where ter make enquiries,' she said. 'I s'pose I could ask the police. They come round 'ere once lookin' fer 'im. 'E could be in prison by now for all I know.'

Sally found she had little advice to offer Ginny, except to suggest that maybe she should talk to the Salvation Army, since she had heard that they traced missing relatives and next of kin when an unidentified blitz victim was discovered. Ginny decided to make a start by writing to her husband's brother to find out if he could tell her anything.

Sally kept an eye on the Almond children whenever Ginny went to the pub or to the pictures with George, and she was taken more and more into her friend's confidence. Ginny was completely uninhibited and she often spoke of her unhappy marriage and of the joy she had found with her new man. Sally recalled the night Ginny had come home at two o'clock in the morning and with a satisfied smile on her broad face announced that she was going to marry George. Sally had intended to leave after eleven as Ginny had suggested but she had fallen asleep in front of the fire and been aroused by Ginny's hand on her shoulder. They had sat drinking tea and Ginny was beaming.

'I couldn't believe it, Sal,' she said. "E jus' come right out wiv it. Well, I tell yer, I was so shocked I nearly fell off the chair. We 'ad a few more drinks ter celebrate, then we 'ad a last drink in the Railway before they shut. We went back ter George's place an' the pair of us were like a couple o' kids. We was gigglin' an' talkin about what the neighbours were gonna say when they 'eard, an' it just 'appened.'

'What 'appened?' Sally asked with a show of innocence.

Ginny looked over her teacup. 'We went ter bed tergevver. Yeah, we did. It just seemed ter be the fing ter do. Mind you, we was like a couple o' fumblin' youngsters. George got all embarrassed an' I was tryin' ter tell 'im it was all right. Bloody 'ell, I was shakin' meself. It's bin so long now. Still we finally managed it, wiv a lot o' difficulty. Christ! I almost forgot what it was like. George said 'e's gonna buy me a real engagement ring. Ain't that nice of 'im? I never 'ad an engagement ring. I didn't 'ave a weddin' ring fer long eivver. I used ter pawn it when fings was bad an' it was in "uncle's" when me ole man left me. As a matter o' fact I never did get round ter redeemin' it. I bought an imitation in Woolworth's. Yer used ter be able ter buy imitations at one time. I dunno if yer still can. Anyway, we're gonna name the day soon as we get ourselves straight. It's only gonna be a registry office do, but you can stand fer me, Sal. After all, yer should know what ter do, yer stood fer Vera.'

The fire had burned low and Ginny had poured them out some more tea. She seemed too excited to sleep and Sally had found herself yawning with tiredness as Ginny went on at length. 'It was really good wiv George. It wasn't

346

ever like that wiv my ole man. 'E'd come in from the pub and demand it. There was no consideration fer me feelin's, an' 'e was never careful. It didn't matter to 'im that every time 'e slipped 'is braces over 'is shoulders I got pregnant. I got ter dread 'im comin' 'ome drunk 'cos I knew what it meant, but I never refused 'im even though I got sick ter me stomach the way 'e be'aved at times. It's strange when yer come ter fink of it. There was me prayin' me ole man would come 'ome sober, an' now fer the past few months I've bin 'opin' George 'ad drunk enough ter get all necessary. Still, it all worked out right in the end, at least I fink it 'as.'

Sally smiled at the recollection of that chat. Ginny deserved a man like George, she thought, and she hoped everything would work out well for the two of them, but the happiness she felt for her friend made her anxiety over Jim's silence all the more sharp.

In the second week of June Ernest Cox went for his army medical and passed A1. He was eager now to get into uniform, despite the depressing and frightening picture of war-time service life painted by Lofty. Ernest had bumped into Muriel on a few occasions and she invariably gave him a big smile and a sly wink. The young man felt very grateful to Muriel for that special evening, and he held her in high esteem. Whenever he heard whispers about the girl's morals he turned his back and shut his ears. Muriel might be a woman of the streets who sold her body for money, but for him she could do no wrong. She was a warm person who had made him feel a man. She had been patient with him and let him make love to her out of friendship and understanding. One thing was certain, he told himself. No one was going to know of his affair with her. He had promised Muriel faithfully that he would not tell anyone, and he intended to keep the secret between them.

A few of Ernest's young friends had already gone into the Army and he was aware that he would receive his calling-up papers very soon. He felt that he would like to do something for Muriel to show his appreciation and affection. He considered taking her a bunch of flowers, but he decided that everyone probably did that. Perhaps he should buy her a small present, he thought, but then what could he get? Ernest was not familiar with brands of perfume or toiletries, and he decided that maybe he should buy Muriel something to wear. He had heard the older men at work talking about buying women frilly underwear and saying that they really appreciated that sort of gift. Ernest recalled that when Muriel undressed in front of him she had been wearing black frilly underwear. She would no doubt be pleased with that kind of thing, he reasoned.

Ernest scratched his head. He dare not ask anyone else to buy the underwear. He would have to do it himself. It shouldn't be too difficult, he told himself. He could say he was buying it for his sister as a wedding present, or something. Maybe he could get it done up in some fancy wrapping-paper and put a little note inside. But where on earth could he buy black frilly underwear? There was that shop in the Tower Bridge Road. He had seen some bras and knickers on display in the window.

When Ernest finished work at midday on Saturday he went directly to the Tower Bridge Road Market and walked casually along until he came to the shop. Not wanting to be seen gaping at the fineries he strolled past leisurely, quickly taking note of the various items on show. Once he was satisfied the shop had what he was looking for Ernest turned back and walked up to the entrance. He was just about to go in when he saw that there were quite a few customers in the shop. He felt a sudden panic and turned on his heel. He was being silly, he told himself. There was nothing wrong in buying ladies' underwear. I bet Lofty buys his wife's underclothes, he thought, smiling to himself as he imagined his pal getting the shop assistant to turn the place inside out until he found just what he was looking for. Lofty was like that. He wouldn't dilly-dally outside the shop with sweaty palms and a red face. Ernest took a deep breath and without further hesitation he walked purposefully into the shop.

'Hello, young man. What can I do for you then?' a soft voice sounded in his ear.

Ernest turned to see a thin character standing beside him. The man was in his thirties at least, although he reached just up to Ernest's shoulder. His pale mauve shirt was open at the neck to display a thin gold chain, and he smelt

349

of perfume. His thick black hair was combed back from his forehead and he regarded the young man with a mocking grin hovering on his lips.

'I wanna buy some underwear – black,' Ernest faltered.

'We only sell ladies' undergarments in here, dear,' the man said, putting a slender hand to his forehead.

'That's what I want. It's a present fer me sister. She's gettin' married,' Ernest blurted out, aware that the rest of the customers were looking at him.

'Well, let me see now,' the assistant said, pinching his chin and eyeing Ernest in a peculiar way. 'We do camisoles, camiknickers and French knickers in black lace, satin and silk. We do a nice line in boned bras, too. The choice is yours, young man.'

Ernest felt his face getting hot. He had not realised that buying women's underwear would be so difficult and the mocking shop assistant was not helping at all.

'Erm – erm, the cami-ones,' Ernest said in a low voice.

'Lace, silk, cotton?'

'Better make it lace.'

'What size?' the assistant asked, enjoying the young man's embarrassment.

Ernest bit on his bottom lip and raised his open hands in an effort to describe the size. 'Medium, I fink,' he almost groaned in his growing discomfort.

The assistant raised his eyes to the ceiling and

sighed. 'The garments come in hip sizes. How tall is she, this sister of yours?'

'About this size,' Ernest answered, holding up his hand. 'About up ter me shoulder.'

'Is she slim, or fat?' the man asked, sighing noticeably.

'She's in between,' Ernest gulped, wishing the floor would open beneath him.

The assistant walked quickly around the counter and took down a large cardboard box which was tied loosely with twine. He hummed tunelessly to himself as he undid the knot and took off the lid. 'There we are, size thirty-eight,' he said. 'These are nineteen and eleven. These are more expensive at twenty-two and six, and these are very nice at twenty-nine and eleven.'

While Ernest stared at the lingerie the assistant looked at him with a bored expression on his angular face. 'You only need two clothing coupons for these,' he remarked, putting a hand on his hip.

Ernest pointed to the most expensive of the items. 'I'll take that,' he said quickly, anxious to get out of the shop as the perspiration started to run down his red face.

When he had got back out into the street Ernest took a deep breath and wiped the sweat from his forehead. He hoped that he had got the right size and that Muriel would be pleased with his choice. Perhaps she would ask him round to do another little job, he thought to himself with a smile.

Back in the shop an elderly lady customer was passing comment. 'I fink it's nice ter see young men buyin' their lady friends underwear. They're pretty fings, those cami-what-d'yer-me call-its, ain't they?'

The assistant nodded, running a forefinger across his brow. 'Yes, they're very nice,' he said. 'I've been wearing them for years.'

On Saturday afternoon Sally was standing over a steaming copper, pressing down a pair of sheets into the boiling water and feeling bad-tempered. She had taken her mother a midday meal but Annie had merely picked at it and said she felt too ill to get out of bed. Charlie had gone to work that morning and had evidently stopped off at the pub. Sally was keeping his meal hot in the oven and it was beginning to brown. She slammed down the copper lid and gathered up the freshly ironed clothes, thinking of all the chores that still remained to be done, and as she went out into the passage Charlie walked in. Sally was about to scold her father for being late when she noticed a strange look on his face. He went into the parlour and took off his coat, hanging it behind the door without uttering a word. Sally looked at him as he flopped down into the easy chair.

'You all right, Dad?' she asked, putting the ironing down on the table.

Her father took up his pipe and flipped open the top of his tobacco-pouch. 'I don't like bein' the bearer o' bad news, gel, but I reckon yer gotta know,' he said with a heavy sigh.

'Gotta know what?' she asked, a puzzled look on her flushed features.

352

'I'm afraid it's Ben, Sally.'

'What's 'appened, Dad?'

''E 'ad an accident at work this mornin'.'

'Is 'e 'urt bad?' Sally asked, feeling icy fingers clutch at her stomach.

'Yeah, it's pretty bad by all accounts,' Charlie replied, looking down at his pipe. 'I 'eard about it in the pub. Apparently Ben slipped an' fell down a ship's 'old. They took 'im ter the 'ospital.'

'Where's 'e at, Guy's?'

'Yeah. The bloke who told me reckons it's 'is back. 'E was all strapped up when they got 'im out on the stretcher. The bloke said Ben was unconscious.'

Sally took off her apron and ran a hand over her hot forehead. 'I'll 'ave ter go in an' see 'im, Dad,' she said quietly. 'I couldn't rest ovverwise.'

Charlie looked at his daughter for a moment, then he dropped his eyes and nodded. 'Yeah, OK, luv. You get yerself up there, I'll see ter me dinner.'

Sally was hurrying to the tram stop in Jamaica Road before she had really had time to think about what she was doing. Although she had decided that her marriage to Ben was finished for good, the thought that he might suddenly die cut her like a knife.

After what seemed a long time a tram finally arrived, but Sally had barely settled herself before it stopped again at the junction with Tower Bridge Road while the conductor got off to switch the points and have a prolonged conversation with his driver. At last the rattling conveyance shuddered to a stop at the foot of Duke Street Hill and Sally jumped down and hurried through the long railway arch which led to the hospital gates.

Sally's footsteps sounded loudly as she walked along the tiled corridor to the admission desk. She stood clasping her bag tightly, biting on her lip while the dreamy-looking receptionist consulted a large open ledger, and finally directed her to a ward on the first floor.

The ward sister took her into a small room and bade her sit down. 'Your husband's in the theatre now,' she said kindly. 'He'll be coming into this ward. As far as we know he's suffered a fractured pelvis and ribs. He has a broken leg, too. Of course you understand we won't know just how bad the injuries are until he comes up from theatre. I should wait until tomorrow before coming in again.'

'Was 'e still unconscious, sister?' Sally asked.

'He was conscious when he went down,' the ward sister replied, patting Sally's arm. 'That's always a good sign.'

Sally walked out of the hospital into the slanting sunlight, her troubled thoughts running wild inside her head. She was confused and worried, and as her conflicting emotions pulled her in opposite directions it felt as if they would tear her apart. She was desperate for a letter from Jim, and yet now her concern for Ben made her feel guilty. Her excitement at the thought of seeing her soldier again was suddenly dulled by a dread feeling that Ben was going to die. She had

354

often formed a picture of Jim in her mind, but all she saw now was the image of Ben walking out of the pub the evening she had asked for a divorce. Tears rose in her eyes as she crossed the street and walked slowly through the deserted railway arch.

Chapter Seventeen

SALLY was deaf to the constant drum of the machinery and the feverish activity around her as she leaned forward over her noisy contraption and worked on the batch of back seams. As she sewed mechanically her mind became detached and her thoughts wandered. She was carried back to the hospital ward and she saw Ben lying there with his eyes closed, deathly white. His fair hair was dishevelled and there was a wide red graze on his forehead. The foot of the bed was tilted up and Ben's plastered leg was supported by straps and pulleys counterbalanced with a heavy weight. His hands and arms were resting above the bedclothes and a saline drip fed into his bare forearm. He opened his eyes and smiled weakly as she touched his arm softly, then he slipped back into his drugged sleep. She sat beside the bed for some time, watching his even breathing and the steady pulse in the side of his neck, until the curtains were pulled around the bed and nurses came to tend to him.

When she spoke to the doctor he told her that

Ben was out of danger but that the healing process would take a long time. Beside the fractured pelvis and shattered leg he had sustained rib fractures and severe concussion. He was young and strong, though, the doctor said, and he should make a full recovery. Sally recalled how she had left the hospital early on Sunday afternoon and walked slowly home, unable to stop thinking about Ben lying there so badly injured. Her father had found out a little more about how the accident had occurred and he told her that some cases had slipped out of a sling and one of them caught Ben, knocking him into the ship's hold. Fortunately the unloading of the cargo had only just started and his fall had been broken. Had he fallen into an empty hold he would most certainly have been killed.

Charlie was aware that his daughter had felt in some way responsible for Ben getting drunk and landing himself in prison, and he worried that she might feel the same way about his accident. For that reason he had been at pains to impress on his daughter that it was pure chance and it could have happened to anyone. He mentioned his fears to Annie. 'I don't want that gel blamin' 'erself in any way,' he said with a worried frown on his face. 'Accidents like that often 'appen in the docks. It can be a dangerous place ter work at times, 'specially now there's always a rush ter get the ships turned round. Our Sally's a feelin' gel. Even though the two of 'em are split up it don't stop 'er finkin' about 'im.'

Annie sat in the armchair with a dressing-gown wrapped tightly around her thin body and she stared moodily into the empty grate. 'I dunno, it's all trouble,' she groaned. 'Jus' as she was gettin' 'erself sorted out wiv that new bloke of 'ers this 'as ter go an' 'appen.'

Charlie looked at his ailing wife and thought how she had aged over the past few months. Her hair had gone completely grey and it was untidily gathered up into a hairnet. Her thin face looked gaunt and colourless and her shoulders had sagged. Annie seemed to do very little except sit around in her dressing-gown or take to her bed whenever she felt miserable. She was taking tablets to help her sleep, and more tablets that Doctor Bartholomew had prescribed for her anaemia. Charlie was worried. Most of the chores now fell on Sally. She did the family washing and ironing as well as keeping the place clean, and she often got the tea ready when she came home from work, with little or no help from Lora.

Charlie slumped down in the chair with a thoughtful expression on his face and filled his pipe. 'Why don't yer get dressed an' take a bit of air?' he said presently. 'It'll do yer better than sittin' around the place all day.'

Annie gave him a cold look. 'I ain't up ter goin' out,' she replied flatly. 'In fact I might go back ter bed yet, the way I feel. Yer don't seem ter understand. I'm far from well.'

Charlie lit his pipe. 'You'd better 'ave a word wiv Lora. She don't do much about the place. It's all left ter our Sal. She don't complain much an' . . .'

'That's it, keep on about Lora,' Annie

357

interrupted. 'She does 'er share. Yer never 'ave a good word ter say about the girl. Sally's always bin yer favourite. If I wasn't feelin' so rough I'd do everyfing meself. I wouldn't 'ave ter ask neivver of 'em.'

Charlie felt it was little use pursuing the subject and he got up and put on his coat.

'I s'pose you're orf ter the pub again,' Annie moaned, rocking forward in her chair.

'That's right,' he growled. 'No point in me sittin' 'ere. I might as well go fer a pint.'

On Monday evening Sally went to the hospital again to see Ben. He gave her a wan smile as she leaned over and kissed him gently on his forehead. His pained eyes stared at her as she pulled a chair to the bedside and seated herself.

'I'm pleased yer come in, Sal. I've bin finkin' about yer,' he said in a hoarse voice.

''Ow yer feelin', Ben?' she asked, reaching for his arm.

He turned his head slightly and winced. 'Like I've bin run over by a steamroller. I feel 'elpless. I can't move.'

'I came in yesterday, but yer was sleepy,' she said, holding on to his arm lightly.

'I remember yer bendin' over me, but I thought I must 'ave bin dreamin'. Sorry ter be a nuisance,' he smiled.

Sally looked at his pale face and felt a wave of compassion surge through her; he looked so helpless lying there. She averted her eyes from his, not knowing what to say.

'What about you?' he asked, staring at her

closely. 'Is everyfing all right?'

She removed her hand from his arm and leaned back in her chair. 'Yeah, everyfing's fine,' she replied nonchalantly.

''Ave yer bin goin' out on any dates, Sal?' he asked quietly.

Sally looked into his tired blue eyes and saw his concern. There would be plenty of time for him to be told, she decided. It would not help him to know about Jim while he was fighting his injury. 'No, I've not bin datin' anybody,' she said.

His eyes closed for a few moments. 'Are yer in pain, Ben? D'yer want me ter go?' she asked.

He opened his eyes and held her with a steady gaze. 'No. It's very nice ter see yer,' he said slowly. 'Will yer come in again?'

She nodded. 'Course I will.'

Ben looked up at the pulley ropes and grinned mirthlessly. 'I s'pose this means I'll be finished at the docks,' he said with some disgust. 'They don't employ cripples.'

Sally reached out and touched his arm again. 'Look, you're gonna be all right. I was talkin' ter the doctor yesterday. 'E said you'll be fine. It's gonna take time, though. You'll be back at the docks, but you'll 'ave ter learn ter dodge those cases next time.'

He grinned and winced slightly with a sudden pain. 'Look, yer don't 'ave ter come in if yer don't want to,' he told her. 'I'll understand.'

She smiled. 'I want to. We're still friends, ain't we?'

He nodded slowly. 'We're still good friends.'

A nurse walked up to the bed pushing a trolley. 'It's time for your jab, Mr Brady,' she said, smiling.

Sally got up as the nurse pulled the curtains around the bed. 'I'll come in again soon,' she said, touching his arm gently. 'Take care.'

Sally walked quickly from the ward out into the long corridor, thinking about how Ben had been curious to know if she was dating anyone. Could he tell? she wondered. Vera had said she looked different. No, it was impossible, she decided. It could not possibly show. He was just asking a question. Things had not changed, he must know that. He was just being curious, and lying there must give him too much time to think.

Sally was preoccupied with her thoughts and she did not see the two heavily built men until they were level with her.

"Ello, Sal,' the one nearer to her said. 'We're just goin' in ter see Ben. 'Ow is 'e?'

"E's doin' well,' Sally stammered, taken by surprise on seeing Ben's brothers.

Nobby Brady looked at Sally closely. 'It's good of yer ter go in ter see 'im,' he said, touching her arm gently.

'It's the least I could do,' she replied quickly, feeling her face going red under the men's gaze.

Jack Brady caught his younger brother's eye. 'We'd better get in, Nobby,' he said. 'That ward sister's a stickler fer time.'

As the two men moved away Nobby winked at Sally. 'See yer around, luv. Mind 'ow yer go.'

She watched the two walk smartly along the

360

corridor. How alike the three brothers were in looks, she thought. Jack was surly and much like Ben in his ways, but Nobby was different. He had a cheerful disposition and had always been friendly towards her. He had seemed genuinely sorry when she and Ben split up and had taken the trouble to say how much he hoped they would get back together again one day.

The bright evening light made her blink as she stepped from the shaded entrance out into the main courtyard. It would be many months before Ben was fit again, she thought. She would continue to go in and see him, but she knew that it would be easy for him to start building up false hopes. She would have to be careful, she told herself. That part of her life was over, and there could be no going back.

On Wednesday morning the postman called into the square and as Sally left for work he handed her a letter. She glanced at the handwriting and with a sweet thrill of excitement she recognised Jim's spidery scrawl. Sally was tempted to go back into the house and open it but she resisted the urge, as if to savour its arrival. She was late already and it would be nice to read it during the morning tea-break. As she reached the tram stop Sally felt the excitement growing within her. The letter had been a long time coming. Maybe Jim had waited until he knew about his leave before writing, or perhaps he had had second thoughts about seeing her again. Whatever was in the letter would have to wait until break-time, she told herself. Then there would be time to read it slowly.

As she entered the factory and got ready for work Sally felt the tension. Harrison's Government contract was running behind schedule and the whole place seemed to be buzzing. The workforce were feeling the pressure as the supervisors toured the factory floor heaping piles of unfinished battledress blouses on to the benches beside the machinists. Maggie Chandler worked away at top speed and even she could not keep abreast of the quotas. Brenda Foster had little to say as usual, and she leaned over her sewing-machine with a sly smile on her face as the pile of battledress blouses beside her appeared to diminish faster than those of her workmates. The hands of the factory clock seemed to stand still, and when the tea-trolley was finally wheeled on to the factory floor Sally leaned back in her seat and reached into her handbag for the letter.

Dear Sally,
Sorry for the long delay in writing.
We've been on exercises and moving from place to place most of the time. I really enjoyed our time together and look forward to seeing you this weekend if you can make it. I'll be at our special meeting-place in the church gardens at 7 p.m. Friday. I've got two tickets for a Forces show up west. I think you'll like it. Hope you're keeping well and not working too hard. Can't write more, it's lights out in a few minutes.
Can't wait to see you. Have been thinking

of you all the time. Please give my regards to
your family.
Yours,
Jim.

Sally read the letter through twice and then
tucked it into her breast pocket. It seemed an
age since their last meeting and in just a few
days' time she would be with him again. Her
heart beat faster as she thought of his goodnight
kiss and the way he had held her in his strong
arms. The next few days would not seem so
monotonous and dull now that she had the
coming weekend to look forward to.

During June there were a few unusual callers to
Paragon Place. One day Maudie Cox took
delivery of a case of tinned corned beef and she
lost no time in distributing it amongst her grateful clients. Harriet Carey had seen the delivery
from behind the lace curtains of her front-room
window and she remarked on it when her sister
came home from work that evening.

'The man walked into the square with a case
on his shoulder, Juliet,' she said, astonished at
the apparent cheek of it. 'I'm sure it's some of
that black-market food. Who would have
thought it? Mrs Cox seems such a respectable
lady.'

Juliet groaned to herself. That previous weekend at Mr Lomax's home she had dined on red
salmon, and he had told her that it came from a
good friend of his who was in the provision
trade. He had said that everyone dabbled in the

black market and it was nothing to be ashamed of.

'Well, it's no concern of ours, Harriet. As long as we're not involved we've nothing to worry about,' she said firmly.

'But that's not the point,' Harriet went on. 'If there weren't any black marketeers there would be more food to go round. I was listening to a broadcast only the other evening. Do you know that hundreds of tons of food go missing from the docks and wharves every week? And where does it go? To the black-market people, that's where. I think people should report any instances of that sort of thing. It's our duty.'

Juliet had visions of their neighbours lying in wait for them as they left for work and she shook her head. 'We can't get involved, Harriet. And in any case we might be a little presumptuous. It could have been something entirely honest and above board. Let's not jump to conclusions.'

Harriet was adamant. 'It was clearly marked "Swift's Corned Beef". I could see it quite plainly. Then there was the man who delivered it. He looked very shifty. He kept glancing over his shoulder as he stood at Mrs Cox's door. When he walked back out of the square Mrs Cox stood watching him and then she started knocking on some of the front doors. I saw her with my own eyes. It looked so suspicious.'

Juliet sighed deeply. 'Did she knock here?'

'I should think not,' Harriet snorted. 'I'd have soon told the woman just what I thought of her.'

The younger sister watched as Harriet set

about polishing the tiny china ornaments. She's getting worse, she thought. First it was Muriel and her nymphomania, then it was Mr Porter planning to poison her, and now it's Mrs Cox and the black marketeers. What will she dream up next? And what would Harriet say if she knew her own sister was engaged in a passionate and long-standing love affair with Mr Lomax? She would no doubt have one of her turns and never recover. Poor Harriet. She really doesn't belong here, Juliet sighed.

The following morning another stranger to Paragon Place knocked on Ginny Almond's front door. She was a large woman with a tight-fitting coat and a large hat perched on the top of her head. Her raven hair was pulled tight about her ears and fixed into a bun at the nape of her wide neck. The woman cuddled a large handbag to her ample bosom and her coal-black eyes stared out at Ginny in a hostile manner as she opened the front door.

'Are you Mrs Almond?' she boomed.

Ginny nodded, slightly taken aback by the woman's approach. 'Yeah, that's right,' she said.

'Mrs Virginia Almond?'

'Yeah.'

The large woman pursed her lips and opened up her handbag. 'This is you, then,' she said, taking out a faded photograph and pushing it towards Ginny.

'Yeah, that's me. 'Ere, where d'yer get that from?' Ginny asked, staring hard at the woman.

'Well, it's a long story,' she replied in a somewhat lower voice.

'You'd better come in, then,' Ginny said, standing back from the doorway.

The large woman walked into the parlour and Ginny motioned her into a chair. 'Now what's this all about?' she asked, her eyes narrowing suspiciously.

'Is your 'usband's name Francis 'Erbert Almond?' she asked.

Ginny nodded. 'Yeah, that's right.'

Her visitor leaned back in her chair. 'I thought as much,' she said quietly.

Ginny sat down opposite the large woman, her face growing hot with anger. 'Now look, missus. I've answered yer questions ter the best o' me ability, now what about yer tellin' me what all these bloody questions are in aid of?'

The woman's shoulders slumped and she gave Ginny a quick smile. 'I'm sorry, but I 'ad ter know,' she said quietly.

''Ad ter know what?' Ginny asked, becoming more perplexed.

'I 'ad ter know if yer was really Frankie Almond's wife,' the woman said.

'Why?'

'Let me introduce meself. I'm Mrs Elizabeth Almond. I'm Frankie Almond's wife, too.'

Ginny almost fell back in her chair. 'Yer mean my Frankie married you? While 'e's still married ter me? I don't believe it. 'E wouldn't. 'E couldn't.'

''E did,' Elizabeth said, opening her handbag and taking out a folded sheet of paper. 'There it is in black an' white. It's me marriage lines.'

'Why, the no-good, dirty whore-son!' Ginny

raved.

'Them's my sentiments entirely. I kicked 'im out as soon as I discovered what 'is little game was,' Elizabeth said, rocking back and forth in her chair. 'The police are lookin' for 'im so I thought it best you should know. Besides, us women 'ave gotta stick tergevver against the Frankie Almonds o' this world.'

Ginny stood up. 'Would yer like a cup o' tea?' she asked politely. 'I need one ter steady me nerves.'

They sat sipping their tea and Ginny listened while Elizabeth explained. 'I met Frankie about three years ago,' she began. 'It was at our local pub over in Poplar. 'E said 'e'd jus' moved in the area and that 'e was a widower. Course, me bein' a silly cow I felt sorry fer 'im. I tell yer, I got took in good an' proper. Anyway, ter cut a long story short we finally got spliced. Fings was very nice at first. Me first 'usband 'ad died years ago an' I'd took over 'is grocery business in Crisp Street. Frankie worked in the shop an' seemed ter get on well wiv all me customers. Everybody liked 'im. As a matter o' fact 'e brought trade in, but I began ter get a bit wary when me takin's started ter drop. It went on fer a couple o' months, an' I made a point o' keepin' me eye on the till. There was nufing I could put me finger on, but I knew somefing was wrong. It all come ter light when one o' me cousins got married. We all went ter the weddin' an' it was at the reception when I over'eard this fella talkin' ter Frankie. The bloke was from this side o' the water an' 'e seemed surprised at seein' that whore-son o' mine at the reception. I 'eard Frankie say 'e was mistaken, but I seen the look on 'is face. I managed ter button-'ole this fella later an' 'e told me Frankie was a dead ringer fer this bloke what lived in Bermondsey an' who was married wiv five kids. Well, that night I went down Frankie's fings. 'E was pissed as an 'andcart so 'e was none the wiser. I found that photo an' I got this address from an old envelope that 'ad some papers in it. Yer can see it says Mr and Mrs Almond. The bastard's a bigamist. I'd never gone down 'is fings before, an' I know 'e didn't expect me to. I tell yer, though, it was a good job I did. The dirty git was robbin' me blind. That's what 'e married me for. I can see it all now. I must 'ave bin bloody stupid.'

Ginny had been listening intently and her face had taken on a look of astonishment. 'Well, I know 'e's a no-good bastard, but I didn't fink 'e'd turn out ter be a bigamist,' she gasped. 'I'm glad yer come ter see me, luv. I'm courtin' at the moment, an' I wanna get shot o' the ugly git.'

Elizabeth stood up and straightened her coat. 'Well, my advice ter you is, go an' see a solicitor,' she said. 'You should 'ave no trouble. As fer me, I already 'ave. I tell yer this, though. If I get me 'ands on 'im 'e won't need no brief. 'E'll need a bloody undertaker!'

Chapter Eighteen

VERA and Joe had returned from their week's holiday in Margate and Sally took the opportunity to inform her friend of all that had happened while she was away. They sat comfortably chatting in the front room early on Saturday afternoon. Joe had gone for a drink with a few of his pals, and Beryl, along with her husband Fred, had taken young Joey to the park.

Vera welcomed the quiet break and she listened intently while Sally told her about Ben's accident, the letter she had received from Jim, and Ginny's visitor. 'You'll 'ave ter be careful, Sal,' she said when her friend had finished. ''Specially now you're gonna be seein' Jim again. It's easy ter get caught up in it all again. It's natural ter feel sorry fer Ben, an' yer might let yer pity get the upper 'and. I don't wanna interfere, but you're standin' real close. I can see it from a different angle. If it's finished, it's finished. Yer can't go back. I know it mus' be 'ard for yer. If yer fink there's a chance wiv you an' Jim then grab it. Don't let yer pity fer Ben get in the way. Yer don't 'ave ter tell 'im straight away. Let 'im get on 'is feet again before yer break it to 'im. 'E's gotta understand. After all, 'e sowed the seed, 'e's gotta reap the 'arvest.'

Sally laughed briefly. 'If Ben 'ad sown the seed it might 'ave bin different!'

Vera clapped her hand against her forehead. 'I said somefing then, didn't I? Anyway, yer know what I mean. Don't chuck it all away fer pity.

You'll regret it.'

Vera refilled the teacups and made herself comfortable again. Outside the sun was shining from a clear sky and children's voices carried up into the quiet room.

'Are yer lookin' forward ter seein' Jim again?' Vera asked, her eyes fixing Sally over her cup.

Sally nodded. 'Yeah, I am. 'E's a real nice fella, an' 'e's bin on me mind a lot lately. I really wanna see 'im again.'

Vera laughed. 'Well, 'e's certainly a nice-lookin' bloke. I could fancy 'im meself. No, I shouldn't say that, should I? Me an' Joe's got a good fing goin'. I wouldn't change 'im.'

'What's 'appenin' about Joe?' Sally asked.

Vera sighed and shrugged her shoulders. 'I've bin on ter 'im ter get out o' the merchant service. It's no job fer a married man, 'specially while the war's on.'

'Couldn't Joe get a job in the docks?' Sally asked. 'All 'is family are dockers, ain't they?'

Vera nodded. 'Joe's ole man an' 'is four bruvvers all work in the docks. Course, dear Joe 'as ter be different. Trouble is, the sea's in 'is blood. I don't fink 'e'd settle fer doin' anyfing else. Joe reckons the docks is a dangerous place ter work anyway, an' 'e said the short time we're tergevver makes up fer all the time we're apart. 'E's got a simple outlook on life, 'as my Joe, but I can't really argue wiv what 'e sez. It's great when we're tergevver, an' we don't 'ave a chance ter get in a rut. Before we get fed up wiv each ovver 'e's off. It's only the fear of 'is ship gettin' torpedoed that scares me. That's what makes the

370

partin's so 'ard.'

The two friends lapsed into silence, and in the comfort of each other's company they became absorbed with their own thoughts. The clock ticked loudly and the small room was bright with the afternoon sunlight that slanted through the lace curtains. A distant tug whistle sounded and the faint clatter of a London Bridge-bound train reached their ears.

Vera shifted her position and crossed her legs. 'Poor ole Ginny,' she said, breaking the silence. 'I bet she's choked.'

Sally nodded. ''Er an' George are plannin' ter get married soon as possible. She's worried in case the weddin' gets delayed over this bigamy fing. I feel really sorry fer 'er. She's really nice, an' George too. By the way, don't let on I've said anyfing. Ginny don't want anybody in the square ter know fer the time bein'.'

'Mum's the word,' Vera replied, holding her hands up in front of her. 'Now c'mon, let me take those curlers out. We've gotta make yer all sexy fer Jim ternight.'

At number 8 Maudie and Arthur Cox sat in their front parlour and Maudie was attempting to console her dejected-looking husband. 'Look Arfur, it wasn't yer fault,' she said. ''Ow was yer ter know? I mean ter say, yer was only doin' yer job.'

Arthur shook his head. 'I know that, Maudie, but Councillor Catchpole don't fink so. 'E reckons I made 'im look stupid an' 'e's gonna report me. I didn't know it was 'im. I jus' saw

371

this bloke stagger up the steps like 'e'd 'ad too much ter drink an' I saw 'im go in the lib'ry. I thought ter meself, that looks like Alf Porter up ter 'is tricks again. I wasn't near enough ter see prop'ly. I sez ter meself, 'old tight, Arfur, play it careful. I didn't approach 'im right away. I watched from the lib'ry door an' I see 'im fetch this great big book an' sit down at a table. Now I've bin told ter keep me eyes skinned, so I stands by the door an' looks over at the counter. I couldn't see that Carey woman but the ovver ole chap was there. 'E was busy an' I guessed 'e 'adn't spotted this queer-lookin' bloke who'd jus' walked in, so I keeps watch fer a few minutes. Anyway, this bloke ain't turned the pages o' the book an' 'e's got 'is 'ead in 'is 'ands. It looked ter me like 'e was fast asleep. Right, I sez ter meself, 'ere we go.'

'So what did yer do, Arfur? Did yer chuck 'im out?' Maudie asked.

Arthur hooked his thumbs through his braces and stuck out his chest. 'I walked over an' 'e didn't even look up. "Righto then, Alf, no sleepin' in 'ere. Let's 'ave yer outside," I sez. Well, soon as 'e looked up I could see it wasn't Alf Porter. "Do you know who I am?" 'e says. Well, when 'e told me I could've fell frew the floor. 'E reckons 'e's gonna get me transferred ter road-sweepin'.'

"E can't do that,' Maudie exclaimed.

Arthur stroked his bushy moustache and looked balefully at Maudie. 'Listen, luv. Thomas Catchpole is the leader of the council. If 'e wants me road-sweepin' that's where I'll end up.'

Maudie shook her head sadly. 'Oh, Arfur. Yer won't be able ter wear yer nice suit any more. I do like yer in that suit.'

As the summer sun dipped down over the chimney-pots Sally walked out of the square and made her way to the church gardens. She felt a sharp sense of excitement in the pit of her stomach. She was eager to see Jim once more. Her thoughts turned to what Vera had said that afternoon. She must not let pity get in the way of her new-found freedom. She was beginning a new, exciting affair with Jim and she felt good with him. It was early days yet, she admitted to herself, but he had brought her out of her shell. Sally could not help recalling how difficult the visit to the hospital on Thursday evening had been. Ben had already recovered enough of his spirit to talk about getting on his feet once more. He had chatted familiarly and wanted her to stay longer. Vera was right and Sally reminded herself that she would have to be careful. Ben was going to be in hospital for some time yet, and he would become more and more used to her visiting him. She would have to tell him soon about Jim. It would be difficult, but he had to be made aware that nothing had changed. She felt anxious at the thought of talking to Ben about it and tried to put the problem to the back of her mind as she reached the garden gate.

Summer flowers bordered the gravel path and as Sally walked through the entrance she could see the secluded seat with its canopy of green. The garden was deserted, and when she reached the chosen spot she stood for a few moments and looked around her. Jim was nowhere to be seen. Sally was seized with a sudden dread. Maybe he would not show up, she thought. Perhaps he could not. She walked slowly along the path, glancing at the neat flower beds and gazing up at the vine-covered old church. She had walked the length of the path and turned back towards the seat, her anxiety growing, when she heard footsteps behind her. Sally turned and saw the uniformed figure hurrying towards her. Jim had a wide smile on his flushed face and as he caught up with her he reached out his arms and clasped her shoulders. He kissed her briefly in his breathlessness.

'I'm sorry I'm late. Bin waitin' long?' he said, taking her by the arm as they walked out of the garden.

Sally looked up into his handsome features and smiled. 'I thought you'd changed yer mind,' she said.

His face was serious. 'I've bin lookin' forward ter seein' yer again, Sally. I wasn't goin' ter miss ternight, even if I 'ad ter go absent.'

They strolled through the backstreets towards London Bridge station, Sally holding on to Jim's arm as he walked on her outside next to the road. She looked slim in her figure-hugging cotton dress, and her black high-heeled shoes sounded loudly on the flagstones. As they crossed the road into Tooley Street they exchanged glances and Jim smiled at her in his disarming way. The wharves were shut and bolted and the railway arches were quiet and deserted as they passed by. A torn war poster flapped from a hoarding above their heads and barrage balloons floated high in the clear blue sky. They walked past the sandbagged entrance to a surface shelter and climbed the steep flight of stairs to the station and when Jim had bought the tickets they made their way to the platform.

Uniformed personnel stood around beside kit-bags or sat quietly on the hard benches, smoking and talking among themselves. Jim eyed the scene and smiled reassuringly as they waited for the train to Charing Cross.

'When yer look at all those faces and all those uniforms it's like lookin' at a giant jigsaw puzzle,' he said. 'Everybody's got a place ter go, an' everybody fits in ter the picture. Soon all the pieces'll be in place, an' then everybody'll be able ter see the result. When all those faces an' all those uniforms are in the right place it's gonna be a sight ter see, Sally. All 'ell's gonna break loose then.'

She looked at him closely, surprised at the way he was talking. 'Is it gonna be soon, Jim?' she asked.

He nodded. 'I'm sure it won't be long. We've bin on exercises, manoeuvres, night schemes. It's all buildin' up. That was why I couldn't write. At one time it looked like we was off, but everyfing was put back. That's not fer repeatin', Sally. I could get shot fer tellin' yer all this,' he laughed. 'When it's all ready we might get leave, or we might be off like thieves in the night.'

Sally clasped his arm tightly. 'Are yer scared?' she asked.

375

He gazed down at his shoes and then looked up to meet her inquiring gaze. 'When I was at Dunkirk I was terrified,' he said. 'At times I thought I'd never get back ter England in one piece. Later, when I saw the ruins of me 'ome an' realised I wasn't gonna see me wife an' baby ever again I couldn't feel anyfing. It was like I was ice. D'yer know, I wanted ter get back ter the fightin'. Maybe it was revenge. Maybe it was a death wish, I dunno. Anyway, I was sent ter this trainin' battalion. I was made up ter sergeant an' put in charge o' trainin' new recruits. A lot of 'em are jus' kids. Some of 'em don't even shave yet but they're soldiers, an' they're gonna be in action before long. I realised that they 'ad the right ter the best trainin' possible. That's what 'elped pull me tergevver. Now I'm scared again. I'm scared because I've got somebody ter fink about. Somebody ter come back to.'

Sally felt herself melting as she looked into his eyes. His urgent stare held her transfixed and she wanted him to wrap his arms around her and kiss her breathless.

He relaxed suddenly and a smile played about his lips. 'I'm sorry fer gettin' all serious, Sally,' he said. 'Let's forget the war an' 'ave a good evenin', shall we?'

The train shuddered to a halt and they climbed aboard for the short journey. They remained silent as the carriage slid past the ancient Southwark Cathedral and clattered along above the bomb-damaged Borough Market. As the train trundled on to Hungerford Bridge they looked down over the wide river and the white stone buildings that flanked either side, and they saw the thin church spires and the broad dome of St Paul's rising over the city before the train slowed into Charing Cross Station.

Saturday evening crowds thronged Trafalgar Square and Pall Mall as the two made their way to the Palladium Theatre. Sally smiled happily as they joined the long queue and waited for the line to move forward. When they finally found themselves inside the large auditorium the show started almost immediately. The band struck up and dancing girls moved swiftly across the wide stage. The sketches and jokes catered to the tastes of the predominantly military audience and loud laughter and occasional cheers soon began to fill the theatre.

Sally was too aware of Jim's closeness to concentrate on the show, and she felt a shiver run down her spine as his hand found hers in the darkness. She was drawn to him, to the way he spoke and the crooked smile that played almost mockingly on his expressive lips. She had looked briefly behind the barrier he had put up around himself to hide the pain of the tragedy that haunted him. She wanted to hold him in a tight embrace and let him open his heart to her completely, and as his hand stroked hers gently she slipped down in her seat and slowly rested her head on his shoulder.

When the show was over Jim took Sally's hand as the audience crowded through the foyer and moved out into the cool night. The young couple found a small coffee-house and sat at a table next to the window, watching the elegant revellers and servicemen passing in the street outside.

'Did yer enjoy the show?' Jim asked, sipping his coffee.

Sally nodded and smiled into his eyes. 'It was smashin'.'

Jim put down his cup and let his eyes wander over her short, dark hair, her smooth neck and her full, shapely lips. 'Would yer like ter go somewhere termorrer?' he asked suddenly, his gaze held by her large brown eyes. 'I can get the late night train back ter camp.'

Sally leaned forward, her hands clasped on the table. 'Let's get out of London fer a few hours, Jim,' she said, a note of excitement in her voice. 'If the weavver's nice we could go ter Farnborough.'

He laughed. 'OK. Let's do it.'

After spending some time in the coffee-house, chatting and laughing together, they walked out into the Saturday night crowds and strolled slowly to Charing Cross. By the time they reached London Bridge and walked out of the station the sky was strewn with stars and a full moon shone down on the grim wharves. Jim slipped his arm around Sally's waist as they walked through the quiet, narrow backstreets and she leaned her head against his tall shoulder.

Ahead of them they saw the tall church spire silhouetted against the velvet night sky. They walked into the gardens along the gravel path and as they reached the secluded seat Jim pulled her to him. Her arms curled around his neck and she let her body mould to his as their lips met in a long, lingering kiss. Sally shivered with excitement as his hands moved along her back and his lips sought her smooth neck. She felt his body press more tightly against her and the warm breath of his whispered words in her ear. 'I've bin wantin' ter do this all evenin,' Sal. Yer look lovely.'

Sally brought her hands down on to his and eased back slightly. 'Will yer get any more leave before yer go overseas, Jim?' she asked quietly.

He straightened up and gripped her elbows, holding her at arm's length. 'I shouldn't be tellin' yer this but we're gettin' kitted out soon,' he said, a serious look appearing on his face. 'That means we're due ter go. I don't know when, but it won't be long. Unless there's a change o' plan we should get seven days' embarkation leave. I'll try an' drop yer a line, soon as I know fer sure.'

She suddenly threw her arms around his neck and kissed him hard on the mouth. 'I don't want yer ter go,' she groaned and she buried her head in his chest.

'Don't worry,' Jim said softly, smiling in an attempt to reassure her. 'We've got termorrer tergevver.'

He held her close and felt her warmth, the smell of her hair and her lips against his neck. It was happening so fast, he thought. He had found someone who had managed to get inside the shell he had protected himself with, someone who was warm and good to be with. She aroused him and he knew he wanted her, wanted to make love to her. As he held her close and stroked his hand along her back a sudden panic seized him. He should check his emotions, he told himself, not get drawn into a relationship. He would be going off to fight very soon and it would be too great a distraction to be yearning after someone, to have someone who would yearn for him, and maybe when it was all over to mourn for him.

He kissed her ear softly. 'C'mon, let's walk yer 'ome, Sally.'

The tenants of Paragon Place awoke to a bright Sunday morning. Children got out of bed and went out to play in the sunshine and sit beneath the sycamore tree trading glass marbles and cigarette cards, women scraped new potatoes and sliced large leafy cabbages for the Sunday meal, and the menfolk cleaned their shoes and made ready for their visit to the pub. Doorsteps were clean, and crisp lace curtains fluttered in the cool breeze.

At number 3 a serious discussion was going on behind Ginny's back.

'Why was Mummy cryin' last night?' Sara asked.

'I dunno. Fancy askin' me,' Billy replied. 'Somebody's upset 'er, I s'pose.'

Frankie looked up from cleaning his shoes. 'I 'spose she was cryin' over Dad,' he said. 'I 'eard Mum talkin' ter Sally next door about 'im the ovver day.'

Sara did not remember her father and she pulled a face. 'Why should Mummy cry over 'im? 'E don't live 'ere any more.'

Arthur, the eldest, had only vague recollections of his father and he scratched his head. 'P'r'aps she wants ter get divorced. P'r'aps she wants ter marry George Tapley.'

Billy snorted. 'Why should that make 'er cry? Gettin' divorced is nufing ter make yer cry over.'

'Look, if yer wanna divorce yer gotta get permission,' Arthur said knowledgably, rolling a dart between his thumb and forefinger and taking aim at a buzzing bluebottle. 'Yer can't jus' get one. P'r'aps Dad won't let 'er get divorced.'

'What's divorced mean?' piped Jenny.

Sara handed her younger sister the rag doll she had just dressed. 'You're too young ter understand,' she said. 'Wait till yer seven.'

'Well, I don't mind if Muvver marries George Tapley,' announced Billy.

''E's all right,' said Frankie. 'At least 'e don't moan when we play ball outside 'is door.'

'I like Mr Tapley,' Jenny said, poking her finger in the doll's eye. ''E pulls funny faces an' makes me laugh.'

Arthur missed the bluebottle and the dart stuck in the door. 'I reckon we should find out about what 'appened to 'im,' he said, looking at Frankie.

'Yeah, let's,' Frankie answered, his eyes opening wide. 'We'll 'ave ter do some detective work. 'E might be in a gang or somefing.'

'Us too,' Sara shouted. 'We wanna 'elp.'

Arthur yanked the dart out of the door. 'Detective work ain't no good fer gels,' he said.

'It's dangerous. Besides, you're both much too young. Me an' Frankie's gonna do it.'

'What about me?' piped in Billy. 'I'm not too young. Besides, I was the one who 'eard Mum tellin' Sally about Dad.'

Arthur stroked his chin the way he had seen George Tapley do it. 'Yeah, all right then. We'll 'ave ter start by findin' out a few fings.'

'What fings?' Frankie asked, wiping a blob of Cherry Blossom Boot Polish from the sole of his shoe.

Arthur signalled his brothers to follow him. They walked out into the backyard and Arthur sat down on the only available chair. 'Right, Billy, this is what yer gotta do,' he began.

When Ginny got back from chatting to George she looked at Sara. 'Where's the boys gone?' she asked. 'I told 'em they couldn't go out till I got back.'

'It's all right Mum, they're in the backyard,' Sara told her.

'What they doin' out there?'

'Detectifin' I fink,' Sara answered, grinning at Jenny.

Ginny raised her eyes to the ceiling. 'I bet that Frankie ain't done 'is shoes yet. Right, you two, out yer go. It's a nice day, but don't leave the square, understand?'

A few minutes later Billy walked into the room and sat down in a chair.

Ginny looked at him curiously. 'Why ain't yer outside playin'?' she asked him. 'I don't want yer sittin' round me all mornin'. I've got work ter do.'

382

Billy sat back in the chair and picked at the loose sole of his shoe. "'Ere, Mum, I 'eard yer talkin' ter Sally Brady the ovver day,' he said. 'Are yer gonna marry George Tapley?'

Ginny was about to give her son the sharp edge of her tongue but she checked herself. He had the right to know, she thought. They all did. George was a lovely man and he would give them the love their own father had denied them.

She sat down opposite Billy and leaned forward. 'Look, yer was too young ter remember yer Dad,' she said quietly. "'E left when Jenny was a baby. I've not seen 'im since, an' 'e's not troubled 'imself ter find out 'ow you kids are gettin' on. Mr Tapley an' me are good friends. 'E finks the world o' you kids an' 'e's bin good ter me when the money was short. 'E'll make yer all a very good farver. Trouble is, I can't marry 'im, Billy. Not yet, anyway.'

Billy nodded. 'Yer gotta get divorced first, ain't yer, Mum?'

She smiled at him and ruffled his hair. 'You're growin' up fast, Billy. Yeah, that's right. I gotta contact yer farver. I gotta find out where 'e is an' tell 'im I wanna get a divorce.'

'Will 'e say all right, Mum?'

'I fink 'e will now. Trouble is I don't know where 'e is.'

Billy sat up straight in the chair. 'Ain't yer got any idea where 'e could be?'

Ginny shook her head and looked at her son for a few moments before going on. 'Look, Billy, yer farver met a lady an' they got married. What 'e's done is breakin' the law an' it's called bigamy. 'E can go ter prison fer bigamy. This lady came ter see me from Poplar. She's got a grocery shop in the market there. That's where yer farver was livin'. 'E might still be somewhere in Poplar, I just don't know.'

'Is Poplar miles away, Mum?' Billy asked, feeling that Arthur and Frankie would be very pleased with his detective work.

'It's over the water, in the East End,' Ginny replied.

Billy got up and walked to the door. 'Well, I 'ope yer find 'im, Mum. We all like Mr Tapley,' he said, walking out of the room with a satisfied look on his young face.

The Railway Inn was busy as usual on that fine Sunday lunchtime. The square's two elderly citizens were sitting in the snug bar sipping Guinness and attempting to discuss the latest snippets of news, but Daisy was finding it difficult to make herself heard and she pointed to Lil's ear.

'Why don't yer go an' see ole Doctor Bartholomew?' she suggested. 'Get 'im ter syringe yer ears out. 'E did mine a treat.'

Lil shook her head vigorously. 'I don't 'old in wiv them there syringes. Ole Mrs Carmody got 'er ear'oles done an' it wasn't long after that when they took 'er away. She went right orf 'er 'ead. Terrible turn out it was. She tried ter chuck 'erself under a tram an' if it 'adn't bin fer ole Albert on the veg stall she woulda done it. 'E grabbed 'er just in time.'

Daisy nodded. 'I remember that. It wasn't

384

nufing ter do wiv 'avin' 'er ears syringed, though. She 'ad water on the brain. Swelled up it did. They reckon it was ter do wiv 'er ole man runnin' orf wiv that flighty piece who worked in the butcher's.'

Lil was watching Daisy's lips closely. 'Butcher's? Yer don't mean that German butcher's in Dock'ead, do yer? What was 'is name? Kellermann's, wasn't it?'

'Yeah, that's right,' Daisy said, sliding her hands up the sleeves of her coat and rocking backwards and forwards in her chair. 'D'yer remember when we used ter go ter Kellermann's on Friday evenin's fer them saveloys an' pease-pudden? And what about that tripe an' onions?'

Lil nodded and stared at her Guinness. 'I used ter like those 'alf a sheep's 'eads. Shame 'e got bombed, wasn't it? There ain't a butcher's round 'ere wot does that sort o' stuff any more.'

Daisy took her hand from the sleeve of her coat and patted at her tightly pinned-up hair. 'I 'ad some skate's eyeballs last night, Lil,' she said, a look of relish in her eyes. 'Our Ginny brought 'em from the market. Smashin', they was. I cooked 'em nice an' steady an' sprinkled 'em wiv a drop o' vinegar an' pepper. Went down a treat, they did. She's a good girl, is Ginny. She knows I like skate's eyeballs.'

Lil leaned forward in her chair. ''Ere, talkin' of eyeballs, did yer see them two from the end o' the square clockin' ole Mrs Cox when she was takin' that there corned beef round? Nosy ole cows was whisperin' tergevver. I see 'em from me front-room winder.'

385

Daisy pulled a face. 'That Maudie Cox wants ter be careful. Yer get put away fer floggin' that black-market stuff.'

Bert Jackson was polishing glasses on a grimy-looking cloth and he turned to Elsie. 'Can yer 'ear them two?' he asked with an exasperated laugh. 'They go from the sublime ter the Gor blimey. Water on the brain, skate's eyeballs, an' now they're on about black-market corned beef. I should fink 'alf the pub knows about Mrs Cox by now. I dunno what ter make of 'em. They're gettin' worse as they get older.'

Elsie grinned. 'Trouble is, Daisy's gotta shout. That Lil's as deaf as a post.'

Bert had noticed Alf Porter walk in the public bar and he nudged Elsie. ''Old tight, 'ere comes trouble.'

Alf walked to the counter and puffed hard as he put one elbow on the polished surface. 'Gissa pint o' bitter, Bert, an' while you're at it 'ave one yerself,' he said.

Bert declined the offer with a smile. 'I was beginnin' ter wonder where yer'd got ter. Yer ole mates 'ave bin 'ere since we opened.'

Alf looked over and saw Charlie sitting with Frank and Ted. They had not spotted him and he turned his back on the trio. Alf was still smarting over the trick they had played on him and he had no wish to get into their company.

'I 'ad a late 'un last night,' he said, pulling a face as he sipped the froth from his drink.

Bert breathed on a glass and gave it a quick polish. 'Well, yer timed it right, Alf,' he laughed. '*They've* bin in 'ere again this mornin',

386

rattlin' the collection boxes an' sellin' the *War Cry*. I fink they upset yer pals.'

'What yer talkin' about, the Salvation Army?' Alf asked, sipping his drink. 'Was them mates o' mine too tight ter put a few coppers in the box? I fink the Sally Army does a good job, what wiv 'elpin' the bombed-out people an' everyfing.'

'No, it wasn't that. They put in the box all right, but there was a bloke goin' round' wiv the woman collector. 'E was doin' recruitin'. Charlie got a bit shirty when this bloke asked 'im if 'e wanted ter join. 'Is two mates wasn't too 'appy neivver. Ted as good as told 'im ter piss orf.'

Alf leaned on the counter and rested his chin on a cupped hand. 'Well, I'd always buy the *War Cry* an' put a couple o' bob in the tin. I dunno what them three got all narky about.'

Bert shrugged his shoulders. 'You know Charlie. This bloke was tryin' ter tell 'im that 'e'd be a soldier o' Christ an' some o' the customers started sniggerin'. Charlie 'ad ter get rid of 'im quick.'

'What did 'e say ter the bloke, Bert?'

'Charlie told 'im ter clear orf round the saloon bar. 'E told 'im there was a few call-up dodgers roun' there. Matter o' fact the bloke's still in there. I wonder 'ow many 'e's signed up.'

'Not many, I should fink,' Alf grinned, a thoughtful look appearing on his thin face.

'Well, yer ain't lost yer chance ter put in the tin,' Bert said, moving away to serve a customer.

Alf glanced over to where his friends were sitting; they were talking and laughing together, unaware that he was eyeing them. Alf quietly slipped out through a door that led into the saloon bar. A few people nodded to him and the blonde barmaid gave him a funny glance. Alf saw the uniformed figures talking to a group at the end of the bar. He whistled to himself as he sidled up, a florin held in his hand.

'There you are, my dear,' he said, thrusting the coin into the box with a gesture of conviction.

The Salvationist gave him a sweet smile and handed him a copy of the *War Cry*. 'God bless you,' she said, rattling the box.

'Yer do a good job,' Alf said in a loud voice, looking at her companion.

The tall, distinguished-looking man turned to him. 'As a matter of fact I'm looking for new soldiers,' he said in a friendly voice. 'Have you thought about joining us? I'm sure you wouldn't regret it.'

'No I don't s'pose I would,' Alf said, scratching his head. 'Trouble is, I've got somewhere ter go now an' I'm late already.'

'That's quite all right,' the man replied. 'We don't want you to make yer mind up right away. If you'd care to give me your name and address we can come along to see you one evening and explain a little more about the Salvation Army and the work we do.'

Alf put on a show of indecision by stroking his jaw, then he nodded. 'OK, yeah. It sounds like a werfwhile idea.'

'Jolly good!' the recruiting officer said happily. 'And could I have your name, please?'

'Charlie Robinson,' Alf replied. 'An' I live at

number 4 Paragon Place.'

The Salvationist scribbled into a note pad, not noticing the ghost of a smile on Alf's lined features.

'By the way, mister. 'Ow about me two friends?' Alf added.

'Your two friends?'

'Yeah. Yer see, we've bin mates fer years. We always do fings tergevver. I reckon they'd like ter join. In fact I'm sure they would. Shall I give yer their addresses?'

The tall man smiled broadly as he wrote some more notes on his pad. It was proving to be a very good Sunday morning, he thought. 'Right, now what evening and what time would be convenient?' he asked.

Alf thought for a few moments. 'I reckon Monday, about eight o'clock, if that's all right wiv you?'

The man nodded. 'That will suit us fine. Until then, Mr Robinson,' he said, holding out his hand.

Alf slipped quietly back into the public bar and bought himself another drink. It was not long before Charlie walked up to the counter with empty glasses clutched in his large hand.

''Ello, Alf. I didn't know yer was in 'ere,' he said, his eyes already glassy from the amount of beer he had drunk.

'I've just this minute walked in,' Alf replied.

Back in Paragon Place the smell of cooking and sounds of music from blaring wirelesses drifted out through open windows. Children's happy

389

voices filled the square and folk stepped over their whitened doorsteps to pass the time of day and chat with their neighbours. Ada and Clara stood together discussing the war, the rationing, and the retail price of corned beef. At number 1 the Carey sisters dusted and polished their tidy room and listened to the wireless, while in the flat below Muriel hummed happily to herself as she stood in the backyard and fed freshly boiled bedsheets through a rusting wringer. She had reason to feel pleased with herself. She had been wined and dined by a tall, broad and handsome American soldier who had brought her home by taxi and been content with a simple goodnight kiss. The square's siren had put on her respectable face that evening and acted the innocent. Her soldier was eager to see her again and Muriel was determined not to spoil what she thought could be the start of a beautiful friendship.

At the far end of the square Joey was propped up in his pram beneath the shade of the sycamore, chuckling at the antics of Danny Fuller who was stalking a cat with a peashooter. At Ginny's front door three young lads sat huddled in conference, discussing their plans to invade Poplar. And across the square at number 8 Arthur Cox sat on an upturned crate in the backyard polishing his work shoes, a look of dejection on his large features. Maudie had been optimistic and pressed his blue serge suit ready for another week, but her dutiful husband had serious doubts about wearing it for much longer. He saw himself pushing a broom through the backstreets with folk shaking their heads sadly and passing whispered remarks about how Arthur Cox had come down in the world. Overhead a warm sun shone down from a cloudless sky as the menfolk returned for their Sunday meal. Last of all the drinkers came Alf Porter, staggering into the square whistling tunelessly to himself, a look of wry satisfaction on his gaunt face.

Chapter Nineteen

SALLY BRADY left the square before eleven o'clock on Sunday morning and walked the short distance to the church gardens. The sun was already high in a clear sky and there was just a hint of a breeze. She had left behind a moody Lora, who was unhappy at having to prepare the Sunday meal. Annie had been up and about since midweek, but she made it clear to everyone that she was far from well. Charlie had puffed on his pipe without much comment and was obviously looking forward to opening time at the Railway Inn. Sally had slipped out of the house glad to be away from the strained atmosphere and eager to see Jim again. She had lain awake for hours thinking about their evening together and of her growing feelings towards him. She felt a little guilty at suggesting they might go to Farnborough for the day and she hoped Jim would not get the idea she was being bold with him. She recalled the strong sexual feelings she had experienced when he kissed her and cuddled her close and she had been aware of the struggle within him as he held her in his arms; he had not taken advantage of her feelings towards him. She liked him for that.

Thoughts about the day ahead tumbled around in Sally's mind. She remembered Farnborough and the surrounding area of the Kentish countryside very well from pre-war days. It was quiet and peaceful, and there were many secluded spots and open paths. She could be alone with Jim and maybe get him to talk a little more about himself. As she turned into the church gardens she saw him walking towards her. He had forsaken his uniform and wore instead grey trousers and a white open-necked shirt with the sleeves folded back from the wrists. Sally thought it made him look younger and she smiled into his eyes as he reached her and took her by the shoulders.

His kiss was soft and brief. 'You look very nice,' he said, glancing at the pretty cotton dress which suited her colouring and at the neat dark hair which reached down to her shoulders.

'Thank you, kind sir,' she laughed. 'Yer look very smart yerself.'

They walked out into Jamaica Road and within a short while they caught a number 47 bus. The journey was leisurely, and from their back seat on the upper deck they watched as the houses and factories gradually gave way to a more spacious suburbia. Soon after the bus climbed Bromley Hill they saw the first open fields and the beginning of the rolling country-side, a patchwork of greens and yellows undulating into the distance, and it was not long before the bus reached Farnborough and pulled into the gravel forecourt of the George public house.

They sat at a wooden table in a shady corner of the pub garden, eating thick cheese sandwiches and sipping their beer, both feeling relaxed and contented in the rural atmosphere. Jim refilled their glasses and for a while they were happy to sit chatting and laughing together, breathing in the scent of red and yellow roses in the garden border near them. The next buses to arrive brought more customers, and as the pub began to fill up Jim and Sally finished their drinks and strolled off slowly down the quiet country lane that led towards the open fields.

After a while they came upon a small, grey stone church with a square tower and ivy-covered walls, and they walked through the overgrown churchyard past the lichen-stained gravestones and the more recent marble memorial pots. At the end of the churchyard they came to a stile and Jim climbed over first, holding out his arms for Sally to jump down. For a moment as he caught her they remained together unmoving, their bodies touching, their eyes fixed on each other as secret, unspoken thoughts seemed to pass between them.

Jim slipped his arm around her waist and they followed a narrow path which ran alongside a cornfield. The pale yellow stalks waved slightly in the gentle breeze and a hot sun beat down on their heads.

Jim undid another button on his shirt and ran his hand around his neck. 'Phew, it's hot,' he said, pulling off a corn-stalk and chewing on it.

Sally felt the warmth of his arm around her waist and the palm of his hand on her side. She leaned into him as they sauntered along to the end of the field. Paths led off left and right beside fields of high corn and Jim looked at her.

'Well? Which way shall we go?' he asked.

'That way,' she said, pointing to the sloping path on her right.

They walked downhill in the hot sunshine and before long they saw a ragged-looking barn ahead of them. Parts of the roof were missing and the rotting timbers hung down in criss-cross fashion. They looked inside and saw a spread of hay and smelt the sweet, animal smell of a stable.

Sally pointed to a rusted horseshoe that was nailed over the entrance and as Jim reached up to touch it she suddenly tickled his ribs. He laughed and made to catch her but she dodged his grasp, moving just out of his reach. He stood for a moment, his eyes widening, then he pounced and grabbed her around the waist. She felt herself being lifted and dumped unceremoniously into the pile of sweet-smelling hay. They giggled like children as she twisted beneath him, and then suddenly all pretence at play was forsaken as they found each other's lips in a passionate kiss. Sally gasped at his breathless passion and responded eagerly. His strong hands were stroking her body, moving urgently yet gently over her round breasts and her smooth thighs. She sighed deeply and closed her eyes as his hands moved across her dress and slowly undid the buttons. His head came down and she ran her fingers through his thick curly hair and pressed him to her as she felt his lips move softly over her breasts. Suddenly they froze. A loud raucous sound carried into the barn. Jim rolled over in time for Sally to see a large bird rise up noisily into the clear sky from just outside the barn.

He blew hard and laughed with relief. 'It's all right, it's only a crow.'

They sat facing each other in the hay, feeling a little awkward and irritated that their loving had been suddenly interrupted. Sally looked into his eyes and felt the unfulfilled desire pulsing within her. She stood up and, holding the front of her dress together, glanced out of the ruined barn. Sweeping fields of corn stretched in every direction and she could see that they were completely alone. Sally turned and looked down at him. A faint smile played on her lips as she slowly and deliberately undid the rest of the buttons and stepped out of her dress as it fell to her feet. Jim gasped. Her hands went around her back and unhooked her bra strap. She let the bra fall to the floor and his eyes widened as he gazed at her small round breasts and hard pink nipples. She slipped her panties down her thighs and straightened up, standing proudly before him. His eyes travelled slowly down her naked body and then he reached out his hands to her. She sank down beside him and reached for him, helping him off with his shirt and fumbling at his belt-buckle with shaking hands. Very soon he was naked with her, holding her to him in a close embrace, caressing her soft skin. She moaned with pleasure and her fingernails dug into his shoulders as they met together at last in pleasure.

They dressed quickly, a little alarmed at their own daring, and for a while they lay close together in the hay. Sally's head rested on Jim's chest and she could feel his fingers gently running along her spine. She heard his now even breathing and the steady beat of his heart and she closed her eyes, a delicious feeling of utter contentment flowing over her body. They did not speak for a time as they held each other, dwelling in their thoughts on the joy of their passionate lovemaking. Finally she moved, raising herself on one elbow and gazing into his pale blue eyes.

'D'yer love me, Jim?' she asked, quickly stifling his answer by placing her fingers over his lips. 'I'm sorry, I shouldn't 'ave asked.'

He took her hand away and pulled her head down until their lips were almost touching. 'Yer was right to ask, Sally,' he whispered. 'I do love yer. I fink I've loved yer from the start. D'yer believe in love at first sight?'

In answer she touched her lips to his.

They walked back through the yellow corn, his arm around her waist and his fingers gently pressing into her side. They were silent until they reached the stile, then Jim leaned on the gate and turned towards her. Sally smiled and slipped into his arms.

'I won't forget terday, Jim,' she said. 'It was special.'

His face had become serious and he looked into her dark eyes. 'I wanna tell yer somefing, Sally,' he began. 'I didn't plan ter fall in love again. I didn't fink I could, but it's 'appened. I didn't want ter go overseas wiv the knowledge that there was somebody waitin' fer me back 'ome.'

'But why?' she said, staring into his troubled eyes.

'It's difficult to explain,' he answered, averting his gaze. 'I can remember the terrible feelin' when I come 'ome an' found everyfing that was dear ter me 'ad gone fer ever. I don't want yer ter know that feelin' if I don't come back.'

Sally felt tears rising in her eyes and she moved closer to him. 'Now listen, Jim,' she said in a low voice. 'I never expected ter meet somebody like you. Fings just 'appen. Nobody can turn round an' say it won't 'appen, or it will 'appen. Fings don't work that way. We've met, an' we fell in love. I don't know what's gonna 'appen in the future, nor do you. One fing I do know, an' that is yer can't go around organisin' ovver people's feelin's. When yer do go away ter fight you'd better realise that there is somebody who's very much concerned about yer, an' who'll be prayin' fer yer ter come back in one piece, so there.'

Jim squeezed her hands and planted a soft kiss

on her lips. 'You've turned me upside down an' inside out, d'yer realise that?'

She laughed. 'You've got me all confused, too, d'yer realise that?'

They climbed the stile and walked on along the narrow path that led back to the churchyard. The sun had dipped down and it was cooler now. A few evening strollers passed them as the lovers made their way along the country lane to the pub forecourt. The bus was waiting, almost full up with passengers already, and as soon as they climbed aboard the conductor rang the bell. The double-decker drew slowly out on to the road and started its journey back to Bermondsey. The upper deck was filled with couples wearing their Sunday best and tired children holding on to fishing nets and jam-jars full of tiddlers and other tiny swimming creatures. Sally yawned and leant against Jim.

'It's bin a lovely afternoon,' she whispered into his ear. 'Did yer really enjoy it?'

'I'll never forget it,' he smiled. ''Ow could I?'

Sally felt her face redden slightly, hoping his whispered words had not been overheard by the other passengers. She closed her eyes, snuggling up to his warm body and letting her thoughts roam free. She had surprised herself by the way she had seduced him in the barn. He had been a wonderful lover, and a warm, glowing feeling of fulfilment still lingered deep down inside her. It had been a long time since she had experienced a man's love and she sighed deeply. She wanted to stay with Jim forever. It was a futile wish, she knew. Soon he would be leaving her to go to war, and even if they were fortunate they would only have a few days together before he sailed.

When the bus arrived back in Bermondsey they alighted and strolled along a cobbled lane that led down to the river. On either side warehouses and wharves loomed above them and the smell of spice hung on the summer air. Directly ahead there was a gap between the riverside wharves, and a flight of old stone steps led down to the foreshore. The tide was out and they could see barges lying in the mud and freighters at anchor further away. To their left Tower Bridge rose high above the water and on their right the river turned and became hidden behind the shabby wharves on the east shore. The sky was changing, and shades of red and gold tinged the vast expanse of deepening blue. Gulls wheeled and dived, squealing loudly at the pigeons that strutted along the barges and fed from the split cornhusks and seed.

Sally looked away down the sweep of the river, a faraway look in her dark eyes. 'When yer get embarkation leave let's go somewhere, Jim,' she said suddenly.

His arm tightened around her waist as they stood at the top of the steps. 'Yeah, that'd be really nice,' he said, looking at her. ''Ave yer got anywhere in mind?'

She shook her head. 'I don't mind. Anywhere, as long as we can be tergevver. I jus' wanna be wiv yer.'

He leaned his head down and rested his cheek on her dark hair. 'We've still got an hour. Let's find a nice quiet pub.'

They retraced their steps and followed the course of the river, passing the grim wharves until they came upon a little pub at the end of a cobbled street which led back down to the water. They went into the saloon bar and found a secluded spot beneath large oaken beams and flaking plaster. It was cool in the dark interior as they sat together, drinks at their elbow, glancing into each other's eyes and touching hands across the table. Around them the few customers who leaned on the bar or sat at iron tables were wrapped up in their own thoughts and ignored the lovers smiling at each other and linking fingers in the corner. Sally was silent, her eyes appraising Jim as he glanced around at the pictures of sailing ships hanging from the discoloured plaster walls. His square face had the look of an enquiring child and his blue eyes seemed to dart here and there, as though he wanted to take everything in and remember it. She noticed how his short fair hair had become dishevelled and thought that it added to his boyishness.

She smiled at him as his eyes met hers. 'Do we 'ave ter go?' she said, sadly aware of the time and wishing that the day would last for ever.

Jim nodded. 'Yeah, I fink we'd better.'

They walked the short distance to the quiet Jamaica Road and turned off into the backstreets. Soon they reached the old church and walked slowly along the gravel path to their secluded bench beneath the hanging vines. He took her to him, his lips seeking hers as he held her tightly in his arms.

'Don't be away too long,' she whispered as their lips parted. 'I love yer terrible, Jim.'

He nuzzled her ear and kissed her neck and her chin, then his lips found hers again in a long, lingering kiss. He eased back at last from the close embrace and looked down closely at her.

'I love yer, Sally,' he said, gazing down into her dark eyes. 'I love yer very much.'

They strolled slowly to the far gate and he took her by the shoulders and kissed her softly.

'I'll see yer soon, Sally,' he said, and with a last lingering look he turned and set off along the street.

As she watched after him her thoughts were racing and a feeling of exhilaration still lingered in her belly. It had been a wonderful day. She had given herself to him and they had pledged their love. Soon he would be sent overseas and she might never see him again. Sally realised with a terrible sinking feeling that their next brief meeting might be their last, and she vowed to make it one they would both remember.

Chapter Twenty

ON Monday evening Annie Robinson answered a knock on the door and was surprised to see two elderly Salvation Army workers standing on the step. The man carried a clipboard and the woman had a batch of papers in her arms.

'We've called to see Mr Robinson,' the man said, smiling.

'I'm sorry, 'e's 'avin' a doze,' Annie replied, eyeing the couple suspiciously.

The man looked disappointed. 'Oh dear. Mr Robinson did say to call round tonight.'

''E did?' Annie queried. 'Why should 'e do that?'

'Well, as a matter of fact Mr Robinson did indicate that he was thinking of joining us,' the man said, glancing down at the clipboard in his hand. 'We've been asked to call on Mr Robinson, Mr Mynott and Mr Bromley. We're seeing them all tonight. We're going to explain a little more about our movement and what it means to become a soldier of Christ.'

A look of disbelief had been growing steadily on Annie's face. 'Well, I s'pose I'd better wake 'im then,' she said, 'although I'd better warn yer, my Charlie's not very 'appy when 'e's woke up out of a doze.'

She hurried in and shook Charlie roughly by the shoulder. 'Wake up, Charlie, there's a couple o' people ter see yer from the Sally Army.'

Charlie rubbed a hand over his face, his bleary eyes staring up at Annie. 'What yer say?' he growled, yawning widely.

Annie jerked her thumb in the direction of the front door. 'Don't leave 'em standin' there. Go out an' see 'em,' she said urgently.

'See who?' Charlie asked, still trying to pull himself together.

Annie gave her husband a blinding look and

walked back to the front door. ''E won't be a minute,' she said. ''E's 'ad a few ternight an' 'e's tryin' ter wake 'imself up.'

The Salvationists looked at each other, frowning at what they had heard, and then they saw Charlie. He came to the door yawning, with his shirt half out of his trousers.

'What d'yer want?' he growled.

'Good evening, Mr Robinson. I'm Major Tweedy,' the Salvationist began in a zestful manner. 'I understand you told my colleague Major Winston that you were thinking of joining the Salvation Army. We've called round to give you a bit more information before you make up your mind. We like to give you plenty of time to consider. It is a big step, Mr Robinson.'

Charlie's eyes narrowed. 'Yer bet yer life it's a big step,' he growled. 'An' I can tell yer 'ere an' now, it ain't one I'm planning ter take.'

'You've reconsidered then, Mr Robinson?'

'I ain't reconsidered nufing,' Charlie said, his voice rising. 'Yer must 'ave made a mistake. I didn't tell Major what's-'is-name anyfing. Now, if yer don't mind, I'm gonna get back ter me kip.'

The major glanced at his partner, then back at Charlie. 'We've got two more names on our recruiting list,' he said frowning. 'A Mr Mynott and a Mr Bromley. Do you know them, Mr Robinson?'

Charlie laughed aloud. 'You've bin 'ad, pal. If yer get those two on yer books I'm a bloody Chinaman. They're friends o' mine, an' I can assure yer they ain't got no intention o' joinin' up neivver. If yer take my advice you'll give 'em a miss. Goodnight.'

Annie had gone back into the scullery, a puzzled frown on her face. 'I fink yer farver's goin' orf 'is 'ead,' she confided to Sally. ''E's only finkin' o' joinin' the Salvation Army. It's that booze. It's rottin' 'is brain, I'm sure it is.'

Sally laughed. 'It must be a mistake, Mum. Somebody's 'avin' a joke.'

When the front door slammed Annie walked back through to the front room just as Charlie was settling himself back down in the chair, his face scarlet with anger. She peered through the lace curtains and watched the couple walking away up the square.

'It's that Bert Jackson, that's who it is,' Charlie raved. ''E's playin' one of 'is tricks. If I find out fer sure 'e'll be sorry, I guarantee yer.'

'So yer changed yer mind, then?' Annie said, grinning.

'Don't you start,' Charlie growled.

Annie was enjoying the joke. 'I can jus' see yer walkin' roun' the streets wiv a bloody great drum strapped ter yer belly,' she smirked. 'What's yer two cronies gonna play, the cymbals an' the triangle?'

Charlie was about to vent his anger with a well-chosen obscenity but he checked himself. 'I can't 'ave a peaceful nap in this 'ouse,' he grumbled. 'I'm orf up the Railway.'

In the Almond household strange goings-on had caused Ginny to become more than a little curious. The boys had become very secretive,

404

and huddled conversations ended abruptly whenever Ginny or Daisy entered the room. At first Ginny had ignored their peculiar behaviour and put it down to some boyish prank being hatched, but it became more noticeable when the school holidays drew near. The girls, Jenny and Sara, seemed to have been left out of whatever scheming was going on and Ginny began to get anxious.

'They're up ter somefing, Daisy,' she confided to her mother-in-law as they sat together in the scullery. 'They ain't bin playin' up like they normally do. It ain't natural.'

'I wouldn't take any notice, luv. Yer know what boys are,' Daisy replied, glancing through her horoscope in the *Daily Mirror*.

Ginny spat on the hot iron and rubbed it on the coconut matting. 'I've 'ad a word wiv the girls but they don't seem ter know what's goin' on.'

Daisy laughed. 'Yer don't expect young Jenny ter know anyfing, do yer? She's only a mite.'

'Well, I s'pose not, but I thought Sara might know somefing,' Ginny replied, pressing the hot iron on Arthur's school shirt. 'It's puzzlin' me what they've got planned. I 'ope it ain't nufing bad, I don't want the coppers knockin' at my door again. It was bad enough when they come callin' about Frankie.'

Daisy pulled a face. The very mention of her wayward son always gave her a bad feeling. She had never forgiven him for leaving Ginny to fend for their children. It wouldn't have been so bad if he had at least asked after them all, she thought. Now he had taken another woman and been stupid enough to marry her. He was facing a prison sentence, and it served him right.

Ginny had noticed her mother-in-law's miserable expression and she put down the iron. 'I'm sorry ter go on about 'im, Daisy,' she said kindly. 'I know 'ow it upsets yer, but I fink we're gonna 'ear 'is name mentioned a lot more now the police are lookin' fer 'im.'

The Almond boys did nothing to allay any of Ginny's fears by their continued secrecy, and when Billy came home from school and announced that he had got a Saturday job helping out on Sullivan's vegetable stall at the market Ginny became more anxious.

'You'd better be careful, Billy,' she said in a worried voice. 'I don't mind yer doin' a Saturday job but I don't like the idea of yer workin' in that market. It's 'eavy work 'umpin' those sacks o' spuds about, an' those trams come right near the stalls. Yer could get knocked down.'

'Don't worry, Mum,' Billy replied cheerfully. 'I'll be careful. Besides, ole Sullivan's OK, an' I need the money.'

'We all need money, Billy. What d'yer need it for?'

The young lad became evasive. 'Oh, nufing,' he said. 'Jus' fings.'

Billy's reluctance to explain why he needed the money left Ginny even more vexed. She remembered Sara telling her that Arthur had sold his cricket bat and cigarette cards to Derek Cox, and she had also recently caught Frankie sliding pennies from his money-box with the aid of a kitchen knife. His excuse had been that he only wanted to count them, but Ginny found that a little hard to believe.

The day before the school term ended Ginny felt that she had to confide in George.

'D'yer know what I fink, George?' she said. 'Those boys o' mine are gonna leave 'ome.'

George laughed and put his arm around her waist. 'Don't talk so silly. They're 'appy enough. P'r'aps they jus' wanna get a few bob saved up fer the 'olidays.'

Ginny shook her head. 'If that was the case they'd jus' tell me. No, it's somefing else. They're so secretive. I caught young Frankie goin' down 'is money-box. 'E's never done that before. 'E saves that money religiously fer Christmas. Talkin' o' which, d'yer remember that cricket bat yer bought Arfur last Christmas? Well, 'e's sold it ter the Cox boy. 'E never said anyfing about it ter me. It was Sara what told me.'

'Did yer ask 'im about it?' George asked, stroking his chin.

'No I never,' Ginny replied.

'Well, maybe yer should 'ave it out wiv 'em. Tell 'em jus' 'ow yer feel about what's goin' on. They're good lads, I'm sure they'll tell yer if yer press 'em.'

Ginny nodded. 'All right, George, I'll give it a try.'

On Friday afternoon the lads came home from school in a happy mood now that term was over and Ginny took the opportunity to confront them.

'Right, you three. Get in the front room, I want words wiv yer,' she said, putting on her serious face.

The boys glanced at each other and followed their mother into the parlour.

'Now look. I wanna know what's goin' on,' she said, looking from one to the other.

'What d'yer mean, Mum? Nufing's goin' on,' Frankie replied, looking suitably innocent.

Ginny sighed and folded her arms. 'What's all this money lark?'

'What d'yer mean, Mum?' Billy asked.

'I'll tell yer what I mean,' she said. 'You've bin workin' on that stall fer the past two weeks, Billy, an' as far as I know yer ain't spent any of yer wages. I know where yer got it stashed, 'cos I come across it when I was cleanin' yer room out. Yer got it wrapped up in an 'ankie and stuffed in yer best shoes, right?'

Billy looked downcast and Ginny glared at him. 'It's all right, I wasn't searchin' the room. I just moved yer shoes when I was dustin' an' I 'eard the money rattle. Now you, Frankie,' she went on, glaring at him in turn. 'I saw yer goin' down yer money-box. You've never done that before. Least I've never seen yer. Why are yer so interested in 'ow much yer got saved up?'

Frankie shrugged his shoulders. 'I jus' wanted somefing ter do. I was bored.'

Ginny turned her attention to Arthur. 'An' you. I 'appen ter know yer sold yer cricket bat and yer cigarette cards ter that Derek Cox.'

Arthur grimaced. 'I bin chucked out o' the school's cricket team fer swearin' an' I don't

408

need it any more. We can't play cricket in the square, Mum, we'd smash the winders.'

'What about yer cigarette cards? What d'yer sell them for? I've seen yer sortin' frew 'em lots o' times. You'd never let the girls touch those cards, an' now yer gone an' sold 'em.'

'I let Jenny look at 'em when she was in bed wiv a sore froat an' she got jam all over 'em. That's why I sold 'em,' Arthur replied, a pained expression on his face.

Ginny's eyes narrowed. 'Right, I've listened ter yer feeble excuses. Now I wanna know what's really goin' on. OK?'

The boys fidgeted and looked from one to the other. Arthur leaned back in his chair and scratched at his chest through the hole in his jumper. 'There's nufing secret, Mum,' he began, glancing quickly at Frankie. 'We jus' wanted ter save up our money fer the school 'olidays. We didn't wanna keep askin' fer money fer sweets an' pictures an' fings. We know yer gonna get married ter George an' we know yer gotta save up fer clothes an' fings so we decided ter get our own money, didn't we?' he concluded, looking at his brothers for support.

Frankie and Billy nodded their heads vigorously, relieved that their leader had got them off the hook.

Ginny sighed and slumped down in the chair, a warm smile on her ruddy face. 'Well, that's a very nice thought an' I appreciate it,' she said. 'I was beginnin' ter fink yer might not like the idea o' me an' George Tapley gettin' married so yer decided ter leave 'ome or somefing.'

Arthur grinned, happy with his performance. 'We like George. We don't mind yer marryin' 'im, Mum, long as you're 'appy.'

Ginny felt the lump rising in her throat and she got up quickly, brushing an imaginary crumb from the tablecloth. 'Well, I'd better get on wiv yer tea,' she said, looking away. 'Don't go wanderin' off, it won't be long.'

Since Jim's leave had ended Sally had been visiting Ben twice each week and she was surprised at his improvement. He seemed to be willing himself to get better. The surgeon said his pelvis had mended well and the bones of his shattered leg had knitted together favourably. At first Sally was happy to see him improving, but then she began to find the visits difficult. Ben chatted away almost incessantly, as though trying to keep her at his bedside for as long as possible, and she had baulked at telling him about Jim. He did not mention the divorce they had agreed upon, and he did not make any suggestions about them making a new start. It was as though he was waiting for her to make the first move. Sally felt guilty as though she were betraying Ben in some way, although she knew she should not be harbouring such feelings any more. She had decided how she was going to lead her own life independently now. She told herself that her visits were nothing more than natural concern, but in moments of doubt she felt deep down inside that she was in danger of becoming involved with Ben again.

Sally began to feel more and more

apprehensive about each visit and she considered telling Ben that it would be better for them both if she stopped seeing him. As much as she thought about it and tried to convince herself that it would be the most honest thing to do, she knew she could not bring herself to do it. If her visiting him had anything to do with his determination to get well quickly then it would be worth it, she decided. There would be time enough to tell him when he was stronger.

Nevertheless, Sally could not help being troubled by the thought of Jim's impending leave. She was hoping they would be able to go away for the whole week and then Ben would have to be told about him. The prospect gave her sleepless nights and she cursed herself for not being able to face up to the inevitable. Ben was going to find out about Jim some time, and the longer she delayed telling him the worse it would be.

Sally received two letters from Jim within a few weeks but he did not mention anything about his expected leave. During the middle of July the news came over the wireless that the allied armies had invaded Sicily and she became anxious. Vera was quick to reassure her friend that she would be able to see Jim before he went to war.

'They don't send 'em straight overseas wivout givin' 'em embarkation leave, Sally,' she told her. 'That's what me dad an' Joe both said.'

Sally sighed as she helped Vera at the wringer. 'I don't fink it'll be long now before Jim goes,' she said. 'I'm scared.'

Vera turned the creaking wringer handle. 'I know 'ow yer feel. I feel like that every time Joe goes back ter sea.'

Sally caught the mangled bedsheet and put it in the galvanised bath-tub. "As Joe 'eard anyfing more about goin' back, Vera?' she asked.

Vera wiped her hand across her forehead. "E's goin' fer anuvver medical next week,' she replied. 'If 'e passes 'e'll be off wivin a couple 'o days. I've bin on to 'im ter get a shore job, but it's no good. Joe's got really moody this last few weeks. It didn't 'elp when I told 'im I was over-due again.'

Sally looked at her friend curiously. 'Yer might jus' be late,' she said. 'It could be the worry o' Joe an' everyfing.'

Vera shook her head. 'No, I've got that feelin'. It was the same last time. I could tell.'

The pile of mangled washing had built up in the tin bath and the two friends sat in the sunlit backyard drinking tea. Vera was being very inquisitive about Sally's relationship with Jim and she was a little annoyed at her friend's reluc-tance to go into details. She was determined to prise a little more information out of Sally.

'When yer know fer sure about Jim's leave are yer gonna go away wiv 'im, Sal?' she asked, a cheeky smile hovering at the corners of her mouth.

Sally shrugged her shoulders. 'I dunno, I expect so.'

Vera stared down into the tea-leaves. 'Well, I would if it was me. Yer can get a week off work, can't yer? If I was you I'd find a nice quiet place somewhere an' 'ave a sexy week.'

Sally smiled, defensively, feeling a little irritated. 'I might,' she said.

Vera laughed. 'I dunno what ter make of yer sometimes. Yer got a real tasty bloke an' no ties ter worry about. Go away an' 'ave some fun. Let 'im put a sparkle in yer eye. Don't let fings get in yer way, Sal.'

'There's nufing in me way, Vera,' Sally rejoined quickly.

Vera put down her cup and stretched. 'You're not lettin' Ben's accident make any difference, are yer?'

Sally stared down at her feet. Vera's question had taken her aback and she tried to hide her confused feelings. 'Ben's accident ain't made any difference at all,' she said. 'I'm not worried about 'im findin' out about me an' Jim. In fact I'm gonna tell 'im, soon as 'e's a bit better.'

Vera leaned back in her rickety chair and propped her feet up on an empty beer-crate, eyeing Sally in a quizzical fashion. 'D'yer know what, Sally?' she said.

'What?'

'I fink you're still carryin' a torch fer that no-good 'usband of yers.'

Sally sighed in resignation. 'You're a persistent cow, Vera,' she said, narrowing her eyes malevolently. 'All right. I'm in love wiv Jim. We 'ave made love an' I can't wait fer 'im ter get leave. Yes, we're gonna try an' get away fer a week an' yes, I'm lookin' forward to a sexy week. As far as Ben is concerned, I'm gonna carry on seein' 'im until 'e's prop'ly better, as a

413

friend. There's nufing mysterious about any of it whatsoever. Does that answer yer questions?'

Vera took her feet down from the crate and leaned forward, a smile breaking out on her face. 'Well, well. Who'd 'ave guessed? Our Sal's took 'erself a lover. Well, good fer you. I've bin tellin' yer fer ages ter do it, an' I'm really pleased. Yer ain't cut out ter be a crotchety ole maid.'

'Don't age me, Vera. I'm thirty, not sixty,' Sally laughed, relieved that they had cleared the air. 'D'yer know, I can't wait ter see Jim again,' she added with an excited grin. ''E's special. I feel all weak at the knees when 'e touches me.'

Vera nodded, surprised at the depth of feeling in her friend's voice. 'I know what yer mean. It's the way it is wiv Big Joe. 'E ain't the 'andsomest feller in the world, an' 'e certainly wasn't at the front o' the queue when brains was given out, but I tell yer, 'e certainly knows what button ter press where I'm concerned. I jus' can't say no when 'e gets 'old o' me,' she said, grinning as she touched her stomach. 'I 'ope this one's a girl. I've always wanted a pigeon pair before I was thirty.'

Sally shook her head in mock disgust. 'Vera, you're a terrible woman. I'm off ter get a letter wrote ter Jim. Take it easy, I'll see yer later.'

Vera laughed. 'Sally!'

'Yeah.'

'Don't ferget ter swalk the envelope. You know, sealed wiv a lovin' kiss.'

Monday morning dawned bright and the clear sky augured another hot day. In Paragon Place the children were out early, eager to make the most of their holidays. Clara Botley was standing at Ada Fuller's front door talking with her.

'I tell yer, Ada,' Clara said, shaking her head. 'I dread the 'olidays comin'. I'll be glad when they're over. My kids drive me up the pole when they're roun' me arse all day.'

Ada nodded. 'Yeah, mine's the same. They're in an' out all day long fer slices o' bread an' jam. They eat me out of 'ouse an' 'ome.'

Clara leaned forward and spoke behind the back of her hand. 'Did yer see 'er new bloke come out o' there last night?' she whispered, nodding her head in the direction of number 1.

'No.'

''E's a Yank. Nice-lookin' fella, too. Dead smart, 'e was. She was all over 'im.'

Ada slipped her hands into the arm-holes of her apron. 'Well, it certainly makes a change from the usual blokes she brings 'ome, I must say.'

Clara nudged her friend. ''Ere, look at the three musketeers. I bet they're up ter no good.'

Ada turned to see the Almond boys marching out of the square. Arthur was whistling tunelessly and Frankie strode along at his side, a brown paper parcel tucked under his arm. Billy was hurrying to keep up. 'Wait fer me,' he moaned.

Clara shook her head. 'Gawd 'elp somebody.'

Ada nodded. 'I tell yer, Clara, I'll be glad when the 'olidays are over.'

The Almond boys set off through the backstreets

and threaded their way to Dockhead. Arthur had worked out that they had to cross the river and make for the Aldgate bus station, and he said that they would have to walk that part of the journey to save the fare money. Frankie and Billy fell in with the plan and the three walked briskly into the narrow, cobbled Shad Thames, heading for the steps that would take them up on to Tower Bridge. Overhead, crane-jibs swung back and forth as cargoes were unloaded, and bales and cases were lowered down on to waiting lorries and horse-carts. Carmen cursed and shouted instructions to the dockers and the rivermen returned the colourful language with choice words of their own. Horses snorted into their nose-bags and stamped their heavily shod hooves on the greasy cobbles as the three lads hurried by. Normally it would have been a fascinating place for them to loiter but today there were more important things to do, and there was only time for a few passing glances as they made for the steps. The smell of hops and beer being brewed at the Courage factory lingered in the air as they hurried up on to the bridge. They could see the Tower of London up ahead on the left as they marched quickly across, stopping once or twice to gaze down at the murky water of the Thames as it flowed beneath them. At St Katherine's Dock ships lined the wharves, cranes dipped and swung in wide arcs and in midstream barges rode at anchor, and the lads tarried awhile at the end of the high bridge to watch the busy scene until Arthur hastened them all along on their important mission.

By the time they had passed the big tea ware-house and reached the high-walled Royal Mint Billy was feeling the effects of trying to keep up with his elder brothers, and he stopped as they passed beneath a railway arch.

'I'm not goin' any furver till yer slow down a bit, I'm gettin' tired,' he groaned.

Arthur puffed. 'All right. We'll soon be at the bus station anyway. Yer can 'ave a rest then.'

A few minutes later the three lads walked into the station forecourt and scanned the destination signs on the fronts of the buses.

'Cor! I've never bin on a trolley bus,' Billy said excitedly, looking up at the twin arms which reached from the top of a waiting bus to the overhead power-cables.

'I've bin on 'em fousands o' times,' Arthur announced, beckoning his brothers to follow his lead.

They joined the queue and climbed aboard a Poplar-bound trolley bus, taking their seats near the door.

'Can't we go up the front?' Billy asked.

Arthur pulled a face. 'Stay 'ere,' he growled. 'We might 'ave ter get off quick.'

The bus jerked away from the terminus and was soon speeding along Aldgate High Street, and in a short while it swung into the Commercial Road. Frankie and Billy were look-ing out of the window, but Arthur only had eyes for the conductor. He bit on his lip anxiously as the man climbed to the upper deck to collect the fares and glanced quickly out of the window. When the bus was approaching the second stop the conductor started down the stairs and Arthur nudged his two brothers. 'Quick! We're gettin' off 'ere.'

As the bus pulled up at the stop the conductor reached the lower deck. 'Oi! What about yer fares?' he called out.

'We got on the wrong bus,' Arthur shouted as the three jumped down and ran off up the road.

They reached the Poplar Market with the aid of three 'wrong' buses and the curses of three angry conductors still ringing in their ears, and Arthur decided they had earned some refreshment. He led the way into Carlson's Coffee Shop and stared at the proprietor over the high counter.

'Three mugs o' tea, please,' he said.

Sammy Carlson looked at the tousle-haired lad. ''Ave yer got any money?' he asked suspiciously.

Arthur pulled a handful of coins from his trouser pocket. 'Course I 'ave. 'Ow much is it?'

Sammy grabbed a large metal teapot. 'Tuppence a small un an' fourpence a large un. Small uns'll be big enough fer you lot.'

Arthur was feeling pretty confident after the free journey to Poplar. 'Give us large uns, mister,' he said, counting the coins and banging them down on the counter.

Sammy filled three enormous mugs and pushed them towards the boys.

''Ere we are. They're big enough fer you whippersnappers ter wash in,' he grinned.

The three travellers slipped into the bench seats and Frankie unwrapped the brown paper

418

parcel and passed a thick slice of crusty bread smeared with dripping to each of his brothers. 'What're we gonna do next?' he asked, biting into his thick slice.

Arthur gulped down his mouthful of bread and dripping and reached into his coat pocket. 'Don't get all grease on this,' he said, laying a dog-eared photograph down on the wooden surface. ''Ave anuvver look an' then we'll start 'untin' fer 'im.'

Billy clasped the large mug between his two hands and took another swig. 'I can't drink no more,' he said, puffing.

Arthur finished his mug of tea and burped loudly as he eased out of the seat, leading the way out into the busy marketplace. 'Right,' he said, breathing deeply. 'We know that lady what come an' see Mum owns a shop in Poplar Market, so we'll look round an' see if we can find 'er shop first.'

'Will Dad be in there?' Billy asked.

Frankie shook his head. 'I shouldn't fink so. The coppers are lookin' fer 'im, don't forget.'

''Ow will we know it's 'er shop?' Billy asked, becoming confused.

'It's simple,' Arthur replied. 'When we see a grocery shop we'll jus' go in an' ask if Mr Almond's in.'

'But yer jus' said 'e won't be,' Billy said, looking perplexed.

'I know that, but if it's the lady what come an' see Mum she'll guess who we are. Anyway, we can tell 'er. She might be able ter give us a clue where ter look.'

'Why don't she look 'erself?' Billy asked.

'Women ain't much good at that sort o' fing,' Frankie butted in. 'Besides, she's prob'ly too busy in the shop.'

Arthur was getting impatient. 'Look, we've bin all over this. We know what we've gotta do, so let's get on an' do it.'

The three Almond boys walked through Crisp Street Market, eyeing passers-by and looking at the shops. Once or twice Billy tugged on his elder brother's arm. 'That looks like 'im,' he whispered.

After a quick glance at the photograph Arthur shook his head. 'Nufing like 'im.'

Frankie spotted the grocery shop first and he nudged Arthur. The three walked into the shop and Arthur looked up at the elderly proprietor. 'Is this Mr Almond's shop?' he inquired, a serious look on his face.

'What's it say on the board outside?' the man asked, glaring at the young lad.

'Baked beans, eleven pence a tin,' Frankie replied, a mischievous grin on his grubby face.

'Get out o' me shop, yer saucy little gits,' the shopkeeper snarled, waving a butter-patter over his head.

Further along the market they spotted another grocery store. 'Let's try this one,' Arthur said, walking boldly into the green-tiled shop.

The young woman who stood behind the counter was wearing a black-lined headband and a clean white apron. 'Yes?' she asked, smiling at Arthur.

'Does Mr Almond own this shop, miss?' he

asked, feeling a little shy.

'No. As a matter o' fact Mr Pearks owns this shop, an' about 'undred an' fifty more at the last count,' she answered with a grin.

Arthur nodded. 'Sorry ter trouble yer, lady. We're lookin' fer a Mr Almond.'

'An' why would yer be lookin' fer a Mr Almond?' the shop assistant asked.

''E's our farver,' Billy blurted out, with one eye on another assistant who was busy working a bacon-slicer.

Arthur and Frankie exchanged quick glances, while Billy became more engrossed in the bacon-slicing.

''As 'e gone an' left yer, then?' the young woman asked.

Arthur slipped his hands into his trouser pockets. 'The coppers are lookin' for 'im an' we wanna find 'im first,' he told her.

'What's yer farver done then?' she inquired, a serious look on her pale face.

'Bigatry,' Billy blurted out, his eyes still on the bacon-slicer.

'Is that bad?' she asked, hiding a smile.

Arthur felt that nothing more was going to come from hanging around and he turned on his heel. 'Fanks anyway,' he said, leading the way out of the shop.

The sun was high in the sky and the Almond boys took a rest away from the crowded market. They sat on a wooden bench in a nearby church garden, munching on red apples they had filched from a stall while the owner had his back turned. 'I don't fink we'll find 'im,' Billy said,

421

nibbling at his apple core.

'We ain't bin all frew the market yet,' Arthur replied hopefully.

Frankie aimed his apple core at a pigeon. 'I know what. When we've finished searchin' the market let's go ter the police station. The coppers might 'ave got 'im.'

Arthur nodded. 'Yeah, OK. C'mon then, let's get started.'

They walked into the busy market once more and strolled past the line of stalls. At the end of the long street they spotted a small grocery shop, and Arthur walked in first. A large red-faced woman was serving a customer and she glanced briefly at the trio. When she had finished marking the customer's ration-book she looked up.

'What can I do fer you?' she asked.

'We're lookin' fer a Mr Almond,' Arthur said, leaning his arms on the marble counter.

'That's funny, so am I,' the woman answered, her eyes widening suddenly. 'You're not Frankie's kids, are yer?'

Arthur nodded. 'We're lookin' fer our farver so we can tell 'im our muvver wants ter get married ter somebody else.'

The large woman smiled benignly. 'You're a long way from Bermondsey, ain't yer? Does yer muvver know where yer are?'

Arthur shook his head. 'She finks we've gone up the park.'

'Well, I can give yer a bit o' news, young man,' the woman said, leaning on the counter. 'The coppers picked yer farver up last night. I

422

got a phone call from the station early this mornin'.'

'Fanks, lady,' Frankie butted in. 'We can tell our mum where 'e is.'

'Whereabouts is the copper station?' Arthur asked.

'You lot ain't finkin' o' goin' round there, are yer?' she asked. 'They won't let yer see 'im.'

'Why? 'Ave they got 'im chained up, missus?' Billy asked, his eyes growing wide.

'No, I don't s'pose so, although that farver o' yours deserves everyfing 'e gets,' the woman said, smiling at Billy.

'We wanna tell our muvver what copper station 'e's in,' Arthur declared.

The red-faced woman pointed through the shop window. 'It's only round the corner, in the East India Dock Road. Now you three better get off 'ome or yer muvver's gonna be worried where yer got to.'

The three lads hurried from the shop and turned off from the market. 'We goin' 'ome?' Billy asked, beginning to feel that detective work was not all that exciting after all.

'No, we're gonna call in the police station first,' Arthur replied, hurrying along in the lead.

Frankie and Billy exchanged awestruck glances as they tried to keep up with their elder brother. Soon they spotted the blue lamp over a doorway.

'There it is!' Arthur exclaimed. 'Let me do the talkin'.'

They walked up the wide flight of steps and pushed their way through heavy swing doors into a large room. Arthur leaned on the counter and eyed the desk sergeant warily. 'I'm Arfur Almond an' I've . . .'

'Come ter give yerself up 'ave yer, Arfur?' the sergeant said, smiling.

'What for? 'E ain't done nufing,' Frankie cut in.

'Oh, so it's you what done it then?'

Frankie looked the sergeant straight in the eye. 'I ain't done nufing neivver. Nor's 'e,' he said quickly, pointing to a frightened-looking Billy. 'We ain't crinimals. We come ter see our farver.'

'Oh? An' what's yer farver bin up to then?' the sergeant asked, beginning to enjoy the confrontation.

''E's bin doin' bigatry,' Billy answered in a low voice.

The sergeant scratched his head. 'Well, we take 'em in fer a lot o' fings, but I don't fink we take 'em in fer bigotry.'

''E means bigamy. Our farver's bin took in 'ere last night an' we wanna see 'im,' Arthur said, standing up straight.

The sergeant consulted an open ledger and then turned to Arthur. 'Look, son, yer can't see yer farver, but I tell yer what. Let's take a few particulars. We're gonna come along ter see yer muvver anyway. Bermondsey yer live, don't yer? Yer ole man's already told us about yer. By the way, you're a long way from 'ome. 'Ow d'yer get 'ere?'

'We walked all the way,' Arthur said quickly, recalling the fare-dodging episode.

'Not all the way,' Billy piped in. 'We got on a trolley bus.'

'Did yer now,' the sergeant said, grinning widely. 'I 'ope yer remembered ter pay yer fares.'

'Course we did,' Frankie cut in. 'We got pocket-money. We done lots of odd jobs an' Arthur flogged 'is cricket bat.'

The sergeant lifted the desk-flap. 'C'mon then, me beauties. Let's get the business over wiv an' then we'll see if we can find yer a glass o' lemonade an' a couple o' chocolate biscuits.'

Ginny Almond had been through the house with a broom and duster and the washing was hanging out in the backyard. She had given Jenny and Sara their dinners and managed to find time for a quiet hour drinking tea and chatting to George before getting on with a huge pile of ironing. Now as the afternoon wore on and the sun started to dip down behind the leaning chimney-pots Ginny began to get anxious.

'Now where 'ave those boys o' mine got to?' she asked Daisy. 'They should be 'ome by now.'

'I wouldn't worry. They'll be 'ome when they're 'ungry,' Daisy replied, easing her position in the armchair.

Ginny got on with darning one of Billy's socks, her eyes constantly glancing up at the mantelshelf clock. At seven-thirty she got up and walked to her front door, staring towards the end of the square. Finally she knocked at the Robinsons' house. Sally answered the door and beckoned Ginny in.

'No, I won't come in, Sal,' she said, frowning. 'I've bin keepin' me eye out fer the boys. They ain't 'ome yet.'

'Where did they go?' Sally asked, noticing the worried look on Ginny's face.

'They left early this mornin'. They said they was goin' up the park. Somefing must 'ave 'appened. They're never this late.'

Sally rested her hand on Ginny's arm. 'They might 'ave stopped off somewhere on the way 'ome,' she said comfortingly. 'I shouldn't worry, Ginny.'

'I'll give 'em what for when they do come 'ome, you wait,' Ginny said, gritting her teeth.

Sally stepped over the doorsill. 'C'mon. I'll walk up the square wiv yer.'

The Almond boys had left the police station in the East India Dock Road and caught a trolley bus to Aldgate. Although it had been tiring they were satisfied with their day's work and Arthur decided that as they had most of their funds still intact he would play fair with the conductor on this occasion. At Aldgate there were no buses in the station heading for Bermondsey so the three youngsters set off on foot, too impatient to wait. When they reached the tea warehouse at St Katherine's Dock Billy announced that he could not walk another step.

'Well, you're too big fer us ter carry yer,' Frankie said, sitting down on the kerb.

Arthur suddenly brightened. ''Ere. Let's go paddlin' before we go 'ome,' he said enthusiastically.

426

Billy's face lit up and he immediately forgot his tired feet and aching limbs. They hurried on to the Tower Bridge and saw to their dismay that the tide was in.

'Never mind, we can sit on the steps and put our feet in the water,' Frankie said, urging them on as they set off across the river.

When they finally reached the other side of the bridge they turned and walked a few yards along the now deserted Shad Thames and clambered down the few steps to the water. Billy's face took on a look of relief as he lowered his blistered feet into the muddy water and he leaned back on the steps and closed his eyes.

The evening sky was darkening when Arthur pulled his feet out of the water. 'C'mon, we better get 'ome,' he said. 'It'll be dark soon.'

'Me socks!' shouted Billy, reaching down into the water and losing his balance.

Arthur grabbed him by the scruff of the neck and with the help of Frankie pulled him clear of the water. Billy was soaked from his waist down and a look of horror appeared on his face as he watched his socks floating downstream. 'What's Mum gonna say?' he groaned as the three started off towards Dockhead.

Ten minutes later they turned into Stanley Street and hurried through the railway arches. Ginny was standing beneath the lamp post at the end of Paragon Place talking to Sally and she suddenly saw her sons coming along the road.

'Where the bloody 'ell 'ave you lot bin?' she shouted, not knowing whether to laugh or cry at the sight of Billy. 'Where's yer socks? You're all wet too. You lot ain't bin near that river, 'ave yer?'

Sally squeezed Ginny's arm. 'I fink they're ready fer bed by the look of 'em,' she laughed.

Arthur turned to his mother as they all walked into the square. 'It's bin an excitin' day, Mum,' he began. 'First we went ter Poplar, then we went ter the police station an' the copper give us lemonade an' luvverly chocolate biscuits, then we went paddlin' 'cos Billy's feet were sore, then 'e lost 'is socks in the river, then . . .'

'We went on a trolley bus as well,' Billy interrupted.

'I'll give you trolley buses. Get in there an' get those wet clothes off,' Ginny growled, grinning at Sally and raising her eyes to the heavens.

Chapter Twenty-One

DURING the warm, dry August days, folk listened to the daily news broadcasts with a sense of anticipation and renewed optimism. George Tapley heard from his elder son Tony, who indicated in his letter that he expected to get home leave very soon. The news of the Allied landings in Sicily and the expectation that the Italian mainland would soon be invaded left George wondering whether his son's leave would be cancelled. He was also desperately awaiting some news from his younger son Laurie, and he felt sick with worry after reading many articles in the newspapers which described the brutality of the Japanese towards their prisoners and the civilian populations in the invaded countries of the Far East. He had heard that the Swedish Red Cross were trying to get the Japanese authorities to release prisoners' mail, and he prayed that he would hear from Laurie very soon.

Sally waited in suspense for Jim to get his embarkation leave, and by the tone of his last letter she felt it would not be long now. He had talked of how he was looking forward to them being together for a whole week and hoped that they might get down to the West Country. Sally reread his letters over and over and at night she lay thinking of how wonderful it would be when he finally came home again. At work she daydreamed about him, oblivious to the noise and bustle at Harrison's as she bent over her machine. She conjured up visions of Jim hurrying to meet her, his arms open wide, and she wove erotic fantasies around him.

When Sally visited Ben she saw that he was still recovering well. He managed to get about the ward with the aid of crutches and he seemed optimistic about getting home soon. She had still not told him about Jim, although on her last visit Sally left the hospital thinking that next time she would finally make him aware that there was now a new man in her life.

The hot August days were happy ones for Arthur Cox. His dreaded demotion had not taken place, although he had been called into the manager's office to be given a stiff lecture on the responsibilities and required behaviour of Town Hall employees. Thomas Catchpole, the leader of the council, was in benevolent mood now that the elections were drawing near, and he did not want to be seen to be using his position to put Arthur on the broom. Maudie Cox continued to press her husband's blue serge suit every week and warned him about being over-zealous in future. She was also very careful in her own dealings. The black market was flourishing as goods of every description became harder to obtain, and Maudie had had quite a few deliveries during the past month. Her neighbours had benefited from her contacts with the underworld, and Ginny's family had been introduced to real red salmon. Other commodities were smuggled into the Cox household and tins of peaches, pineapple and apricots, as well as pats of butter and cheese, found their way to her customers.

Muriel Taylor had become a regular customer, and on one occasion she bought the length of black pin-stripe worsted material that Maudie had been hiding under the mattress, thinking that it would make up into a nice two-piece costume. One of Muriel's contacts was a Jewish tailor who was not disposed to ask questions, and one day she paid him a visit with the roll of cloth concealed around her middle. When Abe Goldberg had finished measuring her vital statistics he scratched his balding head and sucked on the stub of his pencil thoughtfully, and then he told her that he should do the measurements again just to make sure. Muriel resigned herself to his groping, aware that although Abe Goldberg was a lecherous old goat he was also a very good tailor. When Abe had had his fun he looked over his gold-rimmed glasses as he unrolled the cloth and felt its texture.

'It's a good bit o' schmutter, but vyfor you bring me all dis, young lady?' he asked. 'It's enough for a suit as vell.'

Muriel realised she might be able to recoup some of her outlay and she stroked her chin thoughtfully. ''Ow much will yer charge ter make a man's suit, Abe?' she asked.

'For a friend of yours, a fiver. I tell you, 'e von't be disappointed.'

'Cut us a little sample, then,' she told him. 'I'll come back an' see yer later.'

That evening Muriel knocked on Alf Porter's door. Alf did not normally entertain women in his house but he always made an exception in Muriel's case. When he had shown her into a chair and produced a bottle of whisky Alf sat down and looked at the little sample of cloth.

'It's a nice bit o' stuff, an' I could do wiv a new suit,' he said. 'That one o' mine's bin rolled in the shit so many times it's gone threadbare. 'Ow much yer say it is?'

'Fifty shillin's the cloth, an' a friend o' mine can make it up fer a fiver. I tell yer, Alf, it's a bargain. The cloth alone's werf a tenner.'

'All right, gel. I'll 'ave it!' Alf said, slapping the table with his hand. 'When can I get it made up?'

Muriel smiled with satisfaction. 'I'll take yer ter see 'im on Saturday afternoon,' she said. 'Be

431

ready, an' try an' stay sober. Abe won't be able ter measure yer up if you're fallin' all over the place.'

Alf poured Muriel another tot of whisky. ''Ere yer are. One fer the road.'

Muriel downed the drink in one gulp. 'Now don't get sayin' anyfing about the cloth,' she warned. 'It's under-the-counter stuff, OK?'

Alf nodded, wondering if he should have settled for an off-the-peg suit at the Fifty Shilling Tailors.

Maudie Cox's illegal activities, under Harriet Carey's constant surveillance, were the cause of a bitter confrontation and a lot of soul-searching at number 1. It started one evening after Harriet had finished listening to an organ recital on the Home Service of the BBC.

'Twice this week I saw a strange man knock at Mrs Cox's door,' she began. 'Each time he was carrying a large bag. It looked very heavy, Juliet. I could tell by the way he was holding it. Then I saw Mrs Cox knock at that Fuller woman's door. After that she went next door to Mrs Botley's and then to Mrs Almond's. It strikes me there's something going on. I'm absolutely convinced it's that black-market food she's selling.'

Juliet tried to look suitably shocked, but secretly she wondered if it would be possible to get in on the trading. Maybe Mrs Cox had tins of salmon, or maybe some nice tinned ham. Perhaps Muriel Taylor might know. She would no doubt be in on it. She would have to approach her, Juliet thought.

432

Harriet was not finished. 'There's something else, too,' she went on.

'What's that, Harriet?' her sister asked with a show of interest.

'Well, before I went to work this morning I emptied our waste, and do you know what I saw in that bin?'

'What did you see?' Juliet asked, wishing her sister would not be so melodramatic.

'I saw an empty corned-beef tin. A large tin.'

'But that doesn't mean anything, Harriet. Perhaps Muriel saved up her ration quota for two weeks. People do do that, you know.'

'I'm well aware of that,' Harriet went on, the ghost of a smile showing on her pale, thin face. 'The tin had a Swift's label on it. There's been no Swift's corned beef in the shops for ages, and I saw that man deliver a box with "Swift's" marked on it.'

Juliet sighed. She was becoming irritated by her older sister's obsession with Mrs Cox's seemingly illegal dealings. 'But the girl could have bought the corned beef in another area,' she suggested. 'She gets around, I suppose.'

'Yes, as far as the docks, I should think,' Harriet snorted.

'Really, Harriet. You are hard on that girl sometimes,' Juliet countered quickly. 'Muriel's not a bad sort. We should all have a bit of compassion. It can't be easy for her, the way things are. Anyway, she could be giving up her soliciting. She's got a steady boyfriend now.'

Harriet looked closely at her sister. 'A boyfriend?'

'Yes, he's an American soldier. A very nice-looking lad, too. I've seen him on two occasions recently. They seem very happy together. I've seen them arm in arm.'

Harriet pulled a face. 'Well, I don't think a leopard can change its spots, and we all know what those American soldiers are like.'

Juliet had heard enough. 'Harriet, you're becoming a miserable old prude,' she said sternly. 'What do you know about American soldiers? You're only going by what you read. I think they're very nice. They're friendly, and easy-going, and you have to remember they're a long way from home. If Muriel Taylor has an American boyfriend I say good luck to her.'

Harriet listened open-mouthed to her younger sister's outburst. Juliet was becoming tainted by all that was going on around her, she thought. Maybe she was involved in something herself. She always seemed to be ready to defend that Taylor girl, and she didn't seem to worry over what was going on in the square. Then there was that Sunday business. Juliet was very secretive, and she did appear to look forward to her extra work. Perhaps she should have a word with her about that. If there was something going on she had the right to know.

Juliet had surprised herself with her outspokenness and she buried her head in the newspaper, hoping that she had heard the end of Harriet's moaning for the time being, but it was not to be.

'Do you know, I'm surprised at your attitude sometimes,' Harriet said, eyeing her sister. 'It

434

doesn't seem to worry you at all.'

'What doesn't seem to worry me?' Juliet sighed, putting the paper down.

'Everything,' Harriet almost shouted. 'You only have to look at what's going on around us. There's black-marketeering, drunkenness, street brawls and whoring, and it doesn't seem to worry you in the slightest. I'm really disappointed in you, Juliet.'

Juliet was surprised at Harriet even mentioning the word whoring and she fixed her sister with a hard stare. 'That's where you're wrong, Harriet. I am concerned with what's going on around me,' she replied, her pale cheeks flushing in anger. 'I'm concerned that people have to resort to the black market, and I'm concerned that people choose to get drunk as an escape. I'm concerned that even though people are getting killed and maimed in the war they still choose to fight amongst themselves over stupid things. I'm concerned that a young girl chooses to sell her body to men in order to earn a living, but it's the way of life. When this war's over people will still be the same. They'll still fight amongst themselves and they'll still get drunk, and as for whoring, it's the oldest profession in the world. There will always be women willing to sell their bodies in order to live. I know of so-called respectable married women who consider they sell their bodies to their husbands. Does that shock you?'

Harriet's face showed her disgust. 'That doesn't shock me in the slightest. It's nothing more than I would expect of men. They're disgusting.'

Juliet shook her head sadly. 'Women do the trading as well as men, Harriet. What I'm trying to say is that nothing will change. You seem to be looking for a perfect world. It just won't happen. We've got to live in the real world, not shut ourselves away behind lace curtains in our comfortable little sanctuary and look down on the obscenities of life. Try to see things from a different angle, Harriet. Try to be a little more tolerant of people. After all, we're all the same underneath.'

Harriet felt belittled by her sister's outpouring and she retorted angrily, 'I suppose you think it's all right to be lecherous, evil and deceitful because it's all part of life? Well, I don't put up excuses for that sort of behaviour.'

'Well, you wouldn't, Harriet. Your life is well ordered.'

'I should have thought your life was well ordered, too, but maybe it isn't,' Harriet said, a look of scorn appearing in her eyes. 'Perhaps your life is not such an open book, Juliet. Maybe you've become deceitful and corrupted, too.'

'What exactly do you mean by that?' Juliet said in a low voice, feeling her face grow hot as she glared at her sister.

'Exactly what I say,' Harriet answered, her eyes narrowing. 'I think you've become deceitful. I don't think your Sunday tasks are all they seem to be. I think you've lied to me about delivering those documents.'

It had suddenly become deathly quiet as the

436

sisters faced each other across the room. Harriet stood rigid, waiting for Juliet to respond, and the younger sister bit on her lip in consternation. Juliet's mind was racing. At last it was to be out in the open, she realised. There was no going back now. For years she had kept her secret, more in consideration of Harriet's sensitive feelings than for herself. Maybe she should have told her sister long ago, she thought. Maybe it would have helped her to come to terms with the realities of life instead of hiding behind her high morals.

Juliet took a deep breath. 'All right, Harriet,' she began. 'I'm having an affair with Mr Lomax. I've been his mistress for years now. Ever since his wife became an invalid.'

Harriet sank down in a chair. 'Oh my God!' she gasped. 'You and Mr Lomax! It doesn't seem possible. It's like I'm having a bad dream. You've been deceiving me all these years.'

Juliet laughed bitterly. 'I would have thought that if anyone had reason to feel they'd been deceived it would be Mrs Lomax. I've not deceived you, Harriet. I've kept the knowledge from you simply because of your attitude. Just look at yourself. You have this detestation for men and you've attempted to pollute my thinking with it. You've expected me to share your pure white prison. Well, I wouldn't. I couldn't! Good God, Harriet, I can understand you choosing to lead a celibate life, knowing how much you detest men. I would have understood and sympathised if you'd turned to another woman for love. What I find impossible to understand is why you've tried to impose your will on me. I need a man's love. I need a man's attention and flattery. I can't exist by peeping out on the world through lace curtains. I want to be part of it, as bad as it is.'

Harriet sat upright in the chair, her face ashen. 'I can't believe this is my own sister talking,' she almost whispered, shock showing in her eyes. 'I can't believe you'd be so disgusting. You talk about love with another woman. That's not love, it's filthy perversion. I can't take any more. This conversation is making me feel ill.'

Juliet shook her head slowly. 'Yes, I suppose it is,' she said sadly. 'It's been your way for years, Harriet. You've closed your mind to reality. As far as you're concerned, physical love, any form of physical love, is a filthy perversion. The whole world's perverted, and when you come face to face with the realities of it all, you hide, you try to shut the world out. You're not a child, Harriet. You can't throw the bedclothes over your head any more, you'll suffocate in your own delusion.'

Harriet's head dropped on to her chest and her whole body shook. For a moment or two Juliet sat listening to the pitiful wailing of her older sister, then she got up and walked over to her and put an arm around Harriet's shoulders.

'It had to be said, dear,' she whispered. 'Not in spite of my loving you, but because I love you. Please try to understand.'

On the morning of Sunday the 5th of September Sally walked out of Paragon Place carrying a suitcase. She wore a flowered dress and a single-breasted half coat in powder blue with wide lapels. Her dark hair was loosely permed and cut neatly around her ears; she had taken time with her make-up and her hair, and as she made her way to the tram stop in Jamaica Road she felt pleased with her appearance. The thought of seeing Jim again after what seemed an eternity made her stomach flutter and she breathed in deeply in an effort to control her excitement. There had been several letters between them during the last two weeks and finally everything had been arranged. The holiday destination was still a mystery to Sally, although she knew it was to be somewhere in the West Country. Jim had been secretive about it, simply asking her to meet him at Waterloo Station. He had told her he would be arriving on the noon train and from Waterloo they would take the underground to Paddington.

The tram was nearly empty and the conductor joked with her as he fitted her suitcase under the stairs and clipped a threepenny ticket. Sally sat deep in thought as the rattling vehicle passed Dockhead and stopped at the junction with Tower Bridge Road while the conductor jumped down to switch the points. It had been a telling week and she felt relieved now that she had at last found the courage to tell Ben about the new man in her life. Ben had been cheerful when she visited him on Thursday evening and she had held back until he remarked on her worried look.

'Ben, there's somefing I've got ter tell yer,'

she'd begun. 'I've bin puttin' it off, but I s'pose you've got a right ter know.'

She recalled the look on his face and how he had tried to hide the jealousy in his eyes. 'I've started seein' someone. 'E's a soldier. I met 'im at the firm's dance a few months ago, an' we've bin out tergevver a few times.'

'I see,' he said, looking at her closely. 'Is it serious?'

'Yeah, it is. As a matter o' fact 'e's comin' 'ome on embarkation leave this Sunday an' 'e's asked me ter spend the week wiv 'im.'

Ben was silent for a few moments. 'Well, I s'pose it 'ad ter 'appen,' he said finally. 'I didn't expect yer ter mope around indoors. D'yer wanna tell me about 'im?'

Sally averted her eyes, finding the conversation very difficult. ''Is name's Jim Harriman, an' 'e's a sergeant in the Rifle Brigade.'

''Ow old is 'e?' Ben asked, looking at her quickly.

''E's in 'is thirties.'

'Where's 'e come from?'

''E's from Stepney. 'E was married an' . . .'

'Was?' Ben cut in sharply.

'Yeah. 'Is wife an' baby were killed in an air raid.'

'I s'pose yer felt sorry fer 'im an' . . .'

'It wasn't like that at all,' Sally interrupted. 'I didn't find out until 'e asked me out.'

'Why did yer take so long ter tell me about yer bloke, Sally?' he demanded. 'Yer could 'ave said somefing earlier.'

She looked into his blue eyes. 'Be reasonable,

440

Ben. Yer was in bad pain an' strung up like a chicken. I was scared when I first walked up ter yer bed. At first all I wanted ter do was turn around an' run. I didn't know then if yer was goin' ter pull frew, even. It was only when I started comin' in regular I could see yer was improvin' steadily. I was proud of yer the way yer fought ter get better. 'Ow could I tell yer I was seein' somebody else?'

He nodded, his anger gone. 'So yer knew I'd be upset.'

'Well, of course. I knew yer wanted ter start afresh. Yer told me often enough.'

He had gone quiet, and for a few moments they sat together in tense silence. Sally got up to leave, touching his arm in a friendly gesture.

'Yer still gonna come in ter see me, ain't yer?' he asked quietly.

'Of course,' she replied. 'I jus' wanna see yer get better quickly, Ben.'

She had walked out into the evening dusk and breathed a huge sigh of relief. It had been difficult telling him and she felt a lump rising in her throat, but it was something that she had had to do.

The tram pulled up outside Waterloo Station and Sally jumped down and joined the busy throng of travellers passing through the entrance. She walked up to the large arrival board and saw that Jim's train was due at platform 7 in fifteen minutes. There was just time to powder her nose and buy the morning paper, she decided. She weaved her way through the crowded station and found the ladies' room, taking out her powder compact and looking at herself in the cracked mirror as she dabbed her cheeks lightly. When she had adjusted her hair and satisfied herself of her appearance Sally returned to the main concourse and bought the *Sunday Pictorial* from a small kiosk. She found a vacant seat facing the platforms and looked around.

The whole place was a sea of colour. Dull khaki blended with the lighter shades of airforce blue and navy blue uniforms, contrasted by the brightness of gay cotton dresses and wide flowered hats. Piles of kit-bags and suitcases littered the paved area and audacious pigeons strutted around underfoot. Overhead the large clock showed five minutes to midday as a fierce jet of steam from a departing tender shot up into the grey-painted iron rafters. Sally glanced at the Sunday paper. The headlines announced the progress of the Allied invasion of Italy, and lower down the page there was news of big Russian gains. She folded the paper, her thoughts turning to the days ahead. They would be together for a whole week and then Jim would be going away to fight. Sally glanced up at the clock once more and bit on her lip, trying to rid herself of the niggling worry in her insides.

The large hand moved and she looked down the track. Exactly on time the train approached the platform in a cloud of steam. She walked forward, anxiously eyeing the passengers as they spilled from the carriages, and then she saw Jim. He was in uniform and he carried a suitcase. He was walking upright, his broad shoulders

442

swaying slightly, and when he saw her his face broke into a wide grin. They met at the barrier and he dropped his suitcase and took her in his arms, oblivious to the milling crowds around them. He kissed her hard on the mouth and she felt his arms pressing the breath from her body.

''Ello, Jim,' she gasped with a smile, leaning away from him and resting her hands on his shoulders.

His eyes wandered all over her as he released her from his embrace. 'I say,' he joked. 'Yer look real pretty. What've yer done ter yer 'air, Sally? It's got longer.'

She smiled happily and touched her hair with the palm of her hand. 'D'yer like it? Vera gave me a perm.'

He took her suitcase and together they made their way towards the long flight of steps to the underground, Sally taking short quick steps as she hurried to keep up with his long stride. They crossed London on the busy Bakerloo Line, hardly able to talk to each other with the noisy rattling of the carriage and the other passengers pressing around them. When they eventually reached Paddington Station Jim led her to the buffet and they sat on high stools at the window, watching the crowds of people passing beyond the glass.

Sally was intrigued by Jim's secretive attitude. 'Well? Ain't yer gonna tell me where we're goin'?' she asked, stirring her tea slowly.

Jim had been watching her for a short while and he suddenly laughed. 'D'yer know, yer stir yer tea backwards,' he said, grinning.

'Never mind about the way I stir me tea, what about answerin' the question,' she chided him.

He looked at her with a gleam in his blue eyes. 'We're goin' ter Cirencester.'

'Where's that?' Sally asked eagerly.

'It's in Gloucestershire. I went there a few times when I was a youngster. You'll love it. It's quiet and peaceful, and the countryside is really beautiful, 'specially this time of the year.'

'But where are we gonna stay?' Sally asked.

Jim saw the look of concern on her face and he laughed aloud, squeezing her hand in his. 'It's taken care of. We're gonna stay in an 'otel. I found it in an old travel book an' I phoned 'em from the camp soon as I got me leave dates.'

Her eyes widened. 'I 'ope it's not too posh, Jim.'

'Don't worry. It's a family 'otel,' he said, sipping his tea.

Sally let her eyes travel over his high forehead to his short fair hair, and she noticed how it tended to curl. 'When d'yer 'ave ter report back, Jim?' she asked suddenly.

He leaned his elbow on the wide ledge, his eyes gently mocking her. 'I've only bin on leave two minutes an' you're on about when I'm due back,' he said in a rising voice, raising his eyebrows comically. 'D'yer wanna get rid o' me already?'

She laughed and slipped her arm through his, gripping his muscles as she laid her head against his shoulder. 'Course not, silly. I jus' wanna know 'ow much time we got.'

His eyes appraised her and he felt a yearning

growing inside him. Although she was a very attractive, mature woman, she somehow seemed very vulnerable. He kissed her head and slid his hand around her back. 'C'mon, Sal,' he said. 'We've got a train ter catch, in case you've forgot.'

Beyond the open bay window the green downs dipped gradually into a long valley, rising on the far side to an expanse of tall pines stretching across the rolling countryside. The evening sky was tinged with flaming reds and golds and shadows were lengthening across the green hills. The scent of pine resin and jasmine hung in the air and drifted into the cool bedroom. Jim sat in the window seat, a smouldering cigarette held between his fingers. He stared out over the valley at the faint white mist, his mind troubled with thoughts of the unknown months ahead. It was a frightening prospect to go back into action after the terrible days he had spent at Dunkirk. He had prepared himself by throwing all his energies into the long months of training. He had been put in charge of raw recruits and had helped turn them into trained soldiers who would very soon know the terrors of battle. They were mainly young men who were still struggling with shaving and who often felt homesick. He realised that he had been single-minded and even brutal in his methods at times, but he took comfort from the fact that his charges had benefited from his own experiences and were now more able to look after themselves. He knew, too, that his constant preoccupation with the intensive training programme had helped him through his sad loss. There had been little time to dwell on the past, and his private grief had only troubled him in the few spare moments during the busy days, or at night as he lay in his hard camp bed after the bugler had sounded 'lights out'. He had been satisfied that he was prepared for action, mentally as well as physically, but suddenly his whole life had been turned inside out. The impossible had happened. He had fallen in love again, and the new tenderness of his feelings made him vulnerable to the anxieties and sadness of his past.

Sally had gone to the bathroom and slipped under the hot shower. As the water splashed over her she recalled the exciting day she had spent with Jim. The train had sped through the western suburbs and into the open country. Small towns and hamlets flashed past the carriage window and she realised that she had never been this far from home before. Jim had sat facing her, his eyes constantly meeting hers, a smile sometimes playing in the corners of his mouth. They had left the train at Gloucester and taken a bus to Cirencester, and from there a taxi had brought them to the hotel in a sleepy hamlet two miles out of the town.

Sally had been a little anxious as they drove into the gravel forecourt. The walls of the hotel were covered in vines, and tall, leaded bay windows jutted out from the greenery. The place looked a little forbidding, but once she had gone inside she felt comfortable and relaxed. They had signed the register as Mr and Mrs Wilson, Sally blushing at the lie, and then they were shown up to their room. Once the porter had closed the door on them, Jim took her in his arms.

'Well, what d'yer reckon?' he'd asked her.

'It looks a bit posh,' Sally had said, looking around the room.

She had nestled close to him, her eyes taking in the large, high bed and the dark hardwood furniture. When Jim walked across to open the bay window she noticed that the ceiling beams were only inches above his head.

'It's really lovely,' she gasped, moving towards him to look at the view from the window.

They had hardly had time to unpack and for Jim to slip into a dark grey suit before a loud booming sounded along the corridor. He laughed at her frightened expression.

'It's only the dinner gong,' he said, slipping his arm around her waist.

The evening meal had been a leisurely affair, with an elderly waiter plodding slowly between the diners carrying plates of food balanced precariously along his arms. The lovers had sat at a small table by the large window overlooking the rolling hills. A vase of wild flowers had been placed on the centre of the pure white tablecloth and they ate their meal of grilled plaice, new potatoes and peas from large willow-pattern plates. It had seemed unreal to Sally as she looked around the large dining room. A few couples sat near them and at the other side of the room two groups sat around large tables. Jim had been very attentive, making small talk and smiling at her over the flowers. The proprietor, a large middle-aged woman with a ruddy face and friendly smile, came over when they had finished their meal and apologised for the slow service.

'It's the war, I'm afraid,' she said, sighing. 'We find it difficult to get the staff. Old Mr Peters was with us for years until he retired and we've managed to talk him into giving us a hand until we can get someone permanent. I do hope you've not had to wait too long?'

Jim had given the woman a friendly grin and waved away her apologies. 'We can't 'elp the war, can we,' he had laughed.

Sally wrapped a large bathtowel around her and wiped her hand across the steamy mirror. 'One whole week,' she whispered, glancing at her reflection.

Jim heard the bedroom door open and he turned to see Sally standing in the opening. She was wearing a black satin nightdress that reached down to the floor, hugging her slim figure and accentuating her firm, pointed breasts. He stood up as she walked towards him and went to her, and as they met in the centre of the room he reached down and swept her up into his arms, carrying her to the bed.

Around them the night was closing in, and in the dimness of the room his hands sought her body, stroking her slim thighs and gently caressing her breasts. She sighed deeply, clasping her hands around his neck and brushing his face with her lips. Their kisses became breathless, urgent as they moved together in a passionate embrace.

A bright Sunday morning light flooded the room. Sally shielded her eyes and turned over. Jim was lying on his back, one arm bent over his head, his other arm lying across his middle. She lay for a while looking at him and thinking. It had been a wonderful week, but how quickly it had flown past. They had taken long walks in the narrow lanes, stopping at village pubs, climbing stiles and strolling along paths, lying together in the high grass and whispering words of love. They had strolled through the narrow streets of Cirencester, idly looking at the shops and taking refreshment in quaint tea-rooms, and one day they had taken the bus back to Gloucester and climbed the many winding steps to the top of the church tower, standing close together as they looked down over the peaceful countryside. Sally remembered with poignant pleasure their leisurely and romantic evening meals together and their short moonlit strolls afterwards in the scented air. She had looked up at the stars and remembered the old man who had lodged with her family. One night she had noticed a sudden streak of light across the velvet sky and she had clenched her fist and closed her eyes tightly. Jim had looked at her curiously and laughed loudly at her explanation. She felt a little sad as she remembered urging him to make a secret wish next time, but there had been no more falling stars to claim. Now their day of parting had arrived, and Sally slipped her arm around Jim and snuggled close to him. There was so much to remember, but most of all she wanted to remember their nights of love.

Chapter Twenty-Two

ONE Saturday morning at the end of September Alf Porter collected his new three-piece suit from Abe Goldberg's unpretentious little tailor's shop and took it home in a large carrier-bag.

'What yer got there, Alf?' Ada called out from her front door, nudging her friend Clara.

'It's me new whistle an' flute,' Alf replied, grinning. 'I'll come knockin' when I've got it on an' take yer out fer a drink if yer like.'

Ada grinned, and as soon as Alf was out of earshot she turned to Clara. 'Dirty ole git,' she said. 'I bet that won't last 'im five minutes. 'E'll be rollin' it around in the 'orse shit before long, mark my words.'

Alf cast a warning glance at the sycamore tree as he reached his front door. 'Nosy, boss-eyed ole cow,' he mumbled, fishing for his key. 'Take 'er out? She should be so lucky.'

''Ello, Alf. What yer got there?' Daisy called out as she crossed the square.

Alf pretended he had not heard her question and let himself into his house. It was nearing one o'clock and he realised he had not yet had a drink. He quickly changed into his new suit and looked at himself in the dusty bedroom mirror.

It's certainly a good fit, he thought. Maybe I should keep it on for the pub. At least it would give the nosy neighbours something to talk about. Better put a clean shirt and shoes on, though. I can't wear a new suit with a grubby shirt and brown boots.

Alf fortified himself with a stiff measure of whisky, then set about getting ready. A problem soon presented itself, for when he pulled his only pair of shoes from under the bed he saw that one of the leather soles was hanging off. 'Christ! I meant ter get them mended,' he said aloud. 'Oh well, I'll 'ave ter keep these on.'

After he had applied a liberal amount of brown polish and given his boots a brisk rub with a stiff brush Alf turned his attention to finding a clean white shirt, but all he found was a working shirt that had a detachable collar. 'Where's that bloody collar?' he shouted. 'The poxy pub's gonna be shut time I get there.'

At last Alf was ready. He put on his brown trilby and stared into the mirror once more. Well, that will have to do, he thought, adjusting the knot of his red scarf and glancing down at his polished boots.

Ada was still talking to Clara when Alf walked proudly along the square.

''Ere, get a load o' this, will yer,' she mumbled out of the corner of her mouth.

Clara put a hand up to her mouth. 'Whatever does 'e look like?'

Ada giggled. ''E looks like a pox doctor's clerk.'

In his eagerness to show off his new suit Alf

451

had forgotten to take Abe's pinned memo from the coat sleeve. It was not missed by the two women, however.

'What's that 'e's got pinned on 'is sleeve, a pawn ticket?' Ada chuckled.

Alf raised his trilby to the two women and walked blithely out of the square with the scribbled message 'Mr A Porter £5 to pay' clearly visible on his coat sleeve.

At the Railway Inn the regulars had gathered and when Alf walked through the door Charlie Robinson looked him up and down.

'That's a nice whistle, Alf. I bet that cost yer a nice few bob,' he said, trying to keep a straight face as he caught sight of the memo ticket.

Ted Bromley was on his way to get a round of drinks. 'What yer 'avin', Alf? It is Alf, ain't it?' he mocked. 'I like yer whistle. It's a bit of all right.'

'I'll 'ave a pint o' bitter, please,' Alf answered, slipping his thumbs into the pockets of his waist-coat and grinning at the gathering.

Ted walked to the counter and ordered the drinks. 'Ain't yer gonna tell 'im about that ticket?' Bert asked as he pulled down on the beer-pump.

'Not me,' Ted said, shaking his head and trying not to laugh.

Charlie had never been able to discover just who was responsible for the visit paid to him by the Salvation Army, and the suspicion had shifted to the square's drunk. Alf had vigorously denied any involvement but Charlie was not convinced of his innocence and was always on the lookout for ways to get his revenge. As he slid along the wooden bench to make room for Alf he looked over to his companion.

''Ere, Fred. One o' the lads at work told me 'e 'ad a suit made the ovver day,' he said, darting his eyes towards Alf. ''Ow much d'yer fink 'e paid fer it?'

'No. 'Ow much?' Fred asked, grinning widely.

'Five quid. True. Five quid 'e paid fer it,' Charlie went on.

Fred Mynott shook his head. 'Yer can't get a good suit made fer five quid, can yer, Alf?'

'Nah. A good suit would cost yer fifteen guineas at least,' Alf replied. 'Mind yer, this suit o' mine cost a sight more than that.'

'I should fink you'd get at least a fiver fer it in "uncle's",' Ted remarked as he put the refilled glasses down on the table.

Alf was puzzled by his friends' preoccupation with the price of suits, and their childish giggling went on until it was his turn to buy a round of drinks.

'Oi, Alf. What yer got stuck ter yer coat sleeve?' Daisy Almond called out to him as he stood at the counter.

Bert looked up from filling a glass. 'You gone in the advertisin' business then, Alf?' he laughed.

'What d'yer mean?' Alf asked, quickly tearing the slip of paper from his sleeve and staring at it.

Bert merely shook his head sadly and finished pouring the drinks. As he handed over the change he leaned across the counter, a grin on his face. ''Ere, Alf, ask Charlie if 'e knows the name o' the Salvation Army's regimental march, will yer?'

During the first week of October Tony Tapley came home on leave. George was surprised how lean and tanned his son looked, and his joy at seeing Tony again showed in his face as he proudly accompanied him to the Railway Inn for a celebration drink. Sally and Vera were quick to call in on their old friend, and Tony sat with them in his front parlour as they informed him of everything that had happened in Paragon Place while he'd been away.

When Sally asked him about his time in North Africa Tony was dismissive. 'It wasn't too bad,' he replied to her questions. 'Apart from the flies an' the 'eat. I fink they was more of a nuisance than Rommel.'

'Will yer 'ave ter go back there?' Sally asked.

The tall fair-haired soldier shrugged his shoulders. 'I dunno really. They're re-formin' our regiment. We might go on ter Italy, or they might keep us ready fer the big one. We don't know yet, Sal.'

'Yer mean the invasion?'

'That's right,' he replied. 'It's all very secret at the moment.'

'I wish Big Joe could 'ave bin 'ome ter meet yer, Tone,' Vera butted in. 'Still, 'e might get back in time ter see yer. Maybe we could all go out fer a drink. It'll be nice jus' ter talk about when we was all kids tergevver.'

'Yeah, that'll be good,' Tony said, glancing at

Sally as he remembered how Ben had often played with them. 'It was a long time ago now, wasn't it?'

Vera smiled wistfully. 'It wasn't so long ago, Tony. It only seems like it. I fink the war's suddenly made us all a lot older.'

'Well, you two don't look much older,' Tony laughed.

Vera prodded him playfully. 'You're only sayin' that 'cos yer fancy me. D'yer know, yer was the first boy I kissed.'

Tony flushed slightly. 'Was I?' he said in surprise.

Vera winked at Sally. 'D'yer remember when we used ter go an' play in that ole swing park in Dock'ead, Sal? Well, ter tell yer the trufe, Tony took me in the shed and gave me a peck on the lips. It was really nice.'

Tony was trying to hide his embarrassment. 'Glad yer liked it,' he laughed.

'It's all right, Tone, yer was only seven,' Vera went on. 'If I remember rightly yer was eatin' a toffee-apple at the time. Sweetest kiss I ever 'ad!'

During the autumn months Muriel Taylor and her American boyfriend became the talk of Paragon Place. It was now apparent to everyone in the little Bermondsey square that Muriel had forsaken her profession for the love of her 'big Yank'. Private first class Conrad Polaski of the Second Corps, US Marines was now a regular visitor to number 1, and he had made himself known by his easy-going nature and willingness

455

to chat to everyone he met. The children got on very well with him, and from Danny Fuller's first tentative approach with 'Got any gum, chum?' a rapport had developed between Conrad, or Con, as he became known, and all the children of the square. Whenever he strolled up to Muriel's front door the youngsters invariably ran up to him and gathered around while Con handed out sticks of chewing-gum and candy sweets. He had made himself popular with the two most senior residents of the square and Daisy sang his praises to her friend Lil.

'What a nice young fella, Lil,' she said one day. 'Whenever yer see 'im 'e touches 'is cap an' passes the time o' day. 'E's a big 'un, an' very smart wiv it.'

Lil strained to hear her friend's words. 'What yer say?' she asked loudly.

'I said 'e's a big 'un, an' very smart wiv it,' Daisy shouted.

Lil nodded her agreement. 'Yeah, 'e's a nice fella. D'yer notice the way 'e touches 'is cap an' passes the time o' day? That Muriel's done 'erself a bit o' good. Since she's bin goin' out wiv 'im I ain't see 'er bring any fellas back, 'ave you?'

Daisy shook her head. 'I fink she's give it up altergevver,' she shouted.

'Well, I should reckon so too,' Lil snorted. 'She was givin' the place a bad name, an' besides, it wouldn't be right, would it? Not while she's courtin'.'

Daisy gave her friend a toothless grin. 'I bet it's pleased the Carey gels. That 'Arriet's bin on ter the landlords about 'er carryin's-on, by all accounts.'

'Oh, an' where d'yer 'ear that, Daisy?' Lil asked.

'Alf Porter told me. 'E got it from the Taylor gel 'erself. Apparently it was some time ago. Somebody come round ter see 'er an' told 'er she could get evicted if she kept bringin' blokes 'ome. They was on about 'er usin' the 'ouse fer moral purposes or somefing.'

The Careys were indeed pleased with the way things had developed with regard to their down-stairs neighbour. There had been a very strained atmosphere between the sisters since Juliet's dis-closures about her relationship with Mr Lomax, and Harriet had maintained a certain aloof detachment. She felt she had been badly let down by her sister, and once the initial shock had passed she had given the whole matter very care-ful thought. Juliet had told her that she had no intention of ending the relationship. In fact she had made it clear that if her lover were free to marry her he would do so. Harriet realised the prospect was a real possibility, given the physical condition of Mrs Lomax, and in that eventuality she would be left alone. She would have to make her own plans for the future. Her retirement was only two years away and there would be a small pension to go with her modest savings. Harriet knew that she could not continue to live in Paragon Place alone and she decided she would leave London altogether. Maybe she could find somewhere in Surrey or Sussex. Brighton would be nice once the war was over, she thought.

Harriet's immediate fears had been lessened,

however, by the change in Muriel Taylor's behaviour. She could sleep more peaceably in her bed now that there were no nocturnal visitors to the house. The young American had proved to be a very well-behaved and polite young man, she felt. He would always lift his cap whenever he passed and he had even made a kind remark about the new hat she had worn for church. He obviously came from a respectable and well-to-do family, she decided. It showed in his general demeanour. Maybe she had been a little too harsh in her assessment of American soldiers.

Had Harriet Carey known of Conrad Polaski's background she would have been distinctly shocked. The US Marine's grandparents were poor immigrants from Poland who had settled in New York. His father had worked in the clothing trade until his health failed and his mother had struggled to bring up Conrad and his two brothers and two sisters after their father's death. Conrad had grown up in the Bronx and had run with the gangs until he was caught stealing from a liquor store. Two years in the state reformatory had hardened Conrad and he had continued with his life of crime until a kind Irish priest took him under his wing. Father O'Shaughnessy ran a boys' club and it was there that Conrad was introduced to boxing. The sport proved to be a natural outlet for his aggressive tendencies and it was not long before he turned professional. Conrad's promising career was halted, however, when he enlisted in the Marines the day after Pearl Harbour. Finding himself in England had been a strange experience for the Polish-

American boy from the Bronx, but meeting the pretty young Cockney girl from Bermondsey had made him very happy, and he was hoping she would agree to marry him in the near future.

The autumn proved to be a worrying time for Vera. Big Joe's homecoming had been delayed after his ship was damaged by enemy action in the North Atlantic and had to make a stop-over for repairs. Joe had arrived too late to meet up with Tony Tapley, who had rejoined his regiment and was preparing to embark for Italy, but just in time to see young Joey take his first faltering steps. Vera was beginning to show signs of her pregnancy and she was delighted when Big Joe slipped his arm around her and said, 'I've 'ad a bellyful o' gettin' me feet wet, Vera. Now we got anuvver one on the way I'm gonna get me discharge.'

'What yer gonna do when yer leave the sea, Joe?' she asked, barely concealing her excitement.

'Me ole man said 'e'll get me in the docks,' he replied. 'At least I'll still be near the water. Mind you, though, I'm gonna miss those little birds in Maggie May's.'

Vera gave him a stern look. 'Oh, an' what's Maggie May's?'

'It's a brothel in Liverpool,' Joe replied straight-faced. 'I used ter go there a lot. It was only 'alf a quid a time, but yer 'ad ter join the queue.'

'Hmm. I s'pose I'll 'ave ter make some changes, too,' Vera sighed. 'One fing's fer sure, I
459

won't be able ter go out wiv Muriel any more. Mind you, those merchant seamen are a right rough crowd. They expect it fer next ter nufing.'

Joe pulled her to him. 'We're not such a rough crowd. Now give us a kiss, before I belt yer one.'

The smile left Vera's face and she looked up into his eyes. ''Ow about me an' you 'avin' an early night, Big Joe?'

Autumn saw the departure from the square of Ernest Cox. He had received his call-up papers and was to report to the Royal Artillery at Catterick. It was an embarrassing morning for Ernest as he stepped out of the house gripping a small suitcase. His mother and father stood at the front door together with his younger brothers. Maudie gave him a peck on the cheek and told him not to forget to dry himself properly, while Arthur shook his hand vigorously and slipped him a ten-shilling note. As he left the square Ernest was surprised to see Muriel hurrying towards him. She gave him a big hug and kissed him on the cheek.

'Take care, Ernest,' she said softly. 'Fink o' me sometimes.'

'I will, Muriel – an' fanks again,' he whispered.

As the autumn chill became more pronounced Sally's worries grew. The days at Harrison's were now more unpleasant than ever and the general mood of the workforce was becoming militant. Government contracts were renewed and the quotas of work became almost impossible to maintain. The pressure on the supervisors made them more irritable and less understanding of the employees' problems, and the workers themselves began to consider taking action to obtain a better deal.

Sally was preoccupied with her own problems. Ben had now left the hospital with his leg still in plaster and was walking with the aid of crutches. He had gone back to their original home in Potter's Lane, a little backstreet that led from Jamaica Road to the river, and he had asked her to visit him there. Sally felt that she should call round on him but the thought of seeing the house again made her sad. There were so many happy memories that remained with her as well as bad ones. The house had been their first and only home, and she knew that it would be difficult to walk through that front door without being affected. She did not know what to do.

There was something else for her to think about now, something that filled her thoughts every minute of the day and brought her both elation and dread. Jim had gone away to fight and she had not yet received a letter from him. She remembered how small and alone she had felt as she sat down in the waiting-room on Friday morning. She had waited anxiously for what seemed ages before being called into a white-painted room and motioned into a chair. Sally remembered clearly how the woman had pushed a pile of papers to one side and leaned forward on the desk. Clasping her hands together she had looked over her metal-rimmed spectacles and said simply, 'You're pregnant, m'dear.'

461

PART THREE

1944–1945

Chapter Twenty-Three

THE new year started with snow flurries and cold winds, but the Paragon Place folk did not find the inclement weather, the severe food shortages and the long queues at the market shops as burdensome as previous wartime Januarys had been. Everyone believed that '44 was going to see the invasion of Europe and maybe the end of the war. In pubs and factories and on front doorsteps everyone was discussing the Second Front. At the Railway Inn the regulars from Paragon Place had gathered around their usual table on the first Saturday of the year and were having a lively debate.

Bert Jackson had joined the group and he leaned forward on the table. 'Well, it won't start till the spring, that's a dead cert, Charlie,' he said. 'They've gotta get 'undreds o' fousands o' troops and supplies over the Channel an' they can't get moving till the weavver breaks. They'd all be bogged down.'

'Yeah, I make yer right,' Charlie Robinson replied, nodding his head. 'I reckon it'll be about May or June. It could all be over by Christmas.'

Fred Mynott took a swig of beer and wiped the froth from his lips with the back of his hand. 'Yeah, I fink it'll be this summer. You've only gotta look at what's goin' on in the docks. The

465

ships are queuin' up fer berths an' there's all sorts o' stuff comin' in. They're landin' 'undreds o' fousands o' Yanks every week an' they say yer can't move fer troops and tanks along the South Coast. I fink this year's gonna be the big one.'

Alf Porter had been listening to the debate and after draining his glass he banged it down on the table. 'Well, it can't come soon enough fer me,' he said, looking at the landlord. 'Maybe we'll be able ter get a decent drop o' beer then.'

Bert glared at him. 'There's nufing wrong wiv my beer, Alf.'

Alf snorted. 'It's like gnat's piss. All the bloody beer's bin watered down. It's gettin' 'arder than ever ter get pissed on it.'

'Well, yer don't seem ter 'ave much trouble,' Bert countered.

'I don't get drunk on yer bloody beer, Bert, that's fer sure. I need a couple o' shorts ter start me orf,' Alf replied.

Bert gave the square's drunkard a withering look. 'Start yer orf? Finish yer orf, more like it.'

Before Alf could think of a suitable reply Elsie Jackson leaned over the counter. 'Oi, Bert, get yerself round 'ere,' she called out. 'Daisy wants two Guinnesses an' she won't let me pour 'em.'

Daisy Almond had been standing at the snug-bar counter waiting and she cast a critical eye over the landlord as he carefully poured the Guinness.

'I bin listenin' ter that silly ole sod goin' on about yer waterin' the beer down,' she said in a stern voice. 'I 'ope there's no trufe in it.'

Bert looked crestfallen. 'I ain't bin waterin' no

466

beer down. It's that silly git's idea. I don't brew it, I only sell it.'

'Well, yer better not tamper wiv our Guinness, or I'll ave the Pope on ter yer,' Daisy said, picking up the two glasses.

'What's 'e got ter do wiv it?' Bert asked, trying to keep a straight face.

'Well, Guinness comes from Dublin, don't it? An' as far as I'm aware the Dublin people are Catholics, or they was when I went ter school,' Daisy went on, her eyes widening. 'The Pope drinks Guinness an' 'e wouldn't be too pleased ter know yer bin waterin' 'is favourite drink down, I'll be bound.'

Bert nodded. 'I see. Well, next time yer see the Pope, Daisy, tell 'im from me that Bert Jackson wouldn't dream o' messin' about wiv 'is Guinness, OK?'

At Harrison's the new year brought no change to the bad feeling and tense atmosphere in the factory. The January days seemed never-ending to Sally and she tried to blot out all that was going on around her, concentrating her thoughts on Jim and the baby that she carried inside her. She had received just one letter from him since he had landed in Italy. It was a short letter, and he had said simply that all was well and the happy memories of their time together would help to sustain him until they were reunited. When she had replied Sally had decided not to tell him she was pregnant, knowing that he would be worried. She thought of the baby growing inside her, and she could not help

467

feeling sad when she remembered how she had been desperate to get pregnant by Ben. Their failure to have a child together had been the main reason for their marriage breaking up and it had left her feeling unfulfilled. She had given up all hope of ever becoming pregnant, and now she was carrying Jim's baby. She felt elated and excited, although it had come as a shock when her pregnancy had been confirmed. Her family had taken the news well, although her mother's reaction had been predictable.

Sally thought of the evening she had broken the news to her family. Her father had been late in from work and her mother was moaning about his after-work drinking. Sally had waited until the meal was over, then before Lora disappeared Sally had looked tentatively at her mother.

'I've got somefing ter tell yer,' she had said quietly. 'I'm goin' ter 'ave a baby.'

Annie stared at her daughter, as though unable to understand what she had said. 'Oh my Gawd!' she said finally. 'You're not?'

Charlie had been caught in the act of lighting his pipe and the match burned his fingers. 'Bloody 'ell!' he uttered, throwing the match into the hearth and blowing on his fingers. 'You're pregnant, Sally?'

Sally nodded. 'Yeah, I am,' she said simply, looking at the faces of her family and not really knowing what else to say. 'I'm not gonna tell Jim yet, though. 'E'd only worry.'

There was an awkward silence. Lora leaned back in her chair. 'Well, yer finally got

468

pregnant, Sis,' she said. 'Are yer pleased?'

'Pleased?' Annie snorted. 'What about the finger-waggin' an' the snide remarks she's gonna 'ave ter put up wiv from the neighbours? Wait till those two at the end find out. They'll put it all roun' Bermondsey.'

Sally looked at her mother and saw the pained expression on her thin, lined face. 'I'm not worried what the neighbours fink, Mum,' she said with quiet determination. 'I'm pleased I'm 'avin' Jim's baby. We wanna get married one day. The neighbours can fink what they like.'

Charlie had been staring into the fire and he looked up suddenly. 'Sod the neighbours,' he said in a loud voice. 'Let 'em talk.' He looked closely at Sally, a sudden kindness in his eyes. 'Yer want the baby, Sal?'

'Course I do,' she answered. 'It wasn't planned, it just 'appened, but I'm glad all the same.'

Lora studied her fingernails. 'I wonder 'ow Ben's gonna take it?' she said suddenly.

Sally shrugged her shoulders and looked down at the floor. 'I don't know. If 'e still 'opes we can get back tergevver again it's gonna be a shock an' I don't s'pose 'e'll be very 'appy about it, but it's one o' those things. 'E knows about Jim an' me.'

Charlie put down his pipe and stood up. 'Well, if I'm gonna be a grandfarver I fink it calls fer a pint.'

Annie gave her husband a blinding look and picked up her knitting.

Sally realised that the conversation was over

469

and she exchanged glances with Lora. 'Well, I'd better get on with the washing-up,' she sighed.

Lora started to gather up the dirty plates. 'All I can say is, I'm glad it's you an' not me,' she said, grinning.

Annie dropped a stitch in her agitation as she looked over at Lora. 'Don't yer get pregnant fer Gawd's sake,' she admonished her. 'I can't stand any more shocks. You lot'll put me in an early grave.'

Sally smiled to herself at her family's reactions. Her father had been surprisingly kind, while Lora appeared to find it enjoyably scandalous, and her mother would no doubt spend a few weeks agonising over her bad luck and dreading what the neighbours would make of it all, then she would side with father and become very protective of Sally. That was her way.

As the drumming of the machinery and the feverish activity went on around her Sally recalled telling her friends Vera and Ginny about her pregnancy. They were the only two she had told outside of the family and both had reacted in the way she had expected. Vera knew how much having a baby meant to her and she had thrown her arms around her and congratulated her excitedly, pointing out that their babies would be born within a few months of each other and would be able to grow up together. Sally smiled at the recollection. Everything was so uncomplicated and straightforward where Vera was concerned. Ginny's own experiences had made her react in a slightly more subdued way, but she had been quick to point out that what the neighbours thought was of no consequence. 'Now listen gel,' she had said. 'Yer can spend a lot o' time worryin' about what the neighbours might fink, but when yer sit down an' realise just 'ow much time they do spend finkin' about you an' yer problems you'll come ter realise it ain't worth bovverin' about, d'yer see what I'm sayin'?'

Sally was not so sure but she was grateful for being able to confide in the older woman. Ginny was a big, motherly person, and her warm smile and round open face bespoke an honest nature that drew Sally to her. She faced her own problems with a great deal of fortitude and she was never miserable for long. It was good to know that there would be two sympathetic neighbours, two she could count on.

During January there were many comings and goings at the Cox household. One day a rather large consignment of corned beef and tinned ham arrived and Maudie decided she would have to spread her net to include Stanley Street and the adjoining side turnings, and she would put a few coppers on the price for her trouble. It would have to be a case of recommendation only. A few of the Paragon Place folk knew of acquaintances who could be relied on, and once approached the new customers added their own friends' names to Maudie's growing list. The arrangement seemed to work well and Maudie very soon got rid of her consignment. Her supplier was pleased with the way the produce was moving and at the end of January Maudie took delivery of two cases of Swift's prime corned beef. Normally she would set about selling her black-market produce as soon as her supplier left, but on this occasion Maudie had a problem. It was Friday and only a few days since she had been on her rounds. There was only one thing for it, she reasoned. The two cases would have to be hidden away in the house until the following week. Maudie's problem was compounded by the fact that Arthur was ignorant of what was going on and she wanted to keep it that way. Under the bed was the best spot to hide her contraband, she decided. It was one place Arthur would not look.

On Saturday morning Maudie cleaned her front doorstep and swept beneath her window, then she hung her clean net curtains and scrubbed the passage. The shopping was done, the copper was coming up to the boil and most of the week's ironing was finished. Maudie hummed contentedly to herself as she gathered up the bedsheets, unaware that in Page Street, a little side turning off Stanley Street, things were going very wrong.

Mrs Chambers had bought two tins of ham from Maudie and had stored them in her larder. On Saturday morning her husband Ted walked home from the lead mills with a couple of ingots tied around his waist. Pilfering had become a problem at his place of employment and it was Ted Chambers' bad luck to be followed home by detectives who, armed with a search warrant, found not only a hoard of metal but two large tins of ham in the house. Mrs Chambers had broken down in tears, and when the detectives threatened to charge her with being a member of the area's flourishing black market she named Maudie Cox as her supplier.

At four o'clock on Saturday afternoon a police car pulled up at the end of the square and two burly detectives marched across to number 8.

'Mrs Cox?' the first detective inquired as Maudie opened the door, staring at her with a hard look in his eyes. 'We're from Tower Bridge Police Station and we've got a search warrant.'

Maudie looked at the detectives, her mouth hanging open in surprise. 'What d'yer wanna search my place for?' she gasped, feeling her heart pounding.

'We've got reason to think you've been selling black-market foodstuffs. Now stand aside, if you please.'

Maudie felt the tears rising. She would be charged and sent to prison, she told herself fearfully. It would be in the local papers and poor Arthur would most certainly lose his job. The boys, too, would suffer. The whole family would be disgraced.

The two detectives were going through the house thoroughly and when they had finished downstairs they went up to search the bedrooms. In Maudie's room the policemen looked around quickly and one got down on his hands and knees and reached under the bed with a torch. Maudie shut her eyes, waiting for the worst. She racked her brains for something to say, but it was no use. There was no way out of her predicament. She would have to take her medicine. It was her own fault, anyway. Why did she not have the sense to refuse the deliveries?

The detective hauled himself up on his feet and finished his search. 'Sorry for the mess, madam, but we were acting on information received,' he said perfunctorily.

Maudie felt as though she were dreaming. They couldn't have missed the cases, she thought to herself. It was impossible.

She followed the policemen down the stairs and as they stepped out of the house she saw Alf Porter coming into the square wearing his new black pin-stripe suit. 'Oh my Gawd, no,' she muttered under her breath.

'Maudie!' Alf called over, grinning widely. ''Ello, Lady. Like the suit?'

Maudie opened her mouth to speak but the words would not come. She clenched her fists in anxiety as she glanced fearfully at the policemen, but they gave Alf only the briefest of glances as they hurried out of the square.

Maudie saw lace curtains twitch at number 1 and she knew that her visit from the law had not gone unnoticed. She watched Alf as he sauntered along unsteadily, puffing out his pigeon chest in a dandified gesture, and he gave her an exaggerated wink. The man's a bloody fool, she thought. It's a miracle those coppers never spotted that bit of cloth. I knew Muriel shouldn't have sold it to him.

Gathering herself together she hurried inside and rushed up the stairs to the bedroom. Getting down on her hands and knees Maudie peered under the bed. The cases were gone.

She sat with her head resting against the bed and sighed deeply. That was too close for comfort, she thought, trying to steady her racing heart. She wondered what could have happened to the corned beef. Maybe young Derek had found the cases and sold them. No, he wouldn't do that, she told herself. Richard wouldn't either, not without asking. It couldn't have been Arthur. He would have asked her what they were doing there.

The sound of the front door opening and shutting made her jump and she got up quickly. 'Arfur? Is that you?' she called down.

'Yes, dear.'

Maudie hurried down the stairs. 'Oh, Arf. I've just 'ad a terrible shock,' she groaned.

'What's the matter? Yer look like you've seen a ghost,' he said, eyeing her closely.

'The police 'ave bin round.'

'The police?'

Maudie nodded. 'They come lookin' fer the corned beef.'

Arthur sat down in the chair and shook his head. 'I knew it. I knew they'd be round. I was talkin' ter Mr Dangerfield yesterday mornin'. 'E's a dustman at the Council.'

'What's Mr Dangerfield got ter do wiv it?' Maudie asked, puckering her face up.

''Is boy 'Erbert plays wiv our Derek,' Arthur went on. 'Mr Dangerfield's gotta go ter court over 'is son. 'E's bin nickin' off the back o' lorries. Course when I see those cases o' corned beef under the bed last night I said ter meself,

475

that's Derek's stuff. Eivver 'e's nicked it, or 'e's mindin' it fer 'Erbert Dangerfield. So I got rid of it.'

Maudie was by now totally confused. 'Now wait a minute, Arfur,' she said, frowning. 'Yer say yer found it. 'Ow comes yer looked under the bed?'

Arthur looked a little sheepish. 'I wasn't lookin' under the bed,' he said with a little smile. 'I was puttin' somefing under there.'

'Puttin' somefing under there?'

Arthur looked down at his shoes. 'Well, it's our weddin' anniversary termorrer an' I got yer a little present. I got it yesterday in me dinner-hour an' I brought it 'ome under me coat. I went ter put it under the bed 'cos I know yer don't look under there till yer do the cleanin' on Monday mornin's, an' that's when I found the cases o' corned beef.'

Maudie's shoulders shook as she tried to control her laughter. 'Oh my good Gawd! Oh no! Arfur, you're a diamond!'

It was Arthur's turn to look bemused. 'Wait a minute, Maudie. If I got them cases out o' the 'ouse wivout yer seein' me, 'ow comes yer knew the cases was under the bed?'

Maudie looked at him a little embarrassed. 'They was mine. I put 'em there.'

Arthur shook his head sadly. 'Maudie, yer shouldn't get mixed up in that black-market game. Don't yer know the penalties? Yer could 'ave gone ter prison. What'd we do if they locked you up?'

'I fink you'd manage all right, luv,' she said

476

softly. 'You're right, though. It was stupid. I'm never gonna do anyfing like that again.'

Arthur looked suitably stern. 'Jus' mind yer don't. That's all I've got ter say on the matter.'

'Yes, dear.'

Arthur reached under the chair-cushion and took out a small parcel. ''Appy anniversary, dear,' he said, handing it to her with a wide grin.

'What is it, Arf?'

'Open it.'

Maudie undid the wrappings and looked down at the bone-handled carving set. 'Arfur, yer shouldn't 'ave. It must 'ave cost yer a packet.'

He grinned happily. 'Well, I know you're always moanin' about the old carver. I thought yer might like a new one. There's a sharpenin' fing as well.'

Maudie planted a kiss on Arthur's cheek and suddenly her face changed. 'Arfur?' she said, looking at him closely.

'Yes, dear?'

'Where did yer take the cases?'

He grinned. 'Well, I waited till Sandy MacPherson come on the wireless. Yer always drop off ter sleep when 'e plays those nice tunes. While yer was snorin' I crept upstairs an' carried 'em down. Yer didn't stir.'

'But where did yer take 'em, Arf?'

'Well, it was funny, really,' he went on. 'I put 'em in the passage ready ter stick 'em on the bombsite when the coast was clear, then I got ter finkin'. Somebody might see me, so while I was ponderin' at the front door I seen Alf Porter

477

comin' in the square.'

'Oh no! Not Alf Porter?'

Arthur looked abashed. 'I asked 'im ter keep 'em fer me till I sorted somefing out. 'E didn't mind – least 'e said 'e didn't. Matter o' fact 'e was a little bit pissed. 'E said 'e was gonna put 'em under 'is bed.'

Maudie had become almost helpless with laughter. 'No wonder 'e was givin' me those big winks terday,' she groaned, holding her sides and grimacing.

Arthur's face remained serious. 'We'll 'ave ter sort somefing out, Maudie. We can't leave 'em there.'

'No, you're right,' she gasped, struggling to pull herself together. 'We'll 'ave ter talk about it later. Now c'mon, let's get yer somefing to eat. What d'yer fancy?'

Arthur's face broke into a grin. 'Seein' as 'ow yer got a nice sharp carvin' knife now, 'ow about a few thin slices 'o corned beef wiv chips?'

By the end of January Sally was showing outward signs of her pregnancy. Her usually flat belly had started to protrude and her angular face had filled out. When she got together with Vera one Saturday afternoon her friend was quick to point out that it was useless to hide her condition any longer.

'Look at yerself,' Sal,' she said, waving her hand towards Sally's belly. 'You're normally slim, and unless yer start wearin' granny clothes yer bulge is gonna show. Yer can't 'ide it now, so don't worry about it.'

478

Sally grinned. 'Fanks fer tellin' me, Vera. You're right, though. It is beginnin' ter show.'

Vera leaned back in her chair and put her feet up on to the brass fender. 'When yer gonna go round ter see Ben, Sal?' she asked.

Sally sighed and shrugged her shoulders. 'I dunno. I can't leave it too long. I did promise ter go, an' the longer I put it off the 'arder it's gonna be.'

It had been just before Christmas when she bumped into Ben quite by accident as she was coming home from the market. She had turned away from the poorly stocked fruit stall and suddenly she saw him limping along with the aid of a stick. He had just come out of the paper shop and he gave her a wide smile.

''Ello, Sally. 'Ow yer doin'?' he asked.

'I'm OK,' she replied. 'What about you? I see yer got rid o' the crutches. 'Ow's the leg?'

He tapped his thigh with the palm of his hand. 'It's mendin' well. I'm gettin' ter bend it better now. A few more weeks an' I'll be back at work, touch wood.'

Sally smiled. 'I'm glad. Yer done very well. Yer goin' back in the docks, then?'

He shrugged his shoulders. 'It's all I know. I couldn't work in a factory, it'd drive me right roun' the bend. All bein' well I'll be back by the end o' January, so keep yer fingers crossed fer me. By the way, I'm stayin' wiv me family over Christmas, Sal. It'll be nice if yer can pop round an' 'ave a chat in the new year, though. It gets a bit lonely sittin' in that 'ouse all day.'

'All right, Ben,' she replied, a note of

resignation in her voice. 'I'll pop round then.'

Sally had been impressed by his appearance. He looked lean and healthy, and she had seen the look of determination on his face. His mention of being lonely had been casual and almost offhand but it had cut into her like a knife, and knowing that Ben was too proud to play on her sympathy only made it worse. She had already made it clear about her feelings for Jim and it seemed as though Ben had now accepted the situation, but becoming pregnant by another man might change all that. She realised that when they did meet it would be immediately obvious to Ben that she was carrying. It was something that Ben would have to face up to alone. She would not be able to help him any more, for now there could be no going back. Her future was with Jim and their baby.

Vera shifted her position and folded her arms across her own bulging middle. 'When yer do go roun' ter see Ben 'e's gonna notice straight away,' she remarked, as though aware of what Sally was thinking.

Sally smiled. 'Well, at least 'e's gonna know I'm serious about Jim.'

'Mm. It's just as well,' Vera said, nodding. 'Ben always was a persistent sort o' bloke, Sal, even when we was kids tergevver. If 'e thought there was a chance of you two gettin' back tergevver again 'e wouldn't give up tryin', that's fer sure.'

Sally stared down into the fire and watched the yellow flames licking around the large knob of coal. 'It's funny 'ow fings work out,' she said

480

almost to herself. 'I was desperate ter get pregnant an' me an' Ben couldn't look at each ovver wivout rowin'. Now I'm 'avin' a baby, an' we're on friendly terms. It seems strange, some'ow.'

Vera sat up straight in her chair. 'I know yer always get a bit shirty when I mention it, Sally, but I'm gonna say it again anyway. I fink yer still got a fing about Ben, despite all what's 'appened. I've always felt that. Jus' be careful 'ow yer tread or you're gonna get yerself in a right ole tangle.'

Sally did not answer immediately. She knew that in a way Vera was right. It was new and exciting with Jim and he was never out of her thoughts for very long, but she and Ben had shared and enjoyed special times together before the war and they were not easily forgotten. Maybe she was more to blame than Ben for their break-up, she thought to herself. If she had not been so determined to have a child and had tried to hide her disappointment things might have been different. Her longing for a baby had changed Ben more than she had realised at the time. She could see more clearly now how his desperation to get her pregnant had made him try too hard, and their love-making had become more clinical than spontaneous. It had affected them both and the joy and excitement had slowly evaporated until there was nothing left.

Sally looked up at Vera and noticed the question in her eyes. 'I don't fink yer ever ferget yer first love, Vera,' she said with a smile. 'It was the first time fer both of us. It was good once. I'd get dizzy wiv excitement at times, an' Ben was a good lover. Yer can't jus' forget the past an' sweep yer feelin's under the mat. There'll always be memories. There'll always be a little bit o' space in me thoughts fer 'im.'

At the end of January Ginny Almond was sitting in the courtroom when the judge sentenced her husband Frankie to five years' imprisonment for bigamy. Accompanied by George Tapley, she went to see a solicitor and started divorce proceedings. George had been made a happy man, for during the first week of the new year he had received a communication from his son Laurie. It was a small plain postcard on which his son had printed his message. It said he was fit and well, and he mentioned Ginny amongst the various neighbours he sent his regards to. At first George thought that the message seemed strange but Ginny understood the thought behind it.

'Can't yer see, George?' she said, palms upturned as if to urge his understanding. 'They're only allowed ter write so many words an' it's all censored. I know that's right 'cos I read about it in the *Sunday Pictorial*. Yer boy's tryin' ter tell yer somefing.'

George looked at Ginny closely. 'What's 'e sayin', Ginny?'

The buxom woman put her arm around his shoulders. 'Look. When you're OK yer can fink straight. 'E's lettin' yer see 'e's still got all 'is marbles. Jus' mentionin' names shows yer Laurie's not ill. It also shows yer 'e wrote it, don't it? That's the fact o' the matter.'

482

George could see the sense in Ginny's reasoning and he felt much happier, although the news broadcasts gave him some sleepless nights. There had been heavy fighting in Italy and now there was a new allied landing at Anzio. George lived in fear of receiving another buff-coloured telegram and there were days when he sank into dark depression. Ginny understood the worry he was experiencing and whenever possible she coaxed him out for a drink, or a visit to the cinema.

George was very grateful for Ginny's concern and encouragement and he decided it was about time he did something to repay her kindness and affection. He gave the matter some considerable thought, and at first he toyed with the idea of taking her out for the evening. Maybe a meal up west and then a show, he thought, but then Ginny was not one for dining out. She had often told him that she did not feel comfortable sitting in a restaurant. Ginny was not one for shows, either. Her idea of a night out was a pub where there was a piano, where she could join in the old songs once the drinks had taken effect. But then they could do that any weekend, he reasoned. No, it would have to be something she would appreciate and enjoy. He next thought of buying her something to wear, but Ginny was an awkward size and his knowledge of women's styles and preferences was very limited. He could always give her the money, but again Ginny would make a song and dance about him wasting his hard-earned cash and refuse to accept it. George pondered long and hard about what to do and one evening Ginny solved his problem.

They had been sitting together in Ginny's parlour drinking tea and chatting amiably when she suddenly looked around the room.

'D'yer know,' she said. 'I was finkin' only the ovver day. It's bin eight years since this room saw a coat o' paint. That ole goat o' mine done this room out before Jenny was born. I never liked the paper but I didn't say at the time or 'e'd 'ave put the lot in the dustbin an' gone out an' got pissed. I'll 'ave ter get around ter doin' this room up before we get married. I feel ashamed ter bring anybody in 'ere, the way it is now.'

'A nice bit o' purple, brown an' cream would look nice,' George remarked.

Ginny shook her head. 'I'd like all the woodwork painted cream, an' some nice flowered wallpaper. Somefink nice an' bright. Mind you, there's the ceilin' as well. It'd need re-linin' an' a couple o' coats o' whitewash. Trouble is I never seem ter 'ave the time. It'd cost a few bob as well.'

George nodded and quickly changed the subject, but he had decided to go along to the oilshop at the first opportunity.

The following week George purchased all he needed to renovate Ginny's front parlour. He had been working over the weekend and he was now off until Wednesday. George watched from behind his curtains and saw the Almond brood leave for school on Monday morning, then at nine o'clock sharp he knocked on Ginny's door.

'Oh my Gawd!' Ginny exclaimed as she set eyes on him.

George was dressed in a pair of overalls and he was carrying a large parcel under his arm. At his feet there was a half-gallon tin of whitewash and a quart tin of Nicholls and Clarke's best oil-paint in cream. He also had a bucket and brushes, and a step-ladder was propped against the wall.

'Is this the Almond residence?' he inquired in an official tone of voice. 'I've come from G Tapley an' Co, followin' complaints about the state o' yer parlour.'

'C'mon in, yer silly bleeder,' Ginny chuckled, helping him in with his bucket and tins. 'Are yer really gonna do me room up, George?'

'Well, I should 'ope so,' he laughed. ''Ere, take a look at the paper I picked out.'

He unwrapped the bundle and Ginny blinked. The pattern was made up of large yellow roses with bold green leaves entwined along the length of the roll.

'It's luv'ly,' she said, not sure whether the pattern would suit the tiny room.

'Right then. You get the kettle on an' I'll make a start,' George announced, rubbing his hands together.

Ginny's workman studied the layout of the room while he sipped his tea and worked out a plan of action. The old paper would have to come off first. Then there was the discoloured paint, which had tears running down it every-where. Can't do nothing about that, he thought. I'll just have to paint over it. The ceiling was going to be the most difficult part. Still, it was

485

only a small room. Maybe Ginny could hold the paper for him. The more he looked the more George wished he had come up with some other idea for a present. 'Oh well, better get started,' he sighed to himself.

Most of the old paper came off in large strips and with the aid of a wet brush and a scraper George soon removed the rest. After another cup of tea he mixed up the wallpaper paste and cut the lengths of lining-paper, laying one strip on the table. He placed the step-ladder in position and gave a portion of the ceiling a liberal coating of paste, then after pasting the strip of paper he gingerly folded it in half and climbed the steps. With great difficulty George managed to open the length of lining-paper and place one end in the corner of the ceiling. It had been many years since he had last hung ceiling-paper and he soon found himself in trouble. As he climbed down the step-ladder to move it across the room the end that was pasted to the ceiling fell down on his head. Ginny was watching from the doorway and she burst into laughter.

'Don't stand there gigglin', Gin,' he shouted. 'Give us an' 'and.'

When George had become detached from the length of paper he took stock. 'Well, that piece ain't no more good,' he growled. 'I'll paste annuvver piece an' when I get the end up you'll 'ave ter 'old it in place wiv the broom while I move the ladder.'

George finally managed to secure the end of the paper to the ceiling with Ginny's help. She stood holding up the broom while her decorator climbed down from the steps and moved them over. Once he had pressed the rest of the lining paper to the ceiling George took a piece of clean rag from his back pocket and started to press out the air bubbles.

Ginny stood back and surveyed his workmanship. 'I don't wanna worry yer, George,' she said hesitantly, 'but there's a great big bubble in the corner.'

'No problem,' George replied, leaning backwards to reach the spot. 'It's just a question of—'

His words were cut off as he lost his balance and toppled from the step-ladder, crashing against the table in his descent. Ginny screamed and rushed to his aid. George was lying in a heap at the foot of the ladder groaning loudly.

'It's me bleedin' back!' he moaned. 'I've done my back in!'

Ginny bent down and touched his shoulder. 'Can yer move? Yer ain't broke it, 'ave yer?' she asked anxiously.

'No, it's me muscle. I fink I've pulled a muscle,' he gasped. ''Elp me inter the chair, Gin.'

With a lot of grunting and groaning George made it to the chair and he winced noticeably as he eased himself down into it. 'I'll be all right in a minute, Ginny,' he said, breathing heavily. 'If I could jus' sit 'ere fer a while.'

When Jenny and Sara came home from school at lunch-time George was still sitting upright in the chair. Ginny had tidied up the room and removed the ladder.

'You two kids be'ave yerself now,' she told them. 'I'm goin' ter fetch Doctor Bartholomew. George don't feel so good.'

'I don't want the doctor, Ginny. It'll be OK in a minute,' George groaned.

'Yer bin sayin' that fer the last two hours. I'm gettin' 'im an' that's final,' Ginny said firmly.

When the door closed behind her Sara sat down facing George. ''Ow did yer 'urt yer back, Mr Tapley?' she asked, folding her arms.

'I fell orf the ladder,' he answered, wincing suddenly.

'What was yer doin' up the ladder, Mr Tapley?' Jenny piped in.

'I was paperin' yer mum's ceiling an' I slipped.'

'It don't look no different ter me,' Jenny said, cupping her chin in the palm of her hand.

'I didn't get very far,' George groaned.

'Would yer like a Beecham's Powder, Mr Tapley?' Jenny asked. 'Mummy gives me a Beecham's Powder when I've got a toofache.'

'No fank you,' George said, gripping on to the edge of the chair with agony written on his face as he tried to smile.

'When I 'urt meself an' I'm brave an' don't cry Mummy gives me a gob-stopper. Would yer like a gob-stopper, Mr Tapley?' Jenny asked, still holding her chin in her hand.

'Leave Mr Tapley alone,' Sara said, taking her younger sister by the arm. 'We'll make 'im a nice cup o' tea. Would yer like a nice cuppa, Mr Tapley?'

George winced as he tried to turn towards the

488

door. 'Don't yer touch that gas-stove. You'll get burned,' he cried.

'Don't be silly, Mr Tapley. Mummy lets me make the tea sometimes. You jus' sit quiet,' Sara answered in her grown-up voice.

When the doctor arrived George was sipping a cup of tea and Sara was busy laying the table.

'Well now, he doesn't look too bad to me,' the elderly doctor boomed, banging his black bag down on the fresh tablecloth.

After pulling and pushing and asking George to grip his hand Doctor Bartholomew made his diagnosis. 'It's a slipped disc,' he pronounced. 'All you'll need to do is spread yourself out on a hard bed for a few days. I'll give you something for the pain. Oh, and by the way, no more decorating, and no strenuous physical activity for the time being,' he concluded, casting a brief glance at Ginny.

Ginny paid the doctor and when he had gone she sat down facing George. 'Look, luv. Don't try ter get up. I won't be a minute, I'm just poppin' next door,' she said, patting his arm.

Later that evening as dusk was settling over the little square Clara Botley was standing at her front door talking to her friend Ada. Suddenly she nudged her. ''Ere, what's goin' on over there?' she said.

The two strained their eyes in the gloom and saw George being carried out of Ginny's house by Charlie Robinson and Fred Mynott. He was strapped to the chair and groaning loudly.

''E's 'ad a fit, I should reckon,' Ada said, popping her hands through the armholes of her apron. 'That's what yer 'ave ter do when they 've a fit. The poor sod always looked a bit peaky ter me. I guessed somefing like this would 'appen. Same as that ole Mr Goodyear. 'E used ter 'ave fits. They 'ad ter stick a spoon in 'is mouth ter stop 'im bitin' 'is tongue when 'e 'ad one of 'is turns. Nasty fing ter see, Clara. Mrs Goodyear used ter give 'im Parish's Food.'

'Did it do 'im any good?' Clara asked.

'Well, it didn't stop 'is fits, but it didn't 'alf give 'im an appetite.'

Chapter Twenty-Four

DURING the early days of February snow fell and settled inches deep. Coke fires were banked up and only the children of Paragon Place enjoyed the wintry conditions. Ginny Almond's children built a snowman in the square and stood back to inspect the work, blowing on their frozen fingers and tucking them under their arms.

'It's gotta 'ave a face,' Jenny moaned. 'That one's nufing like the one in me picture book.'

Sara raided the coal cupboard and found two small knobs. 'That'll do fer the eyes,' she exclaimed, handing them to Arthur.

'What about its nose? It's gotta 'ave a nose,' Jenny said, still not satisfied.

'We could use a rosy apple,' Frankie suggested.

'We ain't got no apples,' Billy piped in.

'C'mon then, let's go down the market. There's plenty o' rosy apples down there,' Frankie said, grinning.

The Almond boys hurried from the square. 'We ain't got no money fer apples,' Billy gasped, hurrying to keep up with his elder brothers. 'What we gonna do, nick 'em?'

Frankie shook his head and grinned at Arthur. 'Let's go an' see Fat Dolly.'

When the boys reached the market they saw the queue at Dolly's fruit stall and Frankie took the lead. Dolly saw them coming and she nudged her young helper. ''Old tight, there's the Almond boys. Watch the fruit, fer Gawd's sake.'

''Ello, Dolly. Got any specky apples?' Frankie asked.

'No I ain't. I don't sell specky apples on my stall. Now piss orf,' Dolly replied, glaring at the lad.

Frankie pulled a face. 'Billy's lost 'is dinner money. We was goin' ter the pie shop.'

Dolly sighed. 'Give 'im an apple, Alice.'

'Can me bruvvers 'ave one?' Frankie asked, looking sad-faced at Dolly.

'Give 'em one each, Alice, fer Gawd's sake. Anyfing ter get rid of 'em,' Dolly groaned.

'Can yer give us rosy ones, please, Alice?'

'You'll get a rosy ear if you're not careful,' Dolly shouted. 'Now take the apples an' piss orf.'

The boys hurried back through the snow to the square, each munching on a juicy apple. Arthur carried a rosy apple for the snowman in

491

his coat pocket, filched from under Alice's nose.

Finally the snowman was completed to Jenny's satisfaction. It now had a rosy nose, a moth-eaten scarf tied around its neck and a clay pipe pressed into the middle of its face.

Sara stood holding her sister's hand as they stared up at their creation. 'There's only one fing missin',' she sighed.

'What, Sara?'

'It should 'ave an 'at ter keep it warm.'

'We could use Mum's old 'at,' Jenny said suddenly, her eyes lighting up.

'Mum ain't got one.'

'Yes she 'as, I see it in 'er bedroom the ovver day. She don't wear it any more, she told me, so there.'

The girls slipped up to Ginny's bedroom and found the navy-blue hat complete with its sequined veil sitting on the dressing-table. Jenny giggled as they hurried down the stairs and out into the square with their prize. 'Our Mr Snowman is gonna be the bestest one in the whole world, I should fink,' she said proudly.

Ginny had been snoozing comfortably beside the fire during the afternoon and the sound of George's voice roused her. 'Yer there, Ginny?' he called out. 'The door was open.'

'C'mon in, George,' she said, sitting up in her chair and yawning widely. 'I was jus' 'avin' a doze.'

'Sorry ter wake yer. Could yer spare us a cup o' sugar?' he asked.

'Sure. Yer know where it is, 'elp yerself, an' while you're at it put the kettle on, will yer?'

Later the two sat drinking their tea and chatting together beside the banked-up coke fire. "'Ere, George, I've 'ad me navy-blue coat cleaned,' Ginny remarked. 'It's come up really nice. I was finkin' o' wearin' me blue 'at wiv it. I ain't wore that bonnet fer years. I dug it out the wardrobe the ovver day an' I was gonna chuck it away but it should come up OK if I give it a good brush.'

George grinned into his cup.

'What's so funny?' Ginny asked, eyeing him curiously.

"'Ere, I wanna show yer somefing,' he said, trying to look serious.

Ginny followed him to the front door.

'Take a look at that,' he laughed.

'That's me bleedin' bonnet!' she cried. 'The cow-sons 'ave ruined it!'

George could see that the hat had been skewered on to the snowman and he turned to Ginny, a wide smile on his thin face. 'I don't fink it would 'ave suited yer, Ginny,' he said. 'It looks better on the snowman.'

Sally turned into the little backstreet that led past the church gardens as she made her way to Potters Lane. The Saturday afternoon was grey, with a carpet of snow underfoot and a cold wind blowing. She pulled her coat collar up around her ears as she walked past the old church. The garden was deserted and Sally could see the vine-covered alcove some way down the gravel path where she had waited for Jim. There was no reason for her to have taken that particular

493

turning as a short cut to Jamaica Road, for it added to the journey, but Sally had known she would be able to see that secret place once more. She entered the garden and walked slowly up to the bench, her thoughts taking her back to those few wonderful times she had spent with Jim. It seemed so long ago now, although it was only a few months since he had left. She could almost see him standing there, the tall, broad-shouldered figure with his forage-cap worn at a jaunty angle, and his wide smile that melted her heart.

With a sigh Sally pushed her hands deeper into her coat pockets and walked quickly out of the gardens.

Potters Lane was a narrow, cobbled turning with small houses on either side. Gas-lamps were spaced at intervals along its length and at the far end there was a spice warehouse that overlooked the river. All the front doors were shut against the cold wind but Sally felt her presence had been noted. The clip of her heels would have brought one or two neighbours to the windows, and she smiled to herself as she saw a curtain move aside in an upstairs room. She stopped at number 36 and lifted the heavy knocker. She remembered that Ben had a habit of slamming the knocker down on its pad and she had often told him about it. The front door was looking more weather-beaten, and the crack in the downstairs windowsill seemed to have got wider. Sally took a deep breath as she heard Ben's shuffling foosteps coming along the passage, then he opened the door.

494

His eyes lit up and he stood to one side. 'I wondered if you'd come,' he said, closing the front door behind her as she stepped into the dark passage.

Sally walked into the front parlour and looked around. Everything was as she remembered it. Nothing seemed to have been moved, except that there was a space on the mantelshelf where the rearing iron horse used to stand.

'Let me take yer coat, Sal,' Ben said, hooking his walking-stick on the back of a chair.

Sally watched as he hobbled across the room. 'I see you're gettin' around much better now,' she said.

He hung her coat behind the door and shuffled round to face her. 'It won't be long now. The muscles are comin' back.'

Sally seated herself in the easy-chair and adjusted the collar of her cardigan. 'I see yer got rid of the ornament,' she said, nodding towards the mantelshelf.

He grinned sheepishly. 'Yer know I never did like it. I give it ter Mrs Sullivan. She took a fancy to it.'

While Ben was in the scullery making the tea Sally studied the room. The ornaments and pictures looked dusty and there were old newspapers protruding from under seat cushions. The once-white tablecloth was tea-stained and the linoleum-covered floor needed a broom, she thought. The lace curtains were grey and they hung crookedly. Sally remembered how she had religiously changed her curtains every week and she pursed her lips. 'Who does yer cleanin'?' she

495

called out.

She heard Ben's laugh. 'Mrs Sullivan does me washin' an' ironin'. I give 'er a few bob every week.'

'What about yer curtains? They look rotten,' Sally remarked.

'She's bin on ter me ter take 'em down, but I ain't got round ter doin' it yet,' he replied.

Sally could hear sounds coming from the scullery. 'D'yer want me ter come an' get the tea?' she called out.

'No, I can manage,' he laughed. 'It's all good practice.'

They sat facing each other sipping their tea and Sally became aware of Ben's eyes studying her. She realised that when she'd come in she'd been wearing her loose coat and she had sat down before he'd had time to get a proper look at her. The cardigan was hiding her condition, although he must have noticed the weight she had put on.

'Does yer leg give yer much pain?' she asked suddenly, feeling her face getting hot under his gaze.

He shook his head. 'Only a few twinges. I'm still a bit stiff when I walk, though. The doctor said me 'ips are mended OK.'

'That's good. I s'pose you're eager ter get back ter work now?'

'Yeah I am. It's drivin' me barmy sittin' about.'

Sally put down her cup and looked around, searching for something to say.

Ben sat fingering the horsehair that was

protruding from a hole in the arm of his easy-chair. Suddenly he laughed nervously and sagged back in his seat. 'It's funny,' he said. 'When I saw yer before Christmas I was sort o' taken by surprise. Afterwards when I was walkin' 'ome I thought about yer comin' ter see me an' all the questions I was gonna ask yer. I went over it in me mind but now you're 'ere I don't know where ter start.'

Sally looked into his pale blue eyes and sensed panic there. It was as though he was steeling himself for the inevitable. She sighed deeply and looked down into the low fire. 'We both knew it wouldn't be easy, us meetin' 'ere,' she began. 'I've bin wonderin' if it was the right fing ter do. It's only gonna make fings worse.'

Ben looked down at his clasped hands. 'But yer did come, an' that's tellin' me somefing,' he said, raising his eyes with a brief smile. 'I don't fink yer wanted ter come round 'ere jus' ter slag me off fer messin' about wiv ovver women. It's all bin said. What's more, I don't fink yer come out o' pity. Yer know me too well. I don't want anybody's pity, least of all yours, yer know that. Let's be honest wiv each ovver, Sally. That time yer spent wiv that bloke o' yours. Did it make yer certain in yer mind? Are yer gonna stay wiv 'im? That's what I'd like ter know.'

She looked up from the fire and met his hard gaze. 'I'm 'avin' Jim's baby,' she said quietly.

Ben looked down quickly for a moment and Sally could see his knuckles turning white as he gripped the arms of the chair. When he raised his eyes again they were glassy. 'I thought

497

maybe, jus' maybe, there was a little spark left,' he said quietly. 'I wanted ter believe yer called round because of us, an' what we 'ad tergevver. I must 'ave bin stupid. I can see now yer only wanted ter come so yer could tell me yer was pregnant.'

Sally felt tears stinging her eyes. 'You're so wrong, Ben. I wanted ter see yer because of us. I wanted ter keep a little bit of us alive. I still want yer friendship an' good wishes, but maybe I'm the stupid one. Maybe I should 'ave cut yer dead.'

'Friendship? I don't want yer friendship,' he cried. 'I wanted to win yer back. I wanted yer love, not yer friendship. I can't look at yer, even now, wivout wantin' ter take 'old of yer an' love yer.'

She sighed and blinked against her tears. 'I told yer so many times, Ben. There was no future fer us tergevver. You was the one who destroyed us. I could 'ave stood yer knocking me about, but there's one fing I couldn't take, an' that was sharin' yer wiv anuvver woman. No, Ben, we couldn't pick up the pieces like it was a broken plate. I've got somebody else now. All we've got tergevver is friendship. That's all I've got ter offer yer.'

It had become quiet in the little room as they each sat staring into the flickering coals. After a while Ben got up slowly and walked over to the window, then he turned to face her.

'All right, Sally,' he began. 'I guess it was no more than what I expected. I can't blame yer fer feelin' the way yer do. If it's only yer friendship

498

I can be sure of, well, I'll 'ave ter settle fer that. It's gonna be bloody 'ard, but I couldn't stand yer cuttin' me dead an' passin' me in the street wivout as much as a look.'

Sally gave him a wan smile. 'I couldn't do that, Ben.'

He walked over and picked up the cups. 'Let's fill these up, then we can talk about yer plans,' he said. 'Yer ain't gotta go yet, 'ave yer?'

While he was out in the scullery Sally wiped her eyes and tried to compose herself. It had been said, and now Ben knew about the baby. She knew it must have hurt his fierce pride to learn that another man had replaced him. Another man had taken her love and given her the one thing he could not. Jim was a soldier, too, and that must be eating away at Ben. Maybe that was the reason he had fought to regain his fitness. It was that stubborn streak, as well as his pride. He would never have used those crutches a moment longer then he needed, and his stick would be discarded at the first possible moment. Sally felt that he would never give up fighting to regain her love, and she would have to tread very warily.

Ben came in with the tea and eased himself down into the chair. Sally could see that he was in some pain, although he tried to hide it. He stirred his tea thoughtfully, and Sally had time to study him. He had lost weight about his face, although he was still heavily built and wide in the shoulders. His normally short hair had become longer and hung about his forehead. His mouth was still thin and inclined to make him

499

appear stern, but Sally felt that his most striking feature was still his eyes. They were deep-set and pale blue, almost grey, and they seemed to have acquired a greater sharpness. They sparkled when he laughed and they displayed a wicked glint in anger. Now sadness had given his eyes a cold brightness, and as he looked up at her Sally felt undressed beneath his gaze.

'Did yer parents give yer a bad time when they found out about the baby?' he asked suddenly.

Sally shook her head. 'Me mum went on a bit, but it wasn't too bad. I don't fink the neighbours 'ave noticed yet, but it won't be long.'

'Will yer stay wiv yer parents when the baby comes?' Ben asked.

'I dunno,' Sally replied. 'I don't fink Mum could stand a baby cryin' round 'er. I might end up gettin' a place of me own.'

Ben looked down at the tea-leaves in the bottom of his cup and coughed nervously. 'Listen, Sal. If fings get too bad an' yer decide ter move out yer can always stay 'ere. I – well, yer know what I mean. Jus' till yer got on yer feet. There'd be no strings attached.'

Sally looked at him closely and saw that his face had coloured slightly. 'Thank yer, Ben,' she said softly. 'I know it couldn't 'ave bin an easy fing ter say, the way fings are.'

'Like 'avin' anuvver man's baby? Well, it's somefing I couldn't do fer yer,' he said bitterly.

Sally looked down at her clenched hands. 'Well, I fink it was very nice of yer ter make the offer.'

500

He had flushed noticeably now and he looked away in his embarrassment. 'We can't 'ave yer walkin' the streets, can we?' he said, a hint of a smile on his face.

The early dusk had settled over the narrow riverside turning and the room had become dark.

'Well, I'd better make a move,' Sally said, getting up and pulling her cardigan down self-consciously.

Ben helped her on with her coat and picked up his stick. 'I'll walk yer a little way,' he said.

'No, I'm all right,' Sally replied quickly. 'Yer wanna rest that leg. It's painin' yer, I can see.'

He reached out and gently squeezed her arm. 'Remember what I said. I'll see yer around, then? Take care.'

Sally walked along the quiet turning, her breath coming like a white mist and her footsteps sounding muffled in the soft snow. Ben had taken the news of the baby quite calmly, she thought. He was hurt and angry, she knew, but he had hidden it very well. She had been taken aback by his offer of accommodation. It was the last thing she had expected, after him learning about the baby.

Sally closed her fists tightly as she made her way out into Jamaica Road. She knew that if things were different it would be so easy to become involved with Ben once more. All the anger and all the hurt seemed to return to her mind when she faced him, and yet melt away when he looked at her in that special way of his. It was too late to change anything now, she told herself. She had found a new love with Jim and she carried his baby inside her. What was it he had said? Don't dwell on the past. Let it stay buried.

Sally reached the railway arches and she shivered as the icy wind swirled around her. Ahead the unlit lamp post rose up darkly in the bitter air, and as she turned into Paragon Place it started to snow again.

Chapter Twenty-Five

SPRING flowers were opening up in the church gardens and the winds were mild. An April sun rose higher in the sky giving a pleasant warmth, and the old sycamore tree spread its canopy of leaves over Paragon Place once more. Children skipped in and out of a rope and drew chalk lines for hop-scotch, while the older boys built camps on the Stanley Street bombsite. Folk listened to the news broadcasts and read the daily papers in eager anticipation of the invasion of Europe. Food queues appeared to get longer and supplies shorter. Weeds sprouted from the weather-hardened sandbags at the warden's post in Stanley Street and the lamp posts, kerbs and trees went without their fresh coat of white paint. The rusty shelter sign hung down under the railway arches and cats had their kittens on the shelter bunks.

On the first Sunday in April Sally was sitting

with Vera in her friend's upstairs flat. It was late evening and the lengthy warm spell had been broken by a sudden storm. Rain beat against the window and claps of thunder sounded like gunfire. Vera eased her position in the chair and winced.

'They say storms curdle milk,' she laughed. 'It's turnin' me bloody stomach.'

Sally looked at her friend with concern. ''Ere, you ain't started, 'ave yer?'

Vera shook her head. 'No, it's not due till next week. It's jus' gettin' a bit lively, that's all. Big Joe's bin like a cat on 'ot bricks this last few weeks. Every time I touch me belly 'e jumps out o' the chair. 'E didn't want ter go out ter the pub ternight. If yer 'adn't 'ave come over 'e would 'ave stayed 'ere.'

'Will 'e be disappointed if it's a gel?' Sally asked.

'Yeah, 'e wants anuvver boy,' Vera replied, wincing again. 'I reckon 'e's after a football team, but I've told 'im, this is me lot. Two's enough fer anybody ter be gettin' on wiv.'

Sally was getting worried. 'Shall I call down fer yer mum? Yer don't wanna leave it too long if you're gettin' the pains.'

Vera shook her head. 'No, I'm all right. Turn the wireless on, will yer, Sal. It's about time fer the news.'

The chimes of Big Ben sounded and then the newsreader's voice came on, announcing that heavy fighting was going on at Anzio on the Italian mainland. The women remained silent until the news had finished and then Vera got up

503

and switched off the radio set.

'I know 'ow yer feel, Sal,' she said, noticing the worried look on Sally's face. 'It used ter be the same when Big Joe was away at sea. Every time they said ships were sunk me stomach went over. I wouldn't wanna go frew that again.'

Sally forced a smile. 'It's the waitin' that gets me. Every time the postman comes in the square I 'old me breath. It's bin a while now since I 'eard from Jim, although I know 'e's not gonna be able ter write.'

Vera nodded as she stood up and moved beside the fire. ''E'll write soon as 'e can. I remember—' She suddenly gripped the mantelshelf and bit on her bottom lip. 'Phew! I felt that,' she gasped.

Sally got up quickly and took her arm. 'Sit down, Vera. I'm gettin' yer muvver. I reckon you've started.'

Beryl took charge and soon Vera was made comfortable in the warm bedroom. Sally sat with her until the midwife arrived, then she left the Mynotts and crossed the square, her coat thrown over her head against the heavy rain. Charlie was snoring in his favourite chair but Annie looked up from her paper as Sally walked in.

'You've left it late, me gel,' she said. 'Yer should be gettin' yer rest.'

'Vera's started, Mum. The midwife's jus' come,' Sally said, sitting down heavily in the chair.

Annie was in one of her black moods and she folded up the paper and threw it down at her feet. ''E's bin like that fer the past two hours,'

504

she said, nodding towards Charlie. 'I dunno 'ow I stand it, sometimes. 'Is snorin' gets right on me nerves.'

'I don't s'pose it'll be long,' Sally said, ignoring her mother's remarks.

'The second one always seems ter come quicker,' Annie said, folding her arms and leaning back in her chair. 'Long as there's no complications. Yer never can tell wiv babies. Yer take that Mrs Arbuckle what used ter live in Stanley Street. Seven, she 'ad. 'Er ole man delivered most of 'em 'imself. She 'ad the last one while she was down the market. Little boy, it was. She carried the little mite 'ome 'erself. Wrapped in a bit o' tarpaulin, 'e was. It didn't do it any 'arm, though. Young Freddie Arbuckle works in the docks alongside yer farver. Mind you, some 'as a bad time. I remember ole Mrs Axford. Now she was . . .'

'Yer ain't gonna tell me one o' them gory stories, are yer, Mum?' Sally cut in.

Annie looked over her reading glasses. 'Sorry, I was forgettin',' she said with a weak smile.

'Well, it's pretty obvious now, Mum,' Sally replied, rubbing her hand over her large middle.

Annie got up and took off her glasses. 'You sit there an' I'll put the kettle on,' she said. 'I'll be glad when yer confinement's all over. It's all bloody worry.'

Sally leaned back in the chair and sighed. The baby had been moving during the last few hours and her stomach felt tender. She looked over at her father, whose head was now hanging over the side of the chair. He had aged lately, she thought. Sleep and the pub seemed to be his means of escape these days. A few years ago he would have given her a hard time about her getting pregnant. Her mother had not remained shocked for very long either. She seemed to have lost the capacity to smile lately. Maybe a new life coming into the household would give them both something to latch on to, Sally hoped. It would be their first grandchild, after all.

The clock had struck midnight and still Sally sat beside the fire. She had put another few knobs of coal on the flames when her parents went off to bed, knowing Beryl or Fred would knock with the news of Vera's baby if they could see a chink of light showing through the blackout curtains. She re-read the Sunday papers and made herself yet another cup of tea. The clock moved on to the hour and Sally started to slip into a light slumber.

At one-thirty she heard a light tap on the window and she hurried to the door. Beryl stood framed in the doorway, her facing beaming.

'It's anuvver boy!' she exclaimed proudly. 'Eight pounds an' kickin' like mad.'

'Oh, luv'ly!' Sally cried. 'Is Vera all right?'

Beryl nodded. 'She's exhausted but she's OK. The baby was a long while comin'. Little Joey woke up an' we let 'im 'ave a peep.'

'Fanks fer lettin' me know, Beryl,' Sally said. 'I'll pop over before I go ter work, if that's all right.'

The rain had ceased now and as she watched Beryl cross the quiet square Sally heard the baby cry.

As soon as Ada Fuller and Clara Botley heard the news of Vera's new baby they got together on Ada's doorstep.

'She 'ad ter get married yer know,' Clara said, looking left and right in case she was overheard.

Ada's eyebrows rose. 'Is that a fact?'

Clara nodded. 'She was only married eight months when she 'ad 'er Joey. It don't wanna lot o' workin' out, Ada.'

The ginger-haired woman put on her shocked face. 'It makes yer wonder if it was Joe's baby,' she said, lowering her voice. 'I mean ter say, 'e was always away, wasn't 'e? She was always gallivantin' about while 'e was at sea. I see 'er meself. Remember that night 'er an' Annie Robinson's daughter went out all dolled up?'

Clara nodded. 'I remember. They 'ad lipstick an' powder on, an' Vera was wearin' that short skirt. Yer can bet yer life they was orf ter meet a couple o' fellas.' Clara pinched her lips together and frowned. 'I was really surprised when I see Annie Robinson's daughter was carryin', Ada,' she went on. 'She's such a quiet girl, too.'

Ada adopted her usual position when there were important things to discuss. 'Them sort are the worst, Clara. Yer never know what they're up to.'

Clara nodded and copied Ada's pose by putting her hands through the armholes of her apron. 'Yer never can tell. I mean ter say, fer all we know, it could be 'er 'usband's.'

Ada was adamant. 'Nah, it can't be. She's left 'im, an' accordin' ter Annie Robinson she ain't seen nufing of 'im since, so I don't s'pose 'e 'ad

507

anyfing ter do wiv it.'

Clara snorted. 'Well, I don't fink the 'Oly Ghost 'ad anyfing ter do wiv it eivver. 'Ere, she ain't bin knockin' around wiv that Muriel Taylor, 'as she?'

Ada laughed aloud. 'I shouldn't fink so. Not now she's got that nice Yankie fella in tow.'

'P'r'aps that Sally's got a fella where she works,' Clara went on. 'I fink I'll 'ave a go at pumpin' Annie. I'd love ter find out whose it is.'

Ada stuffed her arms deeper into her apron. 'I dunno, it's gettin' like whore's alley down 'ere.'

Alf Porter felt much happier once winter was over. The cold weather was a problem for him, and when he was on one of his binges and it was slippery underfoot it became positively dangerous. There were occasions when he had lost all sense of direction and finally settled down in a doorway or on a park bench to sleep off the effects, only to wake up frozen stiff and aching all over from the tumbles he had taken. Sometimes he had been roused by a patrolling policeman and moved on, which most probably saved him from freezing to death. When he reached home without mishap Alf crawled into his cold bed which had old coats thrown on top of the bedclothes and prayed for spring. The square's inebriate led a charmed life, and apart from a few bumps and bruises he survived the winter without injury or illness.

Each year when the weather broke Alf gave thanks and did his yearly spring-clean. The old coats were removed from his bed and stored away for the duration, the house was swept and scrubbed, and all the junk collected during the year was thrown out. It was in April when Alf started his spring-clean and while he was gathering up the many empty whisky bottles he came across two cases of corned beef under his bed. He had intended to sell the tins at work after doing a deal with a worried Maudie Cox back in the winter. She had said it would be safer to dump them on the bombsite but Alf had persuaded her not to, saying that he could sell them without any problems and that all the local bobbies knew him and were not likely to give him any trouble. Now that he was having a thorough sort-out Alf thought it would be a good idea if he finally got rid of the tins.

On Saturday morning Alf paid Dave Collins a visit. Dave ran a café in Dockhead which was a favourite eating place for the local dockers and carmen. Lately the café had been attracting the attention of the local police. It had been visited by the law on a few occasions following tip-offs, but nothing had been found. Dave always seemed to be one step ahead of the police, thanks to his cousin's husband who was a detective sergeant at the local station, and the café-owner was in a position to supply him with joints of beef, large pieces of cheese and pats of butter for services rendered. The arrangement was mutually satisfactory, since the detective's family ate well and Dave Collins stayed out of the magistrates' court. Alf Porter knew Dave from their younger days and it did not take him long to do a deal with the café-owner regarding two cases of black-market corned beef. Dave Collins struck a hard bargain and although Alf did not make a profit he was pleased that at last he would be rid of the produce.

'We'll 'ave ter be careful,' Dave said, wiping his hands down his grubby apron. 'The bloody law won't leave me alone. They're always watchin' the gaff.'

'Why's that, then?' Alf asked.

'It's the ovver café-owners, I reckon,' Dave went on. 'They're jealous of me trade. I do a nice roast beef an' two veg, an' me sandwiches are the best around 'ere. Yer can bet yer life one o' the monkeys 'as bin shoutin' 'is mouth off ter the law. Bloody jealous, that's all it is. They begrudge a bloke gettin' an honest livin'.'

'P'r'aps we'd better forget it, then,' Alf said, beginning to get nervous.

'Don't worry. We can get round it,' Dave replied, grinning knowingly. 'Yer jus' let me worry about the delivery. I'll send somebody round ter pick the cases up. Now what about a nice bacon sandwich on the 'ouse?'

Clara Botley and Ada Fuller were in their customary position on Ada's front doorstep when Alf walked home and Clara nudged her friend. ''Ere, I reckon 'e mus' be ill or somefing,' she said.

'Why's that, Clara?'

'Well, 'e ain't pissed. 'E's walkin' as straight as me an' you.'

Ten minutes later a large woman walked into the square pushing a bassinet.

''Ere Ada, who the bloody 'ell's this?' Clara

510

exclaimed. 'I ain't seen 'er before.'

The two watched the woman walk up to Alf Porter's front door and Ada turned to her friend. 'Blimey, 'e's at it an' all.'

They watched the woman push the bassinet into Alf's house. 'She's called round fer 'er maintenance, I should fink,' Ada said, grinning.

'Gawd 'elp us, I shouldn't fink 'e could raise a gallop,' Clara laughed.

'I dunno about that,' Ada said. 'Look at the time 'e exposed 'imself ter the Careys. 'E's a dirty ole goat if yer ask me.'

When the stranger emerged from Alf's house a few minutes later and bent over the pram to adjust the covers Ada nudged her friend. ''Old tight, 'ere she comes.'

Alf stood at his front door waving as the woman pushed the pram along the square. She turned as she drew level with the viragos. 'Bye, Alf,' she called out. 'See yer soon, darlin'.'

Ada and Clara stood open-mouthed as the woman pushed the bassinet out of the square.

'The brazen bitch,' Clara gasped. 'I dunno what this square's comin' to. They're all at it.'

'I told yer, Clara. I told yer 'e was a dirty ole goat, didn't I?' Ada said, tucking her hands into her apron.

Clara had become serious-faced. She would have to keep her eye on Patrick, she decided, the way things were. He had been quiet lately, spending a lot of time with his rabbits and chickens and not talking much. Maybe he was hiding something. It might be a good idea to keep her eye on Ada, too, she thought. She could be a bit deep at times.

When Alf's visitor reached home she parked the bassinet outside the side door and pulled back the covers. Gently she lifted the tiny bundle into her arms and cuddled it to her lovingly as she stepped inside. Once in the parlour she threw the bundle into a corner and returned for the bassinet.

"Ow did yer get on, Dora?' Dave asked, peering into the pram.

'There's forty-eight sixteen-ounce tins there. One more trip should do it,' she grinned.

Muriel Taylor's notoriety had grown during the few years she had practised her chosen profession. Wagging tongues had been busy, and stories of the street girl's carryings-on had quickly spread from the limited confines of Paragon Place. Gossipers were quick to point Muriel out to their inquiring friends from the neighbouring backstreets and the story became coloured and exaggerated, so exaggerated that the newly informed folk who passed by the square glanced at number 1 as though expecting to see a red lamp hanging over the front room window. Muriel had always conducted her business discreetly indoors, but the gossip had folk believing that merchant seamen left their ships as soon as they berthed and hurried to line up outside Muriel Taylor's front door. Young girls who were starting out on their romantic adventures and who had incurred the wrath of their worried parents were told in no uncertain terms that if they were not careful they would end up like Muriel Taylor.

Some of the Paragon Place folk felt sympathy for the girl, aware of the circumstances which had caused her to go on to the streets, and they had retained a nodding acquaintanceship with her. Alf Porter, aware that he himself was a target for the gossipers, looked upon Muriel as a friend. So, too, did Ernest Cox, who had now transferred to the Royal Marines and had taken the trouble to drop her a few lines now and then. One visitor to number 1 who had gone back to her place of employment and prayed for the young woman's salvation would have been encouraged by the power of prayer had she seen Muriel Taylor's recent transformation. Other less pious folk put the startling change down to the presence and influence of a mere mortal who hailed from across the Atlantic.

Conrad Polaski had written home to the ageing Father O'Shaughnessy and informed him that he had met a young lady in London whom he intended to marry. He had gone on to say that his proposal of marriage had been accepted and he was now in the process of liaising with the army authorities, who would no doubt be in touch very shortly. Conrad knew that time was paramount as he would soon be part of the invasion forces, and with that in mind he took Muriel to a jeweller's in Aldgate and together they selected a modestly priced engagement ring. Muriel was ecstatic and she decided that the event should be properly celebrated.

'I don't wanna go up west, Con,' she said. 'I

wanna show yer off. Let's go ter the Railway Inn fer a celebration drink.'

Conrad raised his eyebrows with surprise, aware of Muriel's reasons for not taking him there before. 'If you're sure, honey,' he said.

'I'm sure,' she smiled, hugging him tightly. 'They've all gotta know about us. It's somefing I wanna do, an' it's very important ter me, Con.'

He held her close and kissed her ear. 'OK then, let's do it.'

Muriel was feeling happy when she met Sally in the square on Friday evening. 'You're lookin' good, Sal,' she remarked, copying Conrad's mode of speech. ''Ow yer feelin'?'

'Well, apart from feelin' a bit limited I'm fine,' Sally replied, puffing with the exertion of her walk from the tram stop.

'When yer packin' up work?'

'Next Friday, an' it can't come quick enough, ter tell yer the truth,' Sally grumbled.

Muriel glanced down at Sally's rounded belly. ''Ave yer bin gettin' the eye treatment?' she asked.

'The neighbours, yer mean?'

Muriel nodded. 'Yeah. You'll get used to it. They give yer a sickly grin an' then before you're out o' sight they're on about yer. Still, while they're sortin' yer out they're leavin' some ovver poor prat alone.'

Sally laughed. 'It don't worry me none, an' I can see it don't worry you eivver.'

Muriel shrugged her shoulders. 'It did at first, but I soon got used ter the looks an' the whispers. It was ter be expected, I s'pose. Still, I
514

don't need ter worry any more. I'm engaged ter Conrad. We're gettin' married soon as 'e gets the nod from 'is CO.'

Sally squeezed Muriel's arm. 'That's smashin'. I'm so glad fer yer.'

'Fanks, Sal. I appreciate yer sayin' so. Mind you, there's some who's gonna be glad ter see the back o' me.'

'Will yer be goin' ter America?' Sally asked, holding her side and wincing as the baby moved.

'Well, it's early days yet,' Muriel answered. 'Conrad reckons the invasion won't be long now an' 'e'll be in on it. Please Gawd when the war's over 'e'll take me back ter the States wiv 'im. I don't exactly know what's what yet. 'Ere, wanna see me engagement ring?' she added, holding out her hand.

'Cor! It's luvverly,' Sally exclaimed. 'I bet you're proud. 'E's certainly a good-lookin' fella. Where'd yer find 'im?'

Muriel smiled. 'I picked 'im up! Yeah, it's true. I gotta tell yer the story. It was a Saturday night. I'll never forget it. I was on me usual manor an' it started ter get a bit dodgy. I was sittin' in the Red Lion wiv one o' the girls when these merchant seamen came over. Apparently they was off a Spanish ship. They started gettin' a bit loud-mouthed so we decided ter take a walk roun' the block. Anyway, one o' the Spanish fellas followed me out. It's funny, Sal, but in my game yer get ter know the nonsense-cases. Yer can sense 'em, an' believe me this fella looked the part. Anyway, I did the usual tricks, like crossin' the road an' watchin' what 'e was doin'

515

out the corner o' me eye, an' I started ter get frightened. I could see that 'e was definitely followin' me. I was desperately lookin' out fer one o' the regular coppers. They're OK as long as yer don't tout on the streets, an' when yer tell 'em there's a nonse trailin' yer they usually warn 'em off. Well, that night I couldn't see a copper anywhere. I was gettin' really scared, an' I tell yer it takes a lot fer me ter get scared. Well, I stopped ter cross the road again an' this Spanish bloke come up an' took 'old of me arm. I could feel 'is fingers pressin' in an' 'e jus' sort o' pulled me. I knew what 'e was after. 'E wanted ter take me down by the wharves.'

'Christ! I bet yer was terrified, wasn't yer?' Sally exclaimed.

'Yer bet I was,' Muriel went on. 'I tried ter pull me arm away but it was like it was in a vice. 'E was as strong as an ox. It was then that I see Conrad. 'E was standin' on 'is own outside the Warrior pub. Suddenly 'e was standin' in front of us. "Is this guy troubling you, little lady?" 'e said. Well, I can't tell yer 'ow I felt right at that minute. I could see this tall, broad-shouldered Yank wiv cropped 'air an' a mean look on 'is face, an' I melted. This nonsense-case said something in Spanish an' before yer could blink my Con grabs 'im by the scruff of 'is froat an' lifts 'im off 'is feet. 'E brought 'is face right up close to 'im an said somefing in a really quiet voice, an' then 'e slowly lowered 'im down. Well, this bloke 'as it away as fast as 'e can. I'm shakin' like a leaf. Well, ter cut a long story short, 'e buys me a drink, gets a cab an' insists on

516

escortin' me 'ome. What d'yer fink o' that?'

Sally grinned. 'That's better than the stories yer read in the magazines. Did yer tell 'im about yerself?'

Muriel smiled. 'I wasn't exactly dressed like a vestal virgin an' I 'ad me war-paint on. I thought ter meself the fella's earned a free bash, so when I got ter me front door I invited 'im in.'

Sally had forgotten her tender stomach and aching limbs as she listened to Muriel's saga. 'Did 'e take up the offer?' she asked.

Muriel chuckled. 'I tell yer, Sal. 'E calmly lit two fags, jus' like yer see 'em do it in the films, an' 'e 'anded me one of 'em. "I gotta get back," 'e said, all apologetic, then 'e gave me a peck on me cheek an' asked if I was free fer a date. I tell yer, that fella slaughtered me. 'E made me feel like I was somefing special. I don't remember the last time any fella give me that sort o' treatment. After 'e left me at the door I went inside an' bawled me eyes out. I dunno why I did it. Maybe it was reaction, or maybe it was jus' 'cos 'e treated me like a lady, I dunno. Anyway, I swore then that I was gonna give up whorin'. I 'ave, Sally. I really 'ave.'

Sally smiled and pressed the young woman's hands in hers. 'Well that's smashin', Muriel. I'm really pleased fer yer. The neighbours are gonna 'ave ter find somebody else ter gossip about now.'

'They already 'ave, Sal. Welcome ter the club.'

They laughed together and then Sally arched her back and sighed deeply. 'Well, I'd better get

517

in. It's bin nice talkin' ter yer.'

Muriel touched Sally's arm in a friendly gesture. 'By the way. Me an' Conrad are goin' up the Railway termorrer night fer a celebration drink. Why don't yer look in? Bring yer friend Vera, if she's up to it, an' we can all 'ave a nice chat.'

Sally made her way along the square and walked into her house, still thinking about the chat she had had with Muriel. It suddenly seemed strange to her that they had both grown up in the little community without getting to know each other very well until now. Muriel had always kept her own counsel and had not made any real friends in the square, apart from Alf Porter. Her mother's suicide had been a cruel blow and Muriel had coped with the tragedy in her own way. Now it seemed she had put her old life behind her and had a happy future to look forward to, God willing. She would be able to start a new life in America after the war, away from the gossip and the pointing fingers.

As Sally walked into the parlour her thoughts were interrupted by her mother's acid comments. 'I looked out fer yer farver jus' now an' I see yer talkin' ter that little whore,' she said, a hard look in her eyes. 'What's she want?'

Sally sighed as she eased herself down into a chair. 'Muriel's not on the game any more, Mum. She's gettin' married ter that American fella.'

Annie snorted. 'Once a prosser always a prosser, that's what I reckon. A leopard can't change its spots. It's in 'em. I feel sorry fer that

518

bloke of 'ers. 'E'll 'ave ter keep a tight rein on 'er, that's fer sure.'

Sally looked at her mother's tired face and saw the unhappiness reflected in her eyes. 'Are yer all right, Mum?' she asked. 'You're not doin' too much, are yer?'

Annie sighed and put down the plates she was holding. 'I'm all right, but I'd feel a bit better if everybody showed me a little bit o' consideration once in a while. There's yer farver late again. I know where 'e's gorn. Up the pub, that's where. Why 'e can't come straight 'ome like anybody else I'll never know. Then there's Lora. She's come in wiv the 'ump an' gorn straight up to 'er room. I dunno, I'm just about fed up wiv the lot of it.'

'What's the matter wiv Lora?' Sally inquired, kicking off her shoes and rubbing the soles of her feet.

'Yer guess is as good as mine,' Annie replied, laying the table places with exaggerated care. 'If yer ask me it's that bloke she's knockin' around wiv. She ain't bin 'erself fer a few weeks now. Gawd, I 'ope she ain't gorn an' got 'erself pregnant.'

When Sally tapped on Lora's bedroom door and walked in she found her sister sitting on the edge of her bed. 'Anyfing wrong, Lora?' she asked.

Lora shook her head. 'Nufing fer yer ter worry about,' she replied offhandedly.

'Anyfing yer wanna talk about?' Sally asked her quietly. 'I can listen. I've done a bit o' that already ternight.'

519

'Oh, an' who's bin cryin' on your shoulder?' Lora asked, showing a mild interest.

'I bin 'earin' about Muriel Taylor's boyfriend. They're gettin' married, would yer believe. She told me she's give up the game.'

Lora smiled mirthlessly. 'That's a turn-up fer the book.'

'Well, she seems adamant,' Sally went on. 'Mind you, 'e's a nice-lookin' fella. 'Ave yer seen 'im?'

Lora nodded. 'Yeah, I've seen 'im.'

Sally shrugged her shoulders. 'I can see yer don't wanna talk. I'll leave yer alone.'

Lora looked up at her sister for a moment, then she patted the bed beside her. 'I'm sorry,' she said, attempting a wan smile. 'It's jus' me. Sit down, Sal.'

'Is it man trouble?' Sally asked, smiling kindly as she walked over and sat down next to her.

'Yeah, yer could say that,' Lora sighed. 'I've decided I've finished wiv 'em. They're more trouble than they're worth.'

'You're not pregnant, are yer?' Sally said, mimicking her mother's voice. 'Mum said yer better not be.'

Lora forced a grin. 'No fear. We 'ad a big bust-up an' I told 'im I didn't want ter see 'im any more, that's all.'

'That's all?' Sally queried. 'It can be a bad experience, dependin' 'ow deep the feelin' is.'

'Oh, 'e was all right, I s'pose,' Lora said, picking away at the eiderdown. 'I fink it's jus' me. We're turnin' out ter be a right pair, you an' me. When I look around an' see ovver girls I

520

used ter know settled down I wonder if there's somefing wrong wiv me.'

'There's nufing wrong wiv yer, Lora. You're just impossible, that's all.'

The joke was lost on the younger woman. 'Well, if not wantin' to 'ave babies or live like a drudge is unnatural then I'm unnatural,' Lora went on. 'It's not what I want, Sal. I want ter get out o' this mousetrap. I wanna nice place an' enough money ter do the fings I wanna do. Is that bein' unnatural?'

Sally sighed. 'I dunno. I wanted babies, lots of 'em. Sad ter say, Ben couldn't supply me needs an' now I've got a fella that can. I don't worry about 'avin lots o' clothes an' a place in the country, although it would be nice. I jus' want this bloody war ter end an' me an' Jim back tergevver again.'

Lora looked at her sister closely. 'That's the difference between us two,' she said with a friendly smile. 'Yer seem to accept fings the way they are. I can't. I don't know who's right. P'r'aps we both are. I fink it's the way you're made.'

Sally shrugged her shoulders. 'P'r'aps you've jus' bin unfortunate in yer choice o' men.'

Lora nodded. 'Yeah, I do pick 'em, don't I? 'Ere, by the way, d'yer remember Bernard? Well, 'e's got 'is wings. 'E's bin on bombin' raids over Germany, so 'is sister told me. Who would 'ave thought it of Bernard?'

Sally laughed. 'Yer did give 'im a bad time, Lora. The poor bloke didn't know wevver 'e was comin' or goin' wiv you.'

521

'Yeah I was a bit 'ard on 'im, I must admit. Still, I expect Bernard's grown up by now. 'E's prob'ly 'avin' a passionate affair wiv one o' those Waafs.'

The sound of the front door opening and closing carried up the stairs. 'C'mon, Lora, it's Dad,' Sally said quickly. 'We'd better get down there. Mum's bin waitin' ter serve up.'

When they entered the parlour the girls exchanged brief glances. Their father looked the worse for drink and he had slumped down in his favourite chair, his tobacco-pouch and pipe held in his hand.

'Well, ain't yer gonna wash yer 'ands?' Annie moaned. 'I've bin waitin' fer ages ter dish up.'

Charlie gave her a cold stare. 'I'm not all that 'ungry. Leave mine in the oven.'

Annie's face took on a look of disgust. 'Yer bin in the pub, I know. Can't yer come 'ome straight away like anybody else? There's me slavin' over the 'ot stove an' there's you guzzlin' pints. I'm just about sick of it.'

Charlie packed his pipe methodically, his eyes heavy-lidded. 'Don't keep on, Muvver,' he said slowly. 'If yer mus' know I've 'ad a few extra terday. We stopped work at one o'clock. One o' the lads got killed this mornin'.'

Annie sat down heavily. 'Oh my Gawd,' she said sadly. 'Who was it? 'Ow did it 'appen?'

Charlie shrugged his shoulders and stared into the empty grate. ''E was one o' the casuals,' he began. 'I didn't know the bloke meself. It was similar ter Ben's accident. A load o' cases slipped out of a sling an' sent 'im over the side o' the ship. Young Dickie Arnold dived in an' 'eld on to 'im but the bloke was dead when they got 'im out o' the water. Mind you, if it wasn't fer one o' the lightermen stickin' a pole over the barge Dickie would 'ave gorn as well. The currents are strong when the tide's runnin' full.'

Annie had been mollified by what Charlie told her and she felt guilty for losing her temper. 'Put yer feet up, luv,' she said softly, putting her hand on her husband's shoulder. 'Lora, get yer farver a nice cuppa. Don't worry about yer dinner, Charlie. I'll keep it warm till later.'

While Lora poured the tea Sally went into the scullery to help her mother strain the vegetables. 'I remember Ben tellin' me 'ow they stop work fer the day when somebody gets killed in the docks,' she said.

Annie nodded. 'They do it as a mark of respect. Yer farver was sayin' only the ovver night 'ow dangerous it's gettin' lately. Trouble is, there's so much stuff comin' in an' they try ter turn the ships round as quick as they can. Workin' like that I s'pose there's bound ter be accidents. I worry sick over yer dad. 'E ain't gettin' no younger. None of us are, come ter that.'

'Yer still lookin' pretty good, Mum,' Sally grinned.

Annie snorted as she turned off the gas-taps, then suddenly she straightened up, putting a hand to her mouth.

'What's the matter, Mum?' Sally said quickly.

523

Annie's hand went up to her temple. 'Sod it! I've forgot ter salt the greens.'

Chapter Twenty-Six

SALLY held on to Vera's arm as they made their way out of the square and strolled along Stanley Street. Ahead the sombre railway arches loomed up and the sounds of the pub piano carried out into the quiet turning.

'It makes a nice break ter get out fer a couple of hours,' Vera said. 'Mind you, I've 'ad a sermon off me mum. "What ever yer do, stick ter lemonade. Drinkin' can affect the baby while yer breast feedin'." Mind you, I can't complain. Me mum's always ready ter look after the baby. She loves doin' it.'

Sally laughed. 'You'll 'ave ter be careful drinkin' too much lemonade. You'll give the baby wind.'

Vera pulled a face. 'I tell yer, Sal. It ain't much fun when they're on the breast. It's bloody painful, too, at times. Still, I s'pose it's better if you've got enough milk. It saves gettin' out o' bed an' warmin' bottles.'

Sally had also been given a sharp lecture before she left for the pub. 'I reckon yer wanna job, goin' up the pub in your condition,' Annie had said. 'After all, it ain't as though you're friends wiv the girl. Mrs Corrigan got drunk a few weeks before 'er baby was due an' she nearly lost it. Yer gotta be so careful.'

The public bar had filled by the time Sally and Vera arrived and as they walked in Muriel immediately came over. 'No fella ternight then, Vera?' she remarked.

''E's gone fer a drink wiv some of 'is mates,' Vera replied. ''E said 'e might pop in later.'

Muriel gripped the girl's arms. 'Come an' meet Con,' she said with a huge grin. 'We got some seats saved fer yer.'

They squeezed through to the far corner of the bar, and the tall American stood up and smiled. Muriel made the introductions and Vera looked the Marine up and down. 'Cor! Where d'yer get 'im?' she said. 'Is there any more like you back at camp?'

Conrad laughed and moved aside as Sally slipped into a vacant seat. ''E's got good manners, too,' Vera remarked to Muriel. ''E's as big as John Wayne. Are yer a cowboy, Conrad?'

He laughed aloud. 'No. I'm an Easterner. I come from New York.'

Vera winked at Muriel and leaned forward on the table, resting her chin on her clenched fists. ''Ave yer bin in films, Conrad?' she asked.

He laughed and turned to Muriel. 'I'd better get the drinks.'

At the other side of the bar Charlie Robinson was sitting with his drinking-partners and Alf Porter sauntered over to join them. ''Ave yer seen that Yank? Blimey, 'e ain't 'alf a big 'un,' Alf exclaimed.

Ted Bromley leaned forward over his glass of ale. 'It's the food they eat, an' all that fresh air.

It's bloody great steaks out there. They're entitled ter be big.'

Alf took a swig from his glass, then set it down carefully on the table. 'James Cagney ain't so big,' he said, looking at Ted with a mischievous glint in his eye. 'Nor is George Raft, come ter that.'

'Yeah, well p'r'aps they don't eat steak,' Ted grinned.

Charlie was studying his near-empty glass. 'I don't go a lot on Yanks,' he said without looking up. 'They got a lot ter say fer themselves, if yer ask me.'

Ted exchanged glances with Fred Mynott. Their friend had been drinking heavily that lunch-time and he was in a dark mood. They knew that the accident in the docks the previous day had upset Charlie and he had become very surly. 'Ole Nosher plays that pianer well, don't 'e?' Ted remarked, nudging Alf.

The square's drunkard ignored him and looked across at Charlie. 'Them Yanks are all right. Now, yer take that Conrad.'

'You take 'im. I don't want 'im,' Charlie growled.

Alf disregarded Charlie's comment. ''E's a real gentleman. Muriel's got a good un' there.'

'What's 'e doin' in 'ere, anyway?' Charlie said, a nasty edge to his voice.

'They've got engaged,' Alf went on. 'They're 'avin' a bit of a celebration.'

'Well, what did they 'ave ter come in 'ere for?' Charlie growled. 'This ain't the only pub round 'ere, is it?'

Alf's red-rimmed eyes narrowed as he looked at the docker. 'Why yer so set against the Yankie fella, Charlie?' he asked.

Ted's eyes flashed a message to Alf, then he looked across to Charlie. 'Take no notice of 'im, Chas. Let's get a drink in. Same again?' he asked, getting up.

Charlie did not feel inclined to ignore the question. 'I jus' don't like Yanks,' he growled, his eyes boring into Alf. 'Take the last war. They didn't get in to it till 1917. Then they 'ad the gall ter say they won the bloody war. What about all our poor bleeders what got killed and maimed from 1914 onwards?'

Alf was not to be shut up so easily. 'There's gonna be a lot o' them Yanks killed and maimed as well as our blokes before this lot's over, I can tell yer,' he retorted.

Ted had picked up the empty glasses. 'C'mon, Alf,' he urged him. 'Give us a bit of 'elp, an' let's change the subject, fer Gawd's sake.'

When the glasses had been refilled Alf took his and sauntered over to Muriel's table. The women were chatting together and Vera's loud laugh rang out above the piano music. Conrad was sitting back, his arms folded and a blank look on his handsome features. 'Hi ya, Alf,' he grinned. 'Can I get you a drink?'

Alf shook his head and turned to Muriel. ''Ere, can I borrer yer fella? I wanna introduce 'im ter me pals.'

Conrad stood up, towering over the older man. 'Lead on, Alfred,' he grinned.

Alf led the way to his table and stood with his

hands hooked into his waistcoat pocket. 'Fellas, I want yer ter meet a good friend o' mine,' he said proudly.

When the introductions had been made the American sat down at the table and was soon chatting amiably to Charlie's two friends. Alf listened as Ted talked of life in the London docks, and Conrad explained that two of his uncles were longshoremen in New York, where, like in England, there was a close affinity amongst the rivermen.

Throughout the conversation Charlie remained aloof. He had tried to blot out the memory of the previous day's tragic accident by drinking heavily and he had staggered home that lunch-time only to be berated by Annie. He had slept the afternoon away and woken up still feeling depressed. During his long years in the docks Charlie had seen quite a few accidents, some of which had been fatal, and he was always affected in the same way. As he got older witnessing such accidents did not become any easier. Instead it seemed to affect him more deeply.

The public bar was now packed to capacity and the piano player was running through his repertoire of popular songs. Folk were joining in and it became hard to hold a conversation. At the far table Muriel was recounting some of her wilder experiences to her friends and loud laughter rose above the singing. At the other end of the bar the drinks were flowing and Alf was now very drunk. He finished his pint in one long swig, stood up with considerable effort and then staggered off through the throng to order another round of drinks.

Conrad watched his progress with a huge grin on his face. 'I think the old feller needs a hand,' he said, getting up and making his way to the counter.

Alf was trying to attract the landlord's attention, to the displeasure of two young men who stood beside him.

'Take it easy, old man. 'E's servin' us first,' one of them said in a loud voice.

Alf fixed his bleary eyes on the young man. 'Who yer callin' an ole man?' he slurred. 'Don't yer be so lippy, yer young pup.'

The young man turned to his friend and grinned. "Ark at this ole goat, Patsy. They get worse as they get older.'

Alf turned on the young man. 'Listen, flash 'Arry. I 'eard what yer said an' . . .'

'What's the trouble, pop?' Conrad asked as he reached the counter.

The young man rounded on the American. 'Take 'im away, Yank. 'E's makin' a nuisance of 'imself.'

Conrad grinned briefly. 'I wouldn't say that.'

The second man stepped in front of his friend, a hard glint in his eyes. 'I would.'

The big American's face changed suddenly. 'Ease off, fella.'

The young man looked Conrad up and down. 'You Yanks do like chuckin' yer weight around, don't yer?'

The American's face was set hard. 'You got something against Yanks, then?' he said quietly.

Bert had been alerted by the barmaid and he quickly interrupted the argument. 'Look, I don't want no unpleasantness,' he said firmly, leaning across the counter and staring hard at them. 'Everybody's 'avin' a good time, so let's keep it that way. Right?'

The glasses had finally been replenished and Alf was relating the incident to his friends. 'It was those Dougan bruvvers,' he said loudly, twisting his face in disgust. 'Bloody flash gits. Mind you, Con sorted 'em out. Yer told 'em, didn't yer, son?'

Conrad shrugged shyly. 'You'd better pick on someone your own size in future, Alf,' he said with a grin.

Ted glanced over to the counter and then back to the American. 'Them Dougans are a dodgy crowd,' he remarked. 'There's about five bruvvers in that family, an' when yer upset one yer upset the lot.'

Charlie nodded grudgingly. 'I don't go a lot on that crowd. They're all a load o' villains. I've seen 'em cause a few upsets in this pub.'

'Why don't that soppy bleeder of a landlord bar 'em?' Alf asked.

''Cos they're good customers, that's why,' Charlie replied. 'They use the saloon bar most o' the time, especially when they're wheelin' an' dealin'.'

Fred nodded. 'The connivin' bastards are in everyfing. I wouldn't trust 'em as far as I could see 'em.'

Muriel reclaimed Conrad and a little later Big Joe put his head round the door. 'I'm lookin' fer

530

that drunken missus o' mine. Anybody seen 'er?' he asked.

Fred pointed to the far corner. 'She's over there,' he said, looking up at his son-in-law with an amused smile. 'Come on, mate, sit down an' 'ave a drink, fer Gawd's sake, before yer join that cacklin' lot.'

A few minutes later Big Joe came back looking serious-faced. 'Bert just pulled me,' he said. "E reckons the Dougan bruvvers are out fer trouble. 'E said they've bin round the saloon bar talkin' amongst themselves. 'E reckons they're gonna jump the Yank when the pub turns out.'

Fred winced. 'They usually work mob-'anded. 'E won't stand a chance on 'is own.'

Big Joe picked up his pint, a mean look on his wide features. 'Well, I fer one ain't standin' back. Our Vera's wiv 'im an' Muriel, an' there's Sally, too. They could get 'urt if there's trouble. Besides, I ain't forgot the time that Patsy Dougan tried ter chat Vera up while I was away at sea.'

Charlie had been staring into his beer and suddenly he looked up. 'I don't go a lot on Yanks meself, but I don't like ter see anybody took advantage of. I'm in.'

Ted and Fred looked at each other and Fred grinned. 'I'm in, too. What about you, Ted?'

Ted looked at Charlie. 'Remember that time we was in the King's Arms an' that crowd come in lookin' fer a knuckle, Chas?'

Charlie smiled. 'That was a night, wasn't it. I couldn't eat fer a week after that set-to. I cracked me jaw on somebody's boot.'

531

Alf rolled his shoulders and pulled a face. 'Count me in. I like that Yank.'

Big Joe winked at Fred, then turned to Alf. 'I tell yer what. I'll claim 'em one at a time an' yer breathe on 'em, Alf. That should do it.'

The pianist had rounded off the evening by playing 'We'll Meet Again' and Bert had called time. As folk started to leave Charlie nodded to Alf. 'Right, way yer go.'

Alf staggered over to Muriel, a sly grin on his lined face. 'Can you gels go on in front?' he said, holding on to the table for support. 'Me mates wanna 'ave five minutes wiv Conrad.'

Muriel shook her head. 'Now I've got 'im I ain't lettin' 'im go, so yer can tell yer mates they'll 'ave ter wait till next time.'

Alf scratched his balding head. 'Look, Muriel, this is man's talk. Yer gotta let 'im orf the 'ook fer a few minutes or everybody'll fink 'e's right under the thumb, an' yer wouldn't want that, would yer?'

Muriel sighed. 'Alf, you an' yer mates are bloody pests. All right, but don't keep 'im too long.'

Soon after the women had left in a group Bert came over. 'They're outside waitin',' he said urgently. 'There's the five Dougans an' they've got a tasty-lookin' team wiv 'em so yer better be careful.'

''Ow many?' Charlie asked.

'There's about nine or ten in all. Yer better watch Mutton-eye Dorkins. 'E always carries a brass knuckle-duster in 'is pocket.'

'Well, there's five of us, includin' the Yank,'

532

Charlie said, looking round the table. 'Yer can't count pissy Alf. We'll give 'em a run fer their money, I should fink.'

Bert shook his head sadly. 'I dunno, as if there ain't enough trouble in the world wivout Bermondsey 'avin' its own civil war.'

Conrad had joined the men and when Charlie explained the situation the big American nodded, serious-faced. 'That sounds like good tactics. I'll go along with that.'

Charlie tapped the American on the shoulder. 'Right-o then, mate, way yer go. We're right be'ind yer.'

Overhead a full April moon lit up the street and the rumble of a passing goods train echoed through the arches. Conrad Polaski stepped out from the pub, warily glancing left and right. A few people were hanging around talking and one or two wished him good night as he started off in the direction of Paragon Place.

Ahead, Patsy Dougan was standing in the doorway of the corner shop and he turned to his companions who were waiting in the side street. ''Old tight, 'ere 'e comes. It's okay, 'e's on 'is own.'

As Conrad neared the corner Charlie and his friends slipped out into the street one by one and walked in a single file close to the wall and some way behind the American. Conrad guessed that the attack would occur as he reached the corner and he clenched his fists.

As Patsy Dougan jumped at him from the dark doorway Conrad stepped back suddenly and then spun round and swung a punch. His clenched fist caught Patsy Dougan on the side of the face and he fell as though poleaxed. At once the American was surrounded and he staggered against the shop shutters in a desperate attempt to keep his feet against the onslaught of flailing punches and boots.

The men were running now and Big Joe reached the fight first. He hit one of the Dougans on the back of the neck and grabbed at the second attacker, spinning him around and cracking him on the jaw. Ted and Fred were close behind and they swiftly piled into the fray, lashing into the mob and booting two of them into the gutter. Conrad had regained his balance and he was now swinging punches again, but one of the assailants had grabbed Ted's arm and another was punching him in the stomach. By the time Charlie reached the fighting he was panting heavily and he held his head low and charged into the man who held Ted's arms behind his back, smashing him sideways into the shop shutters. Ted threw a hard punch at the other attacker and Conrad grabbed him from behind and threw him head first into the road.

It was soon over. The battered attackers picked themselves up and ran off along the side turning, leaving Mutton-eye Dorkins facing the American. Charlie was panting and wheezing loudly as he staggered to his feet. Together with Conrad, Ted, Fred and Big Joe had gathered in a circle around the most dangerous of the attackers, who had his fingers through a thick brass knuckle-duster. Mutton-eye was crouching like a cornered animal, his face contorted with rage.

'Grab 'im, then,' Charlie gasped.

Conrad raised his hand as he faced the bear-like man. 'Leave him, he's mine!' he shouted, lifting his clenched fists and swaying slowly from the hips.

Mutton-eye was not lacking in courage. He glowered at the American, confident of his own strength, and his face broke into an evil grin. 'Come on then, Yank,' he sneered. 'Let's see 'ow tough yer really are.'

He charged forwards suddenly and Conrad shot out his fist and caught the man between the eyes. Mutton-eye staggered back a pace, blinking in surprise. He rushed the American again and Conrad crashed a heavy blow into him just below the ear, felling him. Mutton-eye shook his head and slowly dragged himself up on to his feet. As he straightened Conrad hit him again, a full-blooded blow on the man's chin. Mutton-eye dropped to his knees and fell backwards, his bulging eyes glazed.

Patsy Dougan had been dazed earlier by Conrad's fist and he was still lying in a heap beside the shop doorway, forgotten by the spectators who had gathered around the fight. Slowly he pulled himself together and glanced at the group. Big Joe was nearest, standing with his back towards him. Patsy felt in his pocket and his fingers closed around the folded knife. Quietly he pulled himself up on all fours and crawled forward slowly, flicking open the razor-sharp blade. When he was only a few feet behind

Big Joe he suddenly lunged upwards.

The men heard a scream and turned to see Patsy Dougan lying full stretch on the pavement. Muriel was standing over him with a heavy wooden rolling-pin held in her hand.

''E was goin' fer yer, Joe,' she said, her voice shaking with emotion.

Charlie looked down at the prone figure and chuckled. 'Yer laid 'im out, gel.'

He went over to Mutton-eye and slipped the knuckle-duster from his hand. 'I reckon yer should 'ave this,' he said, handing the implement to Conrad.

Muriel had picked up the knife. 'I fink I'll keep this,' she said, smiling at Conrad as he slipped his arm around her shoulders.

Ted and Charlie pulled Mutton-eye to his feet. 'Take yer pal 'ome, Dorkins,' Ted said calmly. 'I fink it's all over, don't you?'

The victorious group strolled along to the square. Conrad walked between Charlie and Big Joe, his arms around their shoulders, and Muriel walked between Ted and Fred, still holding on to the rolling-pin.

When they reached the old gas-lamp Charlie turned to the group following behind. ''Ere. Where the bloody 'ell's Alf Porter?' he said suddenly.

Fred brought the palm of his hand up smartly to his forehead. 'Christ! I forgot all about 'im. I got Bert ter lock 'im in the carsey. I thought 'e'd be more of an 'indrance than 'elp. Remember that time we moved 'is pianer?'

536

Charlie chuckled. 'Let's leave 'im there. At least 'e'll be Bert's first customer termorrer.'

Chapter Twenty-Seven

THE pleasant May days were a time of anxious anticipation for Sally as she sat at home awaiting the birth of her baby. She had left Harrison's in the last week of April, and she said goodbye to her workmates during a period of surprising change at the factory. The growing problems at Harrison's had been skilfully dealt with by the management, who had engineered a morale-boosting visit by a travelling team of military top brass. On Monday the lunch-hour had been extended to two hours and the workforce gathered in the canteen to hear themselves eulogised. They learnt that their firm was one of the local factories which was instrumental in winning the war through tremendous effort and self-sacrifice. Newspaper reporters were allowed to sit in on the talk and in their write-ups the scribes heaped praise upon the embarrassed workers. The local papers carried glowing reports of targets surpassed and of happy workers singing merrily as they worked the machines at break-neck speed to reach the quotas. The travelling military spoke of the coming Second Front and the inevitable victory, the sacrifices made by servicemen and women, and the indomitable spirit of the factory workers. When the army officers had finished, the managing director had got to his feet and announced that as a reward for their tremendous effort over the past few hectic months the early Friday finish was to be brought back on a trial basis.

Aware of the sentiment and excitement generated, the factory activists had realised they were fighting a losing battle in their efforts to bring the management to heel and the threatened strike did not take place. Another nail in the coffin of anarchy was the sudden installation of new sewing-machines and canteen equipment, and the announcement that there were to be lunch-time concerts arranged by the BBC. All in all the management had done a masterful job and the workers had been left with guilty feelings over their unpatriotic rumblings of discontent.

It was against this background that Sally took her leave, and when the factory whistle sounded on Friday evening and the noise of the machines ceased she was presented with a bunch of flowers and a yellow layette. In addition to the congratulatory comments there were a few asides and innuendos, made in hope of gleaning some information as to the identity of the father. Sally had always avoided discussing her personal life, and rumours of her separation had never been substantiated. Factory gossip had made her the victim of a certain manager who had recently left in suspicious circumstances, but one particular worker, who was engaged in a shameless and adulterous association with a supervisor, made a wild guess and openly asserted that the factory dance had something to do with the girl's condition.

Sally remained secretive until the end and she left the factory with the parting words of Maggie Chandler ringing in her ears. 'I'm gonna miss yer, Sally,' she had said, tears coming to her eyes. 'Yer was me best friend an' yer always stuck up fer me.'

The waiting days were proving to be long and anxious ones. Sally had received just one short letter from Jim during the last two months and she was beginning to despair for his safety. Every day she listened to news broadcasts which told of the bitter fighting going on in Italy and every week she pored over the published casualty lists with mounting dread. Sally's thoughts went back to the week they had spent together and to the last evening when Jim had suddenly turned to her as they strolled together in the gathering dusk. 'I'm gonna make yer my next of kin, Sal,' he had said. 'There's no family so I thought yer should be the first ter know should anyfing 'appen.'

Sally recalled his words and how they had struck fear into her heart. The war had seemed a million miles away that balmy evening but she had suddenly been brought back to reality by what he said. She remembered feeling suddenly cold and Jim wrapping his protective arms around her, warming her and laughing away her fears. Now she was alone, the baby growing inside her belly, and time was weighing heavily upon her.

The fracas in Stanley Street had left the Paragon Place pugilists feeling apprehensive. The Dougans and their cohorts had been given a bloody nose and Charlie was quick to voice his worry when the group met in the Railway Inn one evening.

'All right, so they ain't bin in the pub since, but that don't mean we've 'eard the last of it,' he warned his friends. 'They're a devious load o' bastards an' we'll 'ave ter watch out.'

Ted and Fred were of the same opinion. 'They'll bide their time an' come back at us when we're not expectin' it,' Fred declared. 'We'll jus' 'ave ter be careful, that's all.'

Alf was still upset about being incarcerated while the rout was taking place and he glared at Fred. 'Well, don't expect me ter get involved. It's your worry, not mine.'

'Don't yer be so sure,' Charlie snorted. 'It all started over yer givin' that Patsy Dougan a load o' lip. Now the Yank's not around they'll jus' as likely pick on 'is friends, an' yer told 'em 'e was a good friend o' yours.'

Ted grinned. 'Yer watch yerself, Alf. You're in it just as much as we are.'

Alf picked up his beer and took a large swig. 'Well, they don't scare me,' he said, wiping his hand across his mouth. 'If yer 'adn't 'ave locked me in the piss-'ole I'd 'ave 'ad a go at 'em as well. I only wish I'd 'ave bin there when that Yank pasted Mutton-eye Dorkins. The ugly git was well overdue fer 'is comeuppance.'

Charlie stroked his chin, a thoughtful expression on his ruddy face. 'That Taylor gel
540

will 'ave ter watch 'erself an' all,' he remarked. 'Patsy Dougan's gonna remember that clout she give 'im.'

June had hardly arrived when Sally had the first contractions late on a Monday evening, and when the midwife called she shook her head and said it would be some time yet. Annie wore her most worried look as she fussed over Sally, and Charlie was warned that he was to keep himself on hand ready to dash up to the phone box at a minute's notice. As midnight approached Annie frantically roused him from his slumber beside the unlit fire and ordered him to make the call quickly.

Early on Tuesday morning Sally gave birth to a daughter. She weighed seven pounds, and as Annie remarked, the baby had been in no hurry to make its appearance. Vera had seen the midwife going in and out of the Robinsons' house and she was the first to visit Sally. As she went into the bedroom she was struck by the change in Sally's expression. She was leaning back against the pillows, exhausted by the long birth, but there was a beautiful smile on her face as she held the tiny bundle to her breast, and her eyes were liquid and shining.

'It's a girl, Vera!' she laughed. 'I've got a baby girl!'

'Oh, I'm so pleased for yer,' her friend said, sitting down next to her. 'Let's 'ave a look at 'er. Oh, isn't she beautiful! 'Ow d'yer feel?'

'Wonderful. An' tired, very tired,' Sally said with a radiant smile.

Vera left after a short time, worried that she would tire her friend too much. Soon after, Ginny called in to congratulate Sally, and she remained downstairs for a while chatting to Annie.

'I'm really pleased fer 'er, Annie,' Ginny said, sipping her tea. 'I know 'ow much yer Sally wanted a baby.'

Annie still wore her anxious face. 'I'm worried fer 'er,' she frowned. 'She ain't 'eard from 'er bloke fer some time, Ginny. I 'ope 'e's all right.'

Ginny nodded. 'Yeah, it's worryin'. George is scared sick over the boys. There's only bin that card from Laurie an' nufing at all from Tony. I'm only fankful none o' mine are old enough ter be called up. It must be terrible ter see yer kids go off ter the war.'

Annie nodded. 'I'm glad I never 'ad sons. Charlie always wanted a boy but I fink 'e's glad now we never did. By the way, did yer 'ear about that Mrs Beaumont? She lost 'er boy last week. 'E was in the navy. She's gone grey. Then there was that Sheila Argent. 'Er boy's a prisoner o' war. 'E got shot down over Germany.'

Ginny was beginning to wish she had not stayed for a chat. Annie was guaranteed to spoil anyone's day with her depressing snippets of information.

'I was talkin' ter that fat cow at number ten the ovver day,' Annie went on. 'She told me a terrible story about this woman she knows. Apparently this woman's friend's sister's boy got took prisoner in Singapore. Anyway, the muvver finally got a card from 'im an' she noticed that the stamp wasn't stuck down prop'ly so she peeled it orf an' under the stamp was the message, "They cut me tongue out." It sent 'er stark ravin' mad by all accounts.'

Ginny puffed loudly in exasperation. 'Annie, I don't know why yer listen ter them sort o' stories. There's a lot o' wicked people about who make 'em up. Ain't yer got any 'appy bits ter talk about?'

Annie got up from her chair and turned on the wireless. 'There ain't many 'appy fings ter talk about, is there?' she moaned. 'What wiv one fing an' the ovver.'

'Well I 'ope yer don't tell George that story. 'E's worried sick over Laurie as it is,' Ginny growled.

The wireless crackled and band music filled the room. Annie lowered the volume and sat down again. 'Mrs Cox was tellin' me 'er boy's gorn in the Marines,' she began. 'She's worried sick over 'im.'

Ginny decided it was time to leave, but as she was getting up the music on the radio cut out and the announcer's voice came on the air. Annie was about to furnish her friend with a parting anecdote of misery when Ginny waved her quiet. ''Ang on, Annie. 'E said somefing about an important announcement.'

The two women sat down again as the solemn words came over the air. 'Under the command of General Eisenhower, Allied naval forces, supported by strong air forces, began landing Allied armies this morning on the northern coast of France.'

Ginny jumped up quickly. 'My Gawd! It's started!' she shouted. 'Annie, we've invaded 'em.'

Annie clasped her hands together as if in prayer. 'I knew it wouldn't be long,' she cried, her usually mournful face lighting up. 'I've 'ad that feelin' fer a couple o' weeks now. Me stomach's bin goin' over. I'm goin' up ter see if Sally's awake. I gotta tell 'er the good news.'

Ginny made for the door. 'I'm gonna wake George up,' she said excitedly. ''E was at work last night but 'e'd wanna know.'

People were gathering in the square talking excitedly. Alf had been on late shift at the newspapers and he came to the door wearing an old coat over his striped pyjamas, their bottoms tucked into his thick woollen socks.

'I 'eard it, Lil!' he called out to Granny Allen. 'I was jus' gettin' up when it came over the wireless. Gawd Almighty! It's finally 'appened!'

Lil chuckled as he jigged on the spot. 'Get dressed, yer silly git, or you'll catch yer death.'

Alf was always looking for excuses to celebrate and he hurried inside his house to find his current bottle of whisky. 'Alf, me ole son, yer gonna get pissed as an 'andcart terday,' he told himself aloud.

Clara was on her doorstep talking to Ada in an excited voice. 'I was doin' me dustin' an' I 'eard the bloke on the wireless,' she said quickly. 'It could all be over this year.'

Ada tucked a loose strand of bright ginger hair into her turban and raised her eyes to the sky. 'Jus' fink of it. No more blackout an' no more

544

bloody ration books. I'll 'ave Maurice 'ome fer good. Please Gawd it won't be long now.'

At eleven o'clock Granny Almond and Granny Allen made their way along the square. Daisy was talking loudly into Lil's ear. 'As I said ter my Ginny, I don't normally 'ave a drink in the daytime, but terday ain't yer normal day, is it? I mean ter say, it ain't every day the invasion starts. She don't like me drinkin' durin' the day. Says it makes me sleepy an' then I'm awake 'alf the night, but I told 'er. "Ginny," I said. "Yer old muvver-in-law's gonna get lit up ternight." Course, she went on a bit, but as I said to 'er, "Look, gel. I know yer mean well, but jus' shut up, will yer?" She's a good gel, my Ginny, but she does go on at times.'

Lil chuckled and tightened her grip on her handbag. 'Well, you're lucky, Daisy. My Rene's glad ter get me out from under 'er feet. I don't get a lot o' sympafy from that one. 'Er Ted gives me more consideration. Sometimes I fink I'm in 'er way.'

The grannies had reached the Railway Inn and already the public bar was unusually busy. Workmen had called in and Bert was laughing with a group of council roadworkers who had left a large hole in Stanley Street unattended. Bert's wife Elsie was kept busy in the saloon bar and as Daisy reached the snug bar counter she rattled on the polished surface.

'Oi! Ain't there anybody at 'ome?' she called out impatiently.

Bert came over, a wide smile on his face. 'No Guinness, I'm afraid, gels,' he said. 'Our boys

545

'ave took it all ter France wiv 'em.'

Daisy waved away his excuses. 'If I thought that was the case I wouldn't mind, but you're a lyin' ole goat, Jackson. Now give me an' Lil a Guinness or I'll be over that counter after yer. An' mind 'ow yer pour it.'

Bert reached under the counter and fished out two bottles. 'Yer startin' a bit early, ain't yer, Daisy?' he said, grinning at her.

Daisy looked down at her friend who had already made herself comfortable in a chair and then looked back to the landlord. 'I tell yer, Bert, I've lived frew the First World War an' the blitz, an' please Gawd I'm lookin' forward ter livin' long enough ter see the end o' this one, so I'm gonna 'ave a good drink terday, an' so's Lil. We're gonna drink our boys' 'ealth, an' if me an' my ole mate Lil get drunk jus' remember we've give yer fair warnin'.'

Bert smiled as he placed the frothing Guinness down in front of the old lady. 'Well, if that's yer attitude, Daisy, 'ave this one on the 'ouse, an' if yer wait a minute I'll take a drink wiv yer.'

Daisy watched as Bert poured himself a full measure of whisky. ''Ere's ter you, gels, an' 'ere's ter the end of the war,' he said, clinking glasses. 'May we all live long enough to see it.'

Daisy had soon finished her Guinness and she glanced at Lil. 'Drink up, gel, I'm gonna get the next one. Oi, Bert. Give us anuvver one, will yer? An' while you're at it pour yerself one. I got anuvver toast ter make.'

They stood together at the counter, drinks in hand, and Daisy raised her glass. 'Wiv all the excitement I forgot ter tell yer, Annie Robinson's daughter 'ad a little gel this mornin', Bert, an' I fink we should drink a toast to the little mite.'

They clinked glasses once more, and Lil wiped a tear away with the corner of her lace handkerchief.

Muriel Taylor had left the square just after the invasion news came over the air. She had been determined to put her past behind her since meeting Conrad and her decision to visit the labour exchange had been made with that promise in mind. Before she left her house she had torn up her exemption certificate and thrown it into the empty grate. There could be no going back now, she told herself. The certificate had been deviously obtained and it represented a way of life she wanted no more part of. She owed it to her American boy. He was now fighting in France and she was going to do her bit as well.

When Muriel reached the labour exchange she was shown into a small room and motioned into a chair. The employment officer, an elderly woman with grey hair and heavy-lidded eyes, looked over her spectacles and sighed.

'Yes, young lady? What is it you want?' she said coldly.

Muriel leaned back in her chair and gave the woman a friendly smile. 'I wanna join up,' she replied enthusiastically.

The smile was lost on the woman. 'Are you exempt? Have you got an exemption certificate?' she asked, a suspicious look on her thin face.

'I'm workin' fer John Fisher an' Sons as a secretary,' Muriel replied.

'Yes, I know the firm. They're an engineering firm on war work,' the woman stated. 'All their employees are registered as exempt, so I'm afraid I can't help you.'

Muriel gritted her teeth. 'Look, missus. I wanna join up. I tore me certificate up before I came out, so there.'

The officer adjusted her glasses. 'Well, that was a silly thing to do. If the police want to see your particulars and you haven't got them you'll most likely spend some time in the police station while they check up. You're registered with us as exempt.'

Muriel puffed. 'Look, the firm said it's all right ter leave, so why can't I join up?'

The woman sighed and pulled a notepad towards her. 'I'll need a few particulars,' she said in a tired voice.

Muriel rattled off her name and address and the official looked at her over her glasses.

'How old are you, Miss Taylor?'

'Twenty-six next week,' Muriel said brightly.

The woman sighed once more and scribbled into her notepad, then she got up and took off her glasses. 'Wait here, young lady. I won't be long.'

Muriel glanced around the office and saw the posters of smiling Wrens and Air Force girls, and there was a large poster showing a young woman in army uniform sitting behind the wheel of a lorry. Another poster caught her eye. It showed women serving tea to soldiers and

548

everyone in the poster had a beaming smile. 'Join the NAAFI' it said. Muriel stroked her chin thoughtfully and was still staring up at the posters when the officer came back into the room.

'Take this release form back to your employer and get him to fill it in, then come back here and we'll see what we can do,' the woman said in a tired voice.

'Christ! What a bloody rigmarole,' Muriel groaned.

'There's a war on, my dear,' the officer said icily, looking over her glasses at Muriel. 'Before we can release you from exemption we have to be sure that the work you're doing can be done equally well by an older person. Fortunately there are a lot of retired women who will be only too glad to take over your job. Actually they have to submit to a job test, but it's not exhausting work and most older people rise to the occasion. On the whole they're very adaptable, so I shouldn't worry. I think you'll be able to secure your release.'

Muriel left the labour exchange smiling to herself at the deception. As she reached the end of the turning and waited to cross the road she felt a sudden pressure on her arm. She turned to see Patsy Dougan leering at her.

'I'll be seein' yer soon,' he said quietly, then he was gone.

After the first few days of June the weather changed suddenly. Leaden skies, high winds and driving rain replaced the warm sunshine, and in

Paragon Place there was a mood of apprehension. The unseasonal weather took second place as a topic of conversation, for there was another more urgent and worrying item to discuss now. The excitement of the invasion and the hopes for an early ending to the war were dulled by the ominous sound of air-raid sirens and the distant crash of falling bombs.

On a Saturday morning in mid-June, as heavy rain was falling outside, Sally and Vera sat together at the Mynotts'.

'It sez 'ere it's a pilotless bomber,' Vera said, looking sideways at the morning paper as she fed Stephen.

Sally was relaxing in an easy chair, the baby sleeping peacefully in her arms. 'I thought we'd 'eard the last o' that siren,' she said regretfully, looking down at her daughter's tiny face. 'It woke Ruth up. We all sat under the stairs till it went quiet.'

Vera placed Stephen over her shoulder and patted his back. 'We did the same, except fer me dad. 'E wouldn't get up. I was terrified, an' me mum kept on about me dad sleepin' frew it all. I wish I could 'ave slept frew it.'

Sally was staring down at her sleeping baby, a sad expression on her face. 'I 'ope I get a letter from Jim soon,' she said suddenly. 'It's bin ages since I've 'eard anyfing.'

Vera gave her a smile of encouragement. 'You'll 'ear soon, Sal. Wiv all this fightin' goin' on in France everyfing's gettin' delayed. By the way, 'ave yer seen anyfing o' Ben lately?'

Sally shook her head. 'I saw 'im a few weeks

ago but 'e didn't see me. I was goin' down ter the clinic on a tram. 'E was walkin' pretty fast. Yer wouldn't 'ave thought 'e'd bin all smashed up just a few months previous. I fink 'e's done very well.'

Vera grinned. 'Yeah, I s'pose yer gotta give 'im credit fer that. Mind you, I reckon they was glad ter get rid of 'im at the 'ospital. 'E can be a right cantankerous so-an'-so, can't 'e?'

Suddenly the loud shrill whine of the siren sounded above the noise of a passing train. Sally grabbed her bag and stood up quickly, Ruth cradled in one arm.

'Bloody 'ell, it's off again,' she groaned.

'Don't go outside!' Vera shouted. 'Come under the stairs wiv us.'

Beryl came into the room holding Joey, fear showing on her face. 'C'mon you gels, don't 'ang about. Get yerselves under the stairs.'

It had gone quiet, and only the sound of water splashing into the back-yard from a broken drainpipe interrupted the stillness. The women looked at each other, their eyes wide with fear.

'P'r'aps it's a false alarm,' Vera said, trying to smile.

The distant growl of the flying bomb grew into a menacing roar as it flew low over the railway sidings. There was a spluttering sound and then silence. Beryl started to count silently, her lips forming the numbers and as she reached ten a loud explosion shattered the stillness. A spray of dust fell over the women and the babies started to wail.

'My Gawd! That wasn't far away,' Vera cried,

551

cuddling Stephen tightly.

'It looks like it's the docks copped it,' a man shouted outside.

People were emerging from their homes to stare up at the sky. 'It's one o' them there flyin' bombers,' someone shouted.

Alf Porter was walking towards the railway arches and heard the sound of fire-bells. It seemed as if the many people rushing past him were being drawn towards the rising smoke. A cyclist wearing an ARP battledress passed him pedalling furiously, a steel helmet perched on the back of his head and a service gas-mask strapped around his middle. Alf walked through the arches and saw the dust cloud hanging in the sky beyond the Jamaica Road.

'It's Potters Lane!' a man called out to him as he hurried past. 'A row of 'ouses copped it!'

Alf shook his head sadly and walked back through the arches. There was no point in going any further, he thought. There would be dead and dying, and people buried beneath the rubble. It wasn't right to stand around watching like some depraved ghoul.

As he reached the Railway Inn Alf heard a roar and looked up. He saw the flying bomb below the clouds, travelling fast with flame spurting from its engine. Alf stood rooted to the spot, his hand on the pub door. Suddenly the flame spluttered and went out. For a brief moment the machine seemed to falter, then it dipped and dived over the rooftops. Alf gritted his teeth and waited for the explosion. A giant ball of flame rose up as the deafening crash echoed through the arches, then black smoke drifted up, billowing out like a giant mushroom.

The terrified man hurried into the Railway Inn and staggered to the counter, his legs shaking. Customers were picking themselves up, looks of terror and disbelief written on their ashen faces. Bert and Elsie stood together behind the counter.

'Gawd Almighty! It's all startin' again,' Elsie wailed. 'Whatever's it all comin' to?'

Bert patted her shaking hands. 'It's all right, luv. It's all right.'

'Give us a double, Bert,' Alf gasped, looking down at his feet as though reassuring himself that he was still in once piece.

The all-clear siren had sounded and folk stood at their front doors, talking in low voices. Vera and Sally stood beside the two prams at Sally's front door and Big Joe was holding Joey in his arms. Ginny Almond was standing with George, one eye on her brood as they played in the square.

'Don't you lot go wanderin' off or yer'll get the back o' me 'and,' she called out as Frankie and Arthur drifted towards the Stanley Street end.

Frankie turned to his elder brother. 'We never get ter do anyfing, Arf,' he moaned. 'Ovver kids can see where the bomb fell but we've gotta stop 'ere wiv the stupid gels.'

Arthur looked along the square. 'We'll wait till Mum looks the ovver way then we'll creep away. We could 'elp dig the people out. There must be fousands buried, what wiv all that smoke.'

Frankie sat down on the paving-stones and opened his penknife. 'I better give this a sharpen,' he said, rubbing the blade back and forth over the stones. 'This fing could come in 'andy. There's a corkscrew an' a saw blade, an' this fing's good fer digging fings wiv.'

Arthur looked up to see Alf Porter walking unsteadily back into the square. 'Cor! Look at 'im, Frankie,' he laughed. ''E's an alcolic.'

'What's an alcolic, Arf?'

'It's when you're drunk all the time,' Arthur told him, his eyes following Alf's slow progress. 'Yer forget fings an' yer 'ave ter get a drink or yer go mad.'

'Who told yer that?' Frankie asked, gingerly feeling the sharpened blade with his thumb.

'I 'eard Mum talkin' ter George. She reckons Alf Porter don't know what day o' the week it is, an' she said 'e 'as ter get a drink or 'e goes potty.'

Frankie was watching Alf closely and suddenly he nudged his brother. 'Quick, Arf! 'E's talkin' ter Mum. Let's go.'

Alf had reached the group of women and he jerked his thumb in the direction of Stanley Street. 'That last one caught the gas-works be all accounts,' he said. 'Somebody come in the Railway an' said there's a big fire at the gas-works. That first one dropped on Potters Lane. A row of 'ouses copped it.'

Sally stared at Alf, her face suddenly drained of colour. 'Potters Lane?' she gasped.

554

'That's what this bloke told me, Sal. 'E was comin' from that direction.'

Vera gripped Sally's arm. 'Yer don't know fer sure, Sally.'

'I gotta find out, Vera. I must go an' see.'

Annie was standing with her hand held up to her face as she looked at her daughter. 'The baby'll be all right, Sally,' she said. 'She's 'ad 'er feed, ain't she?'

Sally nodded. 'I'll be as quick as I can, Mum. I must find out.'

She buttoned up her coat and left the square, hurrying under the railway arches and out into Jamaica Road. When she reached Potters Lane her heart jumped. The row of houses facing Ben's side of the street were a mangled heap. Men were clambering over the rubble, moving timbers and mounds of bricks in an effort to reach the trapped. A policeman stood on duty at the entrance to the turning and he held his hand up as she reached him.

'I shouldn't, lady. It's not a pretty sight,' he said quietly.

'My 'usband's down there. I gotta see 'im,' Sally protested.

'Well, you be careful. We've got enough casualties as it is,' the policeman replied, biting on his chinstrap.

As Sally walked hesitantly along what was left of Potters Lane she felt her heart banging loudly. All the houses facing the pile of rubble had their windows broken and front doors were hanging from broken hinges. The street was filled with glass, roof slates and pieces of brick,

555

and there was a sickly smell of cordite hanging in the air. Sally saw an elderly man who she knew to be an acquaintance of Ben's and she hurried up to him.

''Ave yer seen Ben around, please?' she asked anxiously.

The man pointed over to the rubble. ''E's over there, luv. Look, there 'e is.'

Sally followed his pointing finger with her eyes and she caught sight of Ben perched on top of a mound of bricks and splintered timbers. He was bending down, pressing his ear to the rubble, his hand held aloft for silence. Sally saw his hand suddenly drop and heard his urgent voice. 'Directly below. It's faint, though.'

She watched as Ben quickly took off his coat and wriggled into the narrow tunnel, his feet scraping the bricks as he burrowed his way further down. He quickly disappeared out of sight and the helpers stood silently, holding onto the large timbers. There was a shout from behind them and a nearby wall collapsed in a pile of dust. 'Keep a grip on them timbers or 'e'll be buried as well!' one of the men shouted.

It seemed an eternity to Sally before a shout rang out. ''E's got 'er! Make way!'

Hands reached down and gently pulled a young girl up out of the tunnel. Her hair was caked in brickdust and she was crying. 'You're all right now, luv. C'mon, we got yer,' a voice said gently.

As soon as the girl was free from the debris she was placed on a stretcher and covered with blankets. A woman wearing the uniform of the

WVS bent down over the sobbing young girl and gently wiped her face clean with a wet towel. Ben had emerged from the tunnel, covered from head to foot in dust. His matted hair hung limp over his forehead and he slumped down on his haunches. 'Yer done good, Ben lad,' one of the men said, patting his back. 'That was the last one. They're all out now, accordin' ter the copper.'

Sally waited until she was sure that Ben was all right, then she turned and started off along the street. She heard him call her and she looked around to see him hurrying towards her.

'Jacko told me yer was 'ere, Sal,' he said breathlessly as he came up to her.

Sally looked at him, trying to hide her anxiety. 'I 'eard about the bomb,' she said. 'I wanted ter see if yer was OK.'

He smiled, his white teeth gleaming in his blackened face. 'What about you? Are yer all right?' he asked, touching her arm gently.

Delayed shock and fear for Ben's safety finally overwhelmed her and tears started up in her eyes. She swayed and Ben took her by the shoulders. 'Yer need ter sit down awhile,' he said softly. 'Let's get out of 'ere.'

Ben led Sally out of the street into St James's churchyard. Overhead the sky was grey with thick cloud and the gravel path through the grounds was still wet from the heavy rain. They found a sheltered bench and sat down beneath an overhanging bush, gazing out at the weathered tombstones covered with moss and lichen.

557

'Are yer feelin' better now?' Ben asked, his eyes searching her pale face.

She nodded. 'I can't stop fer long. I left the baby wiv me Mum.'

Ben looked down at his boots for a moment then his eyes met hers. 'I 'eard about the baby,' he said quietly. 'A girl, wasn't it?'

'Yeah. I've called 'er Ruth,' Sally replied, averting her eyes.

Ben was silent for a few moments. He leaned back on the bench, his arm resting on the rail. ''Ave yer 'eard from Jim?' he asked.

She shook her head. 'It's bin a few months now. I'm worried.'

Ben looked up at the church tower, his eyes narrowing. 'I expect 'e's OK. Letters are gonna take a time now. Anyway, I don't s'pose 'e's got time ter write.'

'Yeah, I expect you're right,' Sally answered, sighing.

Ben leaned forward, his eyes staring into hers. 'Look, Sal. D'yer remember when yer called roun' ter see me an' I told yer about stayin' at my place if fings got awkward for yer? Well, the offer still goes. Jus' remember what I said.'

She smiled wanly. 'Fanks, Ben. I appreciate it. Now I better get goin' or I'll 'ave the baby screamin' fer 'er tea.'

They stood up and walked slowly to the gates. 'D'yer want me ter see yer ter the square?' he asked.

'No it's all right,' Sally replied. 'You rest up. Yer look all in.'

He watched her walk away, his eyes following

her until she turned the corner and disappeared from sight, then he thrust his hands deep into his pockets and set off towards his shattered house.

The afternoon wore on and Ginny went to her front door yet again and glanced down the square.

'I'll give them boys what for when they come back,' she grumbled to her two girls. 'If I told 'em once I told 'em 'undred times not ter leave the square.'

Jenny started to cry and Sara put her arm around her younger sister.

'What's the matter wiv 'er?' Ginny groaned.

'Jenny said she's frightened 'case we get bombed, Mum. We won't get bombed, will we?'

Ginny bent down and took her two daughters in her arms. ''Course we won't. The war's gonna be over soon, then yer can go up the park all day if yer like.'

Jenny stopped crying and Sara slipped her arm around Ginny's neck. 'I fink I know where Arfur an' Frankie went, Mum,' she said.

'Where'd they go, Sara?'

'I 'eard Frankie say they wanted ter see the gas-works fire.'

'Oh my Gawd! That's in the Old Kent Road. Jus' wait till they get back, I'll tan their 'ides,' Ginny exclaimed, dreading what her boys might be getting up to.

The Almond boys had reached the gas-works in time to see the fire tenders leaving. The flying bomb had missed the gasometers and landed

559

instead on the large block of offices. A small fire had been put out and a rope had been thrown across the entrance to the site.

Frankie's face dropped when he saw the ruined buildings. 'Ow, look, Arf. They've put the fire out,' he moaned.

Arthur looked warily at the huge policeman who was standing beside the rope. 'Did anybody get killed, mister?' he asked.

'Not yet,' the policeman replied, rocking backwards and forwards on his heels.

Frankie gave the constable a cheeky look. 'What d'yer mean, mister?'

The policeman put his thumbs through the buttons on his breast pockets and looked down sternly at the young boy. 'Little lads who 'ang around bomb-damaged buildin's are more than likely ter get buried under fallin' walls, so if I was you I'd get orf 'ome where yer belong.'

'We come 'ere ter see the fire,' Frankie said, aping the policeman by stuffing his hands into the top pockets of his shirt.

'Well, there ain't no fire, but I tell yer some-fing,' the policeman said, glancing at the rubble. 'There'll be a load o' rats comin' out o' that ruin before long. Big as cats, they'll be. They live in the cellars an' they're gonna be lookin' fer a new place ter live. I shouldn't 'ang around if I were you. Them rats ain't a pretty sight.'

The Almond boys looked wide-eyed at the policeman and Frankie gulped. 'Big as cats, yer say?'

'Yup. Some of 'em are even bigger.'

The boys backed away from the rope barrier

and then turned on their heels and hurried off home. The policeman grinned to himself as he turned and glanced over at the bomb-damaged building. Suddenly his eyes bulged and the smile left his face. When he had recovered his composure he picked up a stone and aimed it at the big black cat that was sniffing around the base of the rubble.

Chapter Twenty-Eight

DAY and night throughout June the flying bombs came over, their fiery trails and terrifying roar sending people diving for shelter. The air raid siren wailed constantly and people went back to the disused shelters and sat in dank, dark caverns, often with their feet in evil-smelling water. There was feverish activity reminiscent of the blitz as rusting shelter signs were replaced and white paint was urgently applied to trees, kerbsides and lamp posts. Street wardens wore their steel helmets once more and policemen dashed through the backstreets on bicycles, sounding their whistles as the flying monstrosities roared overhead. When the air-raid siren started up the Paragon Place folk hurried under the stairs or sat huddled in their front parlours, listening for the evil roar and waiting for the explosion as the engine spluttered and the flying bomb dived to earth. The bombs seemed to come in batches and they suddenly appeared overhead, almost without warning. People were caught out doing their shopping or walking in the streets, and one tenant from the little square suddenly found himself in an embarrassing position.

Alf was on his way to visit one of his old friends who owned a sweet shop near the river, and as he strolled towards Dockhead his mind was far removed from war. The day was bright and the light breeze rustled the leafy plane trees. It was Saturday morning and he was looking forward to a pleasant lunch-time drink. He had backed two winners at New Cross on Thursday evening and with the winnings he had replaced his rapidly diminishing supply of whisky. Muriel Taylor had popped in to see him that morning and had given him a pair of almost new bed-sheets, saying that she had gone off the colour. Dame Fortune seemed to be smiling on him, he thought, and he whistled tunelessly as he crossed the Jamaica Road. Suddenly the air raid sirens wailed and almost immediately the distant sound of a flying bomb grew into a deafening roar. Alf looked up and saw the evil-looking thing flying along towards him. For a few moments he stood transfixed as it drew near. It was almost directly overhead when the engine spluttered. He could see the spurt of flame, like a giant blow-torch that had run out of paraffin. The cigar-shaped monster dipped and Alf threw himself down against a brick wall, covering his ears with the palms of his hands as he waited to be blown into eternity.

The crash of the explosion was muted, and

562

after waiting for a few seconds Alf slowly picked himself up. It must have crashed into the river, he thought, dusting himself down and replacing his trilby. He could feel his heart pounding and decided that a double whisky would soon put that right. The Crown public house was only a short distance away and Alf sauntered along to call in for his medication.

It was just after three o'clock when Alf emerged from the Crown and staggered into the sunlit street, wondering if the all-clear had sounded. He blinked a few times, trying to adjust his eyes to the brightness and the floating pavement, then he set off in the opposite direction to his friend's shop. As he reached a small building he heard the familiar roar. 'The bastards are back again,' he shouted aloud, looking fearfully into the sky and tottering backwards a few paces. The roar grew louder and with a supreme effort Alf staggered up a few steps and in through an open door. The noise stopped and after a few seconds of silence a loud explosion seemed to rock the building.

Alf found himself in a white-painted vestibule and he sat down on a low wooden bench to compose himself. It seemed very quiet in the building and Alf sat in silence for a while, unable to guess in his befuddled state where he might be. After a minute or two he heard footsteps. The wide door at the end of the hallway opened and a tall, lean figure approached him.

'I think the danger's past,' the man said, rubbing his hands together in a washing motion.

'Would you care for some refreshment? We're all here and we'll be starting soon.'

Alf stood up, wondering if he should say what his preference was, but the man turned on his heel and beckoned for him to follow. Alf licked his lips as he entered the large room, imagining the taste of a nice double whisky guzzled straight down with no water. He looked about him and saw that there were people sitting around on benches and standing beside a table laden with cups and saucers.

'Do you take sugar, friend?' his host asked.

Alf groaned to himself. He never ever indulged in light refreshment of that sort during opening hours but he did not want to upset the man.

'Four, please,' he replied, looking around and thinking that maybe he should make a bolt for the door.

'There we are, friend. I'm sure this will help to steady your nerves,' the man said, handing Alf a cup of insipid-looking tea. 'We are all going through a bad time but I'm sure we have the strength to overcome. We must all be strong. What do you say?'

Right at that minute Alf was not sure what to say. They all looked harmless enough, but there was something strange about the group. His host was smiling at him and people were staring. Alf thought it would be better to sit down before he fell down and he tottered across to a vacant seat. He sipped his tea, trying to hide his revulsion at the taste of it as he concentrated on the antics of a large woman dressed in tweeds who seemed to be flitting around the gathering, laughing loudly. Alf groaned to himself as he saw her approaching him. She came over and looked at him closely, her eyes going up to the top of his head. He suddenly realised he still had his trilby on. With a sheepish grin he took it off and placed it beside him on the bench.

The tall, lean character who had brought Alf into the hall caught the woman's attention as he waved over to her. 'Five minutes, Miss Abernethy. We're just gathering the cups,' he called out.

The large woman chuckled, bouncing from side to side. 'Righty-o, Norman,' she yelled back in a cheery voice.

Alf eased sideways as Miss Abernethy flopped down beside him, squashing his trilby. 'Some of us will be renewing and others taking,' she said to him with a big smile, her eyes wide with enthusiasm. 'Are you a renewer or a taker, Mr – em . . .?'

Alf bit on his bottom lip. 'I'm Alf Porter. I'm a – a—' he dithered.

'Shy, are we?' Miss Abernethy laughed. 'Well, never mind. You won't be alone. We're all pledging today, praise be. We'll all be thinking about Frederick Charrington, too. His name is synonymous with our movement, you understand.'

Alf did not understand any of it and he felt it was high time he made his getaway, once the woman got up off his hat.

Escape proved impossible, however. Alf found himself sitting in the front row, placed there by

565

Miss Abernethy as she flitted and bounced around, dragging people from one place to another and then rearranging them with loud laughs and much waving of her arms. Alf slumped despondent and apprehensive as the large woman took her place in front of the group and raised her hands for silence.

'Let us begin with a short prayer,' she said, smiling at him.

'Gawd Almighty!' Alf groaned aloud.

'Praise be!' the man next to him cried.

Alf lowered his head and when the prayer had been said he looked up to see Miss Abernethy standing, legs astride, with her hands held out in front of her and her eyes staring up at the rafters. 'Just picture it, friends,' she began. 'A public house in the East End of London.'

Alf licked his lips. He could picture the Railway Inn right at that moment and he sighed deeply. 'I wish it was their front door I'd walked frew instead o' this bloody lunatic asylum,' he muttered to himself.

'It's cold and dark,' she went on. 'A poorly dressed young woman comes along, her worn-out shoes sounding on the wet cobblestones. She carries a baby who is crying with hunger. The young woman looks warily into the door of the public house. "Food," she cries. "I must have food for the baby." Suddenly she reels back from a cuff around the head and she falls into the gutter, still clutching the baby. Her assailant stands over her. "Get home, woman. I paid you last week. There's no more money, so go," he cries. The woman sobs as her evil husband goes back into the pub, but help is at hand. A well-dressed young man helps her to her feet and presses a sovereign into her raw palm, sending her on her way with a kind smile.'

Alf was staring at Miss Abernethy, wondering what she was talking about. Her face was flushed with passion and her eyes narrowed suddenly. She raised her hands slowly until they were held high above her head.

'The young man was shocked and angered,' she went on. 'Above the public house was the sign, Rising Sun, but what had caught his eye was the name of the brewery. It was Charringtons. His own family business. Yes, my friends. The name of the young man was Frederick Charrington and his own father was the owner of the public house. The terrible scene he had just witnessed horrified the young man, and from that day onwards Frederick Charrington did not allow a single drop of strong drink to pass his lips. He had also decided that everyone should know of the evils of strong drink.'

Alf gasped. 'I don't believe it,' he groaned aloud.

'It's true. Every word of it,' the little man next to him whispered in his ear.

Miss Abernethy's arm went out and her finger pointed over the listeners' heads. 'Frederick Charrington set up a tent in the Mile End Road,' she continued. 'He campaigned vigorously for people to sign the pledge and thousands followed his example and renounced the evils of strong drink. That one sorry sight in an East End alley had so affected the young man that he started the temperance movement – the movement we are continuing to this day. That's why we are here, friends. We are going to reaffirm our pledge. The newcomers here today will sign on to march joyously away from the temptation of alcohol and take the path of total abstinence.'

'I should fink so,' Alf mumbled sarcastically in disgust.

'Glory be! I've seen the light,' the little man next to him called out.

Miss Abernethy raised her hands again for silence. 'Our founder was a humble man,' she said, her voice wavering with emotion. 'Frederick Charrington was a good, sensitive man who was inclined to stutter when excited, and his assertion that abstinence had to be total led him to cry out, "T – total abstinence." It became his rallying cry, and the word "teetotal" found its way into the English language. We are all pledged teetotallers, my friends. Let us reaffirm, and to those of you who have not already done so, I say, let us sign the pledge.'

The little man next to Alf jumped to his feet. 'Lead me to it! Let me sign the pledge!' he cried.

Alf rammed his battered trilby down on to his head and stood up warily. People were rising from their seats and pushing to the front of the hall, eager to sign.

'C'mon an' sign, bruvver,' the little man cried out, pulling on Alf's coat sleeve.

'Let me go, yer silly ole sod,' Alf growled, pulling his arm away and making for the exit.

Suddenly the roar of a flying bomb rumbled through the room and Alf looked around him in desperation. The milling crowd did not seem aware of the peril as they pushed forward. 'They're all roun' the bloody twist,' he gasped aloud, staggering through the door and down the steps into the street.

The roar grew and Alf looked up. He could see the machine spurting flames as it approached and with a gasp he started running away from it as fast as his legs could carry him. He crossed the Jamaica Road without looking and a speeding tram narrowly missed him as he stumbled across its path. When he reached the pavement safely he heard the motor of the flying bomb splutter.

'Get down!' a voice shouted to him.

Alf dived down in the gutter. The explosion lifted him from the ground and he felt a blast of hot air sweep over him.

People were running now. 'It's the Temperance 'All! It's a direct 'it!' someone shouted.

Alf stood up slowly and dusted himself down, looking over at the mangled ruins. Smoke was still rising as people scrambled over the bricks, digging with their bare hands. He turned and walked slowly home, his stomach gripped by an unearthly iciness. Miss Abernethy, Norman, and the little man who only a few minutes ago was tugging at his sleeve urging him to stay were all under that pile of debris, Alf told himself, almost unable to believe what had happened, and a lump rose up in his throat.

At the end of June Sally got a letter from Jim. It was three weeks old and looked as though it had been written in a hurry. In quiet moments she sat with young Ruth cradled in her arms and reread the letter, trying to imagine Jim's voice as he told her that he was fit and well, and how much he was looking forward to being with her again. The letter helped to ease her fears, although she knew that according to the news broadcasts and daily papers the fighting in Italy was very bad. Jim would not have known about the flying bombs when he wrote, she thought. Sally looked down at the tiny bundle in her arms. 'Yer daddy doesn't know anyfing about yer, neivver,' she whispered.

The new danger from the skies had been totally unexpected and the suddenness of the attacks had made the Paragon Place folk reluctant to wander far from their homes. Sally and Vera did not visit the park or the church gardens any more, instead they pushed the prams only as far as the market. After his recent experience Alf Porter had decided to forego visiting his friends for the time being and he used the Railway Inn as his base. A close watch was kept on the children of the square and Ginny had been careful to lay down the law to her brood, especially her three boys. Arthur and Frankie were less than happy about being confined to the immediate vicinity.

'There's nufing ter do round 'ere,' Frankie groaned. 'We can't even go down the docks an' see the ships, an' we can't play on the barges. It ain't fair.'

Billy was less angry with the new restraints. Frankie and Arthur usually left him behind when there were dangerous things to do. He was never allowed to accompany his brothers when they went off to raid the barges or climb into the bomb-damaged houses to scrounge for bits and pieces, and detective work really tired him out. Now they had to stay together in the square, and it suited Billy.

★　★　★

Muriel had been eager to get things sorted out at the labour exchange and she quickly got her bogus employer to sign her release form. After some thought she had decided to join the NAAFI and had filled in the necessary forms. It was only a matter of time now, she told herself, and when the medical appointment arrived Muriel stopped Sally in the square.

'I'm joinin' up, Sal,' she grinned. 'I'm goin' in the NAAFI.'

'So you're gonna be servin' tea an' buns ter the troops, are yer?' Sally grinned, gently rocking the pram.

Muriel nodded. 'The silly ole cow at the labour exchange tried ter get me ter work in a munitions factory but I told 'ere I was allergic ter noisy machinery an' after a lot o' rigmarole she agreed ter let me apply fer the NAAFI.'

'When will yer be leavin'?' Sally asked.

Muriel shrugged her shoulders. 'It shouldn't be long. I've gotta 'ave a medical first, though. I'll be a livin' in the barracks. They've got

571

quarters fer the girls. It'll make a change, an' there's a chance ter go abroad, too. Ter tell yer the trufe I won't be sorry ter get away from this place, an' I could name a few people round 'ere who won't be sorry either.'

Sally touched the young woman's arm in a friendly gesture. 'Me an' Vera are gonna be sorry ter see yer go, Muriel. The square won't be the same once you've gone.'

'That's nice o' yer ter say so,' Muriel replied, looking along the square. 'I'm gonna miss yer an' Vera – and Alf Porter – but it's somefing I gotta do. Besides, it might be a bit safer than Bermondsey – away from the flyin' bombs and ovver troubles.'

Sally looked at the Taylor girl closely. 'Yer mean that business at the pub? Me farver told me the Dougans 'ave stopped goin' in the Railway since the fight.'

Muriel's face became serious. 'I bumped inter Patsy Dougan when I was comin' 'ome from the labour exchange last week. 'E mumbled somefing about sortin' me out, or words ter that effect.'

'Surely 'e's not still 'arbourin' a grudge, is 'e?' Sally queried. 'That trouble at the pub was months ago. I should 'ave thought 'e'd 'ave forgotten it by now.'

Muriel smiled wanly. Things had happened concerning her, things she did not feel able to talk about, and she knew that Patsy Dougan was not going to let her forget. 'They're an evil crowd, Sal,' she answered.

Sally saw fear in Muriel's eyes. 'You just be

572

careful,' she said quickly.

Muriel shrugged her shoulders. 'Trouble is, I've jus' started a part-time job as a barmaid at the King's Arms in Dock'ead. I wanna get a few bob tergevver while I'm waitin'. I do a couple of evenin's a week an' I get a bit frightened o' comin' 'ome when it's gettin' dark. I tell yer, Sal, I've started lookin' over me shoulder now. I wouldn't put anyfing past that 'orrible git.'

Sally winced. 'Did Patsy Dougan know it was you what crowned 'im that night?' she asked her.

Muriel nodded. ''E wouldn't 'ave known, 'e was out cold, but Mutton-eye told 'im. 'E saw me whack 'im.'

Sally laughed. 'I wish I'd've bin there. I bet 'e didn't know what 'it 'im. P'r'aps it's fer the best you're goin' away. Will yer keep yer flat on?'

Muriel nodded. 'Yeah. I need somewhere ter live when I get me leave. I don't fancy spendin' it at the barracks. I might be in some 'orrible little dump. Mind you, I could always do a bit o' toutin' in me spare time, what wiv all them lonely soldiers.'

Sally looked at the young woman quizzically. Muriel laughed. 'I'm only jokin', Sal,' she said reassuringly. 'I wouldn't go back ter that life fer anyfing. I'm jus' waitin' fer Con ter come 'ome so we can get married. Who knows, I might get posted abroad an' meet 'im out there.'

Ruth had started bawling and Sally rocked the pram. 'I'd better get 'ome,' she sighed. 'It's gettin' near 'er feedin' time. You be careful,

Muriel. Jus' keep yer eyes open, an' watch them dark streets.'

Muriel laughed nervously. 'Yeah, I will. It's funny, though. When I was on the game dark streets didn't worry me. I used ter carry a load o' protectives in me 'andbag. Now, I jus' carry one – a pair o' sharp scissors.'

Throughout July the flying bombs came over in increasing numbers and Bermondsey was badly hit. Rows of houses, factories and schools were destroyed, and Paragon Place had a near miss when one flying bomb dived low over the rooftops and hit a leather factory in the next street. The weather remained dismal for the time of year, with heavy clouds and rain that seemed never-ending.

On a wet Sunday in July Sally took Ruth to be christened at St James's Church. It was a quiet family affair, with Lora standing as godmother. Later that evening Charlie went to the Railway Inn to celebrate the event. He had finally managed to persuade Annie to join him and she wore her new hat for the occasion. Lora had declined her father's invitation to go for a drink, as her romance was blossoming once more and she was going off with her beau to see a show in the West End.

While her parents were at the pub Sally sat in her small parlour chatting to Vera. Outside the rain had started to fall again and distant thunder rolled as the conversation switched to Muriel. 'She's leavin' on Tuesday, so she told me,' Sally was saying. 'I bet she's feelin' a bit nervous.'

574

Vera leaned back in the chair and stretched out her slim legs. 'I still can't believe 'ow she changed all of a sudden,' she remarked. 'Mind you, I'm glad fer 'er. It mus' be an' 'ard life bein' on the game. I mean, yer can't pick an' choose, can yer? Well, I s'pose yer can, but yer wouldn't earn all that much. I know I wouldn't if it was me.'

Sally shrugged her shoulders. 'I s'pose it's like any ovver job. Yer gotta take the rough wiv the smooth.'

Vera chuckled. 'It's all right if yer like a bit o' rough. Me, I'd be too fussy. Cor, jus' fancy some ugly great bloke comin' up an' askin' yer ter go off wiv 'im. I reckon girls like Muriel 'ave gotta be 'ot-natured. 'Ow else could they do it?'

Sally laughed. 'I s'pose they jus' shut their eyes an' imagine they're wiv a right tasty fella.'

Vera was not impressed with her friend's reasoning. 'What about them dirty ole gits?' she said shuddering. 'I wouldn't fancy old age creepin' all over me.'

'I don't fink Muriel brought any old blokes 'ome,' Sally replied. 'She used ter work the dock area. She 'ad regular clients.'

Vera looked thoughtful. 'What about the risk o' catchin' a dose? Them sailors visit a lot o' foreign ports. Joe was sayin' it's rife in some countries. One o' them sailors could bring some-fing back.'

'Well, I s'pose yer 'ave ter take precautions,' Sally said. 'Like makin' yer clients wear a letter an' gettin' regular check-ups.'

Vera pulled a face. 'I changed me mind, Sal. I
575

don't fink I'll go on the game after all.'

The rain was falling heavily and Muriel pulled her coat up around her ears as she walked along the dark street. She had been rather late leaving the pub that Sunday night, for the landlord had insisted she stay behind for a farewell drink as it was her last night there. Muriel had been contemplating her new job away from the square as she walked home, but now as she saw the railway arches rising up ahead she heard the sound of heavy footsteps behind her. Muriel became anxious. The dark cloud had obscured the moon and the light from the little torch she held in her hand was very poor. Her high-heeled shoes sounded loudly as she walked quickly under the gloomy arches, not daring to look back, and as she increased her speed Muriel suddenly felt a presence behind her. She had no time to run as a large hand was placed over her mouth, stifling her scream, and an arm was wrapped tightly around her middle. She tried to struggle and kick out but her assailant was far too strong. An ugly feeling of terror and panic gripped her as she found herself being dragged across the empty street towards the bombsite and she could hear his heavy breathing.

'Don't struggle or I'll kill yer!' a voice hissed into her ear.

She could feel hot breath on her neck as she was dragged into the derelict house beside the bombsite and forced down on to the dusty floor among pieces of splintered timber and broken bricks. She tried to break away from her

576

attacker but it was hopeless. Sheer terror made her whole body stiffen and her heartbeats pounded in her ears. The man's body pressed down on her making it difficult to breathe and a large hand squeezed her throat. She could feel his free hand tearing at her clothes and a red haze grew in front of her eyes.

Chapter Twenty-Nine

ARTHUR COX had never relished the thought of weekend work but he had known there was little choice. Councillor Catchpole's grandson was getting christened that Sunday and the family party was to be held at the Town Hall. Arthur had been called into the manager's office late on Friday afternoon and asked if he would be available for duty on Sunday. Remembering only too well that he had fallen foul of Councillor Catchpole once in the past Arthur had felt it would not be a very good idea to say he was not available.

It had been a long day that Sunday. The party had gone on until ten-thirty, then there had been chairs and tables to be packed away, and after that the final ushering out of guests reluctant to leave. During the evening the air raid siren had sounded, but mercifully no flying bombs had fallen in the area. By the time Arthur had locked up and slipped the keys through the letterbox it was approaching midnight. The rain was falling heavily as he turned into the maze of backstreets and walked wearily home.

As he plodded through the darkness Arthur thought of young Ernest, who was now with the invasion forces somewhere in France. The army had been the making of him. Ernest had put on weight and looked the picture of health when he came home on embarkation leave, wearing his Marine shoulder-flashes with pride. Arthur said a little prayer for the boy's safety as he walked under the Stanley Street railway arches.

Suddenly Arthur heard a scuffle up ahead, and as he drew near he saw the dim outline of a young woman being half carried, half dragged across the empty street by a large figure who was snarling at her. Arthur broke into a trot as the woman was dragged through the broken doorway of a derelict house. When he reached the crumbling front wall he could hear the young woman's stifled screams and without hesitating he took a deep breath and charged in past the hanging door. He stumbled over the attacker's feet and quickly reached out and grabbed him by the coat, pulling him backwards away from the young woman. The attacker flailed his arms wildly as Arthur swung him round and crashed his body into the bare brick wall. He broke free with a curse, blood running from a wound on his head as he stumbled frantically out from the house. Arthur heard him running off along the street, and as the footsteps faded he bent over the sobbing victim. He gasped with surprise as he saw it was Muriel. Her eyes were wide with terror as she stared up at him and her whole body was shaking. Arthur gently slipped an arm under her head. 'It's all right,' he said softly. 'Can yer stand up?'

Muriel leaned heavily on Arthur as they made their way across the street and into the square.

'Did yer know 'im? Would yer reco'nise the bloke, Muriel?' he asked.

'I never saw 'im before,' the young woman gasped, her body still shaking violently.

Arthur took the key from her trembling hand. 'I'll let yer in, then I'll send Maudie over,' he said. 'She'll look after yer, luv.'

Muriel felt her legs giving way as her rescuer took hold of her arm and led her into the parlour. 'It was 'orrible,' she sobbed. 'I thought I was gonna die. I couldn't breathe.'

'You sit quiet, I'll fetch Maudie, then we'll get the police,' he whispered.

Muriel turned her tear-stained face up to him suddenly. 'I don't want the police called,' she said quickly.

In the flat above a light was burning in Harriet's bedroom. The librarian put down her copy of *Pride and Prejudice* and leaned against the raised pillow. Late footsteps in the square always worried Harriet and she glanced nervously towards the window. She heard the front door opening and muffled voices. There was the familiar creak as the front-room door opened and then it went quiet. 'My God! The girl's brought a man back,' she said aloud to herself. At first Harriet thought of waking her sister, but then she decided that Juliet would take her usual detached attitude and most probably go back to

579

sleep. It was so worrying. She had voiced her opinion when Juliet remarked how nice it was to see the change in the young woman. She had told her sister that she had doubts about Miss Taylor's sincerity and that time would tell. She had been right. After all, it was predictable. The Taylor girl had slipped back into her old ways and was now bringing men home again. What was to be done?

Harriet sighed as she slipped out of bed and put on her dressing-gown. 'With all this worry it's impossible to sleep,' she groaned to herself.

The sound of footsteps crossing the square made Harriet hurry on tiptoe to the window and as she eased back the heavy drapes and peered through the lace curtains she saw Mr Cox trotting over to his house. Whatever's going on? she wondered. As Harriet paced up and down the room there were more hurried footsteps and the front door opened and closed again. 'The house is becoming a right of way,' she groaned. What would she do if Juliet decided to leave? She couldn't face staying in the flat alone, not now that the Taylor girl seemed to be back to her old tricks. Juliet had been very mysterious about her intentions since telling her of the deterioration in Mrs Lomax's condition. It was very likely her sister would go to live with her lover, should the worst happen, although she had not said as much. Why did that man have to come between them? Why couldn't things be as they were? Maybe it was her own fault. If she had not been so inquisitive Juliet would probably have gone on with her deceit. Would it have been better that way, or was it preferable to have everything out in the open? Why had her sister been so gullible to fall for that despicable man? He was merely using her, the way all men used women. They were all despicable rogues who preyed upon the frailties of the weaker sex. Juliet had been so brazen about her affair when things came out into the open. She had said things that evening which were inexcusable and her reference to lesbian love was disgusting. Was there any reason for her to make that comment? Surely she didn't think that her own sister harboured such feelings? There was no reason for her to think so.

Harriet bit on her bottom lip in anguish. Love with another woman would be preferable to giving herself to a man, it was true, but the thought was revolting nevertheless. Could she ever get to like a woman enough to engage in that sort of behaviour? Could she ever contemplate doing such things? Of course not. The thought was preposterous. Harriet felt her face flushing at her secret thoughts and she shuddered as she slipped back beneath the bedclothes.

It was early on Tuesday morning when Muriel said goodbye to her few friends in Paragon Place. She wore a scarf over her bruised throat and carried a small suitcase as she walked out of the square. Sally and Vera stood, babies held in their arms, as they watched her leave.

'She's a poor cow, 'avin' a fing like that 'appen to 'er,' Sally remarked, a sad look on her pale, angular face. 'I really liked 'er. She was always 'appy-go-lucky.'

Vera laughed. 'Anybody would fink she was goin' fer good to 'ear you talk, Sal. She'll be 'ome on leave soon.'

Sally nodded. 'Yeah, you're right, but I'm still sorry ter see 'er go.'

Vera leaned against the doorpost. 'I wonder why she wouldn't let Maudie Cox call the police?' she said suddenly. 'D'yer fink it was Patsy Dougan who attacked 'er?'

Sally shook her head. 'Muriel reckons she never seen the bloke before, an' Arfur told Maudie that it was a big bloke. Yer can't call Patsy big. Anyway, I don't s'pose 'e'd do it 'imself, even though 'e threatened 'er. I reckon 'e got one of 'is mates ter do it for 'im. If Muriel's fella ever gets to 'ear what 'appened 'e'll give that Patsy a real good 'idin', yer can bet yer life.'

Vera nodded her agreement and jerked her thumb towards Alf's house. ''E was upset about Muriel goin', wasn't 'e? Ain't it funny 'ow birds of a feavver stick tergevver. Alf ain't exactly everybody's cup o' tea but 'im an' Muriel got on well, didn't they?'

Sally laughed aloud. 'Poor Alf. I'll never forget that night 'e got me dad's chamber-pot over 'im. An' what about that night Alf gave the Carey sisters an eyeful?'

Vera chuckled. 'What about when they got that pianer out in the square an' Alf fell down the floorboards?'

Sally looked suddenly pensive. 'I sometimes
582

fink it's more like a big family than jus' neigh-bours in this little square.'

Vera laughed. 'Yeah, you're right. Every-body's in one anuvver's pockets an' anyfing that goes on 'ere is roun' the square in five minutes. Then there's the bitchin' an' tittle-tattlin'. It's jus' like families. I'd like ter be be'ind a few of 'em sometimes. I can jus' picture it, can't you? "Look at them girls. Ain't they disgustin'? There's Sally Brady 'ad a baby by Gawd knows who, an' that Vera. What a trollop. I bet 'er kids don't belong ter that nice young Joe. I bet she's bin 'avin' a right ole game while 'e's bin away at sea. They could be anybody's. Then there's that prosser from number 1. No, not Harriet, the woman underneath. She brings 'em 'ome four at a time. The Carey sisters 'ave said they'd 'elp out but Muriel's such a greedy cow. Won't give anybody else a chance." '

Sally was reduced to tears by her friend's mimicry. 'Shut up, Vera. I'll wee meself in a minute,' she gasped.

Vera had the bit between her teeth and her eyes flashed. "Ere, what about those two ole dragons at nine an' ten? Can yer imagine them two gettin' tergevver. "I reckon those two are on the game, don't you, Ada?" Then Ada touches 'er 'air an' winks that wonky eye of 'ers. "I could 'ave told yer that long ago, Clara. Yer gotta keep yer eye on those two or they'll 'ave our 'usbands away under our very noses." I tell yer, Sal, yer can bet yer life me an' you are in the bad book, along wiv Muriel an' old Alf Porter, that's fer sure.'

Sally cuddled Ruth to her with one arm while she wiped her eyes with her free hand. 'C'mon, Vera, let's take the prams an' go fer a stroll down the market,' she croaked. 'I can't take any more o' this.'

While the flying bombs were creating havoc the square's two elders did not venture very far, but they had decided from the beginning that it would not be right, nor patriotic, to forego their daily medicine. Granny Almond called on Granny Allen as usual and they strolled arm in arm to the Railway Inn for their beverage. On one of their daily jaunts Daisy had a tasty item of gossip to relate and she had waited until they were seated comfortably in the snug bar before bending her friend's rather lazy ear.

'D'yer remember that ole Mrs Brody, Lil?' she said loudly. 'Yer know who I mean, 'er what used ter live next door ter the corner shop.'

Lil nodded. 'Wasn't it 'er whose ole man got nicked fer smashin' up the pawnbroker's shop in Dock'ead?'

'Yeah, that's 'er,' Daisy went on. 'She pawned 'is suit an' 'e wanted it fer a weddin'. What 'appened was, 'e run up ter the shop an' it was closed. Well, 'e banged on the door an' ole Brownlow told 'im ter piss orf, or words ter that effect. Mind you, 'e couldn't 'ave said it to a worse bloke than Mrs Brody's ole man, not when e'd bin on the turps. Well, ole Mick Brody got a dustbin lid an' aimed it right frew the winder. "Gi'us me bleedin' suit," 'e screamed out. Mrs Frank told me all about it. She lives in

584

the buildin's facin' the shop.'

'Wasn't it 'er what 'ad ter go ter court over the kids?' Lil inquired.

Daisy nodded. 'That's 'er. Well, anyway, ole Brody tried ter climb in the winder an' the police pulled up in a car. 'E was fightin' an' kickin' 'em like a madman an' one o' the coppers got a broken nose. Mrs Frank said there was blood everywhere. They finally put the cuffs on 'im an' I 'eard they gave 'im a right pastin' when they got 'im down the station.'

Lil sipped her Guinness, suddenly wondering what all this had to do with Daisy's original question. 'What was yer sayin' about Mrs Brody, Daisy?' she asked.

Daisy put her drink down and folded her arms. 'Well, when I was down the market yesterday I bumped inter Mrs Brody. "'Ello, Daisy," she said. "I ain't seen yer fer years." Well, we got talkin' about the ole neighbours an' she asked me if ole Bill Freeman still lived wiv the Robinsons. I told 'er 'e died last year an' she was shocked. Apparently it was 'er what sent Bill ter the Robinsons when 'e was lookin' fer lodgin's after 'e retired from the leavver factory.'

'Bill Freeman worked at that factory fer more than firty-five years,' Lil said, pinching her chin.

Daisy nodded. 'Anyway, Mrs Brody was sayin' 'e was livin' over 'er an' when the Council condemned 'er place they all 'ad ter get out. Mrs Brody's family were given anuvver place ter live, but as Bill was a lodger 'e 'ad ter find 'imself a place. She was tellin' me about 'im. 'E done time, by all accounts.'

'No? I wouldn't 'ave believed it,' Lil said, pulling on her bottom lip.

'It's true,' Daisy went on. 'Mrs Brody said 'e used ter get on well wiv 'er 'cos she used ter do all 'is washin' an' ironin' an' get 'is meals. Apparently Bill come from the country when 'e was a young man. 'E'd lost 'is wife an' baby wiv the fever an' this vicar bloke fixed 'im up wiv a job at a leavver factory. Well, after a while Bill got friendly wiv the guv'nor's daughter. Pretty young fing by all accounts. They was gonna run off tergevver, 'cos 'er farver forbid 'er ter 'ave anyfing ter do wiv Bill, 'im bein' an ordinary worker. Some'ow the ole man found out what they intended doin' an' 'e give Bill the sack.'

'Bloody ole goat,' Lil remarked.

'Well, accordin' ter Mrs Brody the guv'nor give Bill a week's wages an' a reference so 'e could get anuvver job in the trade, but 'e told 'im never ter try an' see 'is daughter again,' Daisy went on. 'Bill was besotted wiv the girl an' 'e used ter meet 'er in secret, till the ole man found out. There was a right ter do an' Bill punched 'im. The bloke fell an' cracked 'is 'ead on the kerb. The fall killed 'im an' Bill was 'ad up on manslaughter. They give 'im five years. Bloody shame, if yer ask me.'

'That guv'nor must 'ave bin a right no-good bastard,' Lil said with passion. 'Fancy doin' a fing like that ter yer own daughter. I mean ter say, ole Bill was still a smart man when 'e was wiv the Robinsons. I bet 'e was a good-lookin' fella in 'is time.'

Daisy stared down at her half-empty glass. 'I

586

was sad, really. Mrs Brody said that all the time Bill was in prison the girl never visited 'im once, an' the sad part was, when 'e come out o' the jug Bill found out that the girl 'ad gorn an' died wiv consumption. Terrible shock, it must 'ave bin.'

Lil shook her head sadly. 'That's what I've always said. Yer never know the 'alf of it, do yer?'

Daisy finished her drink and picked up the empty glasses. 'Good job I don't tell anybody about my carryin's-on,' she said, grinning. 'It'd fill the *News o' the World*.'

By the end of August the flying bomb terror had passed. Their launching bases in Northern France had been overrun and the Paragon Place folk breathed easier once more.

Since the bombing of his street Sally had seen nothing of Ben. Her father had obviously seen him at the docks, she knew, but he was not disposed to talk about Ben, and she did not want to ask after him for fear of seeming too concerned. Nevertheless word did reach her sometimes, and Vera once spotted Ben walking slowly along Stanley Street.

'I don't know if you're interested, Sal,' she said tentatively. "E looked deep in thought an' I don't fink 'e saw me. What was 'e doin' down 'ere?'

Sally shrugged her shoulders. 'P'r'aps 'e was meetin' somebody. After all, 'e only lives the ovver side o' Jamaica Road.'

Although her friend casually dismissed the news Vera felt that Sally still thought a lot more about Ben than she cared to admit. 'Maybe Ben was jus' checkin' ter make sure Paragon Place was still standin', Sal,' she laughed, unaware that her remark bore a great deal of truth.

Sally felt strangely moved by what she heard, although she tried to appear uninterested. Ben seemed to have matured since their parting, and he had even swallowed his fierce pride by offering her and Ruth a home with him. It must have been hard for him to bring himself to make such a gesture, she thought, even though he had strong feelings of guilt and remorse. Maybe Vera was right and Ben had been checking to see if everything was all right, the way she had when Potters Lane was bombed. Ben was soft-hearted under his brash, masculine exterior. Her family had often accused him of insensitivity and off-handedness, but Sally knew the real Ben. His was an act to keep people at a distance. He was basically a shy person who found it very difficult to express himself. It had been that way even when they first married and it had taken some time for her to break down his defences.

Vera was chatting on and Sally found herself nodding and agreeing without really listening. Why was she thinking this way? she wondered suddenly. Why were thoughts of Ben uppermost in her mind when she should be worrying about Jim and praying for his safety? There had been no letters from him recently and heavy fighting was still taking place in Italy. Maybe he was wounded, or maybe he had been killed. Sally shuddered at the thought. Perhaps dwelling on Ben was an attempt to convince herself that she did not really care so much about Jim, and was not terribly worried about him. Jim might never come back, and the thought of a life without him was something that was just too painful to face.

★ ★ ★

During the early days of September the Paragon Place folk were talking of the new 'dim-out' regulations that had come into force, and Ada Fuller scratched at her ginger hair in perplexity. 'The black-out's finished, then?' she asked her neighbour.

Clara nodded hesitantly. 'Well, it is an' it ain't. It's gonna be a dim-out instead.'

'Are they gonna put the street lights back on again, Clara?' the big woman asked.

'Yeah, but it'll take a time, an' they won't be full on. The shops are gonna be lit up but they can't show too much light.'

'Well, what about the blackout curtains, Clara? Can't we take 'em down?'

'I s'pose we can, but I'm keepin' mine up till I see what everybody else is gonna do,' Clara replied.

Ada scratched her head again. 'I fink I'll keep mine up, too. I don't wanna be fined. They took ole Mrs Barlow ter court. She got fined forty shillin's. The poor ole cow was cleanin' 'er winders an' the bloody lot fell down. She asked 'er ole man ter tack 'em back up again but yer know what 'e's like. Lazy bastard wouldn't lift a finger ter 'elp 'er. That night when she put the light on it shined out frew the curtains an' a copper come past an' nicked 'er.'

'Bloody shame,' Clara said, shaking her head. 'I bet 'er ole man didn't pay the fine.'

'No fear. All 'is money goes up the boozer. If my Maurice was like that I'd spifflicate 'im, I know I would.'

During the second week in September a telegraph boy cycled into the turning and knocked on number 2. George Tapley opened the telegram with shaking hands and then panic seized him. He hurried next door with an ashen face. 'It's me boy, Ginny. Tony's missin', presumed killed,' he cried out.

Ginny hugged the pathetic figure to her and cried with him as he shook in her arms. 'Don't give up 'ope, George, 'e might be captured,' she said, helping him into a chair. 'A lot of our boys turn up in prison camps, like Laurie. Yer mustn't give up.'

George was inconsolable. 'That's both of 'em are gorn now,' he sobbed. 'I'm never gonna see eivver of 'em again.'

'Yes yer will, George. I got that feelin' it's gonna be all right,' Ginny said softly. 'Remember I 'ad that feelin' about Laurie an' I was right, wasn't I?'

He nodded his head slowly. 'You're right, Gin. I mustn't give up 'ope. My Tony's always bin able ter look after 'imself. 'E'll be all right.'

Ginny made him a cup of strong tea and the two sat together in the quiet room. She listened patiently while George recalled memories of his two sons when they were both children, and she was still sitting with him when her brood came in from school. Their childish view of things had been tempered and sharpened by growing up in wartime and they immediately sensed that something was wrong. Ginny felt pride in the way they slipped quietly into the background, their usual high spirits contained.

It was later that day when Ginny was talking to Sally about George's tragic news that the sound of a distant explosion rumbled into the square. The two women looked at each other in surprise.

'It can't be a bomb, Sal. There's bin no air raid warnin',' Ginny remarked, her ears cocked.

Sally bit on her lip. 'P'raps it's a gas-main gone up.'

Another, louder explosion sounded and Ruth started to cry. Sally cuddled the baby to her. 'Whatever is it?' she asked anxiously.

'Surely it can't be anuvver gas-main exploded,' Ginny replied, going to the window and peering through the lace curtains. 'P'r'aps it's more o' those flyin' bombs.'

Sally shook her head. 'I don't fink so. The warnin' always goes first. Besides, it said on the wireless all the sites 'ave bin overrun.'

Ginny sat down in a chair, an anxious look on her ruddy features. 'Gawd, I 'ope it ain't anuvver o' those secret weapons,' she said. 'I don't fink we could take any more.'

Sally held Ruth up on to her shoulder and gently patted her back. The news of Tony Tapley had left her feeling depressed and apprehensive. She had been trying to fight off a
591

feeling of dread for a few days and now it had been heightened. The empty, nervous feeling in the pit of her stomach would not go and she knew instinctively that it would not be long now before that telegraph lad made another call in Paragon Place.

Sally's anxious thoughts were interrupted as Ginny got up and straightened her dress. 'I'd better go an' see 'ow poor George is,' she sighed. ''E's gone ter pieces.'

At the Railway Inn the mysterious explosions had become the main topic of conversation as the regulars gathered in the public bar.

Charlie took a large gulp of ale and burped loudly. 'I reckon it's gas-mains goin' up,' he declared. 'I mean ter say, it don't want a lot o' workin' out. Durin' the blitz fousands of gas-pipes got damaged. There mus' be tons o' gas escapin' under the ground an' when it builds up it's deadly. You've only got ter 'ave a spark an' whoosh!'

'I make yer right,' Ted chipped in. 'Anyfing could set it off. It could be a tram spark, or a fag-end somebody's chucked away. Even an 'orse an' cart could do it. Yer know yerself 'ow the sparks fly from 'orses 'ooves when they clump over the cobbles.'

Bert had been leaning on the counter listening to the conversation and he nodded in agreement. ''Ere, Charlie. D'yer remember when that whole street went up? That was a gas-main.'

'That was over in Poplar, way back in the early firties,' Charlie replied. 'They said it was

592

the anarchists at first, but it turned out ter be a spark from an electric light. Somebody turned the light-switch on an' the whole street fell down. Apparently there was a leaky pipe underground an' the gas built up.'

Fred's face broke into a grin. 'I can just imagine that. Some poor git comes 'ome from work an' wants ter read the paper so 'e turns on the light an' next minute 'e's got all the light 'e wants. Yer gotta laugh, ain't yer?'

Alf had been listening to the banter and he suddenly banged his near-empty glass down on the table. 'You lot make me laugh,' he scoffed. 'Gas-mains? If they're gas-mains they've gotta be flyin' ones.'

'What d'yer mean?' Bert asked, pausing as he polished a glass.

'What do I mean? I tell yer what I mean,' Alf said, prodding the table with his forefinger. 'It's Gerry's new secret weapon, that's what it is. It's a rocket bomb.'

There was loud laughter and Bert leaned over the counter. 'Leave orf, Alf,' he said. 'You've bin seein' too many o' those Flash Gordon films.'

'That's right, 'ave a good laugh,' Alf growled. 'I bet yer I'm right. You jus' wait an' see.'

Bert struggled to keep a straight face. 'I tell yer what, Alf. If you're right I'll give yer 'alf a dozen free pints, but if you're wrong you'll 'ave ter wash all the glasses fer a week. 'Ow's that fer a wager?'

Alf ignored the laughter and walked over to

the counter. 'You're on,' he said, holding out his hand.

'Looks like yer better dig yer apron out, Alf,' Charlie quipped. 'We're all witnesses ter the bet, so yer can't get out of it.'

'Who wants ter get out of it?' Alf shouted above the laughter. 'Jus' you lot wait. Yer fink you're so clever. I'll be the one who's laughin' when I'm gettin' pissed at that flash monkey's expense.'

Bert's face remained impassive as he faced Alf. 'I'm prepared ter pay up if I lose the bet, but I don't want yer blamin' me if yer walk out of 'ere pissed an' those church ladies in the square aim somefing at yer fer flashin'.'

Alf glared at the landlord. 'Don't yer worry over me gettin' sloshed. I'm pretty careful these days. I remember the time Charlie chucked the pisspot over me jus' 'cos I was singin' under 'is winder.'

Charlie looked aggrieved. 'I tell yer somefing, Alf. It wasn't meant fer you, mate. I come in 'alf pissed meself that night an' my Annie chucked the pot at me. I was a bit too quick fer 'er, though. I ducked an' it went out the winder. It was yer 'ard luck ter be standin' underneath.'

'Pity yer ain't quicker gettin' the drinks in,' Alf countered. 'It's yer turn, an' if we 'ave ter wait any longer we'll all die o' thirst.'

During September the mysterious explosions continued and at the Railway Inn they became known as flying gas-mains. The regulars were beginning to think that Alf was right when he

594

talked about the Germans' new secret weapon, and Bert himself feared that it would not be long before he was forced to pay out on the wager. The frightening realisation that a terrible new object was now falling from the sky had made the Paragon Place folk draw together for comfort, and Daisy commented that the long-overdue confrontation between Ada and her next-door neighbour now seemed very unlikely. 'Those two stick tergevver like treacle to a blanket,' she remarked.

Folk slipped into each other's homes for a cup of tea and a chat at every pretext, and even Harriet Carey was moved to bid Alf Porter good morning as she passed him in the square on her way to morning Mass. Alf was taken aback by the gesture and he thought it would be a good idea to keep an eye on things, now that Muriel was away. After all, the two elderly ladies must be frightened in that house on their own, he thought.

A few hours later Alf was sufficiently fortified to knock on number 1. Harriet opened the door and stood back in surprise. Alf blinked once or twice and rocked forward on his feet.

'I don't wanna sh – sheem presump – presump – forward, luv,' he slurred. 'Would yer like me t-ter do yer a f-favour, now you're – you're in the 'ouse on yer own?'

Harriet recoiled as she caught a whiff of Alf's breath, horrified at what she thought he was suggesting. 'How dare you!' she screeched. 'Go away you dirty man! Do you hear me?!'

Alf staggered back a pace and tried to focus

his bleary eyes on the tall, thin woman before him. 'I jush thought yer – yer might be lonely. There's no need ter – ter get shirty, mishish,' he stuttered.

Harriet stepped back to slam the door in his face and at that very moment there was a deafening explosion. The blast threw Alf into the passageway and he landed on all fours, his head buzzing. He blinked once or twice and then he saw the prone figure of Harriet stretched out beside him. He could hear running footsteps crunching over broken glass outside and Charlie's loud voice. 'They've caught the arches!'

Alf gulped and stared down at Harriet. He could see the rise and fall of her chest and he flopped down beside her, his head resting against the passage wall. The silly ole mare's fainted, he thought, reaching into his back pocket for his hip-flask.

Harriet groaned as he took off his coat and fitted it under her head. 'You're OK, luv. Take a sip o' this, it'll do yer good,' he said softly, easing her head forwards.

Harriet spluttered as the fiery liquid ran down her throat and her eyes fluttered open. 'Oh my God!' she cried, a terrified look on her ashen face.

'It was a rocket. It caught the railway arches,' Alf whispered, putting the flask to her lips once more.

Harriet was not quite sure what was happening to her, but the burning liquid was making her body tingle and she began to feel a little less hysterical.

Alf was now stone cold sober and he took a large swig from the flask to steady his nerves. 'Yer fainted, luv. It was the blast what did it,' he said. 'I was just askin' if yer wanted me ter keep an eye on yer place now that Muriel's gone when the bloody bomb landed.'

Harriet was beginning to rally a little and with Alf's help she struggled into a sitting position, her back to the wall. 'I thought you were making an improper suggestion,' she gasped, pulling her tweed skirt down over her calves in embarrassment.

Alf smiled and handed her the flask. 'I only thought yer an' yer sister might be frightened now you're on yer own an' I was gonna offer ter watch yer place ter make sure nobody annoyed yer, that's all.'

Harriet took another swig from the proffered flask and coughed. 'Is this whisky?' she asked.

Alf nodded. 'It's the finest fing out fer shock,' he grinned.

The noise of people shouting and constant footsteps outside carried up into the Careys' front room. Harriet was sitting back in an easy chair, a handkerchief held to her lips as she watched Alf gathering up glass from the shattered windows. Why did Juliet have to go to that awful man today? she thought. I need her here with me. My poor ornaments. They're all smashed.

Alf stood up holding a handful of broken glass and his elbow caught the one remaining piece of china that was balanced precariously on the shelf. Harriet winced as the ornament fell to the floor and smashed.

'Leave the rest, Mr Porter,' she groaned. 'Juliet can finish clearing up when she gets home.'

Alf laid the broken glass down on a spread of newspaper and looked at Harriet closely. 'If you're sure you're OK?' he asked with concern.

'I'm all right, really. I'd just like to be alone, if you don't mind.'

Alf shrugged his shoulders. 'Right-o, luv. I tell yer what, though. Take this,' he said, holding out the hip-flask. 'I've got plenty more indoors. It'll do yer good. It'll keep all them colly-wobbles away.'

Harriet was not sure what colly-wobbles were, but the strong spirit had made her feel light-headed and dreamy. 'Thank you, Mr Porter,' she answered, dabbing at her forehead with her lace handkerchief. 'I'm grateful for your helping me, and I'm sorry I misunderstood your intentions.'

'That's all right, dear,' Alf said, grinning widely. 'You sit back an' take a few drops 'o the ole fire-water. It'll put 'airs on yer chest – oops, sorry.'

Harriet sighed deeply as Alf left the house. What a crude man, she thought. I really should be grateful though. After all, he did clear up some of the mess. I suppose I shall have to forgive him for breaking Larry the Lamb.

Chapter Thirty

THE rocket attack had left the Stanley Street railway arches a tangled mass of girders, railtrack and masonry. The road was closed and all the houses as far along as Paragon Place had suffered damage. Doors hung from their hinges, roof slates had been dislodged and most of the windows were broken. The Railway Inn had suffered badly. All the shelf stock had been destroyed and all the windows were shattered. The large ornate mirror behind the public bar was cracked and chunks of ceiling plaster lay everywhere. Mercifully the explosion had taken place after closing-time and the publicans had escaped injury only because they had decided to have lunch in the back room before tidying up.

The Robinsons' parlour window had been shattered and slivers of glass filled Ruth's pram, but the baby herself had been with Sally in the back bedroom and she had slept through the horror. There were one or two minor injuries, however. Daisy had cut her foot on a piece of glass, and Lil swore she was now stone deaf. Ada and Clara showed off their injuries to each other. Ada had scalded her wrist on the boiling kettle and Clara had bumped her head as she ducked under the table. All the injuries were adequately treated by bandages and plasters, and when Clara saw her friend proudly sporting a bandaged wrist she scowled and contemplated bandaging the small bump on her forehead. Patrick laughed at the suggestion. 'You'll look like bloody Nelson, woman. Take a Daisy

Powder an' then forget it,' he said derisively as he went out to check on his pets.

On Monday morning workmen called to repair the broken windows and replace the few roof tiles, while others were busy reinforcing the arches and replacing the track. The Railway Inn had not opened for trade on Sunday evening but on Monday the windows were replaced, the stock replenished and the ornate mirror removed from behind the counter. Everything was soon back to normal and when Alf walked in on Monday evening he gave Bert a sarcastic look. 'Anuvver gas explosion, then?' he said with a wry grin. 'I reckon somebody chucked a fag-end orf the train, don't you?'

Bert scowled. 'All right, all right. Don't get lippy, Alf. D'yer want one o' yer free pints now or later?'

Alf waved the offer away. 'No fank you. I'm prepared ter wait till the poxy War Minister tells us jus' what is 'appenin'.'

Bert shrugged his shoulders. 'Please yerself. I reckon it's a disgrace leavin' us in the dark.'

When Charlie walked in he looked around the bar. 'I see yer got yerself sorted out, Bert,' he said with a serious look on his face. 'Those flyin' gas-mains do make a mess, don't they?'

Bert ignored the jest and leaned across the snug bar counter. 'Same again, ladies?'

Daisy put her elbows on the polished surface and glared at the publican. 'That last Guinness tasted a bit orf. I 'ope the bomb ain't curdled it all.'

Bert twisted off the bottle tops and carefully

poured out the Guinness. 'It's a bit frothy, luv. Can't be 'elped, though. It's the blast what done it. Don't worry, though, I'll 'ave a word wiv the Pope soon as I get a chance.'

Daisy turned to her friend. 'It's a bit gassy, Lil. It's the blast.'

Lil pulled a face. 'The last? Bloody 'ell, I never known 'im ter run out o' Guinness.'

'The blast,' Daisy shouted, mouthing the words. 'The blast shook up the Guinness.'

'It shook me up an' all,' Lil answered, digging away at her ear with a hairclip. 'I can't 'ear a bloody fing.'

'Yer wanna get some sweet oil,' Daisy said. 'Warm a drop up on a spoon an' shove it in yer burr'ole. It's very good.'

'It ain't as good as it used ter be, though,' Lil remarked.

'What ain't?'

'Why, Guinness, o' course.'

'She can't 'ear a word I'm sayin' even when I shout,' Daisy complained to Bert. 'That explosion sent 'er stone deaf.'

Bert leaned over the counter. 'Why don't yer try that sweet oil, Lil? It's good fer deafness. Yer put a drop on a spoon an' . . .'

'I've already told 'er what ter do,' Daisy cut in.

Lil pointed to her ear. 'It's no good, I can't 'ear what you're sayin'. I'll 'ave ter get some sweet oil. It's good fer deafness. What yer do is put a drop on the spoon an' stick it in yer ear.'

Daisy shook her head in frustration and Bert smiled sympathetically. 'Never mind, Dais,' he

601

said. ''Ave a drink on me.'

Lil glanced up and quickly drained her glass before banging it down on the counter.

Bert gave her a sideways glance and turned to Daisy. 'I fink she's takin' the piss,' he growled.

On that Monday evening Ben Brady walked into the square and knocked at the Robinsons' house. Annie opened the front door and she stood back in surprise, taking a few seconds to recover.

'Quite a stranger,' she said offhandedly.

Ben looked down at his feet and then glared back up to face Annie's hard stare. 'I 'ope yer didn't mind me callin' round,' he said hesitantly. 'I only just 'eard about the railway arches an' I wanted ter see if everybody was all right.'

Annie looked him up and down. 'Wait 'ere. I'll see if Sally wants ter see yer,' she said coldly.

As Sally came to the door Ben stepped back a pace as though he feared her anger. 'I wouldn't 'ave come round, Sally, but I was worried,' he said quickly. 'I only just 'eard about the railway catchin' it.'

Sally stared at him for a few moments, hardly able to believe that he was standing at her door. 'It's OK, we can talk in my room,' she said finally, beckoning him in.

The bedroom curtains had been drawn against the damp weather and a small bedside lamp spread a warm glow throughout the room. As Sally led Ben into the room she heard Ruth cooing contentedly in her crib at the foot of the bed, and suddenly she realised that Ben had not yet seen her baby. She walked over to the crib and smiled down at the tiny bundle.

'This is Ruth, Ben,' she said, feeling a little ill at ease as she turned to face him.

Ben walked over sheepishly and Sally suddenly felt a wave of pity for him as she saw the strange expression on his face. As he peered over the edge of the crib she felt a lump rise up in her throat, and a hollow feeling opened out inside her as she realised that once, a long time ago it seemed now, Ruth should have been their baby. She was afraid of what Ben might be feeling as he gazed down at her baby but as he looked up she saw a calm, tender look in his eyes.

'She's beautiful,' he said smiling. 'She's got yer features, Sal.'

Sally laughed and looked away quickly before tears came to her eyes. 'Fanks, Ben,' she said quietly. 'Sit yerself down over there an' we can 'ave a chat.'

Sally sat on the edge of the bed facing Ben as he settled himself in the only chair. Ruth was still making small cooing sounds and Ben clasped his hands and studied his thumbnails as Sally recounted the bomb incident. He winced as she told of Ruth's fortunate escape from the flying glass.

'I was shocked when one o' the lads at work told me Stanley Street arches copped it on Sunday,' he began. 'I went ter see old Aunt Vi yesterday an' it was late when I got back. At first I feared the worst but me mate said 'e 'eard nobody was badly 'urt. Bloody 'ell, it was close, though. It's a good job the baby was in this room.'

Sally shivered as she picked Ruth up from the crib and held her close. 'What are those fings, Ben?' she asked, looking at him with concern.

'They're large rockets by all accounts. They drop out o' the sky wivout warnin'. There's no time ter sound the siren. The first yer know of it is when they land. I read in the paper they're gonna give out a statement on the wireless soon. Up until now they've bin put down ter gas explosions. I s'pose the government was waitin' ter see 'ow many come over. There's too many landed now so they've gotta say somefing.'

'Me dad said they call 'em flying' gas-mains at the Railway,' Sally said, a smile appearing on her pale face.

Ben grinned. 'Yeah, I s'pose the regulars at the Railway would 'ave a good name fer 'em. Yer Dad still goes up there, then?'

Sally nodded. 'They all do. Vera's dad, Ted Bromley, an' not fergettin' Alf, o' course. They all congregate at the Railway. Did yer 'ear about the trouble there wiv Muriel Taylor's fella an' the Dougans?'

'Yeah, I 'eard from some o' the lads who use the Railway,' Ben replied. 'It was a bit of a ter-do, by all accounts.'

Sally adjusted her position on the bed and pulled her dress down over her knees self-consciously as she held Ruth against her. 'Did yer 'ear about Muriel gettin' attacked?' she asked.

He nodded. 'I was workin' on the same quay as yer farver an' I 'eard 'im tellin' a couple of 'is

604

mates about it. It wasn't Patsy Dougan that attacked 'er.'

Sally shook her head. 'No, it wasn't Patsy. Muriel said she'd never laid eyes on the bloke before. She said 'e was a great big 'ulk.'

Ben smiled mirthlessly. 'It was a bloke called Gerry Austin. 'E's known as Greasy an' 'e comes from over the water – Stepney, I fink. Anyway, this Greasy Austin's got form. 'E's done time fer assaultin' women an' apparently the law wanna talk to 'im about the murder of a prosser over in Wappin'. I tell yer, Sal, that Greasy's bad news. 'E's a right nutter an' it was a good fing 'e was stopped or 'e'd 'ave killed Muriel.'

"Ow d'yer know it was Greasy Austin that attacked Muriel?' Sally asked, a curious look on her face.

Ben leaned forward in his chair. 'It's a long story, Sally. D'yer wanna 'ear about it?'

Ruth was sleeping peacefully and she did not wake up as Sally gently settled her back in her crib, folding the covers tenderly over her. Sally sat down again on the edge of the bed, looking at Ben intently.

'Well ter start wiv,' he began, 'there's bin a bit o' trouble lately between the Dougans an' my two bruvvers. Yer remember Jack an' Nobby used ter run around wiv the Dougans?'

Sally nodded. 'Yeah, I remember.'

'Well, they fell out wiv Patsy Dougan last year over some money owin' 'em,' Ben went on. 'Ever since then there's bin a cold feud goin' on between my bruvvers an' the Dougan crowd. After the trouble outside the Railway Patsy an'

605

'is mob started usin' the Waterman pub at Dock'ead, an' that's the boozer Jack an' Nobby use. Fings 'ave got a bit awkward, yer can imagine, although the Dougans use the saloon bar. The guv'nor o' the Waterman can't stand 'em an' 'e's bin passin' bits o' news ter me bruvvers. Apparently 'e gets it from one o' their mob who can't 'old 'is drink. Anyway, ter cut a long story short, Patsy Dougan asked one of 'is boys ter get somebody from over the water ter put the frighteners on Muriel. That way it wouldn't come back ter Patsy's door. Trouble was, the bloke they recruited was Greasy Austin, an' now they've found out that Greasy's a nonsense case they're worried sick. Word got out from Stepney that Greasy's got a down on prossers an' the police wanna talk to 'im about a number of attacks, includin' the murder o' that street girl in Wappin'.'

Sally's face took on a puzzled look. 'Yeah, but why should Patsy Dougan wanna go ter all that trouble ter frighten Muriel?' sh asked. 'After all, she only stepped in the fight ter stop 'im stabbin' Big Joe, an' even Patsy must 'ave bin glad afterwards that 'e 'adn't done it, when 'e'd sobered up.'

Ben smiled. 'Patsy Dougan didn't go ter all that trouble jus' because Muriel Taylor gave 'im an 'eadache fer a few days,' he said. 'It's somefing else. Somefing a bit more complicated.'

'Like what?' Sally asked, intrigued.

'Muriel Taylor used ter 'ave a certain client by the name o' Cuthbert,' Ben continued. 'Now this dirty ole git 'appens ter be the manager of an estate agent's, the one what manages this square, in fact, an' 'e's bin doin' some dodgy dealin's on the side wiv bomb-damaged 'ouses. The Dougans were brought in ter bodge the repairs an' tergevver they were earnin' a nice few bob. It was a big fiddle an' everyfing was goin' sweet. The Dougans knew about Muriel 'cos she'd bin in the office on occasions when they'd called on business, and they didn't really take much notice, until one day they found out she 'ad anuvver important client who she was seein' pretty regular.'

'Who was that?' Sally asked quickly.

Ben chuckled. 'Muriel was seein' the Chief Inspector at Dock'ead nick, no less.'

Sally puffed out her cheeks in surprise. 'Crikey! She was always a dark 'orse, was Muriel. She certainly knew 'ow ter pick 'em.'

Ben nodded. 'When Patsy found out 'e went berserk. 'E told Cuthbert ter give 'er the elbow but the dirty ole git wasn't gonna do no such fing, an' 'e wasn't too 'appy about the Dougans dictatin' to 'im, neivver. Apparently there was a right ole bust up. Cuthbert threatened to bring in somebody else ter do the repairs an' Patsy 'ad ter find anuvver way of protectin' 'is interests. Yer see 'e was terrified o' Cuthbert openin' 'is trap ter Muriel an' 'er passin' it all on.'

'Muriel wouldn't do anyfing like that,' Sally said, shaking her head.

'Yeah, but Patsy couldn't take that chance. 'E didn't want ter be linked wiv Cuthbert. Yer see, 'e'd bin careful ter put 'is repair business in anuvver name but 'e still thought it was a right dodgy situation ter be in, so 'e decided ter put the frighteners in,' Ben explained. 'At first 'e jus' told 'er that 'e knew she was seein' the top copper an' 'e tried ter warn 'er off. Yer can guess Muriel's response, Sal. She told 'im she wasn't a grass an' 'e could piss off an' mind 'is own business.'

Sally grinned. 'Yeah, that's just what Muriel would do. The fing that seems strange ter me is, yer got all this from one of Patsy Dougan's crowd.'

Ben laughed quietly. 'All we got from them was that Greasy Austin 'ad bin brought in. All the rest came from Muriel 'erself.'

Sally looked incredulously at him. 'Muriel?'

'That's right,' Ben replied with an amused smile. 'Nobby used ter be sweet on Muriel fer a long time, an' I'm still not really sure what went on between 'em, but when 'e found out that Muriel was in danger of gettin' set about 'e told me an' Jack an' we got in touch wiv 'er ter warn 'er. Course we didn't know then that Greasy was a nonsense case. Anyway, we 'ad a nice long chat wiv Muriel over a few drinks an' she told us everyfing.'

Outside, the rain had started and thunder rolled across the dark sky. Sally sat studying her hands, trying to take in all Ben had told her.

Suddenly she looked up at him, a puzzled look on her face. 'Yer say that Patsy Dougan got this Austin bloke in ter frighten 'er off, but why should 'e 'ave done it now? Muriel's packed up the game. She ain't seein' Cuthbert or the copper any more. Patsy must 'ave known that.'

A smile played in the corner of Ben's mouth and he leaned forward. 'I told yer it was a long story, didn't I? Well, there's more. When Muriel decided ter give up the streets she told Cuthbert that she was finished wiv 'im too. The ole git got upset an' 'e's bin pesterin' 'er ever since. A few months ago 'e met 'er an' told 'er if she didn't oblige 'im 'e'd do 'is best ter get 'er evicted. Muriel said she'd tell everybody 'e'd took advantage of 'er in the first place an' 'e'd tried ter blackmail 'er afterwards, but Cuthbert only laughed. 'E said 'e'd deny everyfing an' 'e'd be believed before 'er. Muriel wasn't finished, though. She'd picked up quite a bit of information about the goin's on durin' 'er time wiv 'im an' she threatened ter tell the police all she knew. Cuthbert started ravin' an' 'e told 'er 'e was gonna warn the Dougans. That's what 'e must 'ave done, an' Patsy must 'ave got scared. They'd both be lookin' at a lot o' bird if they was found out. Muriel told us she regretted threatenin' ter blow the gaff an' she was scared o' gettin' worked over. She was right ter be worried, wasn't she? I tell yer Sal, if it wasn't fer that Cox fella comin' on the scene she'd be lyin' on a slab by now.'

Sally shivered. 'No wonder she was dead keen ter get away from the neighbour'ood. She must 'ave bin terrified. I remember 'er tellin' me Dougan threatened 'er, but she didn't make too much of it. Yer know Muriel, she's not one ter say too much.'

Ben nodded. 'It's just as well she's out o' the way. Greasy must 'ave bin told that she'd bin a

609

prostitute, an' the fact that she's give up the game wouldn't mean nufing to 'im. All the time 'e's on the loose Muriel's in danger, an' I don't wanna scare yer, Sal, but any woman's in danger wiv an' 'ead-case like that prowlin' around.'

'We've jus' gotta 'ope that the law catch 'im soon,' Sally said.

Ben nodded. 'The Dougans want 'im out o' the way, too. While Greasy's in the area 'e's an embarrassment to 'em. Patsy only wanted ter slap Muriel around a bit an' tell 'er ter keep 'er mouth shut. 'E didn't know Greasy would wanna kill 'er. Now 'e's got a mad dog on 'is 'ands, an' Greasy ain't gonna be goin' back ter Stepeney 'cos the law there are after 'im.'

Sally shuddered. 'It's frightenin' ter fink there's a bloke like 'im loose in the neighbour'ood.'

Ben stared at her for a few moments. More than anything he wanted to stay with her and protect her, but he knew that it was too late now. 'Oh well, I'd better get goin' or yer mum'll be gettin' worried,' he said, standing up and stretching. 'Jus' be careful, Sal, an' don't go out on yer own at night,' he added, unable to think of anything that would reassure her.

As they left the room Sally saw Ben look briefly at the crib, a distant, sad expression in his eyes. She went with him to the door and when he turned to say goodbye she could see that he was still trying to hide a sadness as he smiled at her.

'Fanks fer lettin' me in fer the chat, Sally,' he said. 'Look after yerself. Maybe we'll bump inter each ovver again soon.'

She nodded. 'Take care, Ben.'

He walked away, his footsteps echoing with a hollow sound in the empty square, and Sally watched him turn the corner without looking back.

Chapter Thirty-One

IT was a cold October morning when the young lad cycled into Paragon Place and knocked at the Robinsons' house. Annie took the telegram and hurried into the parlour where her daughter was bathing Ruth in a tin bath beside the fire. The noise of the knocker had sent a shock wave through Sally's body and icy fingers had gripped at her insides as she heard the muffled words at the door. When she saw her mother's ashen face she knew that the worst thing possible had happened. Annie stood still, unable to say anything, holding out the little buff-coloured envelope in her shaking hand. Sally grabbed Ruth from the bath and quickly wrapped a towel around her, then took the telegram in her wet hands. Annie stood beside the fire, watching fearfully as her daughter opened the envelope and read the few words.

Sally's face drained of colour and she squeezed Ruth to her. 'Jim's missin', presumed killed,' she said in a voice little more than a whisper.

Annie's hand went up to her mouth and she

burst into tears. Sally sat numb for a few moments, then a teardrop ran down her cheek. Ruth gurgled happily, her tiny hand reaching out to touch her mother's face, unaware of the tragedy unfolding around her.

'I was expectin' it,' Sally said, her voice husky with emotion. 'I jus' knew.'

Annie had wiped her eyes and was trying to compose herself. 'Give me the baby, Sal,' she said. 'Let me take 'er.'

Sally shook her head slowly, still trying to accept that Jim was gone for ever. She looked down at the baby and suddenly all the emotion, all the heartbreak burst out of her in a fit of tears, and sobs wracked her body. Annie felt powerless to do anything as she stood motionless over her daughter's shaking figure. Her hand went out and rested on Sally's shoulders, but she could find no words which might comfort her distraught daughter. She turned and hurried from the house, knowing instinctively that there was only one person in the whole square who would be able to help.

Ginny came into the room behind Annie and stood for a moment looking down at Sally as she sat huddled on the floor. 'Get the kettle on,' she shouted. 'Make 'er a strong cup o' tea. 'Ave yer got any whisky in the place?'

Annie nodded and hurried from the room. Ginny went over to Sally and crouched down beside her. She could see Ruth beneath the large towel, her little face becoming red and contorted as she struggled to free herself.

'Give me the baby, Sal. C'mon now,' Ginny

612

said in a firm voice.

Sally was incapable of understanding and Ginny forcibly pulled the baby from her mother's grasp and set about drying and dressing the child. When she had finished she held the baby in her arms and hurried out into the scullery. Annie was pouring the tea, her face a blank mask. Ginny cuddled the baby to her, rocking gently from one foot to the other. 'Stick a decent drop o' whisky in, Annie, it'll 'elp steady 'er,' she said firmly.

The baby had been fed and was sleeping peacefully in her pram beneath the window. Ginny sat facing the sad figure and watched as she sipped her tea. 'I said the same ter George, Sal. Yer never know, 'e might be found. Yer mustn't give up 'ope.'

Sally shook her head. 'I knew I was gonna get news, Ginny,' she said tearfully. 'I've 'ad that feelin' fer ages now. I knew it was only a matter o' time. Jim's dead an' it's no good pretendin' ovverwise.'

Ginny leaned forward in her chair and reached out, her hand closing on Sally's knee. 'Look, Sal. Yer gotta keep 'opin'. It's the only fing yer can do. Lots o' people get those telegrams an' then they 'ear that their folk are alive. Jim might be a prisoner, yer jus' don't know.'

'I know, Ginny. I know 'e's dead. I jus' know,' Sally said, her voice breaking off as she bowed her head.

'Yer gotta pull yerself tergevver,' Ginny said quickly. 'Yer got the baby ter fink of. Yer mustn't jus' accept yer fella's dead. It's early

613

days yet. Keep 'opin', it's all yer can do.'

The day seemed endless to Sally as she moved about the house slowly in a state of shock. She found herself going over and over the same jobs and willing Ruth to wake up from her naps so that she could hold her. It was as though Jim was still close as she cuddled the baby to her. She could see some of him in Ruth. She had his eyes, and there was the comforting feeling that together they had made her. She heard the howling wind as a wail of grieving around the house and the grey sky was like a veil of mourning, a pale winding-sheet spread across the day. Words of sympathy were spoken around her but nothing could ease the pain except the feel of Ruth's warm, moving body in her arms. A few people called during the day offering their condolences, but when Vera called she was too tearful and upset to be of any comfort and Sally was glad when she left. Annie continually broke down in tears, and when Lora came in from work she sat down and cried with her sister. Charlie picked at his evening meal, affected by the grief around him, and then he sat staring moodily into the glowing fire.

Outside the wind had dropped and spots of rain stained the flagstones. As the evening wore on the drizzle turned to a heavy downpour and streamlets of rain ran swiftly along the gutters as water cascaded down from the roof slates. The darkness of a black, moonless night swallowed up the houses. Rainwater poured from damaged drain-pipes, splashing on to the flagstones. Distant thunder rolled and white lightning momentarily lit the black sky as the Paragon Place folk pulled the bedclothes over their ears.

In two of the little houses lights burned through the night. At number 4, Sally sat slumped in her bedside chair with a blanket wrapped around her shoulders, and through her tortured thoughts memories rose up of the green, rolling countryside and a quaint hotel with ivy climbing up the walls. She saw the open bay window and Jim perched on the window seat, a cigarette held between his fingers and a faraway look on his handsome face. She felt his arms closing around her, his warmth banishing the realities of war, and her deep sigh was choked with a sob. It was a brief, happy moment in time, a dream of love, and so soon over.

At number 2, a light burned in the small parlour as George sat staring up at the photographs of the two uniformed figures. His thoughts travelled out across the oceans and he tried to form a picture in his mind of his sons. Laurie was the younger, the quieter of the two. George wondered where he could be now. It would be daytime in the Far East and Laurie would be sweltering beneath a scorching sun, or maybe sheltering from the monsoon rains. Was he well? George agonised. Was he still alive? Then there was Tony, the big easy-going lad, who had made a few of the young girls' hearts flutter when he strolled through the backstreets, his shoulders rolling and his back ramrod-straight. Was he lying in a shallow grave? George wondered, as despair seized him. Or was he still alive and languishing in a prison camp somewhere in Italy? George tortured himself, as if by thinking over and over again until his energy was gone he could know whether his two sons would ever see Paragon Place again, whether they would both walk back into the square one day when the victory flags were flying and the street-lamps shone out once more. George threw another knob of coal on to the fire and watched as the smoking lump burst into violet flame. He sat alone with his thoughts as the coal burned and crumbled, and as he gazed into the bright light of the fire he saw shapes and figures darting in the flames. He saw jungle and desert wastes, shifting and crumbling, and as his head drooped and the flames died dreams cast their twisted shadows across his troubled mind.

The October days passed slowly and the winter took grip. The tragic news of Tony Tapley had been compounded now by the telegraph boy calling at the Robinsons', and it seemed as though the whole of Paragon Place was in mourning. Laughter was guarded in the quiet square and high spirits became restrained. Folk nodded almost apologetically as Sally or George passed by and they found it difficult to bring themselves to engage either of the two in conversation, for fear of saying the wrong thing or seeming unsympathetic. As a result both Sally and George became isolated by their grief. Only the closest of friends were able to offer any support and consolation. For George, Ginny was a rock of solace and strength. Her unbounding faith that one day Tony would be discovered alive saved George from the dark abyss of despair. Vera proved a great source of comfort for Sally. Her vivacity and humour somehow found their way through to penetrate the darkness of her grief and isolation, and in her blackest hours Sally depended desperately on her friend's support.

With the sad, dark days of October came the realisation that the war was going to last until the new year. Although the Allied armies were sweeping through France and Italy the launching sites of the V2s had not yet been overrun and the rockets continued to fall. The suddenness of the attacks made warning impossible and as a result the air-raid shelters fell into disuse once more. Water seeped in, lying in evil-smelling pools, and the canvas bunks and wooden benches became infested with rats. The Paragon Place folk realised that there was no place to hide now and when an explosion sounded they could do nothing but grit their teeth and try to go about their normal business.

Scatty Whybrow, the local tramp, managed to go about his business. Each day he ambled along Stanley Street, stopping at Paragon Place to lean against the lamp post for support, his tatty bundle of belongings resting at his feet. He was a tall, thin character, with matted black hair, partially hidden beneath a greasy trilby hat, and a full black beard above which two coal-black eyes stared piercingly. He had been coming this way every day for years, come rain or shine, and everyone in the little square simply ignored him.

Once Ada Fuller handed him one of Maurice's old coats and Scatty took it without comment. Later Ada found the coat hanging from a gate post further along the street and decided that the tramp was 'a miserable, ungrateful ole bleeder'. For a while the local children had taken an interest in Scatty, eyeing him intently from a safe distance, but even they had grown used to him being there. Now they totally ignored him as he regularly paused for a few seconds every day, puffing through his black beard before taking up his bundle again and moving along.

Alf Porter had adopted a philosophic attitude and he was quick to pass his thoughts on to the square's volatile pair. 'It's no use you two divin' indoors,' he laughed after a distant explosion had sounded one Saturday morning. 'The one yer don't 'ear is the one yer gotta fear.'

Ada gave him a blinding look and turned to Clara. 'What's that soppy git on about?' she asked.

Clara shrugged her ample shoulders. 'Gawd knows.'

Alf sauntered up to the women and stuck his hands deep into his trouser pockets. 'Them there rockets come down like a flash,' he said, rocking back on his heels. 'Yer wouldn't know anyfing about it if one landed on this square. We'd all be blown ter kingdom come before yer could say Jack Robinson, or Charlie Robinson, in our case.'

Clara looked at the diminutive character with malice. 'That's it, frighten the bleedin' life out of us,' she growled.

618

Alf looked aggrieved. 'I'm only statin' a fact. When yer 'ear the rocket go off yer know you're OK. What's in that ter frighten yer?'

Ada mumbled an obscenity and turned to Clara. "Ow's young Sally bearin' up? I ain't seen much of 'er,' she said, hoping Alf would go away if she ignored him.

'I see 'er the ovver mornin',' Clara replied. 'She did look ill. It's ter be expected, though. It's the same wiv that George Tapley. The fella's walkin' around in a bleedin' daze. I see 'im the ovver mornin' an' I was gonna say 'ello but yer don't know what ter say, do yer?'

Ada nodded. 'Mind you though, there's a lot o' them fellas what's missin' got captured. George's boy might be a prisoner like 'is ovver boy, although a lot o' comfort that is. There's some terrible stories in the papers about them Japs.'

Alf had not gone away. He had been listening to the women and suddenly he prodded Ada in the back. "Ere, you know everybody in the square,' he said. 'Why don't yer see if they'd be interested in puttin' a few coppers away each week fer a victory party?'

Ada rounded on him, a malevolent look in her convergent eyes. 'I thought you'd gone,' she told him coldly. 'A party, yer say? What, wiv the bloody rockets comin' down an' people gettin' killed? Leave orf.'

Alf was not to be put off. 'Look, luv. The war's gonna be over next year, yer can bank on it, despite the bloody rockets an' whatever else our Adolf Schikelgrauger's got up 'is sleeve. I know a few streets what's already started ter get organised wiv collections. We could do the same 'ere. Yer don't 'ave ter knock on George Tapley's or Sally Brady's door, but everybody else wouldn't mind puttin' in a few coppers, surely ter Gawd.'

Clara was stroking her chin. ''Ere, come ter fink of it, it ain't a bad idea. There's enough kids in the square fer a party. We could get a few bottles o' beer in as well.'

'Yer could borrer me pianer again,' Alf said, beaming.

Ada nodded. 'All right. I'll talk it over wiv Clara an' let yer know.'

Alf turned on his heel without replying and walked along the square, whistling tunelessly.

In the Robinsons' home the evening meal was finished and Annie sat beside the fire, glasses perched on the end of her nose as she struggled to thread a needle. Charlie had finished the evening paper and his eyelids started to droop. He eased down in the armchair and spread out his legs.

Annie looked over at him. 'Ain't yer goin' out ternight?' she asked.

Charlie shook his head. 'It was perishin' on the quay terday. I got it right across me back. I ain't up ter goin' out.'

Annie finally managed to thread the cotton through the eye of the needle and she knotted the ends around her forefinger. ''Ave yer seen anyfing o' Ben at work, Chas?' she asked suddenly.

620

Charlie nodded, still staring into the fire. 'Ben's gang was workin' next ter mine day before yesterday. First time I've seen 'im fer weeks. I 'ad a quiet word wiv 'im, much as I don't like talkin' ter the bloke.'

'What did 'e say?' Annie asked, putting down Charlie's torn shirt.

'Well, ter tell yer the trufe, Ben looked genuinely sorry ter 'ear of it,' Charlie answered, picking up his pipe and tapping it on the heel of his boot. 'I didn't fink 'e'd 'ave bin too upset, considerin' what 'appened wiv 'im an' Sal, but I must say I didn't see any look o' that sort on the boy's face.'

Annie leaned back in her chair and sighed. 'I dunno what ter make of it all. I'm jus' wonderin' if them two will get back tergevver, now Jim's gone. I'm sure Ben still finks a lot of 'er, despite Sally leavin' 'im. I mean, 'e come round 'ere after the railway arches got bombed ter see if she was all right.'

Charlie looked at Annie, a hard glint in his eye. 'Despite Sally leavin' 'im yer say? It sounds like you're blamin' our Sally fer what's 'appened.'

'All right, keep yer voice down. Yer don't want Sally ter 'ear yer,' Annie chided. 'All I'm sayin' is, a lot's 'appened and I'm not takin' sides. It's usually six o' one an' 'alf a dozen o' the ovver. Yer can tell Ben still wants 'er back. That's all I'm sayin'.'

Charlie finished packing his pipe in silence, then he looked across to Annie. 'Look, gel, I don't condone our Sal gettin' 'erself pregnant.

621

All right, we can't interfere, an' we don't know the rights of it, but I tell yer this. If Sally decides ter get back wiv Ben I wouldn't say nufing ter put 'er off, even though I don't go a bundle on the bloke. Anyway, it's early days yet. Besides, there's the little mite ter fink of. She ain't Ben's kid an' there's always gonna be that ter come between 'em if they ever did get back tergevver again.'

Annie nodded and picked up the shirt she was mending. 'I dunno, it's all worry, what wiv one fing an' anuvver. There's our Lora gaddin' about wiv that fella from work. I've asked 'er time an' again ter bring 'im 'ome, but she keeps puttin' it orf. I fink she's ashamed of us, if yer ask me.'

'Ashamed of us?' Charlie repeated. 'Gor blimey, gel, what's she got ter be ashamed about? Anybody would fink we eat wiv our fingers an' live in shit. I'm workin' class an' proud of it. This family's workin' class, an' so is she – in case she's forgot it. I s'pose if I wore a bowler 'at an' a bloody tie an' we moved out o' Bermondsey it'd be all right. Well, I ain't gonna wear a poxy bowler, an' I ain't intendin' ter move away from 'ere, so there.'

'All right, Charlie, don't get yer blood pressure up,' Annie said slowly, looking at him over her glasses. 'Nobody's askin' yer ter move out, nor ter wear a bowler. I wouldn't wanna move away meself. This is where I was born an' this is where I expect ter stay. I ain't ashamed o' the 'ouse neivver. All right, we've only got the tin barf an' we ain't got an inside lavatory, but the place is clean an' tidy. I keep me curtains

622

changed an' me step whitened. I'm always dustin' an' cleanin' an' I always try ter put a good meal on the table. Mind you, though, it's a bloody worry, what wiv the rationin'. I fink I manage quite well, considerin'.'

Charlie had already shut his ears to his wife's soliloquy and he leaned back in his chair, his eyes straying up to the clock. Annie caught his glance and she looked down at the shirt in her lap.

'I was talkin' ter ole Fat Tits Ada this mornin',' she said. 'She was sayin' somefing about gettin' a collection up fer when the war's over. She said they was finkin' of 'avin' a party fer the kids an' a bit of a knees-up in the square. I said I'd put a couple o' coppers in every week but I still reckon the war's gonna go on fer a long time yet.'

Charlie nodded. 'Anuvver year at least,' he mumbled.

'Could be two years, the way fings are goin',' Annie remarked. 'They're still sendin' them rockets over, an' Gawd knows what else they've got in store fer us. It's a wonder they ain't dropped any o' that there poison gas. Still, it ain't too late.'

Charlie cursed under his breath and looked up at the clock again. 'Me back feels a mite easier now,' he said slyly, moving his shoulders. 'I fink I'll slip up the Railway fer a quick pint. It might 'elp me ter get a good night's sleep.'

'You'd be better orf wiv a cup o' cocoa an' a couple of Aspros,' Annie snorted.

Charlie got up and slipped on his coat. 'I fink

623

I'll give Fred an' Ted a knock,' he said. 'They might fancy a pint.'

'Why, 'ave they got trouble sleepin' as well?' Annie said sarcastically.

Early in November all speculation about the mysterious explosions was finally ended when an official announcement stated that the Germans had developed and were using a new weapon which carried a ton of explosive, and that some degree of damage had been sustained. Descriptions of the 'V2s' were in all the newspapers and in the Railway Inn the wager was paid in full. Alf Porter took his first free pint without gloating and he sat sipping it quietly. The announcement had come as no surprise following the devastation wrought on the railway arches in Stanley Street. Even the most gullible of Bert Jackson's regulars had had to admit that the mangled girders and rail-tracks and the damage to the houses could not have been caused by an exploding gas-main.

The new weapon had brought about a change of thinking and the Paragon Place folk realised that as there was no warning and no chance to take shelter there was no point in staying close to the square. They had become fatalistic, and when they heard the distant rumble of explosions they gritted their teeth and went about their business. Alf started to venture from the immediate area and he paid visits to a few of his old cronies. The women went to the market without bothering to hurry back and even Ginny felt that it was unfair to tie her three lads to the square, although her two daughters were not let out of her sight. Vera and Sally wheeled their prams to the local park and the church gardens when weather permitted and they sat together, muffled up against the cold, and talked. Sally was grateful for her friend's patience and understanding. The sense of loss was weighing heavily on her and there were times when fits of black despair seemed to be pulling her down. The winter days were short and grey with little sunlight, and when night fell and Ruth was tucked up in her crib and fast asleep Sally lay awake, suffering in silence and torturing her mind with thoughts of Jim and what might have been. She saw his face, although it was always misted, never clear, and when she finally slipped into unconsciousness it was a restless sleep of exhaustion.

December arrived with snow flurries and bitter winds. The old sycamore tree lost its last few brown, crinkled leaves and its bare branches shook and rattled against the guttering of Alf Porter's house. The V2s continued to fall with a terrible regularity, and the only one that landed in the area hit a leather factory early one Sunday morning and killed a policeman who was sheltering in a doorway opposite. The shops and market stalls put out their Christmas decorations and the queues lengthened for bread and vegetables. As the dark evenings drew in subdued lights shone out from shops and the stallholders hung up dimmed tilley lamps. People searched for Christmas presents and children became excited at the thought of what they would find in their Christmas stockings. Newspapers published articles about priorities for service demobilisation and showed pictures of the proposed 'demob' suit. Scribes wrote about what direction the peace-time future should take and broadcasters spoke of their ideas for a new world, but still the bitter fighting continued and still the casualty lists filled columns.

During the first week in December Juliet Carey learned that Mrs Lomax had died. Although she had only met the woman on very few occasions Juliet could not help but feel saddened, as well as apprehensive for the future. Basil would of course observe a respectable period of mourning, but he would at some stage approach her about marriage, she felt sure. He had often indicated as much in the past, although she had been quick to change the subject.

Juliet knew that she had a very difficult decision to make. If she accepted his proposal of marriage Harriet would take it badly. She would most definitely not stay alone in the flat. She would be more likely to pine away in some old folks' home. If on the other hand she declined Basil's proposal, she could not expect things to remain as they were now. He could be obstinate at times and he might well put pressure on her by threatening to end their association if she turned him down. It was all so worrying, she sighed.

Ginny Almond had heard from her solicitor that her divorce was making progress and she could expect to be a free woman early in the new year. Ginny felt no surge of elation at the news. George Tapley had become a sad, dejected figure who was slowly losing all hope of ever seeing either of his sons again. Ginny tried her hardest to bring him out of his black depression but she had to admit to her next door neighbour that it was becoming almost impossible.

'I talk to 'im till I'm blue in the face but it don't seem ter make any difference, Annie,' she said sadly. 'George is gonna go down wiv a whimper before long. I can't get 'im ter 'ave a decent meal or change 'is shirt. 'E jus' sits there starin' inter the fire. It's terrible ter see the man go like it.'

Annie slipped her hands inside her apron and shook her head. 'I know 'ow yer feel, Ginny. There's my Sal goin' the same way. She sits up in that room of 'ers fer hours on end, an' when she comes down I can see by 'er eyes she's bin cryin'. It's terrible, but what can yer say? There's nufing yer can say, is there?'

Two weeks before Christmas Vera knocked on Sally's door with a smile on her face. 'Muriel's 'ome on leave,' she said. 'I seen 'er walk into the square this mornin'. She said fer us ter call in. Come on, d'yer wanna go over an' see 'er?'

The two knocked at number 1, and after excited hugs and kisses at the door Muriel showed them into her tidy parlour. Her face became serious as she took Sally's hand in hers.

'I was terribly sorry ter 'ear of yer fella, Sal,' she said quietly. 'Vera told me. I wouldn't give

627

up 'ope, though. 'E could still be alive. 'E could be a prisoner.'

Sally shook her head sadly. 'I don't fink so,' she replied. 'I've come to accept that 'e's bin killed.'

Muriel sighed sadly and looked at Vera for help.

'What about puttin' the kettle on, luv,' Vera said quickly, taking the hint. 'Then yer can tell us all about yer job, an' all those fellas yer bin goin' out wiv.'

Muriel laughed and gestured with her hand. 'It's bin sheer murder. I ain't 'ad a minute's peace. Mind you, it 'elps ter get the NAAFI manager on yer side. 'E's a bit of all right as well.'

Sally sat down and crossed her legs. ''Ow long yer 'ome for, Muriel?' she asked. 'Will yer be 'ere fer Christmas?'

Muriel gave Sally a lopsided grin. 'Seven days' leave, that's all the ole goat allowed me, but I'm sodded if I'm goin' back a week before Christmas.'

'Are yer gonna desert, then?' Vera butted in.

Muriel's grin widened. 'I'm gonna pop round an' see ole Doctor Kelly. I'll take 'im 'alf a bottle of Irish whiskey an' ask 'im ter give me a medical certificate – fer chicken-pox I fink. That should keep me 'ome fer three or four weeks.'

'I can't imagine ole Bartholomew dishin' out certificates that easy,' Vera said above the laughter. ''E's a miserable ole goat at the best o' times, 'specially when 'e gets called out.'

They sat sipping tea, listening to Muriel's

account of her life as a NAAFI girl. 'It's OK, I s'pose,' she told them. 'Mind you, it's 'ard work, but I've put in fer overseas. They're askin' fer volunteers an' I've put me name down. It'll be better than bloody Catterick.'

'What's it like there?' Vera asked.

'Well, ter be honest it's bloody 'orrible, 'specially this weavver. All yer see is uniforms. It's cold up there, too. The bloody wind's enough ter freeze yer vital parts. We live in wooden 'uts jus' be'ind the NAAFI. Some o' the girls 'ave got themselves sorted out wiv fellas an' they wangle 'em inter their quarters, although there's a right ugly ole bitch who's s'posed ter supervise us an' she won't 'ave no 'anky-panky.'

'What about you?' Vera inquired. 'Yer ain't got a fella, 'ave yer?'

Muriel shook her head vigorously. 'No fear. I'm stayin' true ter my Yankie boy. Mind you, it's bloody 'ard bein' faithful. 'Specially when yer climb inter a cold bed.'

Vera wished she had not asked the question and Muriel wanted to kick herself for her unthinking answer as she suddenly remembered Sally's bereavement. She put down her teacup and leaned back in her chair. ''Ere, I gotta tell yer about them upstairs,' she said, changing the subject.

Vera brushed her red hair from her eyes and glanced at Sally. 'Not more scandal,' she said in mock horror.

Muriel crossed her legs and looked briefly towards the room door as though expecting the Carey sisters to be standing there. 'I 'adn't bin in
629

the 'ouse five minutes when Juliet tapped on the door,' she began.

'Which one's that? I always get 'em mixed up,' Vera cut in.

'She's the younger one,' Muriel replied. 'She's all right, really. Anyway, after askin' me 'ow I was gettin' on she suddenly tells me she's got a bloke.' Vera and Sally exchanged glances as Muriel went on. 'Apparently she's bin 'avin' it away wiv 'er guv'nor. It's bin goin' on fer years. 'E's older than 'er but 'e's still got all 'is faculties, accordin' ter Juliet. Well, this bloke's jus' lost 'is wife. She was an invalid fer ages an' now 'e wants Juliet ter go an' live wiv 'im. Trouble is, it's 'er sister. She's a bundle o' nerves an' she don't want ter be left on 'er own. Juliet was sayin' she don't know what ter do fer the best. It's a shame, really. Mind you, I ain't got much time fer that ole bat. It was 'er what reported me ter that Cuthbert.'

Sally had been listening without much interest, but Muriel's mention of the estate agent made her recall the conversation she had had with Ben and the article she had noticed in the *Star* a few days later. She had seen a picture of Greasy Austin staring out at her and an accompanying report stating that he was now wanted for the killing of an East End prostitute. The article had gone on to say that Austin had most probably left the Stepney area and the search for him had widened to other parts of London. Sally realised she would have to tell Muriel that while she was in Bermondsey and Austin was at large she would be in great danger.

Muriel had been chatting away for some time when Vera decided she had to go as her children were due for their feed. When she had left Muriel turned to Sally.

'I'm sorry if I upset yer by goin' on, Sal,' she said. 'It was stupid of me.'

Sally waved Muriel's apologies away with a smile. 'It's OK. Fings are bound ter be said innocently an' I'm always gonna be reminded one way an' anuvver. I gotta get used ter the idea. I've got Ruth ter fink about now.'

'I bet she's gettin' big, ain't she?' Muriel said, picking up the empty cups. 'I mus' see 'er.'

Sally smiled. 'She's got Jim's eyes.'

Muriel refilled their cups, and when they were sipping the fresh tea Sally broached the subject of Greasy Austin. 'I saw Ben after you'd left,' she began. "E was tellin' me 'e warned yer about that Austin bloke.'

Muriel looked over her cup. 'Did 'e tell yer we 'ad a good long chat?'

'Yeah, 'e did,' Sally replied. 'Ben explained what was be'ind the attack. You'll 'ave ter be careful, Muriel. I don't wanna frighten yer but the fella who attacked yer killed a street gel over in Wappin'. I read it in the papers. Apparently the bloke's a nonsense case. The police are lookin' fer 'im but so far they 'aven't caught 'im.'

'Christ! I didn't know that,' Muriel exclaimed, her face becoming anxious. 'I 'ope the 'orrible git ain't still 'angin' aroun' this area. Maybe Patsy Dougan's 'idin' 'im.'

Sally shook her head. 'No, it's unlikely. Ben

told me that Patsy wants 'im out o' the way. 'E didn't know the bloke was a maniac when 'e 'ired 'im.'

Muriel leaned back in her chair and puffed out her cheeks. 'That Cuthbert was the cause of all this. 'E put Patsy up ter gettin' me set about. I wish I'd never gone ter see that ugly ole goat. I thought I was bein' so clever at the time. It looked like I was gonna get notice ter quit an' I worked a deal wiv 'im. Yer can guess what 'is payment was wivout me goin' inter details, Sal.'

A ghost of a smile touched Sally's face and she shook her head slowly. 'I can guess,' she chuckled. 'Anyway, we've jus' gotta 'ope they catch Austin soon. Jus' be careful, though.'

Muriel studied her fingernails for a few moments, then she looked up at Sally. 'Yer was sayin' about Ben. D'yer still see 'im?' she asked.

'As a matter o' fact 'e came round ter see if I was all right after the railway arches got bombed,' Sally replied. 'We've bumped inter each ovver on a couple of occasions lately.'

Muriel was looking at Sally closely. 'Is Ben after gettin' back wiv yer, Sal?' she asked.

Sally nodded. 'Yeah. 'E said I was welcome ter go back ter the 'ouse wiv the baby if fings got too bad.'

Muriel pursed her lips. 'That says a lot. 'E mus' be wantin' yer bad.'

'Ben said there'd be no strings, an' I believe 'im, but it's askin' too much,' Sally said in reply.

'D'yer fink you'd ever consider it, Sal?' Muriel asked her. 'I know it's none o' my business but you an' 'im was tergevver once. At least yer know 'is ways.'

'Yeah, I do,' Sally answered, a hard note creeping into her voice. 'We was 'appy once, but that was a long time ago. Fings changed. I found a new man an' I 'ad 'is baby. I couldn't go back now, even if I wanted to. It wouldn't be fair ter saddle 'im wiv anuvver man's child.'

Muriel shrugged her shoulders. 'Yer can tell me ter shut up if yer like, but I'm gonna give yer a bit of advice, fer what it's worth. I know yer feel terrible now an' yer don't wanna fink about it, but if the day comes when yer wanna go back wiv 'im, do it. The way I see it fellas are like kids. They need ter be Jack the Lad. They need ter feel all important an' in charge. Yer know what I'm sayin', Sal. We've all played their little games fer our own benefit, but there comes a time when it gets ter be more than a game. The stakes go up an' their bluff's called. Some of 'em chuck their 'and in an' ovvers grow up all of a sudden. I don't fink Ben's chucked 'is 'and in. I fink 'e knows the score now, an' 'e's prepared ter play fings your way. What I'm tryin' ter say is, Ben ain't under no illusions, an' don't you be. If it's what yer come ter want, go out an' grab it while yer still can, or you'll 'ave a lifetime of regret.'

Sally smiled briefly as she got up to go. She remembered the advice Bill Freeman once gave her and it seemed as if Muriel was echoing his words. 'Thanks fer the advice, Muriel,' she said quietly. 'There's somefing in what yer say. I'll bear it in mind. You take care now.'

Muriel grinned. 'I still carry a sharp pair o'

scissors in me 'andbag, Sal. I never got a chance ter use 'em last time, but I'll be ready this time.'

Chapter Thirty-Two

TWO heavily built dockers walked into Potters Lane, their caps worn at a jaunty angle, cotton scarves knotted at their necks and their overcoat collars turned up against the biting wind. Their stout steel-tipped boots sounded loudly on the flagstones as the two men hurried along to number 36 and rat-tatted on the front door. Ben Brady stepped out of the house immediately and fell in between his two brothers as they walked purposefully back out of the turning. At forty-two Jack was the eldest of the Bradys. He was a stockily built man with his bulk beginning to turn to fat and his dark hair thinning. Like his two younger brothers Jack was just over six feet tall and broad shouldered. He was a quiet-spoken man, although known for his violent temper. Norman Brady, known to everyone as Nobby, was four years younger. He was the joker of the three, and like Jack he was married with two children. Nobby was a crane driver, an alert, shrewd man whose spare-time money-making schemes had often led him into brushes with the law.

As the three dockers neared the Waterman public house Jack glanced at his brothers. 'We don't go in the saloon, get it?' he reminded them. 'They've approached us, so we do the talkin' in the public bar. Anuvver fing. We don't want their scatty crowd sittin' in neivver.'

Nobby gave Ben a quick glance before eyeing his elder brother. 'As far as I'm concerned, if they don't settle up their debt we give 'em the elbow, Jack,' he said firmly.

The public bar was almost empty as the Bradys walked up to the counter.

'What you lads 'avin?' the landlord asked, looking over his gold-rimmed spectacles at the three brothers.

'Give us three pints o' bitter, Jake, an' we'll need a few minutes before yer tell 'em we're 'ere.'

Jake Collins winked as he lined up the empty glasses on the counter and pulled down on the beer-pump. 'Jus' give us the nod when you're ready, boys. An' do us a favour, will yer?'

'What's that, Jake?' Nobby asked, licking his lips as the first full pint was placed in front of him.

'I know the score wiv you an' the Dougans, so keep it nice an' civilised, will yer? I got me livin' ter fink of.'

Ben laughed as he picked up his pint. 'Don't worry mate. We're 'ere ter talk – unless those monkeys wanna get a bit stroppy.'

Jake grimaced as he picked up the ten-shilling note. When he had given the change to Jack he leaned over the counter, quickly glancing over his shoulder. 'As far as I see it, you're on a winner,' he whispered. 'They're dead worried an' it's in their interest ter get a result. Word's out the nonsense case is still local an' the law's started askin' questions.'

Jack nodded his thanks and led the way to a corner table.

The public bar was beginning to fill by the time Patsy and Shaun Dougan sauntered in. Patsy walked up to the table, his younger brother at his shoulder.

'Evenin', fellas,' Patsy said, smiling. 'Glad yer could make it.'

Jack looked up at the smartly dressed young man who stood with his thumbs tucked into his waistcoat pockets. 'Yer wanna talk business, I understand?' he said coldly.

Patsy nodded and spread his hands in front of him. 'I fink it's about time we sat down tergevver, Jack. I'm after sortin' out our differences in a civilised manner.'

Jack glanced at each of his brothers in turn before fixing his eyes on Patsy. 'Right then. First step is ter get one fing straight, Patsy. Yer turned us over on that last bit o' business. So yer better start talkin' money.'

Patsy Dougan smiled briefly as he sat down in the one vacant chair, leaving his younger brother standing behind him.

Jack fished out a handful of silver from his trouser pocket. 'D'yer wanna drink? You'll 'ave ter get it yerself, though. We've all 'ad an 'ard day.'

Patsy waved away the offer and reached into his coat pocket, taking out a sealed envelope which he slapped down on the table. 'There's a ton in there,' he began. 'I believe that's the

636

figure in dispute. Take it as a sign o' good faith an' we'll go on from there.'

Jack picked up the envelope and slipped it into his pocket without opening it. 'As a sign o' good faith I'm not gonna count it, Patsy,' he replied, eyeing the man with an amused expression. 'The original price was fair, an' yer know yer got a good deal wiv those cases. Now fer the business in 'and. What d'yer want from us?'

Patsy clasped his hands on the table and studied his thumbnails for a few moments before answering. 'There's a certain character loose in the neighbour'ood an' we want 'im outters,' he began.

Nobby took a sip from his pint. 'We take it you're referrin' ter Greasy Austin?'

'Right first time,' Patsy replied, smiling slyly. 'All right I admit we dropped a clanger. We got that nonse in ter do a job an' it turns out 'e's become an embarrassment. We didn't know the proper SP when we pulled 'im in. It turns out the geezer's wanted fer toppin' a brass, an' if we don't get 'im off our backs we're gonna 'ave the Scotland Yard mob swampin' the area. Questions are gonna be asked and it's gonna get naughty fer business. Yer know yerself 'ow they put the frighteners in. When that 'appens nobody's safe.'

'Where do we fit in ter yer plans?' Jack asked.

'You boys 'ave got yer own contacts,' Patsy went on. ''Elp us find Greasy. That's all I'm askin'. If yer do find 'im before us just 'and 'im over. We'll take care of 'im.'

'What yer gonna do wiv 'im?' Ben asked,

glancing quickly at his brothers, then back at Patsy.

'We dump 'im back on 'is own manor an' make sure the Stepney police pick 'im up. It's as simple as that.'

'Ain't yer worried about the consequences?' Jack asked. 'S'posin' 'e blows the gaff about yer 'irin' 'im?'

Patsy smiled slyly. 'There's nufing ter tie us in wiv Greasy. 'E was brought in by a third party. We jus' want that nonse out the way so we can all enjoy a bit o' peace an' quiet. Will yer go along wiv us?'

Jack Brady looked down at his drink for a few moments, then he fixed the young man with a cold stare. 'All right, we'll go along wiv yer, but get one fing straight, Patsy, it's not fer yer benefit,' he said plainly. 'While that evil bastard's runnin' aroun' loose none of our women are safe. We'll put the feelers out, an' if and when we do find 'im you'll be the first ter know. One ovver fing, son. It's down ter you that there's a maniac loose in the neighbour'ood, an' if an' when we do deliver yer better not balls it up. 'Cos if yer do, me an' me bruvvers an' a few of our pals are not gonna take it kindly. I 'ope that's understood?'

Patsy Dougan got up and looked down at the Brady brothers. 'Understood,' he said, a smile playing in the corners of his mouth. Then he turned and walked out of the bar, his younger brother close on his heels.

With Christmas only a week away all but one of

the little houses in Paragon Place had festive decorations hanging in the parlours. Clara Botley got her husband Patrick to put up fairy lights in the front-room window, and it was not long before Ada Fuller approached her neighbour with a friendly smile on her large face.

'I fink they look really nice, Clara,' she said. 'By the way, I've dug some lights out from me cupboard. D'yer fink yer Pat would put 'em up fer us, luv? I could wait till Maurice comes 'ome but yer know what a soppy git 'e is wiv electrisical fings.'

Clara was feeling generous that particular morning and she nodded. 'Course 'e will, luv. I'll send 'im in ternight. It shouldn't take 'im long.'

Alf Porter hung up his decorations as soon as he spotted Clara's lights twinkling in her window. Might as well make a show, he thought, although he knew that he would probably spend little time in the house over the holiday anyway. Among the dusty decorations that he found in a cardboard box under the stairs, Alf discovered a holly wreath which he promptly pinned to the front door with a six-inch nail, splitting the door panel in the process.

At number 4 Annie Robinson stared down at her box of decorations, pinching her chin and frowning. 'I don't know as we should put these up, Charlie,' she said. 'It don't seem right, some'ow.'

Her husband bit on the stem of his pipe. 'P'r'aps yer should 'ave a word wiv Sally first,' he suggested. 'It is a bit awkward.'

Annie approached her daughter with more guile than tact. 'I see those two at the end o' the square 'ave got lights in the winder,' she said casually. 'Bit of a show, if yer ask me. I was lookin' at our decorations the ovver day. They look a bit tatty. I was wonderin' if I ought ter chuck 'em away.'

Sally shrugged her shoulders. 'Get Dad ter put 'em up, Mum. It makes no difference ter me one way or the ovver.'

Only at number 2 was the parlour left bare. George Tapley was adamant when Ginny called in to see him. 'I know it's Christmas, but I'm not puttin' anyfing up this year, Ginny,' he said. ''Ow could I? I don't know if Tony's dead or alive, an' there's young Laurie sufferin' in a prison camp. It'd be wicked.'

Ginny nodded in agreement. 'I understand 'ow yer feel, George,' she said softly. 'Please Gawd next Christmas yer'll be able ter put 'em up. I ain't give up about Tony an' nor should you. I got that feelin' you'll 'ear some good news soon. I can't explain, it's jus' somefing I feel.'

On Friday morning the postman delivered a parcel to number 4 addressed to Sally. The brown-paper parcel contained a china-faced doll with eyelids that opened and shut as the doll was moved, and a furry teddybear, which had a folded slip of paper tucked into its red satin collar. Sally unfolded the note and read the few words.

640

Dear Sally,

Just a little something for Ruth. Your father told me the sad news about Jim. Please accept my deepest sympathy. Should you need anything please call round. I'm always glad to see you.

Ben.

PS: I'm in the Waterman most evenings.

Later, when she had washed, dressed and fed Ruth and the baby was sleeping peacefully, Sally sat on the edge of her bed and re-read the note. It was a nice gesture, she thought. She remembered the look she had seen in Ben's eyes when she first showed him the baby. Ben had been very restrained then, but she could feel that he still wanted her to go back to him.

Sally sighed. It was only two months since that fateful October morning when the telegram had arrived, and she could still remember vividly feeling that a part of her had died, as if a piece of her heart had been torn out of her. It was more than fifteen months since she had seen Jim now, and their affair together, the wild passionate nights of love they had shared, had become like a dream, a starry romance that she had once imagined a long time ago. It was hard for her now to picture Jim's face in her mind, and only the baby who had grown inside her reminded her that it was all real. Ever since Ruth was born Sally had been alone, and it seemed hard to believe sometimes that she had not created the baby all by herself. Instead of yearning for a lost lover now she felt a kind of numb detachment, a distressing sadness that someone she had been so close to for such a short time had lain dead somewhere in cold darkness far away from her.

A knock on the front door interrupted Sally's troubled thoughts. She heard Vera's voice and then her footsteps on the stairs.

Her friend popped her head around the door. 'Yer mum said yer was up 'ere,' she said breezily, her voice dropping suddenly as she noticed the sleeping figure of Ruth in the crib. 'Me mum's mindin' the kids an' I'm off down the market. Fancy a stroll?'

The two walked briskly out of the square, passing Ada and Clara, who were, as usual, engaged in earnest conversation. The late morning was cold and bright, with a chill wind whipping up pieces of dirty paper and brittle brown leaves from the pavement. People came by carrying laden shopping-baskets, and a road-sweeper pushed his wide broom along the kerbside, humming to himself. The two had their coat collars turned up against the wind, their hands buried deep in their pockets. After a few minutes they saw the bustling street-market and main-road traffic up ahead. Vera was chatting away incessantly but her words seemed to flow over Sally's head as she pulled her coat tighter around her against the sharp cold.

They had crossed the main road and were walking along the line of stalls when Vera suddenly pulled on Sally's coatsleeve. ''Ere, see that?' she said quickly, pointing to a placard beside a paper-stand.

Sally shuddered as she saw the banner and quickly fished into her purse for some coppers.

When the two finally got back to the square they went into Sally's house and sat together in the parlour sipping tea.

'She might 'ave already seen it,' Vera said, picking up the midday edition of the *Star* which her friend had left lying open on the table.

Sally put down her cup. 'We'll 'ave ter make sure,' she said. 'She's gotta be put on 'er guard.'

Vera picked up the paper and re-read the story which was printed inside the first page.

ANOTHER PROSTITUTE MURDERED

The body discovered on a bombsite at Rotherhithe early this morning was identified as being that of Elsie Dolan, a known prostitute. She had been strangled with a leather belt and there were signs indicating she had put up a fierce struggle. Detective Inspector Johnson from Scotland Yard stated that there were certain similarities linking this killing with the murder of Gloria Goodyear at Wapping in May. Goodyear was also a prostitute and she, too, had been strangled. Inspector Johnson said that the police were anxious to trace Gerald Austin, a 42-year-old labourer from Stepney, in connection with the two murders. Anyone having information should ring Scotland Yard, Whitehall 1212.

Vera shuddered as she put the paper back down on the table. 'It makes yer go cold jus' finkin' about it,' she said with a horrified expression.

Sally nodded slowly. 'Muriel was very lucky. She's gotta be dead careful now, though. 'E might well come back ter finish the job.'

'Don't,' Vera said, shivering. 'You're scarin' me.'

'Well, it's very likely,' Sally went on. ''E's obviously a maniac, an' accordin' ter the paper they fink it was the same bloke who done the killin's.'

'I tell yer one fing, Sal. I'm not goin' out after dark unless Big Joe's wiv me,' Vera asserted. 'Not while that maniac's loose.'

The Bradys were gathered in the public bar of the Waterman and Jack threw down the evening edition of the *Star*.

'It's in the middle page,' he said, addressing Ben. 'There's a picture of Greasy Austin, too. They're pretty certain it's 'im that's killed 'em both. We've gotta get movin', Ben, or Muriel's gonna be in dead trouble, wiv the emphasis on dead.'

Ben gritted his teeth. 'I could slaughter that Patsy Dougan fer bringin' the bastard in. I dunno why 'e couldn't 'andle it 'imself. What must 'e 'ave bin finkin' about?'

'Well it's done now. It's too late ter argue about it,' Jack replied. 'I've spoke ter the lads on the quay terday an' the word's gone out roun' the local boozers. Arnie's bruvver's puttin' it all roun' the market an' the costers 'ave all got their eyes open. Gawd knows what that soppy git Dougan's doin', but I s'pose 'e's got 'is own contacts.'

Ben sipped his pint and wiped the back of his hand across his mouth. 'I told my lads, too. There's a chance the nonse might show up at the dogs an' we've got that covered. My mate Don never misses a dog meetin' at New Cross an' all the track bookies 'ave bin warned ter keep their eyes skinned.'

Nobby had been listening quietly and he suddenly leaned back in his chair with his arms folded. 'We're missin' somefing,' he said with a frown. 'But what?'

Ben pushed his fingers through his thick fair hair. 'Search me,' he growled. "E's gotta be dossin' down somewhere.'

'That's it!' Nobby exclaimed, thumping the table with his clenched fist. 'There's the doss-'ouse in Tower Bridge Road, an' there's anuvver one in Tooley Street. The bastard could be stayin' at one o' those gaffs.'

Jack shook his head. 'The law's gonna check them places straight off.'

Nobby was not to be put off. 'There might 'ave bin some money changed 'ands,' he suggested. 'Somebody might be 'idin' 'im.'

'Well, in that case we're not gonna 'ave any luck there, are we?' Jack growled.

Ben stroked his chin thoughtfully. 'I dunno so much. Patsy Dougan's fond o' chuckin' 'is weight about. Maybe we should suggest 'e takes a few of 'is boys along ter the two doss-'ouses an' puts the frighteners in. Or maybe that's askin' too much. P'r'aps 'e only puts the frighteners on women like Muriel Taylor.'

645

Jack put his hand on Ben's shoulder. 'Take it easy. I'll 'ave a word in Patsy's ear. It might be a good idea at that.'

It was nearing closing time when Jake Collins hurried over to the Bradys' table. 'I've just 'ad a phone call, Jack,' he said breathlessly. 'A geezer's bin spotted at the King's Arms down by the tunnel. It could be Greasy.'

The Bradys were on their feet in an instant and as Jack made for the door he turned to the landlord. 'Which bar, Jake?'

'Public bar – an' good luck, mate.'

On Saturday morning Ben Brady knocked on Muriel Taylor's front door. The curtains moved aside in the window above and Harriet's anxious face peered down into the square as Muriel showed Ben in.

'I take it you've read the papers?' he said as she stood beside the table.

Muriel nodded, her face serious. 'Yeah. I'm bloody scared, Ben. Your Sal came in yesterday an' showed me. Gawd. I 'ope they catch 'im quick. I'm frightened ter move out o' the square.'

'If it's any consolation we've joined forces wiv the Dougans ter try an' find 'im,' Ben said encouragingly. 'They want the nonse out o' the way quick. 'E's queerin' their pitch, now the Yard's on the manor.'

'Well, they should 'ave 'ad a bit more common sense in the first place,' Muriel said angrily.

Ben shrugged his shoulders. 'Well, that's as it

may be, but at least yer know there's a lot o' people scoutin' the area. As a matter o' fact we thought we got 'im last night, but it was a false alarm. Me an' me bruvvers got the word an' we shot down ter the King's Arms, but the geezer turned out ter be a flasher. Jack knew 'im. 'E was 'armless enough. Still, we're gonna keep on tryin', luv. We'll get 'im, don't yer worry.'

Muriel reached up on tiptoe and planted a quick kiss on his cheek. 'I'm really grateful, Ben. Fank yer bruvvers for me, won't yer?'

'It's a good job yer didn't do that a few years ago,' he said with a grin. 'If Sally 'ad looked in the winder then we'd 'ave 'ad some explainin' ter do.'

Muriel walked with him to the door. 'I fink you two should get tergevver again, Ben,' she said suddenly. 'Sally's a real good 'un an' so are you.'

Ben turned at the doorway. 'I tell yer somefing yer can do, Muriel,' he said quickly. 'I need ter talk ter Sally. Can yer give 'er a message?'

It had been a trying week for Scatty Whybrow. The weather had been playing havoc with his rheumatism and the pickings had not been too good of late. Scatty had lived the life of a tramp for longer than he cared to remember now and when times were as lean as this he knew exactly what to do, even though it involved a certain loss of dignity. It was a simple matter to saunter round to the vicarage just after the morning milk delivery and casually drop one of the bottles on the doorstep. The smashing sound alerted the vicar and when the Reverend Delaney came to the door he sighed, aware of the ritual that was taking place. Scatty then delivered a tirade of abuse and refused to go away, leaving the venerable gentleman no option but to call the police. Scatty had to suffer the indignity of being captured by the beat bobby, who led him away to the station giving him quite a bit of verbal abuse in turn.

Mr Benjamin Terence Whybrow's finances did not run to paying the forty-shilling fine and he would be sentenced to a week in the cells. The magistrate knew what Scatty's game was, as did the local bobbies, and even the vicar played his part to perfection. It was a periodical performance, and the cold weather and scarcity of food seemed to bring out the theatrical talents that Scatty had learnt when he trod the stage. He saw his incarceration as a necessary evil, a respite that gave him a chance to get a good meal and be deloused into the bargain, and he regained his freedom with harsh words ringing in his ears. 'Don't yer come back, Scatty, or next time we'll scrub yer down wiv the yard broom.'

As Mr Benjamin T. Whybrow made his way home to his abode under the arches he was feeling reasonably contented. The hard-faced sergeant at Dockhead had slipped him the usual half crown and Mrs Wellbeloved at the baker's had wrapped up a few stale cakes and passed them to him as he walked by her shop. The wind was getting up and Scatty hurried along, eager to get the brazier going before dark. There was plenty of wood stored away and the cardboard sheets would keep him warm and dry. He hummed tunelessly as he turned into the narrow alleyway that ran beside the railway and scrambled over the bits of rubble, discarded tin baths and rusty bicycle frames.

Scatty's den was a place where nobody ventured, unless they wanted to get rid of bulky rubbish, but on this particular evening the local tramp was feeling uneasy. He could smell woodsmoke, and when he slipped beneath the low arch and reached his hearth he saw that the brazier had been used and the stack of firewood had diminished. 'Well, I'll soon put a stop to that,' he fumed, sorting out a large chunk of wood with a nail protruding from the end.

The wind whistled and swirled around the lonely arches and Scatty huddled closer to the roaring brazier. A pile of wood lay at his elbow and behind him large cardboard sheets were propped against pallet-boards as a shield against the angry wind. Scatty's face glowed with the heat of the flames and he sighed contentedly as he stirred the ashes under the fire. The baked potato will go down well, he thought, shifting his position to ease his aching legs. A sudden sound made him reach for his club, and he breathed a sigh of relief as a large rat scampered over the wood and stood cleaning itself a few yards away. Scatty threw the rodent a piece of stale cake and scooped out the hot potato from the ashes.

When the meal was over Scatty settled down for the night after banking up the fire and covering himself with layers of cardboard. For the first time in a long while he was not worried by lice and he soon fell into a contented sleep. The wind rattling the loose corrugated sheeting on the adjoining fencing did not disturb Scatty's sleep and the Bermondsey tramp slept on, unaware of the stealthy footsteps that were slowly coming closer.

There seemed to be a strange atmosphere about the house, Sally thought, as she sat in front of her dressing-table applying a pale shade of lipstick. Her mother had insisted on clearing away and washing up the tea things and Lora had offered her help without the usual puffing and blowing. Her father, too, seemed relaxed as he sat with Ruth on his knee and made funny noises, much to the child's delight. It felt as though the family were showing their pleasure and indulgence without actually saying anything and Sally allowed herself a wan smile as she opened her powder compact. It was the first time she had worn make-up since getting the telegram and the first time she had worn her best dress since the week she spent with Jim. The family would make their own interpretations about her dressing up, but Sally felt that it was important for her not to appear in widow's weeds. She had decided to wear her best dress as soon as she made up her mind, after much soul-searching, to see Ben.

Annie had taken the message from Muriel and as soon as Sally came in with the shopping she had passed it on before her daughter had had time to take off her coat.

'Ben wants ter see yer,' she said quickly. 'Muriel's bin wiv the message. 'E come ter see 'er this mornin', so the girl said.'

'Ben wants ter see me?' Sally echoed her, hanging her coat behind the door with deliberation.

'Yeah. Ben said can yer try an' meet 'im ternight? Eight o'clock at the end o' the square. 'E said there was fings ter talk about. You'll know what. That was the message,' Annie concluded, sitting down and folding her arms as though waiting for an explanation.

'I was gonna wash me 'air ternight,' Sally replied, testing her mother's reaction.

'Yer never wash yer 'air on Saturday nights,' Annie said quickly. 'It looks all right ter me, anyway.'

Sally was surprised at her own feeling of guarded excitement, and equally surprised at her mother's unspoken wish for her to see Ben. But then it was understandable, she reflected. Her family had been very quiet and subdued since the news about Jim and they had all been afraid to show their feelings properly in case it added to her distress. They had obviously discussed the message from Ben behind her back and had seemingly come to the conclusion that there might even be a chance of reconciliation now. Sally knew that although they did not like Ben very much, her happiness was dear to them. It showed in their manner, in the way that her mother volunteered to look after the baby for the evening while Sally had still been making up her mind whether or not to see Ben. Her father had played his part by staying awake and taking Ruth on his knee, acting like the doting grandparent. It was all so obvious that Sally felt very grateful for their show of concern.

At eight o'clock she left the house, relieved that Ruth was sleeping quietly as she went out. A bright crescent moon lit up the square and she saw Ben already standing beneath the unlit gaslamp, his elongated shadow lying over the flagstones.

As she walked up to him he smiled a greeting. 'Fanks fer comin', Sal,' he said quietly. 'I wanted the chance ter talk. By the way I 'ope the toys were OK?'

She looked into his eyes and smiled. 'They were lovely. It was a nice thought.'

Ben shrugged his shoulders as they walked away from the square. 'Ter be honest Nobby's wife picked 'em out. I wouldn't 'ave known what ter get. It's different when they're older, I s'pose.'

Sally was walking at his side, and she suddenly wondered whether she should take his arm. He had not proffered it, instead his hands were thrust deep into his overcoat pockets.

He glanced at her. 'Would yer fancy a drink at the Waterman?' he asked. 'It's got a nice coke fire an' the public bar don't get too crowded.'

She nodded. 'That'd be nice. I 'aven't bin out since . . .'

Ben winced, and then his face became serious as he looked into her eyes. 'Look, I'm really sorry about Jim, Sally,' he said slowly. 'I mean it.'

Sally smiled wanly. 'Fanks, Ben, I do believe yer. It was a terrible shock, as you can imagine, but some'ow I was prepared fer that telegram. I 'adn't 'eard from him fer a few months an' I jus' knew I was gonna get that news sometime or ovver.'

Ben was quiet for a while and as they crossed the Jamaica Road his hand rested very gently on her back. They turned into the backstreets and as he put his hands into his coat pockets once more Sally took his arm.

'D'yer mind?' she said. 'My shoes are slippery.'

Ben gave her a brief smile. 'I guess Muriel told yer about the chat we 'ad?' he asked.

'I never got ter see 'er,' Sally replied. 'Me mum gave me the message.'

'Wait till we get in the warm an' I'll put yer in the picture,' Ben said, pulling the collar of his coat tighter around his neck.

They entered the public bar of the riverside pub and found a table far away from the door. They sat somewhat ill at ease with drinks in front of them and Sally waited for Ben to start the conversation. He was glancing around the bar, however, as though looking for someone, and she turned her attention to the piano player. He was an elderly gentleman with snowy white hair that hung untidily over his forehead and around his ears. He was tinkling softly on the keys, his head held back and his eyes taking in everything around him.

After a while Ben leaned forward in his seat, his hands clasped on the marble table-top. 'I

653

'ope yer didn't mind me meetin' yer at the square, Sally,' he said quietly. 'I didn't want yer walkin' frew the streets alone, 'specially in the dark.'

Sally shivered. 'I saw that bit in the paper an' I thought it best ter warn Muriel. It's frightenin'.'

Ben nodded, serious-faced. 'Yer remember me tellin' yer about me bruvvers an' Patsy Dougan's crowd? Well, we've got tergevver ter try an' find Austin. They want 'im out o' the way an' Patsy asked fer our 'elp. The money they owed us was sorted out an' we've agreed ter join forces, fer the time bein', anyway.'

'Why did they get that 'orrible bloke in the first place, Ben?' Sally asked, running the tip of her finger around the rim of her glass. 'Surely they know Muriel wouldn't drop 'em in it?'

'They couldn't be sure, Sal,' Ben replied. 'It was only gonna be a back'ander or two an' a sharp warnin' of what could 'appen, but . . .'

'A back'ander or two?' Sally said sharply. 'If it wasn't fer ole Mr Cox she would 'ave bin murdered.'

Ben fixed her with his eyes. 'I know that, Sal,' he said. 'Patsy Dougan knows it, too, now. Like I said, they didn't know who they was dealin' wiv. Anyway, the bloke's still on the loose. The police can't find 'im an' we've 'ad no luck yet. We thought we got 'im last night but it was a false alarm. That was one o' the reasons I wanted ter talk ter yer. Whatever yer do, don't go out on yer own at night – not till we get 'im. And tell yer friends the same. I've already

654

warned Muriel. No woman's safe while that non-sense-case is runnin' loose.'

'P'r'aps 'e's left,' Sally said hopefully. ''E wouldn't 'ang around after killin' that street girl in Rother'ithe, would 'e?'

Ben shook his head. 'I jus' don't know, Sally. 'E could lose 'imself in this area. There's plenty o' places 'e could 'ide. 'E might be finkin' it's safer ter stay in Bermondsey. Anyway, there's a lot o' people on the look out, an' if 'e does show 'is face in the neighbour'ood somebody's gonna see 'im. Let's 'ope it won't be long.'

Customers were filling the bar and a few nodded and waved to Ben. Some of his acquaintances knew Sally, and there were curious glances and sly smiles exchanged.

Sally had noticed it and she turned to Ben. 'I expect there'll be a bit o' gossip, me an' you bein' seen tergevver,' she said.

He smiled. 'I s'pose it's natural. Anyway, it is nice 'avin' the chance ter talk ter yer.'

Sally looked around the bar, a nervous feeling growing in her stomach. 'So this is yer local now,' she said, trying hard to remain cool and detached.

He nodded. 'We get tergevver in 'ere most evenin's. Jack an' Nobby use this pub all the time. They was askin' about yer. They both send their best regards.'

Sally looked into his eyes and felt how searching they were, deep and penetrating. He seemed very calm, although she suspected he was struggling to hold back his feelings. Ben had always been impulsive and quick to anger. She

655

remembered how agitated he would become and how his eyebrows would rise and his eyes open wide, but now his expression was quiet and collected.

She looked down briefly at her drink. 'Was that all yer wanted ter tell me?' she asked.

'No. I wanted ter find out 'ow yer was copin', an' if you'd given any more thought ter movin' in the 'ouse,' he replied, looking down at the glass in front of him.

'I did give it some thought, Ben,' she said quietly. 'It wouldn't be right.'

'Why?' he asked, his eyes lifting to her face and resting on her dark, waved hair. 'I wouldn't expect yer ter live the way we was. I was jus' finkin' o' the problems yer might face. What I said still goes. I wouldn't expect anyfing or put conditions on yer movin' in. It's your choice.'

'I know yer wouldn't go back on what yer said, Ben,' Sally said kindly. 'It's jus' that I couldn't trust meself, ter be honest. There'd be a night when we both felt the need an' neivver of us would be able ter say no. We'd share the same room an' we'd regret it the next mornin'. You'd look at Ruth an' the past would come back ter torture the pair of us. It wouldn't work out, Ben.'

He took her hand in his and felt her gently pulling away. 'Look, Sally. I've never given up 'opin' that one day you'd be able ter put the past be'ind. I've never given up lovin' yer. I feel stronger about yer now than I've ever felt before, an' I've never given up finkin' that there's still a part of us that's always gonna be

656

tergevver, no matter what. Let me jus' say this,' he added quickly, sensing that she was about to cut in. 'I know 'ow much 'avin' a child meant ter yer, an' I know yer was never gonna be 'appy wivout one, but fings are different now. You've got Ruth, an' there's memories, sure, but I'm 'ere, Sally. I don't wanna be just a part of yer past. I want us ter get back tergevver more than I've wanted anyfing in me 'ole life. I still love yer very much, an' I always will.'

Sally sighed deeply. Memories rising up in her mind of what had happened between them were still painful, but she felt no anger towards Ben any more. There was a ghost in her life now, and the baby that she loved dearly would always bring back memories of her lover and the wild, romantic episode in her life. Sally wondered how Ben might be affected by this other man's child, and what secret thoughts might torment him lying awake in the small, still hours of the night. There was the chance that once he had won her back he would become angry with her and grow cold towards the baby. It was too late. If they tried once more and their marriage broke down again it would be too much for her to bear.

The piano player was rendering a popular melody and the bar had filled. Laughter and loud voices echoed around them unheeded as the two faced each other across the small table.

Sally met Ben's gaze, her stomach churning. 'I've always know yer ter be a proud man, Ben,' she began. 'It was that stupid pride that came between us. Yer couldn't accept failure. Yer wanted ter give me a child, an' yer failed. Yer

657

wanted ter join up, an' yer couldn't. Failure wasn't something yer could accept. The trouble was, yer never talked ter me about yer feelin's, the fings that was troublin' yer, till it was too late. We wasn't very good at talkin' about our feelin's, was we? Yer gotta understan,' Ben, I've never thought of yer as a failure. You'll always be a real man ter me. I fink you've proved that by offerin' me an' Ruth a shelter. I know yer wanna 'ear it, Ben, so I'll say it plain an' simple. I've never stopped lovin' yer, despite everyfing that's 'appened, but I need time. It's too soon fer me ter jus' turn me life upside down again. I can't make any decisions now.'

Ben nodded slowly. 'I understand. I wouldn't expect yer to, not so soon after, but I 'ad ter let yer know 'ow I feel about yer. I've changed, Sally. Please believe that.'

It had grown late, and the two walked slowly out of the Waterman with the landlord's urgent plea of 'Time gentlemen, please' carrying out after them into the dark street. She took his arm as they made their way into the main road and then through into the narrow, twisting back-streets. Ahead they saw the sombre arches, still showing the scars of war. The darkened Railway Inn stood silent with its doors closed and they caught sight of Alf Porter staggering home, singing his own version of 'O'Reilly's Daughter'. As they passed him Sally called out goodnight, but it was not until they had reached the gaslamp at the end of Paragon Place that Alf managed to call out a reply. He had stopped short of the square and leaned against the wall for support, fishing into his pocket for his key.

'Shall I give 'im an 'and?' Ben asked, grinning.

Sally smiled and shook her head. 'Leave 'im. 'E's OK. Well, fanks fer the drink, an' fer seein' me 'ome. Goodnight Ben.'

He smiled and stepped back a pace. 'I've enjoyed it. It was very nice ter see yer again, Sally. Look, why don't yer pop round Monday afternoon. The union's sending me up Guy's fer a check-up in the mornin', so I've got no work that day. Bring Ruth, an' if the weavver's not too cold we could take a stroll. The river air'll do 'er good.'

Sally hesitated. 'I dunno, Ben.'

He held up his hands in front of him. 'It's all right, it was just a thought. Goodnight, Sal.'

She watched as he strolled away towards the teetering figure of Alf Porter, and a ghost of a smile played around her lips. The familiar confident swagger seemed more pronounced now. She turned and hurried to her front door, and as she inserted the key she saw Alf turn into the square accompanied by Ben, who was holding him upright.

On Sunday morning Reverend Delaney read the sermon he had chosen with relish. The parable of the good Samaritan seemed apt, he thought, staring down at his flock and rewarding them with one of his benevolent smiles. Reverend Delaney, being a humble and modest servant of the Lord, did not wish to take all the credit, but he allowed himself a small pat on the back for playing his part. He could have walked past on the other side of the road, or gone in and closed the door, to be more precise. Instead, he had summoned help and seen to it that the poor traveller was taken care of. Mr Benjamin Terence Whybrow would surely thank him for playing his part in the ritual charitably and summoning help, even though help arrived in the shape of the local beat bobbie. Benjamin had at least been afforded food and shelter, and a chance to rest his weary bones, just like the traveller in the New Testament. Benjamin would be back in circulation by now and he would wander through the church gardens that Sunday, just as he always did. He would smile his thanks as he rested on a bench, then he would be on his way.

When the morning service was over Reverend Delaney stood on the church steps dispensing smiles and friendly words of comfort until the last of his flock had departed, then he locked up the church and took his stroll through the gardens. He was rather surprised at not seeing Benjamin sitting in his usual spot and he stroked his chin thoughtfully. It was a raw day, but the weather did not normally deter Benjamin from huddling up on one of the benches. Perhaps he was still in custody, he thought, although it was unlikely. He would have a word with Constable Morris when he called in for his coffee that lunch-time. After all, the good Samaritan had made it his job to see that all was well.

It was early evening when Reverend Delaney took the phone call in his study and he slumped back in his cushioned chair, holding a hand up to his forehead. His concern for Benjamin had been relayed by Constable Morris and a check had been made on Benjamin's lonely abode. The Reverend said a silent prayer and then poured himself a stiff brandy, for he now had the task of visiting the mortuary and formally identifying the battered body of Benjamin Terence Whybrow, known locally as Scatty Whybrow the tramp.

Chapter Thirty-Three

WHEN the news broke of Scatty Whybrow's brutal killing Bermondsey folk were stunned. The tramp was known to almost everyone in the riverside borough and the Paragon Place folk had their own stories to tell of the scruffy character who had always gruffly passed the time of day as he shuffled along Stanley Street. People read the accounts of his murder and drew their own gruesome conclusions.

'It's that 'orrible Austin bloke, yer can bet yer life,' Ada remarked to her friend. 'It stands ter reason it's got ter be 'im.'

'It don't say 'e actually done it,' Clara replied, slipping her hands into her apron. 'Mind you, they must 'ave a good idea it's 'im.'

'It's 'im, right enough,' Ada asserted. 'It makes yer scared ter go outside yer front door. 'E could be 'idin' anywhere. They should check all them there bleedin' bombsites. I bet that's where the bastard's 'idin'.'

'Yeah, they should start over the road,' Clara said, glancing fearfully at the Stanley Street ruins. 'That's where 'e dragged the Taylor gel. 'E could be in there right now, fer all we know.'

Ada followed her friend's gaze. 'We could all be murdered in our beds. If my Maurice was 'ere I'd get 'im ter go over there an' 'ave a look. I'd feel safe if I knew 'e wasn't 'idin' over there.'

Clara gave the big red-haired woman a hard stare. 'I s'pose you'd like me ter send my Patrick over there?'

Ada returned the stare. 'Well, it wouldn't 'urt 'im, would it? At least we'd all feel a bit safer.'

'Oh, I see,' Clara said sarcastically. 'I send my Pat over there 'an 'e gets clumped. Who's gonna pay 'is wages while 'e's out o' collar? You?'

'Well, there's no need ter get shirty about it,' Ada replied, her voice rising with anger. 'I know me Maurice would be the first ter do it.'

'Your Maurice? I should fink so. 'E'd be the last one ter volunteer,' Clara snorted, folding her arms and glaring at her neighbour.

Alf Porter had decided to take the day off and he was looking forward to no more than a pint or two at the Railway Inn to liven up the day. He had just set off from his front door when he came across the two large women glaring at each other.

'Mornin', gels,' he called out. 'Terrible about ole Scatty Whybrow, ain't it? I reckon it's that bloody Austin bloke what's done it.'

The two women glared at him as he walked

662

over. 'We was jus' sayin', the bloke could be 'idin' in one o' them bombed 'ouses over there,' Ada remarked.

Alf took off his trilby hat and scratched his head. 'You're right there, come ter fink of it,' he said. 'It might be a good idea if I go an' 'ave a look, just in case.'

Ada could hardly believe what she had heard. 'Take somefing wiv yer, Alf,' she said quickly, before he had a chance to change his mind. "E's a nasty bit o' work.'

'I'll whack 'im wiv me trilby,' Alf laughed, suddenly feeling a little frightened himself.

"Ere, 'old on a minute,' Clara called out, dashing into her house. After a few moments she came back out carrying a small poker.

'Gor blimey! That wouldn't even knock the bleedin' dust orf 'im,' Alf exclaimed. 'Ain't yer got anyfing 'eavier?'

Ada went inside and came out with a large shovel. "Ere, use me coal-shovel,' she said. 'This is bloody 'eavy. One clout wiv it an' you'll open the whore-son.'

Alf whistled to himself as he sauntered over to the bombsite, a nerve-jangling scraping noise coming from the shovel as he dragged it along behind him.

'Anybody at 'ome?' he called out timorously, peering through one of the window-openings.

"Ave a look inside,' Ada shouted from across the street.

'All right, I'm goin' to,' Alf yelled back, wishing he had not been stupid enough to volunteer. 'Bloody boss-eyed ole cow,' he mumbled to himself. 'I could see 'er ole man doin' this. 'E'd be like a plate o' jelly.'

When Alf had briefly inspected the houses and found nothing he sauntered back, rolling his shoulders the way James Cagney would have done.

'It's all clear, gels,' he said, handing back the heavy shovel. 'I'd 'ave demolished the tyke if I'd come across 'im.'

After reading about the murder in the morning papers, Sally intended to drop in on Muriel on her way to the shops. But first, she left the square and walked in the opposite direction to the market. The morning sky was clear and there was a nip in the air as she entered the church gardens. Her feet crunched over the gravel path and when she reached the secluded seat she sat down with a sigh. She felt the need to spend some time alone, and it was here she felt at peace and able to think clearly.

She glanced up at the wet greenery overhead with a sad smile. She would always feel close to Jim in this place. It held so many memories. How little time they had spent together, but how precious that time was. Jim had made her truly happy. He had reawakened her and made her capable of love once more. He had given her Ruth, and now he was gone forever. It was Ruth she must think of now. She must devote herself to her daughter and not allow herself to dwell on the past. It was what Jim would have wanted.

When she arrived back at Paragon Place and knocked on Muriel's front door Sally was feeling calm and composed. There was a longish pause before her friend opened the door, clad in a thick dressing-gown and with an anxious expression on her pale face.

'That's terrible about ole Scatty Whybrow, ain't it?' Muriel said as Sally followed her into the parlour.

Sally frowned and shook her head. 'I reckon it's the same bloke. It's a dead cert,' she said, making herself comfortable in the easy chair while her friend brought in two cups of tea from the scullery.

'I do 'ope the police catch 'im quick,' Muriel said with a shudder. 'It's Christmas next Monday. Imagine 'im bein' on the loose all over the 'oliday. It's really frightenin'. Cor, when I fink of 'ow near the bastard come ter puttin' my lights out.'

Sally nodded slowly with a downturned mouth. 'Yeah. Let's 'ope they 'urry up an' get 'im,' she said. 'Are yer stayin' 'ere over the 'oliday?'

Muriel shook her head. 'I've bin invited ter stay wiv me eldest bruvver an' 'is family. The way fings are I ain't sorry. Stoppin' in 'ere all over Christmas would gimme the 'orrers, 'specially wiv the Careys goin' away fer the 'oliday.'

'Juliet's still livin' 'ere, then?' Sally queried.

Muriel nodded. 'Apparently she told the bloke she's knockin' about wiv that she couldn't leave 'er sister, an' 'e give 'er the elbow. Bin goin' tergevver fer years, an' all. She told me all about it the ovver night. Proper cut up, she was. Mind

665

you, that sister of 'ers is a right ole bat. She's playin' on Juliet's good nature. If it was me I'd piss orf an' leave the ole cow. Still, I s'pose blood's ficker than water. By the way, Sal, 'ow are yer gettin' on wiv Ben lately?'

Sally shrugged her shoulders. 'I'm not sure yet,' she said. 'It's early days. We seem ter get on okay now, but maybe it's 'cos we only see each ovver now an' then. I was finkin' of poppin' roun' ter see 'im this afternoon as 'e ain't workin' terday, I dunno.'

Muriel grinned and crossed her legs. 'You take yer time. Jus' tell 'im all the best fings are worth waitin' for. That's what I'm gonna tell my fella when 'e gets back. I'll keep 'im waitin' fer it – all o' five minutes!'

In the afternoon the weather turned dreary, with leaden skies and a cold dampness that lay on the pavements and hung as a vapour in the air. A damp mist was coming down, mixing with the sulphurous smoke from coke fires and the fog drifting in from the oily river, threatening to thicken into a 'pea-souper'.

After her lunch of pie and mash Sally sat in the parlour for a while, thinking. At first she had decided that seeing Ben again so soon would not be a good idea. They had talked freely, in a way they had never done before, but Sally still felt uncertain. Ben was a proud man, and his eagerness to take her back after all that had happened made her feel a little scared. She felt there should be time for them both to think about what had been said. There was no use in trying to rush things. Nevertheless, she had to admit to herself that she wanted to see him again, though she felt guilty at having such ideas, so soon after losing her lover. But Ben was her husband, the first man she had ever known; Jim was dead now, and he would never return to fill the emptiness in her life.

When Sally took her plate into the scullery to wash up, her mother was already busying herself over the steaming copper.

'You're not gonna take the baby out in this, are yer, Sal?' she asked, turning to her daughter.

'No,' Sally replied. 'I don't like it meself, I daren't take Ruth wiv me.'

'I'll finish orf,' Annie said, taking the plate out of Sally's hands. 'The baby won't be no trouble. She's due fer 'er nap anyway.'

Sally walked out of the square, her heavy coat pulled up around her ears against the fog. The eyes of the skulking figure followed her from where he crouched huddled in the front room of a bombed house, peering through a gap in the broken bricks. It was not chance that had brought him back to Stanley Street. His unsuccessful attempt to kill Muriel Taylor had been tormenting his twisted mind for too long and he knew when he stole into the bombed house the previous night that he would soon have another chance now, although it was dangerous for him here. He had kept watch, creeping out of the way of the stupid man with the shovel, and it had been mid-morning when he first saw the dark-haired girl leave the square and return later with her shopping. That was her, he thought, his senses quickening. It was the same girl he had dragged into the house. She had been lucky that time, but he vowed that next time he would make no mistake. He knew that she deserved to die, they all deserved to die. The voices had told him that prostitutes had to be stopped from spreading their evil disease and corrupting the world. He was leading the campaign, and others would follow his example. The killing of the tramp did not trouble him, for if he had not been silenced he might have jeopardised the whole campaign.

The figure of the dark-haired girl leaving the square and turning into Stanley Street towards him that afternoon was shrouded in the thickening fog but the killer felt confident it was the prostitute. His chance had come. The streets were empty at this time of day and in this fog no one would see him drag her into a dark corner and kill her. Greasy Austin slipped his hand into his coat pocket and felt the leather belt as he made to leave his refuge. Suddenly he cursed and crouched down quickly against the crumbling plaster. Coming towards him was a policeman, walking slowly with his hands clasped behind his back. It seemed an eternity to Greasy before the policeman's footsteps faded and then with a growl he slipped quickly from his hiding-place and hurried after the girl.

Sally walked along quickly, aware that the fog was getting thicker. She had almost reached the main thoroughfare when she thought she heard footsteps behind her. She glanced around and peered anxiously through the swirling haze but she could see nothing. She quickened her pace, feeling suddenly frightened. She seemed to be the only person about on that foggy afternoon, unless there was someone following behind her. She halted for a few moments, straining her ears, and she could hear the footsteps clearly now, hurrying closer. They were getting nearer and Sally walked on quickly, almost running as icy fingers of panic clamped her insides. As she crossed Jamaica Road she looked over her shoulder. She could see the figure now. He was heavily built and dressed in a long overcoat. His shoulders were hunched and his cap was pulled down over his forehead as he lurched along, getting closer with every step.

He was running now. Sally turned and ran, too, and she could hear him gaining on her. Her breath came in gasps of white mist as she reached Potters Lane and dashed along the row of houses. The bombsite loomed out of the mist across the road and Sally suddenly saw herself being dragged into a bombed house the way Muriel had been. She did not dare look over her shoulder as she tore down the street that seemed never to end, trying to scream but unable to make a sound, as if huge fingers had grabbed her throat and were squeezing it shut.

She reached Ben's house and hammered on the door-knocker, her terrified eyes staring back into the fog. She strained her ears for the following footsteps, but it had gone very quiet. The front door opened and when she saw Ben standing there she threw herself into his arms, crying with relief.

''E followed me! 'E was runnin' after me, Ben!' she gasped, holding on to him tightly.

He held her close, his arms encircling her, patting her head and whispering reassurances in her ear.

'It was that Greasy Austin, Ben. 'E nearly got me,' she shuddered. 'I thought I was gonna die.'

'It's all right. There's nobody there,' he said softly, his arms still holding her as he peered along the street into the fog.

'But there was somebody there, Ben,' she gasped. 'I 'eard 'is footsteps an' I see 'im. 'E looked evil.'

Ben closed the front door and slipped his arm around her shaking shoulders as he led her into the parlour. 'Sit down by the fire an' get warm,' he said, releasing her. 'I'll put the kettle on. I won't take a minute.'

The curtains were pulled against the weather and the large chimer ticked loudly on the mantelshelf. They sat together in front of the banked-up coke fire, the warmth beginning to penetrate Sally's ice-cold body. She had taken off her coat and her hands were still shaking as she tried to hold her teacup.

Ben was sitting facing her, his eyes watching her closely. 'D'yer feel better now?' he asked.

Sally nodded, forcing a grin. 'Yeah. I was terrified 'e was gonna get me, Ben.'

'The bastard. We'll get 'im now, Sal. Try not ter fink of it. You're okay now. Finish yer tea an' I'll get yer anuvver,' he said, touching her shoulder as he stood up. 'Ter be honest I didn't expect yer ter come roun' this afternoon, what

670

wiv the weavver.'

'I jus' wanted ter see yer,' she said simply, looking up at him as he stood over her. 'Did yer medical go OK?'

'Yeah, they reckon I'm as fit as a fiddle,' he said with a smile as he sat down again. He looked at her closely. 'I'm glad yer did decide ter come, Sally,' he added softly. 'I've bin finkin' about Saturday night, an' what yer said. I come ter the conclusion we've got a chance. We can be really good tergevver. I fink . . .'

'Don't, Ben, please,' she cut in, a note of panic in her voice. 'Don't misunderstand what I was tryin' ter say that night. It wouldn't be that easy.'

'I know that, Sal. I know it won't be easy, but I know we can be 'appy again.'

The cups had been refilled and they sat sipping the hot tea. Occasionally their eyes met in the embarrassing silence.

Suddenly Sally put down the cup and clasped her hands together. 'I don't want yer ter fink I'm actin' like a stupid child, Ben,' she said quickly. 'We both know the problem. Yer feel the need fer me. I feel the same fer you. I won't try ter deny it, but what about later? What about the mornin' after? Will yer feel the same way, or will yer look at me an' fink you've woken up wiv a woman yer don't know any more? I can't take the chance of us failin' again, Ben. I've gotta be sure we can be 'appy tergevver, an' I don't mean fer the time bein'. I mean fer ever.'

Ben stared down into the fire, biting on his bottom lip. 'I'm sure,' he said in a small voice.

'Are yer really sure, Ben?' she asked.

Ben suddenly leaned across and took her hand. 'I wanna show yer somefing,' he said gently, leading her to the window and pulling the curtains aside. 'See over there? The Grovers lived there. Yer remember 'em. Well, Danny Grover walked out on the family more than two years ago now an' took up wiv a barmaid out o' the Waterman. As far as anybody knew 'e never showed 'is face in this turnin' again, until that flyin' bomb fell on the 'ouses. Somebody told 'im the street 'ad copped it an' Danny dashed inter the turnin'. I saw 'im tearin' away at the rubble wiv 'is bare 'ands till they was raw an' bleedin'. They pulled 'im away an' the bloke sat in the kerb wiv 'is 'ead in 'is 'ands while they dug 'is family out. They were all dead. Danny's wife an' three young children. Yer remember 'em, don't yer? I was there an' I saw Danny sobbin' like a little kid. I knew then, Sal. I knew what was important ter me. I put meself in Danny's place. 'E's got the rest of 'is life ter mourn, ter regret what 'e done. What wouldn't 'e give ter 'ave 'is time over again. I don't want ter be like Danny Grover, Sal. I know now what's important ter me. I've known since the day the bomb fell on the street. You're all I want, an' Ruth, too, 'cos she's part of yer. I can't say it any clearer than that.'

The fog was hanging like a heavy blanket now as Sally stared from the window. Suddenly she turned to face him, her eyes filled with tears. Their bodies were close, almost touching, and he reached out and took her by the shoulders. She

672

stepped forward into his arms and her lips met his. His arms were crushing her and he smothered her with kisses.

'Oh, Ben, Ben,' she whispered breathlessly.

His hands moved down her back and then slid around her until he was clutching her waist. He lowered his head, his lips brushing her neck.

Suddenly she stiffened, as if aware of ghosts from the past that had returned to haunt them, coming between them and filling her with a shapeless fear. She brought her hands up against his chest and pushed him away.

Ben's eyes met hers. 'I'd forgot what it was like ter 'old yer an' kiss yer, Sal,' he said, taking her hands in his.

'I'm sorry Ben. I got carried away. I knew I shouldn't 'ave called round,' she sighed, an apologetic look in her dark eyes.

'There's nufing ter feel sorry about,' he replied, trying to force a smile. 'We both got a bit carried away. It's bin a long time.'

She moved away from him, going back to the chair to collect her handbag. 'I just need a bit more time, Ben,' she said, turning to face him with a gentle expression in her wide eyes. 'Yer do understand, don't yer?'

'Yeah, I understand. I'll still be 'ere,' he answered, helping her on with her coat. 'I'll walk yer 'ome.'

They stepped briskly out of Potters Lane, Sally holding his arm tightly with the memory of being pursued still very much in her mind, and as they crossed the fog-shrouded main road a muffled explosion sounded in the distance.

The soldier stood by the blast-protected window in the hospital corridor and gazed down through the shifting fog. He could just see the bend of the river and the wharves and warehouses along the shore, where tall cranes were moving and dipping, plundering the berthed ships, and a squat, puffing tug was heading downstream past the barges moored at anchor.

The bullet wounds in his left side and leg were almost completely healed now, but the glancing wound he had received on the side of his head ached dully. He could still not remember his name, or anything that had happened before the day he woke up in a peasant's shack with the sharp pain wracking his body and the smell of goats around him.

The local partisans had been suspicious at first, but when the Allies finally took control of the area they had handed him over to the military. From what army intelligence had told him, it seemed that his group had stumbled on a party of Germans caught in an area recently taken over by the Allies. The Germans had stolen their uniforms and identification tags in order to sneak back through the enemy lines, and when the Italian peasant found him in the olive grove he and his comrades had been stripped down to their underpants, all clues to their names, regiment and even nationality gone. He had been badly wounded, but all the other soldiers were dead.

The soldier's head throbbed as he tried hard to remember something about his life before the fighting, but there was nothing. He had been brought to London because of his accent, in the hope that some detail, some sight or sound might trigger his memory, and he recognised the river and the docks along the banks, but he could remember nothing of where he had grown up, or who his parents and friends might be. He sighed as he stood alone at the window staring into the thickening fog, a stranger in his home town.

Chapter Thirty-Four

DURING the few days before Christmas more V2s fell in Bermondsey. One demolished a school only minutes after the last pupil had gone home, and the school caretaker was left badly shaken but otherwise unhurt. The second rocket landed on a factory during the morning and many of the workers were killed. The tragedy sickened the Bermondsey folk, many of whom had friends and acquaintances who perished. With the tragedy in mind folk spent Christmas quietly, and as snow fell silently in the back-streets there was a sad, subdued atmosphere in all the local pubs.

For the folk of Paragon Place Christmas was a time of quiet reflection and high hopes. Alf Porter decided that he would be on his best behaviour over the holiday, and as he walked out of the square over a carpet of snow on Christmas Eve he vowed to get back home from the pub under his own steam and without serenading his neighbours with bawdy songs.

For the Carey sisters, Christmas was a quiet event. They left to stay with friends in a quiet Essex village, and Harriet was happy in the knowledge that her younger sister would not now be leaving the home they had shared for many years. It seemed to her that Juliet had finally come to her senses and realised that she had been the victim of a man's lust. She would soon forget him and return to being the caring, considerate sister she had once been, of that Harriet was in no doubt. For Juliet, the holiday was a sad one. It had been a traumatic experience ending the long association with Mr Lomax. She had decided to stay with her sister, realising that there was little else she could do, but she fervently hoped that Mr Lomax would finally come to his senses. Once he had reflected on her decision to stay with Harriet he might well withdraw his ultimatum, thus allowing them to continue their association in the way they had for the past twenty years.

Christmas was a time of sheer exhaustion for Ginny. There had been presents to buy for all the children and loans to clear up. The extra cleaning job helped and George had given her money as well, without which she would never have managed. Ginny looked forward to the new year with hope. Maybe it would bring good news about Tony, and the end of the war. George tried to put on a brave face but he was still deeply depressed, and Ginny knew that despite all her efforts to inspire him with hope he was convinced that Tony was dead. He had not talked of their future marriage for a long time now, and Ginny prayed for his two sons to be restored to him alive and well against all the odds.

Sally spent a quiet Christmas with her family, caring for Ruth and helping about the house. She shivered when she remembered being chased by Greasy Austin and she dared not venture out alone. Ben was spending the holiday with his brother Jack and his family and he had asked if she would meet him early in the new year for a drink and another chat. Vera was spending all her time with Big Joe and the children, and Sally was glad of the opportunity to be alone with her thoughts. So much had happened in the last few months and she wondered what the new year would hold for her and the baby. She had grown to accept that Ruth would never know her real father, and as she cradled the child in her arms she thought about the important decision that she had to make. She owed it to her child not to make any more mistakes now.

The thin layer of snow in the little square had soon become black with the constant comings and goings. Clara Botley gave her friend Ada Fuller a present and a short while later Ada gave Clara a present, too. The two grannies took their usual Guinness in the snug bar of the Railway Inn, muffled against the weather in woollen scarves and felt hats. Mr and Mrs Cox drank a toast on Christmas night, holding up their glasses of sweet sherry to the photograph of Ernest which had pride of place on the mantelshelf. Alf Porter fell over in the square a little later and then gave a rendition of his own version of 'O'Reilly's Daughter' holding on to the sycamore tree for support. Toasts were drunk to absent friends and to peace in the new year, and many Bermondsey folk were sobered by the thought that the maniac was still at large in their midst.

In the hospital the soldier sat alone, a little wary of mixing with the other patients. His mind was still clouded, and the modest festivities laid on by the staff held no joy for him. He gazed sadly at the little Christmas tree in the middle of the ward, watching the silver balls hanging from its branches as they turned in the yellow light and sparkled with flashes of different colours. He told himself that somewhere in London there were people who knew him, maybe his mother, his father, a girlfriend or his wife. They would be thinking about him, worrying about what had happened to him, and he could remember nothing about them at all.

On the evening of 3 January Ben strolled along to the Waterman to see his brothers. He had not seen them since New Year's Eve and he wanted to find out if they had heard any news about Greasy Austin. When he went into the public bar he found Patsy Dougan and his brother already talking to Jack and Nobby.

"'Ello, Ben,' Jack called out, rising from his seat. 'Sit down, I'll get yer a drink.'

Ben sauntered over and he realised

678

immediately that a heated discussion was taking place.

'We ain't bin sittin' on our arses doin' nufing,' Patsy was saying, glaring at Nobby. 'We've 'ad geezers from the Yard givin' us grief – in the saloon bar, no less, two poxy days after Christmas! It's no joy fer us that the nonse is still around 'ere.'

'Listen, we agreed to 'elp yer, an' we ain't exactly bin walkin' around in a daze feedin' the pigeons eivver,' Nobby replied. 'Yer seem ter be forgettin' you was the ones what brought 'im over the water in the first place. What yer gonna do next time yer 'ave a bit o' trouble wiv a gel yer can't 'andle – send fer Bela Lugosi?'

'I didn't come in 'ere ter 'ave the piss taken by someone like you,' Patsy said hotly. 'An'—'

'An' I ain't sittin' 'ere tryin' ter 'ave a nice quiet drink just so yer can walk in 'ere an' 'ave a go at me,' Nobby butted in. 'In fact . . .'

'Whoa, steady on, gents,' Jack said as he returned with Ben's drink, a wry smile playing about his face. 'Let's all be reasonable. We've told yer where we've checked, Patsy, so all we can do is keep on tryin'.'

'Well, it ain't good enough, Jack,' Patsy grumbled. 'Look, we've bin aroun' the doss-'ouses, the boozers, the waste ground down by the arches where Scatty got done in, an'.' . . .'

'So 'ave we, Patsy,' Jack cut in. 'The dirty git's gone ter ground somewhere we ain't thought of, or else 'e's scarpered out o' the area. The Yard'll 'ang aroun' fer a week or two, then clear off. We've all jus' gotta take it

679

easy fer a while.'

'Easy!' Patsy laughed. 'Them geezers 'angin' about is damagin' me business. It's all right fer you lot not ter give a toss . . .'

Ben had been keeping quiet but he suddenly leaned forward. 'Yer fink I don't give a toss, do yer?' he said angrily, glaring at Patsy. 'My missus only gets chased frew the fog by a nonse tryin' ter do 'er in an' yer sit there tellin' me I don't give a toss. Yer . . .'

'All right, Ben,' Jack cut in loudly, putting his hand in front of his brother. 'Look, Patsy. Do us a favour an' leave it, will yer? We've all got our ole ladies back 'ome an' none of us want a nutter like that on the streets o' Bermondsey one minute longer than we 'ave to, right? We'll keep tryin', an' you do the same.'

When the Dougans had gone back into the saloon bar Jack leaned back in his chair and smiled at Nobby. Nobby took a swig from his pint and then winked at Jack, looking around the bar with an innocent expression on his face.

Ben was still angry. 'You two fink you're bein' funny?' he said, glaring at them.

'What's 'e talkin' about?' Nobby asked, a grin growing on his rugged face.

'Search me,' Jack replied, picking up his pint.

'Yer know very well what I'm talkin' about,' Ben growled. 'Don't take me fer some ole plum. Sally nearly gets done in by Greasy Austin an' you two sit 'ere playin' silly buggers wiv the Dougans. What d'yer fink you're doin'?'

Jack slipped his fingers into his waistcoat pocket and took out a ten shilling note. 'Do us a favour, Nobby,' he said. 'Get a round in while I put our bruv in the picture, will yer?'

When Nobby walked away to the bar Jack leaned forward, his eyes glancing around to make sure they would not be overheard. 'I know you've bin 'avin' an' 'ard time over Sally, Ben,' he began. 'That's why I never said anyfing ter yer about what's bin goin' on. Anyway, it's finished now, so yer can take it easy. Greasy Austin's dead.'

Ben stared at his brother for a few moments without saying anything. "E's dead?' he said finally.

'Yeah,' Jack said, looking round the bar shiftily to make certain no one was listening. 'It was the Colemans who done away wiv 'im, an' it was me an' Nobby who found the bastard.' He smiled self-importantly.

Ben whistled through his teeth. 'The Colemans,' he whispered, still shocked at what he had heard. 'Why should they wanna get involved?'

'Well, as a matter o' fact they 'ad very good reason,' Jack went on. 'The prosser that got murdered in Rother'ithe was Davey Coleman's sister-in-law. That's right. It was 'is wife's young sister. Davey's missus was the one who 'ad ter identify 'er. Apparently the injuries were so bad she fainted when she saw the body. The shock of it turned the poor cow inter a nervous wreck. As a matter o' fact I was talkin' ter Davey terday an' 'e said there's no improvement in 'is wife's condition, even though she knows Greasy's dead. 'E reckons the way she's goin' she could

681

well end up in a mental 'ome. So yer see, the Colemans 'ad very good reasons fer gettin' their 'ands on that evil git before the law got 'im.'

'Yer say you an' Nobby found Greasy?' Ben cut in.

'In actual fact we collected 'im,' Jack replied as Nobby returned with the fresh drinks.

Nobby gave Ben a mischievous smile as he set a pint of bitter down in front of him.

'Jake got a call on New Year's Day from a pal of 'is,' Jack went on, taking a swig from his pint. 'What 'appened was, Austin was payin' the doss-'ouse owner in Bermondsey Lane ter keep 'im out o' sight, but when the news got splashed all over the papers the owner's bottle went. 'E knew 'e'd be pulled in as an accomplice an' 'e made a discreet phone call. The geezer 'e phoned got on ter Jake an' 'e told me an' Nobby.'

'Why didn't Jake tell the Dougans?' Ben asked quickly.

Jack laughed. 'I should 'ave thought that was obvious. Jake Collins knew what would 'appen once Patsy Dougan got 'is 'ands on Greasy, an' 'e didn't wanna be involved in any violence. Jake thought we was gonna 'and Greasy over ter the law, an' so we would 'ave done, if the Coleman family 'adn't bin involved. Yer know the score, Ben. The Colemans all work at the Surrey Commercial. They're dockers, just like us, an' we look after our bruvvers.'

Ben was quiet for a few moments, sipping his beer with a thoughtful expression on his face, then he looked at his brother. 'Did yer 'ave any bad feelin's about 'andin' Greasy over ter the Colemans, Jack?' he asked presently.

'I didn't,' Nobby cut in. 'That no good bastard killed two young women. All right, they were on the game, but they didn't deserve ter get killed. Then there was that Muriel Taylor, not ter mention yer wife, Ben. They both come very close ter gettin' done in. And what about Scatty Whybrow? That poor ole sod never 'armed a fly, an' 'e ended up gettin' 'is 'ead bashed in. All right, s'posin' we'd 'ave 'anded Greasy over ter the law. Imagine the 'eartbreak fer the families o' those girls who got done in. The trial would 'ave bin in all the papers an' at the end of it all some judge would 'ave said 'e was a looney an' stuck 'im away somewhere. Greasy was a devious bastard. 'E might well 'ave escaped an' killed again. No, Ben. I fer one don't lose any sleep.'

'Nor do I,' Jack said quickly. 'An' I tell yer somefing else. Greasy 'ad a quicker endin' than them two girls 'e done in.'

'Did yer 'ave any trouble pickin' 'im up?' Ben asked, still trying to take in what he was hearing.

Jack shook his head. 'Me an' Nobby went ter the doss-'ouse jus' before midnight. It was a foggy night an' we 'ad a taxi waitin' outside. We took young Freddie Anscombe wiv us just in case we needed an extra bit o' muscle, but as it 'appened Greasy didn't give us any trouble. We busted in 'is room an' dragged 'im out o' bed. We told 'im we was the police an' 'e never queried it. 'E got dressed, then we took 'is arm

683

an' walked 'im ter the taxi all peaceful like. Young Freddie wanted ter duff 'im up a bit but we said no. All the time we was in that cab Greasy was mumblin' about riddin' the world of evil, an' 'ow there was ovvers ter carry on the work. Freddie was gettin' a bit agitated ter say the least. 'E wanted ter top 'im there an' then, so we stopped the cab an' told 'im ter get off 'ome. When we got down ter Rovver'ithe Tunnel we paid the taxi off an' walked the rest o' the way wiv Greasy in between us. We knocked at the Colemans' place an' Davey answered the door. We'd already sent word we was comin', but I must admit I was a bit surprised at the bloke's reaction. 'E jus' looked at Greasy fer a few seconds, then 'e called 'is bruvvers. They were all ready. They took Greasy by the arm an' led 'im down the turnin'. As they left the 'ouse I see Davey slip a piece o' lead-pipin' in 'is belt. We didn't 'ang around but I bet it was over in a few seconds. After all, the river runs past the end o' their turnin'.'

Ben shook his head slowly. 'I don't know if I could 'ave done it. I fink I'd 'ave preferred ter 'and 'im over ter the police,' he said quietly.

Nobby shrugged his shoulders and Jack finished his pint, setting the empty glass down on the table with deliberation. Then he looked at his younger brother. 'Yer say yer dunno if you'd 'ave done it,' he said, a thoughtful expression appearing on his face. 'Well, Ben, that's somefing between you an' yer conscience. The way I see it, we gotta take care of our own. I fink I know what you'd 'ave done if 'e'd 'ave got 'old

684

o' Sally. Look 'ow yer copped the needle wiv Patsy a little while ago. All right, we're not s'posed ter be judge an' jury, but in this case we knew the bastard 'ad done it. This is Bermondsey an' we got our own standards. If some flash geezer walked in this pub an' started gettin' stroppy 'e'd soon be took outside an' sorted out. If an ole lady wanted ter cross the road you'd take 'er arm, wouldn't yer? It's the same when there's a case of 'ardship. Somebody always takes the 'at round an' we all chip in wiv what we can afford. It's the way we do fings, an' as far as I'm concerned it's the way it should be. So what do we do when some nonsense-case comes on the manor an' puts our women in danger? We sort it out in the way we know best. Like I said, Ben, I'm not losin' any sleep.'

Ben looked at his brother, a smile growing on his face. 'OK, Jack, I know what yer sayin'. But tell me one fing,' he said, leaning towards him. 'Why ain't yer told Patsy?'

Jack looked at Nobby and grinned. 'Well, yer know. 'E'll find out soon enough. There's no point in rushin' fings, is there?'

Early on Friday morning the soldier woke up at first light and got out of bed quickly, going over to the large window to watch the hazy sun rising. A winter mist hung over the river and he could see that it was slowly lifting. An hour later the view would be uninterrupted, and he knew that beyond the warehouses, wharves and grey buildings the distant high ground would be visible, rising up to the cold blue sky.

685

For a time he stood looking out from the window, excitement growing in his insides. Shapes were beginning to form in his mind, and as his eyes travelled down to the back-streets below he frowned. The rows of little houses with their smoking chimneys seemed to be taking on a new significance. He had been thinking about the hidden hills beyond London, and now his memory was stirring. Although the room was pleasantly warm the soldier shivered as he concentrated his mind on the image of a row of houses which had flashed briefly into his mind during the past few weeks. There was no headache now, only the frustration he felt at not being able to see the picture clearly. He wondered what it could be that was stopping him. Perhaps there was something in his past that he did not want to face.

At eleven o'clock the morning tea-trolley was wheeled in by the pretty nurse, and she joked and laughed loudly at the patients' asides as she poured tea and passed out biscuits. Without realising, the soldier walked towards the trolley and stood nearby as the nurse poured out a bandaged patient's tea and added a spoonful of sugar. She stirred the tea slowly, using her thumb and forefinger, and the soldier stared hard. The patient took the cup in his bandaged hands and the nurse looked at the soldier. She was talking to him but he ignored her, his mind struggling to recall a buried memory. He was sitting in a station buffet and there was a young woman with him. He could not see her

686

face clearly but he could see she was stirring her tea slowly.

'Are you all right, soldier?' the nurse asked, looking at him with concern.

'Yeah, I'm OK,' he replied, sitting down heavily. 'I was miles away then.'

'I was asking if it was one or two sugars,' she said, smiling.

'Two, please,' he said quickly, watching as she placed two sugar-cubes in the saucer and handed over the tea.

'Would yer mind stirrin' it fer me?' he asked, looking into her wide blue eyes.

The nurse gave him a strange look as she dropped the cubes into the hot tea and picked up the spoon. The soldier watched her closely for a moment or two then he slapped the arm of the chair swiftly.

'That's it!' he cried, startling the nurse into slopping the tea over the rim of the cup. 'It's the way yer stir the tea. Yer stir backwards. It's reminded me of somefing – or somebody.' He looked at the nurse and laughed nervously. 'I'm sorry if I scared yer.'

The soldier gulped down the hot tea quickly, wanting to get away from the room and the constant buzz of conversation.

He was walking slowly along a white and black tiled corridor, a part of the large hospital he had not previously been to, his head ringing as he tried to focus his mind. There were bay windows to his right and he could see particles of dust floating in the rays of the sun as they shone down on the tiles.

He was beginning to feel slightly dizzy and he settled himself down in a window seat. It was quiet and peaceful there, with distant sounds echoing along the long corridor. The soldier glanced down at the scene below, his eyes following the maze of backstreets, and suddenly he saw the long gap between the row of houses. Rubble was piled high and shored back from the pavement, and as he stared down tears came into his eyes and he leaned his head against the cold stone wall. It was all coming back now, like a rush of blood to his head. He was back home in Stepney, standing beside the pile of rubble in a bombed backstreet that had once been his home. He recalled the grey, lifeless faces of his wife and child who were lying in the makeshift mortuary, and the look of sadness on the face of the dust-caked beat bobbie as he stood motionless in the little turning.

Memories werre threatening to overwhelm his mind now. The tearful goodbye on the railway station, and then France. The bullets, shells and strafing, as he lay sprawled in the sand on the beach at Dunkirk. The camp in Sussex where the regiment was regrouping, and the tragic homecoming.

His head was beginning to pound as the memories flooded back. He recalled the long dark days of grieving and wide awake, endless nights, praying for the light of day.

He saw her face now. Sally Brady from Bermondsey. The attractive, dark-haired factory girl he had met at her firm's dance. He remembered clearly the times they had spent together, and the summer's day in the ragged barn where they first made love. He recalled the week they had spent together in the Cotswolds, the long walks in the cool of the evening and the nights of love they had shared.

The quietness of the corridor was shattered as footsteps approached and a meal-trolley clattered past, the porter humming loudly to himself. Jim Harriman left his window seat and made his way down the wide stone stairs to ground level. It was cold and windy as he walked along the path beneath leafless trees and saw the patches of crocuses, deep blue in the hard brown soil. The remaining gaps in his memory were filling now. He was on the edge of the olive grove, his platoon spread out and waiting. They had slipped in among the grotesque tree shapes, crouching low and fanning out. The machine-gun fire spurted from ground level and he remembered his squad falling one by one, cut down by the withering volleys of bullets, their screams rending the air. He was bent low and running, firing as he went. He had almost reached the gun emplacement when he felt the hammer blow in his side and the taste of earth in his mouth as he fell face down in the soft soil, unable to move. There were voices, German voices, and then blackness.

The sudden gust of wind shook the bare trees and Jim shivered violently as he sought the warmth of the rest room. The chatter had ceased and only one or two soldiers remained, dozing in the comfortable easy chairs. Jim found a seat by the window and leaned back, closing his eyes. It was just a tiny mannerism which had somehow jogged his memory, he marvelled. It was an unimportant, insignificant little action of Sally's. It had amused him at the time and he had forgotten it, but somewhere in the recesses of his mind it had stayed with him. He smiled as he remembered sitting in the station buffet with Sally. She was talking to him but he was not listening to her. Instead he was watching her hand as it arched gracefully over her cup, stirring her tea backwards.

Chapter Thirty-Five

ON Friday morning, as the red sun struggled through the morning mist, Vera rushed across the square with a newspaper tucked under her arm.

In number 4 Sally was standing in the cold scullery mixing Ruth's feed when her friend hurried in. 'Look, it's on the front page!' she said excitedly.

'What is?' Sally asked, squashing down a Farley's rusk with a teaspoon.

'It's Greasy Austin! They fished 'im out the river last night!' Vera exclaimed, prodding the paper with her forefinger. 'It says 'ere they pulled 'im out at Wappin' Reach.'

''Ow did they know it was 'im?' Sally asked.

'It said they identified 'im from the police files,' Vera replied. 'I s'pose they got it from 'is finger-prints, or a tattoo or somefing.'

Sally took the *Daily Mirror* from Vera and read the account of Greasy's demise. 'It says 'ere the 'ead injuries could 'ave bin caused when 'e went in the water but they're not rulin' out foul play,' she said, looking at Vera wide-eyed.

'Well I don't know about you, Sal, but I say good riddance,' Vera remarked, leaning against the copper. 'I reckon somebody done 'im in, don't you?'

Sally shrugged her shoulders. 'There was plenty o' people on the lookout fer 'im. Somebody could 'ave bashed 'im on the 'ead and dropped 'im in the drink, or 'e could 'ave chucked 'imself in.'

They went into the parlour and Sally sat beside the high-chair, encouraging Ruth to eat the milky mixture.

Vera sat watching with a smile on her face as the child rejected the last spoonful. 'I bet Muriel's gonna be pleased when she reads the paper,' she said presently. 'She was more worried than she let on. I wonder if the police are gonna let it drop? I should 'ave thought they'd be glad ter see the back of 'im.'

Sally wiped Ruth's messy face on the child's bib and undid the straps that secured her in the high-chair. 'I don't s'pose the local police are interested,' she remarked. 'They've prob'ly got a good idea what 'appened, but Ben was sayin' the Scotland Yard police are involved. I don't s'pose they're gonna let up.'

Vera leaned back in her chair and held out her hands. 'Let's take Ruth while yer clear up the

691

mess,' she said, grinning.

Sally had tidied up by the time her mother came in with the shopping. Annie set the bag down by the table and put a hand to her back. 'They've found that Austin bloke in the river,' she said, as soon as she could catch her breath. 'Everybody's talkin' about it in the market. I couldn't get away from 'em. If I got stopped once I got stopped a dozen times. 'Ave yer seen the paper?'

The two nodded. 'I was jus' showin' Sally,' Vera replied. 'They said it could be murder.'

'Well, it serves the dirty ole git right,' Annie said, flopping down into the chair. ''E got 'is jus' deserts, that's what I say. We'll all sleep a bit better in our beds now, that's fer certain.'

When Annie went into the scullery to peel the potatoes Vera turned to her friend. 'Are yer gonna be seein' Ben soon, Sal?' she asked.

'I'm goin' fer a drink wiv 'im termorrer night,' she replied, eyeing Vera curiously. 'What made yer ask?'

'Oh, I jus' wondered,' Vera said, trying to contain Ruth who was fidgeting on her lap. ''E might 'ave 'eard somefing about Greasy Austin.'

Sally took the child and gave her her teddybear before answering. 'If 'e knows anyfing I don't s'pose 'e'd say. 'Specially if somebody did kill Austin an' e' know who it was. Anyway, there'll be ovver fings on 'is mind termorrer.'

Vera noticed the look in Sally's eyes and she became inquisitive. ''Ave yer decided what you're gonna do?' she asked, trying to appear casual.

692

Sally sighed, resigned to the fact that Vera would not give up now. 'I've still not made me mind up,' she answered, after considering for a few moments. 'I know I shouldn't keep 'im waitin' too long fer an answer, it's not right, but I've gotta be sure in me mind. Whichever way I decide it's gonna be by termorrer. I'll tell 'im then an' we'll be done wiv it.'

'It sounds like you're gonna say no,' Vera remarked, a note of disappointment creeping into her voice.

Sally felt irritated by her friend's curiosity. 'I told yer I 'aven't made me mind up yet,' she said firmly. 'I've bin finkin' it over very carefully all week. If it was jus' me it'd be easier, but it's Ruth I'm worried about. It's 'er future, too. If it don't work out she's gonna suffer, so I've gotta be dead sure in me mind that Ben's gonna accept 'er. I'm aware 'ow difficult it's gonna be fer 'im, Vera. Every time 'e looks at Ruth 'e's gonna be finkin' about Jim. I've gotta be sure 'e can live wiv it.'

Vera glanced down at her fingernails for an instant, then she looked across to Sally. 'I fink you're puttin' too much emphasis on what Ben's gonna be finkin',' she said sharply. 'What about you? Don't tell me you're not gonna fink o' those ovver women 'e made love to while yer was sleepin' wiv 'im. That's somefing yer gotta come ter terms wiv if yer do go back to 'im. 'E's gonna 'ave 'is own guilty feelin's,' she went on. 'When 'e looks at Ruth 'e's gonna be blamin' 'imself fer drivin' yer out in the first place. All I'm sayin' is, don't blame yerself too much fer takin' anuvver bloke.'

Sally sighed, wishing Vera would go. 'Don't yer fink I've weighed all that up?' she replied, returning Vera's hard stare. 'That's why I've needed the time. It's fer all those reasons, an' more. If I did go back to 'im an' it didn't work out I wouldn't come back 'ere ter live, I jus' couldn't. It'd mean gettin' a place on me own. Jus' me an' Ruth. I wanna do the best fer 'er. I owe it to 'er.'

Vera got up quickly, feeling that the conversation was beginning to upset her friend. 'Well, you take yer time, Sal,' she said kindly. 'You'll end up makin' the right decision, I'm sure. At the very worst yer won't be on yer own. Remember you've always got a friend ter turn to.'

Dusk was settling down on the cold Saturday evening as the army jeep drove into Stanley Street and stopped short of the railway arches. The driver leaned forward over the steering-wheel, looking curiously at his passenger as he sat staring through the windscreen.

'You OK, mate?' he asked, fiddling with the gear-lever.

Jim Harriman nodded as he eased his legs out of the jeep and pulled himself to his feet. 'It's bin a long time. The place seems different,' he answered.

The driver revved the vehicle and pushed the gear-lever forward. 'Well, good luck, pal. Be seein' yer.'

Jim watched as the jeep roared away through

the arches, leaving behind a trail of exhaust smoke. He stood for a few moments staring up at the newly painted girders, wondering if he had made the right decision. The doctors had wanted him to spend a few more days at the hospital before making the journey to Bermondsey. They had advised him to wait until his next of kin could be informed and a visit to the hospital arranged, but Jim had been anxious to leave. The hospital had provided him with shelter and security while he was struggling to recover his identity, but once the shroud had lifted from his mind he knew that he had to get back into the real world as soon as he possibly could and find the girl he knew that he had loved. Until then he knew that he would be tormented by doubts and fears, and he had become nervous and irritated as he waited for the leave pass to be signed and transport to be arranged.

Jim walked slowly through the arches and saw the small opening some way ahead. He reached the gaslamp and stood beside it, glancing up at the name-sign on the wall. He stood for a moment and gazed into the square. Paragon Place looked neat and tidy. The clean white doorsteps stood out in the failing light, and he could see the tree at the far end of the square with its bare branches reaching out to the grey roof slates. There was no one about except for an elderly man who came out from the end house and walked jauntily towards him. Jim entered the square and returned Alf Porter's nod as he walked up to number 4 and knocked on the door.

He frowned as he heard a baby cry and then the door opened.

'Hello. I'm Jim 'Arriman,' he said simply.

Annie looked at him in total disbelief, her mouth hanging open, and her hand went up to her cheek. 'But yer – you're s'posed ter be dead!' she gasped. 'Me gel got the telegram.'

Jim smiled briefly. 'It's a long story. I . . .'

'Yer better come in,' Annie said, looking past him as though expecting everyone to be at their front doors.

Jim walked into the parlour and immediately he saw the crib.

Annie followed him into the room, fixing her eyes on him. 'Sally's not in. She's gone ter the pub wiv 'er 'usband,' she said, motioning him to a chair.

Jim sat down beside the fire and took off his forage-cap. 'I'm sorry if I upset yer callin' like this but . . .'

The sound of Ruth crying interrupted him and Annie made for the door. 'It's Sally's baby,' she said. 'She's a bit restless. I won't be long.'

Jim stared down at the coconut matting, the woman's words ringing in his ears. He felt suddenly empty inside. They had tried to warn him at the hospital that he should wait, but he had been insistent. 'It's too late,' he groaned to himself. Losing his memory had not only robbed him of his past, it had taken his future happiness too, his and Sally's future together. It was all too late. She was back with her husband, and now she had a baby.

696

The fire was getting hot and beads of sweat started on his brow. Jim got up and stood beside the wooden table. The baby had stopped crying now and he heard Annie's footsteps on the stairs.

She came into the room again and faced him across the table. 'I've settled 'er. The little mite's a bit chesty,' she said, her voice trailing off as she looked into his sad eyes.

'Look, I shouldn't 'ave called,' he said, looking down at the chequered tablecloth. I should 'ave given yer some warnin'. I won't stop. P'r'aps it's better if Sally don't know I've called. I'll leave that ter you.'

Annie felt helpless and she could not decide what to do for the best. Her daughter was seeing Ben again and now her life was going to be turned upside down once more. There was Ruth too. It was for Sally to tell him about the baby, not her. Perhaps she would not want him to know the child was his. Maybe she had already made up her mind to go back with Ben. Why does everything have to be so complicated? she asked herself.

Jim buttoned up his coat. 'I'm sorry fer the trouble,' he said as he walked out of the room.

Annie saw him to the door and watched as he walked slowly out of the square. Her mind was racing as she went back into the warm parlour. Had she done right? she wondered anxiously. Should she have told him about the baby? If she didn't mention that he had called and Sally found out afterwards it would be terrible, she fretted. Annie groaned at her dilemma as she

697

slumped down in the chair, her head pounding with questions and doubts.

She couldn't withhold the news, she decided suddenly. Sally had a right to know. She should have insisted he wait while she sent someone to fetch her daughter from the pub. Why wasn't Charlie there to help her? she moaned to herself. He was always up the pub when he was needed.

Annie stared into the fire for a few moments, then suddenly she got up and took down her coat from behind the door. I'll have to tell her, she thought. It's only right. Sally had said she was going to the Railway Inn with Ben. In any case she would find Charlie there. Maybe he would know what to do for the best.

The Railway Inn was full of jostling, noisy customers and the piano player was warming to his performance. Sally sat with Ben at a corner table, sipping her drink slowly. There was little chance to hold a proper conversation in the bustling, boisterous atmosphere and their attempts to talk were invariably interrupted as Ben returned a greeting or exchanged a few words with some of his friends, all of whom were surprised to see him back in the place.

Suddenly Bert Jackson walked around the bar and leaned over the table to make himself heard. 'Yer mum's in the snug bar, Sal,' he told her. 'She said it's urgent.'

Sally gave Ben a puzzled glance and then hurried through the connecting door.

Annie was leaning against the counter, a worried look on her lined face. 'Sal, I don't know 'ow ter tell yer,' she said quickly. 'I've 'ad such a shock.'

'What is it, Mum?' Sally prompted.

'Somebody called round a few minutes ago, Sal.'

'Who was it, Mum?' Sally asked, gripping her mother's arm.

'That telegram yer got. It was a mistake. Jim's not dead,' Annie said tearfully.

Sally felt her heart jump. 'What yer sayin'? Jim's alive?! Who came roun', Mum? Was it Jim?'

Annie nodded. 'It was 'im. I couldn't believe it. I jus' didn't know what ter say.'

'Where is 'e?!' Sally cried, pressing her mother's arm tightly.

Annie looked into her daughter's startled eyes, aware that Granny Almond and Granny Allen were listening with their mouths hanging open. ''E's gone,' she said softly. 'I wanted 'im ter stop but 'e said it might be better if yer didn't know 'e'd bin.'

'Did yer tell 'im about Ruth?' Sally asked quickly, feeling suddenly faint.

''E 'eard 'er cry, but I didn't tell 'im anyfing,' Annie went on. 'I jus' said it was yer baby cryin'. I told 'im yer was wiv Ben. What else could I do?' Her face had drained of colour.

'Oh my Gawd!' Sally gasped, a distant look coming into her eyes.

''Ere, you two all right?' Daisy asked, getting up from her chair.

Sally nodded, suddenly noticing that her mother looked ill. 'Sit down, Mum. I'll send

Dad round,' she said quickly, her voice shaking.

'No, don't tell 'im. I'll be all right, Sal,' Annie replied, dabbing at her eyes.

Daisy took Annie's arm. 'She'll be all right, I'll get 'er a Guinness.'

Sally hurried back into the public bar, passing her father who was in earnest conversation with Ted, and walked up to Ben.

He stood up, noticing the shocked look on her face. 'What is it, Sal? What's wrong?' he asked quickly.

'It's Jim. 'E's alive,' she said, her voice choked with emotion.

Ben took her arm. 'Sit down. I'll get yer a brandy.'

She shrugged him off. 'I must go, Ben,' she cried, turning away and making for the door.

Ben slumped down in his seat, staring at Sally as she left the bar, unaware of the looks from the people around him. A coldness clutched at his stomach and he lowered his head. 'Why now, after all this time?' he groaned to himself. It had seemed there was hope for the two of them together. Sally had seemed to lose her anger towards him, and the last two times they'd met she had even laughed with him. Now all that was gone. She had dashed from the bar, her thoughts only for the soldier. Maybe he should forget his promise to himself, he felt, as despair seized him. Maybe it was time to get drunk, to drink himself into a stupor, and blot out all the pain and heartache and forget everything. He picked up his empty glass and walked over to the counter.

Sally hurried from the Railway Inn and she stood in the dark turning looking left and right, as though expecting Jim to be coming towards her. The wind was getting up and pieces of paper swirled around her feet. Suddenly she turned and hurried along the street, veering right at the corner shop. There was just a chance, she thought. The only chance she had before he walked out of her life for ever.

The church gardens were dark, illuminated only by the dim light which shone out from the high stained-glass window of the church. She hurried along the dark path unafraid, but her heart was pounding.

As she neared the secluded seat she saw the tall figure walking very slowly towards her. She started to run and then with a leap she was in his arms, her head buried in his chest.

'Jim! Oh, Jim!' she sobbed. 'The telegram. It said yer was missin' an' presumed killed. I waited an' waited. You're really alive! Oh, Jim. I knew you'd come 'ere. I knew I'd find yer 'ere.'

He held the back of her head, pressing her to him, and as her sobs deepened he patted her back gently. 'It's all right. It's all right,' he whispered, leading her towards the wooden bench. 'I wanted ter take one last look at our meetin' place, Sal.'

The wind rustled the few crisp brown leaves, sending them dancing away along the path as they sat holding hands. Sally had composed herself and she sat listening intently while Jim told her of his encounter with the Germans in the olive grove, and how he had been left without any memory of who he was. Her eyes never left his until he had finished, then she looked down at their entwined hands.

'There's somefing yer should know, Jim,' she said, glancing up into his eyes. 'The baby. It's yours. I've called her Ruth.'

He gasped and looked away, his eyes going up to the lighted window of the church. 'I 'ad no idea,' he said quietly. 'I thought the baby was yer 'usband's. Yer never told me in yer letters, Sal.'

'I didn't want ter give yer any reason fer worryin' about us, Jim,' she said, her voice breaking. 'I jus' wanted yer ter come 'ome safely, fer me an' fer Ruth.'

He shook his head slowly, trying to take it in. 'I wish I'd 'ave seen the little one,' he said softly. 'I 'eard 'er cryin'.'

'Yer can come an' see 'er,' Sally said, looking at his lowered head.

A silence grew between them, and then Jim sighed deeply. 'Maybe it's better I don't, Sal,' he said very softly, his eyes lifting to hers. 'Maybe I shouldn't 'ave come callin'. I should 'ave jus' slipped away and left the both of us wiv our memories. It was good, Sally. We were good fer each ovver. I'll never forget the time we spent tergevver.'

'Neivver will I, Jim,' she said quietly, holding back her tears. 'It was terrible when I thought yer was dead. I can't tell yer 'ow much I thought about us. I know it's bin a long time, but there wasn't one day when I never thought about yer.'

He smiled and squeezed her hands tightly. 'I've bin doin' a lot o' finkin', Sal,' he said. 'I

702

wasn't really surprised when yer mum told me yer was wiv Ben. If it's what yer want, it's good fer yer that the two of yer are back tergevver again.'

She smiled briefly, her sad eyes looking down at the ground. 'Ben's bin wantin' me ter go back wiv 'im but at first I wanted ter believe you'd come back. It took me a long while ter accept that it wouldn't 'appen, Jim, an' then I delayed givin' 'im an answer. I was worried about Ruth. I wanted ter be sure Ben would accept 'er.'

''Ad yer made yer mind up, Sal?' he asked quietly.

She sighed deeply. It seemed so unreal. She had given up all hope of ever seeing Jim again, and now they were together once more in their own secret place. It seemed so long ago when he first walked into her empty, meaningless life. He had brought her love and made her feel alive again, like a wild dream come true. And yet, unknowingly, he had led her ever closer to Ben.

'I was gonna tell 'im ternight I'd go back wiv 'im, Jim,' she said quietly.

Jim nodded slowly, then he stood up, pulling her up beside him. 'Look, Sally. We both know it's too late fer us now. We met at a good time fer both of us. We 'elped each ovver ter get our lives back in order. We've both become stronger. Let's be fankful we met. I'll never forget yer as long as I live.'

She was in his arms, feeling his warm body pressed to hers as tears rose up in her eyes. 'I'll never forget yer, Jim,' she sobbed.

He stepped back, gazing deeply into her eyes

703

for a moment, then he released her hands.

'What will yer do, Jim? Where will yer go?' she asked, blinking as she looked up at him.

He smiled. 'I met some Canadian fellas while I was in Italy. They told me a lot about Canada. I was finkin' o' lookin' a few of 'em up. I need a new start, Sal. It's a big, new country. Maybe that's where my future lies. Maybe I'll find what I'm lookin' for in Canada.'

Sally brushed away a tear with the back of her hand. 'Part of me is always gonna be wiv yer, Jim, an' a bit of yer is gonna stay wiv me, too. I'll see yer every time I look at Ruth.'

Their lips met in a brief, soft kiss and then he took her arm and led her from the gardens. 'I'll walk yer 'ome,' he said quietly.

Her heart was heavy with the thought of their imminent parting, the last time she would ever see him. As they reached the corner shop she pulled on his arm. 'Ben's in the pub,' she said, trying to sound cheerful.

Jim glanced towards the Railway Inn and then he looked back at her with a sad smile. 'Goodbye, Sally. Stay 'appy,' he said softly.

'Goodbye, Jim, an' God bless,' she replied, fighting back her tears as he turned away and walked towards the dark arches.

The public bar was hazy with tobacco smoke as she entered. She saw Ben, a pathetic-looking figure as he sat slumped at the table, his eyes moodily studying his empty glass. When he saw her approaching a light came into his eyes and he stood up quickly.

Sally gave him a warm smile, even though a feeling of sadness lingered inside her. Ben's helplessness touched her heart. He reminded her of a young child when he first sees a lighted Christmas tree.

Around them the noise and loud singing carried on, as they stared into each other's eyes.

'D'yer still want me ter come back ter yer, Ben?' she asked.

He gulped. 'I thought ternight was the end of us tergevver, Sally.'

'Will yer still 'ave me back, Ben? Can we be a family?'

He could find no words to answer and suddenly a shadow passed over his face. He hurried past her out into the cold dark street. Sally followed him out, and she saw him leaning against the pub wall, his head resting on his arm and his shoulders heaving as his pent-up emotions overwhelmed him. She walked up to him and put her arm around his waist.

'Come on, Ben,' she said smiling gently up at him. 'Let's see if me mum can look after Ruth fer ternight, then yer can take me 'ome.'

EPILOGUE

1945

THE May sun was already climbing up over the rooftops as Alf Porter walked wearily into Paragon Place with the *Daily Mirror* tucked under his arm. He stood for a few moments staring at the rain-washed square, the freshly whitened doorsteps and the starched net curtains hanging in the cleaned windows, and then his red-rimmed eyes travelled up to the bunting that was stretched between the houses, rippling slightly in the light morning breeze. Alf continued along the square, eyeing the leafy sycamore with caution as he slid the Victory edition of the *Daily Mirror* through the letter-box of number 4 and fumbled in his trouser pocket for his key. Alf's thin face broke into a wide grin as he reached his front door and read the note that was tucked under the knocker.

I've cleaned the step.
Don't tread on it.
Knock for your curtains.
Annie

'Yer better get a few hours shut-eye, Alfie me ole son. The poxy curtains can wait,' he mumbled aloud as he let himself in.

The war was finally over, but not before it had once again touched the lives of the tiny community. Within the space of one week in March, the telegraph boy had twice cycled into Paragon

709

Place. George Tapley had received a telegram stating that his son Tony was alive and well. He had been taken prisoner in Northern Italy and the prisoner-of-war camp had been overrun by the Allies.

The rejoicing was soon stilled, however. On the Friday a telegram was delivered to number 8, and all the folk in the square were deeply saddened to learn that Ernest Cox had been killed in action.

The Cox family had borne their grief bravely, and now, as the bunting was being put up and the women fussed over their curtains and doorsteps, Maudie Cox quietly and sadly whitened her own front step and hung up her starched lace curtains.

Early on Victory morning Muriel Taylor sat at her dressing table thinking of all that had happened during the past two weeks. She had left the NAAFI service to marry Conrad, who had returned from the war with a leg wound. They had only just got back from their short honeymoon and her new husband was due to report back from leave in a couple of days. Conrad was still sleeping and, after glancing at him for a moment, Muriel put down her hair brush and opened the bottom drawer. There, wrapped up in the original brown paper was her present from young Ernest Cox. Slowly and deliberately Muriel removed the black lace undergarment from the wrapping paper and held it to her cheek as her eyes filled with tears.

All day long the victory pyre on the Stanley

Street bombsite had grown. People came laden with bits and pieces, and three young lads from Paragon Place made a contribution in their own inimitable way.

'You sit on the barrer, Billy, an' me an' Frankie'll push yer,' Arthur said, grinning.

'S'posin' the coppers ask us where we got it, Arf?' Billy asked in a frightened voice.

'Don't worry, Billy,' Frankie cut in. 'We can say Fat Dolly lent it to us. Anyway, all the coppers'll be pissed ternight.'

The eager trio reached the air raid shelter and found to their disappointment that all the bunks had already been removed.

'Cor! Some fievin' gits 'ave beat us to it,' Frankie moaned.

Arthur's eyes lit up suddenly. 'You two wait 'ere wiv the barrer.'

'Where yer goin', Arf?' Frankie asked.

'I'm gonna get Mum's screwdriver,' Arthur replied, grinning. 'We're gonna take these doors off.'

The three boys finally reached the bombsite and the adults laughed as a few of the men carried the heavy shelter doors over to the victory pyre. Councillor Thomas Catchpole was preparing to formally light the bonfire when Frankie pushed the barrow up to the high pile of combustibles.

'No, I don't think we ought to burn that, laddie,' he laughed. 'I should take it back where you got it from, there's a good chap.'

Before Councillor Catchpole lit the bonfire he made a short speech, ending with a call for a minute's silence in memory of the fallen.

As heads were lowered Arthur Almond noticed that the Cox boys were standing nearby. Richard had his arm around his younger brother's shoulders and their heads were bowed. Arthur quickly nudged his two brothers and the three of them eased sideways until they were standing next to the Cox boys. The gesture was not lost on Richard, and he smiled sadly as he glanced at his grubby-faced young neighbours.

The Paragon Place folk were out in force. Once again Alf's battered piano had been dragged beneath the sycamore tree, but on this occasion a competent pianist had been recruited from Stanley Street.

When the children had eaten their fill the party tables were moved to one side. Now, as the night sky glowed from the many bonfires across London, folk gathered to celebrate, watched by the Carey sisters who were sitting at the window with their arms resting on cushions, having partaken of two medium-sized glasses of ginger wine.

The sisters exchanged glances and Juliet was rewarded with a wide smile. Harriet was feeling particularly pleased at the way things had turned out since her sibling had mended her ways. They were now able to converse on matters of art and literature just like they had before that despicable Mr Lomax had begun to exert his influence on Juliet; she also liked having her younger sister accompany her to Mass on Sundays. Juliet had decided the new deceit was

712

unavoidable if her sister was to remain happy in her autumn years. Mr Lomax had grumbled about the new arrangement at first, but he had come to understand that there could be no more weekend jaunts, not while Harriet was alive, and had reluctantly settled for the occasional liaison with Juliet during working hours away from the office. On Sunday mornings as Juliet sat with her elder sister at Mass her thoughts sometimes strayed to what she might have been doing at that moment had she not revealed her affair to Harriet.

Muriel Taylor stood beside her brand new husband, her head resting against his chest. Conrad leaned heavily on a walking-stick, his arm around Muriel and a happy grin on his face.

Sally, Lora and Vera stood with Ginny and George, laughing loudly as they watched Alf waltzing Annie around the centre of the square, his shirt-tail showing beneath his coat and his trilby hat perched on the back of his head.

Ginny was feeling particularly happy. The end of the war meant that her boys would not have to go away to fight and she could look forward to peace and some future happiness. Soon she and George would be married and living together in her newly decorated house; George had managed to renovate the place from top to bottom, and without any physical injury to himself.

Ben, Big Joe and Charlie stood chatting together with Ted and Fred, while across the square Patrick was trying to enlighten an inebriated Maurice on the intricacies of rabbit-keeping. Beside them their wives stood talking together. Both had put on their Union Jack aprons and Ada had a paper hat covering her ginger hair.

The overdue explosion of pent-up aggression between the square's two antagonists had not happened. The elation of victory had put out Clara's short fuse and she had to admit that she had probably been a little hard at times on her next-door neighbour. After all, Ada was no oil painting, and she seemed to be getting uglier as she got older. Patrick would have to be blind to have designs on the woman, she thought. Ada herself felt that there had been too much fighting over the past five years and she vowed to ignore Clara's future outbursts. After all, the woman was two pennies short of a shilling, and if she wasn't careful she'd end up in a mental ward.

'I told yer that suit wouldn't last Alf Porter five minutes, Ada, didn't I?' Clara was going on. ''E's knocked the arse out of it already.'

Ada chuckled. 'If 'e keeps on swingin' Annie aroun' like that 'er Charlie's gonna get the needle.'

Clara Botley slipped her hands under her apron. 'The silly ole goat told me 'e's bin takin' dancin' lessons,' she said grinning.

'Who from, the clog dancers?' Ada retorted.

★ ★ ★

The square's two grannies sat together at Lil's front door, bottles of Guinness at their feet. Lil could hear everything now, after her reluctant visit to Doctor Bartholomew's surgery the previous week. She had been convinced that her hearing days were over but the old doctor had taken one look in her ears and tut-tutted. 'They're full of wax,' he shouted. 'It won't take a minute.' She had almost fainted there and then when she saw the size of the syringe, but she had taken a deep breath and decided that it would be worth suffering the torture if it meant she could once again have a sensible conversation with Daisy. Now, as she sat with her old friend, Lil could hear Ada and Clara gossiping at the other end of the square.

'Yer know, Daisy, I still can't believe it's all over,' Lil said, dabbing at her eyes.

'Let's 'ope the Jap war finishes soon, Lil, an' George Tapley's young lad comes 'ome safe,' Daisy said quietly.

Lil nodded. 'I was jus' finkin', Dais. We've seen some ups an' downs in our time 'ere,' she said, picking up her Guinness.

Daisy nodded slowly, then she looked along the square to the raging bonfire across the street and watched the showers of sparks shooting upwards and the silhouetted figures on the bombsite. She glanced around the small square and saw the couples dancing, her neighbours talking and laughing together, and the squealing children as they darted in and out of the light. Her gaze finally came to rest on the old sycamore and she smiled knowingly.

'D'yer remember all those years ago, Lil, when they moved us out o' Salisbury Street?' she said quietly. 'D'yer remember our blokes nicking that tree out o' the church gardens? My

715

Jack an' your Albert always laughed about that, didn't they, Gawd rest their souls.'

Lil dabbed at her eyes with a handkerchief. 'Just a twig then, wasn't it,' she answered. 'I can see ole Isaac Porter now wiv that there waterin' can. Every mornin' 'e was out waterin' that tree. Yeah, we've seen some changes, gel.'

Daisy sipped her Guinness. 'It's nice ter see young Sally an' Ben back tergevver again,' she said. 'They look 'appy, don't they? Our Ginny'll be next. 'Er an' George are gonna tie the knot soon as young Laurie gets back 'ome safe, please Gawd. Terrible about young Ernest Cox, though. I saw Maudie an' Arfur slip out o' the square a while ago. She was tellin' me they was goin' ter the special night service at St James's church. 'E was a nice boy, that Ernie. Terrible shame.'

Lil dabbed at her eyes again. 'Annie Robinson was tellin' me about that young fella 'er Lora used ter knock around wiv. 'E got shot down over Germany. Only a boy, 'e was. Terrible, the loss o' young lives.'

Daisy shook her head sadly. 'Terrible.'

Lil leaned towards Daisy. 'Mind you though, Dais, I don't fink she was wiv that young lad very long. Led 'im on she did, accordin' ter Annie. Bit of a flighty piece what I can make out.'

Daisy looked up and down the square then leaned closer to Lil until their heads were nearly touching. 'They 'ad a right ole bust up last week,' she said knowingly.

'Who did?'

'Why Annie an' 'er Lora.'

'Is that a fact?'

'Annie got upset about 'er Lora not bringin' 'er new boyfriend 'ome,' Daisy went on. ''E's s'posed ter be in a good job in the City, an' Annie reckoned Lora was ashamed ter bring 'im 'ome. Told 'er as much she did. Anyway, Lora broke down in tears an' it all come out. 'Er bloke ain't no big-wig at all. 'E's one o' them there Italian prisoners-o'-war. The bloke's in a camp on Peckham Rye. Lora's bin goin' wiv 'im fer over a year now.'

'Gawd 'elp us,' Lil exclaimed. 'What did 'er an' Charlie 'ave ter say about that?'

Daisy shrugged her shoulders. 'What can she do about it? All she said was that Lora's flesh an' blood an' yer can't turn yer own out on the street. As fer Charlie, 'e's as soft as a dollop o' butter underneath. 'E jus' went out an' got pissed.'

Lil's face broke into a toothless grin. 'I s'pose now the war's over Lora an' 'er Italian'll be goin' in the ice-cream business.'

The two old ladies sat in silence for a time, then Lil put her hand on Daisy's arm. 'Yer know, Dais. I love this ole square,' she said. 'I don't wanna move away, do you?'

Daisy shook her head vigorously. 'We'll see our days out 'ere, luv.'

'I dunno so much,' Lil said. 'They're talkin' about buildin' modern 'omes wiv barfs and 'ot water. These ole 'ouses are gonna go, sure as Gawd made little apples. It won't be the same. No more sittin' in the tin barf in front o' the

717

fire. No more whitenin' the front doorsteps. I s'pose they'll pull that tree down as well.'

Daisy picked up a bottle of Guinness. "Ere, Lil, give us yer glass. You're gettin' me all depressed. We're s'posed ter be celebratin'.'

When the glasses were filled Daisy nodded towards Alf, who was dragging a protesting Ada into the dancing circle. 'I tell yer somefing, Lil. 'E'd miss that ole tree,' she said. 'It's 'eld 'im up a few times.'

'An' knocked 'im down,' Lil chuckled, then she suddenly put down her glass and stood up. 'I won't be a minute, Dais,' she said.

'Where yer goin', Lil?'

'I'm gonna give Muriel's 'usband a big smacker. I've never kissed a Yank!'

MAGNA-THORNDIKE hopes you have enjoyed this Large Print book. All our Large Print titles are designed for easy reading, and all our books are made to last. Other Magna Print or Thorndike Press books are available at your library, through selected bookstores, or directly from the publishers. For more information about current and upcoming titles, please call or mail your name and address to:

MAGNA PRINT BOOKS
Long Preston, Near Skipton,
North Yorkshire,
England BD23 4ND
(07294) 225

or in the USA

THORNDIKE PRESS
P.O. Box 159
Thorndike, Maine 04986
(800) 223-6121
(207) 948-2962
(in Maine and Canada call collect)

There is no obligation, of course.